Morgan's Mercenaries

Three fearless men who've been to hell and back.
Now they're about to fight
the toughest fight of their lives...love!

HEART OF THE WOLF

Wolf Harding thought he'd put
his mercenary past behind him,
but one look at Sarah Thatcher convinced him
to get involved with the lovely spitfire—
for her own safety. But who would protect *him*
from falling for Sarah?

THE ROGUE

Soldier of fortune Sean Killian
was about to face his most dangerous
assignment—safeguarding Susannah Anderson.
The woman who stirred his wounded soul,
Susannah had witnessed a murder and now
only Killian could keep her safe....

COMMANDO

Jake Randolph was no stranger to peril—
he'd faced danger and walked away unscathed.
But his latest assignment, keeping beautiful
Shah Travers from harm, was wreaking havoc
on this brooding loner's heart....

LINDSAY McKENNA

MORGAN'S MERCENARIES:
IN THE BEGINNING

Silhouette Books

Published by Silhouette Books
America's Publisher of Contemporary Romance

SILHOUETTE BOOKS

ISBN 0-373-20185-0

by Request

MORGAN'S MERCENARIES: IN THE BEGINNING

Copyright © 2000 by Harlequin Books S.A.

The publisher acknowledges the copyright holder of the individual works as follows:

HEART OF THE WOLF
Copyright © 1993 by Lindsay McKenna

THE ROGUE
Copyright © 1993 by Lindsay McKenna

COMMANDO
Copyright © 1993 by Lindsay McKenna

Printed in U.S.A.

CONTENTS

Dear Reader,

It is always a thrill to write a letter about my books. I know many of you love Morgan Trayhern just as much as I do. He's a real, modern-day hero in a world where there are few role models anymore. And because he is the epitome of the kind of man I think we all deserve in our lives, I was inspired to write three books that would include him in the background.

Little did I realize that by writing these books, I'd be putting Morgan on a path to fame with all of you! Needless to say, I'm happy that it has happened and plan to keep writing about Morgan and his band of mercenary men and women for a long time to come.

Heart of the Wolf touches upon two areas I know well: Native American knowledge because I'm part Eastern Cherokee, and sapphires. My husband, David, and I used to go up to Montana and work the earth to find these gorgeous gemstones, and I wanted to write about them. *The Rogue* was a character who had been in the background of my mind for some time; I just needed a special vehicle to showcase him, his problems and how the love of a good woman could help heal those livid wounds that haunted him daily. *Commando* touches upon my love of the Amazon basin. I was there for a week, tramping around in the Amazon, looking for orchids in the backwater channels, and was well aware that heartless timber companies were tearing out this beautiful, pristine area of our world.

No matter what book I write, it always comes from experience on my part. A writer can never write outside of herself; she must write from within. I hope you enjoy these books, the start of MORGAN'S MERCENARIES, and our chance to take a peek to see what Morgan is up to next!

Warmly,

Lindsay McKenna

HEART OF THE WOLF

To the "Wolf Pack"—
Ardella Hecht, Marlene Johnson, Bonnie Birnham,
Betty James, Ruth Gent, Karen Durham,
Roni Lee Bell, Karen J. David, Patty Thomas,
Coletta Swalley, Eileen "Tunney" Lunderman,
Laura Dahl, Mary Buckner, Gary Gent,
Glenn Malec, Glorynn Ross and Karen Pietkiewicz

Prologue

"Dr. Shepherd? I'm Morgan Trayhern, from Perseus. You've got two of my men here, Harding and Killian."

Morgan realized he was having trouble controlling his voice. He cleared his throat. Dr. Marlene Shepherd, a pleasant-looking woman whose face was lined with fatigue, looked up at him.

She smiled tiredly and leaned against the nurses' station. "I'm glad you could come, Mr. Trayhern."

"How are they?"

She straightened and gestured for him to follow her to the empty visitors' lounge. At two in the morning, the entire hospital was quiet, with only a skeleton staff on duty. "They arrived only an hour ago, Mr. Trayhern. Mr. Harding is in fair condition, and Mr. Killian is in good condition."

Morgan inhaled a deep, thankful breath. Restlessly he scanned the dimly lit halls, automatically hating Bethesda Naval Hospital's sterile, antiseptic smells. "Then they'll be okay?"

The doctor halted within the spacious visitors' lounge and faced him. She took off her glasses and rubbed the bridge of her nose. "I won't lie to you, Mr. Trayhern. Both men are malnourished, just for starters."

"Starved," he said flatly. It was a statement, not a question. Morgan wondered how much the navy doctor knew about his three-man mercenary team's stint in Peru. Studying her intently, Morgan decided from the worry and confusion on her full, square features that she didn't know much.

"Yes."

"So what's Wolf Harding's condition—specifically?" Wolf had been the team leader in Peru.

"Specifically, Mr. Harding has been, for lack of a better word, tortured extensively, Mr. Trayhern." The doctor's full mouth pursed, and she gave him an incisive look. "So has Mr. Killian—to a far lesser degree."

"You're going to need a microbiologist, a good one," Morgan said grimly. "They've been in the Peruvian jungle for nearly two years. They may be suffering from bacterial infections."

"We've already begun testing for that," Dr. Shepherd said, putting her glasses back on. "No broken bones," she offered.

Broken spirits? Morgan wondered bleakly. The entire Peru venture had been unsuccessful. As he stood listening to Dr. Shepherd continue to list his two mercenaries' lesser medical problems, Morgan forced himself to be patient.

Wolf Harding had been commander of the three-man Perseus team. And his condition was only fair. What had gone wrong? Morgan tried to appear attentive as the soft-spoken doctor completed her analysis of his men's conditions.

"When may I see them, Dr. Shepherd?"

"0800 tomorrow morning, Mr. Trayhern."

"Not any sooner?"

She gave him a sympathetic smile. "I'm sorry. Both men are exhausted and are sleeping deeply right now."

Curbing his impatience, Morgan gave her a curt nod. "I appreciate all your help, Dr. Shepherd."

"Of course. If you'll excuse me, Mr. Trayhern, I have my rounds to complete."

Morgan nodded, then remained standing in the gloomy visitors' lounge as she disappeared down a corridor. The silence ate away at him as his mind traveled back in time. Two years ago, he'd formed Perseus—a security consulting company—and hired twenty mercenaries. His men and women would go anywhere in the world, aiding those in jeopardy who were beyond the help of direct U.S. government intervention. Today, Morgan had more demands for his people's services than he had people to fill those requests. And Perseus had an unblemished record of success—until now.

Rubbing his sandpapery jaw, he decided to stay at the hospital—just in case Wolf took a turn for the worse. He wouldn't abandon his men the way he'd been left— to die alone in some foreign country's hospital. He didn't care whether his men knew he stood guard over them. When he'd started his company, Morgan had made a promise to his people and to himself: He'd treat them the way he'd want to be treated.

Morgan's connections in the upper levels of government meant Perseus lacked for nothing. He had state-of-the-art communications with the FBI and CIA, satellite links, and the eager help of friendly countries. The government had been only too happy to hear he was setting up shop. There were many cases involving American citizens that they couldn't become directly involved in— shadowy political cases that could threaten the progress of diplomacy if the government was implicated. Perseus came in and quietly handled the problem.

Slowly pacing the length of the visitors' lounge, Morgan felt exhaustion tugging at him. He'd had a sixth sense about this long mission, which involved three of his best men. Stopping, he looked around at the gloom and sighed. He was lucky they hadn't been killed. And for that he was grateful. Perseus employees were culled from the top mercenaries in the world. They were at the top of their craft, highly intelligent, loyal, and emotionally stable—unlike many mercenary types, who might have skills, but lacked the stable psychological profile Morgan demanded.

He thought of Laura, his wife, who would still be sleeping soundly in their nearby Washington, D.C., home. She'd become accustomed to him bailing out of bed at ungodly hours to meet his returning mercenaries, arriving from a mission at one of the region's two major airports—or sometimes at the Bethesda Naval Hospital. He'd call and leave Laura a message on the answering service so that she'd know where he was and not to worry.

Frowning, Morgan loosened his paisley tie and unbuttoned his shirt collar. He sank down onto the plastic cushions of a visitors' room sofa, which creaked in protest as he relaxed for the first time in hours. Two of the three men he'd sent to Peru had been injured. Jake, the third—not requiring medical transport—would be returning on a later flight. Morgan would have to wait to hear his version of events. Morgan wished he could get used to this part of his job, but he knew he never would. Once a leader of a company of men, the old Marine Corps saying went, always a leader of a company of men. Well, he'd had his men caught in one hell of a vise. They were lucky they'd survived at all.

With a sigh, Morgan tipped his head back and closed his eyes. He needed to talk to Wolf Harding. He needed to find out what had happened.

A groan pulled Wolf out of his deep, healing sleep. The noise sounded as if it came from faraway, but as he slowly forced his eyes open a fraction he realized he was the one doing the groaning. Pain lapped at the edges of his semiconscious confusion. Where was he? The room was quiet, white and clean. The hell he'd lived in for over a month had been dark, dank and torturous.

I'm alive.

The thought congealed in his groggy mind. Wolf forced his awareness outward. He was in a bed—unshackled. Every muscle in his body felt as if it were on fire. Widening his attention span, Wolf took in two IV's dispensing life-giving fluids into both his arms. Blips of memory from the nightmarish past sped through his mind.

He saw faces, inhaled horrible smells. He heard screams. The scream of a woman. *Oh, God...*

The door to his room slowly opened.

Wolf blinked back the tears that had welled up in his eyes. Though his vision was blurred, he recognized his boss, Morgan Trayhern, who look disheveled, his face darkly in need of a shave, his tie askew over the open collar of his white silk shirt.

A wall of emotion funneled up through Wolf. He opened his mouth to speak, but all that came out was an animal groan. He saw Morgan's pale features grow taut as he approached, his mouth thinning. Wolf knew he must look like death warmed over.

"You look like hell," Morgan said by way of greeting as he halted at Wolf's bedside. Wolf's face was bruised, cut and swollen, the flesh around his eyes puffy, allowing Morgan only a glimpse of gray through the slitted eyelids.

Wolf nodded and dragged in a ragged breath. "Where?" he croaked.

"Bethesda Naval Hospital. The Peruvian police called me, and we sent the jet down for you and Killian. You arrived around midnight last night."

At the mention of his Irish friend's name, Wolf tried to speak, but he found it impossible.

"He's in better shape than you are," Morgan said, reading the question in Wolf's bloodshot eyes. "And Jake is fine. He caught a military flight out of the country and will be arriving here shortly." Morgan frowned. "You're the one we were worried about."

"Yeah?"

"You in much pain?" Morgan recalled all too vividly the times after his own surgery when his pain medication had worn off and he'd sweated in agony for hours before some harried, overworked nurse finally came by to check on him.

Wolf nodded once. He saw Morgan lean over and press the button that would bring a nurse with a shot to numb his physical pain. But as much as he wished there was a shot or pills that could dull the raging pain in his heart, Wolf knew there was nothing to lessen that shattering ache. A clawing sensation tugged at his chest—something he wanted to escape but couldn't. The emotional wall of pain nearly suffocated him as he lay beneath Morgan's concerned gaze. From somewhere, he dredged up the strength to speak.

"Leave," he muttered thickly, his words slurred. "I want to go away, Morgan."

Morgan's eyes narrowed. "Oh?"

"I want to leave the field for a while."

Morgan watched as a parade of emotions crossed Wolf's battered features. "Perseus has an automatic policy to grant returning mercenaries time out of the field after a mission's completed, Wolf—you know that."

"More than a month," Wolf rasped, struggling to speak, struggling to overcome the pain. At least the intensity of the physical pain seemed to temporarily override the emotional pain. That was something.

Morgan looked up toward the window. The bright May sunlight was spilling into the room. "Something happened down there."

Wolf's breath began to come faster, and his heart began to pound, as it thought of— Savagely he slammed the door shut on the too-fresh memories that haunted him. "I...want...time... Need time, Morgan." He forced his eyes as far open as possible. "Get away. Get me a job...any job...away..."

Hearing the desperation in the rising pitch of Wolf's husky voice, Morgan raised his hand. "Just tell me what you need, and I'll make sure it happens, Wolf."

Collapsing against the bed, the tension bleeding out of him, Wolf closed his eyes. His voice was wobbly with raw feelings. "Something safe...quiet... The mountains. Somewhere away from everything."

"People?"

Wolf was always startled by Morgan's insight. Maybe it was because he'd suffered so much himself that he could read Wolf's suffering so easily. "No people. Got…to be alone…"

Rubbing his jaw, Morgan thought for a moment. "Dr. Shepherd said it would be at least three weeks before you can leave the hospital."

"After that," Wolf forced out violently. He had to escape! He had to be alone in order to start dealing with the horrible atrocities he'd managed to survive in Peru— and the emotional ones he feared he hadn't survived.…

"Montana far enough away?" Morgan asked.

Wolf nodded.

"I can get you a job as a forest ranger. I've got the connections. You'd be fairly isolated. Working alone in the wilderness. Interested?"

Again Wolf nodded. He was afraid to speak, afraid that if any noise escaped him it would be a sob—and he'd start crying for all those months of hell he'd endured.

"It's yours, then," Morgan promised. "All I ask is that when you're feeling up to it you write me a report on what the hell happened down there. I'll have my assistant, Marie Parker, have the job ready for you when you walk out of this place." Morgan reached down and gripped Wolf's large, callused hand, which bore many recent pink scars. "Just get well, Wolf. Take the time you need. Perseus needs your talents, your abilities. *I* need you."

Chapter One

Oh, no! Sarah sucked in a sharp breath as the Douglas fir she was working under gave a sharp, splintering crack. Scrambling, she tried to throw herself upward, out of the cavernous hole beneath its twisted roots.

A gasp broke from her as she was slammed back onto the dusty white earth and its carpet of dried fir needles. The sixty-foot tree had arched to one side, missing her head and torso, but pinning her ankles and feet beneath the massive roots. Trapped! She was trapped! And then pain shot up her legs. Groaning, Sarah lay still a moment, reorienting herself, before she struggled to a sitting position. She was in the shallow depression she had dug beneath the fir as she searched for the sapphire gravel concentrate that collected beneath the roots.

"How could I?" she whispered disgustedly, her fingers trembling as she frantically dug in and around the roots, trying to locate her ankles. "This is an amateur's mistake, Sarah Thatcher.'' And then she grimaced and stiffened. The agony was real.

Pushing strands of damp blond hair away from her furrowed brow, Sarah clawed at the loose soil, trying to remove enough from under her legs to free her trapped feet. The sapphire gravel—the gemstones in their natural state, as small, round pebbles—were piled around her with the rest of the debris.

Gasping, Sarah arched back suddenly, her fingers clutching her jean-clad thigh. The pain had increased tenfold. Had she broken one or both of her ankles? Anger at her stupidity warred with her fear of the situation. Glancing up through the fir trees, Sarah could see the clouds building. It was late August, and here in the Rocky Mountains near her tiny hometown of Philipsburg, Montana, it was common for afternoon thunderstorms to pop up, sending furious torrents of rain at a moment's notice.

Her fingers lacerated and bruised, Sarah renewed her digging efforts. Then her eyes widened: The roots of the tree were lodged against a huge black boulder. Her anger gave way to disgust—then real alarm. What if she couldn't escape? What if she really couldn't free herself? Of course, Summers would thank his lucky stars if she was found dead up on her Blue Mountain sapphire claim, Sarah thought bitterly. Gerald Summers, the local land developer, certainly hadn't wasted any time mourning her father's sudden death. But then, Summers had thought she would sell out, and he'd have been too happy to take over her family's claim.

"No way..." she muttered through gritted teeth, stretching as far as her five-foot-three-inch frame would allow. Her prospector's hammer lay mere inches from her outstretched hand. She never traveled without her rifle, a canteen of water, and her mining tools. Her fingers dusty, her nails almost nonexistent from the demands of her livelihood, Sarah groaned as she reached farther—and managed to secure the hammer. Its long, sickle-shaped point was specially designed for digging into rock or dirt.

Sarah kept her blond hair twisted between her shoulder blades in one long, frayed braid so that it was out of the way when she worked, mining the sapphire gravel that lay approximately a foot beneath the thick groves of firs on the slopes of Blue Mountain. Although it was necessary to dig holes around and between the tree roots to find the gravel, any miner knew to dig uphill, away from the tree, so that if the fir fell, it would drop away from where the miner was working.

"Stupid, so stupid, Sarah. Where was your brain this morning?" she chastised herself as she began to chip and strike at the boulder that held her captive. The hard granite gave little beneath her relentless hammering, sparks and tiny chips of the stubborn stone flying from beneath the steel tool's onslaught—not unlike the pressure she endured from Summers. He just kept chipping away at her. First, he'd murdered her father—though the county sheriff, Noonan, had called it an accident. Then her fifty-year-old mother had suffered a stroke upon hearing how her husband had died. The mine was still in her parents' names and Sarah knew Summers would love to get her out of the way. Her mother, Beth Thatcher, was semilucid these days and likely to sign over the sapphire mine to anyone without question, such was the damage the stroke had done to her memory.

"No way," Sarah whispered again, her voice cracking. But this was a stupid mistake on her part, not Summers's work. Frantically Sarah increased the power and strokes of the hammer. Very little of the granite boulder budged.

The sky was darkening, and Sarah glanced at her watch. An hour had passed since she'd gotten herself trapped. Both her legs were now numb from the knees down. *Had* she broken her ankles? Oh, God, it couldn't be! The mortgage payment on the mine was due in two weeks, as was the weighty bill from the nursing home where her mother lived. No, she had to be able to work every day, mining from sunrise until sunset. If she didn't, she'd lose everything. Biting down on her full lower lip, Sarah wiped the sweat from her dusty brow and continued to hammer at the boulder.

After another hour of nonstop pounding, her fingers and lower arms ached with fatigue. She was damp with sweat, and her loose chambray shirt was clinging to her body. Her jeans were filthy with the white, dusty soil.

Sarah eyed her trapped feet beneath the gnarled brown fir roots. No one would miss her. Her isolated cabin was five miles up the road. She couldn't count on her mother. Although Sarah visited her at the nursing home in town nearly every evening, her mother frequently didn't know the time of day, what month it was, or when she had last seen Sarah; time had become meaningless to her since the stroke.

Flopping back on the earth, Sarah closed her eyes, sucking in huge drafts of air, exhausted. Who *would* miss her? Maybe Jean Riva, owner of the small nursing home. But occasionally Sarah missed a visit to her mother in order to facet sapphires for a customer. Pepper Sinclair, a woman smoke jumper with the forest service, was stationed in town. But she rarely saw Pepper—only for an occasional meal. Opening her eyes, Sarah stared up at the turbulent gunmetal-gray sky that boiled above her. Flaring her nostrils, she drank in a huge breath of air, testing it. Yes, she could smell rain in the air. If it rained, her trap would turn into a quagmire. And even though it was nearly September, a thunderstorm could lower the temperature to barely above freezing for hours after the storm had spent itself.

Sarah knew better than to hope it wouldn't rain. She'd lived in Montana all her life, prospecting with her father and helping him mine the sapphire. Groaning, she sat back up. A thought struck her. She took the hammer and started chopping at the thick, long roots, instead of the rock. Why hadn't she thought of this hours before?

"Sarah, you're strung out. You're not thinking straight." The task seemed impossible; the abundant roots directly beneath the fir were the ones that held her captive. And she'd have to hack through the tap root, the main root that the tree sent straight down to find water, in order to free herself. But that wasn't all. Eyeing the massive trunk of the fir, Sarah realized that the roots actually suspended the main bulk of the trunk off her legs. If she succeeded in removing the roots, the tree would smash down, breaking both her legs.

Thunder rumbled, and Sarah shivered in response. Looking around, Sarah stretched out again, got a hold of her rifle and began to use the barrel to pull larger rocks toward her. Perhaps she could build a protective wall of rocks next to where her ankles were trapped to take the weight of the tree once she hammered through the tap root.

Without warning, the rain poured from the torn belly of the sky. Sarah winced as the hard, cold drops struck her sweaty body. The soil would turn slick and sucking if she didn't hurry to get the rocks in place. Her breath coming in uneven gulps, she quickly built her safety net. The hammer's wet handle was slippery in her clenched hand. Gripping it firmly, Sarah tried to ignore the downpour. Rain struck her head, rolling down her face and beneath the collar of her shirt.

The wind increased, bending the tops of the hundreds of firs that surrounded Sarah. Biting, wintry cold clawed at her, and she began to shiver in earnest beneath the sheets of rain. Her muscles trembling with the strain, Sarah worked on. Her hair fell in flat wet strands across her face, blinding her. With the back of her muddy hand, she shoved the strands away from her eyes enough to see what she was doing.

Half an hour later, the storm ceased, as suddenly as it had started, leaving Sarah stranded in a pool of muddy water. She cut a channel away from her through the mud with the butt of her rifle, allowing most of the water to drain away. Then her teeth chattering, she wrapped her arms around her drawn-up knees. Cold. She was so cold.

The wind died down, the forest around her becoming quiet and serene once more. Sarah rubbed her arms, longing for warm, dry clothes. Mud squished around her when she moved. At least half the roots had been destroyed, but she had a good three or four hours of work ahead of her.

Suddenly a sound registered, growing louder. A car? At first, Sarah thought she was hallucinating because of shock and hypothermia. She rarely saw anyone on this back road bordering forest-service land. Tilting her head, she listened. Yes! She could definitely hear the faint growl of a truck making its way up the now-muddy dirt road leading to her cabin. *Impossible!*

Grabbing her rifle, she waited impatiently for the truck to draw nearer. A sudden paroxysm of fear grabbed her

heart. What if it was one of Summers's henchmen come
to check up on her? Once they'd dressed as forest rangers to fool her. The ruse had worked. Sarah had been
caught without her 30.06 rifle nearby, and they had
wrecked her mining camp. She'd managed to knock one
of her assailants unconscious with her hammer, though,
and the other had run, caught off guard by a "helpless"
woman fighting back. Although she'd pressed charges,
neither man had served time in the county jail. Sheriff
Noonan was on Summers's side, and he'd refused to take
her charges seriously.

Her heart pounded in triple time as the truck drew
close, and Sarah gripped the rifle tighter. She *had* to take
the chance! So few people knew about this back road.
Closing her eyes, trying to control her shivering, Sarah
fired the rifle once, twice, three times. She heard the
truck stop and the engine cut off. Sarah opened her eyes
and could barely make out an olive-green vehicle
through the trees and brush below. Who was it? She bit
down hard on her lower lip. She was growing desperate.
No matter who it was, she'd hold the gun on them and
force them to help her get her legs free.

Wolf Harding was sure he'd heard the rifle shots. So
had his half-red-wolf, half-malamute companion, Skeet.
The dog barked once, his tail wagging furiously as he
stuck his head out the window of the truck. Ahead and
to the right, pulled off the road, Wolf saw a battered
white pickup—probably ten years old. The rusty vehicle
was covered with a multitude of dents and scratches.
Putting his truck in park, Wolf got out, his well-worn
cowboy boots sinking into the mud. He took the rifle off
the gun rack on the back seat and placed a round in the
chamber.

Wolf concentrated, focusing on the sixth sense that had saved his life many times before. His gaze ranged across the fir-covered hill, and he breathed in the damp, fragrant air. Suddenly he spotted movement, halfway up the steep slope. Skeet whined.

Walking around the pickup, Wolf opened the door and released the dog.

"Stay," he ordered, quietly.

Skeet was shivering with anticipation, his eyes and ears riveted to the hill. Probably a hunter shooting out of season, Wolf thought. Well, the unsuspecting poacher was going to get a surprise today. Taking out his notepad, he wrote down the license number of the white pickup, then tucked the pad back into his olive-green gabardine jacket.

"Come."

Skeet leaped and whined, but remained at Wolf's side as he quietly worked his way in zigzag pattern up the steep slope. A ground squirrel spotted Skeet, shrieked, and jumped back into the safety of his hole. A blue jay above sounded his warning cry, the call absorbed quickly by the surrounding forest. Wolf's breath came in white wisps in the chilly aftermath of the thunderstorm. A far cry from the jungles of South America, he thought suddenly. The unbidden memory evoked a powerful chill that worked its way up his back and into his shoulders, where an old bullet wound twinged in response. Some things were hard to forget.

Shaking off that all-too-recent memory, Wolf forced himself to concentrate. Hunters frequently shot deer out of season around here, he had been warned by his superior. And more than one forest ranger had been shot *at* because he'd been caught in the same area, as a warning to mind his own business. Wolf's predecessor in the job had taken a bullet in the leg doing the very same thing: stalking poachers in the national forest. Up here in Montana, Wolf thought, these people think they're a law unto themselves. And he was used to teamwork, not working alone. But a lot of things were changing rapidly and drastically in his life. Two months ago, he'd been released from his unhappy three-week hospital stay. Now, with eight weeks of forest ranger training under his belt, he was traipsing through the woods of Montana. Well, he'd wanted to get away....

Skeet growled, the hackles on his red-and-gray coat rising. Wolf froze, his eyes moving to where Skeet was looking. Up ahead he could see a huge mound of recently dug earth. Frowning, he signaled Skeet to remain at his side. He wasn't going to lose his dog to some trigger-happy poacher. His heart started a slow pounding, and he could feel the adrenaline pumping through his system, the familiar friend that heightened his senses and reflexes—perhaps to save his life, as it had before. Wolf didn't want a shoot-out with a poacher his first day on the job.

Sarah gasped as a giant of a man walked into her camp. She hadn't even heard his approach. Out of instinct, she swung her rifle into firing position.

"Hold it!" she ordered. "Don't move or I'll shoot!" He'd crouched into a combat stance.

Frightened and confused, Sarah tried to control her chattering teeth. "Who are you?" she croaked, and she saw his intent gaze soften. Her heart pounded beneath his cursory inspection. The hard line of his mouth relaxed slightly.

"Ranger Harding, U.S. Forest Service," Wolf answered the shivering woman. "You can put the gun

down.'' He set his own beside a tree to show his peaceful intent. She seemed to be trapped beneath a tree, Wolf
saw. She certainly posed no threat to him. She was covered with mud, and exhaustion was evident in her
strained features. Still, she stood out like a yellow but-
tercup, he thought, her blond hair contrasting brightly
with the lush green of the surrounding trees.

"Ranger?" Sarah said challengingly. "You'd better
prove it, mister, or I'll blow your head off before you
come a step closer."

Wolf was nonplussed by her angry response. She appeared to be serious. He looked down at his olive-green
gabardine uniform. "I've got a badge underneath this,"
he offered, slowly moving his hand to open his jacket
and show it to her.

"Don't move!" Sarah stiffened, and the gun's barrel
wavered. Black dots swam in front of her eyes. Did that
mean she was going to faint? She couldn't—not yet!

Wolf scowled. "How am I going to prove to you who
I am, then?" How could something so tiny and bedrag-
gled be so completely distrusting? But very real fear
showed in her huge blue eyes, forcing Wolf to respect
her anxiety, whatever its cause.

"You could have a gun under that jacket," Sarah
hissed.

One corner of Wolf's mouth quirked into a bare sem-
blance of a smile. "Lady, where I come from we hide
our guns in a lot of places, under the jacket's a little too
obvious."

Sarah stared at him hard. Maybe it was the faint curve
at one corner of his mouth that made her want to believe
him. She eyed the dog beside him—just as huge and
intimidating as his master. How could she trust this man?
Sarah had learned the hard way that she couldn't afford

to trust anyone—even the people she loved most had abandoned her in one way or another. No, she could depend only on herself. She had no choice.

"Move slowly, mister. Show me your badge—real slowly. I'm a crack shot."

Wolf suspected that she was in a lot of pain—and possibly in shock. She was extremely pale. Wolf's protective nature reacted strongly. On the team in South America, he'd been the leader and paramedic, and now his caring instincts were aroused, in spite of this unnecessary game she was playing with him. "I'll bet you are," he said, slowly pulling the jacket aside to reveal the silver badge above his left breast pocket.

"Your credentials," the woman bit out. "A badge means nothing. I could go to Anaconda and buy one at a surplus store if I wanted."

Hollow showed beneath her delicate cheekbones, and Wolf could see darkness stalking her eyes. He was certain now that she was in shock, and going deeper by the minute. How long had she been trapped here? And what the hell had she been doing digging into tree roots? He bit back the questions and, lowering his voice, spoke as he would to calm a wounded comrade in battle. "Look, you're in no shape to be playing this silly game. From the looks of things, you're hurt."

Sarah struggled to ignore the soothing tone of his voice. She blinked her eyes several times and tried to shake off the faintness now rimming her vision. "I've got the gun. You're the one in trouble, mister. Now get your ID out and toss it over here. And don't try to pull any funny stuff."

Wolf almost wanted to laugh as he reached into his back pocket. She was so small to have such a large backbone. Carefully he tossed his ID case toward her.

"How long you been trapped?"

"I'll ask the questions!" Her hand shaking badly, Sarah fumbled for the case, then laid it in the mud to flip it open. Her gaze flicked between the ID and the man: Wolf Harding, U.S. Forest Ranger, Philipsburg. *Wolf.* The name fit him well. His features were sharp and accentuated, and there was an alertness to his eyes that she'd never seen in another man. But Philipsburg? Sarah tried for a tone of self-confident disgust. "You're a liar, mister. I've lived in Philipsburg all my life, and I haven't heard of you." Her hands tightened around the rifle.

"This is my first day on the job," he offered easily.

"Where are you staying?"

"I just rented a house over on Broadway."

Sarah wavered. His hair was black as a raven's ebony wing, and cut military-short. And his eyes... She took in a chattering breath. "How do I know I can trust you?"

Wolf shrugged. "Because you don't have a choice. But why should you distrust me?"

The rifle was getting heavy, and her arms were beginning to feel like ten-ton weights. Sarah knew she was getting dizzy from lack of food or water over the past six hours. "Do you know Gerald Summers?"

"No. Should I?"

Sarah probed his gaze, trying to ferret out whether he was telling her the truth. His mouth was now fully relaxed, she noted, the lower lip full and flat. "Summers is a murdering bastard. He hires people to kill for him," she said, her voice quavering. She was so chilled that she was having muscle spasms, and she nearly dropped the rifle. The ranger didn't move. His dog had lain down at his side.

Wolf shrugged. "Look, you're in trouble. You're trapped. I don't know this guy Summers."

"How long you been in Philipsburg?"

"A week."

"Where'd you come from?"

"South America," Wolf ground out, suddenly losing patience. It was a place he wanted to forget. Forever. Just saying the words brought back too many raw, unhealed memories.

Sarah blinked. Harding wasn't a Hispanic, but his skin was brown enough that he could have passed for one. If he weren't so hard-looking, some part of her paranoid brain might have believed him. Instead, to her surprise, it was her heart that shouted strongly for her to trust him.

Licking her lower lip, she whispered, "I—I was mining this morning for sapphires when the tree fell over on me."

"Sapphires?" Wolf shrugged. "Look, you can tell me how it happened later. Let me get you out of there first."

The rifle wavered badly in Sarah's hands. She took in a ragged sigh. "You could kill me. I'm so tired, and my legs are numb. I can't get myself free," she muttered, more to herself than to him. Yet he hadn't moved a muscle. His gaze suddenly warmed with a penetrating care—directed at her?

"I'm not going to hurt you," Wolf told her soothingly. What was she talking about? Who would want to kill her? "Put the rifle down," he urged, "and I'll come over and help you."

"I'll put it down, but not out of my reach, Harding." So much of her wanted to give in, to rest.... Sarah ached to believe what she thought she saw in the man's eyes. Was he really a ranger, or was this just another one of

Summers's men playing a trick on her? She had no choice. She had to let him help her. Reluctantly she put the rifle down in the mud beside her.

It was so natural, Wolf thought as he quickly shrugged out of his gabardine jacket and came forward to where she lay shivering in the mud. Now he was a paramedic again. It was something that came easily to him, the one positive thing left out of the living hell he'd endured in the jungle. Bending down, he brought the jacket around her small, tense shoulders and felt her wince.

"Easy, honey, I'm not going to hurt you. It's all right. Everything's going to be fine," he murmured as he pulled the fabric snugly around her. His long, callused fingers barely grazed her collarbone as he secured the jacket.

The woman jerked back, her eyes wide, her hand darting out for the rifle.

Instantly Wolf's hand clamped over hers. "Take it easy!" he rasped. Her blue eyes were filled with terror. He'd seen both those reactions too often in South America. Gently he loosened his fingers over her muddy ones. "I'm your friend, not your enemy. You've got to believe me if we're going to get you out of here and to a hospital."

Forcing back tears at the suddenly soft expression on his unforgiving features, she pulled her hand from beneath his. "I—I thought you were going to hit me," she muttered.

What the hell had happened to her? Wolf sat crouched for a long minute, digesting her trembling admission and watching her terror parallel her defiance of him. Trying to ease the tension between them, he rasped, "I would never hurt you," and watched with relief as some of the fear on her face subsided. "What's your name?" He eased himself up out of his crouching position. He'd have to treat her like a wild animal, moving very slowly so as not to frighten her again.

"Sarah Thatcher." She watched uneasily as he moved around her to inspect the tree and the roots that trapped her legs.

"Sarah's a pretty name. Soft, but with some backbone to it." Wolf purposely kept up the verbal patter, trying to gain her trust. "Old-fashioned sounding." He got down on his hands and knees to assess the damage to her legs. "Are you?"

She watched him guardedly. "*Old-fashioned* means *double standard,* and I don't buy that crock," Sarah said bitterly. "My mother may have, but I don't." Just his gentle touch on her jean-clad leg made her relax some of her wariness. It was a kind, professional touch, and the sound of his voice was dark and intimate. The man could charm a snake into trusting him, Sarah thought groggily as she pulled the jacket tighter around her.

Wolf turned to face her, his hand remaining on her leg. "Any lady named Sarah is bound to have an old-fashioned side," he teased. Some of the distrust had fled from her taut features. Wolf began to wonder what she would look like if she smiled. Her lips were exquisitely shaped; it was the kind of mouth a man could capture and lose himself in forever. Giving himself an inner shake, he forced himself to take on a more professional demeanor.

"Tell me about your legs. Any pain?"

"No, they're numb."

"Any broken bones?"

"I can still move my toes, so I don't think anything's broken."

Wolf nodded and gazed at the muddied boots caught

beneath the roots. "Probably a lot of tissue damage. You're numb because your legs are swelling from being so bruised."

Tilting her head, her teeth chattering, Sarah stared at him. "What are you? A doctor?"

Wolf grinned self-consciously. "I was a paramedic for many years."

"Thank God," Sarah whispered.

"You believe me, then?"

She eyed him. "You're a stranger," she insisted stubbornly. "For all I know, Summers has paid you to pretend to be a ranger and a paramedic."

With a shake of his head, Wolf rose to his full six feet five inches. Skeet had crept closer, and was now lying right next to Sarah. Wolf felt an unexpected—and unwanted—surge of warmth and tenderness toward Sarah. She was vulnerable, just as— Instantly Wolf slammed the door closed on the memories surging forward. In a way, he felt jealous of his dog's ability to show his feelings openly. As he stood there staring down at Sarah, he fought to suppress the tendrils of longing laced with hope seeping forth from his shattered past. What was it about this Sarah that aroused those dangerous emotions? She was mud from head to toe, and her once-blond hair was caked with fine gray dirt.

"I guess the only way I'm going to prove myself is to get you out of this predicament," he said, struggling to keep his tone light and teasing. Moving to the tree, he retrieved a huge broken limb and shoved it at an angle beneath the trunk. Looking over his shoulder, he told her, "When I push up, I want you to pull yourself out from under there. Understand?"

Sarah gulped. "That tree's huge."

"I know it is. We don't have a choice. Get ready to move."

Turning on her side, Sarah stretched her arms outward. "Do it. Now."

Wolf's olive-green shirt stretched across his powerful back and his broad shoulders as he strained against the makeshift lever. Sarah blinked as the muscles bunched beneath the lightweight fabric. The man was like the Rocky Mountains she loved so much—hard, craggy, and powerful.

The tree began to move. Wolf grunted, digging his boots into the mud and pushing harder. Every muscle in his body screamed for relief as he forced the trunk slowly upward, inches at a time.

"Can you get out?" he rasped.

"Not yet! It's moving, though." Sarah saw the muscles in his face tighten, saw sweat pop out on his brow, giving a sheen to his darkly tanned skin. Suddenly the roots gave way, releasing her. *Now!* To Sarah's dismay she couldn't move her legs. Desperately, she lunged forward, gripping the muddy bank and hauling herself out from beneath the twisted tree, dragging her numb body.

"I'm out!" she gasped.

Wolf didn't dare risk a look over his shoulder. "Sure?" he gasped. If she wasn't completely clear when he let the trunk go, she could be pinned again. And the sudden weight could break her legs.

Struggling to get farther from the trunk, Sarah cried, "Let it go! I'm free!"

Chapter Two

Wolf leaped away as he released his powerful hold on the lever. The fir crashed into the earth, splattering mud in all directions. In one smooth motion, he turned on his heel. Sarah lay on her belly in the mud, her brow resting against her crossed arms. Skeet was nearby, wagging his tail and looking at her anxiously. Wolf felt that way, too, as he made his way to her side.

Leaning down, he closed his fingers over her small shoulders. How tiny she was in comparison to him. Delicate, like a small bird.

"Don't move," he told her gruffly. "I'm going to check you for broken bones."

Sarah lay in a haze of pain. The circulation had returned to her legs with a vengeance. Part of her wanted to remain on guard toward Wolf Harding, but the gentle way he explored her legs for injuries shattered her resolve. Despite his size—one of his hands must have equaled two of her own!—he was amazingly careful. If he *was* one of Summers's men, he could have snapped her neck by now.

Closing her eyes, Sarah groaned as Wolf's hands closed around the hiking boot on her left leg. When he carefully moved her foot, Sarah bit back a cry.

"Hurt?"

"Yes..."

"Not broken, though. That's good." He checked her right foot. Both of the sturdy leather shoes were badly cut and scarred. "You're lucky you didn't break both your ankles," he said when his inspection was complete.

"Can I turn over?" Sarah chattered. Even his warm coat was becoming damp in the mud.

"Let me help you," Wolf said, coming to her side. "My guess is that you have torn muscles or damaged ligaments. Either way, too much movement on your own will worsen your injuries."

Sarah jerked up her head as Wolf slid one hand beneath her left shoulder. "Easy," he crooned, and with one smooth motion he brought her onto her back and into his arms. Then he helped her sit up.

Though she felt his intent gaze on her, Sarah evaded his glittering gray eyes. They were like shards of clear, transparent sapphire, hard and probing. He'd lifted her into his arms as if she were a baby, cradled her for just a moment and then settled her on the drier ground. A deluge of emotions broke loose within Sarah, and she bowed her head, allowing her straggly curtain of dirty-blond hair to hide her expression from Wolf.

"Listen," he told her after a moment, resting a hand lightly on her shoulder. "I need to get you to the hospital in Philipsburg. If I take off those hiking boots, your feet will swell like balloons. You need to have your feet packed in ice—''

''No!'' Sarah lifted her chin. ''I'm not going to the hospital!''

Wolf studied her intently. The jut of her lower lip confirmed something he'd sensed all along about Sarah Thatcher: She was stubborn as hell. ''You'd better have one good reason why—''

''I don't have to have a reason, mister. It's what I *want,*'' Sarah retorted. ''Just take me to my cabin. It's five miles down this road. I'll take care of myself once I get home.''

He eyed her. The silence was brittle between them. ''Look, you've got serious injuries, Sarah,'' he said, trying to keep the exasperation out of his tone. ''You need professional attention. The doc will probably put you on crutches for several weeks to let you heal up.''

Frustration mingled with an inexplicable desire to simply throw herself into Wolf's arms and be held. Sarah was stunned by her reaction. Wolf Harding was an utter stranger to her. Combating her heart's idiotic yearnings, she gritted out, ''Please, just take me home. I'll do everything else.''

Grimly Wolf watched as her face paled even more. Shock was probably the cause of her poor decision. ''I'm taking you to the hospital,'' he said firmly.

''No!'' The cry was animal-like.

Wolf's head snapped up, and his eyes narrowed.

''You don't understand!'' Sarah cried, tears spilling down her cheeks. ''Summers! If he knew I was hurt, if he knew I was in the hospital, he'd jump my claim. I can't stay away from it. If he knows I'm hurt, he'll steal it from me. I can't risk it! I *can't!*'' Sarah threw herself over onto her hands and knees. Making a supreme effort, she awkwardly flung herself upright.

A cry ripped from her as excruciating pain shot up through her legs. Her knees buckled, and blackness engulfed her as she felt herself falling, falling...

Wolf caught her as she crumpled into a heap. With a curse, he scooped her up. Her small form was diminutive against him. Her head lolled against his chest, and her lips parted, telling him she was unconscious.

"Little fool," he whispered, starting down the slope toward his pickup. Wolf debated with himself. Should he take her to the hospital as good sense dictated, or take her back to her cabin? Skeet leaped to Wolf's side as he negotiated the slippery slope covered with pine needles.

Wolf knew a lot about injuries. Torn muscles and ligaments were not unusual in traversing the mountains and jungles. And judging from the black-and-purple bruises showing on Sarah's thin ankles above her hiking boots, her injuries were extensive.

Settling Sarah on the plastic-covered seat of the forest-service truck, Wolf ordered Skeet into the rear of the vehicle. He always carried a wool blanket for emergencies, and now he covered Sarah with it. Hurrying back up the slope of the mountain, Wolf retrieved both rifles and slid back down to the muddy, little-used road.

Hospital or cabin? Wolf's hands tightened on the steering wheel as he turned the vehicle and headed back out. The forest blocked out the stormy sky. The trees reminded him of soldiers standing stiffly at attention. Thunder rolled ominously, and it began to rain again. The already muddy road became worse. The truck didn't have four-wheel drive—and that was exactly what he'd need to make it the eight miles to the main highway.

"Dammit," he whispered, glancing down at Sarah.

Her hair, the color of sunlight, despite the mud, lay limply around her face, her thick braid curving across her shoulders. Once again he was stuck making do with little help. It seemed that every time one of his friends got wounded, there wasn't a prayer of a helicopter rescue or a nearby hospital. And this was no exception. The road was turning ugly, and Wolf knew he couldn't make it many more miles without getting stuck. It looked like Sarah would get her wish. At this point they'd be lucky to make it to her cabin—a hell of a welcome for his first day on the job. He reached for the radio that would link him with headquarters in Philipsburg. Maybe he could get someone out to rescue them. To his dismay, the radio didn't work. Apparently the unit had shorted out.

Wolf slammed his palm against the steering wheel in disgust, then gingerly began turning the truck to head for Sarah's cabin.

Sarah resisted pulling awake until a combination of pain and the crash of thunder forced her to open her eyes. The bare hardwood beams on the ceiling of her cabin met her gaze. Slowly, heeding her stiff, sore body's complaints, she moved one arm from beneath the blanket covering her. Frowning, she realized she was dressed in one of her long cotton nightgowns.

"The thunder wake you?" Wolf asked, rising from the hand-hewn oak rocker nearby. He watched Sarah's drowsy state turn to terror and then subside into a guardedness when she recognized him. Why was she so fearful? What was going on?

"You!"

Wolf nodded and halted by her bed, which occupied a corner of the cabin. He placed his hands on his hips. "Why not me?"

Sarah refused to meet Wolf's cool, steady eyes. "How did I get here?" she demanded, her voice scratchy. Then she realized that not only was she in her nightgown, but she'd been cleaned up, as well. Her hair was wrapped in a towel that smelled like mud. Her alarm growing, she met Wolf's unreadable gray gaze. "And who cleaned me up? And how did I get into my nightgown?"

"Guilty on all counts." Wolf crouched next to her and carefully removed the blanket covering her feet. "You were out like a light, so I did the best I could to clean you up. Your hair still needs to be washed." He noticed that the swelling had gotten worse since he'd removed her boots two hours earlier.

"I don't care about my feet!" Sarah struggled to sit up in bed, her every movement excruciating. "You *undressed* me!"

"I didn't have a choice," Wolf said in a quiet tone, holding her blazing blue gaze. "You were going hypothermic on me. I had to get you out of those clothes and into something warm. But first I had to clean you up."

"You had no right!"

"I had every right, dammit. Why don't you say thank you for saving your neck instead of chewing me out? In case you don't know it, that line of thunderstorms across the mountains is still hanging around. You could've frozen to death out there tonight."

Chastened, Sarah picked nervously at the quilt covering her. Her mother had made it for her long ago. "You didn't have to undress me completely." Even her lingerie had been removed.

Exhaling tiredly, Wolf got to his feet after covering her legs back up. "Women all look the same. Hell, I've helped deliver babies, so don't pretend I've done something wrong."

Sarah watched him stalk out of the room. Looking to her right out the nearest window, she realized it was dusk. Another thunderstorm was lashing the cabin, and above the firs she could see lightning dancing across the gray, turbulent sky. Pulling her covers aside, Sarah examined her feet, which were tightly bandaged. Her mouth dropped open. He'd torn up one of her bed sheets to wrap them! She only had two sets to her name.

The aggravating pain increased as Sarah lifted her legs and swung them across the bed. Her feet barely touching the shining hardwood floor, she groaned.

"What do you think you're doing?" Wolf demanded, appearing at the doorway.

Sarah glared at him. He was carrying a bowl of soup and a cup in his hands. "Getting up. What's it look like?"

"Get back into bed. You try and stand up again and you'll faint again. Is that what you want?" Wolf walked toward Sarah, glowering. He didn't want to growl at her. Why couldn't she be civil?

"No," Sarah muttered belligerently, her fingers digging into the sides of the mattress. "I don't want to faint again. Not ever."

"Well," he drawled, setting the bowl and the cup on her pine dresser, "then I suggest you stay put. You've probably got a few torn muscles in both legs. If you're smart, you'll stick to bed rest and take the help offered."

Giving him a rebellious stare, Sarah whispered, "Help? You're a stranger. You did me a good turn. Thank you. Now why don't you leave?"

With a shake of his head, Wolf looked around the small room. The cabin had been built the old-fashioned way—with mortar and logs. The floor, of reddish-gold cedar, was a masterpiece—a credit to the builder. "You need help, that's why."

Sarah held his hooded look, but couldn't think of a response.

Wolf offered her the cup he'd brought. "It's comfrey tea. I found the herb out in one of your cupboards. My grandmother taught me about herbs when I was a kid, and I know this one's good for muscle and bone injuries. Why don't you drink it?"

Thirsty beyond belief, Sarah took the proffered cup. "Thanks…"

Wolf smiled tentatively, watching her drink the warm liquid down in several gulps. Sarah was becoming civil by degrees. His Cherokee heritage, the wellspring of his patience, would just have to endure her outrageous behavior until he could find out why she behaved so rudely. When she'd finished the tea, she held the cup out to him.

"Want more?"

"No."

But he could see that she did and was too proud to admit it. "I'll get you some."

"I'll get it myself," Sarah said.

"You want to fall flat on your face?"

Glaring up at him, at the rugged features shadowed in the light, Sarah grimaced. Gingerly she tested her left foot, putting a bit of weight on it. The pain was immediate.

"You always learn the hard way?" Wolf demanded, taking the cup out of her hand.

Sarah ignored him and hung her head. When he came back a few minutes later, she took the cup. "Thank you."

"You're welcome." Wolf made himself at home in

the rocker at the end of the bed. Facing Sarah, he noticed the way the light accentuated her soft oval face. With her hair wrapped up in the towel, she looked elegant. Her cheekbones were well shaped, and there was width between her huge blue eyes. Without trying, Wolf's gaze fell to her glistening lips as she unconsciously licked them free of the last of the comfrey tea.

"This cabin belong to you?" he asked.

"Yes. Actually, my father built it. Well, we all did."

"It's a nice place. Had a hell of a time finding it in the middle of a thunderstorm, though."

The soothing quality of his baritone voice lulled Sarah, making her feel cared for—protected. Quickly she snapped herself out of that mode. She didn't know this man. Still, he was being kind. "Dad was always a loner. He wanted a cabin in the woods away from everyone and everything," she explained.

"Was he antisocial?"

Sarah shrugged. The tea was making her feel drowsy, although hot pain throbbed in her legs. "I don't think so," she mumbled.

Wolf smiled. Sarah had a lot of her father in her, he suspected. "What's a young woman like you doing up here in the middle of nowhere? I'd expect to see someone like you living in a city."

"Don't judge a person by their looks, Harding."

"Call me Wolf."

"No."

It was his turn to shrug. "How are your legs feeling?" Wolf asked, realizing how reluctant Sarah was to talk about herself.

"They hurt like hell."

"Come tomorrow morning, the road ought to be good

enough that I can get us out of here. They'll take better care of you at the hospital.''

"I told you, I'm not going to any hospital. My feet feel fine! They just hurt a little.''

"Probably feel like they're on fire.''

"How could you know?'' Sarah probed his darkened face in the dim dusk light that filtered through the window.

"I've had a few pulled and torn muscles myself.''

Silence stretched between them, and Sarah chewed on her lip. It was a nervous habit she'd never been able to get rid of. "What did you mean, 'tomorrow morning'?''

"After you fainted, the storm broke. I was able to drive within a quarter of a mile of your cabin. My truck's down by the creek. When I tried to radio for help, the radio was broken. Then, when we made it here, I found that you had a phone—but it's not working, either.'' Wolf grinned. "By now my new boss probably thinks I've either left the country or am dead.''

His smile sent a sheet of warmth through Sarah. Her gaze was riveted on his mobile mouth, which was curved with faint irony. How incredibly his entire face changed when he smiled. He must not do it often, she thought, noting how few laugh lines surrounded his mouth and eyes. Realizing her privilege in seeing him smile made Sarah feel better for no obvious reason.

"You need a four-wheel drive for this road,'' she agreed. "Still, I'm not going to the hospital tomorrow morning with you.''

"How do you think you're going to get around, then?''

The softly asked question was underlined with amazement. "I'll hobble.'' She shot him a disparaging look. "You act as if a woman can't take care of herself. I've lived up here all my life, and I've weathered some pretty bad things alone.'' She motioned toward her blanketed feet. "I'll get by, don't worry.''

Wolf sat back in the chair, digesting the hurt in her lowered voice. He saw real sadness and pain in her eyes. Perhaps Sarah was trusting him enough to show her true feelings. He was surprised at the feeling of elation that soared through him at the thought.

"Yeah, I know what you mean about being alone and having to handle things,'' Wolf agreed. With a sigh, he sat up and folded his hands between his legs. "You're going to need crutches, Sarah.''

"So pick me up some if you want to help so badly. I'll pay you for them. Anyone in town will accept my checks.''

She was right: He did want to help her, Wolf thought. "I can do that, but...''

Sarah saw a scowl work its way across his brow. "Never mind. Folks back in these mountains don't ask for help. We just get along without. I didn't mean to—''

"Whoa.'' Wolf held up both his hands. "You really jump to conclusions, don't you?''

Sarah frowned.

"Forget I said that. I'll bring you the crutches. I was hesitating because you need medical care, Sarah. I don't think you understand the extent of your injuries. You're going to be laid up for weeks.''

"Weeks!'' Sarah's voice cracked. "That's impossible! It can't happen! I've got bills that need to be paid. My jewelry distributors are waiting for the sapphires I mine....''

The urge to go over and simply fold his arms around Sarah was almost tangible. Wolf sat there digesting that feeling. She was bringing out a weakness in him that he didn't dare indulge. He looked over and saw tears of frustration glittering in her eyes. He grimaced, forcing back his own rising swell of emotion.

"Just what the hell are you doing, living up here by yourself? What mine are you talking about?" he growled.

Sarah gulped back her tears, dismayed by the sudden change in him. Wolf's face had gone hard again, his eyes hooded.

"Blue Mountain is made up of what's known as sapphire gravel," she explained. "The gravel sits about a foot below the soil. The sapphires in their raw state are brownish-white pebbles anywhere from the size of a pinhead to much larger. I dig the gravel out from beneath the fir roots with my prospector's hammer, then put it through three screen boxes to separate the gem from the dirt." She sighed. "I've got some rough sapphires in a tin can on the drainboard out in the kitchen if you want to look at them. It's mostly small stuff—quarter carat to half carat, maybe. Not very big."

"Sapphires?" Wolf shook his head. "I had it in my mind that you had to dig tunnels in the ground and go after that gem with a pick and a sledgehammer."

"Most places around the world you do. But here on Blue Mountain, it's easy to dig them by hand." Sarah shook her head, "Summers's land parallels ours. He owns three-quarters of Blue Mountain. I own the last quarter. His bulldozers and backhoes take tons of the dirt and gravel every day. He makes millions."

Wolf saw the anger and disgust in Sarah's eyes. "Are you making millions?" he asked, looking around the spare, clean cabin.

"No. But then, my quarter of the mountain has fewer sapphires per square foot than anywhere else on the mountain. And one person can only dig and facet so much material. Summers has fifteen men in his employ and ten faceters.''

Sarah shook her head, and Wolf watched the emotions play across her features. ''What's Summers done to you to make you this gun-shy?'' he asked quietly.

Tears stung Sarah's eyes, and she looked toward the darkened wall. ''Six months ago, he murdered my father.''

Wolf sat very still. ''Murdered?''

''Yes. The sheriff says it was an accident, but I know better.'' Blinking, Sarah turned her head and met Wolf's gaze. ''My father bought this mine thirty years ago. He was an explosives expert in construction before that, for a silver mine up near Anaconda. Six months ago my dad was driving a small load of dynamite and caps to our mine when his truck blew up.'' Her voice grew scratchy. ''There wasn't a thing left of him, and not much of the truck. Dad never carried 'hot' explosives. He never wired detonator caps to the dynamite until he was ready to use them at the mine site. The sheriff said he'd wired them before he drove the truck. He said a bump on the road must have caused the dynamite to go off.''

Wolf saw Sarah's small hands clench into fists in her lap. ''Is Summers the local land baron?''

Clearing her throat, Sarah nodded. ''Yes. He's a greedy bastard who wants it all. He owns a silver smelter in Anaconda, and all of Blue Mountain's sapphires except for our small claim. He's already rich beyond anyone's dreams. Why does he have to have our little piece of land?''

The tragedy was clearly mirrored in Sarah's pale features. Wolf got up, resting his hands on his hips. ''You're looking tired, Sarah. Why don't you get some sleep? I'll get a blanket and use the couch in the other room, if you don't mind.''

Wolf paused in the darkness near the doorway, and Sarah thought he looked forbidding. His face was set and impassive again, his mouth a thin line holding back whatever feelings he might be experiencing. Skeet remained on a braided rug next to her bed.

"Good night, Sarah. If you need anything, call. I won't come in otherwise.''

Silence filtered into the growing darkness. Sarah stayed sitting up in bed for a long time afterward. When she was sure Wolf was bedded down on the creaky old couch in the next room, she finally lay down. She fell asleep immediately, her exhausted body finally overriding her overactive brain.

Chapter Three

Sarah struggled awake. Someone was knocking at her bedroom door. Who—? Suddenly her eyes flew open as the memories flooded back: the tree, the storm, the man who'd rescued her. *Wolf.* Light streamed through the window, and she glanced at the clock. Six a.m.

"Come in...." she called, her voice still hoarse with sleep.

Wolf opened the bedroom door, and Sarah's heart slammed against her ribs—but not out of fear. Wolf stood in the doorway, bathed in sunlight, his green cotton shirt open to show a white T-shirt underneath. His feet were bare beneath his muddy green gabardine trousers.

There was something endearing, even vulnerable, about him this morning, Sarah thought. Perhaps it was his tousled black hair, with short strands falling across his now-smooth brow, or his open, peaceful expression.

As her gaze traveled to his mouth, she read an earthiness in his flat lower lip that sent an unexpected wave of heat flowing through her—an unbidden sensual awareness that caught her off guard.

Swallowing against a dry throat as Wolf slipped silently through the door, she met his drowsy gray eyes. Although her legs throbbed with pain, Sarah responded to the warmth smoldering in his gaze and momentarily forgot her discomfort. Taken aback by her heart's response to Wolf, Sarah reminded herself that she didn't have a whole lot of experience with men. Working her father's mine claim and caring for her mother had long overshadowed more personal needs. Was she wrong to think she read an answering longing in his eyes?

Wolf ran his fingers through his hair, pushing the strands aside. Sarah looked like the kind of ethereal spirit that his mind used to conjure up in the jungle after a cool night: Fog would rise in steamy, twisting columns, sometimes taking on human or animal shapes in his imagination.

"Morning…" he mumbled.

How could she have not trusted Wolf? No longer was his face hard and unreadable. Sarah felt his presence powerfully, and her lips parted as he made his way to her bedside.

Wolf longed to reach out and graze Sarah's upturned face. This morning she looked fragile and beautiful, even though her hair was in dried, uncombed strands about her face. The wariness he'd been learning to expect in her huge blue eyes was missing, and inwardly he breathed a sigh of relief. He halted near the bed.

"How do you feel?"

Sarah averted her eyes from his burning, intense ones. The man should have been named Hawk, not Wolf, she thought uncomfortably. Retreating within herself, she attemped to block out the oddly heated emotions buffeting her heart. "Okay, I guess," she offered, struggling to keep her tone impersonal.

Wolf froze internally as he saw Sarah suddenly close down and become distant. A good reminder, he thought, disgusted with himself—he had no need for confusing emotions. "Let me take a look at your ankles and feet," he said, his voice brusque as he leaned over to pull back the sheet and blanket. Sarah tucked her arms against her nightgowned chest at his action, and Wolf winced. She still didn't trust him—but why did it matter? Unwillingly Wolf admitted to himself that he knew why. A bitter taste coated the inside of his mouth as he struggled with the memories. Leaving South America should have been enough. Now this waif of a woman was reminding him of what he desperately needed to forget.

Wolf's eyes narrowed as he removed the loose bandages around her right ankle. His gaze held her hostage. "You're okay?" he ground out, disbelief in his voice.

Sarah shrugged. "I've been hurt before, Harding. Pain's something everyone experiences, don't you think?"

"I won't argue that with you," he whispered. As the bandages came off her slender feet were revealed, looking like bloated black-and-blue sausages. "Look, Sarah, you've got to go to the hospital," Wolf said, his tone no-nonsense. "Your feet are worse. You won't be able to walk on them this morning."

Stiffening, Sarah reached down and jerked the blankets back over her feet. "I *can't* leave!" she cried. "I told you why. If Summers finds out I'm in the hospital, he'll send his men in to start stealing my sapphires." Her voice cracked. "I can mine just enough sapphires monthly to pay my mother's nursing-home bill and the mortgage on this mine. Don't you understand? I'll lose everything if I go to the hospital! I don't have any money saved. I live month to month. My mother's depending on me. What if I can't pay her nursing-home bill? They'll throw her out. And then what will I do?''

Wolf straightened, her pain cutting through him. The despair, the fear, in Sarah's voice and eyes shook him as nothing had in years. He actually *felt* her desperation and anguish. It was disturbing to realize he was feeling deeply again since meeting Sarah.

He held out his hands. "All right, slow down. What's this about your mother?"

Fighting back welling tears—something she hadn't done since her father's death—Sarah rasped out, ''When my dad was murdered, my mother suffered a stroke the same day. She's only fifty, but the shock of having my dad die so suddenly was too much for her to cope with. She was very dependent on him. The stroke affected her memory, so if she isn't watched closely, she'll wander off. She was in the hospital for a month, and it ate up our savings. We couldn't afford health insurance, so it took everything we'd saved.''

"When I got Mother out of the hospital, I tried to keep her at the cabin. That first night when I returned from the mine, she was gone. I found her wandering around in the woods, frightened and confused.'' Sarah took a huge, ragged breath. She would never make the same mistake her mother had—becoming dependent on someone she loved. The price of leaning on another person was just too high. "I tried to keep her with me out at the mine, but half the time I was watching her and not working. Sapphire production fell off. I knew if I didn't do something, I wouldn't be able to make the money I needed to pay the mine mortgage." Her eyes hardened. "Summers is just waiting. If I default on one payment, he's going to have the bank foreclose on my mine so he can buy it."

She rubbed her wrinkled brow. "I didn't know what to do. Eventually I figured out that if I worked seven days a week, dawn to dusk, I could make the money it took to keep Mother in a nursing home and pay the mortgage." Sarah looked away, biting on her lower lip. "I know it's not the whole answer, but it's the best I could come up with. At least she gets three square meals a day, and is taken care of..."

Wolf stared at Sarah's profile, aware of the suffering she was valiantly trying to handle by herself. How brave she was in the face of such overwhelming odds. He allowed his hands to drop to his sides. "How long has this been going on?"

"Six months."

"And you're making ends meet?"

Sarah nodded. "I'm a little ahead. I've got a bit of money in the bank, but I have to get more to help us make it through the winter. I can't mine during winter and early spring. The ground freezes and then turns muddy. The dirt has to be dry for me to sift the gravel."

Wolf looked around the quiet cabin. He'd felt at home in its comfortable simplicity as soon as he'd entered it yesterday. Blue-and-white calico curtains at the windows enhanced its hominess. The handmade furniture was of the same cedar as the floors. A few framed pictures of wildflowers hung on the walls. His gaze returned to Sarah, who was watching him with open curiosity. The wariness came back into her eyes, but not as much as before.

"Why are you entrusting me with all this information?" he asked. His tone was gentle.

Sarah shrugged. "I don't know." She sighed. "Maybe you don't look as threatening to me this morning as you did last night." She gestured to his bare feet.

For the first time, Wolf genuinely smiled. The people of South America had always regarded him as a giant and stood in awe of him. He was sure he looked far more human this morning, barefoot and out of uniform.

"Big feet," he noted ruefully.

"They sure are. What size do you wear?"

His smile widened, and an ache seized him. Sarah's mouth was pulled tentatively into a smile. It was the first time he'd seen her lips in something softer than a tight line or frown. "Thirteen," he admitted. "I have to have my shoes specially made."

"I'll bet."

"They keep me upright, though."

Sarah leaned back against the brass headboard and studied Wolf. The smile had eased the harshness from his darkly tanned features, and she felt her heart opening to him. She didn't know this man, she tried to remind herself. A huge part of Sarah, the inexperienced woman, longed to know Wolf better, to find out why that haunted look remained deep in his eyes. But she'd already learned the hard way the folly of putting her trust in anyone but herself, and she tamped down her unruly heart's yearnings.

"Now you see why I can't go to the hospital," she said quietly.

"As bad as your feet are, Sarah, you can't afford not to be in the hospital for a couple of days."

"I can't afford it."

"I can."

She snapped a look up at him.

"I've got money, so don't worry about it."

Her mouth flattened. "I don't take money from anyone. Especially strangers."

Wolf reined in his impatience. "It'll be a loan, until you can get on your feet again, so to speak."

Sarah ignored his pun. "The bottom line is, if I leave the mine unattended, Summers will send his men to steal everything I own."

"No, he won't," Wolf said smoothly, "because I'll check up on it. Most of my duties involve patrolling the forest area, the creeks, and checking for licenses. It will be easy to run by your cabin a couple times a day."

Her eyes grew huge. "What?"

"You heard me. I'll be your guard dog while you're recuperating." Wolf felt a tightening in his chest at his own confident words. Him, a guard dog. *Sure.* He'd failed miserably at that once before. So why was he reaching out to protect Sarah? Caught in his own damning trap, Wolf wrestled with his conflicting emotions.

The offer sounded too good to be true. Sarah hedged. "I don't want your money."

"Fine. Use your own, then."

"If Summers finds out I'm hospitalized, he will send his men up here, Harding."

"I'll deal with it," Wolf said with a shrug. Moving over to her dresser, he rummaged through the drawers until he found a tank top, lingerie and a pair of jeans for her. He brought them over to the bed. "Get dressed, and I'll take you in."

Sarah held on to the clean clothes in her lap. "I made a promise never to trust anyone again," she flung back heatedly.

Wolf turned at the door and studied her grimly. He

was sure Sarah sensed that he was incapable of protecting her, but somehow he had to try. "You don't have a choice." There was a sadness in his voice that he wished he could have disguised. "You're caught between a rock and a hard place."

With a shake of her head, Sarah muttered, "I don't want your help!"

"Too bad. You're getting it."

Sarah sat there, tense and frustrated. She wasn't willing to listen to her instincts, which were whispering that Wolf was trustworthy. Not after all that had happened in the past six months of her life. How many times had she dreamed of someone coming to help her defend what was rightfully hers, rightfully her family's? But no one had come.

Angrily she said, "Knights on white horses don't exist. They never did! Didn't you know that?"

A gutting pain shattered through Wolf. "Yeah," he whispered rawly. "No one knows that better than me." He turned and left the room as quietly as he'd come.

The silence wrapped around Sarah as she sat digesting the awful sound of his words, the horror that had been banked in his eyes. Then she slowly began to dress, her mind ranging from her own predicament to Wolf's admission. The anguish in his gray eyes had touched her even more than her own dire situation. Who was he? What was he doing here? And what terrible secrets weighted down those magnificent shoulders of his? And, more importantly, why did she care?

By the time they reached Philipsburg Hospital, it was 9:00 a.m. Sarah sat on the passenger side of the truck, with Skeet as a barrier between her and Wolf. She had to give Wolf credit: He knew how to drive the truck through the muddy mire of the road. Was there anything he didn't do well? Didn't know about? She stole a look at him. His profile could have been chiseled from the rugged Rockies of Glacier National Park. But somehow the unforgiving set of his mouth made her heart ache for him. Sarah kept replaying his last words, about not being a knight in shining armor. What had happened in his past to make him believe that? *Because, like it or not, Sarah, right now, he rescued you,* her conscience taunted.

With a ragged sigh, Sarah closed her eyes. For the first time in a long time, she had put herself in someone else's hands. It was a disturbing thought—a paralyzing one. But what else could she do?

As they neared the hospital, the truck radio unexpectedly crackled to life, so Wolf called his boss to explain the situation, saying he'd report in shortly. Arriving at the emergency entrance, Wolf carried Sarah into the hospital. But as he prepared to leave, he saw fear in her eyes that she obviously was trying to hide.

"I'll try to drop in and see you late this afternoon, before I go up to your cabin," he said, trying to sound more cheerful than he felt. Sarah sat on a gurney in a cubicle, her long legs dangling over the side. Her bare feet bruised and swollen. Her hair desperately needed to be washed and brushed, the mud from yesterday's accident still clinging to the golden strands. Her head was bowed, and Wolf started to reach out, to graze her pale cheek to reassure her, but he couldn't even do that. Nothing was for sure in life. Absolutely nothing. His hand stopped in midair.

"Thanks," Sarah whispered, unable to look up. Just having Wolf standing beside her, she felt so much safer, as if everything really might work out—and the knowledge that he was leaving brought her ridiculously near tears.

The urge to hold her, to whisper that things would be okay, needled Wolf. But he, of all people, had no right to guarantee that. *To hell with it.* He gripped her hand momentarily, squeezing it gently. "You worry too much, Sarah. I'll be back later," he said with all the confidence he could muster, and he released her hand. But not before her head snapped up and those glorious blue eyes of hers flared with disbelief and some other tangible but indecipherable emotion. As Wolf turned away, he tried to figure out what it was that he'd seen reflected in her lovely gaze, then shook himself, putting it firmly out of his mind. Once he'd thought he could understand a woman, but experience had taught him differently. He knew he didn't dare trust his sense of the situation with Sarah—as much as his heart bid him to do just that.

Wolf glanced at his watch. It was nearly four o'clock, the day still bright with sunshine after last night's storms. The hospital, a small two-story brick building, stood out against the side of the green mountains that surrounded the small valley town. He pulled the truck into the visitor's parking lot and left Skeet sitting obediently in the cab, his head out the window, his tongue lolling out of his mouth.

Unaccountably, Wolf's spirits lifted as he entered the hospital. All day, she'd been on his mind and lingering in his heart.

Room 205 had two beds in it, but only Sarah was there, the other bed unoccupied. Wolf halted, and his breath caught. Sarah was on crutches, looking out the west window, and sunlight bathed her form. Her once muddy hair was clean, reminding him of the golden corn silk that had tassled the green ears on his father's farm every August. It waved softly down around her shoulders like a cape. She wore a blue tank top that emphasized her small form. As Wolf's gaze moved downward, he saw to his satisfaction that Sarah's feet and ankles were snugly wrapped in elastic bandages, although they still were obviously swollen.

"Sarah?" His throat was dry, his pulse erratic, as he said her name. As she slowly turned her head, Wolf felt as if sunlight were bathing him for the first time in this last dark year of his life; a strange warmth flowed through him, easing some of the pain he carried within him twenty-four hours a day. Delicate bangs framed Sarah's gently arched eyebrows. Today she looked like a beautiful woman, not a waif. The change was heart-stopping.

Sarah turned at the sound of her name—and froze beneath Wolf's unexpectedly hot, hungry gaze. Never before had she been silently caressed like this. Automatically her gaze dropped to Wolf's mouth. What would it be like to kiss him—to feel that dangerous high-voltage power that seemed to throb around him?

Shaking off the strange, heated languor that threatened to engulf her, Sarah frowned. "You!"

Taken aback by the sudden change in her, Wolf halted halfway across the room. "Me?"

"Yes, you!" Sarah watched as he took off his ranger's hat and held it in his long, callused fingers. She hobbled around, hating the crutches and especially hating the fact that she had to rely on them. "Do you know how much just one day in this place has cost me? Four hundred dollars!" She halted a foot from him and glared up into his face. "Four hundred dollars! I can't believe it! I've got to get out of here. I want you to take me home!''

Wolf gripped her gently by the arm. ''Come on, sit down while we discuss this.''

''There's no discussion, Wolf. I want you to take me home. You brought me here, and you can take me back. You owe me that much.''

He nodded and released Sarah's arm as she crossed with some difficulty and sat on the edge of the bed. Grabbing a nearby chair, he turned it around, swung his leg over it and sat down.

''What did the doctor say about your feet?''

Wrinkling her nose, Sarah muttered, ''Same thing you did. No broken bones, just a lot of smashed muscles and skin. I've got to stay on these lousy crutches a week.''

Despite her belligerent tone of voice, the distraught quality in her eyes made Wolf wince. ''I thought so. How do you feel now?''

''Four hundred dollars poorer.''

Wolf grinned, silently applauding her spunk. ''I told you—I'll help you out. A loan you can pay back with no interest.''

Adamantly Sarah shook her head. ''I don't accept help from strangers, Harding.''

Wolf sighed. There was such turmoil and anguish in Sarah's face. And there was turmoil within him, too. He had no right to offer her help, but he couldn't seem to help himself. ''You'll never be able to take care of yourself up there right now, Sarah,'' he warned.

Her name rolled off his lips like a whisper of wind, and it sent a warmth through her. ''Yes, I can! Quit treating me like I'm some breakable piece of glass. I've survived out there all my life just fine without you!''

''But not with two injured feet.''

"Stop it!" Sarah awkwardly rose to her feet again. "I'm checking myself out and leaving right now—with or without your help! If I have to walk back to my cabin, I will!"

"What's going on in here?"

Sarah jerked a look toward the door. Her doctor, Bruce Evans, stood in the doorway in his white coat, running a hand through his gray hair.

"I'm leaving, Dr. Evans."

Wolf stood up, replacing the chair against the wall. He looked at the doctor.

"I'm Ranger Harding, Doctor. I'm the one who found Sarah on Blue Mountain and brought her here. Can she make it on her own?"

Evans smiled ruefully. "About ten minutes on your feet, Sarah, and all that pain will return." He looked over at Wolf. "The answer's no. At least for a week. She needs enforced bed rest to allow those feet to heal."

"I'm sorry, Doctor, but that's not an option." Sarah made her way slowly to the door. "Now stand aside. I'm checking myself out. I can't afford the bill that comes with this rest you're talking about."

Evans's fatherly face gave Wolf a pleading look.

Grimly Wolf stalked over to where Sarah stood.

"Get her a wheelchair," he ordered Evans. "I'll take her home with me for a week."

Sarah's mouth dropped open. "What? Go home with you?" Shock made her voice come out squeaky, not at all in keeping with the confident image she was trying to project.

"That's right." Wolf's tone brooked no argument.

Sarah's eyes grew huge.

"It's me or the hospital, Sarah. Make up your mind." Damn, but she was stubborn.

Evans smiled, placated. "Wonderful solution, Ranger Harding. I'll get the nurse to bring you a wheelchair, Sarah."

Once they were alone, Sarah whispered fiercely, "I'm not going home with you! You take me back to my cabin or else!"

In that moment, Wolf saw just how fragile Sarah really was. Instead of losing patience, he said softly, "Honey, you're in need of a little care right now." He hitched one shoulder upward, his voice turning apologetic. "I'm not the best of caretakers, but I'll do the best I can for you. I've got a small house with one bedroom. I can sleep on the couch in the living room. I'm not such a bad cook—and it's a place for you to rest and heal up." He held up his hands. "Do we understand each other? I'm a friend doing a favor for a friend. Nothing more or less."

Stunned, Sarah couldn't say anything for several moments. She just didn't have the money to stay and pay a huge hospital bill. And right now, her feet were aching as if they were being smashed all over again. The pain was nearly unbearable. But worse than that, when he'd called her "honey," a dam of feelings, both good and bad—emotions she'd held onto so long by herself—flowed through her unchecked.

Sarah realized she had no other friends. She didn't dare have friends. Still, she knew in her heart that she needed help. But her recent past caught up with her, and her voice shook with anger. "You promised to drive by my cabin a couple times a day. Why not take me there instead—you can still check in on me."

Wolf felt as much as heard Sarah's panic. She didn't want to lean on anyone for help. That much he understood, but when he caught and held her distraught gaze, he didn't really see anger, he saw vulnerability.

"The doctor said you had to stay off your feet for an entire week, Sarah. Checking on you twice a day isn't going to do it. I can see it in your eyes. You don't really believe what you're saying."

Fear struck deeply within Sarah. Wolf had seen through her anger and knew her true feelings! Grasping at straws, she snapped, "I'm not going to be your house-keeper, Harding!"

"I'll keep house for both of us."

"Then what do you want out of this?" she demanded. "Everybody always expects something."

Wolf smiled gently. "Where I come from, we were taught to offer our home, food and the roof over our heads to total strangers. This isn't out of the ordinary for me, Sarah, even if it is for you."

Warily Sarah demanded, "Where do you come from?"

"The Eastern Cherokee reservation in North Carolina. I was born and raised there. My father's a full-blooded Cherokee. He met my mother when she came to the reservation to teach. The native American way is to offer help when it's needed, Sarah." He held her mutinous blue gaze. "And you need help."

Sarah was losing the struggle to stay independent, and she knew it. No matter how much she wished her feet hadn't been injured, there was no contradicting the doc-tor's diagnosis. It would take at least a week for them to heal enough that she could walk again. Silently Sarah vowed never to let her guard down around Wolf Har-ding. She sensed that to do so could be devastating—in ways she couldn't even imagine. "Okay," she muttered defiantly.

Wolf felt Sarah's disappointment at giving in. And she had every right to be wary of him, as harsh experience had taught him in South America. Still, a strange light-heartedness flowed through him. "It's not a prison sentence, Sarah," he said, and his voice came out almost teasing.

Sarah struggled to rally, knowing Wolf didn't deserve her anger. "But my cabin...the mine..."

"I've already been up to your mine and cabin twice today. Everything's quiet. Don't worry."

"I'll need stuff from the cabin," Sarah said unhappily.

"I'll drive up there tonight and get clothes and anything else you want for your stay with me."

Sarah moved aside when the nurse brought in the wheelchair. She needed no nudging to sit down in it and take the pressure off her throbbing feet. Wolf was immediately at her side to take the crutches. Just his nearness sent an unexpected sheet of warmth through her, and for just a split second, she wavered. The absurd urge to simply open her arms and move into Wolf's arms was nearly overwhelming. Confused, Sarah sat awkwardly in the silence, unstrung by him. Her entire world was unraveling, and it was all she could do to continue to hold herself together. But, whether she liked admitting it or not, Wolf's quiet, steadying presence was shoring her up.

Skeet barked once in greeting when Sarah climbed into the truck with Wolf's help. The dog thumped his bushy tail.

Sarah rallied at Skeet's enthusiasm, offering a slight smile as she patted the dog's huge head. "I'll bet you thought you'd gotten rid of me, huh?"

Wolf climbed in the driver's side and shut the door. "He won't mind the company. In fact, he'll like it."

"Will *you?*" Sarah asked sourly as Wolf drove away from the hospital.

With a shrug, Wolf glanced over at her, feeling the tension building between them once again. "Does it matter what I think?"

Sarah set her lips and stared straight ahead. "Yes."

Wolf didn't want to lie to her, but he couldn't tell her the truth, either. It was just too painful to talk about. "It will take some getting used to," Wolf admitted, "but I'll handle it."

Inwardly Sarah sighed. Living with Wolf was going to be like living with a wild animal. He was so unpredictable. And so were her wildly fluctuating emotions whenever he was near her.

"We have some talking to do now that we're alone," Wolf said seriously after a few minutes of driving in silence.

Sarah looked at him. She was trying to hold herself apart from him—trying to pretend she didn't care what he would say. "About what?"

"I snooped around your mine this afternoon and took a closer look at that tree that fell on you yesterday."

"Yes?"

Wolf held her gaze. "The tap root and half the roots on the other side of the tree had been sawed through. Did you know that?"

His words sunk in, and Sarah gasped. "Someone deliberately sawed through those roots?"

Sarah folded her arms defensively against her breasts as Wolf nodded confirmation. "Summers," she bit out. "It was that bastard Summers! He sent some of his hired guns up there to do it.'' She closed her eyes, suddenly feeling very alone and afraid.

Wolf forced himself to pay attention to his driving. ''Look, I'm filing a police report on this with the sheriff's office, Sarah. Something has to be done about it. Before, I figured you were blowing things with Summers out of proportion.'' His straight black brows dipped. ''Now I know you aren't.''

''Sheriff Noonan will circular-file your report, just like he did mine on my dad's murder, Wolf.''

The sound of Sarah saying his name moved through Wolf like a heated wave, thawing his once-frozen emotions. ''You're paranoid, but in some ways, after looking at what someone did to that tree, I don't blame you.'' And then, trying to lighten the darkness he saw in her fearful eyes, he said, ''I kinda grow on people like moss on a rock. This week at the house won't be too bad on you.'' He desperately wanted Sarah to believe he could help her through this period. But could he? He didn't know. He'd failed before—and a life had been lost. But as he stared over at Sarah, painfully aware of her situation, Wolf knew he'd never wanted to protect anyone more.

Sarah sighed, fighting the emotions his gruff kindness aroused in her. ''When are you going to file the report?''

''Tonight. I'll get you comfortable at the house, then drive up to your cabin. My last stop will be at the sheriff's office.''

The news of the cut roots had shattered Sarah, although she fought to appear calm. She not only felt the fear, she could taste it. Summers was out to get her claim—one way or another. Never had she felt so nakedly alone. But Wolf's voice was a balm to her raw nerves. His nearness enforced a sense of safety she desperately knew she needed, even as she struggled against it. With a shake of her head, Sarah muttered, "I'd just never have believed a stranger would come into Philipsburg and help me out so much." She looked deep into his gray eyes. "Are you sure there isn't a reason why you're doing this?"

Wolf didn't want to think about reasons. Was it to atone for—to somehow try to change—what had happened in South America? Could he really help Sarah? Even as he wrestled with his own uncertainty, Wolf still saw clearly that if he didn't reach out to help her, Sarah would be in even more immediate danger. He tried to smile to reassure her. "Like I said before—I'm Cherokee, and we'll open our homes to a stranger who needs help."

Sarah stared out the window of the truck, not convinced by Wolf's explanation. She sensed that there was more that he hadn't said. She saw the turmoil in his eyes, and felt the sudden tension around him. Wolf was an enigma, hiding behind something she couldn't identify—yet.

Frustrated, Sarah forced her focus to the town they were driving through. Philipsburg was a small, hundred-year-old silver-mining town that had gone bust. The streets were narrow but paved. Most of the buildings were of wood-frame construction, not more than two stories tall. Many needed a coat of paint from weathering the harsh Montana winters where the wind swept down off the rugged Rockies and through the small valley.

On Broadway, at the edge of the town, they pulled up in front of a yellow one-story house. Red geraniums lined the walk, but the grass was predominantly brown, in dire need of water because of the scorching summer heat. Wooden stairs led up to a wide, screened porch with a swing. Wolf turned off the truck engine and motioned to the house.

"We're home."

The words sounded so good that Sarah's throat tightened. Once she'd had a home. And two parents. Now she lived in an empty cabin. The loneliness of the past six months cut through her. Sarah's imagination caught fire, and she wondered what it would be like to wait for Wolf to come home every night.

"Yes," she whispered, her voice cracking. "We're home."

Chapter Four

"Ranger Harding, I think you're making a mountain out of a molehill." Sheriff Kerwin Noonan eased back in the creaking leather chair and held Wolf's opaque stare.

"Aren't you interested in who sabotaged Sarah Thatcher's mining claim? You know, if I hadn't taken a wrong turn and gone down that road, she could have died out there." Wolf was quickly getting the impression that Noonan abused his power. He had a cockiness, a know-it-all attitude, that automatically rubbed Wolf the wrong way. He had to struggle to keep his voice neutral and hide his mounting anger.

Noonan stroked his steel-gray mustache. "Sarah's always been a precocious thing, Harding. I watched her grow up from a skinny kid who was always in trouble and fighting with someone at school into a young woman who still had axes to grind. She ain't got the sense God gave a goose, jumpin' at shadows and accusin' Mr. Summers.'' With a shrug, Noonan added, "She's always been a troublemaker. If you're smart, you won't get mixed up with her.''

Wolf dropped his written report on Noonan's cluttered desk. The jail was quiet, with only a lone drunk in one of the two cells. "I don't think," Wolf said softly, "that Ms. Thatcher's personality has anything to do with the fact that someone sawed through those roots. She certainly didn't do it to herself.''

Eyeing the report, Noonan sighed. "All right, Ranger, I'll look into it. But I can tell you right now—ain't nothin' gonna come from my investigation. She pulled the same stunt when her daddy blew himself up with that box of dynamite in the back of his pickup. That girl came loose at the hinges, a wild banshee swearin' up and down that Mr. Summers had murdered him. Well, wasn't no such thing. Thatcher blew himself to smithereens all by himself. Pure and simple.''

"I'm interested in anything you find, Sheriff," Wolf said, settling his hat back on his head.

"How's the girl doin'?''

It was obvious to Wolf that Noonan didn't respect women. Nor, plainly, did he see Sarah as the woman she had become. "She's going to be on crutches for a week.''

Noonan's eyebrows rose a bit. "Too bad. I suppose she's heading back to her cabin out there in the middle of nowhere?''

Wolf shook his head. "No, I've offered her a place to stay until she can get mobile again. The doctor wants her off her feet for a while.''

"Harding, the town'll talk.''

"Let them.''

"Your landlady, Mrs. Wilson, won't take kindly to that sort of arrangement."

Giving him a flat stare, Wolf said, "The only arrangement Ms. Thatcher has with me is that I've offered her a roof over her head and some food to eat."

With a grin, Noonan nodded his head. "Just remember, Harding—you've got a wildcat living under the same roof with you. Better watch it, or she'll turn around and bite the hell out of you. Anybody who gets mixed up with her is courtin' big trouble."

Wolf said nothing, turning on his heel and leaving the small, cramped jail facility. Sarah's paranoia about people in general—and especially strangers like himself— was becoming more understandable all the time. No wonder she feared trusting anyone but herself. What the hell had happened to her? Grimly he walked back out to the forestry pickup, where Skeet was waiting in the cab. He'd already picked up Sarah's clothes—what there was of them.

She'd also had him pick up some of her lapidary equipment. There was a large grinding machine with several wheels attached that would polish a stone to perfection. And the faceting machine, about as large as a dinner plate, with a round, movable surface, would allow her to continue working and bringing in some income while she stayed off her feet. Faceting was easy, she'd assured him.

As he'd moved through her cabin, collecting her few belongings, the financial deprivation Sarah suffered became very clear to Wolf. She hadn't embellished the reality of her situation.

Driving out of the parking lot, Wolf headed home. How good that word sounded to him. *Home*. Having Sarah there made it seem like one. Wolf couldn't hide from the fact that for many years he'd dreamed about a home and a family. But his life had veered off in another direction, one that he'd never forget, not until the day he died.

Twilight washed Philipsburg in an apricot hue as the sun dipped behind the mountains. The orange color softened the aging Victorian buildings, built during the silver and copper boomtown period so many years before. It was a town that had relied on mining to keep it alive. Now that the mining, for all intents and purposes, had been stolen from the earth and sold, Philipsburg had died. But, like many towns Wolf had seen, this one was resurrecting itself slowly, one new building at a time, because of tourism and Montana's nationwide reputation as a hunter's and fisherman's paradise.

With a grimace, Wolf thought how his own life paralleled that of the town. So much of him had died down in South America. The rebuilding had barely begun. Taking leave from Perseus had been the first step. Wolf knew instinctively that Sarah was touching the new, emerging chords within him as a man, touching his soul in some wonderful yet undefined way.

Perhaps it was the wildness Noonan had accused Sarah of that appealed to his primal nature, the part of him that, although wounded, had survived. Wolf didn't really perceive Sarah as wild. She'd merely used her instincts to survive—just as he had done.

Hope sprang in his heart, new and fragile. Sarah was untamed, and that excited him. He'd seen too many women beaten down, submissive beneath men's needs and society's expectations. Somehow, Sarah had not conformed in the way most women did.

His mouth was set in a grim line as he turned down the street that would lead him to the house. The price

Sarah had paid thus far for not bowing under pressure had been heavy. Did the other townspeople feel as Noonan did about her? If so, Sarah had been an outcast all her life, and the thought tore at Wolf's emotions.

Then, at the thought of seeing her, his heart began to beat a little harder in his chest. The feeling was delicious, and he savored it like a man starved too long for emotional sustenance. How long had it been since he'd felt these gentle tendrils take root to remind him of a less harsh and demanding world? He frowned. Could he afford to let himself get close?

Sarah heard the key in the lock and sat up tensely on the overstuffed couch. Her swollen feet rested on an upholstered stool. It was 6:00 p.m.—and Wolf had said he'd be home later. Was it him, or one of Summers's henchmen? Her breath caught as the door opened and Wolf entered, his height and build making the doorway look small in comparison. The instant his gaze met hers, she saw an incredible change come over his face. The thin line of his mouth softened perceptibly. The fatigue in his gray eyes lifted, replaced by something warm that made her feel welcome in his home. Relaxation replaced harshness. She gave him a nervous half smile of welcome.

"See? I'm being a good patient," she offered. "My feet are up where you told me to keep them."

Wolf grinned as he closed the door and ambled into the small living room. The couch was a boring beige, but he'd thrown a quilt made by his grandmother across the back of it. The colors woven into it were red, blue, yellow and black, to denote the major directions as seen by the Cherokee. It made the room come alive with vibrancy.

"Why do I get the feeling that you hobbled over and put your feet up two minutes before I arrived?"

Sarah's uneasiness increased. "Are you psychic or something?" she croaked.

Wolf placed his keys on the cherrywood desk and dropped his hat on top of them. "I've been accused of being that from time to time."

"You're downright scary."

"So I'm right?" he asked, coming over and halting beside her. Sarah's hair was plaited in two long braids, and the style suited her. Her cheeks, once waxen, were flushed, and she fiddled nervously with her fingers in her lap. Disappointment flowed through Wolf. Sarah still didn't trust him.

"I can't lie," she said softly. "Yes, I was hobbling around here a couple of minutes before you pulled up."

"So why bother to look like you'd been following my orders?" he teased, starting to grin.

His melting smile seemed to embrace Sarah, and she suddenly felt beautiful beneath his searching, hooded gaze. Wolf was making her hotly aware for the first time in her life, that she was a woman. She saw the interest in his eyes—and the discovery as exciting as it was scary. Sarah had no experience with a man like Wolf. "I guess I didn't want to disappoint you." And then, disgusted by the admission, she muttered defensively, "I don't know."

"Well," Wolf told her, "I appreciate it. I was worrying all day you'd be resting and bored out of your mind."

"I wasn't *that* good."

Wolf lifted his chin and looked around. He noticed that small things, such as the vase full of wildflowers, had been moved slightly. "You dusted."

Sarah wrinkled her nose. "I can't stand a dirty house." Then she quickly amended herself. "I just picked up here and there, tried a little vacuuming, that was all. Your house really isn't dirty."

"Just messy," Wolf agreed. He tilted his head when he saw the wariness come back in her eyes. "What's that look for?"

"Aren't you going to chew me out for doing all that walking around?"

"Why should I? I'm not your keeper. Everyone's responsible for themselves."

"You mean that?" Sarah's gaze probed his laughter-filled gray eyes.

"Sometimes. The Cherokee part of me believes it thoroughly. My white side doesn't."

"I hate men who treat me like a half-wit," Sarah agreed. "Just because I have blond hair doesn't mean I'm dumb or helpless."

"I'd never make the mistake of thinking that," Wolf said wryly. "Hungry?"

"Starved." Sarah was suddenly eager to share the evening with Wolf. There was so much she didn't know about him, and so much she wanted to know. She'd had time alone to feel her way through her reactions to Wolf. All her life she'd been wearing male clothes, and she worked in a male occupation. No one had ever really looked at her as a woman until she'd seen that awareness in Wolf's eyes. He seemed to delve beyond the clothes she wore and the way she made a living to truly see the woman she was. That realization aroused something in Sarah, and she wanted to explore Wolf further, curiosity driving her as never before.

"How about a steak, a baked potato and a salad?"

Wolf asked over his shoulder as he headed for the kitchen.

Sarah grabbed her crutches. "Finc with me. I'll eat anything."

Wolf turned. "Why don't you sit and rest?" He noticed at the entrance to the kitchen that not only had Sarah done his three days' worth of dishes, but the counter was shining, and the table was neat and clean.

"I don't sit or rest very well." Sarah placed the crutches beneath her arms and followed him out to the kitchen. Wolf's bulk seemed to fill the room. She sat down at the table, resting the crutches against the wall. There was something pleasant in just watching him move about the kitchen. Despite his size, he had a catlike grace, never bumping into things the way she did.

"I called over to the nursing home and checked in with the supervisor," Sarah told him. "They know I'm going to be laid up and won't expect me to visit Mom this week."

Wolf glanced over his shoulder as he placed two huge potatoes in the microwave. "Did they tell your mother what happened to you?"

"No," Sarah whispered. "She won't even miss me not being there."

The pain, her pain, stabbed at him. Wolf closed the microwave door and took two steaks from the refrigerator. "Doesn't she recognize you even a little bit?"

"No. Usually when I visit her she reacts to me as if I'm a stranger."

"That must be hard on you." Wolf turned, seeing the hurt in her huge blue eyes.

"Yes...it is...."

Placing the steaks in an iron skillet, Wolf turned up the gas flame on the stove. "My mother died of a heart

attack. I guess in some ways we were lucky. She died
instantly.'' Wolf caught himself. He never spoke about
his past or his family. Perplexed, fighting an inner battle
to remain detached from Sarah, Wolf castigated himself.
Just one look at her and all his intentions melted like ice
beneath sunlight.

"How old were you?" she asked softly.

Uncomfortable, he muttered, "Twelve."

"Oh, dear." Her heart twinged with pain—his pain.
Wolf knew loss. That was why he could understand her.
Her determination never to trust anyone softened even
more as she watched him working over the stove.

Wolf turned when he heard the tone of her voice.
Sarah looked so unhappy that the urge to sweep her into
his arms and hold her tightly against him was nearly
overwhelming. "That was a long time ago," he told her
gruffly. "Save your feelings for someone who counts."

Sarah scowled as he quickly turned away again, busy-
ing himself with kitchen duties. "As if you don't
count," she muttered. "Who rescued me from under that
tree? And took me in for a week because I couldn't
afford the hospital? You count a lot in my book."

The fervency in her voice broke through another painful barrier in Wolf. He turned and mercilessly met her
soft blue gaze. "Honey," he growled, anger vibrating in
his voice, anger aimed at himself, "I'm not worth caring
about. I'm no one's ideal."

Sarah winced at the cold blade of anger in his voice.
Why was Wolf so down on himself? Hurt by his unex-
plained harshness, Sarah sourly reminded herself that
they weren't friends. Friends could confide in one another. Still, curiosity ate at her, and she choked out,
"You're a man with a lot of secrets, aren't you?"

Wolf's scowl deepened. Panic surged through him.

Sarah unerringly sensed that he was hiding a great deal from her. Well, wasn't he? Hell, he was desperately trying to hide it from himself. His voice was clipped with warning as he retorted, "You've got the curiosity of a cat."

"And that isn't going to stop me from finding out why you think so little of yourself," she answered steadily.

Wolf's gut tightened, and he tasted fear. "If you're doing it for curiosity's sake, don't try and unlock me." Wolf stared at her, the challenge in his gaze backed up by the growl in his voice. "I don't play those kinds of games with anyone."

Sarah gave him a tight smile, feeling shaky and euphoric at the same time. The potential thrill of knowing Wolf on a more intimate level was exciting, despite her fear. Sarah felt as if she were walking on a high wire, far above the ground. One small misstep with Wolf and she'd fall to her death—only it wasn't a physical death, but an emotional one. Her curiosity warred with the knowledge of potential danger. Despite her head's warning, her heart demanded to know his terrible secret. "Haven't you noticed yet? I don't play games, either."

"No," Wolf admitted in a rasp, "you don't." He stood at the counter, afraid. Afraid that Sarah was going to gut him of his past.

Sarah felt a bristling kind of power throbbing around Wolf, and decided to back off—for now. "Speaking of games, which one did Sheriff Noonan try to play with you?"

Wolf felt incredibly vulnerable in Sarah's presence. He sensed her tenacity, her determination to reach the very heart of his dark soul. He sighed silently to himself, grateful that she had switched to a more benign topic.

Returning his attention to the stove, he checked the steaks.

"Noonan didn't take my report seriously."

Sarah nodded, feeling a palpable release of the tension that had been building between them, but still wondering why Wolf had gotten so tense and angry. "I figured as much. He never does," she muttered.

"Why?"

"He's on Summers's payroll, that's why. Noonan's a banty rooster, full of himself, strutting around because he's got police power behind him. The folks around here won't buck him." She added grimly, "But I have and will."

Going to the refrigerator, Wolf pulled out salad makings. He divided his time between cutting up vegetables and watching Sarah's darkened face. "What's going on here, Sarah? The sheriff accused you in so many words of being a troublemaker since the day you were born."

"As far as he's concerned, I have been. Wolf, you don't appreciate what I keep telling you—Summers runs this town. Those that are against him are too scared to challenge him."

"Except for you?" Wolf guessed, pleased at the way his name rolled off her lips, low and husky.

"There were others," Sarah admitted unhappily, "but they've moved away. They got tired of butting heads with the bastard."

"And you stayed? Why?"

Sarah idly watched Wolf cut up the carrots. Despite the large size of his hands, he was incredibly skillful, handling the knife with ease. "I'm a fourth-generation Thatcher, that's why. All my family is buried up on the hill behind town. Four generations of my family have given their lives to this life, Wolf. I love this place."

Her voice grew low with emotion. "I love the mountains and the mining. My dad switched from silver to sapphire mining when things went bust around here. Montana is one of the few places in North America where you can find gem-quality sapphires that rival the best in the world."

Wolf set the table, placing the bowls of salad on it. "I never knew anything about sapphire mining."

With a shrug, Sarah leaned over and picked up a small leaf of lettuce and munched on it. "Montana sapphires have the same cornflower-blue color as the ones in Sri Lanka do." When she saw he didn't understand, she added, "Sapphires come in a lot of colors—bright orange, pink, red, green, blue, white and yellow. The ones worth the most money are the dark cornflower-blue ones. The red stones are known as rubies. Corundum is the material they're both made from."

"I didn't realize sapphires came in that many colors."

"Most people don't, because the jewelry industry has pushed blue ones on the public for the last fifty years."

"What do you do with the other colors?" Wolf pulled the baked potatoes out of the microwave and deftly set them on the two plates. Sarah sat at the table, nibbling at her salad and looking as if she belonged there. The sudden thought was heated, filled with promise, but quickly, Wolf pushed the longing away. He wasn't worthy of someone like Sarah.

"You saw all my lapidary equipment when you picked up my faceting machine?"

"Yes."

"My dad taught me how to facet when I was a kid. I facet all the sapphires I find, then sell them to a national gem distributor. He takes the colored sapphires, too.

They become background gemstones in individual pieces of jewelry.''

''Sounds like you could make a lot of money.'' Wolf brought the skillet over and transferred the steaks onto their plates. After setting the skillet in the sink and filling it with water, he joined Sarah at the table.

Sarah hungrily dug into the succulent steak, which Wolf had cooked perfectly. ''That's the rub. The miner gets very little money. It's the middleman, the distributor, who really makes a killing on the sapphires. You have to remember, most of the gemstones aren't of the highest quality. A lot of them have inclusions or fractures, that lower their value. To make good money, I'd have to find a ten- or fifteen-carat sapphire with very few inclusions.'' She smiled across the table at her. ''That hasn't happened yet.''

''It will,'' Wolf promised her. He was starving. Starving for Sarah's bright, spontaneous company. Her enthusiasm was a new side of herself that she was allowing him to see. There was no wariness in her lovely blue eyes now, and for a moment Wolf allowed himself to wonder what Sarah would be like if she let that passionate intensity she held for sapphires to translate into emotions she could share with him.

Chortling, Sarah said, ''You're psychic, so I'll believe you.''

''But you're able to mine enough gems to pay your bills?''

''That's right. But I have to keep at it, Wolf.'' She frowned. ''Being off my feet for seven days is really going to hurt me. The money I had saved went for that damned hospital bill.''

Wolf said nothing, his conscience smarting. ''Why has Noonan got it in for you?''

Sarah poured Italian dressing on her salad. "When I was in high school, I got Rickey Noonan, his only son, in big trouble. Rickey was pushing drugs, Wolf. The sheriff's son. Can you believe it?"

"Honey, there isn't much in this world I haven't seen in twenty-eight years of living. I believe you."

Every time Wolf used the endearment, a giddy sensation flowed through Sarah. She forced herself not to stare at him. What kind of magic did Wolf have over her? She struggled constantly to resist his powerful, quiet charisma. Dismayed at her inability to control her responses to him, she frowned and said, "Rickey was a bully in high school because of his father's power. He talked my best friend, Jody Collins, into taking drugs. Jody tried to commit suicide and I found her just in time. After that, I was so cotton-picking mad that I swore I'd get all drug pushers out of our school. I called the FBI and told them what was going on."

Wolf's eyes widened. "You went to the FBI?"

Indignantly, Sarah said, "Sure! Wouldn't you, if you knew the whole town's legal system was rotten to the core?" Sarah saw his mouth twitch with amusement. "Wolf, it wasn't funny at the time. I was seventeen and scared to death. I didn't even tell my parents what I was doing because I was afraid Noonan would get even. The FBI came and caught Rickey and his gang dead to rights. But when it was all over and done with, my name accidentally got dragged in to it. From that moment on, Noonan had it in for me."

"Did he hassle your parents?" Wolf watched her lick her buttery fingers after wrestling with the baked potato. There was something beautifully sensual and basic about Sarah, and the thought sent an ache surging through him.

"Noonan went after me first. I'd just gotten my

driver's license, and his deputies pulled me over so many times for supposedly speeding that I just quit driving.''

"What did he do to your dad?"

Sarah sighed and pushed her plate away. She'd lost her appetite. "Noonan conspired with Summers, and they went into cahoots,'' she said grimly. "Summers wanted our claim because the majority of our sapphires are the cornflower blue variety. You can take a clear or very light-colored sapphire and heat-treat it to turn it cornflower blue."

"Heat-treat it?"

"Yes, there's a special thermal oven. You put the rough, unfaceted stones in and literally bake them, like a cake, at a certain temperature for a certain length of time to improve and deepen their color."

Wolf shook his head. "Obviously there's a lot to gemstones that I didn't know."

Sarah nodded. "I grew up with it, so I take it for granted. I'm sure if the public knew how many gemstones were heat-treated, they'd be shocked."

"What does heat-treating do to them beside make them a darker blue?"

She gave him a smile. "You ask the right questions."

"In my line of work, my life depended on it," he murmured. Now where did that come from, Wolf wondered. Sarah's mere presence had him revealing pieces of himself. He saw her eyes widen—saw that curiosity burning in them. Before she could ask, he added, "So what does baking do to the sapphires?"

Sarah desperately wanted to pursue his statement. What line of work? But she saw the warning in his eyes and swallowed her curiosity. "It makes them far more brittle than their untreated cousins. For instance, if a woman accidentally banged her sapphire ring on something, it could crack or possibly shatter.''

"So an untreated sapphire is tougher? Less likely to crack?''

"Exactly," Sarah said, pleased with Wolf's quick grasp of her business. "If a gem distributor doesn't have high principles, he'll often pass on heat-treated sapphires along with untreated ones and not tell the jeweler.''

She opened her hands. "There's a lot of difference between jewelers, based on their gem knowledge and experience. They're only as good as their training, Wolf. I've taken courses with the Gemological Institute of America over the years and caught up with what the unscrupulous gem dealers do to gemstones. A lot of jewelers can't afford to get that kind of schooling. It takes money and time to educate and keep up with the guys who would sell you red glass and make you think it was a ruby. Some jewelers can afford the expensive equipment it takes to examine each stone—if you look at it under a microscope, you can see whether a stone's been heat-treated.''

"Fascinating," Wolf murmured.

With a mirthful laugh, Sarah nodded. "If only people who bought gemstones realized some of the things that went on, they'd be a lot more inclined to educate themselves before they bought a stone, believe me. That and question their jeweler about his or her experience and training.''

"So your mine produces more of the industry-standard color, and that's why Summers wants it?''

"Exactly. For some reason, our land had the right chemistry conditions when the sapphires were forming, millions of years ago, and so they tended to clump on that side of the mountain in that deep blue color. Summers is smart enough to know that he can't pass heat-treated stones on to his distributors without telling them.''

''So he's looking at your mine as a source of the higher-paying sapphires?''

''Yes. I get more money per point on the facets of my stones than he does. Heat-treated sapphires are worth less—at least from miner to distributor. Once they hit the retail market, unsuspecting customers could be charged the same amount of money, regardless. Although a good jeweler will use heat-treated stones in a setting like a brooch, pendant or necklace, instead of in a ring, where it's likely to get struck or hit, and will charge less, accordingly.''

''Fascinating.'' Wolf saw her worrying the flesh of her lower lip. ''So when did Summers start wanting your land?''

''About ten years ago. He had some of his hired guns come over and break up our mining equipment. When Dad refused to sell or back down, they beat him up—and again a couple of times after that.''

Wolf saw the fear lurking in Sarah's eyes. ''What else happened?'' he probed softly.

Nervously Sarah muttered, ''They ran my dad off the road, trying to make him wreck. When that didn't work, they broke into our cabin and scared the hell out of my mom. She's a real gentle soul, Wolf, nothing like me. I have my dad's genes. I'm a fighter, and I don't back down when trouble's staring me in the face. Over the years, Summers continued to hassle us. Once he had his men steal all our lapidary equipment. It cost thousands of dollars, money we didn't have, to replace it.''

Wolf set his plate aside. ''What did Summers do to you?''

Squirming in her chair, Sarah whispered, "After Dad died, six months ago, they started putting real pressure on me. A couple of his men showed up dressed up like forest rangers. They knew I carried a rifle with me everywhere I went. I've been known to fire over their heads if I catch them around our property. They disguised themselves so I'd trust them."

Grimly Wolf folded his hands against his chin. "That's why you were so leery of me."

"No kidding. I didn't recognize you, and Summers hires men from out of state to do his dirty work. I'd fallen for the forest-ranger trick once, and wasn't about to fall for it again."

Wolf's throat tightened with barely held emotions. "What happened?"

Refusing to look over at him, Sarah said, "I'm ashamed to talk about it. I mean, I was so stupid, so naive, when they walked into camp. Rangers are around fairly often, since the mine sits in the national forest. I didn't think anything of them coming for a visit...."

Without thinking, Wolf reached over and gripped her clasped hands on the table. He saw the shame in her eyes, and he couldn't stand aside and not try to ease her discomfort. No one should suffer alone. Her head snapped up and he saw the devastation in her features. "Sarah," he told her quietly, "you can tell me."

His hand was rough and calloused on hers. Sarah was wildly aware of Wolf's warmth and strength. It drove tears into her eyes, and she quickly bowed her head. "I'm still angry about it. I believed those two, and let them in my camp. Anyway, they got close enough to haul me out from beneath the roots of this fir I was working under by the scruff of my neck. My blouse ripped..." Sarah shut her eyes. Her voice was low and off-key. She couldn't stand to know what Wolf thought of the next admission. Forcing herself, she whispered, "I—I fought them. They pinned me down."

Automatically his hand tightened around her small ones. Fury, cold and biting, wound through Wolf. Sarah's voice was wobbling, and her skin had gone damp. His mouth grew dry. Terrible scenes from his past blipped in front of him as he held Sarah's wide, frightened eyes. "Did they…rape you?"

Sarah shook her head, still refusing to look up at Wolf. "No. I made a grab for my prospector's hammer and swung it as hard as I could at the guy who had pinned me. It knocked him out for a second. When he let go, I scrambled up. Once I was on my feet, the second guy took off running. By the time I got to my rifle, they'd both hightailed it out of the area."

"When did this happen?"

"Three months ago."

Wolf released a shaky breath, feeling perspiration collect on his brow. He consciously forced himself to relax. "No wonder you didn't trust me."

Sarah lifted her lashes just enough to risk looking at his features. There was harsh anger in his thundercloud-gray eyes, and the fury was translated into the gravelly snarl in his voice. "I survived," she said quietly. "That's what counted."

The urge to gather Sarah into his arms and protect her nearly undid Wolf. He gently squeezed her fingers, then reluctantly released them. A flashback overcame him: He was walking into the village, seeing the dead and dying, hearing the screams of unprotected children and the cries of women. He squeezed his eyes shut. "No," he managed to say hoarsely. He shook his head, forcing the memory away. "There's more than just surviving something like that, Sarah. A hell of a lot more."

The rawness of Wolf's voice forced Sarah to make eye contact with him. Something tragic, something terrible, had happened to him. His face was twisted with pain, and his eyes were filled with such anguish and understanding that tears leaked out of hers.

"Then, I don't know what it is," she whispered, self-consciously wiping the tears off her cheeks. "I survived. I'm alive."

Wolf sat back, wrestling with an array of unexpected emotions from the past that were now coupled to the present. "Women and children who've been victimized wear the scars for the rest of their lives, Sarah, unless something's done to help them undo the trauma."

Tilting her head, she held his gray gaze, which was still dark with tortured secrets. "Ever since it happened, I've been really jumpy," she admitted.

"I'm sure. Do you get nightmares?"

Sarah hesitated, the need to share her worst fears with Wolf outdistancing her usual shell of self-defense. "Yes...sometimes.... Usually, I can't get to sleep." She gave a small shrug and looked away. "It's stupid. I see their shadows on the walls in my bedroom. I'll just be falling asleep, and I'll see them moving toward me."

Wolf nodded. He knew the litany all too well. "Insomnia, nightmares, and a special kind of wariness."

"I call it animal awareness. My hearing's sharper now—my senses are alive like never before since it happened," Sarah said. She rubbed her arms, suddenly chilled.

Wolf frowned and slowly got to his feet. "Let's get those feet of yours soaked in warm water and ice-pack them before you go to bed," he said gruffly. He didn't want to talk any more about violence. He walked toward the counter, a terrible sinking feeling stalking him as he realized that he hadn't been able to escape what had happened in South America. It was here, all over again, right in front of him. The place was different—and the names—but the situation was all too familiar.

Wolf rested his hands against the counter and bowed his head, feeling torn apart inside. Sarah, so small and spunky, had more backbone, more guts, than he did. She hadn't run. He had. A wrenching sigh tore from him. What was he going to do? Run again? Leave Sarah to fight her battle alone?

"Wolf? What's wrong?"

He shook his head. "Nothing."

Sarah slowly got to her feet with the help of the crutches. She swung herself to the counter, a few feet from him. Although she could see only his harsh, unforgiving profile, the set of his mouth shouted of some inner pain he was carrying within him like a living thing. "Look, my troubles and problems are my own. You don't have to take them on—or even get involved. I really appreciate you giving me a place to heal for a week, but you don't owe me anything." With a little laugh, Sarah added, "I owe you, if the truth be known. You saved my life and gave me care when no one else would."

Something old and hurting snapped within Wolf. He turned to her, his breathing harsh. "This time," he gritted out, "I'm not running. Sorry, Sarah, but you're stuck with me. We're going to push Summers and Noonan until they get the message to leave you and your mine alone."

Sarah's lips parted beneath the vehemence in his

voice, the agony and anger in his eyes. "But...why? I'm nothing to you."

"You don't understand. I don't expect you to. Once, a woman gave me a place to heal, and I paid her back by failing her." Sarah's eyes grew huge, and he held up his hand. "I don't want to talk about it, Sarah. I can't ever go back and change the past, but I can change the present for the future. I'm being given a second chance, and I'll be damned if I'm going to fail this time. No, you're stuck with me for the duration, whether you like me or not. We'll find out who did this to you, and we'll bring them to justice."

Sarah stared up at him. The vibrating emotion coming out of Wolf made her want to cry—not for herself, but for him. She was right: Something awful and terrifying had happened to him, to those he cared for. Swallowing, she gave a jerky nod of her head. "Okay, I can use the help. I can't pay you..."

Wolf managed a twisted smile that didn't reach his eyes. "Honey, you don't owe me a thing, and never will. By Cherokee tradition, this situation is seen as a test. I failed the first time. Now the Grandparents are giving me a second chance." Softly he added, "And I'm not going to blow it this time, not this time...."

Chapter Five

Shaken by the intensity of their conversation, Sarah placed the crutches aside and awkwardly moved to the kitchen sink. She saw Wolf frown, his gray eyes turning molten with concern, and it unstrung her badly.

"What do you think you're going to do?" he demanded.

"Wash dishes before I soak my feet."

"No way. You can't stay on your feet that long." Wolf grabbed her arm before he could think what he was doing. Sarah's skin felt firm and velvety beneath his grasp, and he froze.

With a gasp, Sarah stared up at him. His hand seemed to brand her where it touched her arm. Never had she been more vividly aware of herself as a woman. Her heart beating erratically, she felt the burning heat of his stormy gaze upon her. The longing she felt was so intense that it took her breath away, and she was drowning, mesmerized by the changing color of his eyes, with all her being, Sarah felt Wolf's need of her.

The discovery was molten. Unconsciously she swayed forward, and at the same moment, excruciating pain shot up both her legs. With a little cry, she tried to grab something, anything, to take the pressure off her injured feet and ankles. Instantly Wolf's arms went around her and she felt the shock of his strong, unyielding body meeting the softer curves of her own. Her eyes shuttered closed as the pain swept upward, making her light-headed. Sarah allowed herself, for the first time in a long time, to lean against a man. Only Wolf wasn't just any man. She knew that as surely as she could feel her heart pounding in her breast.

Her cheek pressed against the fabric of his shirt, Sarah heard the drumlike beating of Wolf's heart. The smell of him, a man who worked in the fragrant pine forest she loved so much, was Sarah's undoing. Absorbing his male strength, the care of his arms as they swept around her, she surrendered to him in every way—if only for a brief moment. As he held her snugly against him, a small sigh escaped her lips. How long had she gone without any support? Just this once, her heart pleaded with her, let someone else help. Let someone else care.

Wolf released a groan as Sarah collapsed against him. Instantly he realized what had happened. His surprise at her surrender was followed by a massive desire to protect her that tunneled up through him as she sagged against him. She was so small—small and strong at the same time. He felt her capitulation to him, stunned by it, euphoric over it.

For just that moment spun out of time and reality, Wolf allowed Sarah to rest against him. Knowing her past, knowing how strong she'd had to be for so long, he understood her need to lean on him. But it was more than that, as he savored her lithe form. He could feel the birdlike beating of her heart, wildly aware of her small breasts pressed to his chest, of her slender arms moving around his waist.

He inhaled her womanly scent, deeply, raggedly. The memory of a woman seared him, and, fighting himself, he leaned down and pressed his lips to Sarah's sunlight-colored hair. The strands were thin and fine, like her. He could smell the fragrance of her shampoo, the fragrance of her as a woman, and it shattered his efforts to remain detached.

"Sarah...no..." he growled, and gripped her arms. Gently he pushed her away from him and reached for her crutches. It was the last thing in the world he wanted to do. He saw her head snap up, saw her pain-filled eyes widen with shock, then hurt. He knew she wouldn't understand why he was breaking their embrace.

"No..." he said, trying to soften the growl in his voice as he helped her place the crutches beneath her arms. Helplessly he watched as a flush stained Sarah's features. A huge part of him wanted to tell her the truth, the awful, sordid truth. But what would that do? Only make her see him as he saw himself. Bitterness coated his mouth, and he lifted his hands.

Humiliated, Sarah realized she should never have tried to walk without the aid of her crutches. Pain throbbed through her feet, and she felt stupid. "I'm sorry..."

"Don't be," he rasped.

Sarah touched her brow, dizzied at having unexpectedly found herself in Wolf's arms then abruptly pushed away. In his eyes she saw anger, mixed with the fire of longing, and she became confused. If only she had more experience with men, maybe she could understand what was going on between them. She'd seen the need for her in his eyes. She was sure of it! So why had he shooed her away?

Sarah gripped the crutches more tightly, unable to look up at Wolf, mortified by her own weakness. She had reached out to him trustingly....

"I'm going to go watch some television," she muttered as she moved past him. More than anything, she didn't want Wolf to apologize. It was humiliating enough to be rejected. She didn't want him adding to her shame by mouthing some inane reason for not wanting to hold her.

Scowling, Wolf watched Sarah hobble out of the kitchen. Her head was down, the golden sheet of her hair hiding her expression, but he'd heard the pain in her voice, and it made him feel worse than ever. Closing his fists, he railed at himself for his mistake. His protective side was working overtime with Sarah.

Sarah was far from helpless, he realized harshly. Because of the past, he was overreacting. There was a big difference between Sarah and Maria. But the situation, the danger, was the same. Glumly Wolf moved to the table. He'd told Sarah she wasn't a housekeeper, and he'd meant it.

His conscience smarting, Wolf cleared the table and began to wash the dishes. He could hear the television in the next room—the national news was on—but his heart centered on Sarah. He shouldn't have pushed her away so quickly. He'd hurt her, sending her the wrong message. The past was looming over the present, and Wolf didn't know how to handle the turmoil of emotions raging within him. He was projecting onto Sarah all the pain and failure of his past. It wasn't her problem, he reminded himself tersely. She had enough problems of her own.

With a shake of his head, Wolf concentrated on the dishes. Somehow, the drudgery of the duty soothed some of his fluctuating emotions. Still, he wondered how Sarah was feeling. He tried to block from his memory the awful expression of loss on her face when he'd forced her from his embrace. His mouth tightened. If only he'd been more guarded, more alert.

Closing his eyes, his hands in the warm, soapy water, Wolf realized for the first time that Sarah liked him. Why else would she have willingly fallen into his embrace instead of reaching for the counter or her crutches when her legs gave way? Then his mind—that cold blade of reality—reminded him that maybe Sarah was just feeling emotionally torn apart from sharing her traumatic past. Maybe she'd merely needed a haven, a set of arms to hide in for just a moment, and it had had nothing to do with liking him in a personal or intimate sense.

As he stood there feeling his way through the situation, his heart gently informed him that Sarah liked him a lot more than either he or she honestly realized. Wolf had always had good sense about people—until recently. Now he no longer dared trust the instincts that had always kept him in harmony with himself and the world around him. Peru had proven that his senses, his understanding, were faulty. People had died—*he'd* nearly died—because he'd believed he knew what to do and blindly acted on it.

Sarah had just as blindly acted upon her need to be held, and he'd denied her that safe harbor. Wolf silently chastised himself. Sarah deserved someone a hell of a lot better than him. Why had he been placed in her life?

Swallowing hard, Wolf forced himself to finish the dishes. Somehow he had to apologize to Sarah, to make her understand it wasn't her he was rejecting—it was himself.

In an effort to break the tension strung between them, Sarah asked Wolf to set her faceting machine up out on the porch. They worked out on the porch for nearly an hour after the dishes were done. Sarah sat at the small wooden table where her faceting machine had been placed and plugged in. She was nervous in Wolf's presence. The message he'd given her was that she wasn't worthy of him—as a woman—and it left a very real hurt in her heart. Yet he had been so solicitous after coming out of the kitchen.

They'd taken special precautions not to accidentally bump or touch each other as they worked. Gradually, as all the equipment was put into place, some of the tension drained away, and for that Sarah was profoundly grateful. She looked up at Wolf, glad to see that the heavy scowl across his brow had relaxed.

"Tomorrow morning I'll start faceting these." She took a small plastic container and opened it. At least a hundred rough sapphires spilled out into the palm of her hand. Placing them beneath a lamp that Wolf had moved from the living room to her workbench, she motioned for him to look at them.

"See? Their colors are all different."

Wolf came close and leaned over Sarah's shoulder. He should have been looking at the rough sapphires she'd mined. Instead, he was studying her long, graceful fingers. Their nails practically nonexistent from digging in the dirt and sapphire gravel. He noted a number of small scars on her fingers and hand, too, but nonetheless she had an artist's hands, he thought.

"Nice," he grunted.

Sarah twisted a look up at him, wildly aware of his closeness. There was such sadness in Wolf's eyes now. Something within her reached out to him, and she was helpless to stop it. "Wolf, what's wrong?"

Abruptly he straightened. "Nothing."

Stung, Sarah felt heat rushing into her face. She was blushing—again. No man, not even Philip, who had captured her heart years earlier, when she was young and trusting, had made her blush so often. Casting around for a safe topic as the tension leaped violently to life between them again, she said, "I'm really tired. I think I'll go to bed."

Wolf nodded and moved to the entrance. "Take my bed."

Sarah's head snapped up. "What?"

He saw her cheeks flame a dark red. Shoving his hands in his pockets, he muttered, "I said, take my bed. I'll sleep out here on the living room couch."

Wolf's bed. Panic broke in Sarah. She stood up, nearly tipping the chair over. Catching it, she rattled, "I couldn't possibly take your bed, Wolf. I'll sleep on the couch." The memory of him pressing her to his strong, unyielding body, his arms going around her, the male scent of him, was permanently lodged in her heart. Sarah couldn't sleep on Wolf's bed. It would bring all those wonderful sensations back to the surface.

She forced a light smile as she got her crutches. "It's no problem. That couch is fine, Wolf. Really, I've created enough problems for you already by being here. I don't want to cause more. Keep your bedroom. I'll just sleep out here." She motioned toward the living room.

Frowning heavily, Wolf searched Sarah's features. She was forcing herself to placate him because he'd hurt her. Dammit, anyway! Moving aside as she hobbled toward him, Wolf desperately sought to let her know that he hadn't rejected her. "Look," he grumbled, running his fingers through his hair, "you need a good night's sleep. This couch is lumpy and short. You need to stretch out and give those feet all the room they want."

She brushed by him and went into the living room. It was almost painful to be that close to him. Her heart was beating so hard in her chest that she took a long, ragged breath. She stopped in the center of the room, desperate. "Wolf, I want the couch, okay? No argument."

Turning, he held her guileless blue gaze, which broadcast her anxiety all too well. Wolf felt miserable. If only he could explain... He jammed that thought deep down inside him. "You're right," he snapped. "There isn't going to be an argument on this, Sarah." Pointing toward the hallway and the connecting bedroom, he said, "That is your room while you're here. Understand? And don't give me grief about it. Your feet need to heal, and—" he jabbed his finger at the old, worn couch "—they sure as hell won't do that on this thing."

Sarah moved restlessly around in the queen-size bed. She was used to her small bed, not this rambling expanse of mattress. Wolf's emotional reaction had jarred her. Opening her eyes, she stared sightlessly up at the darkened ceiling of the quiet bedroom. *Wolf's bedroom.* He slept in this bed. Unconsciously she smoothed her hand out across the cool cotton sheet and tried to imagine what it would be like for him to be lying next to her.

The thought stunned Sarah. She just hadn't been drawn to that many men in her life. There was Philip, but that had ended badly. Sitting up, the sheet falling away to expose her thin cotton nightgown printed with tiny violets, she frowned. The clock on the dresser opposite the bed read 2:00 a.m. Her feet were throbbing, but that wasn't why she was restless and unable to sleep.

Wolf's words, the look in his eyes—as if some part of him were dying inside—kept her awake. Kept her thinking. Grasping her crutches, which leaned against the wall next to the bed, Sarah slowly got to her feet. Perhaps a cup of tea would help her sleep.

The light from the street filtered in through the dark orange drapes and the sheers as Sarah made her way slowly down the carpeted hall. At the entrance to the living room, she suddenly realized that Wolf was sleeping on the couch, which was located opposite where she stood.

Leaning on her crutches, Sarah's heart started a slow, heavy pounding in her breast. Wolf was far too long for the short couch. It was very warm in the house, the summer heat lingering without a cooling breeze to push it outside, where it belonged. The white sheet he wore across his naked body had slid down and pooled around Wolf's waist, the outline revealing his narrow hips and long, powerful legs. Both his feet were exposed, as he'd kicked the sheet aside. Her gaze moved appreciatively upward to his slab-hard torso and his dark-haired chest.

A small gasp escaped Sarah as her eyes adjusted to the gloom. Was she seeing things? Was it her overactive imagination? Narrowing her eyes, her heart pounded painfully. Wolf's chest bore a crisscross pattern of puckered pink-and-white scars, as if someone had taken a bullwhip to him. No, that was impossible. Sarah closed her eyes and shook her head. What was happening to her? What craziness descended on her when she was in Wolf's quiet, powerful presence?

She reopened her eyes and studied his chest again. Yes, there were scars there. Too many to count. How on earth had he gotten them? Her gaze moved to his face, and the pain she'd felt for him disappeared. In sleep, his face was tranquil. She gripped the handles of her crutches as he stirred and muttered something in his sleep, turning onto his side. One of his arms hung over the edge of the couch, his curved fingers resting against the carpeted floor. He was bathed in sweat, and the sheen emphasized the muscles across his shoulder and upper back.

There was such a powerful beauty to Wolf. Sarah wavered. Should she go back to the bedroom or try to quietly reach the kitchen for the cup of tea? The tea was terribly tempting; it was the only thing that settled her nerves and imagination enough that she could get to sleep. Moving slowly and quietly forward, Sarah opted for the tea.

Wolf slept lightly, as was his custom. A vague noise awakened him instantly, and he jerked into a sitting position, his fists cocked. Disoriented for a second, he saw Sarah, in a knee-length nightgown, freeze in the center of the room.

"Oh, dear. I'm sorry, Wolf. I thought I was being quiet." Sarah stood there uncertainly. Wolf's eyes were softened by sleep. Black strands of hair hung across his brow.

"Sarah?" he croaked, frowning. "What's wrong? Are you all right?" He rose to his feet without thinking, wrapping the sheet around his waist.

Sarah's eyes widened, and she sucked in a quick breath as Wolf approached, casting a giant shadow in the gloom of the room. "I'm fine...fine..." He moved with such fluid ease. As Wolf drew near, Sarah could easily see the terrible series of scars on his chest, and the sight made her want to cry. What kind of pain had this man endured?

Wolf halted inches from her. The fine, thin blond hair about her face and shoulders was like a wraith's. He searched her eyes for the real answer, knowing that what she said might cover what she was really feeling. "Bad dreams?" he asked gently.

Sarah hesitated. "No...yes...in a way.... I slept for just a little while and then woke up." She managed a sad smile. "I got to thinking about what you said in the kitchen last night...."

"Oh."

The word came out hard and flat. Sarah knew Wolf didn't want to talk about it. "When I get like this, a cup of tea always helps me sleep. I was trying to cross the living room without waking you to get to the kitchen." Unhappily she added, "It didn't work."

Relieved that nothing was seriously wrong, Wolf relaxed. He bunched the sheet around him more securely where it had parted to reveal the length of his hairy thigh. Sarah had a high flush to her cheeks, and he read in her face a mixture of awe, fear and longing that made him acutely sensitive to how he affected her as a man.

"Could you stand some company?" Wolf asked. He wanted to join her but knew better than to push himself on her. Let her decide, he thought. He saw the indecision in her eyes turn to surprise.

"Sure, if you want."

He forced a sleepy smile. "Let me get more decent and I'll join you."

Nodding, Sarah suddenly remembered her own thin

cotton nightgown. It wasn't sheer, but she felt vulnerable in it and wished for her robe. "I'll be right back. I want to get my robe."

"I'll get it for you," he said easily. "My pants are in the bedroom."

"Okay, I'll make the tea," Sarah said, aware of an oddly breathless quality in her voice.

Wolf padded down the hall to his bedroom, allowing the sheet to drop to the floor once he'd entered. With a scowl, he looked at his bed. The blankets were on the floor, the sheet twisted like a rag. Sarah was more than just a restless sleeper. Aching to hold her, but knowing that wasn't the answer Sarah needed, Wolf crossed to the dresser and put on a pair of jeans. He pulled a clean white T-shirt over his head. Maria had been deathly afraid of him without clothes. His uncovered chest had made her shrink back in terror.

Wolf slammed the door on the flow of memories. But since being around Sarah, he couldn't seem to force his feelings and memories away as easily as he once had. "Damn," he whispered, padding out of the room in his bare feet, Sarah's robe in his hand.

They sat at the darkened table, each holding a cup of steaming-hot tea. Sarah was delighted when Wolf found a lemon in the refrigerator and placed a few slices on a small saucer between them. And instead of sugar he'd offered her sweet clover honey.

"When I was a little girl, my mom would fix me tea with lemon and honey when I was sick," Sarah said in a quiet voice. "I loved it. She always said the lemon had lots of vitamins."

Wolf nodded, his arm resting on the table, his large hand curved around his china cup. "Tea won't fix what happened to you, though, Sarah."

"I suppose not," she responded sadly.

"Tell me something. After those two jerks jumped you, did you go get help?"

"What kind of help? I reported it to Sheriff Noonan— but that's like spitting in the wind."

"An abuse or crisis center of some kind?"

She smiled wryly. "Here in Backwater, U.S.A.?"

"Did you talk to anyone about the assault?"

With a shake of her head, Sarah said, "No, but what good would that do, anyway?"

"Talk's part of the healing process to anyone who's been traumatized."

"I wasn't hurt much. I had a black eye for a week, was all."

"You were a victim," Wolf said. "It makes you start behaving unconsciously to protect yourself from another possible similar situation."

"Oh, my jumpiness and paranoia?"

He smiled. "I like your honesty, Sarah Thatcher. It's one of many good traits you have. Yes, your hyperalert state is what I'm talking about."

She turned the teacup around in her hands. "There's nothing wrong with me."

"Oh?"

Sarah eyeballed him.

"Then why did I see fear in your eyes when I got up off the couch and walked toward you a little while ago?"

"Well…" Sarah stumbled over her words. "You came out of the shadows. I told you before, at night, shadows look like those two men coming to attack me again. I wasn't reacting to you."

Wolf held her serious gaze. Did he dare hope that was the truth? He had failed miserably before—failed in a way that had cost the person he loved, first her peace of mind, then her life. He couldn't bear to face the pain of the rejection he'd suffered. But, even more, he didn't dare face the possibly life-threatening consequences for Sarah if he ran. Gruffly he probed Sarah's fear. "Are you very sure of that?"

"Of course I am."

"I don't scare you?"

"No."

He smiled slightly. "Your heart doesn't start pounding when I approach you?"

Sarah lowered her lashes. That was exactly what her heart did, but it certainly wasn't out of fear. It was out of some forbidden, sweet excitement he created within her. "You don't scare me," she assured him.

Wolf couldn't believe the relief he felt at Sarah's admission. Her soft blue gaze made him want to reach out and embrace the hell out of her. "I'm glad," he muttered darkly. "I'm no prize, but maybe I can help make a difference in the situation for you. I hope I can...."

Sarah heard the raw pain in Wolf's tone and noted that he refused to meet her gaze. "You're a prize in my eyes," she admitted unsteadily, her emotions overwhelming her. "I don't know what you see in me, and I guess it doesn't really matter. I'm just grateful you're standing between me and Summers and his men. I've lived with horrible daily fear this last six months." She managed a painful smile as he raised his head. "You're a shield to me, Wolf."

Wolf turned his cup slowly on its saucer. If he told Sarah the truth, how much she touched him, how she made him feel alive again, she might run. Worse, if Sarah knew the truth of his past, she'd probably want him to leave. Clearing his throat, he said, "I've always had a place in my heart for underdogs." That should be nonthreatening enough. Her young face was so young and serious.

"I can use all the help I can get," Sarah admitted, a catch in her voice. "If you want to be my guard dog, I'm all for it."

The light, the hope, shining in Sarah's eyes was so endearing, he kept his doubts to himself. Anyway, he wasn't about to make the same mistake with Sarah that he had with Maria—was he? "I'll do anything I can to help you, Sarah," he vowed. "All you have to do is tell me what you want. Communication is the key." This time things just had to be different.

Sarah thrust her hand across the table. "You've got a deal, Ranger Harding. And you've got my thanks. I don't know how I'll ever repay you."

Wolf gripped her hand gently, amazed all over again at how small, yet how strong, Sarah was. "The native Americans have a saying that you need to take to heart."

"What's that?"

"Expect nothing, receive everything."

"Meaning?"

"Don't set expectations. When you do, you set your own limitations and can't move beyond them. When you expect nothing, you become open to more than you ever thought or dreamed possible. It also means, receive help in whatever form it comes to you. There's no need to pay it back."

His callused grip was strong without hurting. Sarah wanted to continue to hold Wolf's hand, but didn't dare. He was far too vulnerable, and she was far too fragile emotionally. She mustn't read anything into their unexpected agreement. "No matter what anyone says, Wolf, in my eyes, you're a knight in shining armor," she whispered.

He released her slim fingers. "Honey, I'm a failure in so many ways, I can't even begin to tell you."

Stubbornly Sarah shook her head. "In my heart, you're a winner." She slowly got up, placing the hated crutches beneath her arms. The look in Wolf's eyes was a blend of relief and hope and denial. But that was all right. *By the time this is all over,* Sarah promised him silently, *I'm going to get you to realize just how wonderful a person you really are—faults and all.*

Chapter Six

The tantalizing odor of bacon frying slowly woke Sarah the next morning. She had shoved both pillows off the bed during her slumber, and the blankets were tangled hopelessly around her legs and body. With a groan, her feet throbbing, she pushed her blond hair out of her face. Lifting her chin, she squinted at the clock on the dresser. It was 7:00 a.m. Wolf had to be to work at eight.

Sitting up, Sarah rubbed her face sleepily, her legs hanging over the side of the bed. The sensation of knowing Wolf was nearby, and the odor of frying bacon, aroused a homesickness within her. How much she missed her father and mother! She assimilated those feelings as she sat there. Yet, with Wolf having unexpectedly entered her life, she'd never felt safer or stronger. He gave her strength, she realized as she slowly tested her weight on her feet.

"Oww..." She grimaced. Well, pain or no pain, she

had to get to the bathroom. Maybe a nice hot bath and a soak for her poor injured feet would help. Reaching for her robe, Sarah shrugged it across her shoulders. She hated being forced to use these crutches. They were symbolic to her, too, and as she gripped them and stood she understood why. All her life she'd been independent— confident that she could stand alone to handle anything that came along.

As she hobbled to the master bathroom, across from the bed, Sarah realized that some of her shock over the past six months had to do with the fact that she'd come up against something she couldn't deal with successfully on her own. She leaned the crutches next to the door and closed it. The pain made her compress her lips as she leaned down to start the bathwater running.

Later, as she allowed herself the luxury of a long, hot bath, Sarah realized that Wolf was symbolic to her, too. But how far could she trust him? She'd trusted her father to be there for her, and he had been ripped from her life. She'd turned to her mother, and she, too, had abandoned her—in a different way. Wiping the perspiration off her brow, Sarah sat up and scrubbed her pink skin with the lilac-scented soap. Whether she wanted to admit it or not, she did trust Wolf. Did she have any choice? She frowned as she stood up and pulled the plug. Did she want a choice? After toweling dry, Sarah brushed her teeth, combed her hair and pulled on a pair of well-worn denims and a pink tank top. She tried to ignore the horribly swollen and bruised feet sticking out from beneath her jeans. Because Wolf was a paramedic, the doctor had told her to let him wrap her feet morning and night.

Her heart began beating more strongly as she hobbled down the hall on her crutches, Ace bandages sticking out of her back pockets. Skeet met her halfway, his large yellow eyes shining, his huge, brushy tail waving back and forth in greeting. Sarah smiled and stopped to pet him.

"You're looking happy this morning," Sarah told the dog as she continued into the living room. Ahead, she saw Wolf's broad back as he worked in the kitchen. Her stomach growled. She was starving! How long had it been since she was this hungry? A long time, she realized.

Her pulse was doing funny things as she hobbled to the entrance of the kitchen. Wolf was busy working at the counter, cracking eggs as the bacon sputtered in a skillet on the stove. The table was set for two. He glanced over his shoulder, and her heart skittered violently as his gray eyes narrowed on her.

"Morning," Wolf said. "Come and sit down. I've got breakfast almost ready." Wolf tried to keep his voice unruffled. Sarah had never looked prettier. The pink tank top brought out the natural flush in her cheeks. He was glad to see that she looked rested. He hadn't slept at all well last night after their midnight tea, because he'd kept rehashing their conversation in his mind.

Sarah gave him a slight smile of welcome and moved slowly into the kitchen. Wolf's hair was recently washed and combed, the kitchen light bringing out the blue highlights in the shiny strands. His skin was scraped free of the beard that had darkened his face since around 5:00 p.m. yesterday. He looked less forbidding without it, Sarah decided as Wolf pulled out a chair for her to sit on.

"Thanks," she whispered, meaning it. Philip had never been this thoughtful, but then, Sarah reminded herself, Philip hadn't been as old or mature as Wolf, either. She sat down carefully, placing the two huge Ace bandage rolls on the table. She wished her heart would settle down.

"How are the feet this morning?" Wolf asked as he poured the scrambled eggs into the skillet. Glancing at Sarah, he saw her poor feet stuck out in front of her, black-and-blue and swollen.

"Better."

His mouth twisted, and he turned his attention to scrambling the eggs. "Really?"

Sarah heard the irony in his voice. "Well..."

"You can tell me the truth, you know."

She stared hard at his back, which was covered now by his dark green work shirt.

"They hurt," she admitted.

"How much?" Wolf lifted the skillet off the stove and divided the scrambled eggs between the two plates on the table. He saw the darkness in Sarah's eyes. "A lot of pain?"

She nodded.

"After breakfast I'll wrap your feet so you won't be in as much pain," he said soothingly. Placing the skillet in the sink's soapy dishwater, Wolf brought over the plate of fried bacon, as well as some toast. He set them down and pulled up a chair opposite Sarah.

"Dig in," he invited. Suddenly an unexpected rush of happiness filled him, and he marveled at how glad he was that she was here to grace this old kitchen. She had a healthy appetite, and he was glad to see her eat. Skeet sat nearby, thumping his tail, looking for a handout.

"Don't give him anything," Wolf warned.

Sarah grinned over at the dog who sat a foot away from her. "He's got such a wistful look on his face, Wolf. How could you not feed him?"

"Harden your heart and tell him no. He's already been

fed this morning.'' A grudging smile came to Wolf's mouth as he buttered a piece of toast then slathered red raspberry jam across it. He envied Skeet's ability to make Sarah smile. What could he do to make her smile—or maybe even laugh? Hell, ever since they'd met, it had been one crisis after another. Not much room for laughter or play. As Wolf munched on the toast, he realized that in the past year of his life he'd become so accustomed to living in crisis mode that he hadn't even noticed until this moment what he was missing.

With Sarah present, Wolf felt lighter, happier, than he could remember being in a long time. Maybe he was finally ready to come out of that long tunnel of grief. When Sarah looked up at him, laughter dancing in her dark blue eyes, Wolf felt his heart explode with joy.

''Harden my heart? Really, Wolf. I never could get tough with kids or animals.'' She wrinkled her nose and chuckled as she picked up the jar of jam. ''I guess I should include insects, too. I never could smash an ant or get hyper about a spider crawling around, either.''

''Good Indian traits,'' Wolf said, forcing himself to chew his toast. A winsome smile touched Sarah's mouth, and he felt himself drowning in the blueness of her sunlit eyes, and absorbed the moment like a greedy thief. The need to be liked ate away at Wolf. Sarah wasn't afraid of him, didn't look at him with terror in her eyes, as Maria had after... With a sigh, Wolf forced the memories away.

''What are good Indian traits?'' Sarah teased. She couldn't help but enjoy Wolf's company. The cabin had been so lonely for the past six months—she'd been starved for the chance to share with another person. The corners of Wolf's mouth drew into a slight smile at her question, and a sheet of warmth flowed through her.

"Most Indians see the world as connected," Wolf explained. "The Cherokees have a saying—All my relations. It means we honor the connection between the bird that flies in the air and the fish that swims in the water and the beetle that makes her home in the ground. Medicine people say they can see a river of light flowing in and around everything, and for them, that proves this connection theory."

"I like that viewpoint," Sarah said thoughtfully. "I worry about digging sapphires because it exposes the tree roots." She shrugged and sipped the fragrant black coffee. "At least I put the dirt back to save the trees. Summers uses backhoes and bulldozers to rip the trees out to get at the sapphire gravel. He's left a path of destruction all across Blue Mountain."

"I noticed that the other day," Wolf said. "Sure you aren't part Indian?"

She laughed and picked up a strand of her hair. "With this hair, and blue eyes? Give me a break!"

Sarah's laughter touched Wolf's heart like a healing balm. It was a low, husky laugh filled with delight, and Wolf smiled fully in response.

"Where did your folks come from?" he asked as he pushed his empty breakfast plate aside in favor of his coffee cup. Suddenly he was eager to learn every detail about Sarah.

"My dad is a mixture of English and Scottish. My mom is mostly Dutch." She smiled fondly. "I've got Mom's hair and Dad's eyes."

"You have beautiful skin, too," Wolf offered. Sarah's fair complexion was the color of thick cream.

Sarah flushed and raised a hand to her flaming cheek. "Thanks," she said softly. Wolf's eyes burned with a desire that sent a ribbon of heat through her. So why had he pushed her away from him yesterday? Allowing her hand to drop, she pretended to be interested in clearing the plates away.

Wolf felt Sarah's discomfort. Was it because she wasn't used to being complimented? Or was it him that made her uncomfortable? Uncertain, Wolf said, "Time's getting late. I want to wrap your feet before I leave."

"Sure," Sarah muttered, and she pushed her chair away from the table. She watched Wolf unwind from his chair, thinking how stalwart he was. He was a man of incredible strength, not only in the physical sense, but emotionally, too. As she handed him the first Ace bandage, his fingers touched hers. A delightful sensation skittered along her hand, and she swallowed convulsively.

Wolf knelt and gently lifted Sarah's foot. Her ankle was so delicate, yet her calf was firmly developed from her hard physical work. "You're in good shape," he said as he rested the heel of her foot on his thigh.

Shaken by his touch, Sarah struggled to gather her strewn thoughts. "Thanks..." She watched, mesmerized, as Wolf's calloused hand flowed carefully across her foot, examining it intently.

"They look a little better this morning," Wolf commented, feeling like a thief as he ran his hand in a practiced manner across her swollen extremity. He began to wrap her injured foot with the sureness born of much experience.

"You said you were a paramedic," Sarah said.

"Yeah."

Wolf's single-syllable response was cold, but somehow Sarah didn't mind the rebuff. Wolf was obvious about letting her know when she asked the wrong question, but she sensed it wasn't a bluff. "Where were you one?" she persisted.

Wolf glanced up at her, frowning. He returned to wrapping her foot, and the moments dragged by. Finally he sighed and said, "The Marine Corps."

"You're a marine?"

He saw the surprise and pride in her eyes. "Was."

"For how long?"

Wolf felt his gut tighten. "Eight years."

"Did you like it?"

"Yes."

Frustrated, Sarah eyed him. "Wolf, you're about as open as a locked safe, do you know that?"

He had the good grace to blush under her fervent observation. "It just comes naturally, honey. I can't help it," he said, trying to lighten his tone.

"Why not?" Sarah tried to ignore the endearment, although it tugged at her heart.

Wolf realized Sarah wasn't going to back off this time. He finished wrapping her foot, pleased with his handiwork. Then he lifted her other foot and began to work on it. "I was a recon marine, and they specialize in certain areas. I liked the medical area, so I took paramedic school a long time ago," he said quietly, keeping his eyes on her foot.

"Why did you like the Marine Corps?"

His mouth pulled into an unwilling grin. "Are you always this nosy?"

Sarah matched Wolf's grin with one of her own, drowning in his light gray gaze. She could read so much in his eyes: fear, joy, desire—and that haunted expression. "When it's important, I am," she flung back archly.

"I'm not important," Wolf growled, getting serious.

"To me you are."

Wolf shook his head. "You're young and full of idealism, Sarah."

"And you aren't?"

"I feel a hundred years old, and no, I don't have any idealism left in me. It got kicked out of me a long time ago."

"By the marines?"

"By life, honey."

Sarah enjoyed Wolf's tender touch, feeling the ache in her feet lessen as he deftly bandaged her feet. "Are you implying that because I live in isolation here in a very unpopulated area of America that I'm naive?" she retorted.

Wolf finished his task and rested his hands on his thighs as he held her challenging blue gaze. The fire in her eyes, the stubborn set of her mouth, touched him. "I see you as naive, yes."

"I don't know whether that's a compliment or an insult, Wolf."

Wolf slowly straightened, rising to his feet. The pleasure of talking with Sarah was going to make him late for work. He retrieved a sack lunch he'd packed earlier. "It just is what it is," he told her softly.

"You think I'm like a child. Is that it?" Was that why he'd pushed her away? Did he see her as immature?

Wolf groaned and held up his hand. "No, I don't see you as a child." Far from it. If Sarah could look inside his heart, she'd find out how badly he wanted to know her better. "You're a beautiful young woman. And in some ways, because of where you live, you are—" he groped for the right word "—untouched by the world at large."

"Untouched?" Sarah demanded, frowning. Wolf saw her as protected from real life? Oh, come on!

Glancing at his watch, Wolf gave her an apologetic look. "Sarah, I'm going to be late if I don't get going. Let's continue this conversation tonight, all right?"

Her lips compressed, Sarah watched as he quickly slid the breakfast dishes into the soapy water. "You're getting off lucky, Harding," she said, half serious, half teasing.

The urge to walk over to Sarah, lean down and plant a very long kiss on her petulantly set lips was almost Wolf's undoing. The fire in her eyes, he knew, reflected her sensitive roller-coaster emotions. Sarah's world was one of strong, passionate feelings—a world Wolf desperately wanted to explore. A world he knew he must forbid himself.

"I've got to go. Do you want me to leave Skeet at home with you today?" Worry gnawed at Wolf. He'd left Maria undefended, and— Swallowing, he added, "Skeet's a good guard dog."

Home. The word struck Sarah hard. Yes, this was a home. The discovery was bittersweet. "No, I'll be fine. Nothing will happen to me here." She saw the concern in his darkening gray eyes. That haunted look was back. Why? Sarah gave him a confident smile and waved. "Get going or you'll be late for work, Wolf."

"I've got a roast pulled out of the freezer, thawing. Will you—"

"I'll take care of it. Although I'm overly protected, young and naive, I think I can handle putting a roast in the oven so we have something to eat for dinner, Wolf."

His mouth worked into an unwilling grin. "Anyone ever accuse you of having a dry wit, Ms. Thatcher?"

"Only naive men like you, Mr. Harding."

With a laugh, Wolf waved goodbye to her, Skeet at his heels. As he walked onto the back porch and out into the morning sunlight, Wolf thought he had never felt happier. Sarah was far from naive, and they both knew it. As Wolf opened the door so that Skeet could bound into the cab, he smiled. He didn't deserve Sarah. He didn't deserve the feelings of joy coursing through him, but he couldn't help himself. After nearly a year of darkness and despair, Sarah's smile, her feisty courage, were helping him to heal.

As he backed the pickup out of the driveway, Wolf worried about Sarah's safety. He tried to tell himself that she would be safe at his home. Sarah wasn't Maria. Sarah knew how to fight back, how to survive. Still, as he'd put the truck in drive and headed down Broadway, his gut was tight with foreboding.

Sarah decided to leave the damnable crutches in the corner of the porch as she hobbled to the faceting machine. She'd rather endure the pain. Morning sunlight flowed strongly through the screened-in area, and robins sang in the trees surrounding the small, green lawn.

Faceting was second nature to her. She fitted the jeweler's loupe over her eye and inspected each stone minutely. Many of the rough sapphires had too many inclusions. No matter how carefully they were polished and faceted, those stones would always have a dull look to them.

The time sped by as Sarah found fifteen rough sapphires worthy of being faceted. She became lost in the process itself, unaware of the hours passing. The radio was playing in the living room, the music softening the grinding noise that the faceting machine made as the hard surface of the sapphire was polished away.

Sarah's stomach growled ominously. Glancing at her watch, she smiled. Noon exactly. Hobbling without the aid of the crutches, Sarah made it to the kitchen and peeked into the refrigerator.

As she made herself a tuna sandwich, she realized with a start that she felt incredibly happy. Ever since her father's death, she'd felt as if she were in a cocoon of grief.

Sarah sat down at the table, a glass of iced tea in hand, the sandwich on a plate. She frowned. It was as if she could still feel Wolf's presence in the small kitchen. Despite his height and size, he moved deftly around the area, never knocking into anything. As she began slowly chewing the sandwich, Sarah's heart centered on Wolf.

Why had he been so worried about leaving her alone? She knew Summers well enough to know that the bastard would never openly attack her and risk eyewitnesses. No, Summers was careful, waiting until she had her guard down.

Suddenly Sarah wished Skeet had stayed with her. It would at least give her someone to talk to—even if he couldn't answer her back. The wish that her mother was more aware of her made Sarah sigh. Right now she wanted to talk to her about all these crazy feelings alive within her, clamoring for attention. Philip had never made her feel like this. But then, she reminded herself grimly, Philip hadn't really loved her.

Deciding she had more questions than answers, Sarah cleaned up the kitchen and went back to work. As she hobbled through the living room, the phone rang. She hesitated, wondering if she should answer. After all, this was Wolf's home, not hers. But what if it was Wolf calling to see how she was? If she didn't answer, he'd panic and come back to check on her. Or would he?

Sarah muttered under her breath. Her imagination was getting the best of her. She meant nothing to Wolf. Moving toward the ringing phone, Sarah reached out and picked it up.

"Ranger Harding's residence."

"You're dead."

Sarah froze. Her fingers automatically tightened around the phone, and she gasped. Then anger followed quickly on the heels of her shock.

"Who is this?" she demanded.

No answer.

Sarah's breathing became erratic. She knew that whoever was on the other end hadn't hung up. "You bastard! Who do you think you are threatening me? Go to hell!" She slammed the phone down.

Shaking, Sarah stood with her arms wrapped around herself. Her heart pounding, she looked anxiously around the small house. The dainty white lace curtains moved slowly as a summer breeze stirred through the living room.

You're dead.

It had to be Summers! He'd hired someone to call her. To threaten her! Anger and fear warred within Sarah as she stood on her throbbing feet, rooted to the spot, unsure of what to do. Her first instinct was to call the ranger station and tell Wolf. No. She couldn't begin leaning on him. She had to handle this herself.

Gnawing on her lower lip, Sarah shivered involuntarily. This was the first time she'd ever received a threatening phone call. There was no point in calling Sheriff Noonan to report it. Her stomach was tight with terror.

Forcing herself to move, Sarah went back to faceting, far more alert, far warier, than before. What should she do? What *could* she do? Every particle of her being cried out to tell Wolf. Her hands shaking badly, Sarah repositioned the stone on the machine for the next facet.

''No!'' she whispered forcefully as she gently set the stone on the grit-layered wheel. Turning the machine back on, she watched it for a long moment. Summers was just like that grit—he was wearing her down a little at a time. Sarah raised her head, tears stinging her eyes. Everything was closing in on her. The only good thing in her life was Wolf. Her father was dead, and her mother was, too, in a sense. Sarah squeezed her eyes shut, tears running hotly down her cheeks. She couldn't stand if Wolf was hurt or killed defending her. No, she just couldn't put him in that kind of jeopardy.

Wolf noticed that Sarah was jumpier than usual when he got home that evening. During their dinner of pot roast, baked potatoes, gravy and carrots, the phone rang. Sarah jumped, her eyes huge. Wolf answered the call— from the ranger station telling him about a change in his assignment the next day. When he sat down again, he noticed how pale Sarah had become.

''Are you all right?'' he demanded, slicing into the thick, juicy pot roast.

''Yes, I'm fine. Fine.''

''You're as jumpy as I would be if I found myself in the middle of a minefield,'' he noted dryly.

Sarah forced herself to begin eating again, her heart banging away in her throat. ''Are you always this alert?'' she muttered.

''It saves lives,'' he answered darkly, and shoved a piece of potato into the gravy.

Lives. Her life. Maybe Wolf's. Sarah choked down a small piece of beef, not tasting it. The very thought of

Wolf being hurt because of her put a knot in her stomach.

"Aren't you hungry?"

Sarah shook her head, afraid to look up. Wolf read her eyes and face too easily.

"Are your feet bothering you?"

"Yes." It was a white lie, Sarah told herself as she pushed the plate away. If she didn't get out of the kitchen, she was going to tell Wolf about the call. Desperation fueling her, she got up and moved around the table, careful not to engage Wolf's gaze.

"Sarah?"

"I'm okay!" she flared, and left the kitchen.

Scowling, Wolf looked toward the living room. Finally, he returned his attention to the food on his plate. He'd had a long day out in the field, walking along the many local trout streams, and he was more tired than usual. Part of it was due to lack of sleep last night, but the bigger part was from worrying about Sarah's safety all day. He saw Sarah limping down the hall toward her bedroom. She was probably going to soak her feet. He'd wrap them later, before she went to bed.

"Dammit," he growled. Sarah had made a wonderful dinner, but his emotions were in tatters. Just being around Sarah made him achingly aware of how much he wanted her—on all levels. Wolf had given the situation with Sarah a hard, realistic look today.

Pushing his plate away, Wolf got up. The chair scraped back, further testing his already taut nerves. Maybe kitchen duty would help take the edge off him. In some ways, he thought, this was going to be the longest week of his life; in other ways, he had never felt as content. There was no explanation for it. He'd never before looked forward to such small, seemingly meaningless things in his life. But now, the thought of Sarah eating, pushing her spun-gold hair behind her ear, sharing her winsome smile with Skeet or just moving with unconscious grace, made him appreciate living as never before.

All evening Sarah worried that the phone might ring again. She took an early bath, pulled on her cotton nightgown and robe and hobbled back out to the living room. Wolf was sitting on the couch watching television when she came and sat down next to him.

"I'm kind of tired. Would you mind wrapping my feet? I think I'm going to bed early." She handed him two Ace bandages.

Wolf nodded and eased out of his sprawled position on the couch. He could see that Sarah was tired from the darkness beneath her blue eyes. As he knelt down at her feet, he looked up at her. "You never said how your day was."

She shrugged and leaned against the couch, her arms around herself. "I got some stones faceted. That was good." At least that wasn't a lie. Her skin tingled as he gently grazed the skin of her foot.

"They look a lot better tonight."

"I threw the crutches away," she muttered.

Wolf grinned as he placed the heel of her foot across his thigh. "Maybe walking on them increased the circulation and helped reduce the swelling."

Sarah watched, fascinated, as Wolf's large, scarred hands carefully wrapped her feet. She never felt pain when he touched her—only a simmering heat that taunted her like the threat of a thunderstorm on a hot summer day. "You mean you aren't going to chew me out for not using those crutches?"

"Am I your keeper?"

She shrugged and made a wiry face. "No woman should be kept."

"I agree."

"You're really different from the guys I've known," Sarah said. "Why is that?"

The pleasure of touching Sarah was humbling to Wolf. Her feet were delicate, despite their swollen condition. "Must be my Cherokee heritage," he teased. "Women are treated as equals in my tribe."

"Will miracles never cease? At least there's somewhere on this earth where we're not maligned or mistreated."

"Now, don't waste your anger on me. I'm treating you like an equal." Wolf tried not to smile, but he saw the laughter dancing in Sarah's eyes. He liked making her happy.

"You're too smart for your own good, Harding."

"Yeah, I know. But my mother taught me when I was knee-high to a cricket that women were just as strong, bright and resourceful as any man." He captured her other foot and inspected it closely. What would it be like to simply run his hand the length of her slender leg? Instantly he blocked the molten thought and began wrapping her foot.

"I think I'm lucky," Sarah admitted. "Dad showed me how to change tires and put oil in the old pickup, and taught me mechanical things. Mom taught me how to sew, cook and clean."

"There's no reason a woman shouldn't be taught those things."

"Well," she said unhappily, "there are plenty of men who think we're nothing but housekeepers."

Wolf's laughter boomed through the living room. He

sat back, his hands on his thighs, and held her mutinous gaze. His breath jammed in his chest as she began to laugh with him, her husky voice as refreshing as clear, clean water. With a shake of his head, he studied her.

"Were you always this rebellious?" he teased.

Sarah felt heat rushing to her face and knew she was blushing—again. "I don't see it as being rebellious. I see life as one of justice for everyone."

"Yet you willingly made dinner for us tonight."

"That's because you asked," she said pointedly. "You didn't expect it of me."

"I think," he said lightly, "what you're really telling me is that you don't want to be taken advantage of."

Sarah's eyes widened as she held his warm gray gaze. "You understand."

Wolf smiled a little. "I like your courage, Sarah Thatcher. You've got brains and a backbone. You keep fighting for what's rightfully yours. Every step you take opens up doors for other women who might not have your strength, conviction or courage. You're doing a good thing."

"Yeah, and it could get me killed," she muttered, more to herself than him.

A pang went through Wolf's heart and rattled his conscience. "I guess," he began in a low tone, "that the Great Spirit puts tests in front of us to make us stronger."

Sarah wrinkled her nose. "Right now I don't feel very strong." *Just scared. Scared to death.* She ached to confide in Wolf, to tell him about the phone call. But why? To involve him and, perhaps, make him a target, too? No, he was too fine a man, a man who reveled in her independent nature.

Without thinking, Sarah reached out, covering Wolf's

hand with hers. "You're so very special, Wolf. I just hope you know that." Reluctantly she removed her hand as she saw the startled look on Wolf's face, and the stormy quality of his eyes. "Good night," she whispered sadly. "I'll see you in the morning...."

Chapter Seven

You're dead.

Sarah jerked awake, screaming. Breathing hard, she hunched over in the bed and buried her face in her hands. She was shaking badly, and the cry was still echoing in her brain. Perspiration dampened her gown, which clung to her.

"Sarah?" Wolf hesitated fractionally at the door.

The darkness was relieved only by the streetlight outside the curtained window. Sarah gasped at the sound of Wolf's thick, sleep-ridden voice. Before she could raise her head, she felt his callused hand slide across her shoulders in a protective gesture.

"Honey, what is it?" Wolf's heart was pounding unrelentingly in his chest. His mercenary instincts had taken over when Sarah's scream had jolted him out of his sleep. His eyes slitted, adrenaline pumping into his bloodstream, all his senses screamingly alert, he checked out the room, the window, the door to the master bathroom. Nothing. He glanced down at Sarah. It had been a nightmare....

Without thinking, Wolf sat down on the bed next to her, and pulled her into his arms. She was trembling badly, and she pressed her face to his chest, sobbing for breath.

"It's okay...." He tunneled his fingers through her mussed hair. "You're safe, Sarah. You're safe...." Wolf shut his eyes, feeling her begin to cry, although she made no sound. It hurt to think that she couldn't even give voice to whatever nightmare had been stalking her.

Leaning down, blindly following instinct, Wolf grazed her temple with a kiss, gently massaging her neck and her tensed shoulders with his hand. "Go ahead and cry, honey," he whispered raggedly.

Sarah's hands curled into small fists, and she let herself sob, the sound echoing in the room. Just the touch of Wolf's hand, soothing her, allowed the trauma to be given a life of its own in strangled, hiccuping sounds that came from deep within her. She was safe. Safe for the first time in a long time. Wolf was holding her, rocking her, and she felt more like a hurt child than a woman. He was her protector, keeping her safe when the nightmare had stripped her of her defenses, leaving her nakedly vulnerable to the world that wanted her dead.

Dead.

Wolf whispered words of support near her ear, and Sarah surrendered completely to him. To his arms. To his voice. To the warm strength of his body that surrounded her. Her world dissolved in a rush of hot, blinding tears, of animal sounds jagging up through her and making her throat raw, releasing so much that she'd tried to suppress for so long. Only Wolf's voice and the tender touch of his hands upon her existed.

Gradually, with each stroke of Wolf's hand across her hair and down her back, Sarah's inner focus began to lessen. Her peripheral awareness began to return, and as the last sob rattled through her, she unclenched her hand and spread her fingers against the soft, thick hair sprinkled across Wolf's chest. Somewhere in her muddled senses, Sarah felt his muscles tense beneath her tentative exploration, and she felt his arms draw her even more tightly against him.

Wolf leaned down, seeing Sarah's cheeks shining with spent tears in the grayish light. Her glistening lips were parted, pulled into a tortured line of anguish. He smoothed the tangle of blond hair away from her cheek and tamed it behind her delicate ear. With his fingers, he began to dry her cheeks and brush the tears from her lower lip. She sniffed and pressed her face against his chest.

A tender smile pulled at Wolf's mouth. He wanted nothing more than this moment. He was vibrantly aware of Sarah's body, meeting his, fitting against his. Her skin was warm and damp from her weeping, and her fingers now tangled in the hair on his chest. The minutes fled by, and Wolf agonized, not wanting the embrace ever to end. He could smell the fragrance of her recently washed hair, the scent of lilacs filling his nostrils.

More than anything, Wolf was aware of the aching contact wherever their bodies touched. Sarah's knee-length cotton gown was a thin barrier between them. Luckily, he'd found a pair of pajama bottoms and started wearing them since she'd been staying with him. Wolf smiled a little when Sarah licked her lower lip, then

raised a hand to wipe away the beads of tears still clinging to her lashes.

He cleared his throat. "Better?" His voice was thick
and unsteady, betraying how much her tears affected
him. Wolf was no stranger to tears. He'd shed more than
he would ever have thought possible. And he'd once
watched the woman he'd loved cry even as she rejected
his embrace. With a sigh, Wolf realized that Sarah had
allowed him the privilege of holding her while she wept.
Whether or not she would ever realize it, the act was a
healing one for him.

Sarah nodded, not trusting her voice yet. She was
wildly aware of Wolf's massive body, his powerful arms
encasing her, his hand gently moving up and down the
length of her arm, soothing away any last vestige of pain.
His voice was shaky, and so was she. Wolf's male scent
entered her awareness, and she inhaled deeply.

Realizing that she'd trusted—completely surrendered
to—Wolf, Sarah lay in his arms, confused. Her head was
screaming at her to move away from him, But her heart,
which had held so much fear and grief alone for so long,
begged her to remain within his embrace. As Sarah
slowly opened her eyes, she remembered their previous
embrace, and how Wolf had pushed her away.

Not this time, her heart whispered. But her head won
the struggle, and she started to move.

"Stay," he rasped, his arms tightening momentarily.
Wolf held his breath. He knew he had no right to ask
such a thing of Sarah. He hadn't earned this privilege,
but he couldn't help himself. Sarah somehow flowed
around all his rational reasons, leaving him helpless to
deny her anything.

Sarah capitulated, still raw from weeping, in need of
human care and love. Her eyes opened. *Love?* Where

had that word come from? And just as swiftly as the thought had come, Sarah rejected it. Love meant trust, offering her heart to be trampled and destroyed. She sniffed and pressed her hand to her eyes, feeling a fresh flow of tears welling.

Wolf reached over to the bedside table and pulled several tissues from the box there. "Here," he said, placing them in her hand.

"Thanks…" Sarah said brokenly.

"Bad dream?"

Sniffing, she nodded and bunched up the damp tissues, loath to leave Wolf's embrace. "I—" she bit back the truth about the phone call. "I-it was a violent one…"

Wolf nodded and stilled his hand against her arm, content just to hold Sarah. "Yeah, they're all too familiar to me."

"You?"

"Pretty frequently." His voice grew wry. "I almost think I'd miss them if they suddenly went away some night."

Twisting a look up at his deeply shadowed, harsh features, Sarah blinked belatedly remembering the terrible scars she'd seen on his chest and back. "You never told me.…"

Bare inches separated their faces, their lips. Wolf placed a steel grip on his desire. Sarah was wide open and vulnerable. It was wrong to take advantage of her. Completely wrong. He held her wounded-looking gaze. Her eyes were dark with fear. "I don't usually admit to having them," he told her huskily.

Sarah became lost in the turbulence of his gray eyes, at a loss about whatever terror-filled past still remained alive in him. She was too raw herself to deal with whatever Wolf carried, anyway. "They're awful," she managed.

"Yeah, but eventually they lose some of their punch," he said, and captured a stray strand of her hair, moving it away from her face. "It's nightly therapy," Wolf joked. "Cheap and free." It was a lousy joke, and he knew it. The anguish on Sarah's face made him grimace. He didn't want her worrying about him; she needed to focus on her own needs.

"The best therapy," he said, clearing his throat, "is talking."

"Interesting theory, coming from you," Sarah noted in a scratchy voice.

"The shoe's on the other foot, honey. It's your turn. What was the nightmare all about?"

Honey. Sarah melted every time the endearment crossed his lips. It touched her heart, tugged at her lonely soul. She lowered her lashes, unable to hold his burning gaze. He seemed to see right through her. Relaxing in his arms, she sighed and whispered, "Ever since my dad was killed in that explosion—I've never cried."

Wolf's brows moved upward. "Never?" His arms tightened briefly around Sarah. Wolf, too, had hidden his tears, pretended they weren't there or that he was tough enough to take it. But there had been unbidden times when the tears had refused to be held back—and, exploding with rage and helplessness, Wolf had cried alone.

"N-no. I had to be strong for Mom." *For myself.* Sarah sniffed and wiped her nose. "It was such a shock," she went on in a hoarse tone, "my dad dying and all. H-he always dreamed of finding that one huge cornflower-blue sapphire that would haul us out of poverty and make us millionaires." Sarah closed her eyes and absorbed the feel of Wolf's hand briefly grazing her cheek, where fresh tears flowed. "Dad loved us very much. He was my idol. He was an honest man. He worked sixteen hours a day during the summer to make enough money to tide us over during the winter."

"He sounds a little like my father," Wolf said, thinking fondly of his own dad.

"My dad gave me my work ethic, Wolf." Sarah opened her eyes and lifted her head to meet and hold his warm gray gaze. "He taught me to go after what I wanted." Swallowing hard, Sarah dropped her gaze. "After he was murdered, my whole world fell apart. I—I didn't realize how much my mother depended on my dad until she had that stroke. I just didn't realize..." Another sob escaped her.

Wolf nodded and pressed a kiss to her hair, wishing he could take away the fresh pain that had surfaced. "Maybe you weren't aware of the love they had for each other when you weren't around."

Sarah gave a small, helpless laugh. "I guess you're right, Wolf—I'm naive. After Mom had the stroke and I put her in the nursing home, I had to clean out a bunch of drawers at the cabin to take her clothes to her." She picked at the damp tissue still wadded in her hand. "In one drawer I found a whole box of letters my dad had written to her when he was serving in Vietnam."

Wolf felt Sarah tremble and realized intuitively how much she needed to share this with someone—even him. "Tell me about it," he urged gently, stroking her hair with his hand.

The touch of Wolf's hand upon her hair broke the dam that had held back Sarah's grief. "Th-they were love letters—" She choked softly and pressed the tissue to her eyes. "There must have been a hundred of them.

When I first discovered them, I didn't know what they were. I opened one and read it. What my Dad wrote was beautiful. When I realized it was from the sixteen months he'd spent in the army, I sat down on the floor and read every one of them.'' She sniffed. ''That was when I realized just how much they loved each other.''

''That must have been healing for you,'' Wolf murmured, looking down at her flushed features, her bright, tear-filled eyes.

''It was and it wasn't. I just didn't know, Wolf! I never saw them kissing or stuff like that. I never saw my dad come up and put his arm around my mom, or reach over and hold her hand. Nothing...''

''They came from a generation that believed in showing their love behind a closed bedroom door,'' Wolf reminded her quietly.

''I don't ever want that! I want my kids to know I love my husband. I want them to see us kissing, touching and holding. I want them to be hugged, to be touched and held—'' Sarah broke off, realizing what she'd said. Sniffing, she muttered, ''I'm not getting married, anyway. It's not worth it, Wolf.''

''Why not?''

''Marriage is too risky.''

''You mean, loving someone?''

With a quirk of her mouth, Sarah gazed up at him. In that moment, he appeared so wise and understanding. He seemed to see beneath her painful words. ''Yes...I guess so.''

''Why?''

''Because—because if you give your love, it's taken away.'' Sarah realized how lame that sounded.

Wolf nodded. ''Your love for your dad was ripped from you?''

"Yes."

"And then, in a way, your mom abandoned you, too. Right?"

Wolf's insight was startling. Sarah eased out of his arms. She stood up and moved a few feet from the bed. Sarah tried to smooth the wrinkled cotton gown. The silence deepened in the room. Sarah knew she couldn't evade Wolf. He didn't deserve that from her. Finally she clasped her hands in front of her and looked over at him.

"I know she didn't do it on purpose," she admitted in a broken whisper. "But—Mom's gone. All that's left is her body. She rarely ever recognizes me anymore. I'm—" she choked "—a stranger to her."

Rising, Wolf slowly approached Sarah. He placed his hands on her slumped shoulders, hoping in some small way to absorb her anguish. "Love is risky," he admitted thickly. "No guarantees, Sarah. Not ever."

She touched her heart with her hand, feeling the pain. "I-I just don't have any more to give, Wolf."

"I understand better than you think," he rasped. His hands tightened on her shoulders. "Feel like trying to go back to sleep? It's 3:00 a.m."

Sarah heard that awful anguish in his voice again and looked up, seeing clearly the haunted look in his gray eyes. Someday she'd get him to share that pain as he'd convinced her to share hers.... Suddenly, exhaustion descended upon her like a heavy blanket. Her eyes, burning from her many tears, felt heavy-lidded. She nodded, realizing she had to sleep. When Wolf removed his hands, she felt alone as never before. Searching his harsh, unreadable features, she asked, "Will it come back?"

"The nightmare?"

"Yes."

"Probably not." He gave her a slight smile meant to

buoy her. "But if it does, just scream and I'll be here for you. Deal?"

She smiled a little, remembering the deal she'd had with earlier him, and their handshake. Her lower lip trembling, she whispered, "Deal."

Sarah awoke the next morning. It was nearly 10:00 a.m.! With a start, she sat up in bed, her head aching from all the crying she'd done the night before. With a groan, she touched her brow. Slowly her conversation with Wolf floated back to her and, more importantly, his tenderness toward her. Taking in a ragged breath, she tried to push away the feelings he'd aroused. She had to keep her distance—it was a matter of survival!

After washing and dressing in a pair of jeans and a short-sleeved yellow blouse, Sarah hobbled—without the crutches—to the living room. The house was quiet. How she missed Wolf's larger-than-life presence. Skeet was gone, too.

In the kitchen, she found a note near the automatic coffeemaker.

Sarah—
I'm going to drop by at noon and check on you. I didn't want to wake you up this morning to wrap your feet. Just take it easy today, honey. You've been through a lot. Wolf.

Sarah's hand trembled. Her gaze caught on the word *honey*. With a small sound, she dropped the note into the wastebasket. Trusting Wolf meant giving him something in return—her heart. Pressing her hands against her eyes, Sarah stood, feeling torn apart.

The phone rang.

With a gasp, Sarah jerked a look toward the living room. *No!* The phone rang again. And again. Her heart pounding, Sarah stood, unsure whether to answer. It could be Wolf calling to check on her. Or it could be—

Pressing her hands against her ears, Sarah tried to blot out the harsh sound. After fifteen rings, it finally stopped. Her mouth was dry, and her heart was pounding raggedly in her breast. What if it was yesterday's caller? What would he say to her?

"Oh, God..." Sarah whispered, and sat down hard on the chair, her knees buckling with fear. Wildly she looked around the kitchen. Wolf's kitchen. He was in danger, too. She'd placed him in danger. But what if it had been Wolf calling her? Sarah knew her mind was running rampant with dread.

Trying to calm herself, she realized that when Wolf came home at noon, she could ask if he'd called. If he had, it would clear her conscience. But what if he hadn't? Shouldn't she tell Wolf about the threat? Maybe it was meaningless—another of Summers's mind games. Maybe.

Sarah knew she had to get busy. That was the way to drive the fear away. She hobbled to the porch and looked around carefully before stepping through the door. Then, warily, she peered out at the surrounding yard. Finally satisfied, she began faceting her sapphires. But no matter how hard she tried to hold her concentration on what she was doing, she longed for Wolf's return.

When Wolf returned to the house, around noon, Skeet stayed outside, content to sniff the boundaries of the wire fence that enclosed the backyard. Entering the house, Wolf took off his hat and placed it on the desk, calling, "Anyone home?"

"I'm in here," Sarah said from the kitchen.

Wolf smiled uncertainly as he entered the kitchen. Sarah stood at the counter, making sandwiches. She looked feminine in a puff-sleeved yellow blouse. Her hair hung in two pigtails. "You look like a little girl ready to go jump rope," he teased. His heart beat erratically in his chest as memories of holding Sarah flooded him. Hell, he'd thought of nothing else all morning. At the office, his considerable paperwork had stared back at him as he reran the entire sequence from last night.

"Oh, the pigtails," Sarah said belatedly. She looked up at Wolf, and her heart melted. He looked so strong and capable, and she felt none of those things. "Sit down. I made us tuna sandwiches." Nervously, she brought over a jar of sweet pickles and placed a bag of potato chips on the table between them.

"You didn't have to go to the trouble," Wolf murmured, appreciative of her efforts. He sat down and smiled at Sarah. Her face was pale, the flesh drawn around her eyes and mouth, but he wrote it off as the result of the emotional storm she'd weathered last night.

Sitting down, Sarah managed a small smile. "That's what I like about you—you don't take me for granted," she said. She picked at a potato chip, her stomach knotted. Somehow she had to find out if Wolf had called her. "How did you manage to get away? Weren't you out patrolling in the woods?"

"Today was paper-crunch day," Wolf told her, munching on his sandwich. "One day of the week is stay-at-the-office day. Well," he hedged, "sort of."

"What do you mean?"

"Early this morning I took a run by your cabin, just to check on it, before I headed to the office."

"How is it?" Sarah asked quickly, thinking of the threat.

"Quiet. I went in and had a look around. Nothing's been disturbed."

"And the mining area?"

"Fine."

"No evidence of anyone digging?"

"No, everything's quiet." Wolf wondered why Sarah was so nervous.

"D-did you call me this morning. Around ten?" Sarah held her breath.

Wolf shook his head. "No. Why?"

Sarah shrugged. "No reason…" The urge to blurt out the truth nearly overcame her. Maybe it had been one of Wolf's friends calling. But he'd never mentioned anyone. Panic ate at her.

"Maybe the word's got out to Summers that I'm checking your place two or three times a day."

She grimaced. "Knowing Summers, he's just waiting for the right opportunity." Giving Wolf a pleading look, she whispered, "Please be careful out there. I don't trust him, Wolf. He could jump you the way he jumped me."

Wolf saw the terror in her eyes, heard it in her voice. Reaching over, he captured her hand and squeezed it. "I'll be okay, honey. Stop worrying."

Just Wolf's touch momentarily staved off her panic. Trying to gather her strewn feelings, Sarah asked, "Have you heard from Sheriff Noonan?"

"I called him this morning. I can't say he was real happy to talk to me." Wolf scowled. "He doesn't have any suspects. I don't think he's done a damn thing, if you want my gut impression."

Sarah swallowed hard, feeling a lump of fear form in her throat. "Maybe you ought to back off, Wolf."

"Why?" He saw the worry in Sarah's eyes.

"Well...because.... I've pushed Noonan before, and that's when the goons jumped me."

"They won't jump me."

Moving restlessly around in her chair, Sarah whispered, "I just worry about you, Wolf."

Her admission hit Wolf as a pleasant surprise. "You do?"

"Yes," she muttered with a frown. Wrestling with her feelings, she added, "I'd worry about any friend who was tangling with Noonan, that's all." She stole a look at Wolf. "Not that I have friends..."

"Because having friends means reaching out and trusting someone?"

She shrugged painfully. "It sounds stupid when you say it."

"It's not stupid," Wolf murmured. Sarah wasn't eating. She was just sitting there, tense, her hands in her lap. "When you've been hurt repeatedly, it's tough to reach out again." The corners of his mouth curved gently. "I'd like you to think of me as your friend—if you want."

Sarah bit on her lower lip and forced herself to hold his gaze. "You have been a friend to me from the beginning," she admitted hollowly. "I-I've just been afraid to admit it to myself, Wolf."

"Because with the admission come the feelings."

"Exactly."

He stopped eating, his own heart opening to her vulnerability, her honesty. "It's better to have someone to turn to when you're feeling alone," he offered gently. "I know having you here has helped me—in ways you could never know."

Perplexed, Sarah stared at him. "There's so much I don't know about you, Wolf!"

Wolf knew he had to steer her away from his problems; she had enough of her own to handle without becoming entangled in his miserable life.

"How are your feet feeling?" he asked, changing the subject. He took another bite of his sandwich.

"Better, but not good enough." Although Sarah could have sworn that Wolf's magic touch was speeding up the healing of her feet. She removed the Ace bandages and stuck her feet out so that he could see them.

"They don't look as bruised," Wolf said, pleased.

"Thanks to you," she said, with a warm look in his direction.

"Healing comes in many forms."

"Who taught you about healing?"

"My grandmother. Her name was Bear Woman. People with bear medicines have great healing abilities, and she passed a lot of her knowledge on to me when I was a kid."

"Tell me about your life on the reservation," Sarah asked hopefully. So far, he'd gently parried all her attempts to know more about him.

Putting his plate aside, Wolf drew the cup of coffee into his hands. "My grandmother was a medicine woman for our tribe. Besides teaching me healing skills, she taught me a lot about how to survive."

"Oh?" Sarah saw the darkness come back into his eyes, as it did each time she touched on some distant unhealed memory. Instinctively she knew he, too, had to talk if he was to heal.

"When I was twelve, I went on a vision quest. For three days, I fasted and prayed with a pipe my grandmother had given me. On the third day, I had a vision.

I walked back to her cabin—in the Smoky Mountains of North Carolina—and told her about it.'' Wolf smiled softly. ''She was such a wise old woman. I can't tell you about the vision—to do so is to break the power of it. But, in general, she spoke to me about being a warrior, someone who would do battle of one sort or another all my life.''

''And so you went into the Marine Corps?''

Wolf hedged, then softened. To hell with it. It was too hard withholding information from Sarah. ''I spent eight years in the Marine Corps after I got out of high school, Sarah,'' he explained.

''But you're a forest ranger now. Did you get out of the marines and come here?''

Frowning, Wolf knew he couldn't lie to Sarah. Inhaling deeply, he took in the hope and interest shining in her blue eyes. Finally he said, ''No. I got an invitation to join Perseus, so I did.''

''What's Perseus?''

''It's a private security company run by Morgan Trayhern—a man I trust with my life. We work as troubleshooters sent all over the world, and we interface with the U.S. government. I've spent a lot of time in Colombia, Venezuela and Peru.''

Sarah was thrilled that Wolf was finally opening up to her. And then she realized humbly that it was because she had offered her friendship to him. She had finally trusted him; now he was beginning to entrust her with his past. ''Then you're like a soldier?''

''A mercenary,'' he said flatly.

''Did you…did you kill people?''

''My job was to train the police or military of each country. I was an advisor, Sarah.''

''I'm glad,'' she whispered.

He held her gaze. "I have killed."

"In defense of yourself?"

"Myself or others." Wolf shook his head. "I tried to defend—help—others. I failed sometimes...." Just the admission sheared painfully through Wolf, but he knew it was necessary to give it voice.

"I hope I never have to kill another human being." Sarah shivered at the thought. "You don't have the eyes of a killer. Summers does, and so do his hired guns."

"I didn't say I enjoyed killing, Sarah. I've got a conscience." Wolf grimaced. "And it never lets me forget the faces or the situations when it happened."

"And so you quit because you didn't want to kill?" Sarah probed, still not understanding why Wolf was here in Montana. She sensed that something terrible had happened to him, and that was the reason he was here, instead of some more exotic place.

Wolf looked away from Sarah's gaze. The truth tasted bitter in his mouth. The awful need to confide in her was almost overwhelming. But he couldn't tell her—not yet. Sarah was still too vulnerable. He didn't want to dump his problems on her. They had time, and he'd pick and choose when it was right to reveal his past. A terrible fear gutted him. When Sarah found out what he'd done, wouldn't she distrust him? She'd withdraw her friendship—and the hope he saw blazing so strongly in her eyes would disappear.

"I'd had enough killing. Enough fighting. I got wounded in Peru, so I came home to heal. In a sense, a huge part of me died down in Peru."

"When I first met you, Wolf, I could see such darkness in your eyes sometimes, as if you were lost in a black pit."

"You're not far off the mark," he agreed quietly, staring down at his empty coffee mug. "I wanted a quieter life, a life that hinged on helping living things, not fighting drug lords. I told Morgan that I wanted a job as a forester, and he used his influence to get me into the ranger program. They sent me here after training."

"You wanted to be alone," Sarah murmured. "To heal."

Her insight stunned him. Just the way Sarah whispered the words made his heart lurch with awareness of her, of her beauty as a woman with an incredibly understanding soul. "Yes."

For a long time, Sarah didn't speak. "Isn't it funny how we met each other? You came to Montana to get away from everything that had hurt you. I was fighting a battle that I knew I was losing an inch at a time." She shook her head. "Wolf, you're walking right back into the fire by helping me. You know that, don't you?"

He smiled at her candor. "In the Cherokee way, honey, walking through the fire is a part of life. Yeah, I know I'm repeating a cycle I've been through before. But you don't deserve to be abandoned." He stretched his arms out before him. "I'm going to try to help you. I've failed before, Sarah. Badly. But if you'll take a chance on me, I'll try to be there for you." *Please,* Wolf prayed, *this time, I must not fail.*

"How did you fail?" Sarah asked, seeing the haunted look return to his eyes. "You've said that before."

Wolf shook his head. "I don't want to talk about it yet, Sarah."

Sarah sat back. Wolf had divulged far more than she'd thought he would. But whatever terrible secret he carried was still there, eating away at him. A huge part of her wanted to help him—and believed she could. Then Sarah realized just how much of her trust she was willing to give him in order to do it. The thought frightened her, and she retreated. "You don't know Summers," she cautioned. "He's dangerous, and he'll kill." Rubbing her arms, suddenly feeling chilled, she added, "I've got this awful feeling, like he's lying in wait for me. I've been expecting him to raid my cabin, steal my lapidary equipment. Something…"

"Maybe the word's got out that you have a big guard dog," Wolf teased gently, getting to his feet. He took the cups and saucers to the sink to wash them.

Terror, shadowy and powerful, swept through Sarah. She looked up at Wolf, appreciating his strong back and shoulders. What burdens had he carried alone on those broad shoulders? He needed to be held, too, to be kept safe from a dangerous world. The desire to get up, slide her arms around him and do just that nearly overwhelmed Sarah, but she fought the urge.

Still, she couldn't shake the terror leaking through her. Should she tell Wolf about the phone call? But what could he do, anyway? Quit his job and make a bristling armory out of his house, waiting for Summers to try to kill her? It was stupid, she decided. She had to hope that the phone call was only a scare tactic.

"Let's get your feet wrapped," Wolf said as he finished his duties at the kitchen sink, "and then I've got to get back to the paperwork."

Sarah nodded and handed him the first Ace bandage. "Will you check the cabin before you come home tonight?"

Wolf knelt down and examined her foot. "I always do," he assured her. "You can expect me home around six tonight."

The moment Wolf turned into the fir-lined narrow dirt road that led to Sarah's cabin, Skeet started to whine.

The sun had dropped behind Blue Mountain, but pale daylight lingered. Automatically Wolf looked for the cause of his dog's reaction, and as he turned the corner, he got his answer. Two pickups, one black and the other tan, were parked next to Sarah's cabin. The hair on Skeet's neck bristled, and he growled low and deep.

"Easy," Wolf said soothingly, quietly bringing the truck to a halt and pulling off into the trees. Wolf opened the door and got out, leaving Skeet in the cab. He didn't want the dog shot if Sarah's visitors were some of Summers's henchmen. As he walked quietly toward the cabin, Wolf put a round in the chamber of his rifle. Hearing voices inside, he moved quickly to the open door. He saw three men dressed in jeans and cowboy shirts standing inside. Before they realized he was there, Wolf had imprinted their faces on his memory.

"You men got business with Sarah Thatcher?" he demanded, moving into the doorway and blocking any possible escape.

One man, heavyset with a black beard, swung around, a startled expression on his blocky face. Almost as quickly, his two cohorts did the same.

The bearded one sneered. "What's a forest ranger doing here?"

Wolf saw that some of Sarah's lapidary equipment had been piled in several boxes on the floor. The men appeared to be ready to haul the boxes out of the cabin.

"Not the same thing you're doing here, that's for sure," Wolf snarled. He kept the rifle pointed at them. "What the hell do you think you're doing?"

"Get him!" the black-bearded one yelled.

Wolf sensed someone behind him. Too late! Bracing himself, Wolf whirled and threw out his foot, connecting solidly with another of the men, this one blond. His boot sank deep in the man's gut. From behind, Wolf heard a rush toward him. A fist hit him squarely in the right kidney. Groaning, he staggered forward, raw pain radiating through his back. The rifle dropped from his hands.

"Get the son of a bitch!" Black Beard screamed. "Beat the hell out of him! Show him he can't interfere!"

Wolf staggered and turned, parrying another blow and throwing one of his own. His fist connected solidly with the man's square jaw, the tremor jolting up Wolf's arm and into his shoulder. Out of the corner of his eye he saw Black Beard running toward him. Breathing hard, Wolf tried to keep his footing, but the two men leaped at him at the same time. He slammed to the floor, the breath knocked out of him. And then the fists started to come at his face, two, three at a time. Pain arced and exploded through his brain and mercifully, Wolf lost consciousness.

Chapter Eight

It was dark when Wolf regained consciousness. He was lying on the floor of Sarah's cabin. He vaguely heard the sound of Skeet's nonstop barking coming from the truck. Groaning, he lay very still, getting his bearings and wondering if he had any broken bones. He was thankful Sarah hadn't been here when the henchmen had come. Revulsion and disgust flowed through him as he slowly sat up, every bone and muscle in his body protesting. If Sarah had been here, they might have raped her—or killed her. Or both.

The metallic taste of blood in his mouth was overwhelming. Thirsty, Wolf lurched to his hands and knees, then woozily staggered to his feet and over to the kitchen counter. Turning on the faucet, he cupped the cold water in his hands, throwing it on his bruised and puffy face. He winced at the cold—startling and soothing at the same time. Grabbing a towel hanging on a nearby nail, he buried his face in the soft folds of the terry cloth and leaned heavily against the counter.

Taking careful steps across the room, Wolf turned on the light. It hurt his eyes, and he squinted. The two boxes filled with Sarah's lapidary equipment were still on the floor! At least the bastards hadn't managed to steal anything after all.

Looking at the watch on his wrist, Wolf took a good thirty seconds to figure out what time it was: 8:00 p.m. Sarah would be worried. Lurching to the phone on the table next to her bed, Wolf sat down. Thankfully, he'd called the telephone company to repair Sarah's phone several days ago. Grimacing, he dialed his home number. The phone rang and rang. He prayed she'd pick it up. Finally the phone was picked up, and he heaved a sigh of relief.

"Hello?"

Wolf heard the carefully concealed terror in Sarah's voice. "Sarah, it's me, Wolf.... Something's happened up here at your cabin—"

"Wolf? You sound awful! What's happened?"

"Honey, it's okay," he mumbled, discovering several loose teeth on the left side of his face. His cheek had already swollen. He must look like a chipmunk carrying nuts. "I'll be home in an hour."

"You don't sound good. Wolf, what's wrong?" she demanded.

"I'll tell you when I get home. Just have some hot water and bandages ready, Sarah."

Sarah gave a low cry, caught herself, then became more coherent. "Bandages and hot water. Okay, I'll have them waiting for you, Wolf."

He wanted to smile, but couldn't. "Sounds good, honey. See you soon." He placed the phone back on the receiver and sat there a good minute before moving. Sarah had tried to be so brave about the conversation. Rising slowly, Wolf automatically placed his hand against his back where his right kidney was located. The bastard who'd hammered him there had meant to take him out—permanently. Luckily, he was in good shape, and he'd been turning as the blow was delivered, or he might not be walking.

As he pulled the door to Sarah's cabin shut, Wolf saw that the lock had been broken, probably with a crowbar. He'd have to replace it for her. His mind was spongy, and as he slowly put one foot in front of the other his need of Sarah rose with burning intensity. As he pulled open the truck door, Skeet whined and wagged his thick, brushy tail. Giving the dog a reassuring pat on the head, Wolf hauled his tired, aching body onto the seat. Somehow, he had to drive home. Somehow.

Despite the pain in her feet, Sarah walked quickly out the rear door of the house when she saw the lights of Wolf's truck in the driveway. It was dark, and she could barely make out that it was him as the truck pulled to a stop. Her heart hammering, she jerked open the driver's side door.

"Wolf?" Her voice was high and off-key.

The instant her hand settled on his shoulder, Wolf leaned back against the seat. "It's okay, Sarah—"

She gave a little cry. Wolf's face was swollen and bloodied. She should have told him about the phone call! Shaken, Sarah whispered, "Come on, put your arm around me. I'll help you into the house. Her voice was trembling with anger and terror as he reached for her. She bit back a groan as Wolf's weight sagged against her. He was none too steady on his feet, but she managed to guide him up the concrete steps and through the door. Her own feet were screaming in pain, but she ignored them.

"Just get me to the bathroom," Wolf rasped.

Sarah did as she was ordered. He sat down on the side of the bathtub, gripping the side of it for support. Quickly she pressed a cold cloth to his face. One eye was almost swollen shut, the bluish color pronounced around it.

"Who did this?" she asked in a wobbly voice, unable to contain her fear. Gently she dabbed away the blood, which made the injury look a lot worse than it really was.

"Don't know. Three men," Wolf said, his speech slurred. He touched his jaw. "Got loose teeth on this side."

"If you're lucky, they'll tighten up in a couple of days. Hold still—this is going to hurt." Sarah applied a washcloth with a hefty dose of soap on it. Wolf never moved, never flinched, never even showed any expression. Sarah remembered his mercenary duties in Peru.

"Is this what happened to you down in Peru?" she asked, quickly rinsing away the soap with fresh, clean water.

Wolf slid a glance upward, wildly aware of each of Sarah's touches. "Yeah...this was a normal, daily kind of punishment...."

Swallowing against the lump in her throat, Sarah continued to clean up his face. "Tell me what happened to you down there. *Please.*"

His defenses were down, and he knew it. Wolf was hurting too much, needing Sarah too much, to try and fight her request. His voice was low, off-key. "A woman

I knew…that I loved…was raped,'' he admitted finally. "Gang-raped.''

"Oh, God,'' Sarah whispered, "I'm sorry. For her and for you.'' The bleak devastation lingered in his eyes.

"Be sorry for the hell Maria went through, but don't be sorry for me,'' Wolf said roughly, unleashed emotion flowing like a bitter river through his heart.

Sarah sat very still, realizing the agony Wolf was experiencing. In a hushed tone, she said, "Go on.''

A tremor went through Wolf. He shut his eyes. "I've never told anyone about it…about Maria. After it happened… Not even Morgan.''

Sarah felt Wolf's fragility, the secret pain he carried, so evident in his roughened voice. "You told me talking about a trauma was a good thing. Why don't you apply it to yourself? You've already helped me. Maybe you don't realize it, but you have…and I'm grateful for your understanding.''

Wolf glanced up at Sarah. He realized how privileged he was to see the vulnerable side of her, and the thought was like sweet, molten heat flowing through his ice-cold soul. "It's ugly,'' he warned her.

"What about Maria? You said you loved her?''

Wolf cleared his throat—suddenly constricted with tears. "Yeah… She was a beautiful Peruvian woman, your age.'' Wolf stared down at his bruised, swollen hands, his mind and heart going back to that time and place. "We met over a pig drowning in a pond, if you can believe it. She was up to her knees in the water, the red skirt she was wearing hiked up around her hips. The pig was thrashing around out in deep water because a jaguar had chased it into the pond to catch and drown it. Maria was there when it happened. She yelled at the cat, and he took off.''

Wolf tried to smile and failed. "She was so damned angry at that pig because he was swimming farther out into the pond instead of back to the shore. I offered to go get it for her. When I brought the pig out and put it in her arms, she offered me and my men a meal at her village. A real hot meal. I took her up on it in a second. She was one hell of a cook, and I was grateful for village hospitality. But Maria was kind to everyone."

Wolf closed his eyes and then opened them, staring at the opposite wall of the bathroom. "I was stationed near her village for over a year, and eventually, we fell in love. Because I'm part Indian, and her people were of Incan heritage, I was respectful of their laws. I courted Maria. I had plans for us—lots of plans. When my mission was completed, I was going to marry Maria and bring her back to the States with me."

Wolf's gaze moved back to Sarah. There was such compassion and understanding in her shadowed eyes. "Maria's village was surrounded by coca plantations, and there was a lot of drug activity—the making of cocaine from the coca leaves. The head of the village, Juan Renaldo, forbade his people to get involved with the drug trafficking. Instead, they asked for protection from the Peruvian police. It was a clean village, and that's why I was assigned with my team to protect them from the drug armies. More than once, men from the village had shown us caches of cocaine and pointed out those from surrounding villages who were in the drug trade. It made for a lot of enemies and bad blood."

"My team fell for a trap, and we left the village unprotected for the day. When we returned, the village had been burned to the ground, most of the men killed, and the women—raped." Wolf's voice fell. "It was a warning from Ramirez, the drug lord, to the survivors."

Sarah took in a shaky breath. "My God, I'm so sorry, Wolf. Poor Maria."

Wolf nodded dully. "The rape really messed her up in the head. My men and I, along with another U.S. team, helped rebuild the village and get the people back on their feet physically. But the emotional scars it left behind couldn't be erased." He shook his head. "The survivors were scared. They lost their joy, their natural optimism. No one smiled very much after the raid. Even though I loved Maria, she was afraid of me. I mean, really afraid of me."

"Because you were a man, and it was men who'd hurt her?" Sarah guessed.

"Yeah."

The unhappiness in his face was almost too much to bear. "What eventually happened to you and Maria? Did she decide not to marry you?"

It hurt to talk, to feel so deeply again. Wolf squeezed his eyes shut. "I tried to love her the best I knew how, to convince her I loved her. Maria couldn't stand to be touched by me. She couldn't stand being held. It reminded her too much of being pinned down by those bastards who raped her. I tried to understand. I tried..." Wolf stopped, the pain working up through his chest. More than anything, he owed Sarah the last of the story. The real truth that would show him to be the miserable failure he really was.

"Ramirez set us up again, and I fell for it. I fell for all of it," Wolf told her bitterly. "A second time, we left the village unprotected. When we were out chasing Ramirez's men, he came into the village and killed again." Wolf desperately struggled to control his wildly fluctuating emotions. "Maria was murdered by the bastard," he rasped.

Sarah gave a little cry and pressed her hands against her lips. She stared down at Wolf and saw the terrible carnage of what had happened. Suddenly she realized why he'd made all those oblique references over the past week; that he was a failure, that he couldn't protect anyone, including her. Reaching out and placing her trembling hand on his slumped shoulder, she whispered, "Did you feel like you killed her?"

"I did," he muttered harshly. "I lost it after I found Maria dead. I went crazy. Ramirez was still running around loose. I'd already seen the daily fear and agony Maria had gone through. Who knows what she suffered at the end? I was helpless. What were words? Even while she was still alive, I hadn't been able to reach her. I couldn't even comfort her, one human being to another, when she needed to feel safe. I couldn't even do that for her. I failed her. I'd left her unprotected...."

Wolf rubbed his face savagely. "I went on a rampage. I swore I'd kill those bastards who'd murdered Maria."

"Those scars on your chest," Sarah whispered. "Don't tell me—"

"I tangled with Ramirez and his army," Wolf told her. "We fought several pitched battles around his home. I got too bold—I wasn't thinking straight—and Ramirez captured me. Killian, one of my men, tried to rescue me, but they got him, too."

Sarah shook her head. "What did they do to you?"

"Tortured me," he said numbly.

"My God! How did you survive?" she cried.

"One minute at a time. One second at a time. Ramirez had me in his special torture chamber for a month until Jake, the third man on my team, along with the Peruvian police, was able to bust me out and get me to a hospital. Killian was tortured, too, but thank God, not as bad.

Ramirez was paying me back for killing his men. I was the one he wanted, because I was the leader of the team.''

Shakily, Sarah covered her face with her hands. ''And I thought I had problems. My God, I don't. I really don't.''

Wolf forced himself to sit where he was. If he moved, he'd get up, pull Sarah in his arms and hold her. Not because she might need him, but because he needed her. And that wasn't fair. He didn't deserve her comfort. ''Your problems are similar. Summers isn't as overt as Ramirez, but his goals are the same, Sarah.'' With a sigh, Wolf added, ''That's why I promised I'd help you.'' Holding her tear-filled gaze, he continued. ''Summers sees you as a continuing threat to him, and he's going to keep going after you. He doesn't have much to fear from the judicial system here. It's the old-boy network in action. He's got his connections. That's why I'm going to walk at your side through this mess. We'll find your attackers, and we'll find out who wanted you to die trapped beneath that fir. With or without Noonan's help.''

Sarah studied him for a long time in silence. ''I need to tell you about the phone call I got, Wolf.''

Wolf took the washcloth and pressed it to his swollen cheek. He heard guilt in Sarah's voice. ''What call?''

Rubbing her brow, she rattled, ''The phone rang, and I picked it up. A man on the other end said, 'You're dead.'''

Wolf scowled, and it hurt. ''Sarah—''

''I know, I know. I should have told you.'' She reached out and touched his shoulder. ''I'm sorry, Wolf. I thought it was just one more of Summers's harassment tricks to scare me off. Oh, God, if I'd thought he was going to have his men jump you at my cabin, I'd have told you—I was trying to keep you out of it!''

Wolf awkwardly patted her hand. ''It's all right,'' he told her in a gravelly voice. ''We'll get through this.''

Sarah stared down at him, tears in her eyes. ''Why are you doing this for me?''

He shrugged. ''Maybe I'm doing it for a couple of reasons. One of them is guilt. Every night, I see the faces of those who died in Peru. There isn't anything I don't remember about the massacre at the village, Sarah.'' He was loath to give voice to the other reason: He cared about Sarah—one hell of a lot. He'd been given a second chance to rectify his poor choices in Peru. He found it shocking that Sarah hadn't condemned him for his failures. Instead, she seemed to take hope as never before. He knew he couldn't divulge how he felt about her.

''It must be a living hell for you.''

''We all live in a hell of some sort,'' he muttered.

Sarah said nothing, realizing Wolf was living with one of the worst emotions she could name—guilt. ''It wasn't your fault that it happened, you know,'' she finally said.

''What?''

''Maria's rape.''

Wolf shook his head. ''Sarah, I'll go to my grave being sorry about that—for being stupid enough to be tricked by Ramirez into leaving her unprotected. Hell, I left the whole village wide open for a second attack.''

''Still,'' Sarah said softly, ''with time, some of the pain will dull. At least that's what everyone tells me about Dad's death.'' She rubbed the area where her heart lay. ''It felt pretty raw in here, until I cried in your arms last night....''

''At least you cried,'' Wolf whispered huskily. ''That's a good sign the healing process is going on.

While I was recuperating in the hospital, I started doing some investigation on rape and what it does to a person's head and emotions. I had to try and understand Maria's actions toward me. If I'd known then what I know now, I would have gotten her to a therapist in the nearest city. She needed help, and so did I.''

"But you didn't know how to help her," Sarah said, feeling deeply for Wolf. "That's not your fault."

He rallied beneath her warm blue gaze, which was sparkling with unshed tears. How easily touched Sarah was beneath that tough shell she wore to defend her own fragile, wounded emotions. "No, I didn't know," he agreed heavily. "But—" he tendered her an intense look "—I do know now, and that's why I'm treating you the way I do. You're a victim of violence, too. And you need time to heal. I was never able to help Maria. All I did was make things worse for her, and what we shared between us died."

Sarah didn't have the words to help Wolf. Gently she steered him to another topic. "You said there were a couple of reasons for helping me. What's the second one?"

Wolf wrung out the cloth and placed it back against his cheek. If he told Sarah the truth—how much she touched him, made him feel alive again—she might run. Or, worse, tell him to go away, as Maria had. Clearing his throat, he said, "I've always had a place in my heart for underdogs." Wolf glanced up to see what affect his words had on her. Her young face was so grave and serious.

"There isn't a woman alive who isn't an underdog," Sarah said. She'd finished cleaning up his face, and now she treated his scraped, bloodied hands. Her own hands shook slightly as she dressed his wounds, her mouth a tight line, as if she were trying to stop herself from crying. Her reaction moved Wolf deeply.

"Well, we'll see if I can help even out this situation. I don't know if the men who hit me at your cabin were Summers's men—"

"They're Summers's men, all right," Sarah gritted out, washing her hands off in the sink and putting the bandages away. "That's how they work. They sneak up behind you, and they always work in pairs or a trio."

Wolf's face was aching like hell. "There's some aspirin in there, Sarah," he said, indicating the medicine cabinet. "Get me a couple of tablets?"

"Sure." She glanced down at Wolf's features. They looked washed out beneath the harsh glare. It was nearly 10:00 p.m., and he was exhausted. She handed him the aspirin and a glass of water.

"You have to report this to Sheriff Noonan. Tomorrow morning."

Wolf choked down the bitter-tasting tablets and finished off the water. He handed her the glass and thanked her. "First things first. I'm going over to the hospital emergency room tomorrow morning to find out if any of those jokers went over there. I know for sure I busted one guy's nose, and I'm pretty positive I heard the jaw of a second one crack. They'll need X rays and medical help, and the hospital's the only place around here to get them. When I've got their names, I'll start an investigation on my own, before I go to Noonan."

Sarah winced. "Sounds like you gave them worse than you got," she said, pride seeping into her voice.

"We'll see," Wolf rasped. "Look, I need to lie down."

"Yes, you do. On *your* bed." Sarah gave him a hard look. "And don't argue with me, Wolf. Ever since you started sleeping on that couch, you've had circles under your eyes."

Wolf slowly rose to his full height. How beautiful and defiant Sarah looked in her cotton nightgown and robe, her silky golden hair like a cloud around her shoulders. He longed to lose himself in those wide blue eyes.

"No, Sarah, I'll be fine out on the—"

"Damn you!" Sarah grated out. "Don't you dare argue with me, Wolf Harding!" She grabbed him by the arm and used all her strength to haul him out of the bathroom and toward the bedroom.

Wolf gripped her arm and gently drew her to a halt. "Now listen..." he rasped in the darkness of the hall, wildly aware of how close she stood to him. "You sleep on the bed. No argument, Sarah. Your feet are still healing up."

"I thought I was stubborn, but you're worse than I am! I refuse to sleep in your bed tonight!" She jerked out of his grasp and spun around to head for the living room and claim the couch before he could.

His patience thinning, Wolf gripped her shoulder. "All right," he muttered, "we'll both sleep in my bed. Now come on."

Gasping, Sarah was propelled ahead of him into the bedroom. "Wolf, this is ridiculous! I—"

He shut the bedroom door with finality and stared at her through the gloom. The defiance in her eyes made him want to smile, but his face hurt too much for him to attempt it. "Relax, will you? We both need a good night's sleep. I'll be damned if you're going to sleep on that rickety old couch."

Sarah's eyes widened as Wolf stripped out of his blood-spattered green shirt, then pulled his white T-shirt over his head. Her mouth went dry, and her heart started to leap and flutter. The sight of Wolf's powerful chest made her take a step back, but when Wolf turned, she saw a huge black bruise midway down on the right side of his back and gave a low cry of alarm.

Wolf froze at the sound of Sarah's cry. Before he could turn to see what had upset her, he felt the coolness of her hands against his back.

"What happened here, Wolf? Look at this. Look at this! It's awful!"

He stood very still, a groan threatening to rip out of him. Sarah's hands fluttered like a butterfly around the injury. She placed one hand flat against his rib cage beneath his right arm. The other gently touched the bruised area.

"I got hit from behind. The bastard tried to take me out with a kidney punch."

Biting down hard on her lower lip, Sarah explored the bruise. "It's so swollen, Wolf. You ought to go to the hospital. Really, this looks bad...."

Wolf turned and gently placed his arm around her small shoulders, drawing her in front of him. The genuine concern in her eyes melted him, and he ached to cup her small face and kiss those delicate lips.

"Honey," he rasped, "I'll be all right. Just you touching me made the pain less." Without thinking, because Sarah invited his tender side, Wolf grazed her deeply flushed cheek with his lips. Her skin was as firm and soft as a ripe peach. "Look, let's get some sleep. I'm about ready to fall over." The statement was a blatant lie now that Sarah was standing so close to him. Wolf tried to separate right from wrong. She was so damned enticing, yet he saw fear lurking in the recesses of her eyes. He didn't want to hurt Sarah as he'd unthinkingly hurt Maria. He removed his arm from her shoulder.

"Come on," he coaxed huskily. "You get in bed and turn your back to me. You'll be safe, understand?"

Swallowing, Sarah nodded, her cheek tingling where his lips had brushed it. The burning fire in his hooded eyes made her ache with a longing she'd never experienced in her life. Confused she whispered, "Sure..." Turning away from him, she did exactly as he asked and took one side of the bed. She pulled the sheet up to her waist, her back to him.

Sarah lay there, hearing Wolf's clothing drop to the floor beside the bed. She swallowed again, convulsively, unable to contain her vivid imagination, raging over the image of what it would be like to be pulled into Wolf's powerful arms in passion rather than comfort. He could crush her, he was so large in comparison to her. Yet his touch was always gossamer, painfully arousing her needs as a woman.

When the bed sagged and creaked beneath his weight, Sarah stiffened momentarily. And then she relaxed as he spread his weight out across the mattress, leaving plenty of room between them.

Wolf pulled the sheet up across his hip to his waist. He couldn't lie on his right side, his normal side to sleep on, because of the bruised kidney. Instead, he had to lie on his left side, facing Sarah's back. Just the way her golden hair lay in silky abandonment made him want to reach out and thread his fingers through it. Her cotton nightgown was cut low in the back and revealed her long, deeply indented spine. Wolf ached to reach out and pull her against him. He could almost feel her small breasts against his chest, the light warmth of her breath caressing his neck, her hands wrapping around his waist...

Chapter Nine

Wolf awoke with a start, bathed in sweat. Disoriented momentarily, the sudden movement making his body ache, he opened his eyes and blinked away the perspiration. The room, his bedroom, was washed by the early-morning light. His nostrils flaring, he inhaled sharply, a new and unfamiliar scent surrounding him like the caress of a lover.

His muddled senses sharpened, became focused. The scent, delicate and sweet, drifted toward him again. He inhaled deeply, and old, painful memories stirred to life. Then Wolf realized with a start that Sarah lay curled up next to him. Her small hand was pressed against his naked chest, as was her brow. He lay very still, not daring to move, not daring to breathe.

Sometime during the night—and Wolf sure as hell didn't know when—she had left her side of the bed, turned over and curled up in almost a fetal position against him. His eyes narrowed as he surveyed the small form covered with the crinkled white nightgown that had ridden up on her thighs during the night. Her face looked peaceful, her lips parted in sleep, fine strands of blond hair lying against her cheek.

Without thinking, Wolf barely touched her soft skin as he slipped his finger beneath the silky strands and pushed them back off her face. How serene Sarah looked. An explosion of joy rocked through him as he savored the fact that she was touching him. His heart started a hard, powerful thudding. Her hand was warm against him, as was her moist, shallow breath. Unconsciously his breath seemed to be synchronized with hers as she slept trustingly beside him.

Shifting all his awakening awareness to her, Wolf could feel the cool silk of her hair against him where her brow met the wall of his chest. Her position was endearing, telling him that Sarah probably had little experience with men. Her long, coltish legs were tucked up tightly against her body, not touching him at all. Her position was that of a child seeking safety.

Still, Wolf lay there trembling inwardly, grateful that Sarah trusted him that much—even on an unconscious level. In sleep, people showed their true selves, he believed. If she didn't trust him, she wouldn't have found her way into his arms. Savoring Sarah, Wolf closed his eyes tight as tears sprang to them. His mouth moved into a tight line as he fought back the sudden and unexpected deluge of emotion throbbing through him.

A few tears leaked out from beneath Wolf's lashes, making warm tracks down the sides of his face. Sarah didn't see him as a miserable failure, even though he'd admitted the truth of his past. What kind of forgiving heart lay in her breast, that she could grant him that kind of understanding—that she hadn't judged him? He still judged himself harshly—but, at the same time, he savored Sarah's reaction to him. For the first time in a year, hope entwined his heart. Hope for a future—if he could protect Sarah. If he could keep her safe.

Slowly, because he didn't want to awaken Sarah, Wolf lifted his arm from where it rested against his body. He didn't need to open his eyes to know where Sarah lay. He carefully placed his arm across her shoulders.

A sound, like a softened groan, issued from Wolf as his arm rested around Sarah's shoulders. The moment brought exquisite pain from the past, yet simultaneously was freeing to Wolf. Sarah lay sleeping against him, and he absorbed her into him, silently promising her he'd keep her safe—even if he had to give his life to do it.

Sarah awoke slowly. Morning sounds filtered into her awakening consciousness, and she forced her eyes open. Sunlight poured through the sheers at the window, illuminating the bedroom. What time was it? Groggily she raised her head from the mattress, seeing her pillow, as always, on the floor. It was 9:00 a.m.! She'd overslept. The bed was empty, Wolf's larger-than-life presence gone.

Turning over onto her back, Sarah closed her eyes. What crazy dreams she'd had last night! Dreams of Wolf holding her so gently that she'd wanted to cry. Lifting her hand, Sarah realized with a start that her cheeks contained dried tears. Where did dreams end and reality begin? Had she really been in Wolf's arms last night?

Sarah lay there, her gaze on the plaster ceiling as she absorbed fragments of memories, dreams, from last night. Unconsciously she slid her arm across the bed to where Wolf had slept. The sheet was cool to her touch, but a slight depression still existed where he'd lain. Her heart did funny leaps as she felt her way through the possibility that Wolf had held her as she slept. A part of her was disappointed. If he'd held her, he could have gone one step further and kissed her. And then she'd have awakened, and Sarah knew, in the dreamy state between wakefulness and sleep, she would have made love with Wolf.

The thought was as startling as it was heated. With a tremulous sigh, Sarah closed her eyes. Yes, she wanted to love Wolf. The man had had so much taken away from him. So much. She knew instinctively that she could heal some part of him by loving him. Making love was a simple act that could do so much to heal—or to rend apart. Sarah knew that from bitter experience. Her disastrous relationship with Philip had taught her that she didn't have what was necessary to make a relationship work.

Wolf's love of Maria was something she could understand—that special, fierce emotion that overlapped each day's activities, that gave each hour a special meaning. Opening her eyes, Sarah rolled to her side and tucked her hands beneath her cheek. She stared at Wolf's pillow, which had been punched and shaped to cradle his head.

Worry over how Wolf was this morning after the beating made her get up. Pushing her hair off her face, she brought her legs across the mattress and rested her toes on the carpeted floor. Outside the closed bedroom door, she could hear Wolf moving around.

Concerned, she quickly got dressed and brushed her hair. She ignored the crutches in the corner. Today she would walk a lot more on her still tender feet, she decided. She could no longer afford the luxury of remaining crippled. Wolf was in as much danger as she was, and he needed to know she was strong and reliable. Besides, sapphires needed to be dug, faceted and readied for Kirt Wagner, her distributor, by the end of the month. Without the needed money, Sarah knew, she wouldn't be able to make her mother's nursing-home payment. And that just couldn't happen.

She opened the door and discovered Skeet there to greet her. She smiled and patted the dog's broad head. He turned and trotted alongside her as she moved down the hall. Sarah found Wolf in the kitchen, making breakfast. The smell of ham was heavenly. She stood at the entrance watching him cook.

"Morning," Wolf said. He'd awakened a half hour earlier. Now he turned to see Sarah standing uncertainly, her blond hair framing her face and shoulders. Today she'd dressed in well-worn jeans and a green tank top, leaving her feet bare. Her blue eyes looked warm and serene, in sharp contrast to how he felt inside this morning. Getting to hold Sarah had been a double-edged sword, Wolf thought, arousing other, more sensual feelings of longing to plague his wounded heart.

Sarah smiled sleepily and said, "Hi…" She moved slowly toward the gas stove, where Wolf stood, turning the ham in the skillet. "I overslept."

Wolf tore his gaze from hers. The sweetness of her innocent smile, the care in her azure eyes, damn near unglued him. It took everything he had to stop himself from putting down the fork, letting go of the skillet and sweeping Sarah uncompromisingly into his arms.

Scowling, he forced himself to pay attention to the frying meat. "That makes two of us."

"Yes…" Sarah looked at her watch. "It's almost nine-thirty. How are you feeling?"

Wolf tendered her a slight smile. His face was still puffy, and one corner of his mouth hurt like hell. "I've missed something by not seeing you this time of morning," he admitted huskily. When Sarah tilted her head, not understanding his comment, Wolf added, "You look pretty."

Heat suffused Sarah's face, and she quickly avoided his burning look. Had Wolf really held her last night? His voice was low and vibrating, like the earthy growl of an animal. Her heart suddenly pounding, she turned and moved to the opposite counter. His compliment had shaken her. It was as if he could look into her heart and mind and know that she wanted to kiss him, to love him.

"Thank you," she whispered, reaching for two plates from the cupboard. But to love Wolf meant to trust him, to give everything she felt to him. And Sarah couldn't do that—the danger to them was too real. What if Wolf was killed? Sarah hated herself for thinking it, for allowing herself to feel, even for a moment, the terrible pain it created in her heart. Somehow she was just going to have to deny her feelings toward Wolf. Grasping at another topic, she said, "You still didn't tell me how you're feeling."

Wolf's mouth curved again. "How do I look?" he asked dryly.

"Like hell."

"Well, that's about how I feel."

Sarah placed the plates on the table and got out the flatware. "Your face is a mass of bruises, Wolf. Shouldn't you go to the doctor? You've got to be in a lot of pain."

"I'm okay. I called in and told my boss I was taking the day off. I want to do some checking around for those three men." The pain of longing he felt for Sarah at that moment was far greater than the pain from the beating he'd received the night before. He wondered distractedly if Sarah realized how much he wanted her.

After placing two paper napkins beside their plates, Sarah went over and poured them each a cup of coffee. "Are you going to report this to Sheriff Noonan?"

"Yes, I will," Wolf assured her. He saw the fear darken her eyes. "Stop worrying."

"How can I?"

"Because I can take care of myself, that's why." Although not very well, it was obvious, Wolf thought, feeling a deep, cutting doubt that he could keep Sarah safe. He motioned for her to sit down. "How do you want your eggs?"

Eating was the last thing on Sarah's mind. Something had changed between them, something that was now translucent, like a fine blue sapphire revealing its true shimmer in sunlight after merely glowing in indoor light. Sarah stood several seconds longer than necessary, caught in the burning intensity of his gaze.

Wolf saw the look, and his mouth went dry. She was as hungry for him as he was for her. The realization was startling, lush. Never had Wolf wanted a woman more than he did Sarah. Had she known that he was holding her last night? Could that explain the subtle change in her attitude toward him? He was afraid to ask. Afraid of finding that the answer was only some silly dream of his scarred heart.

"Wh-what?"

"Eggs," he repeated gruffly. "How do you want them?"

"Uh...scrambled, please." Sarah quickly turned away, her cheeks burning like fire. Shakily she placed the plate of ham on the table and sat down. What was going on? One moment she'd glanced at him, only to find herself gently snared in his fierce dark eyes, eyes that spoke a silent language of need for her. Rubbing her face, Sarah wondered if it was her overactive imagination. It had to be! But the dream, the exquisite memory of his arm around her, drifted back to her as she sat there, her heart slowly coming back to a normal beat.

Fighting to overcome her powerful feelings toward Wolf, she croaked out, "You know Noonan won't help you. Reporting this will be a mistake."

"Maybe. Maybe not. I want the report, Sarah. When I catch those men and bring them up on charges, Noonan isn't going to be able to sweep it under the rug like he's done in the past."

Her eyes widened considerably. "You're going after them?"

"Yes." Wolf had scrambled six eggs. Sliding half onto her plate and half onto his, he set the skillet back on the stove.

She watched as he sat down and gave her a slice of toast. "You're walking on Noonan's territory. He won't take kindly to you investigating," she warned.

Wolf buttered his toast and took a forkful of scrambled eggs. "Honey, I don't care what Noonan does or doesn't like."

"Oh." Because of her worry for him, Sarah couldn't even taste the eggs or the toast. The silence in the kitchen deepened as they ate. Half the eggs still remained when Sarah finally gave up and pushed the plate away.

"Aren't you going to eat them?" Wolf asked incredulously.

"No."

"Why not? Are you full?"

With a half shrug, Sarah pulled the cup of steaming coffee toward her. "Not exactly."

"Look at me."

Sarah refused.

"Sarah?" Wolf placed his hand on her arm. "What's wrong?"

The gentleness in his voice forced the truth from her. His fingers, long and callused, seemed to brand the skin of her arm where they rested. She ached to fling her arms around him. "I...uh, I'm worried about you. Okay? Those three jerks who jumped you could do it again. Next time..." She looked away. "Next time they might kill you, Wolf."

Wolf's fingers tightened on Sarah's arm. Her forlorn expression wasn't lost on him. She cared for him. The discovery was wonderful. Exhilarating. And he wouldn't play games with her by asking her why that worried her. Instead, he said softly, "I haven't been taken out yet, Sarah. I'll be careful, I promise." When she lifted her chin and looked at him, his heart melted with such fierce love for her that it nearly smothered him. "I've got too much to live for. Do you understand that?" he said roughly.

Sarah wasn't sure what he meant by that statement. She was bathed in the shadowed look from his gray eyes, and his voice, low and soft, flowed across her as if he'd stroked her. Shaken, she could do nothing but nod, words jammed uselessly in her constricted throat.

Wolf nudged the plate in her direction. "Go on, try to finish the eggs."

Touched to the point of tears, Sarah hung her head, her curtain of blond hair hiding her reaction. She ate everything on her plate, not tasting the food, but happier than she'd ever been—and more frightened than she would ever have thought possible.

"What if Noonan plays rough?" Sarah asked Wolf later as he got ready to leave to make out a report.

Wolf shoved his billfold in his back pocket. Today, since he was off duty, he'd dressed in jeans and a blue plaid cowboy shirt, the sleeves rolled up to his elbows. Sarah sat on the couch, worry reflected in her face and voice.

"If Noonan or Summers starts playing for keeps," Wolf said as he turned to face her, "I've got an ace up my sleeve."

"What's that?" How darkly handsome Wolf looked, Sarah thought. He was more cowboy than forest ranger. She could easily envision him astride a horse.

"My friends."

"Your team from Peru?"

"Yeah." Wolf walked over and sat down next to her. Sarah deserved a full explanation. He didn't want to cause her any more worry than necessary, but it was hard not to get distracted. She had left her hair down instead of putting it up in braids today, and he ached to sift his fingers through it.

"Sean Killian and Jake Randolph are my best friends. Jake was in the Marine Corps, like me—we got out at the same time. Killian was in the French Foreign Legion, along with Morgan Trayhern, my boss, and that's where they met, a long time ago.

"I need to give you some background on my work, Sarah," he continued, "and the people I work for. Morgan Trayhern is a Vietnam vet who got shafted by the Marine Corps. They had him up on treason charges for leaving his company when it was overrun by the enemy in Vietnam. Everybody in the States swallowed the cover-up story, except for his family and the woman he fell in love with, Laura Bennett. She began investigating Morgan's past, and together they found out a CIA boss had framed him. It's a hell of a story, and he's a hell of a man.''

''Sounds like Laura isn't too bad herself,'' Sarah said.

Wolf nodded. ''She's a fighter, just like you.''

Eyeing him, Sarah added, ''So Perseus could bring their troubleshooting skills here?''

''That's right.'' Wolf scowled. ''I may ask them to fly into Philipsburg if I can't handle this situation on my own.'' He reached out and caressed her pale cheek. Her eyes were as huge as those of a child being told a scary story. ''They're good men, Sarah, not killers. If I can settle this thing with Summers and his men peacefully, I will. No one hates fighting more than I do.''

She released a breath of air. ''I am glad you have a backup plan,'' she admitted.

He grinned, even though it hurt like hell. ''If I didn't learn anything else in Peru, I learned to rely on my team, to ask for help. I'll be back by noon, and I'll take you to lunch.'' He pointed to her feet. ''Soak them in hot epsom salts and then pack them in ice.''

Sarah felt absolutely bathed in his undeniable caring. ''I will.'' She reached forward and gripped his hand. ''Wolf, be really careful, okay?''

''For you, I will be,'' he promised huskily, forcing himself to leave. It was that or sweep her into his arms. Rising, he said, ''I'm leaving Skeet here with you. My rifle is in the bedroom. Keep the doors locked, and don't answer the phone. Understand?''

Sarah nodded, the reality of her situation burying the

joy of having discovered so many things about Wolf. "I promise," she said solemnly.

When Wolf entered the jail, a man dressed impeccably in a gray silk suit, white shirt and navy tie was talking to Noonan. Noonan gave Wolf a squinty look. The man next to him turned with a calculating glance.

"Looks like you ran into a Mack truck," Noonan drawled.

Wolf closed the distance, his intuition screaming a warning about the man in the suit. He had gunmetal-gray hair, cut short and neat, dark brown eyes that were like bottomless caves, and ramrod-straight posture.

"It wasn't a truck, Sheriff." Wolf threw three photocopies of hospital reports down on the officer's desk. "I want you to make out a warrant for the arrest of these three men. They jumped me last night at Sarah Thatcher's cabin. They made the mistake of going to the emergency room to get treatment after leaving me unconscious on the cabin floor."

Noonan's mouth dropped open. He snapped it shut just as quickly. Glancing at the man in the suit, he hesitantly reached for the hospital records.

"Well, now..." He slowly perused each set of copies.

"You must be Ranger Harding," the other man said smoothly.

Wolf held his cold gaze. "That's right. Who are you?"

"Gerald Summers. I'm a local mine owner."

Wolf didn't extend his hand, and neither did Summers.

"You say three men jumped you?" Summers coaxed in a cultured voice.

"That's right." Wolf wanted to add, *Three of your*

men. But it was too early to indict Summers. He shifted his focus to the sheriff, who was scowling.

"More than likely these three have left town by now," the sheriff told him testily.

"I don't care. I want warrants made out for them. Just give me the papers to sign so that you can put the legal end in motion," Wolf ordered.

Summers smiled slightly. "Sheriff, I'll leave now. Ranger Harding, nice meeting you."

Wolf nodded but said nothing. Summers reminded him of a weasel, as sleek and oily-looking as that bastard Ramirez.

"Like I said before," Noonan repeated, "these boys have probably left town."

"As *I* said before, I don't care, Sheriff. I want them caught."

Noonan's eyes hardened. "No one tells me my business, Harding."

Wolf stared back into the sheriff's belligerent eyes. "And no one gets away jumping me from behind—or trying to steal from Sarah Thatcher."

Leaning forward, resting his palms on his desk, Noonan looked Wolf over. "Kinda chummy with her, ain't you?" he asked finally.

"That has no bearing on this," Wolf growled, pointing at the copies.

"Yep, she's got you wrapped around her little finger. She did that once to a guy name Philip Barlow, you know. Poor fella was all the worse for it. He had to leave town once she got done with him. A real viper, she is."

Gritting his teeth, Wolf leaned across the desk. "Noonan, I don't want to hear one more thing out of that filthy mouth of yours about Sarah Thatcher. Got it? Your job is to track down these bastards. If you don't do it, I'll make sure it happens. Do we understand each other?''

Noonan's eyes grew large, then squinted in fury. He came bolting around his desk and clutched at Wolf's shirtfront.

Instantly Wolf grabbed the sheriff's soft white hand with his own. ''Don't do it if you want to live, Noonan,'' he ground out softly.

Releasing Wolf's shirt, Noonan straightened, his face white with anger. ''Get outa here, Harding. You're bad news, just like that Thatcher woman. A cold wind follows you, mister. A real cold one.''

''I'm coming in here tomorrow to find out what you've done about apprehending those three men, Sheriff.''

''Don't threaten me!''

Wolf walked slowly to the door, then stopped, his hand resting lightly on the doorknob. ''It's not a threat, it's a promise.''

''No one tells me my job!''

''I'll be here at 1:00 p.m.,'' Wolf snarled. He jerked open the door and left.

Outside, the weather was warming quickly. It was eleven o'clock and he had enough time to get home, pick up Sarah and take her someplace special for lunch, Wolf thought. He was looking forward to it. Every minute was precious when it was spent with Sarah. He frowned as he got into his truck. As he drove away from the jail, Wolf wondered who this Philip Barlow character was. Momentary jealousy stabbed at him, and he had trouble shrugging it off. The idea of any man making love to Sarah made Wolf uneasy. His grandmother had always said he had a bit of a jealous streak, but it had never surfaced—not until now. Then Wolf recalled the rest of his grandmother's words—that his jealousy would only rear its head when he fell in love with the woman who would walk with him as his wife.

Rubbing his brow, Wolf replayed his medicine-woman grandmother's prediction. He'd never been jealous of Maria in any way, he had to admit. He'd known that she'd had two lovers before him, and it had never bugged him. But this Philip whoever-he-was bothered the hell out of him. Was he an ex-lover? An ex-husband? Wolf knew so little about Sarah, and suddenly he wanted to know everything.

Chapter Ten

The noontime trade at Francey's Diner consisted mostly of tourists, and for that Sarah was grateful. She didn't want locals who worked for Summers to see her with Wolf or possibly eavesdrop on their conversation. As it was, she and Wolf were seated in a vinyl-covered booth at the rear of the diner, as far from the other patrons as possible, and they kept their voices low.

Wolf sat opposite her, their knees brushing beneath the narrow table. Sarah was hungry, finishing off a hamburger platter with relish, but she noticed that Wolf had left his hot beef sandwich practically untouched.

"What's bothering you?" she asked, blotting her mouth with a paper napkin.

Wolf shrugged. "Not much." He'd told her about the incident with Noonan, but not about Philip Barlow. There was no sense in making Sarah suffer because the sheriff hated her. She'd had enough nasty words flung at her.

Tilting her head, Sarah smiled. "You're brooding. You look like a thunderstorm ready to split open and pour down rain."

Wolf attempted to return her smile. "Good analogy," he told her. Moving his fork absently around the tabletop next to his plate, he added, "It's nothing." It was something, all right, and Wolf was becoming angry with himself, because it seemed that he could hide nothing from Sarah's perception. Jealousy ate at him, although he knew it shouldn't.

"Oh." Sarah sat back and picked up her mug of coffee. "I thought friends could share problems and concerns."

"They can."

"I'll listen if you want to talk," she said softly.

Wolf glanced up at her, on the verge of asking about Philip. He knew he was behaving like some immature sixteen-year-old kid—and it was making him mad. Swallowing, he shook his head. "It's nothing," he repeated.

"For once, I'd like to help you," Sarah whispered. "I'm not a world traveler, and I don't have more than a high school education, but maybe all you need is a set of ears."

"Sarah," he said, scowling, "stop putting yourself down."

"Was I?"

"Yes. You've got so much going for you. You've got drive, energy and brains. You handle a career like gem mining all by yourself. And," he said, "successfully. I've seen college grads and Ph.D.s who were worthless at running a business."

Grinning, Sarah said, "Okay, so I'm a good businesswoman. Thank you."

"You're welcome." Wolf saw a slight flush come to Sarah's cheeks. What she needed was a little care, a little pampering—a focus on her strengths.

"So," he said, moving aside his platter of uneaten food, "how did you manage to get half this town angry at you?"

With a laugh, Sarah said, "It wasn't hard, Wolf. My dad bucked Summers, and after he died, so did I."

"You had a reputation as a troublemaker even back in high school," he said, baiting her.

Frowning, she agreed. "Yes, I did. As my mom said, I don't suffer fools gladly." Sarah brightened. "My mom was always quoting different passages, things that made sense to me." Her happiness faded. "That's one of the things I miss about her since the stroke. She always had the right saying for any occasion."

Wolf hurt for her. "At least she's alive, and there's a part of her left," he said gently. Maybe he should take Sarah to the nursing home to see her mother. "And you love her. She knows that."

Sarah shrugged unhappily and sipped her coffee. "Maybe she does, maybe she doesn't. I just wish…"

"What?" Wolf said softly, absorbing her sad, pensive face.

With a sigh, Sarah forced a slight smile. "I just wish Mom was still here. I really miss talking to her and getting her advice. She sure helped me get through some tough times."

"Such as?"

Sarah gave him an arched-eyebrows look. "My reputation in this town was bad news after the FBI investigation, Wolf. A lot of locals wouldn't have anything to do with me—of course, a lot of them work for Summers. But even those who don't are afraid of him." She gave him an apologetic look. "See what happened to you because you've sided with me? They almost beat you to death."

Raising her hand to his lips, Wolf kissed her fingers gently. The need to give her some solace burned hotly through him, and he watched as her eyes widened at the touch of his lips on her skin.

"I wasn't beaten to death, Sarah. You have a tendency to blow things out of proportion."

Sarah's fingers tingled pleasantly. For a moment, she sat in shock from Wolf's unexpected kiss. Scrambling to find words, she said, "I know."

Smiling, Wolf reluctantly released her hand. "That's one of the many things I like about you, Sarah Thatcher." How much heartbreak Sarah had endured. The look in her eyes was one of warmth mixed with desire. Wolf wondered if it could really be desire for him.

Sarah's heart wouldn't settle down. She had watched his strong mouth gently graze her hand, and the sensation had shone like sunlight through her until she ached to love him. But did he like her enough to want her? She sat digesting those thoughts as she finished her coffee.

Wolf pulled his platter back in front of him and began to eat the now-cooled beef sandwich, potatoes and gravy. Sarah smiled.

"What brought back your appetite?"

"Talking with you."

She gave him a rueful look. "Noonan must have mentioned my name when you went to see him."

"Yes. And not in very pleasant terms."

"I'm sure." Sarah fingered her sweat-beaded water glass. "I'm not a mean person, Wolf, although part of this town may paint me that way. I'm a fair-minded person. And I'm easily touched by sad stories." She gave a little laugh.

"You bluster a lot, but underneath you've got a soft heart, honey," he agreed.

Sarah blushed at the endearment, drowning in the burning gray of his gaze. "Mom always called me feisty," she admitted wryly with a widening smile. "I'd get my hackles up at the drop of a hat, but then, I'd cool down just as quickly."

"You're a woman of fire. I like that."

The words, gritty and low, made Sarah quiver with a hunger she'd never experienced. "Y-yes, I guess you could say I am." The powerful intimacy that had sprung up between them frightened Sarah badly. Each time she held Wolf's tender gaze, more of her trust reached out to him. It just couldn't happen! Inwardly she began to panic. When she was around Wolf, she automatically surrendered to him, to the emotions that blossomed in his presence. Summers posed a physical danger to her, but Sarah felt the danger of being around Wolf becoming even more frightening.

"After lunch I'll take you to see your mom at the nursing home, if you want."

Desperate, Sarah jerked her chin upward and met his gaze. "I—No. I called the nursing home when you were gone, and she's doing fine. She really doesn't miss me." Nervously she moved the water glass around between her hands and tried to prepare herself for the explosion she knew was coming. "Wolf, I want to go back to the cabin today."

Her pleading tone tore at him. Frowning, he muttered, "You're not ready to go back there, Sarah."

"I have to! You know I've got to mine enough sapphires to pay the bills coming up."

Wolf stopped eating and again pushed his plate aside. Sarah had both elbows on the table and was leaning forward, her eyes intense and stubborn-looking. "I can't protect you if you're up there, Sarah."

"I can protect myself. Wolf, take me home—please." Sarah had other reasons for leaving. She knew that if she remained with Wolf she might do something embarrassing and stupid.

Leaning back in the booth, Wolf held on to his patience. "Why can't you work at the house?"

"It's impossible," Sarah said, spreading her hands. "I've got to dig more sapphires."

The conversation was getting too heated. Wolf looked around and dug money out of his billfold. "Come on," he growled. "We'll talk about this on the way home."

Sarah glanced around, realizing she'd become a little too loud. Wolf was right: The diner was no place to discuss the situation. She remained silent until they were on their way home, Skeet sitting between them.

Wolf broke the silence. "Look, if it's the money worrying you, I'll give you whatever you need, Sarah." Holding her pleading stare, he added, "I'll pay your bills. I'd rather have you safe than out on that mountain alone."

Desperation filled Sarah. "No, Wolf. I've never taken anyone's money, and I'm not starting now. Thanks, but—"

"Make it a loan, then."

Tensing, Sarah whispered, "No."

His mouth tightening, Wolf lowered his voice as he

pulled into the driveway of the house. He slammed the truck into park and turned to Sarah. "All right, level with me. Why do you suddenly want to leave?"

Blinking, Sarah whispered rawly, "Because I'm drawn to you, Wolf, that's why." She watched him rear back as if he'd been struck, surprise written all over his harsh features. "Well, you don't have to act like that," she said bitterly. "Don't worry, I'll keep to myself." She climbed out of the truck and nearly ran into the house, Wolf following close behind.

Once they were in the living room, Wolf gripped her by the shoulders. "We need some straight talk," he rasped. He realized how tightly he was gripping her, and eased his fingers a bit. "You're afraid if you stay around me that something will happen?"

Hanging her head, Sarah nodded. Wolf's hands were like brands on hers. "I can't trust myself. It's not you...."

Wryly Wolf said, "Don't kid yourself. This is a two-way street, Sarah. But we can deal with this like adults. You don't have to run away from me, from the protection I can give you." He watched Sarah's head snap up, her eyes huge.

Sarah forced herself to meet and hold Wolf's gaze. There was such tenderness in his eyes that she felt her breath escape in response. As a lover, Wolf would be cherishing with her, Sarah realized instinctively in that moment. All the more reason to leave. But she saw the set of his jaw and knew that Wolf wouldn't let her go— at least not yet.

Driven to a point of desperation she'd never thought she'd feel, she twisted out of his grip. Taking several steps back, she lied to him. "I need time to think this over, Wolf. I—I want to go see my mother and think about it.''

Wolf raised his eyebrows. She'd said she didn't want to visit the nursing home. Sarah's face was flushed, and there was fear in her eyes. Wolf wrestled with the knowledge she'd shared with him. He knew that she was scared. He nodded. "Maybe that would be better," he agreed thickly. Inwardly he breathed a sigh of relief that Sarah was going to remain under his roof.

"Come on," he said, all the emotion draining from his voice. "I'll take you over there."

"Fine," Sarah rattled. "Just let me get my purse." Her mind was racing with alternative plans. Somehow she would find someone—perhaps Pepper Sinclair, the closest thing she had to a friend in this town—to drive her up to the cabin. Once she got there, Wolf would realize too late that she'd meant what she said. She had to get away from him. He moved her as no man had ever done, and Sarah couldn't risk losing the last of her disintegrating self-reliance to Wolf.

Part of her was relieved, but another part was crying out that she would miss Wolf's company, his presence. The feelings she'd had for Philip and those she held for Wolf were chasms apart. Her mother had told her what real love was like, how it felt, and what it meant. Did she love Wolf? The thought was pulverizing, sweet and unsure.

In front of the nursing home, Sarah turned to Wolf. She ached at having hurt him. Dragging in a breath, Sarah said, "I want to meet Pepper Sinclair when I'm done seeing Mom."

"Who's Pepper?"

"She's a smoke jumper for the forestry department.

I'm surprised you haven't met her yet. She's the only woman on the team.''

Wolf roused himself from his unhappiness that Sarah wanted to leave. "No...I haven't met her, yet. I heard her name mentioned once.''

Sarah forced a small smile. "She's a lot like me— independent and a fighter.''

"Are you two friends?''

With a shrug, Sarah said, "I guess Pepper is a friend to me—but I haven't been a very good one to her.''

"Because of the trust issue?'' Wolf guessed grimly.

"Yes.'' Sarah licked her lower lip. "I'll call her from here, Wolf. I...I need some time away from you—from everything.''

"How are you getting home?'' he asked, trying not to feel the smarting pain of her honesty.

"I'll have Pepper drop me off. It'll be a couple of hours, so don't worry, okay?'' She looked up to see the torture in his eyes and felt terrible for her dishonesty. More than anything, Sarah wanted to avoid subjecting Wolf to an argument over her leaving. This way it would be cleaner, less hurtful to both of them.

"Just keep your eyes open, Sarah. I don't trust Summers at all.''

Without meaning to, Sarah reached out and grazed his puffy cheek. "I'll be careful because you care,'' she told him, her voice quavering. And she would.

The tingling dulled the pain in his jaw. Wolf watched her leave the truck. Unhappy, he sat with his hands resting on the steering wheel. There was nothing he could do to stop Sarah. He'd lost Maria through a very stupid mistake; he didn't want to lose Sarah the same way. He tried to tell his hammering heart that she would be safe enough at the nursing home. And he'd heard that Pepper Sinclair was a woman warrior in disguise.

Sighing, Wolf put the truck in gear and backed out of the asphalt parking lot. His entire body ached, but, worse, his heart was in utter turmoil. Sarah had admitted some of her feelings for him. He tried to understand the terrible pressures that must put on her. She didn't want to trust him, didn't want to like him, but she did. Exasperated, Wolf left the nursing home. He'd go take a nap, and maybe, by the time he awoke, Sarah would be home.

Sarah moved guiltily around her cabin. Pepper had just left, and she was alone for the first time in nearly a week. The silence of the cabin was nerve-racking; something it had never been to her before. Nervously, Sarah looked at her watch. Two hours had passed since Wolf had trustingly left her at the nursing home.

Staring at the phone, Sarah knew she should call him. She didn't want Wolf to worry. Perhaps she'd wait another half hour... She dreaded calling him—dreaded his reaction. The cabin needed to be dusted and mopped. She noticed that Wolf had all the lapidary equipment back in place after Summers's henchmen had tried to steal it. One chair—her rocker—was broken. Moving over to it, sadness stole through Sarah as she gently touched the back of it.

Forcing herself to get to work as the evening light began to steal through the cabin windows, Sarah tried to focus her energy on housecleaning. She should be happy to be home, but somehow she wasn't. The vacuum cleaner was a noisy old machine, and Sarah ran it over the burnished cedar floor. Brushing strands of damp hair off her brow, she finally finished cleaning the living room and shut it off.

A car door slammed in the driveway. Sarah jerked up, her heart pounding. Summers? Or Wolf? She froze, the vacuum in hand. She saw the shadow of a man pass the kitchen window, heading for the door. Gulping, Sarah dropped the vacuum handle. Sharp banging on the door made her jump.

"Sarah?"

Her mouth dropped open. Wolf stood at the kitchen door.

Crushing her hand against her breast in relief, she hurried as fast as her healing feet would take her to the back door. She saw the agitation on Wolf's face and tried to emotionally prepare for his righteous anger. Opening the door, she muttered, "How did you know I came home?"

Wolf held onto his anger as he moved into the kitchen. He deliberately shut the door softly behind him. Sarah's face was riddled with guilt. "I got worried," he said, "and I called the nursing home. They said you left with Pepper. When you didn't come to my house, I figured you came up here."

"I—I'm sorry, Wolf."

"You didn't have to lie to me, Sarah," he said sadly.

"Yes, I did!" she cried, moving into the living room. Wolf followed. "Don't you realize you're at risk?" he demanded hoarsely, stalking up to her until mere inches separated them.

Belligerently, Sarah raised her chin and met the fierce thunderstorm of his eyes. "Risk?" she cracked. "Being with you is the biggest risk of all, Wolf! Don't you realize that? I tried to tell you earlier... I tried..." And she took a step back, choking on the words.

Blindly Wolf made a grab for Sarah. He thought she was going to run from him—again. His hands closed around her upper arms, and he drew her against him. "No," he rasped. "Don't run, Sarah. You make yourself a target, and I can't...I can't let you be killed!"

With a whimper, Sarah tried to pull away. Wolf was too close, too overpowering, and his masculinity was undoing her in every way. Raw emotions flowed through her, ribbons of need entwining with heat and longing. Tears stung her eyes as she lifted her hands to push at him.

It was impossible!

Instinctively Wolf cupped Sarah's face with his hands. There was such love radiating from her eyes—mixed with her fear of her feelings for him—that he couldn't stop himself. His breathing suspended as he barely grazed Sarah's parted, waiting lips. A soft moan came from her. His hands tightened imperceptibly on her face, and he made contact with her again, feeling her lips move shyly beneath his. There was such uncertainty coupled with the need in her kiss. Her mouth opened as a flower opens to the sun's rays, lush and questing. This time, Wolf's control disintegrated, and he met and melded hotly with her lips. A groan reverberated through him like thunder. Sarah's returning kiss was hungry, inciting a fire within him. Despite her awkwardness, her shyness, Wolf drowned in the heat and fire of her offering. The spicy scent of her hair and velvety feel of her skin filled his senses, dizzying him.

Sarah drowned in the splendor of Wolf's fiery kiss. His mouth was strong and coaxing. Her nostrils flaring, she drank in the scent of Wolf, a combination of pine and fresh air and pure male. Her fingers tensed against his barrel chest, and she felt one of his hands slide down the length of her spine and tightly capture her hips against his. The contact was shocking, pleasurable. Gasping, Sarah broke the kiss, gulping for air.

Instantly Wolf released her. She swayed. He caught her gently by the arm and allowed her to lean against him. They were both trembling.

"Sweet," he breathed against her hair, his arm going around her shoulder as she sank weakly against him, "you make a man tremble like a willow in a thunderstorm."

Sarah couldn't talk, she could only feel. She burrowed her head against his chest, hearing the wild beating of his heart. His arms swept around her, and she surrendered to his superior strength. After a moment, Sarah lifted her head and gazed up into his stormy eyes—and what she saw there was a combination of savage hunger and tenderness.

The kiss should never have happened, her mind screeched at her. But, somehow, Sarah couldn't fight herself any longer. Wolf was just as stunned by the kiss as she was, she was sure. It had happened like lightning striking them, leaving them shaken in its wake.

Wolf gently eased just far enough away from Sarah to see her flushed features. As her lashes lifted to reveal lustrous blue eyes, he groaned silently. Her lips were glistening from the power of his kiss, and he reeled with need of her. Trying to grapple with the situation, he rasped, "I never want to share anything but honesty about how we feel about each other." His voice was low as he lightly removed strands of golden hair from her cheek. "You give me hope, Sarah. I felt dirtier than hell before meeting you, and you make me feel clean inside." He continued to stroke the crown of her hair, marveling at the way the light changed and danced across the strands. "I'm still carrying a lot of guilt about Maria, about what happened. When you started living with me, I started feeling differently about myself, maybe about the world in general." He gave her an embarrassed look. "You have that kind of effect on me, honey. You're one of a kind, a special woman. Magical."

Sarah clung to his words. They were spoken with such reverence. "It shouldn't have happened, Wolf."

"We both wanted it."

Wincing, Sarah bowed her head. "I felt so terrible lying to you, Wolf. I'm scared...so scared..."

The tremor in her voice deeply affected him. "I know, honey. So am I—for different reasons." He grazed her cheek. "You're afraid to trust outside yourself, and I'm afraid I can't protect you well enough to deserve that trust."

Sarah nodded, but she knew Wolf was questioning his own ability to love, too. "Let me stay here, Wolf. Give me the time I need," she pleaded.

"Sarah—"

"No, hear me out—I have a gun. I know how to use the thing! I'm a crack shot, and believe me, I've shot at Summers's men before." She pulled out of his arms, hating herself for it, hating the loss she saw in Wolf's eyes. "You've got to understand, Wolf. Being around you is a special kind of hell for me! I—I can't keep my mind on Summers while I'm trying to deal with the emotions you pull out of me." Opening her hands, her voice dropping, she whispered, "Please, let me stay here. I'll be okay. I know I will."

Wolf's gut warned him that Sarah wasn't safe at all. But what could he do? He couldn't kidnap her. He wouldn't force himself on her in any way. The hot memory of their explosive kiss seared him. Maybe Sarah was right: The emotions that leaped to life between them were too much for either of them to deal with right now. Maybe they needed a cooling-off period.

"Okay," he growled, finally. "I'll go back to the house and pick up your clothes and the faceter."

Relief tunneled through Sarah. "I know how hard it is for you to let me go...."

Grimly Wolf held her tearful gaze. Words choked in his throat, and all he could do was nod.

Drowning in his lambent gaze, Sarah whispered, "It's nice having someone in my corner who believes in me."

"I've got to get going," Wolf heard himself say. "Are you sure you want to do this?"

Sarah nodded and took a step back from his imposing height. "I have to, Wolf."

"I'll be back in about two hours," he promised. Fear for her safety ate away at him. He felt completely helpless. "Be careful," he warned, and then he left.

It was almost nine in the evening when Sarah got ready to take her shower. Wolf had been gone almost an hour, and she knew he'd be home by now, packing her clothes. The kiss still hovered hotly on her lips, she caught herself touching them, feeling the power of Wolf's mouth molding against her own. Never had she been kissed like that. She'd tasted him, felt his heart thudding in unison with her own. Most of all, she'd felt as if she were merged with him, all the way to his tired, wounded soul.

Absently Sarah touched the broken rocking chair, caught up in her escaped feelings for Wolf. The kiss had ripped away her pretenses, her lies to herself about not trusting Wolf. Standing there, she shut her eyes and felt a new kind of pain drift through her vulnerable heart. Did she know what real love was? She wished she could talk to her mother about the wildly fluctuating feelings she had for Wolf. In comparison, the relationship she'd had with Philip had been tame.

Opening her eyes, Sarah chastised herself for thinking too much. Her mother had always told her to flow with her feelings and not let her head interfere. But if she allowed her feelings to flow, they would wrap around Wolf in every way. It wasn't that she couldn't live her life without Wolf's presence; it was simply that her life was better with him around. He somehow enhanced her, and it made her feel awakened as a woman, made her feel that she possessed sensual longings she hadn't known existed.

As she walked across the living room toward the bathroom, Sarah glanced up. She jerked to a halt, thinking she must be imagining things. Out of the corner of her eye she saw the shadow of a man cross the darkened window. Her heart started a slow, uneven pounding. Was it her overactive imagination playing tricks on her? Ever since Wolf had left, she'd felt nervous and vulnerable.

Licking her lower lip, Sarah stared hard at the curtained window. There! Another shadow! A small cry broke from her. It wasn't her imagination. It was Summers's men! Because her feet were healing, Sarah couldn't turn quickly. Awkward in her movements, she lurched toward the bedroom to get the rifle that sat in the corner. Hurry! The door in the kitchen was being jimmied. Her throat constricted.

A cry broke from Sarah as she saw three men with bandaged faces rush through the door into the cabin. The cedar floor was highly polished, and she was in her stocking feet. Rattled, she slipped in the hallway and fell.

She heard one man grunt as he came closer to her. Sarah scrambled to her knees. Forgetting the rifle, she lunged to her feet and ran toward the front door of the cabin. Jamming her hand around the doorknob, she tried to pull the door open. Escape! She had to escape!

"Hold it!" a man snarled, settling his hand on her shoulder and gripping her hard.

Blindly Sarah lashed out with her elbow as she was dragged backward. Pain and light exploded along the side of her face and jaw. She slammed against the door and crumpled to the floor.

"Don't move."

Gulping for breath, Sarah opened her eyes. Three men dressed in cowboy shirts, jeans and boots were hunkered over her. They moved aside when a fourth man entered the cabin.

"Summers," Sarah hissed.

Chapter Eleven

Shakily Sarah pressed her hand against her smarting cheek. It was bloody. Trying to steady her breathing, she glared up at Summers as he approached. He wore a suit, and, as always, he appeared freshly groomed. In his hand he held a sheaf of papers.

"Sign this."

"Like hell I will."

Summers's mouth curled. "It's an agreement, Sarah, that you're turning over the mine to me for the tidy sum of fifty thousand dollars. Now, that's not a bad profit for a quarter of this mountain, is it?"

Sarah pushed herself to her feet, using the door as a support because her knees were wobbly. Looking around at the hardened faces of Summers's men, she realized that two of them were the same men who'd attacked her before. One grinned at her. She shrank back against the door.

"You can kill me, Summers, but I'll never turn this place over to you. Never!" she cried.

Summers gave a one-shouldered shrug. "Billy here said he owes you for cold-cocking him with that prospector's hammer." Summers smiled evenly. "You've always been wild, Sarah. Your reputation precedes you. Billy, wouldn't you like to even the score?" He turned to the man, who nodded, his angry gaze riveted on Sarah. Summers smiled a little more. "If you sign, we'll leave right now, Sarah."

Her heart pounding in her chest, Sarah crouched, fear overcoming her. Billy's large nose was bandaged. Wolf must have broken it the day before.

"What if I don't sign?"

"Well, first I'll let Billy even the score with you, and then we'll leave. But we'll be back tomorrow night. The boys might get bored fighting you and want some other kind of fun." Summers looked around the cabin. "Be a shame if this place went up in smoke..."

"No!" Sarah's voice cracked with fury and disbelief.

He lost his smile. "And if you refuse even after you've got cinders at your feet, Sarah, we'll keep harassing you until you do sign. Understand?" He held out the paper and pen once more. "Make it easy on yourself. Sign now."

Rage exploded violently within Sarah. Without thinking, she pushed away from the door and lunged for Summers. He barely dodged her flailing fists, knocking over the other man as he stumbled backward to dodge her attack.

"Get her!" Summers roared as he fell to the floor.

Sarah scrambled toward the kitchen. Throwing herself out the back door, she dug her toes into the pine needles and dry soil, disappearing into the darkness. Pain shot through her feet and ankles, but she ignored it as she raced away from the cabin. No one knew this mountain more intimately than she did. Two of the men were coming after her. The night was bathed in black. Sarah swerved to the left. There was a ten-foot drop-off just ahead. If she could make it without breaking an ankle or her leg, she could lose her pursuers.

Wind tore past her as she stretched her stride to the maximum. Both men were bearing down upon her, and she heard them cursing and gasping for air. Just a few more feet! The edge of the rock ledge was coming up fast. Sarah threw herself off it, bending her knees to take the impact of landing.

She hit the ground hard, automatically flexing and rolling to absorb the jarring shock. Quickly she scrambled to her hands and knees, then pushed to a standing position. A scream lurched from one of the men above her. There was no time to take satisfaction in the thought of the two men falling over the cliff. Sarah ran to the right and crouched down, pushing through several bushes. Behind the shrubbery was a small cranny in the rock, a cavelike depression.

Sarah pressed her hands across her nose and mouth to try to soften the sound of her breathing. She heard both men strike the forest floor, one groaning loudly. The other cursed. She sat very still, her knees jammed against her chest and chin. Rock wall bit into her back, but she ignored the discomfort. Anything was better than being beaten or raped. Anything. Shaky with adrenaline, Sarah concentrated on trying to breathe quietly.

The cursing grew louder. Sarah hunched down as one of the shadowy figures came close to her hiding spot.

"Son of a bitch!" Billy yelled. "She got away!"

"Screw the bitch," the other one groaned. "Come

back here and help me. I think I busted my ankle, Billy. Dammit to hell!''

Sarah's eyes had adjusted to the darkness, and she saw Billy hesitate near the bushes where she hid, then turn back to help the other man. Burying her head in her arms, Sarah breathed through her mouth, trying to stay quiet. Both men hobbled off, and in a few minutes the forest had grown quiet again.

How long Sarah waited, she didn't know. Finally, the urgent need to warn Wolf that Summers and his men were at the cabin got the better of her. Disregarding her painful feet, she slowly extricated herself from the depression and carefully moved along the cliff wall. A deer path led back toward the cabin and the road, she knew. She had to warn Wolf before he ran into Summers and his gang!

By the time Sarah made it back to her cabin, Summers and his men were gone. She stood just inside the tree line, wondering if it was a trick. No trucks were in her driveway. It was quiet. Deathly quiet. Beginning to tremble in earnest, Sarah wrapped her arms around herself. The summer nights were always cool in the mountains, and sometimes chilly. Her keen hearing picked up the sound of a truck being driven at high speed down the dirt road toward her cabin. Was it Wolf, or was it Summers returning?

Sarah waited, positioning herself so that the headlights wouldn't flash over her and give away her position. As the truck drove into the driveway and braked to a halt next to the cabin, she realized it was Wolf.

With a little cry, Sarah lurched out of the forest. Sobbing Wolf's name, she ran toward him, her arms open.

Wolf emerged from the pickup and heard Sarah's cry. Startled, he jerked around toward the sound. His eyes

widened enormously. Sarah's shadowed features were
twisted with fear, and blood was smeared along her
cheek. Wolf grabbed his rifle off the rack and loaded a
round in the chamber. Skeet leaped down, remaining at
his side. His breathing was strangled, and his heart was
beating hard in fear. Terrible flashbacks of finding the
Peruvian villagers slaughtered slammed into Wolf as he
stood frozen for that moment.

"Sarah!"

A cry broke from her as she staggered into his arms.
Instantly she was surrounded by Wolf's strength, by the
protection of his arms and massive body.

"Summers was here!" she sobbed.

Wolf's senses were screamingly alive. He held Sarah
as she collapsed against him, but his gaze never stopped
roving around the area.

"What happened?" Wolf rasped. "Honey, are you
okay? Talk to me! Are you okay?"

Sarah nodded, burying her face in his shirtfront, shaking so hard that her knees were threatening to give out
from under her. "It was Summers. He came when you
left, Wolf. I—I'm all right. I was so scared…so
scared…"

Getting a better hold on Sarah because she appeared
faint, Wolf guided her toward the cabin and the open
kitchen door. "Hang on," he growled. "Are they
gone?"

"I—I think so." The light hurt Sarah's eyes as Wolf
led her up on the wooden porch and into the kitchen.

Wolf placed her against the counter. "Stay here," he
ordered tightly. "If you hear firing, drop to the floor and
then get the hell out of here. Understand?"

Sarah looked up at him. This was a side of Wolf she'd
never seen before: the mercenary. His face was impas-

sive, covered with a fine sheen of sweat, and his eyes
were merciless. The ease with which he held the rifle
made her tremble with fear. She gave a jerky nod of her
head, and he turned away to search the rest of the house.

Unable to move because she was afraid she'd fall,
Sarah leaned against the counter until Wolf returned.
Skeet had remained at her side, guarding her fiercely.

"It's safe," Wolf announced as he returned to the
kitchen. All his attention swung to Sarah, and he placed
the rifle on the counter. The blouse she wore had been
torn open, her jeans were dust-covered and she wore no
shoes. His gaze moved up to her face. A long scratch
had bloodied her cheek and temple. The terrible realization that he'd failed to protect Sarah from danger
sheared through him. He'd left her undefended for two
hours, and Summers had capitalized upon the opportunity. Anger surged through Wolf.

"Come here," he ordered tightly, "and sit down."
He pulled a chair out from the table.

Sarah collapsed into the chair as Wolf moved to the
sink and wet a cloth. When he returned, he moved her
and the chair so that she was facing him. Kneeling down,
he placed the cold cloth against her cheek and gently
began to clean away the blood.

"Tell me what happened," he said gruffly. Sarah's
eyes looked haunted and shocky. Her pupils were dilated
and black, and her flesh was cool and translucent.

Stuttering and stammering, Sarah told him everything.
When she mentioned Billy and told him he'd intended
to beat her up, Wolf winced visibly. His hand tightened
momentarily on her arm. Then, becoming aware of the
pressure, he released some of his hold.

"I—I had to escape, Wolf," Sarah rattled as he continued patiently cleaning her face, neck and arms.

"They could have killed you," he agreed in a shaken tone.

Miserable, Sarah held his tortured gaze. "You were right," she whispered, "I was wrong to come back here alone. This was my fault, Wolf. I'm so sorry...." And she reached out to him, because right now she needed to be held more than ever before.

Wolf pulled Sarah out of the chair and into his arms. He shakily pushed the hair away from her eyes and face. "It's okay, honey. It's my fault. All my fault. I shouldn't have left you alone...."

Sarah slid her hands upward to frame his bruised and swollen face. "No," she choked out. "Don't do this to yourself, Wolf. I was the one who tricked you, who lied to you." She saw the haunted wildness in his gaze. Tears glittered on his short black lashes. A small cry escaped her as she threw her arms around his broad shoulders and held him as hard as she could. Sarah understood his tears; they were for the past, which had come back to haunt Wolf in this very moment. He had loved Maria, and despite her shock she knew he was vividly recalling that time in his life. To lose her as he had Maria would have been too much.

Wolf buried his face in Sarah's hair and felt all her woman's strength go around him, holding him, caring for him. Tears leaked from his tightly shut eyes. His mouth moved into a tight line, fighting back a sudden and unexpected deluge of emotions that tunneled up through his chest. How many times had he ached to have Maria come to him and hold him like this. After the rape, she'd tried to sleep with Wolf, as she had before, but it was impossible. The six months following her terrible ordeal had been agonizing, the nights spent tossing sleeplessly, knowing she lived in her parent's hut and not with him. They'd carved a scar on Wolf's heart he'd thought would never disappear.

The driving need to give Maria solace against the fears that stalked her day and night had nearly driven Wolf insane. He'd fall asleep for just a little while, then jerk awake, his arms wrapped around him, as if Maria had been there, as if he'd been holding her as he had before the rape.

Tears trickled down Wolf's face, and he tightened his embrace around Sarah's slender form. He'd failed abysmally, and he was once again overwhelmed by the grief he'd never released over Maria's murder. As Sarah's arms held him, a sob worked its way up and out of Wolf. His entire body shook, his focus narrowing on the pain rushing up through him.

"It's all right," Sarah whispered brokenly, caressing Wolf's shoulder. Tears touched her eyes. She'd never seen a man cry before, and it tore her apart. Sarah understood the source of Wolf's weeping, and she had never wanted to help someone as she did him. He hadn't left her since that day he'd found her. He'd been loyal and unswerving in his devotion to her, and to her safety. Pressing small kisses against his cheek, temple and neck, Sarah allowed herself to trust Wolf as never before. He deserved nothing less.

A soft groan issued from Wolf as Sarah's small kisses grazed his flesh. The moment was exquisite as the internal anguish dissolved and freed Wolf. He'd never been able to console Maria. Now, with Sarah holding him with all her strength and courage, he released the woman he'd loved and lost so long ago.

Sarah felt the emotional storm within Wolf diminish. She felt his entire body lose its tension. All she wanted to do was console Wolf—the touch of her hand upon his thick black hair, a reassuring embrace with her arms, or the soft whisper of her voice near his ear. At least that she could do. After what she'd put him through because of her own fears and lack of trust, Sarah hoped her presence, her care, would be enough.

Feeling gutted, Wolf slowly loosened his hold on Sarah.

"Let's go into the living room, to the couch," Sarah urged softly, and led him through the cabin to the cedar couch. Sitting down close to Wolf, she felt her heart burst with compassion as he raised his hand and dried the tears on his face. His gray eyes looked wounded, and Sarah framed his face with her hands, gazing deeply into his dark eyes.

"I didn't mean to hurt you like this," she choked out. "It's my fault. I put you through your past all over again, Wolf. I'm sorry...so sorry..."

Wolf took in a deep, ragged breath as he drowned in her blue eyes, eyes that were swimming with tears. He was wildly aware of Sarah's small hands on his face, of the care she was giving him so unselfishly. Despite a roller coaster of emotions he'd been through, Wolf understood what it cost Sarah to extend her care to him. She hadn't wanted to trust again, to give her love to another living human being.

Removing her hands and putting them in her lap, Wolf nodded. He brushed the tears coming down her pale cheeks. "You didn't do it on purpose," he rasped, then managed a lopsided smile.

Sarah bowed her head, feeling guilty. "The only thing to come out of my stupid decision was that you got to release so much grief from the past." She raised her head, and when she spoke again, her was voice scratchy.

"You needed to cry for Maria. For yourself. I understand, Wolf."

And she did. He gazed at her, unable to believe that anyone could see that far into his scarred, tortured soul. "I did," he admitted brokenly. "This whole thing tonight triggered it, Sarah. I got scared when you came running out of the woods. I saw the blood on your face." He groaned and shut his eyes. "Everything from the past was suddenly superimposed on the present, and I was back there again. A flashback."

"But I'm alive, Wolf, and I'm fine." Sarah tried to smile and failed. "At least you cried. That was important." Shyly she added, "I never saw a man cry before. I—I didn't know what to do. I felt so useless, but I knew crying was healing for you." Sarah sniffed, closing her eyes and pressing her cheek into the palm of Wolf's hand.

"You did everything right," Wolf said hoarsely, continuing to graze Sarah's cheeks. "Everything." He slid his hands around her shoulders. The driving need to kiss her, to reassure her, forced him forward. As his mouth met and moved against Sarah's, he took her hungrily, starved for her taste, her texture. The grief of the past evaporated beneath Sarah's equally hungry response, her lips moving, molding to his.

Sarah was drowning beneath the searching heat of Wolf's mouth, aching to find a way to tell him how very much he meant to her. His hands, roughened by outdoor work, moved upward to capture her face as he deepened the kiss. As his tongue seared her lower lip, she drew in a gasp of air. Sensation was moving through her like lightning. Following pure instinct, Sarah placed her hands on Wolf's chest and felt the powerful beating of his heart beneath her palms. His breath was hot against her face as she responded guilelessly to his needs.

Wolf broke their kiss gradually. Sarah was in his arms, resting against him, her lips wet and pouty from his exploration of her. With a trembling hand, Wolf smoothed her mussed hair. Her eyes were the color of a foggy morning sky in North Carolina. Molten heat burned through him as the corners of her soft mouth pulled into a shy smile.

"You're healing," Wolf whispered, and pressed a kiss to her brow. *And I love you for your unselfishness. I know what it cost you.* Wolf looked deeply into her eyes, never wanting to say those words to anyone but Sarah. "I thought they'd shot you or something," Wolf said in a strained tone. "I care deeply for you, honey. I don't know what I'd do if you'd been hurt."

His words moved Sarah to silence, and all she could do was stare up at his rugged features, which were awash with grief. "I—I care for you, too, Wolf."

He pressed his finger to her lips. "Shh... You don't have to say anything, Sarah. I know what it cost you to reach out to me."

She captured his bruised and scarred hand and kissed it gently. "I'm not saying it because you want to hear it. I'm telling you how I feel, Wolf."

He nodded, absorbing her quavering admission. "Look," he said with an effort, "we need to get cleaned up and go to bed." Looking around, Wolf added, "I don't think Summers will try anything more tonight. I'll stay with you. Skeet will alert us if anyone tries to get within a mile of this place."

With a sigh, Sarah nodded. "Let me get a quick bath." She looked down at her dirty clothes. "I smell like fear.''

"You're in good company," Wolf mused.

Sarah had just changed into her cotton nightgown when Wolf knocked lightly at the bedroom door.

"Come in."

Wolf walked in, narrowing his gaze on Sarah. She looked small and vulnerable as he approached. He missed nothing, from her distraught features to the shadowed darkness lingering in her eyes as she put a damp towel across the back of a wooden chair. He'd just taken a hot, cleansing shower himself, but before he climbed onto the couch to sleep, he wanted to make sure Sarah was all right.

"How are you feeling?" Wolf wanted so badly to reach out and pull her into the safety of his arms.

Sarah stood uncertainly by her bed. "I feel like I could fall asleep on my feet."

Wolf nodded and crossed to the bed, pulling back the covers. "Get in," he ordered softly.

"Where will you be?"

"I'll sleep on the couch," Wolf promised. Sarah was slurring her words with fatigue. "Come on, climb in and I'll tuck you in." Wolf wanted to do much more than that. He wanted to lie beside Sarah and hold her.

Stumbling to the bed, Sarah slipped off her robe and set it aside. "Thanks," she whispered wearily, getting into bed. She no longer questioned her heart, which was clearly ruling her fuzzy brain. She reached up and caught Wolf's hand. "Come to bed with me? Hold me?" She saw surprise flare in his darkened eyes and feared he'd say no. "Please, Wolf. I—I don't want to be alone tonight...."

He squeezed her hand, shattered by her honesty.

"Okay," he rasped. "Let me make one more tour of the cabin, and then I'll join you."

Nodding, Sarah moved over in the double bed and brought the sheet and blanket back. She watched as Wolf turned and left. Skeet came in and lay down on the braided oval rug, his chin resting on his crossed paws, his eyes and ears alert. When Wolf returned, he carried the rifle in his hand. He shut the bedroom door and locked it. Then he placed the rifle on his side of the bed, where he could get ahold of it in a hurry. The lights were already off, but a slice of moonlight filtered through the lacy curtains at the east window.

Sarah's heart pounded briefly as Wolf divested himself of his shirt. He gave her a sheepish look.

"I'll wear my briefs," he said.

Sarah nodded, her mouth going dry as he pulled off his jeans, dropping them in a heap on the floor near the bed. The moonlight accentuated his powerful build. Sarah had never felt such a keen longing.

Wolf got into bed, bringing up the sheet and blanket. It was so easy to turn onto his side, slide one arm beneath Sarah's shoulders and draw her against him. She nestled her head in the crook of his shoulder, her arm going around his waist. With a sigh, Wolf closed his eyes, the exhaustion torn from him. The cool cotton of Sarah's nightgown was such a thin barrier between their bodies. Yet he controlled his need of her. Tonight he could give Sarah the protection he'd never been able to give Maria. It had nothing to do with sex. It had to do with unselfish love.

He pressed a chaste kiss to her damp hair. "Go to sleep, honey. I'll hold you."

Wolf's deep, vibrating voice drifted through Sarah, and she felt safe. All the panic died within her as Wolf grazed her arm with his hand, as if to reassure her. His lips against her hair stirred her senses, but the exhaustion and shock of the attack overwhelmed her.

"Thank you..." She fell into a deep, spiraling sleep.

Wolf kissed her temple. The words *I love you* wanted to escape. He whispered instead, "Sleep, honey. You're safe...."

His rough, low voice lulled Sarah to sleep almost immediately. She vaguely remembered his lips pressed to her temple, and the gentle strength of his hand on hers.

The sun was shining brightly into the bedroom when Sarah awoke. She sat up, groggy and disoriented. Looking at the clock on the bedside table, she saw that it was nearly ten in the morning! The odor of sausage frying heightened her senses as she scrambled to get out of bed. Every muscle in her body protested, and she groaned.

"Slow down," she reprimanded herself, standing. Touching her cheek where she'd been slapped the night before, Sarah found it puffy. It hurt to open and shut her mouth. First she'd wash up, then she'd get dressed. Sarah could hear Wolf moving around in the kitchen, and she relaxed.

After a hot shower to take away some of the soreness, Sarah chose a short-sleeved white blouse and pair of jeans. Although her feet were getting better, she still couldn't put on her mining boots, and she had to settle for a pair of sandals instead. She brushed her hair, then headed for the kitchen.

"Hi," Sarah whispered, halting at the entrance. Wolf wore the same jeans and shirt he had the night before. When he lifted his chin and met her eyes, Sarah saw how bloodshot his were. Hadn't he slept?

Wolf looked up, stunned by Sarah's natural beauty as

she stood uncertainly in the doorway. He smiled tenderly, remembering last night, remembering the softness of her against him, of her shallow breath against his chest. "Come on in. I'm fixing us pancakes and sausage." He transferred a stack from the oven to two plates on the table. Placing the links in a basket between them on the table, he asked, "How'd you sleep?"

Self-consciously Sarah shrugged. She was hotly aware of the light burning in Wolf's eyes. It made her feel a keening ache that centered in her lower body, as if she were missing something and didn't know what. Yet Wolf's gaze made her feel whole, made her feel like a woman. "Like the dead," she said, then grimaced as she sat down. "Scratch that. I slept like a log. 'Dead' sounds terrible to me right now."

Wolf poured them coffee and joined her. The color had returned to Sarah's face. Her blond hair was freshly washed and dried, falling about her shoulders like a golden frame. He wanted to say so much, yet didn't know where to begin. Or end. He loved her. It was that simple, and that complex. But Sarah appeared so tentative, so fragile, after last night's attack that he didn't know what to say. "I understand."

"You look awful."

"I kept watch last night," Wolf said gruffly, handing her the maple syrup.

"Watch?"

"Yes. I'm treating this situation like a wartime one. One person sleeps, the other stays awake in case the enemy comes around."

Shivering outwardly, Sarah set the syrup down on the table. "This is like a nightmare, Wolf."

"It's getting messy," he agreed. "This morning I called Morgan and filled him in on the situation."

"What do you mean?"

"I wanted to put him on alert and let him know what was happening out here." Wolf saw the color drain from Sarah's face. "I intend to handle this, but just in case, I want someone from outside this area to know what the hell is going on." -

Sarah felt her stomach shrink in terror. "What can he do?"

Wolf tendered a smile to ease her fear. "Honey, they're professional soldiers. We've got a sheriff who's in cahoots with Summers. And he's got a lot of men on his payroll if he wants to attack us. If I can't handle this, then we're going to need help, and the only help I can count on is from Perseus."

"Summers wouldn't like that. Wolf, he's got a lot of men."

"I know that," he said patiently. "And don't worry, I'm not going to drive into Philipsburg like a posse, shooting up the town. I'm going into town this morning to try and negotiate a settlement on this with Summers."

Fear shot through Sarah. Wolf could be killed—just like her father. An icy coldness bathed her. "I never thought it would come to this. I thought Summers would just harass me off and on."

Wolf shook his head grimly. "He'll never lay another hand on you. That's a promise."

The words, spoken in a low, menacing growl, made a chill work its way up Sarah's spine. Her world was coming apart at the seams, and Wolf was all that was keeping it from completely collapsing around her. "If you weren't here, Summers would already have the mine," she murmured.

"And you might possibly be dead."

The thought was sobering. She gave Wolf a sideways

glance. For a few awkward minutes, she pushed the pancakes around on her plate, forcing herself to eat. Who knew what lay ahead today? Keeping up her strength had to be primary, so she forced the food down.

Wolf watched Sarah through hooded eyes as he ate. He didn't taste the food. All his senses were focused on her. Her brow was drawn in a frown, and he saw the tension around her soft mouth. A mouth he wanted to worship, to kiss reverently, for the rest of his life. He knew he didn't deserve this kind of second chance—not with someone as courageous as Sarah. She was a match for him in every way—proud, independent, unselfish, and generous to a fault. What had last night meant to her? His mind returned to Sheriff Noonan's remark about Philip Barlow.

His mouth tightening, Wolf put his fork and plate aside. He had to know. "Sarah?"

She raised her head. Wolf's entire demeanor had become dark and serious. Her heart started a dreadful pounding. "Yes?"

"Maybe I don't have any right to ask you this, but I need to know about a guy named Philip Barlow. Noonan said he was your boyfriend?"

"Oh." She pushed the plate aside and opted to slip her fingers around the ceramic mug filled with coffee. "I imagine he didn't have anything good to say about me in relation to Philip, either?"

Wolf shook his head. "No."

With a slight shrug, Sarah whispered, "When I turned Ricky Noonan in to the FBI, my boyfriend, Philip, got really furious with me."

"Why?" Wolf's heart beat a little harder.

"I didn't realize Philip was tied up with Noonan, too. He was selling drugs for him. When I found out, it just tore me apart. I thought—'' She grimaced and avoided Wolf's probing gray eyes. "I thought Philip loved me. I sure loved him...."

"First love?" Wolf ventured softly.

"Puppy love was what Mom called it," Sarah said with a slight, pained smile. "When the FBI finished their investigation and indicted Philip along with Ricky Noonan, I was heartbroken. Philip accused me of setting him up, of...so many things. The evidence against him wasn't that strong, so the FBI let him go, and he left town. I haven't seen him or heard from him since. He said I'd ruined his life."

Relief rushed through Wolf. Reaching over, he captured Sarah's work-worn hand. "Honey, you didn't ruin his life. He ruined it for himself."

Wolf's touch was so right, and Sarah shyly returned his squeeze. Her hand was engulfed by his, and it gave her an overwhelming sense of protection. "I know that—now. Years ago, I didn't. My mom really helped me get through the heartbreak." She held his warm gaze. "I thought I loved him, Wolf." Then, quietly, she added, "He was the first and only boy to ever like me."

"I don't believe that," Wolf said, and he meant it. Couldn't they see beyond Sarah's clothes and her mining job? They were all crazy, Wolf decided. Clothes and a career didn't make a woman.

Sarah frowned. "My reputation in this town was bad news after the FBI investigation, Wolf."

Raising her hand to his lips, Wolf gently kissed her fingers. The need to give back to Sarah some of what had been cruelly taken from her burned through him. He watched her eyes widen beautifully as he brushed the kiss over her skin.

Wolf grinned and reluctantly released her hand. Now

that he knew the truth about Philip Barlow, his jealousy had subsided. The look he saw in her eyes was one of warmth mixed with desire. Wolf wondered if it was desire for him. He'd never wanted a woman more than Sarah, but it had to be her decision; he'd never force her into bed with him.

Her hand tingled, even after Wolf let it go. Was it possible? Did the care he spoke of last night mean he might love her?

Sarah considered while she finished her coffee in the comfortable silence of the kitchen with Wolf. The robins chirping their songs outside the window eased some of the tension she unconsciously held in her shoulders.

"When will you see Summers?" she asked.

Wolf got up and put the dishes in the sink. "I'm going in now," he said grimly.

"May I come with you?"

"No." Wolf turned and faced her. He leaned against the counter and crossed his arms against his chest. "The safest place for you is here. You'll keep Skeet with you, and you've got a rifle." His brows fell. "I don't think Summers will try two days in a row. He's probably going to wait to see if you're going to run into town to sign those real estate papers of his."

"He said he'd come back tonight, Wolf." Her voice was hollow with fear.

"If I get to him today, he won't be back," he promised darkly.

"Why can't I come with you?"

Wolf didn't want to say, but he didn't know how to evade Sarah. "You're safer here," he repeated with more authority.

"Because if Summers sees your truck he could have his men fill it with bullet holes?"

Wolf's mouth tightened. At least Sarah was a realist. Unwinding from his position at the counter, Wolf straightened. "Exactly. Better a single than a double target."

Sarah winced, her hands tightening around the mug.

Wolf came around behind her and placed his hands on her shoulders. He gently kneaded her tight muscles until she began to relax. "Look, I know this is tough on you, but you're safest here. You already evaded Summers's men once, and you know this area, honey. Once I find Summers, I'll settle this thing with him once and for all."

"How?" Sarah twisted a look up at him, glad that he was standing behind her, glad that his hands were on her shoulders.

"I'll tell him about Perseus and our connections with the FBI and the CIA, and I'll tell him that if he doesn't leave you alone once and for all we'll have him investigated." Satisfaction rang in Wolf's voice. "He's the kind of slimy bastard who wants to avoid public notice and a trial at all costs."

Sarah couldn't help but shiver. She tried to be brave, not only for Wolf but for herself. "I—I just worry about you, that's all."

Wolf leaned over and placed a kiss on her cheek. "Your worry isn't for nothing," he told her huskily. "I'll be all right." Straightening, he forced himself to move. The last thing he wanted to do was to leave Sarah for any reason. "What I want you to do is form an escape route in case Summers does come back. Tell me where I might find you if you have to make a run for it."

"I'd rather be out on the mountain working, not here at the cabin." Sarah gave him a narrow look. "I'll work at the new mine site. That way, I'll have a chance to hear them coming. Besides, there's a series of caves down on the other side of Blue Mountain," Sarah whispered, her hand touching her throat, where a lump was forming. "I could hide there and they'd never find me."

"Good. I know the area you mean." Wolf glanced down at her feet. "Are you sure you can work?"

"I want to work, Wolf. I'll go crazy if I have to sit here waiting for you to come home. You know that."

"Yeah, I guess I do." Wolf felt more sure now that Sarah had a plan in place. "Draw me a map of the cave area, and I'll take it with me when I leave." He gave her a slight smile meant to buoy her. "We'll get out of this alive and together," he promised her.

Together. Sarah nodded jerkily and got to her feet. She wanted to cry, because she'd just discovered Wolf— the first man she'd truly loved in her life. And now he was going into a town bristling with enemies who carried weapons that could all too easily be aimed at him. Everything was moving too quickly for Sarah. Her emotions were in shreds, and she knew they didn't have time to sit down and talk about all the new discoveries cascading through her.

Forcing herself to think, she went into the living room and picked up a notebook to draw Wolf a map of the caves.

Chapter Twelve

Sarah waited tensely at the cabin. It was exactly noon, the time Wolf promised he'd be home. Her heart rate rising, Sarah gasped as she saw the dark green forest service truck turn into the driveway. It was Wolf, and he was safe! Moving off the porch, Sarah met him as he parked the truck and shut off the engine. She tried to read his rugged, closed features as he opened the truck door and stepped out. Skeet rushed up and wedged between them.

"How did it go?" Sarah asked. What she wanted to do was throw her arms around Wolf in welcome. She wasn't sure what to do, or how to act; her nerves were stretched to the breaking point, her emotions frayed by the hourly unknowns of her life.

Wolf absently patted Skeet, then devoted his attention to Sarah. He heard the fear in her voice, and saw it in her eyes. Automatically he placed his arms around her.

The softness of her parting lips made him ache with need as she came against him without resisting.

"Summers couldn't be found," he told her as he walked with her to the cabin. "I talked to Noonan."

Sarah pressed her head against his shoulder, content, a feeling of safety enveloping her once again. "Is that good or bad, Wolf? You look worried."

Wolf released Sarah once they entered the kitchen. "I don't feel good about it, honey." He scowled and settled his hands on his hips as he studied her. "Summers is playing a game. I think he'll be back here again. Maybe tonight, if not sooner."

Gulping, Sarah's eyes widened. "What are we going to do?" Her voice was strained.

Wolf smiled, but the smile didn't reach his eyes. He saw the sandwiches on the table and motioned for her to join him. "When I was in Philipsburg, I called the airport at Anaconda." He held her frightened gaze. "I'm taking you out of here, tonight. You've got an airline ticket to Washington, D.C., Sarah. I've talked to Morgan, and he's agreed to put you up at one of the condos the company owns until this thing gets resolved."

"We're leaving?"

"No, you are. I'm staying." Wolf saw stubbornness come into her face. "Sarah, please, don't argue with me on this. I want you safe. I'm not going to keep you here in the line of fire."

"I'm not going anywhere if you're not going with me, Wolf!" Her voice was strident and off-key. Sarah suddenly stood up and gripped the back of her chair as she held Wolf's weary gaze. "This is my fight!"

"It's our fight," Wolf agreed, trying to calm her down. Didn't Sarah realize he loved her? That he wanted her safe and out of harm's way?

"But this isn't fair, Wolf! You're in danger, too! It isn't just me!"

He held up his hands. "Honey, I'm more equipped to deal with it than you."

"How?" she demanded, shaken. "I've been shot at, Wolf. I've been beaten up by Summers's goons. I've shot at them to scare them off."

"But you've never killed, Sarah."

Stunned, Sarah heard the haunted quality of Wolf's voice. His eyes were tired-looking, his mouth was a tight line. There was such pain mirrored in his face that Sarah froze.

"You think it's coming to that?" she asked hollowly.

Wolf rubbed his face gently. A lot of the swelling had gone down, but the dark bruises remained to remind him of Summers's way of dealing with situations. "I do."

"Oh, God." Sarah sat down. She clasped her hands on the table and stared at Wolf. "Did Noonan say that?"

With a twist of his mouth, Wolf said, "Noonan turned white, red, and then plum-colored. I told him about Perseus, and the fact that Morgan would call in a head honcho from the FBI to begin investigating Summers if he didn't leave you and your mine alone once and for all."

"What did he say?"

"He got angry and accused me of threatening him." Wolf shrugged and pushed the plate bearing the sandwiches around and around with his fingers. Finally he looked up at Sarah. "I know what's going to happen. Summers is hiding out—for now. Noonan will take the information to him, and I know in my gut that Summers will hit us either tonight or tomorrow."

Trembling, Sarah sat down again. "Then that's all the more reason for you to come with me, Wolf. You can't stay here and fight it out alone."

"You're a gutsy lady," Wolf said, "but there are times when you need to know when to retreat. This is one of those times. The only flight out of Anaconda to Washington is at midnight. I wish it was sooner. It's not exactly a hub airport, so I don't have any choice in the matter." Worriedly Wolf held her blue eyes, and saw them shimmering with unshed tears. "I need you to leave, Sarah. I lo—I care for you too much to keep you here." He reached out and gripped her hand. "I can't let what happened to Maria happen to you," he told her fervently. "I can't lose you." Wolf sat tensely. He'd nearly slipped and said he loved Sarah. Her face had blanched white, and he wondered if she'd caught his faux pas.

Love? Sarah sat there, very still, very much aware of Wolf's warm, strong hand around hers. She was sure that was what he'd stopped himself from saying. Her mouth grew dry. As she clung to his darkened gaze, Sarah realized that Wolf did love her. The tenor of his voice shook her as nothing else could have. The desperation in his eyes verified his fear for her life.

She pulled her hand from his grasp. "Wolf, I'm not leaving you here alone to fight it out with Summers," she began in a low voice. "I'm sorry, but I'm not abandoning you. I can't—" And her voice cracked.

Wolf unwound from the chair and came around the table. He placed his hands around her arms and pulled her upward, emotionally devastated by Sarah's tears. "Now listen to me," he rasped thickly. "You're not abandoning me. No argument on this, Sarah. I'm taking you to Anaconda tonight. Now, I don't care if you agree with my plan or not." His hands tightened on her arms, and his voice became hoarse. "*I won't lose you.* And I don't care if you curse me, hate me, or never want to see me again—you're leaving.''

Tears blurred Sarah's vision, and her lips parted. She couldn't stand the agony in Wolf's eyes. "You don't understand!" she cried. "You just don't understand!"

Grimly Wolf pulled Sarah against him. He'd needed her closeness, her warmth, all morning. With a groan, he buried his face in her hair. As her arms twined around his waist, he released a shuddering sigh. "I understand a lot more than you'll ever know," he rasped, and he held her as tightly as he dared.

The inky cape of night had fallen across the valley by the time Sarah was ready to leave the cabin. Wolf had helped her pack, extraordinarily tense and hyperalert to any sound that seemed out of the ordinary. He kept his rifle nearby and watched Skeet for warnings.

Sarah closed her only suitcase, a small one, and Wolf took it out to the pickup. She stood in the center of the living room, torn. When Wolf appeared, she was startled; he'd come back without her having heard him. His face looked grim as he approached her.

"What about my mother?"

He placed his hands on her small shoulders. "I know you're worried about her," he said soothingly.

"Summers has gone to her a number of times in the past, Wolf, and tried to get her to sign papers that would give him our mine. If I'm gone, he could try it again."

He shook his head. "I've talked to Jean Riva, the owner of the nursing home, and told her to call me if anyone wants to speak with your mother." Wolf saw the anguish in Sarah's eyes. "She'll be fine," he told her. But would she? He couldn't promise Sarah anything except safety for herself—once he got her out of this hell-hole.

"Look at it another way," Wolf said, gently caressing her shoulders, "if Summers did get her to sign over the mine, you could contest it in court and win. Your mother isn't of sound mind, and the doctor would make it clear that because of her stroke she wouldn't really know what she'd been coerced into signing."

"Maybe you're right," Sarah murmured. She placed her hands on Wolf's powerful chest. "Please let me stay."

Just the touch of her hands upon him sent a hot longing through every level of Wolf. He leaned down and kissed her wan cheek. "I can't..."

It was time to go, and Sarah eased out of his hands. Fighting back tears, she turned to him as he followed her out the door. "What if you're wounded? Who would care for you, Wolf? You're one man against all of Summers's men."

"If I need help, I'll call Morgan," he told her, capturing her hand as they walked to the truck. "I just think we need to get over the next couple of days and we'll be okay. You've got to trust me on that, Sarah."

She did trust him—with her life. With her heart. The words begged to be torn from her, but she swallowed them. Wolf opened the passenger side of the truck. Skeet jumped in first, and Sarah followed. The silence was ominous as she watched Wolf looking around, alert and wary, as he moved around the truck. Before getting in, he placed the rifle on the gun rack across the back seat.

He got in and started the truck. His gut was screamingly tight. This was a bad time of night to be leaving. He couldn't drive without lights on the twisting, turning dirt road. The moon was concealed by the thick clouds overhead. It looked as if it might rain. Wolf backed out and put the truck in gear, gravel crunching beneath the wide tires. He glanced over at Sarah's strained face.

"You'll be safer away from here," he told her.

She shyly slid her hand across Skeet's broad back and touched Wolf's shoulder. It was Wolf's past that was making him react this way. "I feel as if you can't trust me to hold up my end of this fight, Wolf. Just because I'm a woman."

Wolf winced, his mouth tightening. Sarah had a good point, but he didn't dare capitulate to her rationale. "Honey, one thing I learned the hard way was to retreat instead of just charging blindly ahead. When Maria was murdered, I lost it. I wasn't thinking clearly, for myself or my men. I got myself captured, and Killian, too. And for what?" He glanced over at Sarah's shadowed features. "This has nothing to do with you being a woman. This has to do with me trying to deal differently—better—with the same situation all over again. Do you see that?"

Torn between what she felt was right for her and her all-too-clear understanding of Wolf's past, Sarah shrugged. "Yes," she whispered, "I know what you're trying to do. What if you just got me a hotel room in Anaconda and stayed a few days? Wouldn't that be good enough, Wolf?"

He shook his head. "What if Summers's men are tailing us? What if they found out where you were staying?"

The grimness of the scenario Wolf outlined made Sarah realize he was right. "I worry for you...."

"I'm worried for me, too." Wolf tried to smile for her benefit. He placed his hand across hers momentarily, keeping his eyes on the road. The headlights stabbed through the night. ''Maybe because I've got a woman who takes me as I am. You've allowed me to open up and talk, Sarah. I've never done that before, and I've got to tell you, it feels damn good. You've taken away a lot of the load I carried.''

Her throat constricted. ''It's because I care for you, Wolf. Mom always said love makes carrying a problem less.''

Surprise at her softly spoken admission sent Wolf's heart skittering. Just as he opened his mouth to speak, he saw the winking of rifle fire to the right, on Sarah's side of the truck. His words turned to a croak of warning, and he jerked Sarah down off the seat just as the bullets slammed into the truck.

Hitting the brakes, hearing glass shattering and flying all over the cab, Wolf ducked. Son of a bitch! They were being bushwhacked! He knew why, too. The threat of an FBI investigation had gotten to Summers. This was his answer to the problem: Kill Wolf and Sarah, the two eyewitnesses, and there could be no trial. Noonan and Summers would be free.

''Stay down!'' Wolf yelled, jerking the wheel of the truck to the left. The pickup shrieked and skidded down the loose gravel road. More rifle fire poured into the cabin. Skeet howled. Sarah screamed.

Jamming his foot down on the accelerator, Wolf kept low. The bastards! They were out in the middle of nowhere, too far from the main highway, from Philipsburg, from civilization, for anyone to report gunshots. They were alone.

The truck coughed and strained. The gunfire stopped. They were out of range for now. At the top of small knoll, the truck's engine coughed, sputtered and quit. Cursing, Wolf pulled over onto the berm of the dirt road.

"Sarah, are you okay?"

"Y-yes." She raised her head, realizing what had happened. Skeet was squeezed in beside her on the floorboards of the passenger side of the truck. "I—I think Skeet's okay, too."

"Good." Quickly, Wolf pulled the rifle down off the gun rack. "Get out! Hurry! They'll be coming to see if we're dead!"

Bailing out the door, Sarah fell, her knees giving way out of fear. With a little gasp, she forced herself to stand. Skeet leaped out of the cab, growling deep in his throat. The night was black, with no moonlight to help guide them. She squinted, unable to see what Skeet must either see or hear.

Wolf came around the truck, putting a bullet into the chamber of the 30.06 rifle. "Come on," he rasped, gripping her by the arm, and they hurried down the embankment and into the fir trees below. Luckily, there was little brush to hamper their escape, and Wolf kept Sarah at a steady run back toward the cabin.

"Who?" Sarah gasped.

"Noonan and Summers," he ground out, jogging alongside her. Skeet moved ahead of them, his tongue lolling out the side of his mouth. "We're lucky they didn't kill us."

"Wh-what are we going to do?" Sarah gasped between breaths, not used to such violent exercise. Wolf moved fluidly, as if running were the easiest thing in the world for him. Although her feet were healing, Sarah could already feel them beginning to throb from the exertion.

"We're three miles from the cabin. I don't remember any houses along the way where we could stop and make a phone call. I want to try to make it back to the cabin so we can call for help.''

Sarah gasped when car lights about a mile away suddenly flashed on and headed toward them. Wolf saw them, too. He gripped her arm and propelled her more deeply into the woods. She stumbled, caught herself, and ran on.

''They'll kill us, Wolf.''

''Only if they catch us.'' Worriedly Wolf realized that Sarah didn't have the physical stamina to outrun Noonan and his bunch. She was already gasping loudly, sucking in huge drafts of air. Dammit! He loved Sarah, and there was no way she was going to be taken from him. No way in hell! Keeping a firm grip on her arm so that she wouldn't fall, he rasped, ''Run as far as you can, and then we'll stop and rest, Sarah.''

The headlights flashed through the dense fir. Sarah heard several vehicles screech to a halt. Men's voices, loud and angry, punctuated the air. They were still at least a mile ahead of them. Skeet had dropped to the rear, as if to protect them. But nothing could protect them from bullets.

''How many bullets have you got?''

''Two boxes. Enough to take them out one at a time if I have to,'' Wolf told her. ''No more talking, Sarah. They might hear us. Just concentrate on running.''

Tears jammed unexpectedly into Sarah's eyes. She sobbed for breath, her legs beginning to feel like strings of rubber. Wolf jogged easily at her side, strong and seemingly impervious to the harsh conditions. She'd admitted her love to him in the truck and had seen the surprise, and then the tenderness, in his face. There was no question in Sarah's bursting heart that Wolf loved

her, too. Now Noonan and Summers were out to kill
them. And how could one man with a rifle and an injured
woman stop them?

Chapter Thirteen

Sarah was running hard, occasionally slipping on the pine needles only to be caught and steadied by Wolf, who never left her side. She knew she was slowing him down with her injured feet. Behind her, she could hear men crashing through the underbrush, not far behind them. Flashlights stabbed through the blackness toward them. Her lungs were burning. Her throat was raw and felt as if it were going to tear apart.

The level floor of the valley was starting to slope gently toward the mountains ahead, where her cabin was situated. Each foot flung in front of the other made her labor harder. Then her toe caught on a small rock and she was thrown off her feet.

Wolf caught her before she slammed to the ground. Gasping, she clutched at his arms as he dragged her upright.

"Wolf...go on without me. I...I can't run anymore!"

Looking around, his eyes now adjusted to the darkness, Wolf glared back at the men following them, realizing there must be three to five of them.

"Hold on," he rasped, sliding his arm under her arms and supporting her. Taking Sarah to a depression behind a huge black boulder, he placed her there. "Get down on your belly, Sarah, and don't move."

"What are you going to do?"

"I'm going to try the wounded-bird-with-a-broken-wing routine." He gripped the rifle in one hand and forced her to lie down. "Cover your head with your hands. I'll lead them away from you. Whatever you do, don't move. Don't speak. Understand?"

Sobbing for breath, she nodded. "B-be careful!"

"Don't worry, honey, I will." He gripped her shoulder hard. "I love you. I'm not about to lose you."

Sarah jerked her head up. Wolf was gone like a silent shadow, and Skeet with him. Had she heard wrong? Wolf loved her? Her heartbeat wildly erratic, she hugged the rock with her body. Luckily, she wore dark clothes and couldn't be easily seen. Cries and curses drew closer. What if they found her? What if they shot Wolf?

Concentrating on being silent, Sarah opened her mouth and breathed through it. She pressed against the boulder, hugging it like a snake. Blond hair was a detriment, she thought suddenly. Its color standing out in even the worst darkness. If the men didn't come around the boulder, she'd be safe. If they did... Sarah gulped, not wanting to think about it.

As the group grew closer, the flashlights were like floodlights to Sarah. She recognized Noonan's raspy voice and that of the red-haired man who had attacked her previously. Adrenaline plunged through her when she recognized Summers's voice.

"She can't run that far. Not with those feet in the condition they're in," he growled.

"Well, hell," Noonan exploded. "Where are they, then?"

"I don't know. Fan out! Thirty feet between each man," Summers ordered, out of breath. "We can keep track of one another by watching where our lights are."

"Anything makes a sound, shoot!" Noonan added angrily. "I want them dead!"

Sarah heard a distinct rustling in the distance, as if someone were bulldozing through a heavy patch of brush. All five men stopped talking. It had to be Wolf deliberately making noise to get their attention.

"It's them!" Noonan exploded harshly.

Within seconds, all five men were running toward the sound. Sarah crumpled wearily against the rock. She was safe—for now. Lifting her head, she slowly got to her hands and knees. The men were crashing through the forest, not even trying to be quiet. A far cry from Wolf's stealthy retreat, Sarah thought as she got to her feet.

Her knees were still rubbery, and she was shaking with fear. Pushing the hair off her face, Sarah remained by the boulder, waiting...waiting.

A hand snaked around, jerking her backward and off her feet. A scream caught in her throat. Sarah stumbled, off balance, and fell against the hard body of a man. The smell of sour sweat struck her nostrils. Closing her eyes, she bit down as hard as she could on the fingers clamped over her mouth.

"Ow! You little bitch!"

It was Noonan! Sarah managed to twist around. She kicked, hit and bit, blindly striking out at the sheriff. His hand caught her by the neck, his fingers sinking deeply into her flesh. With a small cry, Sarah felt herself being slammed to the forest floor.

Noonan was breathing harshly, his hand splayed out across her chest and collarbone. He shoved his face down into hers and grinned.

"Not too smart having blond hair, Sarah." He grinned and put his rifle next to him on the ground. "Don't move." He reached into his back pocket for handcuffs.

Sarah saw the handcuffs and struggled wildly. "No!" she shrieked. If he got those cuffs on her, she was dead, and she knew it. Lashing out with both feet, she connected solidly with Noonan's chest. The sheriff grunted, rolling over backward.

Scrambling to her feet, Sarah dived into the darkness.

"Come back here!" Noonan roared.

Sobbing, Sarah struck a tree, bounced off it and hit the ground. She had to think! She had to stay calm! Noonan was after her! Get up! Get up!

Rifle fire suddenly split open the darkness. Bark from a nearby tree exploded, flying in all directions. Sarah ducked and cried out. She had to remain silent! Getting to her feet, she concentrated on avoiding the trees in the darkness. Noonan was close! The rifle fired three more times. Bullets whined around Sarah.

To her left, she heard a shout. The night suddenly flared with the muzzle blasts of several rifles. Wolf! Oh, God! Sarah dived headlong up the slope, climbing hard, tripping and catching herself. Had Summers found Wolf? Tears squeezed from her eyes. Sarah knew she had to reach the cabin. She had to get to Wolf's friends to get help. Was Wolf injured? Dead?

Cresting another hill, Sarah found a huge boulder and hunched down behind it. She'd lost Noonan long ago, and had maintained a steady walk or trot for another hour, even as the pain in her ankles increased. The watch on her wrist read midnight. Shaking from fear as much as from the drop in temperature, Sarah felt her heart breaking into pieces. Had Wolf been captured? Wounded? What had happened back there? Tears came, this time in earnest. Wolf loved her. He'd said words she'd never thought to hear.

Shakily wiping her dusty, damp face, Sarah looked up through the shadowy firs at the sky, which was lit with stars now. Meager light shone from pinpoints that looked like tiny white sapphires to her. Trying to think where she was in relation to the road, and which way was north, so that she could find her cabin, she continued to study the stars. Long ago her father had taught her to navigate at night by them alone, without a compass.

Sitting there for a good fifteen minutes, Sarah began to relax. Still trembling from the chilliness of the mountain air, she wrapped her arms around herself. The thin nylon windbreaker she wore wasn't enough. Sarah realized she had strayed off in a northeasterly direction and would have to make a correction. How many miles out of the way had she come? In her hysteria to escape Noonan, she'd become disoriented and had run to save her life.

A twig snapped. Inhaling sharply, Sarah tensed, her fingers digging into the soft, fir-needled ground. Who? What? Her heart was beating so hard that she couldn't hear anything else in her ears. Frustrated, fear crawling up her spine, she slowly eased to her hands and knees to look around the rock. The light was practically nonexistent, but she prayed she would be able to see what had caused the sound. Maybe something had dropped from a tree. That was possible.

Nearly paralyzed with fear, Sarah peeked out from behind the rock. Probing the darkness, she could see nothing, but that didn't mean no one was there. She remained crouched by the rock, ready for flight.

A dog whined.

Sarah's eyes grew huge. It was Skeet! Or was it? Coyotes regularly prowled the mountains. She tried to ferret out some movement in the direction of the sound, her mouth dry. She was torn. Should she call out Skeet's name? What if Summers had a dog along with him?

Another whine.

Shaking, Sarah got to her feet, her fingers digging into the boulder. The sound was much closer this time. A rustle came from the right. Sarah whirled around.

"Skeet!" she cried out softly.

The dog stood there on three legs. He whined once more.

Sarah dropped to her knees and carefully touched the dog's massive head. His right front leg was lifted up. She spoke in a crooning tone as she used her fingers to trace the injured leg. The dog winced.

Warm, sticky blood met her touch. Skeet sat down, panting heavily as Sarah tried to find the extent of damage to his paw.

"You're okay," she whispered in a trembling tone. Taking off her jacket, she quickly tore off one sleeve, then took several strips of nylon to wrap his paw in a makeshift bandage. The work took her long, tortuous minutes, because her hands were shaking so badly that a knot was impossible.

Looking around after dressing Skeet's paw, Sarah choked back tears. "Where's Wolf?" she asked the dog. The animal whined soulfully, as if he understood her question.

Just the feel of Skeet's thick, soft fur gave Sarah a faint sense of safety. Skeet would protect her. Wolf had trained him to attack, and he'd taught Sarah the commands. If Skeet was shot, there was a good chance that Wolf had been similarly injured. Man and dog had left her together.

Sarah couldn't contemplate such an awful thing. Yet she knew Summers and his men played for keeps. Killing was perfectly acceptable to them. Patting Skeet, she peered down at the animal.

"Find Wolf!" she whispered. "Go find Wolf!"

Instantly Skeet raised himself to his three good legs and began hobbling off in the direction he'd come from. Sarah followed, as quietly as possible. From time to time, the dog would stop, turn his head to check on her progress, then continue. The slope was steep, and Sarah slipped and fell a number of times on the pine needles. With every step she took, Sarah prayed that Wolf was alive.

Wolf bit back a groan of pain. He lay beside a fallen fir twice his height, his hearing keyed for Summers and his henchmen. Sticky wetness spread across his shirtfront, where a bullet had grazed him an hour earlier. The stray shot had knocked him off balance, and he'd fallen over a fifteen-foot cliff. Looking up, Wolf knew he was lucky to be alive after tumbling over that ledge. Careful not to make a sound, he tested his limbs and his reflexes. Nothing was broken.

His mind returned sluggishly to Sarah. He'd heard her scream. Did Summers have her? If so, where were they? Wolf lay on his side, hugging the fallen tree for safety, as well as for camouflage. There were no sounds to indicate that Summers was still in the area. Had they captured Sarah and left? Wolf felt a cry welling up from deep within him, begging to be released. It was a cry of pure rage and denial. If Summers had captured Sarah... Vignettes of Maria, of her raided village, pummeled Wolf's senses.

From his left, he heard a whine. Skeet! When he'd fallen over the ledge, he'd lost his dog. Getting shakily to his hands and knees, Wolf saw the animal appear out of the darkness, limping toward him. His eyes narrowed. *Sarah!* Her name nearly tore from his lips as he rose unsteadily and turned to meet her. An incredible avalanche of relief shattered through him, ripping away at his raw feelings and exposing his love for her.

Sarah jerked to a halt as a hulking shadow rose from the darkened ground. A scream nearly left her throat. And then she recognized Wolf. With a little cry, she flung herself forward, her arms open.

The instant Sarah hurled herself into Wolf's awaiting arms, she realized he was injured. She heard him groan her name close to her ear, his arms going around her like tight bands of protection. He held her close, and she pressed her head against his chest wall, a sob coming from her.

"It's all right," Wolf rasped thickly. "It's all right...." And it was. Just the special scent of Sarah, and the feel of her thin but strong arms going around his waist in welcome, was enough. Wolf pressed a series of hungry, quick kisses against her tangled hair, her cheek, then searched wildly for her mouth. The instant she turned her face upward and their lips met, Wolf hungrily claimed her.

The world, the danger, ceased to exist, if only for a few moments. Sarah lost herself in Wolf's searching, heated mouth. Immersed in a kaleidoscope of surprise and pleasure, she sank against him.

"I love you," he said hoarsely, pulling back and drowning in her tear-filled eyes. There was no need for further words, Wolf realized humbly as tears streaked down Sarah's grimy features. He framed her face with his shaking hands, touching her as if he didn't know whether she was real or a fevered figment of his tortured imagination.

"You're alive...." Sarah choked out. "Oh, Wolf..."

He touched her lips with his fingers to silence her. Holding her tight, he lifted his head and began to search the darkness. Wolf was relying on his dog's acute hearing and smell more than anything else. Skeet sat nearby, alert, through his silence telling them they were safe— if but for a moment. Removing his fingers from her lips, Wolf touched Sarah's hair. There were so many pine needles in the fine golden strands that they'd have to be removed by hand, not with a comb.

The moment Sarah's hand came to rest on Wolf's shirt, she gasped. The wet, sticky stuff was blood. Her eyes widened enormously as she drew away from him and saw the dark stain across his belly.

"You're hurt...."

"Just a graze. I'm okay. Sarah, we've got to get out of here."

Shaken, Sarah couldn't tear her gaze from his wound. A graze? Half the shirt was bloodied, and it was torn where the bullet had ripped into the fabric. She remembered that Wolf was a mercenary by trade, that his soldiering instincts were finely honed, but nevertheless he was surely in pain.

Taking Sarah's hand, Wolf squeezed it to get her attention. "Your feet?"

"Th-they're fine."

"Sore?"

"A little."

"What do you mean, a little?"

Wetting her lips, Sarah tried to think coherently. "I— They hurt, Wolf, but I can walk on them."

Convinced she was telling the truth, Wolf looked around. "I don't know where Summers and his gang are anymore. I blacked out after I fell over that ledge."

Sarah eyed the jagged rock far above them. A chill swept through her. Wolf was far tougher, and far luckier, than any man had a right to be, and she was grateful for that. Holding his hand tight, she whispered, "I don't know where Summers is, either. I haven't heard them for over an hour."

Nodding, Wolf checked out Skeet. The dog remained passive, and he was sure none of their enemies were close. "Are you hurt in any way?"

Sarah shook her head. "No... Noonan jumped me from behind, but when he tried to cuff me I broke free." She gave a wobbly smile. "I was never so scared.... But I was more scared for you. They were firing those rifles in your direction, Wolf."

Relief came on the heels of Wolf's terror over Sarah's trembling admission. More than anything, he wanted to hold her and keep her safe. She was shaking like a leaf. But then, so was he. There were several small scratches across her brow and cheek, plus a bruise on the side of her neck. He wanted to kill Noonan. Realizing that he was gripping Sarah's small hand too tightly, Wolf released her.

"We have to get to the cabin."

"Yes."

"I don't know how far we are from it," Wolf admitted.

"It doesn't matter. We have to make it."

His mouth pulled into a sour grimace. "We'll go slow and quiet, honey. Skeet will be our ears and nose." Stroking her hair, he saw her rally at his barely whispered words. Sarah had courage, true courage.

"Let's go," she said, and gripped his large hand once again.

Wolf swiveled his head and caught Skeet's attention. Instantly the dog was on his feet and hobbling out in front of them. There was little brush between the huge Douglas firs, so it was relatively easy to walk hand in hand with Sarah. Slowly Wolf's heart settled down into a steady rhythm again. He still had his rifle and ammunition. The odds were against them, but they definitely had a chance.

As Wolf guided Sarah through the maze of darkened trees, his thoughts moved back in time. Back to Peru, to the fact that Maria and her people hadn't stood a chance against Ramirez and his men. At least Sarah was alive and had escaped. A resolve more powerful than any emotion he'd ever felt in his life tunneled through him. Even if he had to die in the process, he was going to make sure that Sarah wasn't hurt or captured by Summers. This time, things were going to work out.

They were resting beneath a huge tree when the muted sound of gunshots echoed in the distance. Sarah stiffened, and instantly she felt Wolf's arm tighten around her shoulders. Both of them looked toward where the sounds had originated from.

"What do you think?" Sarah asked in a low voice. They'd taken a break from their walking to catch their breath. She knew Wolf had done it for her, not for himself.

Wolf stirred. "Probably Summers. His men are jumpy, and a deer might have made them start shooting."

Hope sprang through Sarah as she leaned forward on her crossed legs. "How far do you think we are from the cabin?"

Wolf shrugged. "I don't know." He gazed down at her uplifted features. Exhaustion was written across Sarah's face. "Could be a mile or so. We scattered and ran, so it's hard to tell. I want to get to the road, because it'll be easier going." He added grimly, "We can't walk on the road, though, because Summers and his men might be waiting to ambush us again. We'll parallel it from the safety of the tree line."

With a sigh, Sarah relaxed against Wolf's body and pressed her brow against his shoulder. "I wish we could sleep...."

Leaning over, he pressed a kiss to her hair. "I know."

"But we can't." Sarah slid her hand around his waist. The bleeding from the bullet that had grazed his torso had finally stopped, much to her relief.

Getting to his feet, Wolf growled, "No." The last thing he wanted to do was leave. After admitting his love to Sarah, all he wanted was to know her reaction. Had she even heard his words? Wolf felt terribly unsure, and he was trying to combat the feeling of panic deep within him. Gently he helped Sarah stand.

"By the time we get back to the cabin, it's going to be dawn," he told her in a hushed tone. Picking several pine needles from her mussed hair, he smiled and held her shadowed eyes.

Then he placed his arm around her shoulders, drew

her near and whispered, "Let's go. Dawn will shed new light on the situation."

Sarah nodded, feeling numb inside. The shots worried her. Who had fired them? Were Summers and his men hanging around, waiting for them to appear? Everything seemed so tentative, so extraordinarily fragile.

Sarah halted, her heart beating in triple time. "Wolf?"

He frowned and halted. Automatically his hand went to her arm. She looked forlorn. Frightened.

"What? What is it, honey?"

Just the endearment gave Sarah the courage she needed. "Wolf...I...I'm scared, and I love you...." There—the words were out. She stared up into his craggy, drawn features, her breath jammed in her throat. Croaking, Sarah forced out the rest of what had been begging to be said. "I—I know it's too soon, that we haven't known each other very long, but I have to tell you how I feel. I didn't want to trust you, to care about you, but I couldn't help it. I was afraid to admit I loved you, because I was so afraid I'd lose you...." Sarah looked down at the ground and bit her lower lip. "I still might," she said with a sob. "Inside, I feel so vulnerable and frightened that we could die at any moment." Afraid that she'd said too much, or hadn't said it right, Sarah halted. It took every last bit of her courage to lift her head to see the effect her words had on Wolf.

Trying to steel herself against possible rejection, Sarah lifted her lashes to meet and hold his hooded stare. In that instant, she knew that even if Wolf rejected her she would never love another man as she loved him. No one could possibly match Wolf in stature, in his understanding and complete acceptance of her. But was the love he'd professed to her earlier a fleeting thing? An affair? Sarah couldn't stand that thought. Her feelings ran too deep, and she looked at commitment as a long-term thing.

Wolf raised his hands to Sarah's face. There was such hope and anguish in her eyes. Tears jammed his, and he didn't try to hide his reaction to her low, unsteady admission.

"It's me who should be down on his knees to you, Sarah, not you to me."

Confused, tears brimming her eyes, Sarah whispered, "What are you talking about?"

His smile was tender as he caressed her temples and cheeks. "I'm scarred and wounded, Sarah. I have huge chunks of myself that still aren't healed, but you love me anyway." Unshed tears blurred her face in front of him. Choking out the words, Wolf rasped, "Sarah, I love you. I meant what I said tonight. I'd been feeling that way ever since I met you. And, yes, it hasn't been a long time, but it doesn't matter. What matters most is that you gave me your trust and I gave you mine."

Blindly Sarah moved into his arms, a small cry escaping her lips. "We could die at any time. I—I just wanted you to know, Wolf, to know I love you."

With a groan, he took Sarah's full weight against him, holding her, holding her love forever. "I don't deserve a second chance," he said thickly, his lips near her ear, "and I certainly don't deserve you."

"Yes, you do," Sarah said with a little laugh that was partly a sob of relief. She looked up, his glistening eyes melting her heart. "I just wanted you to know, in case something happened to me—to us."

"We'll get through this—together." He leaned down, capturing her tear-bathed lips. "Together..."

Chapter Fourteen

"Wolf, look!" The words escaped Sarah as they neared the cabin. Dawn had come and gone, and the strong morning light was now sending blinding shafts through the fir trees on Blue Mountain. Beside the cabin were several cars, among them a black Jeep. In addition, there were three state police cruisers, and another black car Sarah hadn't seen before. She saw two men in expensive suits, and two other men, in jeans and short-sleeved shirts, who looked dangerous and alert.

"It's Morgan!" Wolf said, coming to a halt, disbelief in his voice. "And Killian. And Jake."

She twisted a look up at him and saw the joy leaking into his exhausted features. "Your boss?" she croaked.

A slow grin started across Wolf's mouth as he looked down at Sarah and brought her hard against him. "Yes, and my team. I'll be damned," he whispered, and kissed her long and hard. As he broke free of her lips and saw her stunned expression, he said, "Morgan must have sensed all hell was going to break loose and decided to come after I called him. If I'm not mistaken, the other guy in the dark suit is a top FBI official. Come on, honey, we're saved!"

Sarah needed no coaxing. She knew they both looked disheveled, and the blood on Wolf's shirt gave the appearance that he'd been wounded much more seriously then he had. The first to sense their approach was a cougar-lean man with black hair. He swiveled around, instantly on guard.

"Wolf!" Killian called to the other men and then trotted toward them. A quarter of a mile separated them. The rest of the men raised their heads, stopped talking and looked with amazement in their direction.

Realizing just how tender Sarah's feet were, Wolf decided to halt on the slope and give her a well-deserved rest. He watched his friend's approach. Although Killian never smiled, Wolf could see his friend's green eyes dancing with silent welcome as he trotted up to them. "We're okay," Wolf said, extending his hand in greeting.

Gripping Wolf's hand, Killian's narrowed eyes swung from Wolf to Sarah, then back to Wolf. "Thank all the saints, you're alive. We were worried. Summers wasn't talking after we apprehended him and his men earlier this morning down the road from the cabin. We figured, with the arsenal they were carrying, that they'd been hunting you."

Wolf nodded. He kept his eyes on the group of men at the base of Blue Mountain. "That's exactly what happened. Who's with Morgan and Jake?"

Killian briefly turned his head. "State troopers, and FBI agent Kyle Talbot."

Relief plunged through Wolf. "Good. When did you arrive? And what the hell's happening? You said you nabbed Summers?"

"Morgan can fill you in on the details, but after you called him yesterday, he rounded us up. We caught the first flight out to Anaconda and rented a car. Kyle came with us. Morgan pieced things together. He figured you'd be at Sarah Thatcher's cabin, so we came up here. We met Summers and his men, running around like idiots with rifles in their hands, about three miles from here. Kyle arrested them, and then after we checked out Ms. Thatcher's cabin, we figured they'd been hunting you." His mouth pulled into the slightest of smiles. "Morgan said if you were still alive you'd eventually show up here at the cabin. He was right."

Sarah sagged against Wolf, dizzy with relief. "It's over," she murmured.

Wolf studied her anxiously and kept his grip firm around her waist. He glanced over at Killian. "Sarah, this is Killian, one of my men."

Killian nodded. "Ms. Thatcher."

Sarah tried to smile, but she was incredibly exhausted. "Hi, Killian. Thank you for coming...."

"Then Summers and his men are in jail?" Wolf demanded.

"That's right. All of them, including Sheriff Noonan."

Sarah pressed her hand against her heart, relieved. "I'm so glad...."

Concerned for Sarah, Wolf glanced at the rest of the men coming to greet them. "We're going to make some fast introductions, and then I want to get Sarah cleaned up. We both need to rest," he told Killian.

"Looks like you may need to go to the hospital,"

Killian warned, pointing at the rust-colored blood staining Wolf's shirt.

"Just a graze," Wolf muttered. "Right now, I need a
hot bath, bed and—" he smiled down at Sarah "—this
lady at my side."

Sarah fought grogginess as she emerged from the
shower and wrapped herself in a thick, fluffy towel. Outside the door, she could hear the Perseus men talking in
low tones in the living room of her cabin. It was over.
All over. Meeting Morgan Trayhern and the other men
had been little more than a blur in her spongy state. She
remembered shaking hands, but that was all.

As she pulled on her cotton gown and donned her
robe, she heard the men leaving. Glancing out the bathroom window, she saw Morgan and his men climb into
the black Jeep. The FBI agent stood talking with Wolf
for a moment before he got into his dark sedan. With a
sigh, she opened the door and stumbled toward the bedroom. What she needed was Wolf to hold her. The need
to be in his arms was overwhelming.

Sarah pulled back the covers and lay down. Before
she could even pull the sheet over her, she fell into a
deep, spiraling sleep.

Wolf rubbed his eyes. They were burning from lack
of sleep. His steps echoed through the cabin. Spotting
the bathroom door open, Wolf moved slowly toward the
bedroom door. At the entrance, he hesitated, a slight
smile tugging at his mouth. Sarah lay on her side, curled
in a fetal position, her hands beneath her cheek. She was
fast asleep. Just the soft parting of her lips stirred him,
made him want to love her as he'd never loved another
woman.

Quietly he tiptoed into the room and pulled the sheet

and blanket across Sarah's sleeping form. Her hair, still damp from being recently washed, framed her face. Gently Wolf touched her cheek and felt the velvet firmness of it beneath his fingers.

Forcing himself to move away from her, Wolf knew he desperately needed to bathe before joining Sarah in bed. As he left the room and closed the door, nothing had ever seemed so right to him. He was drained in a way that left him weaving across the floor to the bathroom, and he knew he'd be lucky to make it to bed and gather Sarah into his arms before he keeled over from sheer exhaustion.

The impertinent chirp of an upset robin outside the raised bedroom window awakened Sarah first. Evening light filtered in the window, telling her it must be close to nine o'clock at night. She'd slept a long time. Wrapped in a sense of being protected, she groggily turned and realized that she was pressed against Wolf's entire length. His arm was wrapped around her shoulders, and her head lay in the hollow of his shoulder. Just his soft breathing, the rise and fall of his massive chest, stirred her. Wolf was alive. She was alive. How close they had come to dying less than twelve hours ago, she thought.

Tentatively she slid her hand across the massive breadth of his darkly haired chest, allowing all of her senses to absorb the exploration. There was such latent power to Wolf, and yet he had been nothing but gentle and sensitive to her, to her needs.

Raising up on one elbow, Sarah gazed down at Wolf's sleeping features. The beard lent his face an even more dangerous quality. She rested her palm against his heart and felt the slow, powerful beat of it beneath her hand.

His hair was tousled, and it gave his face a vulnerable look. Her heart expanded with such joy that she blindly followed womanly instinct and leaned forward.

The first, tentative brush of Sarah's lips on Wolf's mouth eased him out of deep slumber. Was he dreaming again? But this was too real. He barely opened his eyes as he lifted his hands. Her mouth was warm and inviting, softly exploring his. A groan rumbled through him as Sarah artlessly pressed herself to him, a signal to his spinning senses that she wanted much more than just a kiss from him.

Sleep was torn from Wolf as he eased Sarah onto her back against the bed covers. The evening light through the window was muted, giving the room a quiet sense of surrender to the coming darkness. The gold of Sarah's fine, silky hair as he ran his finger through the strands satisfied Wolf even more. Her eyes were lustrous with allure, and his body hardened in response.

"Sarah..." he rasped, cradling her cheek. "Honey, wait..."

Sarah's hand skimmed Wolf's bearded cheek. She took pleasure in his sweetly sleepy state. There was such unexpected vulnerability in him. "We've waited long enough," she whispered.

Wolf saw the longing in her blue eyes, eyes that were drowsy with desire. Every fiber of his being wanted to love her. With his thumb, he traced her parted lips, lips he wanted to ravish. "I love you," he rasped, his heart pounding in time with the urgent throbbing of his need. Her hands skimmed his arms, shoulders and neck like a tantalizing breeze.

She framed his face with her hands. When she spoke, her voice was low and quavering. "I love you, Wolf. I trust you. I was so afraid about how I felt toward you."

She smiled a little. "I know your love can help me across whatever fears might be left." Sarah felt the sting of tears and blinked them away. She felt the massive, potent power of his barely controlled body above her, felt a fine trembling shudder pass through him as she spoke those words.

Love. Wolf pressed his brow against Sarah's. He tried to find the words, but couldn't. Only her hands, moving across his body, brought him out of the turmoil within him. Finally he eased back enough to hold her shimmering gaze.

"I love you, Sarah. When I told you that last night, in the heat of battle, I meant it."

"I was scared then, and I'm scared now," Sarah quavered, "but in a different way."

He nodded and closed his eyes. "That makes two of us." When he opened his eyes again, he added, "I'm afraid that I'll go too far too fast and scare the hell out of you, or make you push me away. And," he added sadly, "I'm afraid I'll see fear, see fear of me, come into your eyes..."

Whispering his name, Sarah eased upward, grasping his shoulders. Wolf had taken a terrible emotional beating in many ways, and as she pressed a kiss to his jaw, Sarah knew she could help him. She would welcome his advances, reassure him with herself, with her body and, most of all, with her heart. It was thrilling to discover that she could give Wolf back a huge piece of himself that had been crushed by the events in Peru.

"You can't hurt me," she whispered. "Just love me, Wolf. Please...I want you..."

Wolf nuzzled her cheek, found her mouth and gently trapped her against the bed as he claimed her. There was such lushness to her eager, exploring lips against his.

It took real courage to reach out and live life, Wolf realized, to love despite the possibility of rejection. As he drowned in the splendor of Sarah's welcoming mouth and touch, Wolf knew he had to risk himself, and place his damaged hope once more on the line. As Sarah came willingly into his arms, her strong, loving body pressing urgently against his, Wolf surrendered to his heart as never before.

As he drew the flowery printed nightgown off Sarah and gazed down at her, Wolf transcended his own fear; perhaps it was Sarah's fearless approach to wanting to love him. Wolf wasn't sure, and in that golden, heated moment it no longer mattered.

Sarah closed her eyes as she felt Wolf's strong hands caress her shoulder, her waist, and on down to outline the shape of her hips. There was such tenderness in his exploration of her that she felt herself unraveling. His touch was like sunlight skimming silently across the land. When he leaned over, his mouth capturing hers at the same moment that his hand caressed her breast, she moaned.

The world spun to a halt as Sarah drowned in the heat, the fire, of Wolf's mouth, and when his lips settled on the peak of her breast she gave a small cry of pleasure. Her fingers kneaded his broad, damp shoulders as he drew her deep into his arms, pressing her hotly against him, his mouth bringing a new kind of fire that raced through her. The ache centered in her lower body, and as she moaned, Sarah lost herself in all the sensations of Wolf as a man.

She tasted the perspiration of his taut shoulder, felt him tremble as she caressed him intimately. Her boldness, her need to show just how much she loved him, broke through whatever barrier continued to hold him a prisoner of the past. As she lifted her lashes, she saw his burning gray eyes meet and hold her own as he covered her with his body.

The moments suspended. Sarah held her breath as she felt Wolf's knee guide her thighs apart. His hands framed her face, and she clung to the hooded, heated look in his eyes, to the tension mirrored in his rugged features. There was still a thread of fear in Wolf's eyes, and instinctively Sarah allowed her feminine heart to guide her as she arched upward to meet him, capture him, pull him deeply within herself.

She immediately felt Wolf's fingers tighten around her face, and she not only heard, but felt, a deep animal growl come from within him as she enclosed and held him within her molten, silky confines. It was as if something snapped within Wolf as he arched and tensed within her, and Sarah smiled softly as she felt him surge forward, taking her, claiming her for the first time.

In those golden, spinning moments, moments that seemed so far removed from the real world, Sarah surrendered herself to Wolf in every possible way, for the first time in her life. As he slid his hand beneath her hips, giving back the same pleasure she was giving him, she understood what real love was all about. It was about sharing—giving, taking, allowing the fear to fall away in order to love fully. Whatever issues of trust she'd had also dissolved beneath the cherishing strength of his mouth, the worship of his hands across her body that made it sing like the most beautiful bird she'd ever heard. There was such beauty being shared, such care and love, that tears matted her lashes.

The lightninglike heat grew deep within Sarah as he moved with her, making her his own. The sudden current of release shot through her like a lush explosion, catching Sarah by surprise. Arching into Wolf's arms, pressed against his length, absorbing his strength, she cried out and threw her head back as the waves of sensation overwhelmed her. The intense pleasure went on and on, and Sarah could only helplessly sponge up the wild, fiery feelings that Wolf prolonged for her.

As Sarah began to slide back into the molten fire afterward, she felt Wolf tense and grip her hard to him. In those moments, as she held him, her face pressed to his shoulder, Sarah willingly received Wolf's gift of himself to her. All she was aware of was his damp, hot skin, his ragged breath against her face and neck, and his hands wrapped lovingly in the length of her blond hair.

Opening her eyes, she smiled up at Wolf. All the tension and fear had been drained away from him by her vessel of a body, by her love fearlessly reaching out to him. Extending a hand, Sarah gently caressed his darkly bearded cheek.

"I love you with my life," she told him, her voice quavering.

Much later, they stirred in each other's arms. The small night-light on the wall broke the hold of darkness in the bedroom as Sarah roused herself. She realized that Wolf was already awake, at her side, his hand resting against her as he studied her in the silence. There was such peace and serenity in Wolf's face that Sarah was stunned by the change in him. She smiled sleepily up into Wolf's rugged, shadowed features.

"I slept again," she whispered, her hand moving across his chest, luxuriating in the soft, dark hair there.

"We both did," Wolf murmured, running his hand slowly up and down the length of her strong spine. "I woke up first, though." He tendered a slight smile to show her how much he loved her. Wolf caressed Sarah's shoulder and arm, feeling like a thirsty sponge absorbing everything about Sarah. Earlier, she had been damp and slick against the hard planes of his body. Now her skin was like velvet beneath his touch.

"You were wonderful," Sarah told him as she sat up facing him. The covers pooled around her hips, and she captured his hand. "We were wonderful."

Wolf nodded, absorbing the shining luster in Sarah's eyes as she smiled. She fed his soul. Reaching out, he sifted strands of her gold hair through his fingers. "You weren't afraid like I was," he told her. "You had the courage to go all the way. I knew I was holding back..."

Leaning forward, Sarah laughed softly and captured his mouth to let him know how much she loved him. Wolf's response was instant and heated. As she reluctantly broke the kiss and gazed into his molten gray eyes, she whispered, "Maybe because we love each other so much, that helped us get past our own fears."

He gave her a lazy smile and eased her upward until she lay over him. Instantly he saw the change in her eyes and felt the heat of her stir the fires within him again. "I feel like life is going to start getting good again," he confided. "For both of us, honey."

Sarah delighted in her contact with Wolf. "We have the time, don't we?"

Sarah leaned down and nuzzled Wolf's cheek, then gave him a swift, hot kiss on the mouth before laying her head on his shoulder. "All the time in the world," he said. He brought his arms around her. He wanted to discuss marriage, but it was too soon. Or was it?

"Wolf?"

"Hmmm?"

Sarah smiled tentatively and brushed his short, dark

hair away from his furrowed brow. "Will you stay here until Summers goes to trial?"

Wolf stilled and held her serious look. "Sarah, I'm not the kind of man who does well at one-night stands or even living together." He scowled and pushed his fear of rejection aside. "Loving you was a commitment," he told her gravely. "I don't want to stay just for Summers's trial. I want what we have to be the start of a commitment that works toward marriage."

His words were like a sweet dream flowing through her. Sarah swallowed against her tears. "I wasn't sure, Wolf.... I don't want a one-night stand, either. And I'd like you to come and live with me, if that's what you want." She saw his face become gentle with emotions, and it gave her the courage to dive headlong into what really lay in her heart.

"I know we haven't known each other very long, and I know we need the time. With Summers going to jail, we'll have it. I just need you to know how much I love you. It's not a passing thing, Wolf. You opened yourself up and let me give you my trust. It was something I never thought I could do again, but you made it easy." She leaned over and kissed him.

"I love the hell out of you, Sarah Thatcher," Wolf whispered thickly, fitting his mouth against her parted lips. He loved her fiercely, for her goodness, her thoughtfulness toward others—and for the fact that she moaned and returned his kiss with all the womanly fire she possessed. He cupped her cheek and held her lustrous blue gaze. Her eyes were shining with love for him alone. "I'd like to move in here, to live with you."

"Good..." Sarah sniffed and gave him a trembly smile.

Smiling softly, Wolf pressed a kiss to her salty, wet

lips. So much had been taken away from each of them, and yet, as they held one another, he realized that despite their individual scars, together they achieved a wholeness that would give them a new lease on life.

Wolf eased Sarah into his arms and wiped the tears from her cheeks with his fingers. "We'll have the time now," he told her, "to grow and know each other. We've got some tough times ahead with the trial, but we'll take that together." His voice went deep with raw feeling. "When the time's right, I want to marry you, Sarah. I want you to carry our children, if that's what you want. We're going to take life together, on our terms. You hear me?"

She did, and she closed her eyes as she uttered Wolf's name. As his arms closed around her, Sarah knew, at last, that with love, anything was possible.

* * * * *

THE ROGUE

To my husband, David,
who has stuck with me through thick and thin,
making each year better than the last.

Prologue

"Killian, your next assignment is a personal favor to me."

Morgan Trayhern was sitting with his friend and employee in a small Philipsburg, Montana, restaurant. The situation with Wolf Harding and Sarah Thatcher had been successfully wrapped up, and now it was time to pack up and go home. Morgan grimaced apologetically, as Killian's features remained completely closed, only a glitter in his hard, intelligent blue eyes suggesting possible interest.

Morgan picked up a fork and absently rotated it between his fingers and thumb. They'd already ordered their meals, so now was as good a time as any to broach the topic. "Look," he began with an effort, purposely keeping his voice low, "whether I want to or not, I'm going to have to put you on an assignment involving a woman, Killian."

Killian sat relaxed, his long, spare hands draped casually on his thighs as he leaned back in the poorly padded metal chair. But anyone who knew him knew he was never truly relaxed; he only gave that appearance. He stared guardedly at Morgan. ''I can't.''

Morgan stared back, the silence tightening between them. ''You're going to have to.''

Killian eased the chair down and placed his hands on the table. ''I told you—I don't deal with women,'' he said flatly.

''At least hear me out,'' Morgan pleaded.

''It won't do any good.''

Exhaustion shadowed Morgan's gray eyes. ''Just sit there and listen.''

Killian wrestled with an unexpected surge of panic that left a bitter taste in his mouth. He held Morgan's gaze warningly, feeling suddenly as if this man who had been his friend since their days in the French Foreign Legion had become an adversary.

Morgan rubbed his face tiredly. ''The assignment deals with Laura's cousin from her mother's side of the family,'' he began, referring to his wife, who'd managed to befriend Killian—at least as much as Morgan had ever seen him allow. ''This is important to me—and to Laura—and we want to know that you're the one handling the situation. It's personal, Killian.''

Killian's scowl deepened, and his mouth thinned.

''Laura's cousin, Susannah Anderson, came to visit us in D.C.'' Morgan's eyes grew dark and bleak. ''From what we've been able to piece together, on the way home, Susannah was at the bus station in Lexington, Kentucky, when a man came up and started a conversation with her. Moments later, he was shot right in front of her eyes. We think Susannah saw the murderer, Killian—and he shot her, too, because she was a witness. The bullet hit her skull, cracked it and exited. By some miracle, she doesn't have brain damage, thank God. But the injury's swelling left her in a coma for two months. She regained consciousness a month ago, and I was hoping she could give us a lead on her attacker, but she can't remember what he looked like. And another thing, Killian—she can't talk.''

Morgan rubbed his hands together wearily, his voice heavy with worry. ''The psychiatrists are telling me that the horror of the experience is behind her inability to speak, not brain damage. She's suppressed the whole incident—that's why she can't describe the killer. Laura went down and stayed with Susannah and her family in Kentucky for a week after Susannah was brought home from the hospital, in hopes that she'd find her voice again.'' Morgan shrugged. ''It's been a month now, and she's still mute.''

Killian shifted slightly, resting his hands on the knees of his faded jeans. ''I've seen that mute condition,'' he said quietly, ''in some of the children and women of Northern Ireland.''

Morgan opened his hands in a silent plea to Killian to take the assignment. ''That's not the whole story, Killian. I need you to guard Susannah. There's evidence to indicate that the killer will go after Susannah once he finds out she survived. I think Susannah was an innocent bystander in a drug deal gone bad, but so far we don't know enough to point any fingers. Susannah's memory is the key, and they can't risk her remembering the incident.

''Susannah was under local police guard at the Lexington hospital while she was there, and I had one of my female employees there, too. Since her release, I've told Susannah to stay on her parents' fruit farm in the Kentucky hills. Normally she lives and works down in the small nearby town of Glen, where she teaches handicapped children.''

Morgan grasped the edge of the table, and his knuckles were white as he made his final plea. ''She's family, Killian. Laura is very upset about this, because she and Susannah are like sisters. I want to entrust this mission to my very best man, and that's you.''

Glancing sharply at his boss, Killian asked, ''I'd be a bodyguard?''

''Yes. But Susannah and her parents aren't aware of the possible continued threat to her, so I don't want them to know your true capacity there. They're upset enough after nearly losing their daughter. I don't want to stress them more. Relaxation and peace are crucial to Susannah's recovery. I've contacted her father, Sam Anderson, and told him you're a friend of mine who needs some convalescence. Sam knows the type of company I run, and has an inkling of some of the things we do. I told him you were exhausted after coming in off a long-term mission and needed to hole up and rest.''

Killian shrugged. The story wasn't too far from the truth. He hardened his heart. ''I never take assignments involving women, Morgan.''

''I know that. But I need you for this, Killian. On the surface, this assignment may look easy and quiet, but it's not. Stay on guard. I'm trying to track the drug deal right now. All our contacts in South America are checking it out, and I'm working closely with the Lexington police department. There's a possibility it could involve Santiago's cartel.''

Killian's jaw clenched at the name of José Santiago,

the violent Peruvian drug kingpin they'd finally managed to extradite and get behind bars.

Morgan gave Killian a pleading look. "Susannah's already been hurt enough in this ordeal. I don't want her hurt further. I worry that her family could become a target, too."

Cold anger wound through Killian as he thought about the mission. "Picking on a defenseless woman tells you the kind of slime we're dealing with."

Morgan gave Killian a probing look. "So will you take this assignment?"

Morgan knew that Killian's weakness, his Achilles' heel, was the underdog in any situation.

"One more thing," Morgan warned as he saw Killian's eyes thaw slightly. "Susannah isn't very emotionally stable right now. Her parents are Kentucky hill people. They're simple, hardworking folks. Sam owns a two-hundred-acre fruit farm, and that's their livelihood. Susannah ought to be in therapy to help her cope with what happened to her. I've offered to pay for it, but she's refusing all help."

"Frightened of her own shadow?" Killian asked, the face of his sister, Meg, floating into his memory.

Morgan nodded. "I want you to take care of Susannah. I know it's against your guidelines for a job, but my instincts say you're the right person to handle this situation—and her."

His own haunted past resurfacing, tugging at his emotions, Killian felt his heart bleed silently for this woman and her trauma. Avoiding Morgan's searching gaze, he sat silently for a long time, mulling over his options. Finally he heaved a sigh and muttered, "I just can't do it."

"Dammit!" Morgan leaned forward, fighting to keep

his voice under tight control. "I *need* you, Killian. I'm not *asking* you to take this assignment, I'm *ordering* you to take it."

Anger leaped into Killian's narrowed eyes, and his fist clenched on the table's Formica top as he stared at Morgan. "And if I don't take this assignment?"

"Then, whether I like it or not, I'll release you from any obligation to Perseus. I'm sorry, Killian. I didn't want the mission to come down to this. You're the best at what we do. But Susannah is part of my family." His voice grew emotional with pleading. "Whatever your problem with women is, put it aside. I'm begging you to help Susannah."

Killian glared at Morgan, tension radiating from him, every joint in his usually relaxed body stiff with denial. He *couldn't* protect a woman! Yet, as he stared at Morgan, he knew that if he didn't take the assignment his boss would release him from his duties with Perseus, and the money he made was enough to keep Meg reasonably well-off. If he hadn't come to work for Perseus, he'd never have been able to free her from the financial obligations brought on by her tragedy.

His need to help his sister outweighed the risk of his own pain. The words came out harshly, bitten off: "I'll do the best I can."

Relief showed on Morgan's taut features. "Good. My conscience is eating me alive on this situation, Killian. But this is the only way I can make amends to Susannah for what's happened. She was innocent—in the wrong place at the wrong time."

"I'll leave right away," Killian rasped as he took the voucher and airline ticket Morgan proffered. No use putting off the inevitable. He'd pick up his luggage at the motel across from the restaurant and get under way. No longer hungry, he rose from the booth. Morgan appeared grateful, but that didn't do anything for him. Still angry over Morgan's threat to fire him, Killian made his way outside without a word. Walking quickly, he crossed the street to the motel, his senses as always hyperalert to everything around him.

What kind of person was this Susannah Anderson? Killian wondered. He'd noticed Morgan's voice lower with feeling when he'd spoken about her. Was she young? Old? Married? Apparently not, if she was staying with her parents. A large part of him, the part that suffered and grieved over Meg, still warned him not to go to Kentucky. His soft spot for a woman in trouble was the one chink in his carefully tended armor against the pain this world inflicted on the unwary.

Yet, as he approached the motel on this hot Montana summer morning, Killian felt an oblique spark of interest that he hated to admit. Susannah was a melodic name, suggestive of someone with sensitivity. Was she? What color was her hair? What color were her eyes? Killian could read a person's soul through the eyes. That ability to delve into people, to know them inside out, was his greatest strength. On the flip side, he allowed no one to know him. Even Morgan Trayhern, who had one of the most sophisticated security companies in America, had only a very thin background dossier on him. And Killian wanted it kept that way. He wanted no one to know the extent of the pain he carried within him—or what he'd done about it. That kind of information could be ammunition for his enemies—and could mean danger to anyone close to him. Still, his mind dwelled on the enigmatic Susannah Anderson. She could be in more danger with Killian around than from any potential hit man. Why couldn't Morgan understand that? Killian hadn't wanted to tell Morgan his reasons for refusing to take assignments involving women; he'd never told anyone. A frown worked its way across his brow. Susannah had been a victim of violence, just like Meg. More than likely, she was afraid of everything.

Arriving at his motel room, Killian methodically packed the essentials he traveled with: a long, wicked-looking hunting knife, the nine-millimeter Beretta that he wore beneath his left armpit in a shoulder holster, and his dark brown leather coat.

When he'd placed a few other necessary items in a beat-up leather satchel, Killian was ready for his next assignment. He'd never been to Kentucky, so he'd have a new area to explore. But whether he wanted to or not, he had to meet Susannah Anderson. The thought tied his gut into painful knots. Damn Morgan's stubbornness! The woman was better off without Killian around. How in the hell was he going to handle his highly volatile emotions, not to mention her?

Chapter One

"We're so glad you've come," Pansy Anderson gushed as she handed Killian a cup of coffee and sat down at the kitchen table across from him.

Killian gave the woman a curt nod. The trip to Glen, Kentucky, and from there to the fruit farm, had passed all too quickly. However, the Andersons' warm welcome had dulled some of his apprehension. Ordinarily, Killian spoke little, but this woman's kindness made his natural reticence seem rude. Leathery-looking Sam Anderson sat at his elbow, work-worn hands clutching a chipped ceramic mug of hot black coffee. Pansy, who appeared to be in her sixties, was thin, with a face that spoke of a harsh outdoor life.

As much as Killian wanted to be angry at everyone, he knew these people didn't deserve his personal frustration. Struggling with emotions he didn't dare explore, Killian whispered tautly, "I'm glad to be here, Mrs. Anderson.'' It was an utter lie, but still, when he looked into Pansy's worn features he saw relief and hope in her eyes. He scowled inwardly at her reaction. He couldn't offer hope to them or to their daughter. More likely, he presented a danger equal to the possibility of the murderer's coming after Susannah. Oh, God, what was he going to do? Killian's gut clenched with anxiety.

''Call me Pansy.'' She got up, wiping her hands on her red apron. ''I think it's so nice of Morgan to send you here for a rest. To tell you the truth, we could sure use company like yours after what happened to our Susannah.'' She went to the kitchen counter and began peeling potatoes for the evening meal. ''Pa, you think Susannah might like the company?''

''Dunno, Ma. Maybe.'' Sam's eyes became hooded, and he stared down at his coffee, pondering her question. ''My boy, Dennis, served with Morgan. Did he tell you that?''

''No, he didn't.''

''That's right—in Vietnam. Dennis died up there on that hill with everyone else. My son sent glowing letters back about Captain Trayhern.'' Sam looked up. ''To this day, I've kept those letters. It helps ease the pain I feel when I miss Denny.''

Pansy sighed. ''We call Susannah our love baby, Killian. She was born shortly after Denny was killed. She sure plugged up a hole in our hearts. She was such a beautiful baby....''

''Now, Ma,'' Sam warned gruffly, ''don't go getting teary-eyed on us. Susannah's here and, thank the good Lord above, she's alive.'' Sam turned his attention to Killian. ''We need to warn you about our daughter. Since she came back to us from the coma, she's been actin' awful strange.''

"Before the tragedy," Pansy added, "Susannah was always such a lively, outgoing young woman. She's a teacher over at the local grade school in Glen. The mentally and physically handicapped children are her first love. She used to laugh, dance, and play beautiful music." Pansy gestured toward the living room of the large farmhouse. "There's a piano in there, and Susannah can play well. Now she never touches it. If she hears music, she runs out of the house crying."

"And she don't want anything to do with anyone. Not even us, much of the time," Sam whispered. He gripped the cup hard, his voice low with feeling. "Susannah is the kindest, most loving daughter on the face of this earth, Killian. She wouldn't harm a fly. She cries if one of Ma's baby chicks dies. When you meet her, you'll see what we're saying."

"The violence has left her disfigured in a kind of invisible way," Pansy said. "She has nasty headaches, the kind that make her throw up. They come on when she's under stress. She hasn't gone back to teach, because she hasn't found her voice yet. The doctors say the loss of her voice isn't due to the blow on her head."

"It's mental," Sam added sadly.

"Yes…I suppose it is.…" Pansy admitted softly.

"It's emotional," Killian rasped, "not mental." He was instantly sorry he'd spoken, as both of them gave him a strange look. Shifting in his chair, Killian muttered, "I know someone who experienced something similar." Meg had never lost her voice, but he'd suffered with her, learning plenty about emotional wounds. He saw the relief in their faces, and the shared hope. Dammit, they shouldn't hope! Killian clamped his mouth shut and scowled deeply, refusing to meet their eyes.

Pansy rattled on, blotting tears from her eyes. "You understand, then."

Pansy gave him a wobbly smile and wiped her hands off on the towel hanging up on a hook next to the sink. "We just don't know, Killian. Susannah writes us notes so we can talk with her that way. But if we try and ask her about the shooting she runs away, and we don't see her for a day or two."

"She's out in the old dilapidated farmhouse on the other side of the orchard—but not by our choice," Sam offered unhappily. "That was the old family homestead for over a hundred years 'fore my daddy built this place. When Susannah came home from the hospital last month, she insisted on moving into that old, broken-down house. No one's lived there for twenty years or more! It's about half a mile across the hill from where we live now. We had to move her bed and fetch stuff out to her. Sometimes, on a good day, she'll come join us for supper. Otherwise, she makes her own meals and stays alone over there. It's as if she wants to hide from the world—even from us...."

Killian nodded, feeling the pain that Pansy and Sam carried for their daughter. As the silence in the kitchen became stilted, Killian forced himself to ask a few preliminary questions. "How old is Susannah?"

Sam roused himself. "Going on twenty-seven."

"And you say she's a teacher?"

A proud smile wreathed Pansy's features as she washed dishes in the sink. "Yes, she's a wonderful teacher! Do you know, she's the only member of either of our families that got a college degree? The handicapped children love her so much. She taught art class." With a sigh, Pansy added, "Lordy, she won't paint or draw anymore, either."

"Nope," Sam said. "All she does is work in the orchard, garden and tend the animals—mostly the sick ones. That's what seems to make her feel safe."

"And she goes for long walks alone," Pansy added. "I worry. She knows these hills well, but there's this glassy look that comes into her eyes, Killian, and I sometimes wonder if she realizes where she's at."

"Have there been any strangers around, asking about Susannah?" Killian asked offhandedly. Now he understood why Morgan didn't want to tell these gentle, simple people the truth of the situation. But how the hell was he going to balance everything and keep a professional attitude?

"Oh," Pansy said with a laugh, "we get lots of folks up here to buy our fruits, nuts and fresh garden vegetables. And I'm known for my healin' abilities, so we always have folks stoppin' by. That's somethin' Susannah took to—using herbs to heal people with. She's a good healer, and the hill folk, if they can't get to me because I'm busy, they'll go to Susannah. We have a huge herb garden over by the old homestead, and she's making our medicines for this year as the herbs are ready for pickin'."

"That and using white lightning to make tinctures from those herbs." Sam chuckled. And then he raised his bushy eyebrows. "I make a little corn liquor on the side. Strictly for medicinal purposes." He grinned.

Killian nodded, reading between the lines. Although the Andersons were farm people, they were well-off by hill standards. When he'd driven up earlier in the brown Land Cruiser he'd rented at the airport, he'd noted that the rolling green hills surrounding the large two-story white farmhouse were covered with orchards. He'd also seen a large chicken coop, and at least two hundred chickens roaming the hundred acres, ridding the land of insect pests. He'd seen a couple of milking cows, a flock of noisy gray geese, some wild mallards that made their home in a nearby pond, and a great blue heron walking along the edge of the water, probably hunting frogs. In Killian's mind, this place was perfect for someone like him, someone who was world-weary and in need of some genuine rest.

"Why don't you go out and meet Susannah?" Pansy asked hopefully. "You should introduce yourself. Maybe what she needs is someone her own age to get on with. That might help her heal."

White-hot anger clashed with gut-wrenching fear within Killian. Anger at Morgan for forcing him to take this mission. Fear of what he might do around Susannah if he didn't maintain tight control over his emotions. Killian kept his expression passive. Struggling to keep his voice noncommittal, he said, "Yes, I'll meet your daughter. But don't get your hopes up about anything happening." His tone came out harder than he'd anticipated. "I'm here for a rest, Mrs. Anderson. I'm a man of few words, and I like to be left alone."

Pansy's face fell a little, but she quickly summoned up a soft smile. "Why, of course, Mr. Killian. You are our guest, and we want you to feel free to come and go as you please."

Kindness was something Killian had *never* been able to deal with. He stood abruptly, the scraping of the wooden chair against the yellowed linoleum floor an irritant to his taut nerves. "I don't intend to be lazy. I'll help do some work around the place while I'm here."

"I can always use a pair of extra hands," Sam said, "and I'd be beholden to you for that."

Relief swept through Killian, at least momentarily.

Work would help keep him away from Susannah. Yet, as a bodyguard, he'd have to remain alert and nearby—even if it was the last thing he wanted to do. But work would also help him get to know the farm and its layout, to anticipate where a threat to Susannah might come from.

Sam rose to his full six-foot-five-inch height. He was as thin as a spring sapling. "Come meet our daughter, Mr. Killian. Usually, this time of day, she's out in the herb garden. It's best I go with you. Otherwise, she's liable to start 'cause you're a stranger."

"Of course," Killian said. Everything about the Anderson home spoke of stark simplicity, he noted as he followed Sam. The floors were covered with linoleum, worn but clean, and lovingly polished. The handmade furniture looked antique, no doubt crafted by Anderson men over the generations. A green crocheted afghan covered the back of the sofa. Pansy had mentioned when he arrived that it had been made by her mother, who had recently passed away at the age of ninety-eight. Evidently, a long-lived family, Killian mused as he followed Sam out the creaky screen door onto the large wooden porch, where a swing hung.

"Now," Sam warned him, "don't take offense if Susannah sees you and takes off for her house. Sometimes when folks come to buy our produce they mistakenly stop at the old house. She locks herself in and won't go near the door."

Not a bad idea, Killian thought, with her assailant still on the prowl. Sometimes paranoia could serve a person well, he ruminated. He looked at himself. He was paranoid, too, but with good cause. As they walked down a well-trodden path lined with fruit trees he wondered how much Susannah knew of her own situation.

"Now," Sam was saying as he took long, slow strides, "this here's the apple orchard. We got mostly Gravestein and Jonathan varieties, 'cause folks are always lookin' for good pie apples." He gestured to the right. "Over there is the Bartlett pears and Bing cherries and sour cherries. To the left, we got Alberta and freestone peaches. Ma loves figs, so we got her a row of them, too. Susannah likes the nut trees, so I ended up planting about twenty acres of black walnuts. Darn good taste to the things, but they come in this thick outer shell, and you have to wait till it dries before you can even get to the nut. It's a lot of work, but Susannah, as a kid, used to sit around for hours, shelling those things by the bucketful. The black are the best-tasting of all walnuts."

Killian nodded, his gaze never still. The surrounding rolling hills, their trees bearing nearly mature fruit, looked idyllic. A variety of birds flew through the many branches and he heard babies cheeping loudly for their parents to bring them food. Still, the serene orchard was forestlike, offering easy cover for a hit man.

After about a fifteen-minute walk up a gentle slope, Killian halted beside Sam where the orchard opened up into an oblong meadow of grass. In the center of the open area stood an old shanty with a rusted tin roof. The sides of the ramshackle house were grayed from years of weathering, and several windows needed to be repaired, their screens torn or rusted or missing altogether. Killian glanced over at Sam in surprise.

"I told you before—Susannah insists upon living in this place. Why, I don't know," Sam muttered. "It needs a heap of fixin' to be livable, if you ask me." He stuffed his hands into the pockets of his coveralls. "Come on. The herb garden is on the other side of the house."

* * *

Susannah sank her long fingers into the welcoming black warmth of the fertile soil. Then, taking a clump of chives, she placed it in the hole she'd dug. The inconstant breeze was dying down now that dusk had arrived. She heard the singing of the birds, a peaceful reminder that no one was nearby. A red-breasted robin flew to the white picket fence that enclosed the large herb garden. Almost immediately he began to chirp excitedly, fluttering his wings.

It was a warning. Susannah quickly looked around, feeling vulnerable with her back turned toward whoever was approaching. Her father rounded the corner of the house, then her heart began beating harder. There was a stranger—a man—with him.

Ordinarily Susannah would have run, but in an instant the man's steely blue gaze met and held her own, and something told her to stay where she was. Remaining on her knees in the soil, Susannah watched their progress toward her.

The man's catlike eyes held on hers, but instead of the naked fear she usually felt at a stranger's approach since coming out of the coma, Susannah felt an odd sizzle of apprehension. But what kind? His face was hard-looking, revealing no hint of emotion in his eyes or the set of his mouth. His hair was black and military-short, and his skin was deeply bronzed by the sun. Her heart started to hammer in warning.

Her father greeted her with a smile. "Susannah, I've brought a friend to introduce to you. Come on, honey, come over and meet him."

The stranger's oddly opaque gaze held her suspended. Susannah gulped convulsively and set the chives aside. Her fingers were stained dark from the soil, and the jeans she wore were thick with dust. Slowly, beneath his continued inspection, Susannah forced herself to her bare feet. The power of the stranger's gaze, the anger she saw in the depths of his eyes, held her captive.

"Susannah?" Sam prodded gently as he halted at the gate and opened it. "Honey, he won't hurt you. Come on over...."

"No," Killian said, his voice hoarse. "Let her be. Let her get used to me."

Sam gave him a quizzical look, but said nothing.

Killian wasn't breathing. Air seemed to have jammed in his chest. Susannah was more than beautiful; she was ethereal. Her straight sable-colored hair flowed around her slender form, almost touching her breasts. Her simple white cotton blouse and jeans enhanced her figure. Killian could see no outward signs of the violence she'd endured, although at some point in her life her nose had been broken. The bump was prominent, and he wondered about the story behind it. Her lips were full, and slightly parted now. But it was her eyes—large, expressive, dove gray—that entranced him the most.

Who is he? Why is he looking at me like that? Susannah looked down at herself. Sure, her jeans were dirty, but she had been gardening all day. Her feet, too, were covered with soil. Automatically she raised a hand to touch the front of her blouse. Was one of her buttons undone? No. Again she raised her head and met those eyes that, though emotionless, nonetheless drew her. There was a sense of armor around him that startled her. A hard, impervious shell of self-protection. She'd often sensed the same quality around her handicapped children when they first started school—a need to protect themselves against the all-too-common hurts they were subjected to. But there was more than that to this man's bearing, Susannah realized as she allowed her intuition to take over. She also sensed a darkness, a sadness, around this tall, lean man, who was probably in his mid-thirties. He felt edgy to her, and it set her on edge, too. Who was he? Another police detective from Lexington, come to grill her? To try to jar loose her frozen memory? Susannah's hands grew damp with apprehension. This man frightened her in a new and unknown way. Maybe it was that unexpected anger banked in his eyes.

Killian used all his senses, finely honed over years of dangerous work, to take in Susannah. He saw her fine nostrils quiver and flare, as if she were a wary young deer ready for flight. He felt the fear rise around her, broadcast in every line of her tension-held body. Meg's once-beautiful face floated in front of him. The terror he'd felt as he stood at her hospital bedside as she became conscious for the first time since the blast slammed back into him. Smiling didn't come easily to him, but he'd forced one then for Meg's benefit, and it had made all the difference in the world. She'd reached out and weakly gripped his hand and begun to cry, but to Killian it had been a good sign, a sign that she wanted to live.

Now, for Susannah's benefit, Killian forced the corners of his mouth upward as he saw terror come to her widening eyes. Although he was angry at Morgan, he didn't need to take it out on her. Almost instantly he saw the tension on her face dissipate.

Fighting the screaming awareness of his emotional response to Susannah, Killian said to Sam in a low voice, ''Go ahead and make the introduction, and then leave us. I don't think she's going to run.''

Scratching his head, Sam nodded. ''Darned if I don't believe you. For some reason, she ain't as afraid of you as all the rest.''

Killian barely nodded as he continued to hold Susannah's assessing stare. Her arms were held tightly at her sides. Her fingers were long and artistic-looking. She seemed more like a girl in her teens—barefoot and in touch with the magic of the Earth—than a schoolteacher of twenty-seven.

"Honey, this is Mr. Killian," Sam said gently to his daughter. "He's a friend of Morgan's, come to stay with us and rest up for a month or so. Ma and I said he could stay. He's a friend, honey. Not a stranger. Do you understand?"

Susannah nodded slowly, never taking her eyes off Killian.

What is your first name? The words were there, on the tip of her tongue, but they refused to be given voice. Frustration thrummed through Susannah. How she ached to speak again—but some invisible hand held her tongue-tied. Killian's mouth had curved into the barest of smiles, sending an odd heat sheeting through her. Shaken by his presence, Susannah could only nod, her hands laced shyly together in front of her. Still, she was wary. It wasn't something she could just automatically turn off.

Killian was excruciatingly uncomfortable, and he wanted to get the social amenities over with. "Thanks, Sam," he said brusquely.

Sam's gaze moved from his daughter to Killian and back to her. "Honey, supper's in a hour. Ma would like you to join us. Will you?"

Susannah felt her heartbeat picking up again, beating wildly with apprehension over this man named Killian— a male stranger who had come to disrupt the silent world where she'd retreated to be healed. She glanced down at her feet and then lifted her chin.

I don't know. I don't know, Pa. Let me see how I feel.

Susannah was disappointed with herself. All she could do was shrug delicately. Ordinarily she carried a pen and paper with her in order to communicate with her folks, or friends of the family who stopped to visit. But today, not expecting visitors, she'd left her pad and pen back at the house.

"Good enough," Sam told her gruffly. "Maybe you'll let Killian walk you back afterward."

Killian stood very still after Sam disappeared. He saw the nervousness and curiosity reflected in Susannah's wide eyes—and suddenly he almost grinned at the irony of their situation. He was normally a person of few words, and for the first time in his life he was going to have to carry the conversation. He spread his hand out in a gesture of peace.

"I hope I didn't stop you from planting."

No, you didn't. Susannah glanced sharply down at the chives. She knelt and began to cover the roots before they dried out. As she worked, she keyed her hearing to where the man stood, outside the gate. Every once in a while, she glanced up. Each time she did, he was still standing there, motionless, hands in the pockets of his jeans, an old, beat-up leather jacket hanging loosely on his lean frame. His serious features were set, and she sensed an unhappiness radiating from him. About what? Being here? Meeting her? So many things didn't make sense to her. If he was one of Morgan's friends, why would he be unhappy about being here? If he was here for a vacation, he should be relaxed.

Killian caught Susannah's inquiring gaze. Then, dusting off her hands, she continued down the row, pulling weeds. The breeze gently blew strands of her thick hair across her shoulders, framing her face.

Although he hadn't moved, Killian's eyes were active,

sizing up the immediate vicinity—the possible entrances
to the shanty and the layout of the surrounding meadow.
His gaze moved back to Susannah, who continued acting
guarded, nearly ignoring him. She was probably hoping
he'd go away and leave her alone, he thought wryly.
God knew, he'd like to do exactly that. His anger toward
Morgan grew in volume.

"I haven't seen a woman in bare feet since I left Ireland," he finally offered in a low, clipped tone. No, conversation wasn't his forte.

Susannah stopped weeding and jerked a look in his
direction. Killian crossed to sit on the grassy bank, his
arms around his knees, his gaze still on her.

As if women can't go with their shoes off!

Killian saw the disgust in her eyes. Desperately he
cast about for some way to lessen the tension between
them. As long as she distrusted him, he wouldn't be able
to get close enough to protect her. Inwardly Killian
cursed Morgan.

Forcing himself to try again, he muttered, "That
wasn't an insult. Just an observation. My sister, Meg,
who's about your age, always goes barefoot in the garden, too." He gestured toward the well-kept plants.
"Looks like you give them a lot of attention. Meg always said plants grew best when you gave them love."
Just talking about Meg, even to this wary, silent audi-
ence of one, eased some of his pain for his sister.

You know how I feel! Weeds in her hands, Susannah
straightened, surprised by the discovery. Killian had seen
her facial expression and read it accurately. Hope rushed
through her. Her mother and father, as dearly as they
loved her, couldn't seem to read her feelings at all since
she'd come out of the coma. But suddenly this lanky,

tightly coiled stranger with the sky-blue eyes, black hair and soft, hesitant smile could.

Are you a psychiatrist? I hope not. Susannah figured she'd been through enough testing to last her a lifetime. Older men with glasses and beards had pronounced her hysterical due to her trauma and said it was the reason she couldn't speak. Her fingers tightened around the weeds as she stood beneath Killian's cool, expressionless inspection.

Killian saw the tension in Susannah's features dissolve for just an instant. He'd touched her, and he knew it. Frustrated and unsure of her reaction to him, he tried again, but his voice came out cold. "Weeds make good compost. Do you have a compost pile around here?"

Susannah looked intensely at this unusual man, feeling him instead of listening to his words, which he seemed to have mouthed in desperation. Ordinarily, if she'd met Killian on a busy street, he would have frightened her. His face was lean, like the rest of him, and his nose was large and straight, with a good space between his slightly arched eyebrows. There was an intense alertness in those eyes that reminded her of a cougar. And although he had offered that scant smile initially, his eyes contained a hardness that Susannah had never seen in her life. Since the incident that had changed her life, she had come to rely heavily on her intuitive abilities to ferret out people's possible ulterior motives toward her. The hospital therapist had called it paranoia. But in this case, Susannah sensed that a great sadness had settled around Killian like a cloak. And danger.

Why danger? And is it danger to me? He did *look* dangerous, there was no doubt. Susannah couldn't find one telltale sign in his features of humanity or emotion.

But her fear warred with an image she couldn't shake, the image of the sad but crooked smile that had made him appear vulnerable for one split second out of time.

Chapter Two

Killian watched Susannah walk slowly and cautiously through the garden gate. She was about three feet away from him now, and he probed her for signs of wariness. He had no wish to minimize her guardedness toward him—if he could keep her at arm's length and do his job, this assignment might actually work out. If he couldn't...

Just the way Susannah moved snagged a sharp stab of longing deep within him. She had the grace of a ballet dancer, her hips swaying slightly as she stepped delicately across the rows of healthy plants. He decided not to follow her, wanting to allow her more time to adjust to his presence. Just then a robin, sitting on the fence near Killian, took off and landed in the top of an old, gnarled apple tree standing alone just outside the garden. Instantly there was a fierce cheeping, and Killian cocked his head to one side. A half-grown baby robin was perched precariously on the limb near the nest, fluttering his wings demandingly as the parent hovered nearby with food in his beak.

Killian sensed Susannah's presence and slowly turned his head. She was standing six feet away, watching him pointedly. There was such beauty in her shadowed gray eyes. Killian recognized that shadow—Meg's eyes were marred by the same look.

"That baby robin is going to fall off that limb if he isn't careful."

Yes, he is. Yesterday he did, and I had to pick him up and put him back in the tree. Frustrated by her inability to speak the words, Susannah nodded and wiped her hands against her thighs. Once again she found herself wanting her notepad and pen. He was a stranger and couldn't be trusted, a voice told her. Still, he was watching the awkward progress of the baby robin with concern.

Unexpectedly the baby robin shrieked. Susannah opened her mouth to cry out, but only a harsh, strangulated sound came forth as the small bird fluttered helplessly down through the branches of the apple tree and hit the ground roughly, tumbling end over end. When the baby regained his composure, he began to scream for help, and both parents flew around and around him.

Without thinking, Susannah rushed past Killian to rescue the bird, as she had yesterday.

"No," Killian whispered, reaching out to stop Susannah. "I'll do it." Her skin was smooth and sun-warmed beneath his fingers, and instantly Killian released her, the shock of the touch startling not only him, but her, too.

Susannah gasped, jerking back, her mouth opened in

shock. Her skin seemed to tingle where his fingers had briefly, carefully grasped her wrist.

Taken aback by her reaction, Killian glared at her, then immediately chastised himself. After all, didn't he want her to remain fearful of him? Inside, though, his heart winced at the terror he saw in her gaze, at the contorted shape of her lips as she stared up at him—as if he was her assailant. His action had been rash, he thought angrily. Somehow Susannah's presence had caught him off guard. Infuriated by his own blind reactions, Killian stood there at a loss for words.

Susannah saw disgust in Killian's eyes, and then, on its heels, a gut-wrenching sadness. Still stunned by his swift touch, she backed even farther away from him. Finally the robin's plaintive cheeping impinged on her shocked senses, and she tore her attention from Killian, pointing at the baby robin now hopping around on the ground.

"Yeah. Okay, I'll get the bird," Killian muttered crossly. He was furious with himself, at the unexpected emotions that brief touch had aroused. For the most fleeting moment, his heart jumped at the thought of what it would feel like to kiss Susannah until she was breathless with need of him. Thoroughly disgusted that the thought had even entered his head, Killian moved rapidly to rescue the baby bird. What woman would be interested in him? He was a dark introvert of a man, given to very little communication. A man haunted by a past that at any moment could avalanche into his present and effectively destroy a woman who thought she might care for him. No, he was dangerous—a bomb ready to explode—and he was damned if he was going to put any woman in the line of fire.

As he leaned down and trapped the robin carefully

between his hands, the two parents flew overhead, shrieking, trying to protect their baby. Gently Killian cupped the captured baby, lifting the feathered tyke and staring into his shiny black eyes.

"Next time some cat might find you first and think you're a tasty supper," he warned sternly as he turned toward the apple tree. Placing the bird in his shirt pocket, he grabbed a low branch and began to climb.

Susannah stood below, watching Killian's lithe progress. Everything about the man was methodical. He never stepped on a weak limb; he studied the situation thoroughly before placing each foot to push himself upward toward the nest. Yet, far from plodding, he had an easy masculine grace.

Killian settled the robin in its nest and quickly made his way down to avoid the irate parents. Leaping the last few feet, he landed with the grace of a large cat. "Well, our good deed is done for the day," he said gruffly, dusting off his hands.

His voice was as icy as his unrelenting features, and Susannah took another step away from him.

Thank you for rescuing the baby. But how can such a hard man perform such a gentle feat? What's your story, Killian? His eyes turned impatient under her inspection, and Susannah tore her gaze away from him. The man had something to hide, it seemed.

How much more do you know about me? What did my folks tell you? Susannah felt an odd sort of shame at the thought of Killian knowing what had happened to her. Humiliation, too, coupled with anger and fear—the entire gamut of feelings she'd lived with daily since the shooting. Out of nervousness, she raised a hand to her cheek, which felt hot and flushed.

Killian noted the hurt in Susannah's eyes as she self-consciously brushed her cheek with her fingertips. And in that moment he saw the violence's lasting damage: loss of self-esteem. She was afraid of him, and part of him ached at the unfairness of it, but he accepted his fate bitterly. Let Susannah think him untrustworthy—dangerous. Those instincts might save her life, should her assailant show up for another try at killing her.

"I need to wash my hands," he said brusquely, desperate to break the tension between them. He had to snap out of it. He couldn't afford to allow her to affect him—and possibly compromise his ability to protect her from a killer.

Unexpectedly Susannah felt tears jam into her eyes. She stood there in abject surprise as they rolled down her cheeks, unbidden, seemingly tapped from some deep source within her. Why was she crying? She hadn't cried since coming out of the coma! Embarrassed that Killian was watching her, a disgruntled look on his face, Susannah raised trembling hands to her cheeks.

Killian swayed—and caught himself. Every fiber of his being wanted to reach out and comfort Susannah. The tears, small, sun-touched crystals, streamed down her flushed cheeks. The one thing he couldn't bear was to see a woman cry. A weeping child he could handle, but somehow, when a woman cried, it was different. Different, and gut-wrenchingly disturbing. Meg's tears had torn him apart, her cries shredding what was left of his feelings.

Looking down at Susannah now, Killian felt frustration and disgust at his inability to comfort her. But that edge, that distrust, had to stay in place if he was to do his job.

Turning away abruptly, he looked around for a garden hose, for anything, really, that would give him an excuse to escape her nearness. Spying a hose leading from the side of the house, he turned on his heel and strode toward the faucet. Relief flowed through him as he put distance between them, the tightened muscles in his shoulders and back loosening. Trying to shake pangs of guilt for abandoning her, Killian leaned down and turned on the faucet. He washed his hands rapidly, then wiped them on the thighs of his jeans as he straightened.

He glanced back toward Susannah who still stood near the garden, looking alone and unprotected. As he slowly walked back to where she stood, he thrust his hands into the pockets of his jeans. "It's almost time for dinner," he said gruffly. "I'm hungry. Are you coming?"

Susannah felt hollow inside. The tears had left her terribly vulnerable, and right now she needed human company more than usual. Killian's harsh company felt abrasive to her in her fragile emotional state, and she knew she'd have to endure walking through the orchard to her folks' house with him. She forced herself to look into his dark, angry features. This mute life of pad and pencil was unbelievably frustrating. Normally she believed mightily in communicating and confronting problems, and without a voice, it was nearly impossible to be herself. The old Susannah would have asked Killian what his problem with her was. Instead she merely gestured for him to follow her.

Killian maintained a discreet distance from Susannah as they wound their way through the orchard on the well-trodden path. He wanted to ask Susannah's forgiveness for having abandoned her earlier—to explain why he had to keep her at arm's length. But then he laughed derisively at himself. Susannah would never understand. No woman would. He noticed that as they walked Susannah's gaze was never still, constantly searching the area, as if she were expecting to be attacked. It hurt him to see her in that mode. The haunted look in her eyes tore at him. Her beautiful mouth was pursed, the corners drawn taut, as if she expected a blow at any moment.

Not while I'm alive will another person ever *harm you,* he promised grimly. Killian slowed his pace, baffled at the intensity of the feeling that came with the thought. The sun shimmered through the leaves of the fruit trees, scattering light across the green grass in a patchwork-quilt effect, touching Susannah's hair and bringing red highlights to life, intermixed with threads of gold. Killian wondered obliquely if she had some Irish blood in her.

In the Andersons' kitchen, Killian noted the way Susannah gratefully absorbed her mother's obvious care and genuine concern. He watched the sparkle come back to her lovely gray eyes as Pansy doted over her. Susannah had withdrawn into herself on their walk to the farmhouse. Now Killian watched her reemerge from that private, silent world, coaxed out by touches and hugs from her parents.

He'd made her retreat, and he felt like hell about it. But there could be no ambiguity about his function here at the farm. Sitting at the table now, his hand around a mug of steaming coffee, Killian tried to protect himself against the emotional warmth that pervaded the kitchen. The odors of home-cooked food, fresh and lovingly prepared, reminded him of a far gentler time in his life, the time when he was growing up in Ireland. There hadn't been many happy times in Killian's life, but that had been one—his mother doting over him and Meg, the lighthearted lilt of her laughter, the smell of fresh bread baking in the oven, her occasional touch upon his shoulder or playful ruffling of his hair. Groaning, he blindly gulped his coffee, and nearly burned his mouth in the process.

Susannah washed her hands at the kitchen sink, slowly dried them, and glanced apprehensively over at Killian. He sat at the table like a dark, unhappy shadow, his hand gripping the coffee mug. She was trying to understand him, but it was impossible. Her mother smiled at him, and tried to cajole a hint of a reaction from Killian, but he seemed impervious to human interaction.

As Pansy served the dinner, Killian tried to ignore the fact that he was seated opposite Susannah. She had an incredible ability to communicate with just a glance from those haunting eyes. Killian held on tightly to his anger at the thought that she had almost died.

"Why, you're lookin' so much better," Pansy gushed to her daughter as she placed mashed potatoes, spareribs and a fresh garden salad on the table.

Susannah nodded and smiled for her mother's sake. Just sitting across from Killian was unnerving. But because she loved her mother and father fiercely she was trying to ignore Killian's cold, icy presence and act normally.

Sam smiled and passed his daughter the platter of ribs. "Do you think you'll get along with Killian hereabouts for a while?"

Susannah felt Killian's eyes on her and refused to look up, knowing that he was probably studying her with the icy gaze of a predator for his intended victim. She glanced over at her father, whose face was open and readable, and found the strength somewhere within herself to lie. A white lie, Susannah told herself as she forced a smile and nodded.

Killian ate slowly, allowing his senses to take in the

cheerful kitchen and happy family setting. The scents of barbecued meat and thick brown gravy and the tart smell of apples baking in the oven were sweeter than any perfume.

"I don't know what you did," Pansy told Killian, "but whatever it is, Susannah looks so much better! Doesn't she, Sam?"

Spooning gravy onto a heaping portion of mashed potatoes, Sam glanced up. "Ma, you know how uncomfortable Susannah gets when we talk as if she's not here."

Chastened, Pansy smiled. "I'm sorry, dear," she said, giving her daughter a fond look and a pat on the arm in apology.

Susannah wondered glumly how she could possibly look better with Killian around. Without a doubt, the man made her uncomfortable. She decided it was just that her mother wanted to see her looking better. Aching inwardly, Susannah thought how terribly the past three months had worn down her folks. They had both aged noticeably, and it hurt her to realize that her stupid, failed foray into the "big" world outside Kentucky had cost them, too. If only she hadn't been so naive about the world, it might not have happened, and her parents might not have had to suffer this way. Luckily, her school insurance had covered the massive medical bills; Susannah knew her folks would have sold the farm, if necessary, to help her cover expenses.

"Let's talk about you, Killian," Pansy said brightly, turning the conversation to him.

Killian saw Susannah's eyes suddenly narrow upon him, filled with curiosity—and some indefinable emotion that set his pulse to racing. He hesitated, not wanting to sound rude. "Ordinarily, Pansy, I don't open up to anyone."

"Whatever for?"

Sam groaned. "Honey, the man's got a right to some privacy, don't he?"

Pansy laughed. "Now, Pa..."

Clearing his throat, Killian moved the mashed potatoes around on his blue-and-white plate. He realized he wasn't going to be able to get around Pansy's good-natured probing. "I work in the area of high security." The explanation came out gruffly—a warning, he hoped, for her to stop asking questions.

"Surely," Pansy said, with a gentle laugh, "you can tell me if you're married or not. Or about your family?"

Tension hung in the air. Killian put down his fork, keeping a tight rein on his reaction to what he knew was a well-intentioned question. Sam shot him an apologetic look that spoke volumes, but Killian also saw Susannah's open interest. She'd stopped eating, and was waiting to hear his answer.

Killian felt heat creeping up his neck and into his cheeks. Pain at the memory of his family sheared through him. He dropped his gaze to the uneaten food on his plate and felt an avalanche of unexpected grief that seemed to suck the life out of him momentarily. Unwillingly he looked up—and met Susannah's compassionate gaze.

Killian shoved his chair back, and the scraping sound shattered the tension. "Excuse me," he rasped, "I'm done eating."

Susannah saw pain in Killian's eyes and heard the roughness of emotion in his voice as he moved abruptly to his feet. The chair nearly tipped over backward, but he caught it in time. Without a sound, Killian stalked from the kitchen.

"Oh, dear," Pansy whispered, her fingers against her lips. "I didn't mean to upset him...."

Susannah reached out and gripped her mother's hand. She might not be able to talk, but she could at least offer the reassurance of touch.

Sam cleared his throat. "Ma, he's a closed kind of man. Didn't you see that?"

Pansy shrugged weakly and patted her daughter's hand. "Oh, I guess I did, Sam, but you know me—I'm such a busybody. Maybe I should go after him and apologize."

"Just let him be, Ma, and he'll come around," Sam counseled gently.

"I don't know," Pansy whispered, upset. "When I asked him about his family, did you see his face?"

Susannah nodded and released her mother's hand. As she continued to finish her meal, she ruminated on that very point. Killian had reacted violently to the question, anguished pain momentarily shadowing his eyes. Susannah had found herself wanting to reach out and reassure him that all would be well. But would it?

Morosely Susannah forced herself to finish eating her dinner. Somehow she wanted to let her mother know that there had been nothing wrong with her questions to Killian. As she had so many times these past months, she wished she could talk. Pansy was just a warm, chatty person by nature, but Susannah understood Killian's discomfort over such questions. Still, she wanted to try to communicate with Killian. She would use the excuse that he could walk her home, since it would be nearly dark. Her father never allowed her to walk home alone at night. At the same time, Susannah felt fear at being alone with him.

What was there about him that made her want to know him? He was a stranger who'd walked into her life only a few hours ago. The fact that he was Morgan's friend meant something, of course. From what her cousin Laura had told her, she knew that Morgan Trayhern drew only loyal, responsible people to him. Still, they were hard men, mercenaries. Susannah had no experience with mercenaries. In fact, she had very little experience with men in general, and especially with men her own age. She felt she wasn't equal to the task of healing the rift between her mother and Killian, but she knew she had to try. Otherwise, her mother would be a nervous wreck every time Killian sat down to eat. No, something had to be done to calm the troubled waters.

Killian was sitting in the living room, pretending to watch television, when he saw Susannah come out of the kitchen. He barely met her gaze as she walked determinedly toward him with a piece of paper in her hand. He saw uncertainty in her eyes—and something else that he couldn't have defined. Knowing that his abruptness had already caused bad feelings, he tensed as she drew close enough to hand him the note.

Walk me home. Please?

Killian lifted his head and studied her darkly. There was such vulnerability to Susannah—and that was what had nearly gotten her killed. Killian couldn't help but respond to the silent plea in her eyes as she stood waiting for his answer.

Without a word, he crushed the note in his hand, got

to his feet and headed toward the door. He would use this excuse to check out her house and the surrounding area. When he opened the door for her, she brushed by him, and he felt himself tense. The sweet, fragrant scent of her perfume momentarily encircled him, and he unconsciously inhaled the subtle scent.

It was dusk, the inky stains across the early-autumn sky telling Killian it would soon be dark. As he slowly walked Susannah back to her house, his ears were tuned in to the twilight for any out-of-the-ordinary sounds. He needed to adjust his senses to the normal sounds of this countryside, anyway. Until then, he would have to be even more alert than normal. There were no unusual odors on the fragrant air, and he couldn't ferret out anything unusual visually as he restlessly scanned the orchard.

When they reached her home, Killian realized that it had no electricity. He stood just inside the door and watched as Susannah lit a hurricane lamp filled with kerosene. She placed one lamp on the wooden table, another on the mantel over the fireplace, and a third in the living room. The floorboards, old and gray, creaked beneath her bare feet as she moved about. Uneasy at how little protection the house afforded against a possible intruder, Killian watched her pull open a drawer of an oak hutch.

Susannah located a notebook and pen and gestured for Killian to come and sit down with her at the table. Mystified, Killian sat down tensely at Susannah's elbow while she wrote on the notepad.

When she'd finished writing, she turned the notepad around so that Killian could read her question. The light from the kerosene lamp cast a soft glow around the deeply shadowed kitchen.

Killian eyed the note. ''Is Killian my first or last

name?'' he read aloud. He grimaced and reared back on two legs of the chair. "It's my last name. Everyone calls me by my last name."

Susannah made a frustrated sound and penned another note.

What is your first name?

Killian scowled heavily and considered her request. Morgan's orders sounded demandingly in his brain. He was to try to get Susannah to remember what her assailant looked like. If he remained too cool and unresponsive to her, she wouldn't want to try to cooperate with him. Yet to reveal himself would be as good as opening up his horrifying past once again. That had happened once before, with terrible results, and he'd vowed it would never happen again. Dammit, anyway! He rubbed his mouth with his hand, feeling trapped. He had to gain Susannah's cooperation. Her trust.

"Sean," he snarled.

Susannah winced, but determinedly wrote another note.

Who do you allow to call you Sean?

Killian stared at the note. Despite Susannah's obvious softness and vulnerability, for the first time he noticed a look of stubbornness in her eyes. He frowned.

"My mother and sister called me by my first name. Just them," he muttered.

Susannah digested his admission. Maybe he used his last name to prevent people getting close to him. But evidently there were at least two women in his life who could reach inside those armored walls and get to him.

There was hope, Susannah decided, if Killian allowed his family to use his first name. But she'd heard the warning in his voice when he'd spoken to her mother. She might be a hill woman, and not as worldly as he was, but surely it wasn't unreasonable to expect good manners—even from a mercenary. She held his blunt stare and felt the fear and anger seething around him. That cold armored cloak was firmly in place.

Grimly Susannah penned another note.

My mother didn't mean to make you uncomfortable. If you can find some way to say something to her to defuse the situation, I'd be grateful. She meant well. She didn't mean to chase you from the dinner table.

Killian stared at her printed note for a long time. The silence thickened. Susannah was right; he'd been wrong in his reaction to the situation. He wished he had the words, a way to explain himself. Frustration overwhelmed him. Looking up, he thought for a moment that he might drown in her compassionate gray gaze. Quirking his mouth, he muttered, "When I go back down tonight, I'll tell her I'm sorry."

Susannah smiled slightly and nodded her head.

Thank you. I know so little of Morgan's men. None of us know anything about mercenaries. I hope you can forgive us, too?

Steeling himself against Susannah's attempt to smooth things over, Killian nodded. "Don't worry about it. There's nothing to forgive." He started to get up, but she made an inarticulate sound and reached out, her hand closing around his arm. Killian froze.

Susannah's lips parted when she saw anguish replace the coldness in Killian's eyes as she touched him. She hadn't meant to reach out like that; it had been instinctive. Somewhere in her heart, she knew that Killian needed touching—a lot of it. She knew all too well through her work the value of touching, the healing quality of a hand upon a shoulder to give necessary support and courage. Hard as he appeared to be, was Killian really any different? Gazing up through the dim light in the kitchen, she saw the tortured look in his eyes.

Thinking that he was repulsed by her touch, she quickly released him.

Killian slowly sat back, his heart hammering in his chest. It was hell trying to keep his feelings at bay. Whether he liked it or not, he could almost read what Susannah was thinking in her expressive eyes. Their soft gray reminded him of a mourning dove—and she was as gentle and delicate as one.

My folks are simple people, Killian. Pa said you were here for a rest. Is that true? If so, for how long?

Killian felt utterly trapped, and he longed to escape. Morgan was expecting the impossible of him. He didn't have the damnable ability to walk with one foot as a protector and the other foot emotionally far enough away from Susannah to do his job. The patient look on her face only aggravated him.

"I'm between missions," he bit out savagely. "And I want to rest somewhere quiet. I'll try to be a better house guest, okay?"

I know you're uncomfortable around me. I don't expect anything from you. I'll be staying up here most of the time, so you'll have the space to rest.

Absolute frustration thrummed through Killian. This was exactly what he *didn't* want! "Look," he growled, "you don't make me uncomfortable, okay? I know what happened to you, and I'm sorry it happened. I have a sister who—"

Susannah tilted her head as he snapped his mouth shut and glared at her. He wanted to run. It was in every line of his body, and it was in his eyes. The tension in the kitchen had become a tangible thing.

Who? What?

Agitated, Killian shot to his feet. He roamed around the kitchen in the semidarkness, seesawing back and forth about what—if anything—he should tell her. She sat quietly, watching him, without any outward sign of impatience. Running his fingers through his hair, he turned suddenly and pinned her with an angry look.

"My sister, Meg, was nearly killed in a situation not unlike yours," he ground out finally. "She's disfigured for life, and she's scared. She lives alone, like a recluse. I've seen what violence has done to her, so I can imagine what it's done to you." He'd said enough. More than enough, judging from the tears that suddenly were shimmering in Susannah's eyes.

Breathing hard, Killian continued to glare at her, hoping she would give up. He didn't want her asking him any more personal questions. Hell, he hadn't intended to bring up Meg! But something about this woman kept tugging at him, pulling him out of his isolation.

I'm sorry for Meg. For you. I've seen what the violence to me has done to my folks. It's awful. It's forever.

As Killian read the note, standing near the table, his shoulders sagged, and all the anger went out of him. "Yes," he whispered wearily, "violence is wrong. All it does is tear people's lives apart." How well he knew that—in more ways than he ever wanted to admit.

If you're a mercenary, then you're always fighting a war, aren't you?

The truth was like a knife in Killian's clenched gut. He stood, arms at his sides, and hung his head as he pondered her simple question. "Mercenaries work in many capacities," he said slowly. "Some of them are very safe and low-risk. But they do deal with violent situations, too." He lifted his head and threw her a warning look. "The more you do it, the more you become it."

Are you always in dangerous situations?

He picked up the note, then slowly crushed it in his hand. Susannah was getting too close. That just couldn't happen. For her sake, it couldn't. Killian arranged his face into the deadliest look he could muster. "More than anything," he told her in a soft rasp, "you should understand that I'm dangerous to you."

It was all the warning Killian could give her short of telling what had happened when one woman *had* gotten to him, touched his heart, made him feel love. He'd sworn he'd never tell anyone that—not even Meg. And he'd vowed never to let it happen again. Susannah was too special, too vulnerable, for him to allow her to get close to him. But she had a kind of courage that frightened Killian; she had the guts to approach someone like him—someone so wounded that he could never be healed.

"I'll see you tomorrow morning," he said abruptly. He scanned the room closely with one sweeping gaze, then glanced down at her. "Because I'm a mercenary, I'm going to check out your house and the surrounding area. I'll be outside after I make a sweep of the house, and then I'll be staying at your folks' place, in the guest bedroom." He rubbed his jaw as he took in the poor condition of the window, which had no screen and no lock. "If you hear anything, come and get me."

I've been living here the last month and nothing has happened. I'll be okay.

Naiveté at best, Killian thought as he read her note. But he couldn't tell her she was in danger—good old Morgan's orders again. His mouth flattening, he stared across the table into her weary eyes. "If you need help, come and get me. Understand?" As much as he wanted to stay nearby to protect Susannah, Killian knew he couldn't possibly move in with her without a darn good explanation for her and her parents. He was hamstrung. And he didn't want to have to live under Susannah's roof, anyway, for very different reasons. As much as he hated to leave her unprotected at the homestead, for now he had no choice.

At least Susannah would remain safe from him, Killian thought as he studied her darkly. His mind shouted that he'd be absolutely useless sleeping down at the Anderson house if the killer tried to reach her here. But what could he do? Torn, he decided that for tonight, he would sleep at the Andersons' and ponder the problem.

With a bare nod, Susannah took in Killian's vibrating warning. He had told her he was a violent man. She sensed the lethal quality about him, and yet those brief flashes she'd had of him without his defenses in place made her believe that deep down he longed for peace, not war.

Chapter Three

As she bathed and prepared to go to bed, Susannah tried to sift through her jumbled feelings. Killian disturbed her, she decided, more than he frightened her. Somehow she was invisibly drawn to him—to the inner man, not the cold exterior he held up like a shield. She pulled her light knee-length cotton gown over her head and tamed her tangled hair with her fingers. The lamplight cast dancing shadows across the opposite wall of the small bathroom. Ordinarily, catching sight of moving silhouettes caused her to start, but tonight it didn't.

Why? Picking up her clothes, Susannah walked thoughtfully through the silent house, the old planks beneath the thin linoleum floor creaking occasionally. Could Killian's unsettling presence somehow have given her a sense of safety? Even if it was an edgy kind of safety? Despite his glowering and his snappish words,

Susannah sensed he would help her if she ever found herself in trouble.

With a shake of her head,* Susannah dumped her clothes into a hamper in the small side room and made her way toward the central portion of the two-story house. At least four generations of Andersons had lived here, and that in itself gave her a sense of safety. There was something about the old and the familiar that had always meant tranquility to Susannah, and right now she needed that sense as never before.

She went into the kitchen, where the hurricane lamp still threw its meager light. Pictures drawn in crayon wreathed the walls of the area—fond reminders of her most recent class of children. Last year's class. The pictures suggested hope, and Susannah could vividly recall each child's face as she surveyed the individual drawings. They gave her a sense that maybe her life hadn't been completely shattered after all.

Leaning down, Susannah blew out the flame in the lamp, and darkness cloaked the room, making her suddenly edgy. It had been shadowy the night she'd walked from her bus toward the brightly lit central station—she could remember that clearly. She could recall, too, flashbacks of the man who had been killed in front of her. He'd been sharply dressed, with an engaging smile, and he'd approached her as if she were a longtime friend. She'd trusted him—found him attractive, to be honest. She'd smiled and allowed him to take the large carryon bag that hung from her shoulder. With a shudder, Susannah tried to block the horrifying end to his brief contact with her. Pressing her fingers against her closed eyes, she felt the first signs of one of the massive migraines that seemed to come and go without much warning begin to stalk her.

As she made her way to her bedroom, at the rear of the house—moving around familiar shapes in the dark—Susannah vaguely wondered why Killian's unexpected presence hadn't triggered one of her crippling headaches. He was dangerous, her mind warned her sharply. He'd told her so himself, in the sort of warning growl a cougar might give an approaching hunter. As she pulled back the crisp white sheet and the worn quilt that served as her bedspread, Susannah's heart argued with her practical mind. Killian must have lived through some terrible, traumatic events to project that kind of iciness. As Susannah slid into bed, fluffed her pillow and closed her eyes, she released a long, ragged sigh. Luckily, sleep always cured her headaches, and she was more tired than usual tonight.

Despite her physical weariness, Susannah saw Killian's hard, emotionless face waver before her closed eyes. There wasn't an iota of gentleness anywhere in his features. Yet, as she searched his stormy dark blue eyes, eyes that shouted to everyone to leave him alone, Susannah felt such sadness around him that tears stung her own eyes. Sniffing, she laughed to herself. How easily touched she was! And how much she missed her children. School had started without her, and she was missing a new class of frightened, unsure charges she knew would slowly come out of their protective shells and begin to reach out and touch life.

Unhappily Susannah thought of the doctors' warnings that it would be at least two months before she could possibly go back to teaching. Her world, as she had known it, no longer existed. Where once she'd been trusting of people, now she was not. Darkness had always been her friend—but now it disturbed her. Forcing herself to shut off her rambling thoughts, Susannah concentrated on sleep. Her last images were of Killian, and the sadness that permeated him.

A distinct click awakened Susannah. She froze beneath the sheet and blanket, listening. Her heart rate tripled, and her mouth grew dry. The light of a first-quarter moon spilled in the open window at the head of her old brass bed. The window's screen had been torn loose years ago and never repaired, Susannah knew. Terror coursed through her as she lay still, her muscles aching with fear.

Another click. Carefully, trying not to make a sound, Susannah lifted her head and looked toward the window opposite her bed. A scream jammed in her throat. The profile of a man was silhouetted against the screen. A cry, rooted deep in her lungs, started up through her. Vignettes of the murderer who had nearly taken her life, a man with a narrow face, small eyes and a crooked mouth, smashed into her. If she hadn't been so frightened, Susannah would have rejoiced at finally recalling his face. But now sweat bathed her, and her nightgown grew damp and clung to her as she gripped the sheet, her knuckles whitening.

Breathing raggedly, she watched with widening eyes as the silhouette moved. It wasn't her imagination! The shriek that had lodged in her chest exploded upward. A sound, a mewling cry fraught with desperation, escaped her contorted lips. *Run!* She had to run! She had to get to her parents' home, where she'd be safe.

Susannah scrambled out of bed, and her bare feet hit the wooden floorboards hard. Frantically she tore at the bedroom door, which she always locked behind her. Several of her nails broke as she yanked the chain guard off and jerked the door open. Blindly she raced through the living room and the kitchen and charged wildly out the back door. Her bare feet sank into the dew-laden grass as she raced through the meadow. Her breath coming in ragged gulps, she ran with abandon.

The shadows of the trees loomed everywhere about her as she sped onward. As she sobbed for breath, she thought she heard heavy footsteps coming up behind her. Oh, God! No! *Not again!*

Killian jerked awake as someone crashed into the back door of the farmhouse. At the sound of frantic pounding he leaped out of the bed. Wearing only light blue pajama bottoms, he reached for his Beretta. In one smooth, unbroken motion he slid the weapon out of its holster and opened the door. Swiftly he raced from the first-floor guest room, through the gloomy depths of the house, to the rear door, where the pounding continued unabated.

The curtains blocked his view, but Killian knew in his gut it was Susannah. Unlocking the door, he pulled it open.

Susannah stood there, her face twisted in terror, tears coursing down her taut cheeks and her gray eyes huge with fear. Without thinking, he opened his arms to her.

She fell sobbing into his arms, her nightdress damp with perspiration. Killian held her sagging form against him with one hand; in the other was his pistol, safety off, held in position, ready to fire. Susannah's sobs were a mixture of rasps and cries as she clung to him. Killian's eyes narrowed to slits as he dragged her away from the open door, pressing her up against the wall, out of view of any potential attacker. Rapidly he searched the darkened porch beyond the open door, and the nearby orchard. His heart was racing wildly. He was aware of Susannah's soft, convulsing form trapped between him and the wall as he remained a protective barrier for her, in case the killer was nearby. But only moonlight showed in the quiet orchard and the countryside beyond.

Seconds passed, and Killian still could detect no movement. Susannah's sobs and gasps drowned out any chance of hearing a possible assailant. "Easy, colleen," he whispered raggedly, easing away from her. The feel of her trembling body beneath him was playing havoc with his carefully controlled emotions so much so, he'd called her colleen, an Irish endearment. Fighting his need to absorb the softness of her womanly form against him, Killian forced himself away from her. Shaken, he drew her into the kitchen and nudged the door closed with his foot. "Come on, sit down." He coaxed Susannah over to the table and pulled the chair out for her. She collapsed into it, her face filled with terror as she stared apprehensively at the back door. Killian placed a hand on her shoulder, feeling the terrible tension in her.

"It's all right," he told her huskily, standing behind her chair, alert and waiting. The kitchen had only two small windows, just above the counter and sinks, and the table was in a corner, where a shooter wouldn't be able to draw a bead on them. They were safe—for the moment. Killian's mind ranged over the options a gunman would have. He could barge into the kitchen after her, or leave and wait back at her house. Or he could leave altogether and wait for another opportunity to kill Susannah.

Susannah shook her head violently and jabbed her finger repeatedly toward the door. She glanced up at Killian's hard, shadowy features. Her eyes widened even more when she spotted the pistol that he held with such casual ease. He was naked from the waist up, she realized, the moonlight accentuating his deep chest and his taut, leanly muscled body. Gulping, Susannah tore her attention back to the door, waiting to hear those heavy footsteps that had been pursuing her like hounds from hell. Her breathing was still harsh, but Killian's hand on her shoulder made her feel safer.

Killian looked around, his hearing keyed to any strange noises. Surprised that the Andersons hadn't awakened with the amount of noise Susannah had made, he glanced down at her. Undiminished panic still showed in her eyes. One hand was pressed against her heaving breast. She looked as if every nerve in her body were raw from whatever she'd just experienced.

Leaning down, he met and held her wide, searching gray eyes. "Susannah, what happened? Was someone after you?"

She nodded her head violently. Her mother always had a pencil and paper on the kitchen table for her. She grabbed them and hastily scrawled a message.

A man! A man tried to get in the window of my bedroom!

Killian's eyes narrowed.

Susannah gasped raggedly as she held his burning, intense gaze.

He patted her shoulder, hoping the gesture would offer her some sense of security. "You stay put, understand? I'm going to try and find him. I'll go back to your house and have a look around."

Susannah gave a low cry, and the meaning of the sound was clear as she gripped Killian's arm and shook her head. *No! No, don't go! He's out there! He'll kill you! Oh, please, don't go! He's after me, not you!*

Killian understood her silent plea for him to remain with her. But it was impossible under the circumstances. "Shh... I'll be all right," he said soothingly. "I want you to stay here. You'll be safer."

Gulping unsteadily, Susannah nodded, unwillingly releasing him.

With a look meant to give her solace, Killian rasped, "I'll be right back. I promise."

Shaking badly in the aftermath of her terrified run, Susannah sat huddled in the chair, feeling suddenly chilled in her damp cotton gown. Killian moved soundlessly, like a cougar, toward the door. But as he opened it and moved out into the night, Susannah felt a new wave of anguish and fear. Killian could be murdered!

Weaving in and around the fruit trees, the dew-laden grass soaking his bare feet and pajama legs, Killian quickly circled the Anderson house. If the killer was around, he wasn't here. Moving with the soundlessness of a shadow, he avoided the regular path and headed for Susannah's house. As he ran silently through the orchard, a slice of moon and the resulting silvery light allowed him to penetrate the night. Reaching the old homestead, his pistol held upward, Killian advanced toward the rear of the house, every sense screamingly alert. His nostrils flared, he inhaled, trying to get a whiff of any odor other than the sweet orchard fragrances.

Locating Susannah's bedroom at the rear, Killian saw nothing unusual. Remaining near a small grove of lilac bushes that were at least twenty feet tall, he waited. Patience was the name of the game. His original plan to remain at the Anderson house obviously wasn't a good one, he thought grimly as he waited. Frustration ate at him. He'd have to find a way to stay at Susannah's home in order to protect her. The chill of the predawn air surrounded him, but he was impervious to it.

His gaze scouted the surrounding area, his ears tuned in to pick up any sound. *Nothing.* Killian waited another ten minutes before moving toward the house. The killer could be inside, waiting for Susannah to return. His mouth dry, he compressed his lips into a thin line and quietly stole toward the homestead. His heart set up a sledgehammer pounding in his chest as he eased toward the open back door, the only entrance to the house. Wrapping both hands around the butt of his gun, Killian froze near the door frame. Susannah had left so quickly that the screen door was ajar, as well.

Still, there was no sound that was out of place. But Killian wasn't about to trust the potentially volatile situation. Moving quickly, he dived inside, his pistol aimed. Silence. His eyes mere slits, he remained crouched and tense as he passed through the gloomy kitchen, his head swiveling from side to side, missing nothing, absorbing everything. The living room was next. Nothing.

Finally, after ending the search in Susannah's bedroom, Killian checked the windows. Both were open to allow the fresh early-fall coolness to circulate. One window's screen was in place; the other screen, on the window behind her brass bed, was ripped and in need of repair. Going outside, Killian checked carefully for footprints around either of the bedroom windows, but the grass next to the house was tall and undisturbed. He noticed that as he walked distinct footprints appeared in the heavily dew-laden grass. There were no previous footprints to indicate the presence of an intruder.

Grimly Killian headed back toward the Anderson house, still staying away from the path, still alert, but convinced now that Susannah had experienced a nightmare about her assailant. Relief showered over him at the realization. Still, the incident had put him on notice not to allow the idyllic setting to relax him too much. Dawn was barely crawling onto the horizon, a pale lavender beneath the dark, retreating mantle of the night sky. A rooster was already crowing near the chicken coop as Killian stepped lightly onto the wooden porch.

Susannah met him at the screen door, her eyes huge with silent questions.

"There wasn't anyone," Killian told her as he entered the quiet kitchen. He noticed that Susannah had put a teakettle on the stove and lit the burner beneath it. He saw her eyes go wider with shock at his terse statement. Her gaze traveled to the pistol that was still in his hand, and he realized that it was upsetting her.

"Let me put this away and get decent. I'll be out in a moment. Your folks awake yet?"

Susannah shook her head. Despite her fear, she felt herself respond to the male beauty of Killian's tall, taut body. Black hair covered his chest in abundance, a dark strip trailing down across his flat, hard belly and disappearing beneath the drawstring of the pajamas that hung low on his hips. Susannah gulped, avoiding his narrowed, burning gaze.

In his bedroom, Killian quickly changed into jeans and a white short-sleeved shirt. He pulled on dark blue socks and slipped into a pair of comfortable brown loafers, then ran his fingers through his mussed hair, taming the short strands back into place. Then he strapped on his shoulder holster and slid the pistol into place.

Rubbing his hand across his stubbled jaw, Killian

moved back to the kitchen, still amazed that the Andersons had slept through all the commotion. All the more reason, he warned himself, to stay alert for Susannah's sake.

When he entered the kitchen, he saw that she had poured him a cup of tea in a flowery china cup. She was sitting at the table, her hand gripping the notepad and pencil, as if she had been waiting for his return. Killian sat down next to her.

"You had a nightmare," he told her. "That was all."

Susannah rapidly wrote a note on the pad and turned it around for Killian to read.

Impossible! I saw his shadow!

Killian picked up the tea and sipped it, enjoying the clean, minty taste. "There was no trace of footprints around either of your bedroom windows," he explained apologetically. "I searched your house carefully and found nothing. It was a dream, Susannah."

No! Susannah sat back, her arms folded across her breasts, and stared at his darkly etched features while he drank the tea. After a moment, she scribbled on the pad again.

I saw him! I saw the face of the man who nearly killed me!

Killian saw the bleak frustration, and fear in her gray eyes. Without thinking, he placed his hand over hers. "You remember what he looks like?" Before, she'd been unable to identify her assailant.

She nodded.

"Good. The police need an identification." Realizing

he was gently cupping her cool hand, Killian pulled his
back and quickly picked up his teacup. What the hell
was going on? Couldn't he control his own actions? The
idea frightened him. Susannah seemed unconsciously to
bring out his softer side. But along with that softer side
lurked the monstrous danger that could hurt her. He took
a sip from the cup and set it down. His words came out
clipped—almost angry.

"When you settle down over this, I want you to draw
a picture of his face. I can take it to the police—it might
give them a lead."

Hurt by his sudden gruffness, Susannah sat there, still
taking in Killian's surprising words. *A nightmare?* How
could it have been? It had been so *real!* Touching her
forehead, which was now beginning to ache in earnest,
Susannah closed her eyes and tried to get a grip on her
rampant emotions. Killian's warm, unexpected touch
had momentarily soothed her apprehension and settled
her pounding heart—but just as quickly he'd withdrawn.

Opening her eyes, she wrote:

I'll draw a picture of him later, when I feel up to
it.

Killian nodded, still edgy. One part of him was keyed
to Susannah, the other to the door, the windows, and any
errant sound. He knew his shoulder holster disturbed her.
She kept glancing at him, then at the holster, a question
in her eyes. How much could he tell her? How much
should he tell her? He sensed her curiosity about him
and his reasons for being here.

Feeling utterly trapped, Killian tried to think clearly.
Being around Susannah seemed to scramble his emotions. He'd been too long without softness in his life.

And, Killian lectured himself, *it would have to remain that way.* Still, he couldn't let go of the memory of the wonderful sensation of her pressed against him. He should have thrown her to the floor instead of using himself as a human shield to protect her, he thought in disgust. That way he wouldn't have had to touch her, to be reminded of all that he ached to have and never could. But he hadn't been thinking clearly; he'd reacted instinctively.

Grimly he held her gaze. ''From now on, Susannah, you need to stay here, in your folks' home, where it's safer.''

I will not stay here! I can't! If it was just a dream, then I'll be okay out there. I don't want to stay here.

He studied her in the silence, noting the set of her delicate jaw and the flash of stubbornness in her eyes. With a sigh, he set the cup down on the saucer.

''No. You'll stay here. In *this* house.''

Susannah shook her head.

You don't understand! I tried to stay here when I got home from the hospital. I had awful dreams! If I stay in my room, I can't sleep. At the other house I feel safer. I don't have as many nightmares. I don't know why. I can't explain it, but I will not come and stay here.

Killian studied the scribbled note, utterly thwarted. No one knew better than he did about the night and the terrible dreams that could stalk it. He understood Susannah's pleading request, probably better than anyone else could. His heart squeezed at the pain in her admission, because he'd too long lived a similar life. With a sigh, he muttered, "All right, but then I'm staying at your place with you until we can get this settled. I need to know for sure whether this guy is real or just a dream."

Shocked, Susannah stared at him, her mouth dropping open. She felt the brutal hardness around him again and saw anger, touched with anxiety in his eyes. Her mind reeled with questions as the adrenaline left her bloodstream and left her shaky in its aftermath. With a trembling hand, she wrote:

Who are you? You carry a gun. I don't think you are who you say you are. Morgan suspects something, doesn't he? Please, tell me the truth, even if you don't tell my parents. I deserve to know.

Killian fingered the note, refusing to meet her challenging gaze. Stunned by Susannah's intuitive grasp of the situation, he realized he had to tell her. Otherwise, she'd never allow him to stay at her house.

"All right," he growled, "here's the truth. Morgan suspects that the man who tried to kill you will come and hunt you down once he knows you survived. You can ID him, and he's going to try to kill you before you can do it." He saw Susannah's eyes grow dark with shock. Angry that he had to hurt her with the truth, Killian snapped, "I'm here on assignment. I'm to protect you. Please don't tell your parents my real reason for being here. Morgan feels they've been through enough. I wasn't going to tell you, dammit, but you're so stubborn, you didn't leave me any recourse. I can't have you staying alone at the other house."

Susannah felt Killian's anger buffet her. Despite her fear and shock, she felt anger toward him even more.

How dare you! How dare Morgan! You should have told me this in the first place!

Killian didn't like being put in the middle, and he glared at her. "Look, I do as I'm ordered. I'm breaking my word in telling you this, and I'll probably catch hell from my boss for doing it. I don't like this any more than you do. If you want all of the truth, I don't even want to be here—I don't take assignments that involve women. But Morgan threatened to fire me if I didn't take this mission, so you and I are in the same boat. You don't want me here, and I damn well don't want to be here!"

Stunned, Susannah blinked at the powerful wave of feeling behind his harsh words. She sensed a desperation in Killian's anger, and it was that desperation that defused her own righteous anger.

I'm sorry, Killian. I shouldn't be angry with you.

He shook his head and refused to meet her eyes. The frightening truth was, every time he did, he wanted simply to find his way into her arms and be held. "Don't apologize," he muttered. "It isn't your fault, either. We're both caught between a rock and a hard place."

Without thinking, Susannah slowly raised her hand and placed it across Killian's clenched one on the table. His head snapped up as her fingers wrapped around his. The anger dissolved in his eyes, and for just a moment Susannah could have sworn she saw longing in his stormy gaze. But, just as quickly, it was gone, leaving only an icy coldness. She removed her hand from his, all too aware that he was rejecting her touch.

All she had wanted to do was comfort Killian. From

her work, Susannah knew the healing nature of human touch firsthand. Killian had looked positively torn by the fact that he had to be here with her. Susannah had wanted to let him know somehow that she understood his dilemma. He didn't want anything to do with her because she was a woman. Her curiosity was piqued, but she knew better than to ask. Right now, Killian was edgy, turning the cup around and around in his long, spare hands.

You don't have to stay out there with me.

Killian made a muffled sound and stood up suddenly. He moved away from the table, automatically checking the window with his gaze. "Yes," he said irritably, "I do. I don't like it any more than you do, but it has to be done."

But it was a nightmare! You said so yourself. You can stay here with my folks.

Killian savagely spun on his heel, and when he spoke his voice was hoarse. "There's nothing you can say that will change my mind. You need protection, Susannah."

With a trembling hand, Susannah touched her brow. It was nerve-racking enough to stay by herself at the abandoned farmhouse. She was desperately afraid of the dark, of the terrors that came nightly when she lay down as her overactive imagination fueled the fires of her many fears. But Killian staying with her? He was so blatantly male—so quiet, yet so capable. Fighting her own feelings toward him, she sat for a good minute before writing on the notepad again.

Please tell my folks the truth about this. I don't want to lie to them about the reason you're staying out at the house with me. It would seem funny to them if you suddenly started living out there with me.

Killian couldn't disagree with her. He paced the room quietly, trying to come up with a better plan. He stopped and looked down at her exhausted features.

"I'll talk to them this morning."

Relief flowed through Susannah, and she nodded.

Morgan was trying to protect us, but this is one time when we should know the whole truth.

"I tried to tell him that," Killian said bitterly. He stood by the table, thinking. "That's all water under the bridge now," he said. "You saw the killer's face in your nightmare. I need you to draw a picture of him this morning so that I can take it to the police station. They'll fax it to Lexington and to Morgan."

Trying to combat the automatic reactions of fear, rage and humiliation that came with remembering, Susannah nodded. Her hand still pressed against her brow, she tried to control the cold-bladed anxiety triggered by the discussion.

It was impossible for Killian to steel himself against the clarity of the emotions he read in Susannah's pale face. "Easy," he said soothingly. "Take some deep breaths, Susannah, and the panic will start to go away." He watched her breasts rise and fall sharply beneath her wrinkled cotton gown, and he couldn't help thinking how pretty she looked in the thin garment with lace sewn around its oval neckline. She was like that lace, fragile and easily crushed, he realized as he stood watching her wrestle with her fear.

Miraculously, Susannah felt much of her panic dissolve beneath his husky-voiced instructions. She wasn't sure. if it was because of the deep breaths or merely Killian's quiet presence. How did he know what she was experiencing? He must have experienced the very same thing, otherwise he wouldn't know how to help her. And he was helping her—even if he'd made it clear that he didn't want to be here.

"Good," Killian said gruffly as she became calm. He poured them more tea and took his chair again. "I'll sleep in the bedroom down the hall from yours. I'm a restless sleeper," he warned her sharply. "I have nightmares myself...." His voice trailed off.

Susannah stared at him, swayed by the sincerity in his dark blue eyes. There was such torment in them. Toward her? Toward the assignment? She just wasn't sure. Morning light was stealing through the ruffled curtains at the window now, softening his harsh features.

Nervously fingering the rectangular notepad, Susannah frowned, uncertain of her own feelings as she was every time he was with her.

"I won't bother you, if that's what you're worried about," he added when he saw the confusion on her face. He prayed he could keep his word—hoped against hope that he wouldn't have one of the terrible, wrenching nightmares that haunted him.

Agitated, Susannah got to her feet and moved to the window. The pale lavender of dawn reminded her of the color of her favorite flowers—the lilacs. Pressing and releasing her fingers against the porcelain sink, she thought about Killian's statement.

Killian studied Susannah in the quiet of the kitchen.

Her dark hair lay mussed against her tense shoulders, a sable cloak against the pristine white of her nightgown. Killian ached to touch her hair, to tunnel his fingers through it and find out what it felt like. Would it be as soft as her body had been against his? Or more coarse, in keeping with the ramrod-straight spine that showed her courage despite the circumstances?

"Look," he said, breaking the tense silence, "maybe this will end sooner than I expect. I'll work on the house over there to stay close in case something happens. I'll paint and fix up the windows, the doors." *Anything to keep my mind off you.*

Turning, Susannah looked at him. He sat at the table, his long fingers wrapped around the dainty china cup on the yellow oilcloth. His body was hunched forward, and he had an unhappy expression on his face. She would never forget the look in his eyes, his alertness, or the sense of safety she'd felt when she'd fallen sobbing into his arms at the back door. Why was she hedging now about allowing him to be near her?

Licking her lips, she nodded. Suddenly more tired than she could remember ever being, she left the counter. It was time to go home. When she got to the screen door, Killian moved quickly out of his chair.

"I'll walk you back," Killian said, his tone brooking no argument. Opening the screen door, she walked out.

Although he wanted Susannah to believe he was relaxed, Killian remained on high alert as they trod the damp path through the orchard back to her home. The sky had turned a pale pink. It wouldn't be long before the sun came up.

Killian felt Susannah's worry as she looked around, her arms wrapped tightly around herself. He wanted to step close—to place a protective arm around her shoulders and give her the sense of security she so desperately needed and so richly deserved. Yet he knew that touching her would melt his defenses. That couldn't happen—ever. Killian swore never to allow Susannah to reach inside him; but she had that ability, and he knew it. Somehow, he had to strengthen his resolve and keep her at arm's length. At all costs. For her own sake.

"Maybe if I patch that torn screen in your bedroom and put some locks on the windows, you'll feel better about being there." He saw her flash him a grateful look. "I'll tell your folks what happened when they get up. Then I'll contact Morgan."

Susannah nodded her agreement. She longed simply to step closer to Killian, to be in his protective embrace again. She couldn't forget the lean power of his body against hers, the way he'd used himself as a barrier to protect her.

She wrestled with conflicting feelings. Why was Killian so unhappy about having to stay out at the house with her? She couldn't help how she felt. She knew that right now, if she went back to her old room at her folks' house, the nightmares would return. Her life had begun to stabilize—until tonight. If only Killian could understand why she had to be at the old homestead.

"I'll make sure your house is safe. Then I want you to get some sleep. When you get up, you can draw me the face you saw in the nightmare."

Killian saw Susannah's eyes darken.

"Don't worry, I'll be around. You may not know it, but I'll be there. Like a shadow."

Shivering, Susannah nodded. Her life had turned into nothing but a series of shadows. Killian's body against hers had been real, and never had she needed that more. But Killian didn't like her, didn't want to be with her.

She swallowed her need to be held, still grateful that Killian would be nearby. Perhaps her mind was finally ready to give up the information it had seen, and that should help in the long run.

Touching her throat, she fervently wished her voice would come back. At least now she could make some noise, and that seemed a hopeful sign. She stole a glance up into Killian's grim, alert features. She'd welcome his company, even though he didn't want hers. Right now, she needed the human contact. Thinking back, she realized that the anger she'd sensed in Killian had been due to his not wanting to take the assignment. It hadn't really been aimed directly at her. Sometimes it was lonely out there at the homestead. He wasn't a willing guest, Susannah reminded herself. Still, if her attacker was really out there, she would feel a measure of safety knowing that Killian was nearby.

After thoroughly checking Susannah's home again, Killian allowed her into the farmhouse. He'd double-check around the house and quietly search the acreage around it just to make sure no one was hiding in wait. At the bedroom door, Susannah shyly turned and gave him a soft, hesitant smile. A thank-you showed clearly in her eyes, and it took everything Killian had for him to turn away from her. "I'll be over about noon," he rasped, more gruffly than he'd intended.

Susannah waited for Killian's promised noon arrival as she sat at her kitchen table. She questioned herself. Her real home was in town, near the school where she taught. Why didn't she have the courage to move back there? Glumly she admitted it was because she was afraid of being completely alone. At least this broken-down homestead was close to her parents.

Killian deliberately made noise as he stepped up on Susannah's porch, carrying art supplies under one arm. He knew all about being jumpy. He'd decked more than one man who had inadvertently come up behind him without warning. Wolf had been one of those men, on assignment down in Peru. The others on the team had learned from his mistake and had always let Killian know they were coming.

Susannah was waiting for him at the screen door. She looked beautiful, clothed in a long, lightweight denim skirt and a fuchsia short-sleeved blouse. She'd tied her hair back with a pink ribbon, and soft tendrils brushed her temples. Killian tensed himself against the tempting sight of her.

Stepping into the kitchen, Killian sniffed. "You've got coffee on?" He found himself wanting to ease the seriousness out of her wary eyes. The dark shadows beneath them told him she hadn't slept well since the nightmare.

Placing sketch pad, colored pencils and eraser on the table, Killian eased into a chair. Susannah went to the cupboard, retrieved a white ceramic mug and poured him some coffee. He nodded his thanks as she came over and handed it to him.

"Sit down," he urged her. "We've got some work to do."

Looking over the art supplies, Susannah sat down at his elbow. Somehow Killian looked heart-stoppingly handsome and dangerous all at once. His dress was casual, but she always sensed the inner tension in him, and could see some undefinable emotion in his blue eyes when he looked at her. But the anger was no longer there, she noted with relief.

"I'd like you to sketch for me the man you saw in your nightmare," Killian said.

Hesitant, Susannah fingered the box of colored pencils. Her throat constricted, and she closed her eyes for a moment. How could she make Killian understand that since the attack her love of drawing and painting had gone away?

"It doesn't have to be fancy, Susannah. Draw me something. Anything. I have a way to check what you sketch for me against police mug shots." He saw pain in her eyes, and her lower lip trembled as she withdrew her hand from the box of pencils. He cocked his head. "What is it?" He recalled his sister's pain, and the hours he'd spent holding her while she cried after realizing her once-beautiful face was gone forever. A powerful urge to reach out and give Susannah that same kind of help nearly overwhelmed him, but he reared back inwardly. He couldn't.

With a helpless shrug, Susannah swallowed against the lump and shakily opened up the sketch pad. She had to try. She believed in Killian, and she believed he could help her. Suddenly embarrassed, she took her pad and pencil and wrote:

I'm rusty at this. I haven't drawn since being wounded.

He grimaced. "I'm no art critic, Susannah. I can't draw a straight line. Anything you can do will look great to me. Give it your best try."

Susannah picked up a pencil and began to sketch. She tried to concentrate on the task at hand, but she found her senses revolving back to Killian's overwhelming presence. All morning she'd thought about him staying

here with her. It wasn't him she couldn't trust, she realized—it was herself! The discovery left her feeling
shaken. Never had a man influenced her on all levels, as
Killian did. What was it about him? For the thousandth
time, Susannah ached to have her voice back. If only
she could talk!

Quiet descended upon them. Killian gazed around the
kitchen, keenly aware of Susannah's presence. It was
like a rainbow in his dismal life. There were at least
forty colorful drawings tacked to the kitchen walls, obviously done by very young children. Probably her class.
Peace, a feeling that didn't come often to Killian, descended gently around him. Was it the old-fashioned
house? Being out in the country away from the madding
crowd? Or—he swung his gaze back to Susannah and
saw her brows drawn together in total concentration, her
mouth pursed—was it her?

Unconsciously Killian's shoulders dropped, and he
eased the chair back off its two front legs, loosely holding the mug of coffee against his belly. Birds, mostly
robins, were singing and calling to one another. The
sweet scents of grass, ripening fruit and clean mountain
air wafted through the kitchen window. Susannah had a
small radio on in the corner, and FM music flowed softly
across the room, like an invisible caress.

His gaze settled on Susannah's ponytail, and he noted
the gold and red glints between the sable strands. Her
hair was thick and luxurious. A man could drive himself
crazy wondering what the texture of it was like, Killian
decided unhappily. Right now, he knew his focus had to
be on keeping her protected, not his own personal longings.

The sketch of the man took shape beneath Susannah's
slender fingers over the next hour. Frequently she strug-

gled, erasing and beginning again. Killian marveled at her skill as an artist. She might consider herself rusty, but she was definitely a professional. Finally her mouth quirked and she glanced up. Slowly she turned the sketch toward him.

"Unsavory-looking bastard," Killian whispered as he put the coffee aside and held the sketch up to examine it. "Brown eyes, blond hair and crooked front teeth?"

Susannah nodded. She saw the change in Killian's assessing blue eyes. A fierce anger emanated from him, and she sensed his hatred of her attacker.

He reminds me of a weasel, with close-set eyes that are small and beady-looking.

Killian nodded and put the sketch aside. "I'll take this to the police department today. I called Morgan. He knows you've remembered what your attacker looked like, so he's anxious to get this, too. He'll know what to do with it. If this bastard has a police record, we'll be on the way to catching him."

Chilled, Susannah slowly rubbed her arms with her hands.

Killian felt her raw fear. But he stopped himself from reaching out to give her a touch of reassurance. Gathering up the sketch, he rose. "I'll be back as soon as I can. In the meantime, you stay alert."

The warning made another chill move through her as she looked up at him. Somehow, some of the tension around him was gone. The peace that naturally inhabited the farmhouse had always worked wonders on her own nervousness, and Susannah realized that it might be doing the same for him. She nodded in agreement to his orders.

"It would be best if you went down to your parents' house while I'm gone. They know the truth now, and they'll be more watchful for you. In the long run, it's best this way."

Susannah couldn't disagree with him. The more people who were on guard and watchful, the less chance of the killer's finding her. Rising, she left with him.

"Maybe," Killian told her as they walked across the top of the hill, "this will be over soon."

At his words, Susannah's eyes sparkled with such fierce hope, combined with gratitude, that Killian had to force himself to keep from reaching out to caress her flushed cheek.

He'd give his life for her, if necessary, he realized suddenly. Susannah was worth dying for.

Chapter Four

Susannah was helping her mother can ripe figs in the kitchen when she saw Killian return from Glen. She stood at the counter and watched him emerge from the four-wheel-drive Land Cruiser. The vehicle seeming fitting for a man like Killian, she thought, a man who was rugged, a loner, iconoclastic. Though his face remained emotionless, his roving blue gaze held her, made her feel an inherent safety as he looked around the property. Her heart took a skipping beat as he turned and headed into the house.

"Killian's home," Pansy said. She shook her head as she transferred the recently boiled figs to the jars awaiting on the counter. "I'm so nervous now." With a little laugh, she noted, "My hands haven't stopped shaking since he told us the truth this morning."

Wanting somehow to reassure her, Susannah put her arms around her mother and gave her a hug.

Killian walked into the kitchen and saw Susannah embracing her mother. He halted, a strange, twisting feeling moving through him. Mother and daughter held each other, and he remained motionless. It was Susannah who sensed his presence first. She loosened the hug and smiled shyly in his direction.

Pansy tittered nervously when she realized he was standing in the doorway. "I didn't hear you come in, Mr. Killian."

"I should have said something," he said abruptly. Killian felt bad for the woman. Ever since he'd told the Andersons the truth, it had been as if a shock wave had struck the farm. Sam Anderson had promptly gone out to the barn to fix a piece of machinery. Pansy had suddenly gotten busy with canning duties. Staying occupied was one way to deal with tension, Killian realized. His gaze moved to Susannah, whose cheeks were flushed. Her hair was still in a ponytail, the tendrils sticking to her dampened temples with the heat of the day and the lack of breeze through the kitchen. She looked beautiful.

"Did you tell the police?" Pansy asked, nervously wiping her hands on her checked apron.

"Yes. Everyone has a copy of the picture Susannah sketched. Morgan will call me here if they find out who it is. The FBI's in on it, so maybe we'll turn up something a little sooner."

Susannah heard her mother give a little moan, and she reached over and touched her shoulder and gave her a look she hoped she could decipher.

"Oh, I'm okay, honey," Pansy said in response, patting her hand in a consoling way.

Killian absorbed the soft look Susannah gave her worried mother. She had such sensitivity. How he wished he could have that in his life. A sadness moved through him, and he turned away, unable to stand the compassion on Susannah's features.

"Is Sam still out at the barn?" he demanded.

"Yes."

"I'll go help him," Killian said, and left without another word.

An odd ache had filled Susannah as she watched Killian's carefully arranged face give way to his real feelings. There had been such naked hunger in his eyes that it left her feeling in touch with herself as a woman as never before. She tried to help her mother, unable to get Killian's expression out of her mind—or her heart.

"That Mr. Killian's a strange one," Pansy said, to no one in particular, as she spooned the figs into a jar, their fragrant steam rising around her. "He's so gruff. Almost rude. But he cares. I can feel it around him. I wonder why he's so standoffish? It's hard to get close to him, to let him know how grateful we are for him being here."

Susannah nodded. Killian *was* gruff—like a cranky old bear. It was part of what he used to keep people at bay, she thought. Yet, just a few minutes ago, she'd seen the real Sean Killian—a man who had wants—and desires. And her heart wouldn't settle down over that discovery.

Around four o'clock, Pansy sent Susannah out with a gallon of iced tea and two glasses for the men, who were still laboring in the barn. The sunlight was bright and hot for an early-September day, and Susannah reveled in it. Chickens scattered out of her path as she crossed the dirt driveway to the barn, which sat off to one side of the green-and-white farmhouse.

As she entered the huge, airy structure, the familiar smell of hay and straw filled her nostrils. At one end of the barn, where the machinery was kept, Susannah spotted her father working intently on his tractor. The engine had been pulled up and out of the tractor itself and hung suspended by two chains looped around one of the barn's huge upper beams. She saw Killian down on his knees, working beneath the engine while her father stood above him. They were trying to thread a hose from above the engine to somewhere down below, where Killian leaned beneath it, his hand outstretched for it.

Killian had clearly shed his shirt long before, and his skin glistened with sweat from the hot barn air, accentuating his muscular chest and arms. A lock of black hair stuck damply to his forehead as he frowned in concentration, intent on capturing the errant hose.

Susannah slowed her step halfway to them. Her father turned away from the tractor, going to the drawer where he kept many of his tools. Just then, she heard a vague snap. Her eyes rose to the beam that held the heavy engine. Instantly her gaze shifted to Killian, who seemed oblivious of the sound, his concentration centered on threading the hose through the engine.

Sam Anderson was still bent over a drawer, rummaging for a tool.

Susannah realized that the chain was slowly coming undone. At any second it would snap free and that heavy tractor engine would fall on Killian! Without thinking, she cried out a warning. *"Look out, Killian!"*

Her scream shattered the barn's musty stillness.

Killian jerked his hand back and heard a cracking, metallic sound. He glanced to his left and saw Susannah, her finger pointing toward the beam above him. Sam had whirled around at the cry. In one motion, Killian leaped away from the engine.

Susannah clutched the jar of iced tea to her as she saw

the chain give way. She screamed as the tractor engine slammed heavily down on the barn floor. But Killian was leaping away as the engine fell, rolling through the straw and dust on the floor.

Setting the iced tea aside, Susannah ran toward him, unsure whether he was hurt or not. He lay on his side, his back to her, as she raced up to him.

"Killian?" she sobbed. "Killian? Are you hurt?" She fell to her knees, reaching out to touch him.

"Good God!" Sam Anderson hurried to Killian's side. "Son? You all right?"

Breathing raggedly, Susannah touched Killian's hard, damp shoulder. He rolled over onto his back, his eyes narrowed and intense.

"Are—are you all right?" she stammered, quickly glancing down his body, checking for blood or a sign of injury.

"I'm fine," Killian rasped, sitting up. Then he grew very still. He saw the look in Susannah's huge eyes, saw her expressive fingers resting against her swanlike throat. Her face was pale. He blinked. Susannah had spoken. Her eyes still mirrored her fear for him, and he felt the coolness of her fingers resting on his dirty arm.

"You're sure?" Susannah demanded breathlessly, trading a look with her father, who knelt on the other side of Killian. "You could have been killed!" Badly shaken, she stared down into his taut face and held his burning gaze. Killian was like a lean, bronzed statue, his gleaming muscles taut from the hard physical labor.

Sam gasped and stared at his daughter. "Honey, you're talking!"

Gasping herself, Susannah reared back on her heels, her hands flying to her mouth. She saw Killian grin slightly. It was true! She had spoken! With a little cry,

Susannah touched her throat, almost unbelieving. ''Pa, I got my voice back....''

Killian felt Susannah's joy radiating from her like sunlight itself. He felt embraced and lifted by her joy at her discovery. And what a beautiful voice she had—low and husky. A tremor of warning fled through him as he drowned in her shining eyes. This was just one more thing to like about Susannah, to want from her.

Susannah's gaze moved from her father to Killian and back again. ''I can speak! I can talk again!'' Susannah choked, and tears streamed down her cheeks.

''Oh,'' Sam whispered unsteadily, ''that's wonderful, honey!'' He got to his feet and came around to where his daughter knelt. Leaning over, he helped her stand, then threw his arms around her and held her tight for a long, long time.

Touched, Killian remained quietly on the floor. The closeness of Sam with his daughter brought back good, poignant memories of his early home life, of his mother's strength and love. Slowly he eased himself to his feet and began to brush off the straw that clung to his damp skin. Sam and Susannah were laughing and crying, their brows touching. Tears jammed unexpectedly into Killian's eyes, and he quickly blinked them away. What the hell was happening to him?

Turning away from the happy scene, Killian went to retrieve his shirt. Disgruntled and shaken at his own emotional response, he tried to avoid looking at Susannah. It was *her*. Whatever magic it was that she wielded as a woman, it had a decided effect on him, whether he wanted it to or not. Agitated, Killian buttoned his shirt, stuffed the tail into his jeans and gathered up the broken chain, which lay across the floor and around the engine.

''Come on, honey, let's go tell Ma,'' Sam quavered,

his arm around his daughter's shoulders. He gave Killian a grateful look. "You, too. You deserve to be a part of the celebration."

Killian shrugged. "No…you folks go ahead…."

Susannah eased out of her father's embrace and slowly approached Killian. How beautifully and dangerously male he was. Her senses were heightened to almost a painful degree, giving her an excruciating awareness of his smoldering, hooded look as she approached. His chiseled mouth was drawn in at the corners.

"You're okay?" Susannah breathed softly. Then she stepped back, blushing.

Shocked by her unexpected concern for him despite what had happened to her, Killian was at a loss for words. He gripped the chain in his hands. "I'm okay," he managed in a strangled tone. "Go share the news with your mother…." he ordered unsteadily. What a beautiful voice she had, Killian thought dazedly, reeling from the feelings her voice stirred within him.

Trapped beneath his sensual, scorching gaze, Susannah's lips parted. What would it be like to explore that mouth endlessly, that wonderful mouth that was now pursed into a dangerous, thin line of warning? Every nerve in her body responded to his look of hunger. It was the kind of look that made Susannah wildly aware that she was a woman, in all ways. It was not an insulting look, it was a look of desire—for her alone.

"Come on, honey," Sam said happily as he came up and patted her shoulder, "let's go share the good news with Ma. She's gonna cry a bucket of tears over this."

Killian remained still, nearly overwhelmed by his need to reach out and touch Susannah's mussed hair or caress her flushed cheek. He watched as father and daughter left the barn together. Their happiness surrounded him like a long-lost memory. Taking a deep, steadying breath, Killian began to unhook the ends of the chain from the engine. His mind was waging war with his clamoring heart and his aching body. Susannah could now tell them what had happened to her. His emotions were in utter disarray. Her voice was soft and husky, like a well-aged Irish whiskey.

Angrily Killian cleaned up the mess in the barn and put the chains aside. In a way, he felt chained to the situation at the farm, he thought—chained to Susannah in a connection he could neither fight nor flee. Never had a woman gotten to him as Susannah had. His relationships with women had been few and brief—one-night stands that allowed him to leave before darkness came and made an enemy out of anyone who dared get close to him. What was it about Susannah that was different? The need to explore her drove him out of the barn. He slowly walked toward the farmhouse, savagely jamming down his fiery needs. Maybe now he could talk to Susannah about the assault, he reasoned.

Pansy was serving up lemonade in tall purple glasses in celebration. Susannah felt Killian's approach at the screen door before he appeared. What was this synchronicity the two of them seemed to share? Puzzled, but far too joyous over her voice returning to spend time worrying, she gave him a brilliant, welcoming smile as he walked into the kitchen.

"Sit down, son," Sam thundered. "You've earned yourself a glass of Ma's special hand-squeezed lemonade."

Killian hesitated. He'd hoped to come into the house, go to his room, take a cold shower and settle his roiling emotions. But the looks on their faces made him decide differently. With a curt nod, he took a seat opposite Susannah. Her eyes sparkled like diamonds caught in sunlight. He felt himself becoming helplessly ensnared in the joy that radiated around her like a rainbow of colors.

Pansy gave him the lemonade, gratitude visible in every line of her worn face.

"Killian, we're glad you're all right," she said. "Thank goodness you weren't hurt." She reached over and patted Susannah's hand warmly. "Just hearin' Susannah's voice again is like hearin' the angels speakin'."

Killian sipped the icy lemonade, hotly aware of the fire within him, captive to Susannah's thankful gaze. "Your daughter saved me from a few broken bones," he muttered.

Sam hooted and said, "A few? Son, you would've had your back broken if my Susannah hadn't found her voice in time."

Killian nodded and stared down at the glass. If there was such a thing as an angelic woman, it was Susannah. Her skin glowed with renewed color, and her lips were stretched into a happy curve as she gripped her father's leathery brown hand. Killian absorbed the love and warmth among the family members. Nothing could be stronger or better than that, in his opinion. Except maybe the fevered love of a man who loved his woman with a blind passion that overrode the fear of death in him.

"I can't believe it! This is like a dream—I can talk again!" Susannah told him, her hand automatically moving to her throat.

Killian ruminated over the events. He was perfectly at ease with saving other people's lives—but no one, with the exception of his teammates in Peru, had ever saved him from certain death. And he had to admit to himself that Sam was correct: If not for Susannah he'd have a broken back at best—and at worst, he'd be dead.

Killian was unsure how to feel about having a woman save his worthless hide. He had a blinding loyalty to those he fought beside, to those who saved him. He lifted his head and stared at Susannah. Things had changed subtly but irrevocably because of this event. No longer was Morgan's edict that he stay here and protect her hanging over his head like a threat.

Moving his fingers across the beaded coolness of the glass, Killian pondered the web of circumstances tightening around him. Perhaps his sense of honor was skewed. On one hand, Susannah deserved his best efforts to protect her. On the other hand, he saw himself as a danger to her each night he stayed at her home. What was he going to do? He could no longer treat her as a mere assignment—an object to be protected. Not that he'd been particularly successful with that tack before.

"Getting your voice back is going to be a big help," Killian offered lamely.

With a slight laugh, Susannah said, "I don't know if you'll feel that way or not, Sean. Pa says I talk too much." Susannah felt heat rise in her neck and into her face when his head snapped up, his eyes pinning her. She suddenly realized she'd slipped and used his first name. Vividly recalling that Killian had said that only his mother and sister used his first name, she groped for an apology. "I'm sorry, I forgot—you like to be called by your last name."

Killian shrugged, not wanting to make a big deal out of it. "You saved my life. I think that gives you the right to call me anything you want." His heart contracted at her husky, quavering words, and he retreated into silence, feeling that words were useless. Her voice, calling him Sean, had released a Pandora's box of deeply held emotions from his dark, haunted past. When she'd said his name, it had come out like a prayer. A beautiful, clean prayer of thanks. How little in his world was clean or beautiful. But somehow this woman giving him her lustrous look made him feel as if he were both. His head argued differently, but for once Killian ignored it.

With a happy smile, Pansy came over and rested her hands on her daughter's shoulders. "You two young'ns will stay for dinner, won't you? We have to celebrate!"

Killian wanted the safety of isolation. He shook his head. "I've got things to do, Mrs. Anderson." When he saw the regret in the woman's face, he got to his feet. He felt Susannah's eyes on him, as if she knew what he was doing and why he was doing it. "Thanks anyway," he mumbled, and quickly left the kitchen. His job was to protect this family, not to join it. Killian was relieved to escape, not sure how long he could continue to hold his emotions in check. As he stalked through the living room and down the hall to his bedroom, all he wanted was a cold shower to shock him back to the harsh reality he'd lived with since leaving Ireland so many years before. And somehow, he was going to have to dredge up enough control to be able to sleep under the same roof with Susannah. Somehow...

Early-evening light shed a subdued glow around the kitchen of Susannah's small house. Killian sat at the kitchen table and watched as she made coffee at the counter. He had insisted he wasn't hungry, but Pansy had sent a plate of food with him when he'd escorted Susannah back to her homestead. The meal had been simple but filling. Tonight he was more tense than he could recall ever being. He felt as if his emotions were caught in a desperate tug-of-war.

Was it because of Susannah's whiskey laughter, that

husky resonance that made him feel as if she were reaching out and caressing him? Killian sourly tried to ignore what her breathy voice did to him.

"You sure ate your share of Ma's cherry pie, Sean," she said with a teasing look over her shoulder. Killian sat at the table, his chin resting forward on his chest, his chair tipped back on its rear legs. His narrow face was dark and thoughtful.

"It was good."

Chortling, Susannah retrieved the lovely flowered china cups and saucers from the oak cabinet. "You ate like a man who hasn't had too many home-cooked meals in his life."

Killian grudgingly looked at her as she came over and set the cups and saucers on the oilcloth. Her insight, as always, was unsettling to him. "I haven't," he admitted slowly.

Susannah hesitated. There was so much she wanted to say to him. She slid her fingers across the back of the wooden chair opposite him. "Sean, I need to talk to you. I mean really talk to you." Heat rushed up her neck and into her cheeks, and Susannah groaned, touching her flushed face. "I wish I didn't turn beet red all the time!"

Killian absorbed her discomfort. "In Ireland we'd call you a primrose—a woman with moonlight skin and red primroses for cheeks," he said quietly.

The utter beauty of his whispered words made Susannah stand in shocked silence. "You're a poet."

Uncomfortable, he muttered, "I don't think of myself in those terms."

She saw the wariness in his eyes and sensed that her boldness was making him edgy. "Is it a crime to say that a man possesses a soul that can see the world in terms of beauty?"

Relieved that Susannah had turned and walked back to the counter, Killian frowned. He studied her as he tried to formulate an answer to her probing question. Each movement of her hands was graceful—and each time she touched something, he felt as if she were touching him instead. Shaking his head, he wondered what the hell had gotten into him. He was acting like a man who'd been without a woman far too long. Well, hadn't he?

Clearing his throat, Killian said, "I'd rather talk about you than myself."

Susannah sat down, drying her hands on a green-and-white checked towel. "I know you would, but I'm not going to let you." She kept her voice light, because she sensed that if she pushed him too hard he'd close up. She opened her hands to him. "I need to clear the air on some things between us."

Killian's stomach knotted painfully. The fragrant smell of coffee filled the kitchen. "Go on," he said in a warning growl.

Susannah nervously touched her brow. "I'm actually afraid to talk to you. Maybe it's because of what happened, getting shot by that man. I don't know…"

"The hurt part, the wounded side of you, feels that fear," Killian told her, his tone less gruff now. "It was a man who nearly killed you. Why shouldn't you be afraid of men in general?" He had to stop himself from reaching out to touch her tightly clasped hands on the tabletop. Her knuckles were white.

"You seem to know so much about me—about what I'm feeling." She gave him a long, scrutinizing look. "How?"

Shifting uncomfortably, Killian shrugged. "Experience, maybe."

"Whose? Your own?" After all, he was a mercenary, Susannah reminded herself. A world-traveled and world-weary man who had placed his life on the line time and again.

"No...not exactly... My sister, Meg, was—" His mouth quirked at the corners. "She was beautiful, and had a promising career as a stage actress. Meg met and fell in love with an Irish-American guy, and they were planning on getting married." He cleared his throat and forced himself to finish. "She flew back to Ireland to be in a play—and at her stopover at Heathrow Airport a terrorist bomb went off."

"Oh, no..." Susannah whispered. "Is she...alive?"

The horror of that day came rushing back to Killian, and he closed his eyes, his voice low with feeling. "Yes, she's alive. But the bomb... She's badly disfigured. She's no longer beautiful. Her career ended, and I've seen her through fifteen operations to restore her face." Killian shrugged hopelessly. "Meg cut off her engagement to Ian, too, even though he wanted to stay with her. She couldn't believe that any man could love her like that."

"How awful," Susannah whispered. Reaching out, she slid her hand across his tightly clenched fist. "It must have been hard on you, too."

Wildly aware of Susannah's touch, Killian warned himself that she'd done it only out of compassion. Her fingers were cool and soft against his sun-toughened skin. His mouth went dry, and his heart rate skyrocketed. Torn between emotions from the past and the boiling heat scalding up through him, Killian rasped, "Meg has been a shadow of herself since then. She's fearful, always looking over her shoulder, has terrible nightmares, and doesn't trust anyone." Bitterly he added, "She's even wary of me, her own brother." It hurt to admit that, but Killian sensed that Susannah had the emotional strength to deal with his first-time admission to anyone about his sister.

Tightening her hand around his, Susannah ached for Killian. She saw the hurt and confusion in his eyes. "Everyone suffers when someone is hurt like that." Forcing herself to release Killian's hand, Susannah whispered, "Look what I've put my parents through since I awakened from the coma. Look how I distrusted you at first."

He gave her a hooded look. "You're better off if you do."

"No," Susannah said fervently, her voice quavering with feeling. "I don't believe that anymore, Sean. You put on a tough act, and I'm sure you're very tough emotionally, but I can read your eyes. I can see the trauma that Meg went through, and how it has affected you." She smiled slightly. "I may come from hill folk, but I've got two good eyes in my head, and a heart that's never led me wrong."

Killian struggled with himself. He'd never spoken to anyone about his sister—not even to Morgan. And now he was spilling his guts to Susannah. He said nothing, for fear of divulging even more.

"I'm really sorry about your sister. Is she living in America?"

"No. She lives near the Irish Sea, in a thatched hut that used to belong to a fisherman and his wife. They died and left her the place. Old Dun and his wife Em were like grandparents to Meg. They took care of her when I had to be on assignment. Meg can't stand being around people."

"It's hard for most people to understand how it feels

to be a victim of violence," Susannah mused. She looked over at the coffeepot. The coffee was ready to be served. Rising, she added, "I know that since I woke up from the coma I've been jumpy and paranoid. If someone comes up behind me, I scream. If I catch sight of my own shadow unexpectedly I break out in a sweat and my heart starts hammering." She poured coffee into the cups. "Stupid, isn't it?"

Putting a teaspoon of sugar into the dark, fragrant coffee, Killian shook his head. "Not at all. I call it a survival reflex."

Coming back to the table and sitting down, Susannah gave him a weak smile. "Even now, I dread talking about what happened to me." She turned her hands over. "My palms are damp, and my heart is running like a rabbit's."

"Adrenaline," Killian explained gently, "the flight-or-fight hormone." He stirred the coffee slowly with the spoon, holding her searching gaze.

"Morgan only gave me a brief overview of what happened to you," he probed gently. "Why don't you fill me in on your version? It might help me do my job better."

Susannah squirmed. "This is really going to sound stupid, Sean. It was my idea to go visit Morgan and Laura." She looked around the old farmhouse. "I've never gone much of anywhere, except to Lexington to get my teaching degree. A lot of my friends teased me that I wasn't very worldly and all that. After graduating and coming back here, I bought myself a small house in Glen, near where I work at the local grade school. Laura had been begging me to come for a visit, and I thought taking a plane to Washington, D.C., would expand my horizons."

Killian nodded. In many ways, Susannah's country ways had served to protect her from the world at large. Kentucky was a mountainous state with a small population, in some ways insulated from the harsher realities that plague big cities. "Your first flight?"

She smiled. "Yes, my first. It was really exciting." With an embarrassed laugh, she added, "I know, where else would you find someone who hasn't flown on a plane in this day and age. I had such a wonderful time with Laura, with her children. Morgan took me to the Smithsonian Institution for the whole day, and I was in heaven. I love learning, and that is the most wonderful museum I've ever seen. On my way home I landed at Lexington and was on my way to the bus station to get back here to Glen." Her smile faded. "That's when all this happened."

"Were you in the bus station itself?"

Susannah shook her head. "No. I'd just stepped off the bus. There was a row of ten buses parked under this huge roof, and my bus was farthest away from the building. I was the last one off the bus. It was very dark that night, and it was raining. A thunderstorm. The rain was whipping in under the roof, and I had my head down and was hurrying to get inside.

"This man came out of nowhere and began talking real fast to me. At the same time, he was reaching for my shoulder bag and pulling it off my arm. He was smiling and saying he'd like to help me."

"Was he acting nervous?" Killian asked, noticing that Susannah had gone pale recounting the event.

"I didn't realize it at the time, but yes, he was. How did you know that?"

"Because no doubt he spotted you as a patsy, someone gullible enough to approach, lie to, and then use your luggage—probably to hide drugs or money for a later pickup. But go on. What happened next?'' Killian leaned forward, his hands around the hot mug of coffee.

Susannah took in a ragged breath. She was amazed by Killian's knowledge. She was so naive, and it had nearly gotten her killed. ''He said he'd take my bag into the station for me. I didn't know what to do. He seemed so nice—he was smiling all the time. I was getting wet from the rain, and I was wearing a new outfit I'd bought, and I didn't want it ruined, so I let him have the bag.'' She flushed and looked down. ''You know the worst part?'' she whispered. ''I was flattered. I thought he was interested in me....'' Her voice trailed off.

Susannah rubbed her brow and was silent for a long moment. When she spoke again, her voice came out hoarse. ''He'd no sooner put the piece of luggage over his shoulder than I saw this other man step out of the dark and shoot at him. I screamed, but it was too late. The man fell, and I saw the killer move toward me. No one else was around. No one else saw it happen.'' Susannah shuddered and wrapped her arms around herself. ''The next thing I knew, the killer was after me. I ran into a nearby alley. I remember thinking I was going to die. I heard shots—I heard bullets hitting the sides of the building and whining around me.''

Closing her eyes, she whispered, ''I was running hard, choking for air. I slipped on the wet street, and it was so dark, so dark...'' Susannah opened her eyes. ''I remember thinking I had to try to scream for help. But no one came. The next thing I knew, something hit me in the head—a hot sensation. That's it.''

Glancing over at Killian, Susannah saw anger flash in his narrowed eyes. Her voice went off-key. ''I woke up two months later. My ma was at my side when I came around, and I remember her crying."

"It was probably a drug deal gone wrong," Killian growled. He stared down at his hands. He'd like to wrap them around that bastard and give him back what he'd done to Susannah. "You were at the wrong place at the wrong time. There may have been drugs left in a nearby locker that the man who talked to you was supposed to pick up. Or the guy may have been on the run, using you as a decoy, hoping the killer wouldn't spot him if he was part of a couple." He looked at her sadly. "I'm sorry it happened, Susannah."

"At least I'm alive. I survived." She shrugged, embarrassed. "So much for my trying to become more worldly. I was so stupid."

"No," Killian rasped, "not stupid. Just not as alert as you might have been."

Shivering, Susannah slowly rubbed her arms with her hands. "Sean…the other night when I woke up?"

"Yes?"

"Please believe me. There *was* a man outside my bedroom window. I heard him. I saw his shadow against the opposite wall of my bedroom."

With a sigh, Killian shook his head. "There was no evidence—no footprints outside either window, Susannah. The grass wasn't disturbed."

Rubbing her head with her hands, Susannah sat there, confused. "I could have sworn he was there."

Killian wanted to reach out and comfort her, but he knew he didn't dare. Just her sharing the tragedy with him had drawn her uncomfortably close to him. "Let me do the worrying about it," he said. "All I need you to do is continue to get well."

Susannah felt latent power swirling around him as he

sat tautly at the table. Anger shone in his eyes, but this time she knew it wasn't aimed at her; it was aimed at her unidentified assailant.

"I never thought about the killer coming to finish me off," she told him lamely. "That's stupid, too."

"Naive."

"Whatever you want to call it, it still can get me killed." She gave him a long look. "Would this man kill my parents, too?"

"I don't know," Killian said, trying to soothe her worry. "Most of these men go strictly for the target. In a way, you're protecting your parents by not being in their house right now."

"But if the killer got my address, he might think I was at my home in Glen, right?"

"That would be the first place he'd look," Killian agreed, impressed with her insight.

"And then he'd do what?"

"Probably discreetly try to nose around some of your neighbors and find out where you are," he guessed.

"It's no secret I'm here," Susannah said unhappily. "And if the killer didn't know I was out here at the homestead, he might break into my folks' home to find me."

"Usually," he told her, trying to assuage her growing fear, "a contract killer will do a good deal of research to locate his target. That means he probably will show up here sooner or later. My hunch is that he'll stake out the place, sit with a field scope on a rifle, or a pair of binoculars, and try to figure out the comings and goings of everyone here. Once he knew for sure where you were and when to get you alone, he'd come for you."

A chill ran up her spine, and she stared over at Killian.

His blue eyes glittered with a feral light that frightened her. "All the trouble I'm causing..."

"I'm here to protect all of you," Killian said. "I'm going to try to get to the bottom of this mess as soon as possible."

With a sigh, Susannah nodded. "I felt it. The moment you were introduced to me, I felt safe."

"Well," Killian growled, rising to his feet, "I'd still stay alert. Paranoia's a healthy reaction to have until I can figure out if you're really safe or not," he said, setting the cup and saucer in the sink.

Grimly Killian placed his hands on the counter and stared out the window. The blue-and-white checked curtains at the window made it homey, and it was tempting to relax and absorb the feeling. He'd been so long without home and family, and he was rarely able to go back to Ireland to visit what was left of his family—Meg. Sadness moved through him, deep and cutting. Being here with Susannah and her family had been a reprieve of sorts from his loneliness.

"Sean, I really don't feel good about going back to town, back to my house, knowing all this." Susannah stared at his long, lean back. He was silhouetted against the dusk, his mouth a tight line holding back unknown emotions, perhaps pain. Overcoming her shyness, she whispered, "Now that I know the real reason you're here, I'll take you up on that offer to stay with me at night. If you want..."

Slowly Killian turned around. He groaned internally as he met her hope-filled gaze, saw her lips part. The driving urge to kiss her, to explore those wonderful lips, was nearly his undoing.

Susannah took his silence as a refusal. A strange light

burned in his intense gaze. "Well...I mean, you don't have to. I don't want you to feel like a—"

"I'll stay," he muttered abruptly.

Nervously Susannah stood and wiped her damp hands down her thighs. "Are you sure?" He looked almost angry. With her? Since the assault, she'd lost so much of her self-esteem. Susannah found herself quivering like jelly inside; it was a feeling she'd never experienced before that fateful night at the bus station.

"Yes," Killian snapped, moving toward the back door. "I'll get my gear down at your folks' place and bring it up here."

Feeling as if she'd done something wrong, Susannah watched him leave. And then she upbraided herself for that feeling. It was a victim's response, according to the woman therapist who had counseled her a number of times when she'd come out of the coma but was still at the hospital.

"Stop it," Susannah sternly told herself. "If he's angry, ask him why. Don't assume it's because of something you said." As she moved to the bedroom next to her own, separated by the only bathroom in the house, Susannah felt a gamut of insecurities. When Sean returned, she was determined to find out the truth of why he'd been so abrupt with her.

Chapter Five

"Are you angry with me?" Susannah asked Killian, the words coming out more breathless than forceful, to her dismay. He'd just dropped his leather bag in the spare bedroom.

Turning, he scowled. "No. Why?"

"You acted upset earlier. I just wanted to know if it was aimed at me."

Straightening, Killian moved to where Susannah stood, at the entrance to his bedroom. Twilight had invaded the depths of the old house, and her sober features were strained. It hurt to think that she thought he was angry with her. Roughly he said, "My being upset has nothing to do with you, Susannah."

"What does it have to do with, then?"

He grimaced, unwilling to comment.

"I know you didn't want this assignment from Morgan...."

Exasperated, he muttered, "Not at first." Killian refused to acknowledge that Susannah appealed to him on some primal level of himself. Furthermore, he couldn't allow himself to get involved emotionally with the person he had to protect. And that was why he had never before accepted an assignment involving a woman; his weakness centered around those who were least able to protect themselves—the women of the world. Emotions touched him deeply, and there was little he could do to parry them, because they always hit him hard, no matter what he tried to do to avoid them. Men were far easier to protect; they were just as closed up as he was, lessening the emotional price tag.

Susannah wasn't about to let Killian squirm out of the confrontation. "I learned a long time ago to talk out problems. Maybe that's a woman's way, but men can profit from it, too." She lifted her hands and held his scrutinizing gaze, gaining confidence. "I don't want you here if you don't want to be, Sean. I hate thinking I'm a burden to anyone."

The ache to reach out and tame a strand of hair away from her flushed features was excruciatingly tempting. Killian exhaled loudly. "I wish you weren't so sensitive to other people's moods."

She smiled a little. "Maybe it's because I work with handicapped children who often either can't speak or have trouble communicating in general. I can't help it. What's bothering you, Sean?"

He shoved his hands into the pockets of his jeans and studied her tautly. "It's my nature not to talk," he warned.

"It does take courage to talk," Susannah agreed, gathering her own courage, determined to get to the root of his problem with her. "It's easier to button up and retreat into silence," she said more firmly.

His mouth had become nothing more than a slash. "Let's drop this conversation."

Susannah stood in the doorway, feeling the tension radiating from him. He not only looked dangerous, he felt dangerous. Her mouth grew dry. "No."

The one word, softly spoken, struck him solidly. "I learned a long time ago to say nothing. I'm a man with a lot of ugly secrets, Susannah. Secrets I'm not proud of. They're best left unsaid."

"I don't agree," Susannah replied gently. She saw the terror lurking in the depths of Killian's eyes as he avoided her searching gaze. "My folks helped me through the worst of my reactions after I came out of the coma. They understood my need to talk about my fears by writing them down on a piece of paper when I couldn't speak." She blinked uncertainly. "I couldn't even cry, Sean. The tears just wouldn't come. The horrible humiliation I felt—still feel even now—was lessened because they cared enough to listen, to hold me when I was so scared. At least I had someone who cared how I felt, who cried *for* me when the pain was too much for me to bear alone."

Killian lifted his chin and stared deeply into her luminous gray eyes. The need to confide, to open his arms and sweep her against him, was painfully real. His whole body was tense with pain. "In my line of work, there aren't many therapists available when things start coming down—or falling apart. There are no safe havens, Susannah. To avoid trouble and ensure safety, I breathe through my nose. It keeps my mouth shut."

He'd said too much already. Killian looked around,

wanting to escape, but Susannah stood stubbornly in the doorway, barring any exit. Panic ate at him.

Susannah shook her head. "I felt such sadness around you," she whispered, opening her hands to him. "You put on such a frightening mask, Sean—"

Angrily he rasped, "Back off."

The words slapped her. His tone had a lethal quality. Swallowing hard, Susannah saw fear, mixed with anguish, mirrored in his narrowed eyes. The words had been spoken in desperation, not anger. "How can I? I feel how uncomfortable you are here with me. I feel as if I've done something to make you feel like that." She raised her eyes to the ceiling. "Sean, I can't live like that with a person. How can you?"

Nostrils flaring, Killian stared at her in disbelief. Her honesty was bone deep—a kind he'd rarely encountered. Killian didn't dare tell her the raw, blatant truth—that he wanted her in every way imaginable. "I guess I've been out in the field too long," he told her in a low, growling tone. "I'm used to harshness, Susannah, not the softness a woman has, not a home. Being around you is…different…and I'm having to adjust." *A lot.*

"And," he added savagely, seeing how flustered she was becoming, "I'm used to bunking with men, not a woman. I get nightmares." When her face fell with compassion for him, he couldn't deal with it—almost hating her for it, for forcing the feelings out of him. "The night is my enemy, Susannah. And it's an enemy for anyone who might be near me when it happens. The past comes back," he warned thickly. Killian wanted to protect Susannah from that dark side of himself. He was afraid he might not be able to control himself, that terrorized portion of him that sometimes trapped him for hours in its brutal grip, ruling him.

Standing there absorbing the emotional pain contained in his admission, Susannah realized for the first time that Killian was terribly human. He wasn't the superman she'd first thought, although Morgan's men had a proud reputation for being exactly that. The discovery was as breathtaking as it was disturbing. She had no experience with a man like Killian—someone who had been grievously wounded by a world whose existence she could hardly fathom. The pleading look Killian gave her, the twist of his lips as he shared the information with her, tore at Susannah's heart. Instinctively she realized that Killian needed to be held, too. If only for a little while. He needed a safe haven from the stormy dangers inherent in his chosen profession. That was something she could give him while he stayed with her.

"I understand," she whispered unsteadily. "And if you have bad dreams, I'll come out and make you a cup of tea. Maybe we can talk about it."

He slowly raised his head, feeling the tension make his joints ache. He held Susannah's guileless eyes, eyes that were filled with hope. "Your naiveté nearly got you killed once," he rasped. "Just stay away from me if you hear me up and moving around at night, Susannah. *Stay away.*"

She gave him a wary look, seeing the anguish in his narrowed eyes even as they burned with desire. Desire for her? Susannah wished that need could be for her alone, but she knew Killian was the kind of man who allowed no grass to grow under his feet. He was a wanderer over the face of the earth, with no interest in settling down. Much as she hated to admit it, she had to be honest with herself.

Killian wasn't going to say anything else, Susannah

realized. She stepped back into the hallway, at a loss. Lamely she held his hooded stare.

"It's as if you're saying you're a danger to me."

"I am."

Susannah shook her head. "I wish," she said softly, "I had more experience with the world, with men..."

Killian wanted to move to her and simply enfold Susannah in his arms. She looked confused and bereft. "Stay the way you are," he told her harshly. "You don't want to know what the world can offer."

Susannah wasn't so sure. She felt totally unprepared to deal with a complex man like Sean, yet she was powerfully drawn to him. "Should I follow my normal schedule of doing things around here tomorrow morning?" At least this was a safe topic of conversation.

"Yes."

"I see. Good night, Sean."

"Good night." The words came out in a rasp. Killian tasted his frustration, and felt a heated longing coil through him. Susannah looked crestfallen. Could he blame her? No. Darkness was complete now, and he automatically perused the gloomy area. Perhaps talking a little bit about himself hadn't been so bad after all. At least with her. He knew he couldn't live under the same roof without warning Susannah of his violent night world.

By ten, Killian was in bed, wearing only his pajama bottoms. He stared blankly at the plaster ceiling, which was in dire need of repair. His senses functioned like radar, swinging this way and that, picking up nuances of sound and smell. Nothing seemed out of place, so he relaxed to a degree. And then, against his will, his attention shifted to dwell on Susannah. She had a surprisingly stubborn side to her—and he liked discovering that strength within her. Outwardly she might seem soft and naive, but she had emotional convictions that served as the roots of her strength.

Glancing at the only window in his room, Killian could see stars dotting the velvet black of the sky. Everything was so peaceful here. Another layer of tension dissolved around him, and he found himself enjoying the old double bed, the texture of the clean cotton sheets that Susannah had made the bed with, and the symphony of the crickets chirping outside the house.

What was it about this place that permeated his constant state of wariness and tension to make him relax to this degree? Killian had no answers, or at least none he was willing to look at closely. Exhausted, he knew he had to try to get some sleep. He moved restlessly on the bed, afraid of what the night might hold. He forced his eyes closed, inhaled deeply and drifted off to sleep. On the nightstand was his pistol, loaded and with the safety off, perpetually at the ready.

Killian jerked awake, his hand automatically moving to his pistol. Sunlight streamed through the window and the lacy pale green curtains. Blinking, he slowly sat up and shoved several locks of hair off his brow. The scent of freshly brewed coffee and frying bacon wafted on the air. He inhaled hungrily and threw his legs across the creaky bed. Relief flowed through him as he realized that for once the nightmares hadn't come to haunt him. Puzzled, he moved to the bathroom. Not only had the nightmares stayed at bay, but he'd slept very late. Usually his sleep was punctuated by moments of stark terror throughout the night and he finally fell more heavily asleep near dawn. Still, he never slept past six—ever.

But now it was eight o'clock. Stymied about why he'd slept so late, he stepped into a hot shower.

Dressed in a white shirt and jeans, Killian swung out of his room and down the hall, following the enticing smells emanating from the kitchen. Halting in the doorway, he drank in the sight of Susannah working over the old wood stove. Today she wore a sleeveless yellow blouse, well-worn jeans and white tennis shoes. Her hair, thick and abundant, cloaked her shoulders. As if she had sensed his presence, she looked up.

"I thought this might get you out of bed." She grinned. "So much for keeping up with me and my schedule. I was up at five-thirty, and you were still sawing logs."

Rubbing his face, Killian managed a sheepish look as he headed for the counter where the coffeepot sat. "I overslept," he muttered.

Taking the bacon out of the skillet and placing it on a paper towel to soak up the extra grease, Susannah smiled. "Don't worry, your secrets are safe with me."

Killian gave her a long, absorbing look, thinking how pretty she looked this morning. But he noted a slight puffiness beneath Susannah's eyes and wondered if she'd been crying. "I guess I'll have to get used to this," he rasped. The coffee was strong, hot and black—just the way he liked it. Susannah placed a stack of pancakes, the rasher of bacon and a bottle of maple syrup before him and sat down opposite him.

"'This' meaning me?"

Killian dug hungrily into the pancakes. "It's everything."

Susannah sat back and shook her head. "One- or two-word answers, Sean. I swear. What do you mean by 'everything'?"

He gave her a brief look. He was really enjoying the buckwheat pancakes. "It's been a long time since I was in a home, not a house," he told her between bites.

She ate slowly, listening closely not only to what he said, but also to how he said it. "So, home life appeals to you after all?"

He raised his brows.

"I thought," Susannah offered, "that you were a rolling stone that gathered no moss. A man with wanderlust in his soul."

He refused to hold her warm gaze. "Home means everything to me." The pancakes disappeared in a hurry, and the bacon quickly followed. Killian took his steaming cup of coffee and tipped his chair back on two legs. The kitchen fragrances lingered like perfume, and birds sang cheerfully outside the screen door, enhancing his feeling of contentment. Susannah looked incredibly lovely, and Killian thought he was in heaven—or as close as the likes of him was ever going to get to it.

Sipping her coffee, Susannah risked a look at Killian. "To me, a house is built of walls and beams. A home is built with love and dreams. You said you were from Ireland. Were you happy over there?"

Uncomfortable, Killian shrugged. "Northern Ireland isn't exactly a happy place to live." He shot her a hard look. "I learned early on, Susannah, the danger of caring about someone too much, because they'd be ripped away from me."

It felt as if a knife were being thrust down through Susannah. She gripped the delicate cup hard between her hands. "But what—"

With a shrug, Killian tried to cover up his own unraveling emotions. Gruffly he said, "That was the past—there's no need to rehash it. This is the present."

Pain for Killian settled over Susannah. She didn't know what had happened to him as a child, but his words "the danger of caring about someone too much" created a knot in her stomach.

Finishing her coffee, Susannah quietly got up and gathered the plates and flatware. At the counter, she began washing the dishes in warm, soapy water.

Killian rose and moved to where Susannah stood. He spotted a towel hanging on a nail and began to dry the dishes as she rinsed them.

"You're upset."

"No."

"You don't lie well at all. Your voice is a dead giveaway—not to mention those large, beautiful eyes of yours." No one could have been more surprised than Killian at what had just transpired. He hadn't meant to allude to the tragedy. Her empathy was touching, but Killian knew that to feel another person's pain at that depth was dangerous. Why didn't Susannah shield herself more from him?

Avoiding his sharpened gaze, Susannah concentrated on washing the dishes. "It's just that, well, you seem to carry a lot of pain." She inhaled shakily.

"I told you the secrets I carried weren't good ones," he warned her darkly.

"Yes, you did...." she agreed softly.

Disgusted with himself, Killian muttered, "Face it, life isn't very nice."

Susannah's hands stilled in the soothing water. Lifting her chin, she met and held his stormy gaze. "I don't believe that. There's always hope," she challenged.

With a muffled sound, Killian suppressed the curse that rose to his lips. Susannah didn't deserve his harsh side, his survival reflexes. "*Hope* isn't a word I recognize."

"What about dreams?"

His smile was deadly. Cynical. "Dreams? More like nightmares, colleen."

There was no way to parry the grim finality of his view of the world—at least not yet. Susannah softened her voice. "Well, perhaps the time you spend here will change your mind."

"A month or so in Eden before I descend back into hell? Be careful, Susannah. You don't want to invest anything in me. I live in hell. I don't want to pull you into it."

A chill moved through her. His lethal warning sounded as if it came from the very depths of his injured, untended soul. Killian was like a wounded animal— hurting badly, lashing out in pain. Rallying, Susannah determined not to allow Killian to see how much his warning had shaken her.

"Well," she went on with forced lightness, "you'll probably be terribly bored sooner or later. In the end, you'll be more than ready to leave."

Killian scowled as he continued to dry the flatware one piece at a time. "We'll see" was all he'd say. He'd said enough. *Too much.* The crestfallen look in Susannah's eyes made him want to cry. Cry! Struck by his cruelty toward her, Killian would have done anything to take back his words. Susannah had gone through enough hell of her own without him dumping his sordid past on her, too.

"What's on the list this morning?" he demanded abruptly.

Susannah tried to gather her strewn, shocked feelings. "Weeding the garden. I try to do it during the morning hours, while it's still cool. We have to pick the slugs off, weed and check the plants for other insects. That sort of thing.'' Again, tension vibrated around Killian, and it translated to her. She knew there was a slight wobble in her strained tone. Had Killian picked it up? Susannah didn't have the courage to glance at him as he continued drying dishes.

A huge part of Susannah wanted to help heal his wounds. Her heart told her she had the ability to do just that. Hadn't she helped so many children win freedom from crosses they'd been marked to bear for life? She'd helped guide them out of trapped existences with color, paints and tempera. Each year she saw a new batch of special children, and by June they were smiling far more than when they'd first come to class. No, there was hope for Killian, whether he wanted to admit it or not.

Killian methodically pulled the weeds that poked their heads up between the rows of broccoli, cauliflower and tomatoes. A few rows over, Susannah worked, an old straw hat protecting her from the sun's intensity. He worked bareheaded, absorbing energy from the sunlight. Since their conversation in the kitchen that morning, she'd been suspiciously silent, and it needled Killian enormously.

He had to admit, there was something pleasurable about thrusting his hands into the damp, rich soil. Over near the fence, the baby robin that had previously fallen out of its nest chirped loudly for its parents to bring her more food. Killian wore his shoulder holster, housing the Beretta beneath his left arm. Susannah had given him a disgruntled look when he'd put on the shoulder harness, but had said nothing. Just as well. He didn't want her getting any ideas about saving him and his dark, hopeless soul. Let her realize who and what he was. That way, she'd keep her distance. He wasn't worth saving.

Susannah got off her hands and knees. She took the handful of slugs she'd found and placed them on the other side of the fence, under the fruit tree, below the robin's nest. Not believing in insecticides, she tried to use nature's balance to maintain her gardens. The robins would feed the slugs to their babies, completing the natural cycle.

Usually her work relaxed her, but this morning the silence between her and Killian was terribly strained, and she had no idea how to lessen it. She glanced over at Killian, who worked in a crouch, pulling weeds, his face set. Every once in a while, she could feel him surveying the area, his guarded watchfulness evident.

Susannah took off her hat, wiped her damp brow with the back of her hand and walked toward the house. She wanted to speak to him, but she felt that cold wall around him warning her to leave him alone.

Entering the kitchen, Susannah realized just how lonely was the world Killian lived in. It was sheer agony for him to talk. Each conversation was like pulling teeth—painful and nerve-racking. Tossing her straw hat on the table, Susannah poured two tall, icy glasses of lemonade.

Killian entered silently, catching her off guard. Susannah's heart hammered briefly. His face was glistening with sweat, but his mouth was no longer pursed, she noted, and his eyes looked lighter—almost happy, if she was reading him accurately.

"Come on, sit down. You've earned a rest," she said.

The lemonade disappeared in a hurry as he gulped it down and nodded his thanks.

"More?"

"Please." Killian sat at the table, his hands folded on top of it, watching Susannah move with her incredible natural grace.

With another nod of appreciation, he took the newly filled glass but this time didn't gulp it down. He glanced at his watch. "I hadn't realized two hours had gone by."

Susannah smiled tentatively. Casting about for some safe topic, she waved at the colorful pictures on the kitchen walls. "My most recent class did these. Some of the kids are mentally retarded, others have had deformities since birth. They range in intellectual age from about six to twelve. I love drawing them out of their shells." And then, deliberately holding his gaze, she added, "They find happiness by making the most of what they have." Susannah pointed again to the tempera paintings that she'd had framed. "I keep these because they're before-and-after drawings," she confided warmly.

"Oh?"

"The paintings on this wall were done when the children first came to class in September. The paintings on the right were done just before school was out in June. Take a look."

Killian rose and went over to the paintings, his glass of lemonade in hand. One child's first painting was dark and shadowy—the one done nine months later was bright and sunny in comparison. Another painting had a boy in a wheelchair looking glum. In the next, he was smiling and waving to the birds overhead. Killian glanced at Susannah over his shoulder. "Telling, aren't they?"

"Very."

He studied the others in silence. Finally he turned

around, came back to the table and sat down. "You must have the patience of Job."

With a little laugh, Susannah shook her head. "For me, it's a wonderful experience watching these kids open up and discover happiness—some of them for the first time in their lives." Her voice took on more feeling. "Just watching them blossom, learn to trust, to explore, means everything to me. It's a real privilege for me."

"I guess some people pursue happiness and others create it. I envy those kids." Killian swallowed convulsively, feeling uncomfortably as if her sparkling eyes were melting his hardened heart—and his hardened view of the world. Her lower lip trembled under the intensity of his stare, and the overwhelming need to reach over, to pull Susannah to his chest and kiss her until she molded to him with desire, nearly unstrung his considerable control. If he stayed at the table, he'd touch her. He'd kiss the hell out of her.

Susannah wanted Sean to get used to the idea that he, too, could have happiness. "You know, what we did out there this morning made you happy. I could see it in your eyes. Your face is relaxed. Isn't that something?"

Leaving her side abruptly, Killian placed his empty glass on the counter, a little more loudly than necessary. "What's next? What do you want me to do?"

Shocked, Susannah watched the hardness come back into Killian's features. She'd pushed him too far. "I... Well, the screen in my bedroom could be fixed...." she said hesitantly.

"Then what?" A kind of desperation ate at Killian. He didn't dare stay in such close proximity to Susannah. The more she revealed of herself, the more she trusted him with her intimate thoughts and feelings, the more she threatened his much-needed defenses. Dammit, she trusted too easily!

"Then lunch. I was going to make us lunch, and then I thought we'd pick the early snow peas and freeze them this afternoon," she said.

"Fine."

Blinking, Susannah watched Killian stalk out of the kitchen. The tension was back in him; he was like a trap that begged to be sprung. Shakily she drew in a breath, all too clearly recognizing that the unbidden hunger in his eyes was aimed directly at her. Suddenly she felt like an animal in a hunter's sights.

Chapter Six

"Look out!" Killian's shriek careened around the darkened bedroom. He jerked himself upright, his hand automatically moving for the pistol. Cool metal met his hot, sweaty fingers. Shadows from the past danced around him. His breathing was ragged and chaotic. The roar of rifles and the blast of mortars flashed in front of his wide, glazed eyes as he sat rigidly in bed. A hoarse cry, almost a sob, tore from his contorted lips.

He made a muffled sound of disgust. With the back of his hand, Killian wiped his eyes clear of tears. Where was he? What room? What country? Peru? Algeria? Laos? *Where?*

His chest rising and falling rapidly, Killian narrowed his eyes as he swung his gaze around the quiet room. It took precious seconds for him to realize that he was here, in Kentucky. Cursing softly, he leaped out of bed, his pajama bottoms damp with sweat and clinging to his

taut body. Shaking. He was shaking. It was nothing new.
Often he would shake for a good hour after coming
awake. More important, the nightmare hadn't insidiously
kept control of him after waking. The flashbacks frightened him for Susannah's sake.

Laying the pistol down, Killian rubbed his face savagely, trying to force the remnants of the nightmare
away. What he needed to shock him back into the present was a brutally cold shower. That and a fortifying cup
of coffee. Forcing himself to move on wobbly legs, he
made it to the bathroom. Fumbling for the shower faucet,
he found it and turned it on full-force.

Later, he padded down the darkened hall in his damp,
bare feet, a white towel draped low around his hips. His
watch read 3:00 a.m.—the same time he usually had the
nightmares. Shoving damp strands of hair off his brow,
he rounded the corner. Shock riveted him to the spot.

"I thought you might like some coffee," Susannah
whispered unsteadily. She was standing near the counter
in a long white cotton nightgown. Her hands were
clasped in front of her. "That and some company?"

Rubbing his mouth with the back of his hand, Killian
stood tautly, his heightened senses reeling with impact.
Moonlight lovingly caressed Susannah, the luminescence outlining her slender shape through her thin cotton
gown. The lace around the gown's boat neck emphasized
her collarbones and her slender neck. He gulped and
allowed his hand to fall back to his side. Susannah's face
looked sleepy, her eyes dreamy with a softness that
aroused a longing in him to bury himself in her, hotly,
deeply. She remained perfectly still as he devoured her
with his starving gaze.

There was fear in her eyes, mixed with desire and
longing. Killian not only saw it in the nuances of her

fleeting expression, but sensed it, as well. Like a wolf too long without a mate, he ached to claim her as his own. And then, abruptly he laughed at himself. Who was he kidding? She was all the things he was not. She had hope. She believed in a future filled with dreams. Hell, she gave handicapped children back the chance to dream.

"It's not a good time to be around me," he rasped.

Inhaling shakily, Susannah nodded. "It's a chance I'll take." Never had she seen a man of such power, intensity and beauty as Killian. He stood in the kitchen doorway, the towel draped casually across his lean hips, accentuating his near nakedness.

Killian's shoulders were proudly thrown back, and his muscles were cleanly delineated. His chest was covered with hair that headed like an arrow down his long torso and flat belly. The dark line of hair disappeared beneath the stark whiteness of the towel, but still, little was left to the imagination. Susannah gulped convulsively.

Susannah's skin tingled where his hungry gaze had swept across her. Trying to steady her desire for him, she noticed that her hands shook as she turned to put the coffee into the pot.

It had taken everything for Susannah to tear her gaze from his overwhelming masculine image. "I—I heard you scream. At first I thought it was a nightmare I was having, and then I realized it wasn't me screaming. It was you."

Killian remained frozen in the doorway. The husky softness of Susannah's voice began to dissolve some of the terror that seemed to twist within him like a living being.

She shrugged. "I didn't know what to do."

"You did the right thing," he said raggedly. He

forced himself to move toward the table. Gripping the chair, he sat down, afraid he might fall down if he didn't. His knees were still weak from the virulent nightmare. He looked up at Susannah. "Didn't I tell you that I wasn't worth the risk? Look at you. You're shaking." And she was. He wanted desperately to reassure her somehow, but he couldn't.

Rubbing her arms, Susannah nodded. "I'll be okay."

Killian felt like hell. He'd scared her, triggered the fear she'd barely survived months ago, and he knew it. "I walk around in a living death every day of my life. You don't deserve to be around it—or me."

The sweat glistening on Killian's taut muscles spoke to her of the hell he was still caught up in. Susannah forced herself to move through her fear and cross to his side. She reached out and gently laid her hands on his shoulders.

Killian groaned. Her touch was so warm, so steadying.

"Just sit there," she whispered in a strained tone. "Let me work the knots out of your shoulders. You're so tense."

He opened his mouth to protest, but the kneading quality of her strong, slender hands as they worked his aching muscles stopped him. Instead of speaking, he closed his eyes and gradually began to relax. With each sliding, coaxing movement of her fingers along his skin, a little more of the fear he carried with him dissolved. Eventually he allowed himself to sag against the chair.

"Lean on me," Susannah coaxed. She pressed her hand to his sweaty brow and guided his head against her.

How easy it was to have his head cushioned against her as her hands moved with confidence on his shoulders and neck. A ragged sigh issued from him, and he closed his eyes, trusting her completely.

"Good," she crooned softly, watching his short, spiky lashes droop closed. Even his mouth, once a harsh line holding back a deluge of emotions, gradually relaxed.

Susannah felt the steel-cable strength of his muscles beneath her hands. He was built like a cougar—lean and lithe. Her feelings were alive, bright and clamoring not only for acknowledgment, but for action. The thrill of touching Killian, of having him trust her this much, was dizzying and inviting. Susannah ached to lean forward and place a soft kiss on his furrowed brow. How much pain did this man carry within him?

As she stood in the moonlit kitchen with him, massaging his terror and tension away, Susannah realized that Killian's life must have been one of unending violence.

"Two years ago," she said unsteadily as she smoothed away the last of the rigidity from his now-supple muscles, "I had a little boy, Stevey, in my class. He was mentally retarded and had been taken from his home by Social Services. He was only eight years old, and he was like a frightened little animal. The social worker told me that his father was an alcoholic and his mother was on drugs. They both beat up on him."

Killian's eyes snapped open.

"I'm telling you this for a reason," Susannah whispered, her hands stilling on his shoulders. "At first, Stevey would only crawl into a corner and hide. Gradually I earned his trust, and then I got him to draw. The pictures told me so much about what he'd endured, what he'd suffered through, alone and unprotected. There wasn't a day that went by that I didn't cry for him.

"Stevey taught me more about trust and love than any

other person in my life ever has. Gradually, throughout the year that he was in my class, he came to life. He truly blossomed, and it was so breathtaking. He learned to smile, then to laugh. His new foster parents love him deeply, and that helped bring him out of the terror and humiliation he'd endured.

"I saw this frightened, beaten child have enough blind faith in another human being to rally and reach out just once more. Stevey had a kind of courage that I feel is the rarest kind in the world, and the hardest to acquire." Susannah reached out and stroked Killian's damp hair. "Stevey knew only violence, broken trust and heartache. But something in him—his spirit, if you will—had the strength to work through all of that and embrace others who truly loved him and accepted him for who he was."

Killian released a shaky breath, wildly aware of Susannah's trembling fingers lightly caressing his hair. Did she realize what she was doing? Did she know that if she kept it up he'd take her hard and fast, burying himself in her hot depths? Longing warred with control. He eased out of her hands and sat up.

"Why don't you get us that coffee?" he said. His voice was none too steady, and it had a sandpaper rasp. Glancing up as Susannah walked past him, he saw her face. How could she look so damned angelic when all he felt was his blood pounding like a dam ready to burst?

Miraculously, the nightmare and its contents had disappeared beneath Susannah's gentle, questing hands. Killian's eyes slitted as he studied her at the counter, where she was pouring the coffee. What was it about her? Grateful that she wasn't looking at him, Killian struggled to get his raging need back under control. Usually he had no problem disconnecting himself from his volcanic emotions, but Susannah aroused him to a white heat of desire.

With trembling hands, Susannah set the coffee before Killian, sharply conscious of his perusal of her. His words, his warning, kept thrumming through her. She felt danger and intensity surrounding them. Did she have the courage to stay? To be there for Killian? Forcing herself to look up, she met and held his blue gaze, a gaze that was hooded with some unknown emotion that seemed to melt her inwardly.

Gulping, she sat down at his elbow, determined not to allow him to scare her away. Right now, her heart counseled her, he needed a friend, someone he could talk with.

Killian sat there thunderstruck. Susannah couldn't be this naive—she must realize how he wanted her. Yet she sat down next to him, her face filled with determination as she sipped her steaming coffee. Angry, and feeling at war within himself, he snapped irritably, ''Why don't you go back to bed?''

''Because you need me here.''

His eyes widened enormously.

Prepared to risk everything, Susannah met and held his incredulous gaze. ''You need a friend, Sean.''

His fingers gripped his cup, and he stared down at the black contents. ''Talking is the last thing I want to do right now.''

She tried to absorb his brutal, angry words. ''What, then?''

He snapped a look at her. ''Get away from me, Susannah, while you can. Stop trying to get close. I'm not Stevey. I'm a grown man, with a grown man's needs. You're in danger. Stay, and I can't answer for what I might do.''

There was such anguish in his raspy words, and she felt his raw need of her. She sat up, her fingers releasing the cup. "No, you aren't like Stevey," Susannah whispered unsteadily. "But you are wounded—and in need of a safe haven."

With a hiss, Killian jerked to his feet, the chair nearly tipping over from the swiftness of his movement. "Wounded animals can bite those who try to help them!" Breathing harshly, he walked to the other end of the kitchen. "Dammit, Susannah, stay away from me. You've already been hurt by a man who nearly killed you." He struck his chest. "I can hurt you in so many different ways. Is that what you want? Do you want me to take you, to bury myself in you, to make night and day merge into one until you don't know anything except me, my arms, my body and—"

With a muffled sound, Killian spun around, jerked open the screen door and disappeared into the night. If he didn't go, he was going to take Susannah right there on the hard wooden floor. The primal blood was racing through him, blotting out reason, disintegrating his control. As he stalked off the porch, he knew she was an innocent in this. She was the kind of woman he'd always dreamed of—but then, dreams never could stand the test of harsh daylight.

Who was he kidding? Killian walked swiftly, his feet and ankles soon soaked from the trail he made through the dewy grass. Moonlight shifted across him in unending patterns as he continued his blind walk through the orchard. He had to protect Susannah from himself—at all costs. She didn't deserve to get tangled up with his kind. It could only end in disaster.

Gradually he slowed his pace as his head began to clear. The night was cool, but not chilly. He realized with disgust that he'd left without his weapon, and that he'd left Susannah wide open to attack if someone was prowling around. As he halted and swiftly shifted his awareness to more external things, he acknowledged that, although unarmed, he was never defenseless. No, he'd been taught to kill a hundred different ways without need of any kind of weapon.

He stood in the middle of the orchard, scowling. Bats dipped here and there, chasing after choice insects that he couldn't see. The old homestead was a quarter of a mile away, looking broken down and in dire need of paint, and also the love and care it would take to put it back in good repair. Killian laughed harshly. Wasn't he just like that old house? The only difference was that the scars he wore were mostly carried on the inside, where no one could see them. No one except Susannah. Why couldn't she be like everyone else and see only the tough exterior he presented to the world?

Killian stood there a long time, mulling over the story she'd told him about the little boy named Stevey. The boy deserved Susannah's loving care. She was the right person to help coax him out of his dark shell of fear. Her words, soft and strained, floated back to him: "You are wounded—and need a safe haven."

How long he stood there thinking about their conversation, he didn't know. When he glanced at his watch, it was 4:00 a.m. Forcing himself, he walked slowly back to the homestead. As he walked, he prayed—something he rarely did—that Susannah had had enough sense to go back to bed. What would he do if she was still up and waiting for him? His mouth was dry, and he wiped at it with the back of his hand. He didn't know.

Susannah was out in the extensive rose garden, giving the colorful flowers the special food that helped them to bloom. It was nearly noon, and she was hot, even though she wore her straw hat, a sleeveless white blouse and a threadbare pair of jeans. Her mind and heart centered on Killian. She'd gone back to bed around four, and had promptly plummeted into a deep, restful sleep. When she'd gotten up this morning at six, his bedroom door had been shut. Was he in there? Had he gone somewhere else? Susannah didn't know, and she hadn't had the courage to find out.

Taking her one-gallon bucket and the box of rose food, she went back over to the hose to mix the ingredients for the next rosebush. The air was heavy with the wonderful fragrance of the flowering bushes. The rose garden sat on the southern side of the homestead, where there was the most light. There was no fence around it, and the bushes stretched for nearly a quarter of a mile.

Susannah hunched over the bucket and poured the rose food into the pooling water, stirring it with her hand. The water turned a pretty pink color. Pink always reminded her of love, she thought mildly. Then Killian's harsh warning pounded back through her. He *was* dangerous, she thought, feeling the heat of longing flow through her—dangerous to her heart, to her soul. Killian had the ability to touch her very essence. How, she didn't know. She only knew he had that capacity, and no other man she'd ever met had been able to touch her so deeply.

Shutting off the faucet, Susannah set the food aside and hefted the gallon bucket to carry it to the next rosebush, a beautiful lavender one with at least ten blossoms. No longer could she keep from entertaining the idea of loving Killian. Her dreams had turned torrid toward morning, and she vividly recalled images of his hands caressing her body, his mouth ravishing her with wild abandon, meeting her willing, equally hungry lips.

She poured the bucket's contents into the well around the rosebush. What did she want? *Killian.* Why? Because... Susannah straightened and put the bucket aside. She pulled out a pair of scissors and began pruning off old blooms. Was it to help him heal? Yes. To show him that another person could trust him fully, fearlessly, even if he didn't trust himself? Yes. To give him her love in hopes that he might overcome his own fear of loving and losing—and to love her? *Yes.*

Stymied, she stood there, her hands cupped around one of the large lavender roses. She leaned forward, inhaling the delicate fragrance. Life was so beautiful. Why couldn't Killian see that? As she studied the many-petaled bloom, Susannah ached for him. She knew she had the ability to show him the beauty of life. But what then? He would be in her life only long enough to catch the killer who might be stalking her. He'd repeatedly warned her that he wasn't worth loving.

But he was. With a sigh, Susannah pocketed the scissors, picked up the bucket and headed back to the faucet. Her stomach growled, and she realized that it was nearly lunchtime and she was hungry. Placing all the gardening tools near the spigot, Susannah walked back to the homestead. Would Killian be there? And if he was, would he be up yet? Fear mingled with need of him inside her. How would she handle their next confrontation?

Killian's head snapped up at the sound of someone's approach. He was at the kitchen cabinets, searching through them for something to eat. He'd just gotten up and taken a scaldingly hot shower to awaken, then gotten dressed in a dark blue short-sleeved shirt and jeans. He felt like someone had poleaxed him.

Susannah opened the screen door and took off her straw hat. When she saw him, she hesitated.

Killian glared at her.

"Hungry?" she asked, hoping to hide the tension she felt. She continued into the room and placed her hat on the table.

"Like a bear," he muttered, moving away from the counter.

Susannah kept plenty of distance between them. She noticed the stormy quality in his blue eyes, and her nerves grew taut. Scared, but aware that Killian needed courage from her, not cowardice, Susannah said firmly, "Have a seat and I'll fix you what I'm going to have: a tuna sandwich, sweet pickles and pretzels."

Sitting down, Killian tried to soften his growly bad humor. "Okay."

"Coffee or iced tea?"

"I don't care."

Gathering her dissolving courage, Susannah said, "I think you need a strong cup of coffee. Are you always like this when you wake up?" Killian looked fiercely unhappy, his eyes bleak, with dark circles under them. It was obvious he hadn't slept well after their verbal battle last night.

Killian refused to watch her as she moved to the icebox. "I told you I was a bastard."

She forced a laugh and brought bread and a bowl of prepared tuna to the counter. "You really aren't, you know. You're just grouchy because you lost some sleep last night and you haven't had your coffee yet."

"Maybe you're right." Killian watched her hungrily, every movement, every sway of her hips. Susannah had her sable hair swept into a ponytail, as usual, and it shone with each step she took. Her face glowed with the good health of a woman who loved the outdoors. Unhappily Killian folded his hands on the table. Why wouldn't Susannah heed his warning? Why didn't she believe that he was a bastard, someone capable of hurting her badly? He didn't want to hurt her—not her, of all people.

Humming softly, Susannah made coffee, prepared the sandwiches and put together a wholesome lunch. When she turned around, Killian's rugged profile still reflected his unhappiness. He sat tensely, his mouth pursed.

"Here, start on the sandwich. Bears don't do well on empty stomachs."

Grateful for her teasing, he took the sandwich and began eating. But he didn't taste it—all he was aware of was his own intense suffering, and Susannah's sunlit presence. She chased away his gloom, that terrible shadow that always hovered over him like a vulture ready to rip out what little was left of his heart.

Placing the coffee before him, Susannah took her usual seat at his elbow. Her heart was hammering so hard in her chest that she feared Killian might hear it. As she forced herself to eat, the kitchen fell into a stilted silence.

"Earlier, I went down to visit my parents," she offered after a moment, trying to lessen the tension. "They told me my school had called, that the principal wanted me to consider coming back to work sooner." She picked up a pickle and frowned. "I really miss teaching. I have a new class of kids that I've never seen." She watched Killian raise his head, his blue gaze settling on her. Her pulse raced. Trying to continue to sound nonchalant, she added, "So I called Mr. Gains back—that's the principal—and told him I'd like to return."

"When?" The word came out sharp.

Wiping her hands on a napkin, Susannah said, "Next Monday. I feel well enough now."

Relief shattered through Killian. That, and terrible disappointment. Some stupid part of him actually had held out hope that Susannah would stay, would persevere with him and reach into his heart. Putting down the sandwich, he reached for the coffee. Gulping down a swallow, he burned his mouth.

"Does that mean you're moving back into town? Into your house?"

"I—I don't know." Susannah managed a small shrug. "I really miss my kids, Sean. But I don't know if I'm ready to be alone. Do you know what I mean?"

He nodded and dropped his gaze. "Yeah, I know what you mean."

"I've been doing a lot of thinking this morning, and I guess I'll try to go to work full-time. Mr. Gains said if I have any problems I can split the class and work only half days for a while, until I get back into the swing of things."

"Half a day is enough for now."

She shrugged, not sure.

"Susannah, you're still healing."

And the other half of the day would be spent here, in Killian's intense presence, reminding her constantly of her need of him as a man, a lover. "I don't know," she confided in a low voice.

He set the coffee cup down a little more loudly than he'd intended. Susannah winced. "You aren't ready for all of that yet. You've got to pace yourself. Comas do funny things to people. What if you get flashbacks? Periods of vertigo? Or what if you blank out? All those things could happen under stress. And going back into that classroom *is* stress.''

Susannah stared at him, feeling his raw intensity, his care. ''Being here with you is stress, too, Sean.''

Gripping the cup, he growled, ''I suppose it is. I'm not the world's best person to be near. Around you, I shoot off my mouth, and look what it's done.''

A soft smile touched her lips, and she leaned over and rested her hand on his arm. ''Sean, some kinds of stress aren't bad. I like talking with you, sharing with you. I don't consider it bad or harmful. I feel shutting up and retreating is far more damaging.''

''You would,'' Killian muttered, but he really didn't mean it. Just the cool, steadying touch of her fingers on his arm sent waves of need pulsing through him.

''Everyone needs someone,'' Susannah whispered. ''Your needs are no different than anyone else's.''

He cocked his head. ''Don't be so sure.''

She smiled a little, feeling danger swirling around her. ''I'm betting your bark is worse than your bite.''

''Oh? Was that the way it was with Stevey?''

Susannah forced herself to release him. ''At first, every time I came near him, he lashed out at me.''

''And what did you do?''

''I'd lean down, pull him against me and just hold him.''

Killian shut his eyes and drew in a deep, shaky breath. ''I don't know what to make of you, Susannah. Why would anyone put themselves in the line of fire just to let someone else know that they weren't going to be hurt again?'' He opened his eyes, searching her thoughtful gray ones.

''I believe we're all healers, Sean. We not only have

the ability to heal ourselves, but to heal others, too. Stevey wanted to be healed. Each time I approached him, he struck out less and less, until finally, one day, he opened his arms to me. It was such a beautiful, poignant moment.''

''He trusted you,'' Killian said flatly.

''Yes, he did.''

''You're a catalyst.''

''So are you,'' she said wryly, meeting his wary eyes.

Uncomfortable, Killian wanted to shift the conversation back to her. ''So you're going to try class for a full day next Monday?''

''Yes.''

''All right, I'll drive you to work and hang around, if you don't mind. I want to get the layout of your school, your classroom. If they've got a contract out on you— and we still don't know if they do or not—I want to have that school, its entrances and exits, in my head in case something comes down.''

She sat back, surprised. ''Do you really think I'm in danger?''

''Until I can prove otherwise,'' Killian said roughly, ''I'm assuming there's a hit man out there somewhere, just waiting for you. What you can't comprehend is that a contract means anytime, anywhere. A killer doesn't care where the hit takes place. He's been paid to do a job, and he's going to do it. He doesn't care if other lives get in the way.''

The brutal harshness of his words sank into Susannah with a frightening chill. ''What about my kids? Are they safe?''

Killian shrugged. ''I don't know, Susannah. Hit men usually try for a clean one-shot deal. They don't like putting themselves in a messy situation where they could get caught.'' He saw the color drain from her face. ''Look,'' he added harshly, ''let me worry about the possibility of a hit man, okay? I know where to look, I know their usual methods. You'll be safe. And so will your kids,'' he added, softening his voice for her sake.

Getting up, Susannah moved to the counter. ''I—I just didn't realize, Sean....''

''I didn't want you to,'' he muttered. ''It's fairly easy to watch you here, at the farm. But the moment you start driving to work, shopping and doing all the other things normal people do daily, you become more of a target-rich opportunity.''

She shivered at the military jargon. *Target-rich opportunity.* Gripping the cool porcelain of the double sink, she hung her head. ''I can't—I won't—live my life in fear, Sean.''

''Well, then, there's a price to pay for that kind of decision. You deserve to know the chances you're taking. You could stay here, at the farm, and flushing out the hit man would be easier—but it would probably take longer.''

Susannah turned around and held his searching gaze. Crossing her arms in front of her, she shook her head. ''No. If there really is a contract out on me, let's find out. I'd rather get it over with.''

Killian understood only too well. ''You're courageous,'' he said, and he meant it.

''No,'' Susannah told him, her voice quavering, ''I'm scared to death. But I miss the kids. I miss teaching.''

Killian slowly rose and pushed back his chair. He brought over his now-empty plate and coffee cup. ''Okay, Monday you go to work, but I'll be like a shadow, Susannah. Everywhere you go, I go. I'll explain the situation to your principal. He may decide not to let you come back after he knows the potential danger.''

"Then I'll stay away," Susannah whispered. "I don't want to endanger my kids. They're innocent."

He set the dishes in the sink and turned to her. Placing his hands on her slumped shoulders, he rasped, "So are you."

Chapter Seven

Uneasy, Killian walked the now-quiet halls of Marshall Elementary School, which was located near the edge of the small town of Glen. All of the children, from grades one through six, were in their classes, the wood-and-glass door to each room closed, and the teachers were busy with their charges. Killian's heart automatically swung back to Susannah, who was happily back at work. The meeting with the principal had gone well. Killian had actually expected him to turn down Susannah's request after hearing about the possibilities.

The principal obviously didn't believe there could be a contract out on Susannah. Nor did she. They didn't want to, Killian thought grimly as he padded quietly down the highly polished floor of an intersecting hall lined with metal lockers.

Dressed in jeans, a tan polo shirt and a light denim jacket that hid his shoulder holster, Killian had a small blueprint layout of the school and its adjacent buildings. He'd already been in Susannah's room and met her ten handicapped students. The children ranged in age from seven to twelve. He hadn't stayed long—he was more interested in the deadly possibilities of his trade.

At lunch, he planned to meet Susannah and her class in the cafeteria. A story had been devised to explain Killian's presence in Susannah's classroom: He was monitoring the course, a teacher from California who was going to set up a similar program out there. Everyone, including the faculty at the morning meeting, had accepted the explanation without reaction. Killian had discovered that Susannah had, from time to time, had teachers from other states come and watch how she conducted her class, because the children had developed more quickly than usual as a result of her unique teaching methods.

The lunch bell rang as Killian finished circling on the map in red ink those areas where a contract killer might hide. Luckily, there weren't many. He missed Susannah's presence, and he hoped to meet her on the way to the cafeteria with her charges.

Susannah's heart sped up at the sight of Killian moving slowly through the hall, which was filled with hundreds of laughing and talking children. She saw his dark eyes lighten as he met and held her gaze, and she smiled, feeling the warmth of his heated look.

Killian moved to the wall of lockers and waited for her.

"Hi," she said breathlessly.

Susannah's eyes shone with a welcome that reached through Killian's heavy armor and touched his heart. An ache began in his chest, an ache that startled Killian. How easily she could touch him with just a look and a soft smile. "How you doing?" Killian fell in step just behind her.

"Fine." Susannah beamed. "It's so good to be back, Sean! I feel like my life's finally coming back together again." Susannah looked tenderly at Freddy, a seven-year-old boy with Down's syndrome who walked at her side, his hand firmly gripping hers. "I really missed my kids," she quavered, looking up at Killian.

Killian had his doubts about Susannah returning to work, about how it might affect her, but he said nothing. Freddy gave her a worshipful look of unqualified love. No wonder Susannah liked working with these special children. They gave fully, in the emotional sense, Killian noted with surprise.

"Are you done with your walk around the school?" Susannah asked as her little flock of children surrounded her. The double doors to the cafeteria were open. She guided her group through them and down the stairs.

"Yeah, I'm done. What can I do to help?"

She smiled and pointed to several long tables with chairs lined up on either side. "See that area?"

"Yes."

"After we get the kids seated, some of the help will bring over their lunches. You go ahead and go through the cafeteria line and meet me over there. I'm going to be pretty busy the next twenty minutes."

Killian sat with his back to the wall. For security reasons, he was glad that the cafeteria was in the basement with no windows. He didn't taste his food—chili, a salad and an apple—or the coffee he'd poured for himself. Instead, he watched Susannah. She wore a bright yellow cotton skirt today, a feminine-looking white short-sleeved blouse, and sandals. Her hair was loose, flowing over her back. She looked beautiful. And it was clear...that there wasn't one child who didn't adore her and positively glow when rewarded with her smile, a touch of her hand, or a brief kiss on the brow.

"Finally!" Susannah sat down with her tray of food. She tucked several stray strands of hair behind her ear and smiled across the table at him.

"You've got your hands full," Killian commented. Lunch was only forty-five minutes long, and Susannah had been up and helping her kids for close to half an hour. Now she'd have to gulp her food down.

"I love it! I wouldn't have it any other way."

Killian quietly suffered the din in the cafeteria, his senses heightened and pummeled at the same time. He nodded to Susannah, but his concentration was on the faculty. There was a possibility that the hit man could pose as a teacher, slip in and try to kill Susannah in the school. All morning he'd been committing faculty faces to memory, his gaze roving restlessly across the huge, noisy cafeteria.

"Well? Did you find what you were looking for?" Susannah asked, eating her chili.

"I located possible sites," Killian said, not wanting to refer directly to the topic for fear of scaring the attentive, listening children who surrounded them. "I'll discuss it with you tonight, when we get home."

With a sigh, Susannah smiled. "Home. It sounds so nice when you say that."

Avoiding her sparkling gaze, which sent a flush of heat sheeting through him, Killian nodded and paid attention to the apple he was eating but not tasting. Home anywhere with Susannah was a dream come true, he decided sourly. Four o'clock couldn't come soon enough because Killian realized he *wanted* time alone with Susannah. Each moment was a precious drop of a dream that, he knew, must someday come to an end. And, like a man lost in the desert, he thirsted for each drop that she gave him simply by being nearby.

"You're exhausted," Killian told Susannah as they worked in the kitchen preparing their dinner. He'd taken on the salad-making duties, and she was frying some steaks.

"Oh, I'm okay. First days are always that way. I'll adjust."

He glanced at her as he cut a tomato deftly with a knife. Susannah had changed into a pair of jeans and a pink sleeveless blouse. She was barefoot. He frowned as he studied her at the stove.

"Maybe you ought to switch to half days for now."

"No... I'll be okay, Sean. It's just that the first days are overwhelming. The children—" she glanced up and met his serious-looking face "—needed reassuring that I wouldn't abandon them. Handicapped children are so sensitized to possible loss of the people they rely on. They live in a very narrow world, and part of their stability is the fixedness of activity within it. If a teacher or a parent suddenly leaves, it's terribly upsetting to them."

"So you were applying Band-Aids all day?"

She grinned. "You might say that. You look a little tired yourself."

With a shrug, Killian placed the two salad bowls on the table near their plates. "A little," he lied. He'd hardly slept at all last night.

"Is the school a viable target?" she asked as she arranged their steaks on the plates.

Killian heard the quaver in her voice. He sat down and said, "There are pros and cons to it. The only place where you're really a target is the school-bus loading and unloading zone. The gym facility across the street is two stories tall—ideal for a hit man to hide in and draw a bead on you.''

Trying to stay calm, Susannah sat down after pouring them each a cup of coffee. Taking a pink paper napkin, she spread it across her lap. ''This is so upsetting, Sean.''

''I know.'' The strain on Susannah's face said it all. Killian wished he wasn't always the bearer of such bad tidings.

''It's not your fault.'' She cut a piece of her steak and gave him a sidelong look. ''Do these men hit quickly?''

''What do you mean?''

''Well, if a contract's been put out on me, will he try to get it done quickly, instead of waiting months to do it?''

''They like to get paid. They'll do it as quickly as possible to collect the balance of the money.''

Susannah pushed some salad around with her fork. ''Have you heard from the police about a possible identification from the sketch I gave you a few days ago?''

''Not yet. I was hoping Morgan or the Lexington police would call me. With any luck,'' Killian said, eating a bite of the succulent steak, ''we'll have more answers by tomorrow at the latest.''

''And if you find out who my attacker is, you'll be able to know whether or not he's part of a larger drug ring?''

''Yes.''

With a sigh, Susannah forced herself to eat. ''I just wish it was over.''

''So I'd be out of your life.''

She gave him a tender look. ''You're something good

that's happened to me, Sean. I don't want you out of my life.''

With a disgruntled look, he growled, ''If I were you, I would.''

As gently as possible, Susannah broached the subject of Meg with him. ''Has your sister had any therapy to help her through the trauma she endured?''

Killian looked up. ''A little.'' He frowned. ''Not enough, as far as I'm concerned. Ian, her fiancé, wants to come back into her life, but Meg is afraid to let it happen.''

Once again Susannah saw the anguish burning in Killian's eyes, anguish and love for his sister. There was no question but that he cared deeply about her. It was sweet to know that he now trusted her enough to reveal a small piece of his real self. Still, she knew she would have to tread lightly if Sean was to remain open and conversant. What had changed in him to make him more accessible? Possibly today at the school, she thought, cutting another piece of meat.

''Ian still loves her?''

Killian's mouth twisted. ''He never stopped.''

Susannah moved back to the stove. ''You sound confused about that. Why?''

''Because Ian is letting his love for her tear him apart years afterward. He won't forget Meg. He refuses to.''

''Love isn't something that dries up and goes away just because there's a tragedy,'' she said gently, passing him the platter of meat.

Killian placed another piece of steak on his plate, then handed the platter back to Susannah. ''If you ask me, love is a special kind of torture. Ian twists in the wind waiting for Meg to take him back.''

''He loves her enough to wait,'' Susannah noted. She

saw Killian's eyes harden, the fork suspended halfway to his mouth.

Glancing at her, he snapped, "Love is nothing but pain. I saw it too many times, too many ways, growing up. I've watched Ian suffer. It's not worth it."

"What? Loving someone?" Susannah stopped eating and held his turbulent gaze.

"Yes."

Treading carefully, she asked, "Does Meg allow Ian back into her life in any form?"

"No, only me. She trusts only me."

"Why won't she allow Ian to help her recover?"

Flatly he responded, "Because Meg is disfigured. She's ugly compared to what she used to look like."

Suffering was all too evident on Killian's hard features. Susannah ached for both him and Meg. "She thinks that if Ian sees her he'll leave her anyway?"

"Yes, I guess so. But Ian knows she's no longer beautiful, and he doesn't care. I tried to tell Meg that, but she won't listen."

"Maybe Ian needs to go to Meg directly and confront her about it."

With a snort, Killian shook his head. "Let's put it this way. Our family—what's left of it, Meg and me—are bullheaded."

"She's not being bullheaded," Susannah said softly. "She's sticking her head in the sand and pretending Ian and his feelings don't count."

Killian moved around uncomfortably in his chair. "Sometimes," he muttered defiantly, "running away is the least of all evils."

Susannah met and held his dark blue gaze. "I don't agree. Having the courage to face the other person is always better. You should tell Ian to go to Meg and talk things out.''

"If Ian knew where she lived, he'd have done that a long time ago.''

She stared at him. "You won't tell him where she lives?''

"How can I? Meg begs me not to. Do you think I'm going to go against her wishes?''

"But,'' Susannah said lamely, "that would help heal the situation, Sean. Ian wouldn't be left feeling so tortured. Meg wouldn't feel so alone.''

Smarting beneath her wisdom, Killian forced his attention back to his plate. He'd lost his appetite. "You're young, Susannah. You're protected. If you'd been kicked around like my family has been, gone through what we've gone through, you wouldn't be so eager for emotional confrontations.''

She felt his panic—and his anger. "I know I'm naive,'' she whispered.

"Life makes you tired,'' Killian rasped. "Try getting hit broadside again and again and see how willing you are to get up and confront it again. Believe me, you'll think twice about it. If Ian's smart, he'll get on with his life and forget Meg.''

The depth of his belief in running and hiding frightened Susannah. How many other women had wanted to love Killian? How many had he left? Upset, she could only say, "If I were Ian, I'd go to Meg. I'd love her enough to find her on my own without your help.''

Killian saw the flash of stubbornness in her eyes, and felt it in her voice. He offered her a twisted, one-cornered smile. "Idealism doesn't make it in this world, and neither does hope. You've got too much of both, Susannah. All they'll do is hurt you in the end.''

* * *

Susannah was getting ready to take a bath around ten that night when the phone rang. Killian was sitting in the living room, reading the newspaper. His head snapped up and his eyes narrowed. Forcing herself to answer the phone, Susannah picked up the receiver.

"Hello?"

"Susannah?"

"Morgan! How are you?"

"I'm fine. Better question is, how are you doing with Killian there?"

She flushed and avoided Killian's interested gaze. "Better," she whispered, suddenly emotional. "Much better."

"Good. Listen, I need to talk to Killian. Can you put him on?"

"Sure. Give Laura and the kids my love, will you?"

"Of course. Are you doing all right physically?"

Susannah heard the guilt in Morgan's voice and knew that he blamed himself in some way for her problems. Her hand tightened on the phone. "I'm improving every day," she promised.

"The headaches?"

Susannah thought for a moment. "Why," she breathed as the realization sank in, "I've had fewer since Killian arrived. Isn't that wonderful?"

"It is."

"I'll put Sean on the phone. Hold on." Susannah held the phone toward Killian. "It's Morgan. He wants to talk to you."

Unwinding from his chair, Killian put the newspaper aside.

Just the touch of Killian's fingers on her own as he took the receiver sent an ache throbbing through Susannah. Sensing that he wanted to be alone to talk to Morgan, Susannah left to take her bath.

Holding the receiver, Killian waited until Susannah was gone. "Morgan?"

"Yes. How's it going?"

"All right," Killian said noncommittally, keeping his voice low. He continued to watch the doorway that Susannah had disappeared through. If the conversation was disturbing, he didn't want her to overhear and become upset. "What's going on?"

"That sketch you sent that Susannah drew?"

"Yes?"

"We've got a positive identification from the FBI. His name is Huey Greaves, and he was a middleman stateside for Santiago's ring. So my hunch was correct—unfortunately. Greaves doubles as a hit man for Santiago whenever another cartel tries to encroach on his territory. The man who was killed was there to pick up drugs that were later found in one of the bus terminal luggage bins. He was from another drug ring—one that's been trying to move in on Santiago's territory."

Killian released a ragged breath, cursing softly. Susannah was in serious danger. "You've given this info to the Lexington police?"

"Yes. They've got an APB out on him. They've also alerted the county sheriff who covers Glen and the Anderson farm."

Grimly Killian gazed around the living room, which was dancing in the shadows created by the two hurricane lamps. "The bastard will hit Susannah."

Morgan sighed. "It's only a matter of time. Santiago—it figures."

"I've got to talk to her about this," Killian rasped. "She's got to know the danger involved. She started teaching today, and under the circumstances I don't think it's a good idea for her to go in tomorrow morning.''

"No," Morgan agreed. "We know from experience that Santiago will go to any lengths. His people wouldn't care if there are children involved. Keep her at the farm, Killian. It's safer for everyone that way."

Killian almost laughed at the irony of the situation. No place was safe for Susannah—not even with him. "Yeah, I'll keep her here."

"You know Glen doesn't have much of a police department. The county sheriff is the only one who can help you if you get into trouble. Get the number and keep it handy. With budget cuts, they only have two patrol cars for the entire county, so don't expect too much. A two-hour delay wouldn't be unusual, Killian. I'm afraid you're really on your own on this one. The county sheriff knows who you are and why you're there, and if they see this guy they'll call to let you know—and send a sheriff's cruiser in your direction as soon as humanly possible."

"Good." At least the police and the FBI were working together on this. Still, chances were that when the hit went down it would be Killian against the killer.

"Stay in touch," Morgan said.

"Thanks, Morgan. I will." Killian scowled as he hung up the phone. He wasn't looking forward to telling Susannah the bad news.

Susannah couldn't sleep. She was restless, tossing and turning on her ancient brass bed. The night air was warm, and she pushed off the sheet. Her watch read 2:00 a.m. It was the phone call from Morgan that had left her sleepless.

With a muffled sound of frustration, Susannah got up. She didn't want to wake Sean. Just the thought of him sent a flurry of need through her as she padded softly down the hall to the kitchen. Perhaps a cup of hot chamomile tea would help settle her screaming nerves so that she could sleep. But, she warned herself, tea wasn't going to stop the simmering desire that had been building in her for days.

Susannah ran a hand through her unbound hair, then opened the cabinet and took out a cup and saucer. Killian had warned her away from him—told her that he was no good for her. Why couldn't she listen to his thinly veiled threat?

"Susannah?"

Gasping, she whirled around, nearly dropping the cup from her hand. Killian stood in the doorway, his drawstring pajamas barely held up by his narrow hips. His eyes were soft with sleep, and his hair was tangled across his brow. Her heart pounding, Susannah released a breath.

"You scared me."

"Sorry," he muttered, any remaining sleepiness torn from him as he studied her in the shadowy moonlight that crossed the kitchen. Her knee-length white gown gave her an angelic look, and the moonlight outlined her body like a lover's caress through the light cotton fabric. The dark frame of hair emphasized the delicateness of her features, especially her parted lips.

"I—I couldn't sleep." She gestured toward the kettle on the stove. "I thought I'd make some chamomile tea."

"Morgan's call upset you?"

"Yes."

Easing into the room, Killian crossed to the table and

sat down. His head was screaming at him to go back to bed, but his heart clamored for her closeness.

"Make me a cup, will you?"

"Sure." Susannah's pulse wouldn't seem to settle down, and she busied herself at the counter, attempting to quell her nervousness. Killian's body was hard and lean. She wondered what it would be like to kiss him, to feel his arms around her.

As Susannah turned, the cups of tea in her hands, the window at the kitchen counter shattered, glass exploding in all directions.

"Get down!" Killian shouted. Launching himself out of his chair, he took Susannah with him as he slammed to the floor. More glass shattered, splintering in rainbow fragments all around them.

Susannah groaned under Killian's weight, her mind spinning with shock. She could hear Killian's harsh breathing, and his cursing, soft and strained. Almost instantly she felt his steely grip on her arms as he dragged her upward and positioned her against the corner cabinets for protection.

Her eyes wide, she took in the harshness in his sweaty features.

"The hit man," he rasped. *Dammit!* He'd left his pistol in the bedroom. He noticed small, bloody cuts on Susannah's right arm.

"But—how?"

Killian shook his head, putting his finger to his lips. Silence was crucial right now. The hit man had to be on the porch. But why the hell hadn't he heard him? Felt him? A hundred questions battered Killian. His senses were now screamingly alert. He had to get to his gun, or they were both dead!

Gripping Susannah's wrist, Killian tugged and motioned for her to follow him. If they couldn't make it to his bedroom, they were finished. The last thing he wanted was Susannah dead. The thought spurred him into action.

Gasping for breath, Susannah scrambled out of the kitchen on her hands and knees. In the darkened hall, Killian jerked her to her feet, shoving her forward and into his room. Instantly he pushed her onto the floor and motioned for her to wriggle beneath the bed and remain there.

Killian's fingers closed over the pistol on the nightstand. The feel of the cool metal was reassuring. Now they had a chance. His eyes narrowed as he studied the window near his bed and the open door to his room.

"Stay down!" he hissed. "Whatever happens, stay here!"

Tears jammed into Susannah's eyes as she looked up into his taut, glistening features. Here was the mercenary. The soldier who could kill. She opened her mouth, then snapped it shut.

"Don't move!" Killian warned. He leaped lightly to his feet, every muscle in his body tense with anticipation. He tugged at the blanket so that it hung off the bed and concealed Susannah's glaringly white nightgown. Swiftly he turned on his heel and moved to the door, his hands wrapped around the pistol that he held high and at the ready.

Killian was angry at himself—angry that he'd dropped his guard because he cared for Susannah. He pressed himself hard against the wall and listened. His nostrils flared to catch any unusual scent. Morgan Trayhern had called him a hound from hell on more than one occasion because of his acutely honed senses. Well, they'd saved his life more than once. Tonight, he had to count on his abilities to save Susannah.

As he ducked out of the entrance and quickly looked up and down the hall, Killian saw no evidence of the hit man. Then a creak of wood made him freeze. There! The kitchen! His heart was a thudding sledgehammer in his chest, his quiet breathing was ragged. The bastard was in the kitchen.

There! Killian heard the crunch of glass. How close to the kitchen doorway was he? He continued down the hall soundlessly, on the balls of his feet. His hands sweaty, beads of perspiration running down his temples, Killian focused like a laser on his quarry. Susannah's killer. Only two more feet and he'd have enough of an angle to peer into the darkened depths of the kitchen. Every muscle in his body stiffened with expectation.

Another crunch of glass. The sound was directional, giving away where the hit man stood. Instantly Killian launched himself forward, flattening himself against the hardwood floor, both hands in front of him, the snout of the Beretta aimed. Seeing the darkened shape of a man move, he squeezed off two shots. The sounds reverberated through the farmhouse. Damn! He'd missed!

The hit man fired back, a silencer on his gun cloaking the sound to light pops. Killian rolled to the left, the door jamb his shield. Wood cracked and splintered as bullets savagely tore at the barrier. His mind working rapidly, Killian counted off the shots. Six. More than likely the bastard had nine bullets in his clip. Then he'd have to reload.

The scrambling over glass continued. Killian kept low. He realized with terror that the bedroom where Susannah was hiding was directly behind the hit man. If

Killian fired, his shots could go through the walls and hit her. Damn!

Breathing hard, his lips pulled away from clenched teeth, Killian grabbed a piece of wood near his bare feet, and threw it into the kitchen.

Two more shots were fired at it in quick succession. Good! Only one more round before he'd have to take precious seconds to reload. Stinging sweat dripped into his eyes, and he blinked it away.

In those seconds, waiting for the hit man to make his move, Killian realized that he loved Susannah. Where had such a crazy idea come from? Tightening his grip on the Beretta, he rose onto one knee, ready to fire.

An explosion of movement occurred in the kitchen. Before Killian could fire, the table was tipped over, slamming against the doorway and spoiling his shot. The screen door was ripped off its hinges as a dark figure scrambled out. The thudding of running feet filled the air.

Cursing roundly, Killian leaped over the table. The son of a bitch! Sprinting onto the porch, Killian saw the hit man fleeing toward the road, where his car must be hidden. Digging his toes into the soft, wet grass, Killian started after him. The direction the hit man was running was in line with the Andersons' farmhouse, not more than a quarter mile away. Killian couldn't risk a stray bullet hitting the house or its occupants.

Running hard, he cut through the orchard. Ahead, he saw a dark blue car. The hit man jerked the door open, disappeared inside and hit the accelerator.

The nondescript car leaped forward, dirt and clods flying up, leaving a screen of dust in its wake. Killian memorized the license plate number before the car was swallowed up by the darkness. Lowering his pistol, he continued to run toward the Anderson residence. He wanted to report the car's license number to the sheriff and call Morgan. More than likely the vehicle was a rental car, and the hit man had signed for it with an alias at an airport—probably Lexington.

Killian's mind spun with options, with necessary procedures that would have to be instituted quickly.

Reaching the house, he wasn't surprised to find the Andersons still asleep, completely unaware of what had just occurred. Susannah's house was nearly a half mile away with plenty of orchard to absorb the sounds of battle.

Breathing hard, Killian entered the house via the kitchen and found the phone there on the wall. Setting his gun nearby on the counter, he shakily dialed the county sheriff. As he waited for someone to answer, his heart revolved back to Susannah. Was she all right? He recalled the cuts to her right arm, caused by the shattering glass. Anger with himself because he hadn't protected her as well as he should have filled Killian. As soon as he'd reported the incident, he'd get back to the house and care for Susannah.

Lying on her belly, Susannah had no idea how long she remained frozen. Her heart was beating hard, and her fingers were dug into the wooden floor. Sean! Was he all right? What had happened? Did she dare risk coming out from beneath the bed to find out? There had been no sound for about fifteen minutes. Her mind was playing tricks on her. Maybe Sean was bleeding to death on the kitchen floor and she didn't know it. Should she move from her hiding place? Should she stay?

She closed her eyes as tears leaked into them. Sean couldn't be dead! He just couldn't! The attack had ripped away her doubts. She loved Killian. It was that simple—and that complicated. Lying there, shaking badly as the adrenaline began to seep out of her bloodstream, she pressed her brow against her hands. Sean had ordered her not to move—no matter what. But how could she remain here? If he was lying wounded somewhere, how could she not move?

With a little cry, Susannah made her decision.

"Susannah?"

Killian! She gasped as he pulled the blanket away. Her eyes widened enormously as he got down on his hands and knees.

"Sean?"

He smiled grimly and reached for her. "Yeah. I'm all right, colleen. Everything's okay. The hit man got away. Come on, crawl out of there."

Susannah discovered how wobbly she was as she got to her feet. Killian gripped her hands.

"I—I don't think I can stand," she quavered, looking up into his dark, sweaty features.

"I'm not too steady myself," he answered with a rasp. He drew Susannah into his arms and brought her against him. The contact with her was shocking. Melting. Killian groaned as she leaned heavily against him, her arms around him, her head against his shoulder.

"Sweet," he whispered, holding her tightly—holding her so hard he was afraid he was going to crush her. The natural scent of her—a fragrant smell, like lilacs—encircled his nostrils. Killian dragged in that scent, life after the odors of death. He felt Susannah shift and lift her head. Without thinking, he cupped her chin and guided her lips to his mouth.

The meeting was fiery, purging. He felt the softness of her lips, felt them flow open, their heat, their moistness overwhelming his heightened senses. Time ceased to exist. All he was aware of, all he wanted, was her. The warmth of Susannah's breasts pressing softly against his chest, her softness against his hardness, shattered the last of his control.

He groaned, taking her mouth hungrily, sliding against her, absorbing her warmth, her womanliness. His breathing grew chaotic, fevered, as she returned his inflammatory kiss. His fingers sliding into her hair, Killian gripped the silky strands, framing her face, holding her captive as he absorbed her into him like a starving man.

Susannah moaned, but it was a moan of utter surrender mingled with pleasure. She found herself pressed onto the bed, with Killian's tense body against her, driving her into the mattress. The near brush with death— the fear of losing him—overwhelmed her, and she sought blindly to reassure herself that she was alive, that he was safe. There was security in Sean's arms, those powerful bands that trapped her, holding her captive beneath him. With a fierce need, she returned his searching kiss.

"I need you, I need you," Killian rasped against her wet, soft mouth. "Now. I need you now...." He felt her arch beneath him, giving him the answer he sought. He'd nearly lost Susannah to an assailant's bullet. The warmth of her flesh, the eagerness of her beneath him, could have been destroyed in a split second. Sliding his shaky hands beneath her rumpled gown, he sought and found her slender rib cage, then moved upward. The instant his hands curved around her small breasts, he heard her cry out. But it was a cry of utter pleasure, not fear or pain. The husky sound coming from her throat increased the heat in his lower body. Never had he wanted a woman more. Never had he loved a woman as he loved Susannah.

The fierceness of his roiling emotions shattered Killian's ironclad control. He was helpless beneath her hands. They were gliding over his taut back and shoulders as he pulled the gown off her. In moments his pajamas were in a heap on the wooden floor. Her fingers dug convulsively into his bunched shoulders as he leaned down and captured the tight peak of her nipple with his insistent lips. She became wild, untamed, beneath him, moving her head from side to side, begging him to enter her.

The fever in his blood tripled, sang through him as he felt her thighs open to welcome him. He wanted to take it slow, to make it good for Susannah, but the fiery blood beating through him ripped away all but his primal need to plunge deep into her—to bury himself in her life, escaping the death that had stalked them less than an hour earlier.

Framing her face with his hands, Killian looked down into her dazed, lustrous eyes as he moved forward to meet her. He wanted to imprint Susannah's lovely features on his heart and mind forever. The moment he entered her hot, womanly confines, a low, vibrating growl ripped out of him. He couldn't stop his forward plunge—didn't want to. His need for this feverish coupling was like a storm that had waited too long to expend itself.

Killian's fingers tightened against Susannah's face and he stiffened as liquid fire encircled him, captured him, leaving him mindless, aware of nothing but a rainbow of sensations, each more powerful, more overwhelming, than the next. When Susannah moved her hips, drawing him even deeper inside her, he sucked in a ragged breath.

Never had he experienced heaven like this. He leaned down, savoring her lips, drowning in the splendor of her sweet, fiery offering.

Then nothing existed but the touching and sliding of their bodies against each other, satin against steel. Susannah was soft, giving, bending to Killian's needs with a sweet suppleness. He was hard, demanding—plunging and taking. Her lilac fragrance surrounded him as he buried his face in the silky folds of her hair. In moments, an explosive feeling enveloped him, freezing him into an immobility of such intense pleasure that he could only gasp in response. As she moved her hips sinuously against him, he could no more control himself than a rain storm could hold back from spending itself on the lush warmth of the earth.

Afterward, moments glided and fused together as Killian lay spent. He raised his head and realized that his fingers were still tightly grasping the thick strands of Susannah's hair, as if he were afraid she'd slip away from him—as if this were one of his fevered dreams, ready to flee when he opened his eyes. Susannah's lashes fluttered upward, and he held his breath, drowning in the glorious gray of her eyes.

The soft, trembling smile that curved her lips sent another sheet of heat through Killian. He felt her hot, wet tightness still around him, holding him, and he groaned.

"I feel like I've gone to heaven," he rasped against her lips. And then he added weakly, "Or as close as I'll ever get to heaven, because I'm bound for hell."

"You *are* heaven," Susannah managed huskily, held captive by him in all ways, luxuriating in his strength and masculinity.

Carefully Killian untangled his hand from her hair and touched her swollen lips. With a grimace, he whispered,

"I'm sorry, colleen, I got carried away. I didn't mean to hurt you."

Susannah kissed his scarred fingers. "I'm fine. How could you hurt me?"

He shakily traced her smooth forehead and the arch of her eyebrow. "In a million ways," he assured her.

With a tender smile, Susannah framed his damp features. No longer was the man with the hard face staring down at her. No, this was the very human, vulnerable side of Sean Killian. And she reveled fiercely in his being able to shed his outer shell—to give himself to her in an even more important, wonderful way.

Gently Killian moved aside and brought Susannah into his arms as he lay on the bed. "Come here," he whispered, holding her tight for a long, long time. The moments ran together for him. Susannah's arm flowed across his chest, and one of her long, lovely legs lay across his own. He blinked his eyes several times, trying to think coherently. It was nearly impossible with Susannah in his arms.

"You're all a man could ever dream of having," he told her in a low, unsteady voice as he kissed her cheek, and then her awaiting lips. Lying there with her in his arms, he caressed her cheek.

Susannah melted within his embrace, savoring the feel of his fingers moving lightly across her shoulder, down her arm to her hip. He was stroking her as if she were a purring cat. And wasn't she? "I'll never be sorry this happened," she admitted breathlessly. "Never."

As Killian lay there, his mind finally beginning to take over from the lavalike emotions that had exploded in a volcano lain dormant too long, he tasted bitterness in his mouth. There was Susannah, innocent and trusting in his arms, her eyes shining with such adoration that it made him sick inside. She didn't know his sordid past, didn't know the ghosts that still haunted him.

"I shouldn't have done this to you," he rasped, frowning. Yet he couldn't stop touching her, sliding his hands across her satiny flesh and feeling her effortless response.

"No!" Susannah forced herself up onto one elbow. She reached out, her hand on his chest, where his heart lay. "We both wanted this, Sean. *Both* of us."

He grimaced. "It shouldn't have happened," he said, more harshly.

"Really?" Susannah couldn't keep the sarcasm out of her tone, and she was sorry for it.

Unable to meet her eyes, he shook his head and threw the covers aside. "I was to protect you, Susannah!"

"Loving someone isn't protecting them?"

He glanced at her sharply as he forced himself to get up and leave her side. If he stayed, he'd want to love her all over again, with the fierceness of a breaking thunderstorm.

"I was paid to protect you, dammit!" he flared, moving around the bed and going to the dresser. Jerking open the drawer, he retrieved jeans and a polo shirt.

Sitting up in bed, Susannah suddenly felt bereft. Abandoned. Quiet tension thrummed through the room, and a chill washed over her. Killian put on boxer shorts and the jeans. His face was hard again, his mouth set in a thin line.

"Sean, what's going on? I liked what we shared. I like you. Why are you so angry and upset about it?"

"You'd better get cleaned up, Susannah," he told her tautly, pulling the shirt over his head. "Take a shower and get dressed. The sheriff is sending out a cruiser to check out what happened with the hit man. He'll probably be here in a half hour or so.''

Forcing herself to her feet, Susannah moved over to him. His movements were abrupt and tense. She gripped his arm.

''The police can wait,'' she said hoarsely, searching his dark, unfathomable eyes. ''*We* can't.''

Her fingers were like small, exquisite brands burning into his flesh. Killian pulled away from Susannah. ''There is no 'we'!'' he said harshly. It was pure, unadulterated hell looking down at her standing there naked and beautiful before him. ''Look at you! Even now you can't protect yourself against the likes of someone like me. It shouldn't have happened, Susannah! It was my fault. I wanted—needed you so damned bad I could taste it.'' Aggravated, Killian ran his fingers through his mussed hair. ''I broke a cardinal rule that I've never broken before—I got involved with the person I was supposed to protect.'' He gave her a sad look, his voice cracking with emotion. ''I'm sorry. I'm sorry it happened. You didn't deserve this on top of everything else, Susannah.''

Chapter Eight

Susannah had barely stepped out of the shower when the sheriff's cruiser arrived. Going to her bedroom, she dressed in a sensible pair of dark green cotton slacks and a white short-sleeved blouse. Her hair was still damp, and she braided the strands together, fastening the ends with a rubber band. Her hands shook as she put on white socks and a pair of sneakers.

The terror of nearly being killed warred with Sean's reaction to their lovemaking, buffeting her weary senses. Each time she replayed the conversation, it made no sense to her. Why was he sorry he'd loved her? She wasn't. Touching her bangs with trembling fingers, she took one look in the mirror. Her face was pale, and her eyes were dark and huge. And her lips... Susannah groaned softly. Her mouth looked wonderfully ravished, slightly swollen and well kissed.

Entering the kitchen, Susannah saw the damage from

the gunfire for the first time. Killian had set the table upright, and he and the two deputies sat at the table, their faces grim. Across the wooden floor, glass lay splintered and glinting in the lamplight.

Killian glanced up. Susannah stood poised just inside the room. He was struck by her beauty, her simple clothing—the luster in her gray eyes that he knew was meant for him alone. Trying to steel himself against his still-turbulent emotions, he got up.

"Come over here and sit down," he invited, his voice rough. "They've caught the guy who tried to kill us."

Gasping in surprise, Susannah came forward. "They did?"

"Yes, ma'am," a large, beefy deputy volunteered. "Thanks to Mr. Killian's quick reporting, we got him just as he was trying to leave the Glen town limits."

Killian pulled the chair out for her so that she could sit down. It hardly seemed possible, but Susannah looked even paler.

"You want some coffee?" he asked. Dammit, why did he have to sound so harsh with her? He was angry with himself, with his lack of control. It was he who had initiated their lovemaking.

"Please." Susannah tried to ignore Killian's overwhelming male presence—to concentrate on the deputy, whose name tag read Birch. But it was impossible. "Deputy Birch, what can you tell us about this hit man?" she managed to say, her voice unsteady.

"Not much. We're putting him through the paces right now back at the station. I do know he'll get put in jail without bail. The judge won't hear his case until nine this morning."

Susannah looked at the wall clock. It was 3:00 a.m., yet she felt screamingly awake. Was this how Sean felt all the time? Did a mercenary ever relax? As Killian moved around the counter, which was strewn with wood and glass debris, Susannah sensed an explosiveness around him.

"How may I help?" Susannah asked the deputies in a low, off-key voice.

"Just give us your statement, Miss Anderson." Birch threw a look at Killian. "I'd say your guardian angel here saved you."

She forced a smile that she didn't feel. "Yes, well, Mr. Killian is protective, if nothing else." Susannah saw him twist a look across his shoulder at her. His eyes were dark and angry. What had she done to deserve his anger? She hoped against hope that, when the deputies left, she and Sean could sit and talk this out.

Killian moved restlessly around the kitchen. It was 4:00 a.m., and the deputies were wrapping up their investigation. Susannah was looking exhausted, her adrenaline high clearly worn off, a bruised-looking darkness beneath her eyes.

"We'll be in touch shortly," Birch promised as the deputies stood up and ended their visit.

"Thank you," Susannah told them wearily, meaning it. She watched as Killian escorted the officers out to the porch, where they talked in low voices she couldn't overhear. Exhausted, she stood up, feeling as if she'd gone days without sleep. As much as she wanted to wait for Sean to return, to discuss whatever problem had sprung up between them, Susannah knew she didn't have the emotional strength for the confrontation. It would have to wait.

In her room, Susannah set the alarm for seven, so that she could call the principal and tell him she wouldn't be able to teach today. She lay down on the bed, not caring that she was still dressed, and fell asleep immediately. In her dreams, Killian loved her with his primal hunger all over again.

Susannah awoke with a start, her heart pounding. Sunlight was pouring in through the curtains at a high angle. What time was it? Groggily she looked at her watch. It was noon! She barely recalled getting up at seven to make the call and going straight back to bed.

Sitting for a moment, she allowed herself time to get reoriented. Had last night been some terrible combination of nightmare and dream? Killian's words about heaven and hell came back to her. That was what last night had been for her: tasting both extremes. It had been heaven loving Sean, feeling the intensity of his need for her. The hell had arrived earlier, in the form of a killer who'd wanted to take her life. Rubbing her brow, Susannah felt the beginnings of a headache. A heartache would be more appropriate. Why was Sean sorry he'd loved her?

When Susannah went to the kitchen, she found it almost as good as new. The only thing missing was the window over the sink. The floor had been swept clean of debris and mopped, the counters cleared of any evidence of the violent episode. She looked around. The splintered wood in the doorway had been removed. Either Killian or her father was busy making repairs.

What couldn't be repaired as quickly were the bullet holes along the kitchen wall. They were an ugly reminder, and Susannah stood there, rubbing her arms absently, feeling very cold.

"It's almost like new."

Gasping, Susannah turned at the sound of Killian's

low voice. He stood at the screen door, a piece of wood in his hand. "You scared me to death!" She placed her hand against her pounding heart.

Entering, Killian scowled. Susannah looked sleepy, her eyes puffy, and her mouth— He groaned inwardly. Her mouth looked beautifully pouty, the force of his kisses last night still stamped there. The ache to kiss her all over again, to ease the fear lingering in her eyes by taking her into his arms, flowed through him. Savagely he destroyed the feeling.

"Sorry," he muttered. "I didn't mean to scare you." He stalked across the kitchen and placed the wood against the door jamb. It fit perfectly. Now all he had to do was nail it into place.

"That's okay," she reassured him, a little breathlessly, "I'm just jumpy right now."

"Now you know how a mercenary feels twenty-four hours a day." He gave her a cheerless look. Killian wanted to convey in every way possible the miserable life he led—no place for a decent human being like Susannah. He wished she'd quit looking at him like that, with that innocence that drove him crazy with need.

Forcing herself to move, Susannah poured herself some fresh coffee. "Has the sheriff called yet?"

"Yes. Greaves was the man. The same one that nearly killed you at the bus station. He isn't talking, but I spoke to Morgan earlier, and he's working with the sheriff. The FBI are still in on it, too." Killian placed the board against the wall and went to the icebox. He wasn't hungry, but he knew he had to eat.

Biting down on her lower lip, Susannah glanced over at Killian as he brought out whole wheat bread, lunch meat and mustard. "Is it over, then?"

"I don't know. Morgan is sending a message through

a third party to Santiago's cartel in Peru. He's ordering him to lift the contract on you or we'll start extradition procedures against more of the cartel honchos.''

''What makes you think they'll lift the contract?'' Susannah watched him slap some mustard on the bread and top it with several pieces of lunch meat. His features were unreadable, as usual. What was he feeling? Hadn't their loving meant anything to him? He was acting as if it had never happened!

Killian moved to the table and sat down with his sandwich. ''This particular drug family is in plenty of hot water already with the Peruvian government, so they don't need any more attention from the authorities. Besides, Greaves is one of their top men who does dirty work for them in this country. They don't want to risk him spilling the beans to the American authorities on what he knows about the drug shipments to the U.S. He's been in a position to know about a lot of things. No, they'll probably make the deal and take the heat off you.''

Turning around so that her back rested against the counter, Susannah crossed her arms. Killian sat, frowning darkly while he munched on the sandwich. ''How soon will we know?'' she asked softly.

''Morgan says a day or two at the latest. He'll call us.''

Her arms tightened against herself. ''And if they agree to lift the contract, what will you do?''

Forcing himself to meet her gaze, Killian growled, ''I'll leave.''

The words plunged into her heart like a dagger. Susannah felt as if someone had just gutted her. Turning away, she realized she was out of sorts, still waking up, in no mental—or emotional—state to discuss last night.

Killian was biting into his sandwich as if he were angry with it. His blue eyes were turbulent, and he was markedly restless. Misery avalanched Susannah.

"I'm going into town," Killian said abruptly, rising. He'd choked down the sandwich, not tasting it at all, and now it sat like a huge rock in his stomach. The suffering on Susannah's face was real, and he had no control over his response to it. He'd made her this way with one lousy indiscretion—with his selfish need of her. Killian stalked to the screen door, which he'd recently rehung with new hinges.

"I've got to pick up the new glass for that window. I'll be back later."

Hurt, Susannah nodded. When Killian had left, she remained where she was, her head bowed, her eyes shut. Forcing back tears, she realized that even though he'd made wild, passionate love to her this morning, it had been little more than that. She knew nothing of the mercenary type of man. Was this part of their pattern—loving a woman and then leaving her? Susannah laughed derisively as she opened her eyes. There were a lot of men out there like that, unwilling to commit to a real, ongoing relationship, so they used women, then left them. Was Killian like that?

Her heart cried no, but as Susannah moved around the kitchen, she couldn't come up with a more reasonable answer. Still, Killian just didn't seem the type not to be loyal. Perhaps, when he came back with the window this afternoon, both of them would be more settled after the frightening events of last night, and she could talk to him.

Killian stood back, pleased with the new window gracing the kitchen. He was wildly aware that Susannah was nearby. She'd taken care of the bullet holes, filling them with spackling compound. In a day or two, when they'd dried sufficiently, she would sandpaper them smooth and paint over them. No one would realize the bullet holes were there—no one except them. Some things, he thought with disgust, one never forgot.

As Killian poured himself some coffee and went to sit on the front porch swing, he knew he'd never forget loving Susannah. The swing creaked beneath his weight, the gentle back-and-forth motion taking the edge off his screamingly taut nerves and aching heart. Taking a sip of the hot, black liquid, he narrowed his eyes, seeing nothing in front of him. He loved Susannah. How had it happened? When? He shook his head as a powerful sadness moved through him.

It didn't matter. No woman had ever captured his imagination, his feelings, the closely guarded part of him that still knew how to dream, as she had. More than anything, he wanted to spend the whole day loving her, falling asleep with her supple warmth beside him—waking up to love her all over again. But this time he wanted to move slowly, to savor Susannah, to pleasure her. He doubted she'd gotten much pleasure the first time. He'd stolen from her like a thief, because he'd needed her so badly, he thought sourly.

Reality drenched Killian as he swung slowly back and forth. Susannah could never know how he loved her.

"Sean?"

He snapped his head up. Susannah stood uncertainly at the screen door.

"Yes?" He heard the brittleness in his voice and automatically steeled himself.

"I need to talk with you," Susannah said, and pushed

the screen door open. "I was waiting for you to take a break."

His mouth thinning, he picked up his now-empty coffee cup in both hands. If he didn't, he would reach for Susannah, who had come to lean against the porch railing, near the swing.

"The window's in."

Susannah nodded, licking her dry lips. "Yes... It looks good as new." She shrugged. "I wish...I wish we could fix ourselves like that window—be brand-new all over again and not have a memory of what happened last night."

"That's what makes us human, I guess," he answered gruffly. The terrible suffering in Susannah's eyes was beginning to tear him apart.

Susannah nervously clasped her hands in front of her and forced herself to look at Killian. His face was closed and unreadable, his blue eyes narrowed and calculating. "We've got to talk," Susannah began hoarsely. "I can't go on like this."

"Like what?"

Taking in a ragged breath, Susannah whispered, "We loved each other last night, Sean. Doesn't that mean anything to you?"

Wincing inwardly, Killian saw tears forming in her eyes. His mouth going dry, a lump growing in his throat, he rasped, "Dammit, Susannah, it shouldn't have happened!"

"I'm not sorry, Sean, if that's what you're worried about."

He gave her a dark look. "Well, I am. We didn't use protection. For all I know, you could be pregnant."

Startled, Susannah allowed his growling words to sink

in. "Is that what's bothering you? That I might be pregnant?"

With a disgusted sound, Killian lunged to his feet, tense. "Doesn't it worry you?" he snapped. Desperate for anything that might force her to understand that there was no possible future for them, he zeroed in on that argument.

Susannah cringed beneath his taunting words. It felt as if Killian could explode at any moment. He stood next to her, tense and demanding. "Well—"

"I didn't think you were looking ahead," he rasped.

"That isn't the issue," Susannah said, forcing herself to hold his angry gaze. "The real issue is whether or not we have something special, something worth pursuing—together."

No one loved her courage more than he did. For the first time, Killian saw the stubborn jut of her jaw and the defiance in her eyes. He told himself he shouldn't be surprised by Susannah's hidden strength.

With a hiss, he turned away. "There is no us!"

"Why? Why can't there be?"

Killian whirled on her, his breathing ragged. "Because there can't be, Susannah!" He glared at her. "There will be no relationship between us." It tormented him to add, "You got that?"

Her lips parting, Susannah took a step away from Killian. Although his face was implacable, his eyes gave him away. Her womanly intuition told her that at least part of what he was saying was bluff.

"What are you afraid of?" she said, her voice quavering.

Stunned by her insight, Killian backed away. "Nothing!" he lied. His chest heaving with inner pain—and the pain he was causing Susannah—he added savagely,

"Stick with your dreams and hopes, Susannah. I don't belong in your idealistic world. I can't fit into it. I never will." His voice deepened with anguish. "I warned you to stay away from me. I warned you that it wouldn't be any good if you got close to me."

Rattled, Susannah whispered, "But I did! And I don't regret it, Sean. Doesn't that make any difference?"

Killian shook his head, his voice cracking. "Listen to me. I told you, I'm out of your life. I'm here for maybe a day or two more at the most. I'm sorry I made love to you. I had no right. It was my fault." He gave a helpless wave of his arm.

Her eyes rounded. How callous, how cold, he sounded. "I don't believe you mean that," she said, her voice beginning to shake with real anger.

He stared at her, openmouthed. "Don't look at me like that, Susannah. I'm no knight on a white horse."

Hurting, fighting not to cry in front of him, Susannah stared up at him. "What man is?" she cried. "We're all human beings, with strengths and weaknesses. You try to keep people at arm's length by making them think you're cold and cruel. I know you're not! You're bluffing, Sean."

Startled, Killian felt panic as never before. But he loved Susannah enough to allow her the freedom she didn't want from him. If only he could explain it to her... Moving forward, he gripped her arm with just enough force to let her know he meant what he was going to say. "Bluffing? When I leave and you don't hear from me again, that's no bluff, Susannah. I'm sorry I ever met you, because I've hurt you, and I never meant to do that. I swear I didn't." He gave her a little shake. When he spoke again, there was desperation in his voice. "Move on with your life after I leave. Find a good man here—someone who believes in dreams like you do. I've told you before—I'm bound for hell. Well, I got a little taste of heaven with you. It was damned good, Susannah. I'll never forget it, but I'm a realist.'' He released her and stepped back.

With a little sob, Susannah lifted her hand and pressed it against her mouth. Giving her a hopeless look, Killian spun on his heel and stalked back into the farmhouse.

Swaying, Susannah caught herself and sat down heavily in the swing, afraid her knees would give out entirely. Killian's words pummeled her, cut through her. She felt flayed by his anger. Hell was here, right now. It took a long minute for Susannah to wrestle with her unraveling emotions and force herself not to end up in a weeping heap. Miserably, she wiped the moisture from her eyes. In two days or less, they would know from Morgan whether or not the drug cartel would agree to the deal. If they did, Killian was out of her life in an instant. He wanted to run. He wanted to escape.

Killian slowly finished packing his bag. Morgan had just called to let him know the Peruvian cartel had agreed to lift the contract on Susannah. At least now she would be safe. His hand tightened around the handle of his satchel. The badly beaten leather bag had seen better days—like him, he thought wearily.

Right now, Susannah was out in the garden, barefoot, wearing her old straw hat, doing the weeding. Two of the most miserable days of Killian's life had somehow managed to pass. Never had he suffered so much, known agony as devastating as this. Every fiber of his being wanted to go out and say goodbye to Susannah. He hesitated, torn. If he did, he knew there was a good possibility he couldn't continue his charade. Last night, he'd heard Susannah sobbing softly, as if she were trying to hide her pain by crying into her pillow.

Tears jammed into Killian's eyes. With a disgusted sound, he forced them back. No, he didn't dare say goodbye to Susannah in person.

''Dammit,'' he rasped, his voice cracking. He scribbled a quick note, then went into the kitchen and left it on the table where Susannah would see it. He took one last look around the old, dilapidated farmhouse. Capturing the memories, he stored and locked them in the vault of his scarred heart.

Taking one last look toward the garden area, Killian saw Susannah down on her hands and knees, still weeding. Dragging in a deep, painful breath, Killian silently whirled around and left. Forever.

Susannah washed most of the dirt from her hands with water from the hose outside the garden fence. It was nearly four, and she knew she had to prepare supper. Where was Sean? She'd hardly seen him in the past two days. And why hadn't Morgan called? It hurt to think. It hurt to feel, Susannah thought as she slipped the straw hat off her head and entered the kitchen.

Almost immediately, she saw the note on the table. Next to it was a glass containing a freshly cut yellow rose. Frowning, her heart doing a funny skipping beat, Susannah went over to the table. Sitting down, she shakily unfolded the note.

Dear Susannah:
Morgan called about an hour ago to tell me that the drug cartel has promised to leave you alone. You're safe, and that's what is important.

By the time you get this note, I'll be gone. I'm

sorry I couldn't say goodbye. Being with you was heaven, Susannah. And for a man bound for hell, it was too much to take. Cowardice comes in many forms, and I didn't have the courage to say goodbye to you. You deserve better than me, as I've told you many times before.

You were a rainbow in my life. I never thought someone like me would ever see one, much less meet one in the form of a woman. You deserve only the best, Susannah. I'm not a man who prays much, but I will pray for your happiness. God knows, you deserve it. Killian.

A sob lodged in Susannah's throat. She stared at the paper, the words blurring as tears rose then spilled out of her eyes and down her cheeks. She gripped the letter hard, reading it and rereading it. There were so many mixed messages. It hadn't been the hardened mercenary writing this. No, it had been the very human, hurting man beneath his warrior's facade.

Crying softly, Susannah put the note aside and buried her face in her hands. The school had given her another month's leave to recover from the shooting incident. Lifting her head, she wiped the tears from her eyes. She had a month.... Gathering her strewn emotions, Susannah decided to call Morgan and talk to him about Sean. Outwardly, Killian was behaving like a bastard, but a bastard wouldn't have written about her being a rainbow in his life.

Susannah worked to compose herself. She'd gone through so much in such a short amount of time. A huge part of her didn't believe Sean's letter. Never had she felt this way toward a man. She'd been "in love" before, but that relationship hadn't matured. No man had made her feel so vibrant or so alive. Did she even know what real love was? Had Sean touched her heart with genuine love? Susannah didn't know, but one way or another she intended to find out.

She brought the glass containing the yellow rose forward. Touching the delicate petals with her fingers, the fragrance encircling her, Susannah realized that Killian might be tough in many ways, but, like this rose that he'd symbolically left her, he had a vulnerable, fragile underside.

That realization gave Susannah hope as nothing else could have. She'd call Morgan and begin an investigation into Sean and the world he called hell. There was a reason why he'd left her. Something he hadn't told her. Now Sean was going to have to realize that not everything in his life was destined for hell. Nor was every person going to allow him to run away when it suited his purposes—whatever they might be.

Chapter Nine

Morgan stood and came around his large walnut desk as Susannah gave him a slight smile of welcome and stepped into his office. When his assistant, Marie, had shut the door, he opened his arms.

"I'm glad you came, Susannah."

Fighting back tears, Susannah moved into Morgan's comforting embrace. She gave him a quick squeeze of welcome and then stepped away from his towering presence.

"Thanks for seeing me, Morgan. I know how busy you are."

He gestured toward the creamy leather sofa in the corner of the spacious room. "You know you aren't getting out of here without staying at least overnight. Laura insists."

Nervously Susannah sat down. "Yes, I told her I'd stay one night. But she must be terribly busy with this second baby. It's wonderful you have a boy and a girl now.''

Morgan nodded, satisfaction in his voice. ''A year apart. Katherine Alyssa Trayhern will have a big brother to grow up with. We're very happy about it. She's a real spitfire, too.''

Susannah was truly happy for them. Dressed in a navy pin-striped suit, with a paisley silk tie and white shirt, Morgan looked professional, every inch the head of his flourishing company. Susannah and Laura had been close throughout the years, and she knew of Morgan's terrible, torturous past. ''Well,'' she whispered, glancing up at him, ''I'm going to need some of that spitfire personality your daughter has.''

''I know this involves Killian. How can I help you?'' Morgan sat down, alert.

Gripping her leather purse, Susannah held his curious gaze. ''I know I was vague on the phone, but I didn't feel this was something I wanted to talk about in detail to anyone except you. And I wanted to do it in person. As I told you on the phone, the school is giving me a month to get my life back in order, and I intend to use it to do just that.''

Morgan nodded. ''I'm just glad the contract's been lifted. What's this about Killian?''

Susannah's heart contracted in grief. Unable to hold his warm, probing gaze, she felt a lump forming in her throat.

Morgan leaned over and slid his hand across her slumped shoulder. ''What's going on, Susannah?''

Fighting to keep herself together, she whispered, ''I don't know how it happened or when it happened, but I've fallen in love with Sean.'' She gave him a pained look. ''It happened so fast....''

Morgan nodded. "I fell in love with Laura the first moment I saw her, although I didn't know it then." He grimaced. "I fought the attraction, the love she brought out in me, for a long time. It was nearly my undoing. Luckily, she hung in there and refused to let me go my own way."

"Mercenaries must all be alike," Susannah muttered unhappily.

"There's probably a grain of truth to that. I met Killian in the Foreign Legion. Did you know that?"

"No, I didn't."

"He was a corporal in the company I helped run." Morgan shrugged. "Many of the men I employ here at Perseus are old contacts out of the Legion. The women who work for me all have a military background of some sort, too."

"What is Sean running from?"

"I don't know. Did he tell you anything about his past? He's always been more tight-lipped about it than most."

"No, it's like pulling teeth to get any kind of information out of him." Susannah sat quietly, staring down at her clasped hands. Softly she said, "Something happened to me when Sean was there protecting me from that hit man. The night we were almost killed, I discovered that I loved him. The fact that we might both lose our lives clarified my feelings for him."

Frowning, Morgan sat up. "I see...."

"Sean ran away from me, Morgan. He left me a note. He couldn't even face me to say goodbye, and that's not fair to me—or to him."

"Men who join the Foreign Legion are always running from something," Morgan said gently.

"I understand that now, but that's not an excuse for

his behavior. I need some information,'' Susannah said firmly. "About Sean. About his past."

Morgan opened his hands. "When men come from the Legion, you don't ask many questions,'' he said gently. "Each of my employees signs a legal document saying that they aren't wanted criminals in another country before I'll hire them for Perseus. It's their word. I don't make inquiries unless I get a tip-off from Interpol or some other governmental body.'' He shrugged. "And Killian has been one of the most closemouthed of my men. I know very little of his past.''

"Then let me fill you in,'' Susannah whispered, "because when I'm done with my story I want you to tell me where he lives. He and I have some unfinished business to clear up.''

Morgan was scowling heavily by the time Susannah had completed her story. He'd asked Marie to bring in hot tea and cookies, and the tray sat on the glass-topped coffee table in front of the sofa. He'd also had her stop all incoming calls—except for emergencies—and canceled the rest of the day's business.

Susannah couldn't eat, but she did sip some fragrant tea.

"I hate to tell you this,'' Morgan said, sitting down with her again, "but when Killian came in off your assignment he requested leave.''

"Leave?''

"Yes. It's a program I devised when I set up this company. When an operative's out in the field, there are tremendous stresses on him or her. When they come in off a particularly demanding assignment, they can request time off from the company for as long as they need to recuperate. Killian came back from Kentucky and wanted leave. I granted it to him, no questions asked.''

Susannah's heart beat a little harder. ''Where is he, then?''

''Ordinarily, where our people live is top secret. We never give out addresses to anyone, for fear of the information leaking into enemy hands. But in this case, I'm going to make an exception.''

Relief made her shaky. ''He won't be expecting me to show up.''

Morgan smiled grimly. ''There's something about the element of surprise—you might catch him off guard enough to level with you.''

''He never has leveled with me, Morgan.''

Moving uncomfortably, he said, ''Susannah, you're dealing with a lot of unknown factors here.''

''He's hurting terribly, Morgan.''

Rubbing his jaw, Morgan nodded. ''I was hurting a lot when Laura met me,'' he murmured. ''And I can't say I was the world's nicest person around her.''

''But you hung in there—together. And look at you now. You're happy, Morgan.''

Exhaling, he said, ''Susannah, Killian's hurting in a lot of ways neither of us knows. I know you're an idealist, and I know you have a large, forgiving heart. But Killian may not have the capacity to reach out to you, even if he wants to. He may be too afraid, for whatever reason. You have to be prepared to accept that if it happens.''

She hung her head and nodded. ''I'm not so idealistic that I don't know when I'm not wanted, Morgan. But Sean never gave me that chance. He never had the courage to sit down and tell me the truth.''

''I'm not saying what he did was right,'' Morgan said,

frowning heavily. "We all run in our own way. Luckily, I had Laura's steadfast courage, her belief in me that helped me get a handhold on my own internal problems." Then, with a slight smile filled with sorrow, he added, "I still have problems that overflow into our personal life, our relationship. Mostly because of me, because of my past that still haunts me. It's not as bad now, but believe me, Laura has her hands full some days with me when the past hits me like a sledgehammer." He glanced at the gold watch on his wrist. "Come on, it's time to go home. Laura promised me a special meal because you were coming. Let's not be late."

The loneliness Susannah had felt since Killian's abrupt departure was somewhat ameliorated by Morgan and his happy family. Laura, beautiful as ever with her long blond hair, dancing eyes and ready smile, helped lift Susannah's spirits. Her son, Jason Charles Trayhern, had his father's dark black hair and gray eyes. On the other hand, three-month-old Katherine Alyssa was a duplicate of Laura's ethereal beauty. Just getting to hold her was a treat for Susannah.

After the meal was eaten and the children had been put to bed, Susannah lingered over a cup of coffee with Laura in the living room. Morgan discreetly excused himself and retired to his home office in the basement of their large home.

Laura curled up on the flowery print couch and smoothed her long pink cotton skirt.

"So tell me what's going on, Susannah! You barely ate any of that great supper I fixed!"

"I know, and I'm really sorry, Laura. The roast leg of lamb was wonderful. It's just that I've got a lot of things on my mind. Well...my heart, to be more honest.'' She smiled and leaned over, petting Sasha, the family's huge brown-and-white Saint Bernard, who had made herself at home next to Susannah's feet. She'd long since taken off her shoes and gotten comfortable—Laura and Morgan's home invited that kind of response.

"Killian, by any chance?"

"How did you know?"

With a slight smile, Laura said softly, "He's a man who's crying for a woman to help bring him out of his self-imposed exile."

"You've always had such insight into people."

Laura shrugged and smiled. "That's what helped me understand Morgan when I first met him. He was a man trapped in hell, although I didn't understand why for quite some time."

"Well," Susannah muttered. "That's exactly how Sean described himself."

"Chances are," Laura said gently, "he lives in an emotional hell on a daily basis." With a sigh, she sipped the coffee. "Susannah, men who go through a war like Morgan did are scarred for life. It kills a part of them, so they're crippled emotionally, in a sense. But that doesn't mean they can't make the most of what is still intact within them."

"Morgan had you to help him realize all of that."

"We had our love, our belief in each other," Laura agreed quietly. "Sometimes it's still not easy. For Morgan, the war will never really be over. There are days when there's a lot of tension between us." She smiled softly. "Fortunately, we love each other enough to sit down and discuss what's bothering him. Morgan has slowly been opening up more with each year that passes, but it's never easy for us, Susannah."

"You have his trust," Susannah pointed out. "I never

had time to get Sean's trust. It all happened so fast, so soon...."

"I understand better than most," Laura whispered. "Men like Killian and Morgan need a woman with strength, with steadiness, because they've lost those things emotionally within themselves. I hope you're prepared for the kind of uphill battles a man like that will put you through."

Susannah glanced at her. "You're not scaring me off, Laura, if that's what you're trying to do."

Reaching over, Laura touched her shoulder. "No one believes in the power of love more than I do. I've seen it work miracles with Morgan—and with me." She lifted her head and looked toward the darkened hall that led to the bedrooms, her eyes misty. "And we have two beautiful babies that reflect that love."

"Ma didn't raise me to think life was easy," Susannah said. "I know the hell I went through with Sean while he was there. He just wouldn't—couldn't—talk."

"And that's going to be the biggest stumbling block when you see him again. Men like that feel as if they're carrying such a horrendous amount of ugliness within them. They're afraid that if they start to talk about it, it will get out of control."

"So they get tight-lipped about it?"

Laura nodded. "Exactly."

With a sigh, Susannah shrugged. "I don't have a choice in this, Laura. I don't want one, anyway. Sean is worth it."

"Well, tomorrow morning, Morgan's driver will take you to the airport, and you'll fly to Victoria, British Columbia, where he lives. It's on a lovely island off the west coast of Canada. There's quite a British flavor to the place. And flowers!" Laura smiled fondly. "The island is a riot of color and fragrance. I've never seen so many roses! You'll love the island.''

As she listened, Susannah hoped that her lack of worldliness wouldn't be her undoing. She sat tensely, her hands clasped in her lap. All she had to lead her through this tangled web that Sean lived within was her heart. What would he do when she showed up at his doorstep? As Morgan had said, the element of surprise might work for her—but, she thought, it could also work against her.

Susannah had never needed the kind of strength she knew she would need in order to face Sean Killian bravely. Only Sean could show her if what she felt for him was love. But even if it was, there was no guarantee that he would have the courage to admit it.

Kneeling in the triangular flower bed, Killian stared glumly down at the bright yellow marigold in his hands. The gold, red and yellow flowers assaulted the air with their rather acrid odor. Like the flower in his hand, surrounded by the moist, rich soil, he was alone. Alone and bitter.

Resolutely he dug a small hole with the trowel, and placed the marigold in it. With dirt-stained hands, he pressed the moist earth securely over the roots. Gardening had always helped soothe him. *Until now.*

Looking up from the garden, Killian stared at the calm blue of the ocean, three hundred feet away. His green manicured lawn contrasted beautifully with the glassy water. The pale azure of the sky was dotted with fleecy white clouds. Summer in Victoria was his favorite time. Luckily, the money he'd earned over the years had gotten him this small English-style cottage when the couple who'd owned it, up in years, could no longer keep up with its landscaping and gardening demands and sold it to him.

Susannah. Her name hung in front of Killian as he caressed the tiny, frilly petals of a pale yellow marigold. The color reminded him of the hope that always burned in her eyes. Hope. He had none. The feeling had been utterly destroyed so long ago. Closing his eyes, he knelt there, surrounded by the lonely cries of the sea gulls that endlessly patrolled the beach and, off in the distance, the hoarse barks of sea lions.

Killian opened his eyes, feeling the terrible loneliness knife through him as never before. Slowly he looked around. He was surrounded by the ephemeral beauty of many carefully constructed flower beds, all geometrically shaped and designed by him, their rainbow colors breathtaking. But Killian could feel none of his usual response to them. Only Susannah could make him feel.

What was wrong? What had happened to him? He opened up his hands and studied them darkly. He'd made love to other women off and on throughout his life, but never had the act—or more truthfully, the feelings—continued to live like a burning-hot light within his body and heart as they did now.

With a shake of his head, Killian muttered under his breath and got to his feet. Brushing off the bits of soil clinging to his jeans, he straightened. The three tiers of flower gardens culminated with at least a hundred roses of various colors. Their fragrance was heavy in the area nearest the rear sliding glass doors to his house.

And it was a house, Killian reminded himself harshly. Susannah's ramshackle, broken-down old place was a *home*. She'd made it feel homey, comfortable and warm with her life and presence. Killian savored the hours spent with her in that antiquated kitchen. Every night when he lay down to try to sleep, those scenes would replay like a haunting movie across his closed eyelids. And when he finally did sleep, torrid, heated dreams of loving Susannah drove him to wakefulness, and a clawing hunger that brought him to the verge of tears. Tears! He never cried!

Stopping at the rose garden, a long, rectangular area bordered with red brick, Killian barely brushed a lavender rose with his fingertips. *Susannah.* No longer did Killian try to escape her memory. The doorbell rang, pulling his attention from his morbid reverie. Who could it be? His housekeeper and regular gardener, Emily Johnston, had left earlier to buy the week's groceries, and she wouldn't be back until tomorrow morning.

Automatically Killian dropped into his natural mode of wariness. Although his address and phone number were known only to Meg and Morgan, he didn't trust his many enemies not to track him down. As careful as Killian was about masking his movements to preserve his sanctuary, he never fooled himself. Someday one of his more patient and vengeful enemies might locate him.

Padding through the fully carpeted house, Killian halted at the front door and peered through the one-way glass. *Susannah!* His heart thumped hard in his chest. What the hell was she doing here? Could he be dreaming? His mind spun with questions. His heart began an uneven pounding. As he closed his hand over the brass doorknob, Killian felt a surge of hope tunnel through him. Just as quickly, he savagely destroyed the burgeoning feeling.

The door swung open. Susannah looked through the screen at Killian. As usual, his features were set—but his eyes gave away his true feelings. Her palms were sweaty, and her heart was thundering like a runaway freight train. She girded herself for his disapproval.

"What are you doing here?" Killian demanded in a rasp. He glanced around, checking out the surrounding area. Luckily, the street ended in a cul-de-sac, and he knew who his neighbors were and the cars they drove. The white Toyota out front must be a rental car that Susannah had driven.

"We've got some unfinished business," Susannah whispered. It was so hard to gather strength when she felt like caving in and stepping those precious few feet to fall into Killian's arms. The terrible light in his eyes told him he was no less tortured by her unexpected appearance than she was.

"Get in here," he growled, and gripped her by the arm.

Susannah didn't resist. She could tell that Killian was carefully monitoring the amount of strength he applied to her arm. She entered his home. A dusky-rose carpet flowed throughout the living room and hall area, which was decorated with simple, spare, carefully placed furniture. The walls were covered with floor-to-ceiling bookcases. Killian must be a voracious reader.

There were so many impressions she wanted to absorb, to investigate. Each one would give her another clue to Killian. But she didn't have that kind of time. Every word, every gesture, counted. She turned as he closed the door with finality. The grimness in his face made her feel cold. Alone.

"How did you find me?"

"I flew to Washington and talked with Morgan. He told me where you lived." Susannah saw his eyes flare with disbelief.

Killian took a step back, because if he didn't he was

going to sweep Susannah uncompromisingly into his arms. And then he was going to take her to his bedroom and make wild, hungry love with her until they were so exhausted that they couldn't move.

Killian looked down at her vulnerable features. There was real hope in Susannah's eyes, a kind of hope he'd never be able to claim as his own. She was dressed in a summery print blouse—pink peonies against a white background—and white slacks, with sandals outlining her feet. Her lovely sable hair was trapped in a chignon, and Killian had to stop himself from reaching forward to release that captive mass of silk into his hands. His mouth had grown dry, and his heart was beating dangerously hard in his chest.

"All right, what's going on?"

"You and me." Susannah felt her fear almost overwhelming her, but she dared not be weak now. She saw a slight thawing in Killian's narrowed eyes, a slight softening of his thinned mouth. "What made you think," Susannah said in a low, strangled voice, "that you could walk out on me just like that? We made love with each other, Sean. I thought—I thought we meant something to each other." She forced herself to hold his hardening gaze. "You ran without ever giving me the opportunity to sit down and talk to you. I'm here to complete unfinished business." Her voice grew hoarse. "One way or another."

Killian stood stunned. It took him a long time to find his voice. "I told you—I didn't mean to hurt you," he rasped. "I thought leaving the way I did would hurt you less."

Susannah's eyes went round, and anger gave her the backbone she needed. "Hurt me less?" Susannah forced herself to walk into the living room. She dropped her purse and her one piece of luggage on the carpet. Turning, she rounded on Killian. "I don't call running out on me less hurtful!"

Nervously Killian shoved his hands into the pockets of his jeans. "I'm sorry, Susannah. For everything."

"For loving me?"

Killian dropped his gaze and stared at the floor. He heard the ache in her husky tone; her voice was like a lover's caress. He was glad to see her, glad that she was here. "No," he admitted. He raised his chin and forced himself to meet her large, tear-filled eyes. "But I am sorry for the hurt I've caused you."

"You walk around in your silence and don't communicate worth a darn. I'm not a mind reader. Do you know how awful I felt after you left? Do you know that I blamed myself? I asked myself what I did wrong. Was it something I said? Did?" Grimly, her eyes flashing, she said, "I don't have a lot of worldly ways like you. I know I'm a country woman, but I don't question the way of my heart, Sean. You had no right to leave the way you did. It wasn't fair to me, and it wasn't fair to you, either."

Pain knifed through him and he moved into the living room with her. He halted a foot away from her, aching to put his hands on her shoulders, but not daring to. "I was to blame, not you."

To her amazement, Susannah saw Killian thawing. Perhaps Laura was right: He needed a woman to be stronger than him so that he could feel safe enough to open up. Had he never had a woman of strength to lean on? If not, it was no wonder he remained closed, protecting his vulnerability. The discovery was as sweet as it was bold—and frightening. Susannah was just coming out of her own trauma. Did she have enough strength for the both of them? She simply didn't know, but the glimmer in Killian's eyes, the way his mouth unconsciously hinted at the vulnerability he tried so hard to hide and protect, made her decide to try anyway.

"I hope you've got a guest bedroom."

He blinked.

Susannah drilled him with a fiery look. "Sean, I happen to feel that we meant a lot to each other when you were in Kentucky. And after we made love, you ran. I don't know your reasons for running, and that's what I'm here to find out. I intend to stay here, no matter how miserable you make it for me, until we get to the bottom of this—together."

Dread flared through Killian. No woman had ever challenged him like this. "You don't know what you're saying," he warned.

"Like heck I don't! Give me some credit, Sean. I work with special children. I've got to have a lot of insight into them to reach them, to touch them, so that they'll stop retreating."

Killian took another step away, terror warring with his need of Susannah. "You're biting off too much. You don't know what you're getting into," he snapped.

Tilting her chin, Susannah rasped, "Oh, yes I do."

"Now look," he said in a low, gravelly voice, "I don't want to hurt you, Susannah. If you stay here, it'll happen. Don't put yourself on the firing line for me. I'm not worth it."

Tears stung her eyes, but Susannah forced them back. Killian would read her tears as a sign of weakness. "You're wrong. You're a good man, Sean. You've been hurt, and you're hiding. I'm here to show you that you don't need to keep running. You're allowed to laugh, you know. And to cry. How long has it been since you've done either?''

Killian lunged forward blindly and gripped her by the arm. "Dammit," he rasped off-key, "get the hell out of here while you still can, Susannah! I'm a monster! A monster!" He savagely poked a finger at his belly. "It's in here, this thing, this hell that I carry. It comes out and controls me, and it will hurt whoever is around. You've got to understand that!"

She held his blazing gaze, seeing the horror of his past reflected in his eyes, hearing the anguish in his tone. "No," she said. "I'm not afraid of you," she rattled, "or that so-called monster inside of you. For the first time in your life, Sean, you're going to be honest, not only with yourself, but with someone else—me."

Killian took a step back, as if she'd slapped him. He stared down at her as the tension swirled around them like a raging storm. Frightened as never before, he backed away. In place of the panic came anger. He ground out, "If you stay, you stay at your own risk. Do you understand that?"

"I do."

He glared at her. "You're naive and idealistic. I'll hurt you in ways you never thought possible! I won't mean to, but it'll happen, Susannah." He stood there, suddenly feeling very old and broken. His voice grew hoarse. "I don't want to, but I will. God help me, I don't want to hurt you, Susannah."

Swallowing hard, a lump forming in her throat, she nodded. "I know," she replied softly, "I know...."

"This is hopeless," Killian whispered, looking out one of the series of plate-glass windows that faced the flower gardens and the ocean. "I'm hopeless."

Grimly Susannah fought the desire to take Killian into

her arms. Intuitively she understood that it would weaken her position with him. He was wary and defensive enough to strike out verbally and hurt her for fear of getting hurt again. As she picked up her luggage, Susannah realized that her love for Sean was the gateway not only to trust, but also to a wealth of yet-untapped affection that lay deep within her.

"You're not hopeless," Susannah told him gently. "Now, if you'll show me where the guest bedroom is, I'll get settled in."

Killian gaped at her. His mouth opened, then closed. "First door on the right down the hall," he muttered, then spun on his heel and left.

Her hands shaking, Susannah put her week's worth of clothes away in the closet and the dresser. Her heart wouldn't steady, but a clean feeling, something akin to a sense of victory, soared within her. She took several deep breaths to calm herself after having established a beachhead in the initial confrontation. Killian's desperation told her, she hoped, how much he was, indeed, still tied to her. Perhaps Morgan and Laura were right, and Killian did love her after all. That was the only thing that could possibly pull them through this storm together. Any less powerful emotion would surely destroy her, and continue to wound Killian.

Straightening up from her task, Susannah took in the simple, spare room. A delicate white Irish lace spread covered the double bed. The carpet was pale lavender, and the walls cream-colored. A vibrant Van Gogh print of sunflowers hung above the bed. The maple dresser was surely an antique, but Susannah didn't know from what era. The window, framed by lavender drapes and ivory sheers, overlooked a breathtaking view of the ocean.

"Well, Susannah, keep going," she warned herself. As much as she wanted to hide in the bedroom, she knew it wasn't the answer. No, she had to establish herself as a force in Killian's isolated world, and make herself part of it—whether he wanted her to or not. And in her heart she sensed that he did want her. The risk to her heart was great. But her love for Killian was strong enough to let her take that risk. He was always risking his life for others; well, it was time someone took a risk for him.

Killian stole a look into the kitchen. Susannah had busied herself all afternoon in his spacious modern kitchen. Although he'd hidden out most of the time in the garage, working on a wood-carving project, the fragrant odors coming from the kitchen couldn't be ignored. As upset as he was, the food she was cooking made him hungry. But it was his other hunger for Susannah that he was trying to quell—and he wasn't succeeding.

"What's for dinner?" he asked with a frown.

Susannah wiped her hands on the dark green apron she had tied around her waist. "Pot roast with sourcream gravy and biscuits. Southerners love their biscuits and gravy," she said with pride.

"Sounds decent. Dessert?" He glanced at her.

"You really push your luck, don't you?"

He wanted to smile, but couldn't. "Yeah, I guess I do."

"I didn't come here to be a slave who cooks you three meals a day and cleans your house," Susannah pointed out as she gestured for him to sit down at the table. "This food is going to cost you."

"Oh?" Thinking he should leave, Killian sat down.

Susannah seemed to belong in the kitchen—her presence was like sunshine. The bleakness of his life seemed to dissolve in her aura.

Susannah served the meat and placed the pitcher of gravy on the table with a basket of homemade biscuits. Sitting down, she held his inquiring gaze. "My folks and I always used to sit and talk after meals. It was one of the most important things I learned from them—talking."

With a grimace, Killian offered her the platter of meat first. "I'm not much of one for talking and you know it."

"So you'll learn to become a better communicator," Susannah said lightly. She felt absolutely tied in knots, and she had to force herself to put food on her plate. Just being this close to Killian, to his powerful physical presence, was making her body betray her head. When his lips curved into that sour smile, Susannah melted inwardly. She remembered how hot, how demanding and sharing, that mouth had been on hers. Never had she wanted to kiss a man so much. But she knew if she bowed to her selfish hunger for him as a man, she'd lose not only the battle, but the war, as well.

"Okay," he said tentatively, "you want me to talk." He spooned several thick portions of the roast onto his plate, added three biscuits and then some gravy. "About what?"

"You," Susannah said pointedly.

"I'm willing to talk about anything else," he warned her heavily.

With a shrug, Susannah said, "Fine. Start anywhere you want."

The food was delectable, and Killian found himself wolfing down the thick, juicy meat. Still in wonder over this strong, stubborn side of Susannah that he hadn't seen before, he shook his head.

"I didn't realize you were this persistent."

Susannah grinned. "Would it have changed anything?"

The merest shadow of a smile touched Killian's mouth, and the hesitant, pain-filled attempt sent a sheet of heat through Susannah. Taking a deep breath, she said, "I want to know about you, your past, Sean. I don't think that's too much to ask. It will help me understand you—and, maybe, myself, and how I feel toward you."

Again her simple honesty cut through him. He ate slowly, not only hearing, but also feeling her words. He saw Susannah's hands tremble ever so slightly. She was nervous, perhaps even more nervous than he was. Still, his heart filled with such joy that she was here that it took the edge off his terror. "So, if I open up, maybe you'll give me some of that dessert you made?"

Susannah laughed, feeling her first glimmer of hope. She felt Killian testing her, seeing if she was really as strong as he needed her to be. "That coconut chiffon pie is going to go to waste if you don't start talking, Sean Killian."

Her laughter was like sunlight in his dark world. In that moment, her eyes sparkling, her lush mouth curved, Killian ached to love her, ached to feel her take away his darkness. Hope flickered deep within him, and it left him nonplussed. Never had he experienced this feeling before. Not like this. Giving her an annoyed look, he muttered, "I'd rather talk about my flower gardens, and the roses."

"Enough about the roses," Susannah said as she stood up and cleared away the dishes. She saw his eyes darken instantly. Tightening her lips, she went to the refrigerator, pulled out the pie and cut two slices.

"I want you to tell me about your childhood."

Moodily he sat back in the chair, unable to tear his gaze from her. "It's not a very happy story" was all he said.

Susannah gave him a piece of pie and a fork. She sat back down, grimly holding his hooded gaze. "Tell me about it."

With a sigh, Killian shrugged and picked up the fork. "I was the runt. The kid who was too small for his age. I was always scrapping with older boys who thought they could push my younger sister Meg around. He pointed to his crooked nose. "I had this busted on three different occasions in grade school."

"Did you have anyone to hold you?"

Killian flashed her an amused look. "Scrappers didn't fall into their mothers' arms and cry, Susannah."

"Is your mother alive?"

He winced inwardly and scowled, paying a lot of attention to his pie, which he hadn't touched. "Mother died when I was fourteen."

"What did she die of?" Susannah asked softly.

Rearing back in the chair, and wiping his hands absently on his jeans, Killian replied, "A robbery."

She heard the rising pain in Killian's tone, and saw it in the slash of his mouth. "Tell me about it."

"Not much to tell," he muttered. "When I was thirteen, my parents emigrated to America. They set up a grocery store in the Bronx. A year later, a couple of kids came in to rob them. They took the money and killed my parents," he concluded bluntly. Killian bowed his head, feeling the hot rush of tears in his tightly shut eyes. Then he felt Susannah's hand fall gently on his shoulder.

Just that simple gesture of solace nearly broke open the wall of grief he'd carried so long over his parents' harsh and unjust deaths.

Fighting to keep her own feelings under control, Susannah tried to understand what that experience would do to a fourteen-year-old boy, an immigrant. "You were suddenly left alone," she said unsteadily. "And Meg was younger?"

"Yes, by a year."

Susannah could feel the anguish radiating from him. "What did you do?"

Killian fought the urge to put his hand over hers where it lay on his shoulder. If he did, he'd want to bury his head blindly against her body and sob. The lump in his throat grew. So many unbidden, unexpected feelings sheared through him. Desperate, not understanding how Susannah could so easily pull these emotions out of him and send them boiling to the surface, Killian choked. With a growl, he lunged away from the table, and his chair fell to the tiled floor.

"You have no right to do this to me. None!" He turned and jerked the chair upright.

Susannah sat very still, working to keep her face neutral. She battled tears, and prayed that Killian couldn't see them in her eyes. His face was pale and tense, and his eyes were haunted.

"If you're smart," he rasped as he headed toward the garden, "you'll leave right now, Susannah."

Stubbornly she shook her head. "I'm staying, Sean."

His fingers gripped the doorknob. "Damn you! Damn you—"

She closed her eyes and took a deep, ragged breath. "You aren't going to scare me off."

"Then you'd better lock the door to your bedroom

tonight," he growled. "I want you so damned bad I can taste it. I can taste you." He jabbed his finger warningly at her. "You keep this up, and I don't know what will happen. You're not safe here with me. Don't you understand?"

Susannah turned in her chair. When she spoke, her voice was soft. "You're not even safe with yourself, Sean."

Wincing, he stalked out of the house. Maybe a walk, a long, brutal walk, would cleanse his agitated soul and his bleeding heart. He loved Susannah, yet he feared he'd hurt her. No woman had ever unstrung him as easily and quickly as she did. He strode through the beauty of his flower gardens, unseeing.

Chapter Ten

Susannah got ready for bed. She hadn't heard Killian return, and it was nearly eleven. Her nerves were raw, and she was jangled.

Lock the door.

Did she want to? Could she say no if Killian came into her bedroom? Where did running and hiding end? And where did freedom, for both of them, begin? Perhaps it would be born out of the heat of their mutual love.... Her hands trembling, Susannah pulled down the bed covers. The room was dark now. Slivers of moonlight pierced the curtains, lending a muted radiance to the room.

Lock the door.

Dressed in a simple knee-length cotton gown, Susannah pulled the brush through her hair. Her own emotions were jumbled and skittish. What if Sean walked through that door? She stared hard at the doorknob. She hadn't locked it—yet. Should she? Was she hesitating for herself or for Sean?

Lock the door.

Trying to recall the nights with Killian at her farmhouse, Susannah realized that she'd been in such turmoil herself that, except for that one night, she had no idea if he generally slept, had terrible nightmares or experienced insomnia. Making a small sound of frustration, she set the tortoiseshell brush on the dresser. No. No, she had to leave the door open. If she locked it, it was a symbol that she really didn't trust him—or herself. Taking a deep, unsteady breath, she slipped between the cool sheets. Getting comfortable, she lay there, her hands behind her head, for a long, long time—waiting. Just waiting.

Lock the door.

Killian moved like a ghost through his own house. All the lights were out, but the moon provided just enough light to see. He was sweaty and tired, having walked miles along the beach in order to purge himself of the awful roiling emotions that were flaying him alive. The forced hike had taken the edge off him, but he hadn't dealt at all with his feelings.

Susannah.

Killian stood frozen in the hallway and finally faced the full realization: He loved her. His hand shook as he touched his forehead. When? Making a sound of disgust, he thought that from the moment he'd seen Susannah his heart had become a traitor to him. Yes, he'd made love to women in his life, but never had he wanted truly to love them. With Susannah, he wanted to give. He wanted to see that velvet languor in her eyes, and the soft curve of her lips as he pleasured her, loved her so thoroughly that they fused into melting oneness.

His nerves raw, more exhausted than he could recall ever having been, Killian forced himself to go to his room for a cold shower. But as he passed Susannah's room, he stopped. His eyes narrowed on the doorknob. Had she done as he ordered and locked her door against him? Sweat stood out on his tense features as his hand slowly moved forward. For an instant, his fingers hovered. A part of him wanted her to have the door locked. He didn't want to hurt her—didn't want to take from her without giving something back. But how could he give, when he didn't even know how to give to himself after all those years?

His mouth tightening, Killian's hand flowed around the doorknob. He twisted it gently. It was unlocked! He stood there, filled with terror and hope, filled with such hunger and longing that he couldn't move. Susannah trusted him. She trusted him to do the right thing for both of them. Just as quietly, he eased the doorknob back to its original position.

Her heart beating wildly, Susannah sensed Killian's presence outside her room. She lay there gripping the sheet, her eyes wide, as she watched the doorknob slowly turn, trying to prepare herself emotionally. If he entered her room, she wasn't sure what she'd do. Her heart whispered to her to love him, to hold him, to allow him to spend himself within her. Loving was healing, and Susannah knew that instinctively. Her head warned her sharply that he'd use her up and eventually destroy her emotionally, just as he'd been destroyed himself over the years.

The seconds ticked by, and Susannah watched the

doorknob twist back into place. Killian knew now that she was accessible, that she would be here for him, for whatever he needed from her. The thought was as frightening as it was exhilarating. On one level, Susannah felt as if she were dealing with a wild, unmanageable animal that would just as soon hurt her as stay with her. That was the wounded side of Sean. The other side, the man who possessed such poignant sensitivity and awareness of her as a woman, was very different. Somewhere in the careening thoughts that clashed with her overwrought feelings, Susannah was counting on that other part of Sean to surface. But would it? And in time?

When the door didn't open, she drew in a shaky breath of air and gradually relaxed. At least Killian had come home. She'd worried about where he'd gone, and indeed whether he'd return. Forcing her eyes closed, Susannah felt some of the tension drain from her arms and legs. Sleep. She had to get some sleep. Tomorrow morning would be another uphill battle with Sean. But the night was young, her mind warned her. What were Killian's sleeping habits? Was he like a beast on the prowl, haunted by ghosts of the past, unable to sleep at night? Susannah wished she knew.

Sometime later, her eyelids grew heavy, her heart settled down, and she snuggled into the pillow. Almost immediately, she began to dream of Sean, and their conversation at the table—and the look of pain he carried in his eyes.

Susannah jerked awake. Her lips parting, she twisted her head from one side to the other. Had she been dreaming? Had she heard a scream? Or perhaps more the sound of an animal crying out than a human scream? Fumbling sleepily, she threw off the sheet and the bedspread. Dream or reality? She had to find out. What time was it? Stumbling to her feet, Susannah bumped into the dresser.

"Ouch!" she muttered, wiping the sleep from her eyes. Her hair, in disarray, settled around her face as she glanced at the clock. It was 3:00 a.m. The moonlight had shifted considerably, and the room was darker now than before. Reaching for her robe, Susannah struggled into it.

She stepped out into the hall, but only silence met her sensitive hearing. Killian's room was across the hall. The door was partly open. Her heart starting a slow, hard pounding, Susannah forced herself to move toward it.

Just as she reached it, she heard a muffled crash in another part of the house. Startled, she turned and moved on bare feet down the carpeted hall toward the sound. In the center of the gloom-ridden living room, she halted. Her nerves taut, her breathing suspended, Susannah realized that the sounds were coming from the garage. Killian did woodworking out there. More crashes occurred. Fear snaked through her. She knew he was out there. She had to go to him. She had to confront him. Now Susannah understood what an animal trainer must feel like, facing a wild, untamed animal.

Her mouth dry, her throat constricted and aching, Susannah reached for the doorknob. A flood of light from the garage momentarily blinded her, and she stopped in the doorway, her hand raised to shade her eyes.

Killian whirled around, his breathing raspy and harsh. His eyes narrowed to slits as he picked up the sound of the door leading to the house being opened. He'd prayed that his shrieks wouldn't wake Susannah, but there she stood, looking sleepy yet frightened. Sweat ran down the sides of his face.

"I told you—get the hell out of here!" The words, more plea than threat, tore out of him. "Go! Run!"

Susannah's mouth fell open. Killian's cry careened off the walls of the large woodworking shop. Despite her fear, she noted beautifully carved statues—mostly of children, mothers with children, and flying birds. Some had been knocked off their pedestals and lay strewn across the concrete floor. Were those the crashes she'd heard? Susannah's gaze riveted on Killian. He was naked save for a pair of drawstring pajama bottoms clinging damply to his lower body. His entire torso gleamed in the low light, and his hair was damp and plastered against his skull. More than anything, Susannah saw the malevolent terror in his dark, anguished eyes.

She whispered his name and moved forward.

"No!" Killian pleaded, backing away. "Don't come near me! Damn it, don't!"

Blindly Susannah shook her head, opening her arms to him. "No," she cried softly. "You won't hurt me. You won't..." and she moved with a purpose that gave her strength and kept her fear in check.

Stumbling backward, Killian was trapped by the wood cabinets. There was no place to turn, no place to run. He saw blips of Susannah interspersed among the violent scenes that haunted him continuously. In one, he saw the enemy coming at him, knife upraised. Another flashback showed his torturer coming forward with a wire to garrote him. He shook his head, a whimper escaping his tightened lips. He was trying desperately to cling to reality, to the fact that Susannah was here with him. He heard her soft, husky voice. He heard the snarl and curse of his enemies as they leaped toward him.

"No!" He threw his hands out in front of him to stop her. Simultaneously the flashback overwhelmed him. His hands were lethal weapons, honed by years of karate training, thickened by calluses, and he moved into position to protect himself. Breathing hard, he waited for his enemy to come at him with the knife as he met and held his dark, angry eyes.

Susannah saw the wildness in Killian's eyes, and she reached out to touch his raised hand. His face was frozen into a mask devoid of emotion; his eyes were fathomless, intent and slitted. Fear rose in her, but she knew she had to confront it, make it her friend and reach Killian, reach inside him.

Just as she grazed his hand, he whimpered. Her eyes widened as she saw him shift.

"Sean, no!" She threw out one hand to try to stop him. "No," she choked out again.

Where was he? He heard Susannah's cry. *Where?* Slowly the flashbacks faded, and Killian realized she was gripping his arm, her eyes wide and brimming with tears.

"No…" he rasped, and quickly jerked away from Susannah's touch. "God…I'm sorry." Bitterness coated his mouth, and he dragged in a ragged breath. "I could have hurt you. My God, I nearly—"

"It's all right. I'm all right, and so are you," Susannah whispered. Dizziness assailed her. She stood very still. When he reached out to touch her, his hand was trembling. The instant Killian's fingers touched her unbound hair, Susannah wanted to cry. There was such anguish in his eyes as he caressed her hair, as if to make sure she wasn't a part of whatever nightmare had held him in its thrall. Gathering what courage she had left, Susannah lifted her hand and caught his. His skin was sweaty, and the thrum of tension was palpable in his grip.

"It was just a nightmare," she quavered, lifting her head and meeting his tortured eyes.

Killian muttered something under his breath. "You shouldn't have stayed," he rasped. "I might have hurt you...." He gently framed her face and looked deeply into her tear-filled eyes. "I'm so afraid, Susannah."

Whispering his name, Susannah slid her arms around him and brought him against her. She heard a harsh sound escape his mouth as he buried his face against her hair, his arms moving like steel bands around her. The air rushed from her lungs, but she relaxed against him, understanding his need to hold and be held.

"I love you," she whispered, sliding her fingers through his short black hair. "I love you...."

Her words, soft and quavering, flowed through Killian. Without thinking, he lifted his head to seek her mouth. Blindly he sought and found her waiting lips. They tasted sweet, soft and giving as he hungrily took her offering. His breathing was chaotic, and so was hers. Drowning in Susannah's mouth and feeling her hands moving reassuringly across his shoulders took away the terror that had inhabited him. Her moan was of pleasure, not pain.

In those stark, naked moments, Killian stopped taking from her and began to give back. Her mouth blossomed beneath his, warm, sweet and hot. How badly he wanted to love her; his body was aching testimony to his need. Tearing his mouth from hers, he held her languorous gray gaze, which now sparkled with joy.

"It's going to be all right," he promised unsteadily. "Everything's going to be all right. Come on...."

Susannah remained beneath his arm, his protection, as

he led her through the silent house. In the living room, he guided her to the couch and sat down with her. Their knees touched, and he held both her hands. "You're the last person in the world I'd ever want to hurt," he rasped.

"I know...."

"Dammit, Susannah, why didn't you run? Why didn't you leave me?"

She slowly looked up, meeting and holding his tear-filled eyes. "B-because I love you, Sean. You don't leave someone you love, who's hurting, to suffer the way you were suffering."

Killian closed his eyes and pulled her against him. The moments of silence blended together, and he felt the hotness of tears brim over and begin to course down his cheeks. His hands tightened around her as he gathered her into his arms. Burying his face in her sable hair, he felt a wrenching sob working its way up and out of his gut. The instant her arms went hesitantly around his shoulders, the sob tore from him. His entire body shook in response.

"Go ahead," Susannah whispered, tears in her eyes. "Cry, Sean. Cry for all the awful things you've seen and had to do to survive. Cry. I'll hold you. I'll just hold you...." And she did, with all the womanly strength she possessed.

Time drew to a halt, and all Susannah could feel were the terrible shudders racking Killian's lean body as he clung to her, nearly squeezing the breath from her. He clung as if he feared that to let go would be to be lost forever. Susannah understood that better than most. She tightened her grip around his damp shoulders, whispering words of encouragement, of love, of care, as his sobs grew louder and harsher, wrenching from him.

Susannah was no longer feeling her own pain, she was experiencing his. She held Killian as if she feared that to release him would mean he would break into a million shattered pieces. His fingers dug convulsively into her back as the sobs continued to rip through him. Her gown grew damp, but she didn't care. His ability to trust her, to give himself over to her and release the glut of anguish he'd carried by himself for so long, was exhilarating.

Gradually Killian's sobs lessened, and so did the convulsions that had torn at him in her arms. Gently Susannah stroked his hair, shoulders and back. His spine was strong, and the muscles on either side of it were lean.

"You're going to be fine," Susannah whispered, pressing a kiss against his temple. "Just fine." She sighed, resting her head against his, suddenly exhausted.

Killian flexed his fingers against Susannah's back. Never had he felt more safe—or loved—than now. Just the soft press of her lips against his temple moved him to tears again. He nuzzled deeply into her hair, pressing small kisses against her neck and jaw.

Words wouldn't come. Each stroke of Susannah's hand took a little more of the pain away. The fragrance of her body, the sweetness of it, enveloped him, and he clung to her small, strong form, absorbing the strength she was feeding him through her touch and voice.

Susannah had been hurt by his abruptly leaving her life without an explanation, yet now she was strong, when he had never felt weaker. Her fingers trembled against his hair, and he slowly lifted his head. She gave him a tremulous half smile, her eyes huge with compassion and love for him.

Love. He saw it in every nuance of her expression, in her hand as it came to rest against his jaw. How could she love him? When she reached forward, her fingers taking away the last of the tears from his cheeks, he lowered his lashes, ashamed.

"Tears are wonderful," Susannah whispered, a catch in her voice. "Ma always said they were liquid crystals going back to Mother Earth. I always liked that thought. She said they were the path to the heart, and I know it's true." She smiled gently into Killian's ravaged eyes. "You were brave enough to take the biggest step of all, Sean."

"What do you mean?" he asked, his voice thick, off-key.

"You had the ability to reach out and trust someone with your feelings."

"Crying is a weakness."

"Who taught you that?"

"Father. Men don't cry."

"And they aren't supposed to feel. Oh, Sean—" Susannah stroked his cheek gently. "Men have hearts, too, you know. Hearts that have a right to feel as deeply and widely as any woman's."

He shakily reached over and touched her cheek. "I was afraid that if my nightmares came back and you were around, I'd hurt you." Hanging his head, unable to meet her compassionate gaze, he said, "When I was in the Foreign Legion, I met an Algerian woman, Salima, who loved me. I loved her, too." He shook his head sadly. "I kept having nightmares out of my violent past with the Legion, and it scared her. Finally, I left her for good. I feared that one night I might lash out and strike her." Miserable, Killian held Susannah's gaze. "After that, I swore never to get involved with a woman. I didn't want to put anyone through the hell I put Salima through. I saw what it did to her, and I swore I'd never do it again. And then you walked into my life. I've never felt such strong emotions for a woman before, Susannah. Those old fears made me leave to protect you from what I might do some night. My God, I couldn't stand it if I hurt you. I nearly did tonight.''

She caressed his jaw. "You could have, but you didn't. Some part of you knew it was me, Sean. That's what stopped you, darling.''

He lowered his gaze, his voice cracking. "I—I had a nightmare about Peru, about one of our missions. Wolf and I got caught and tortured by a drug lord, and the rest of our team had to go into the estate and bust us out.'' He squeezed his eyes shut. "That was last year. It's too fresh—that's why I get these nightmares, the flashbacks...''

"And you were having flashbacks after you woke up?'' Susannah guessed grimly.

His mouth quirked and he raised his head. "Yes. I was hoping...'' He drew in a ragged sigh. "I started screaming in my bedroom, and I got up, hoping I hadn't awakened you. I went out to the garage, where I always go when these things hit. It's safer that way. A lot safer. I'm like a wild animal in a cage,'' Killian added bitterly, unable to meet her lustrous gaze. His hands tightened around hers.

"A wounded animal, but not a wild one,'' she whispered achingly as she cupped his cheek. Killian's eyes were bleak; there was such sadness reflected in them, and in the line of his mouth. "Wounds can be bound up to heal, Sean.''

He managed a soft snort. "At what cost to the healer?''

Susannah stroked his damp, bristly cheek. The dark growth of beard gave his face a dangerous quality. "As long as you're willing to get help, to make the necessary changes, then I can stay with you, if you want."

He turned to her. "Look at you. Look at the price you've already paid."

Susannah nodded. "It was worth the price, Sean. *You're* worth the effort. Don't you understand that?"

"I don't know what kind of miracle was at work when you reached out for me," he rasped. Killian held up his hands. "I've killed with these, Susannah. And when I mean to defend myself, I do it. The other person doesn't survive."

A chill swept through Susannah as she stared at his lean, callused hands. Swallowing convulsively, she whispered, "Some part of you knew I wasn't your enemy, Sean."

He wanted to say, *I love you, that's why,* but stopped himself. Just looking at her pale, washed-out features told him that he had no right to put Susannah on the firing line. A terrible need to make love with her, to speak of his love for her courage, her strength, sheared through Killian. He gazed down at her innocent, upturned face.

"You're a beautiful idealist," he whispered unsteadily. "Someone I don't deserve, and never will."

"I'll decide those things for myself."

He gave her a strange look, but said nothing. Placing his hand on her shoulder, he rasped, "Let's get you to bed. You need some sleep."

"And you? What about you?"

He shrugged. "I won't sleep."

"You slept like a baby after we made love to each other," Susannah whispered. She reached over and gripped his hand.

"I guess I did."

Susannah held his misery-laden eyes. "Then sleep with me now."

Killian stared at her, the silence lengthening between them. His throat constricted.

"Come," she whispered. "Come sleep at my side."

Chapter Eleven

A ragged sigh tore from Killian as he felt Susannah's weight settle against him. The darkness in her bedroom was nearly complete. Everything was so natural between them that it hurt. Despite how badly he'd frightened Susannah, she laid her head in the hollow of his shoulder, and her body met and melded against the harder contours of his. Her arm went around his torso, and Killian heard a quivering sigh issue from her lips. To his alarm, after he'd drawn up the sheet and spread, he felt Susannah trembling. It wasn't obvious, but Killian sensed it was adrenaline letdown after the trauma she'd endured.

"This is heaven on earth," he whispered roughly against her hair, tightening his grip around her. Susannah was heaven. A heaven he didn't deserve.

"It is." Susannah sighed and unconsciously moved her hand across his naked chest. The hair there was soft and silky. His groan reverberated through her like music.

Stretching upward, Susannah placed her lips softly against the hardened line of his mouth. Instantly Killian tensed, and his mouth opened and hungrily devoured hers. She surrendered herself to the elemental fire that leaped between them wherever their bodies touched.

Sean needed to understand that no matter how bad the terror that lived within him was, her love—and what she hoped was his love for her—could meet and dissolve it. Susannah's fleeting thought was quickly drowned in the splendor of his mouth as it captured hers with a primal hunger that sent heat twisting and winding through her. His hands tangled in her thick hair, and he gently eased her back on the pillow, his blue eyes narrowed and glittering.

"Love sets you free," she said, and reached up and drew him down upon her. Just the taut length of his body covering hers made her heart sing. The gown she wore was worked up and off her. The white cotton fell into a heap beside the bed, along with his pajama bottoms. As Killian settled back against her, he grazed her flushed cheek.

"You're so brave. So brave..." And she was, in a way Killian had never seen in a woman before. Knowing gave him the courage to reach out and love her as he'd torridly dreamed of doing so many times. As he slid his fingers up across her rib cage to caress her breast, he felt her tense in anticipation. This time, Susannah deserved all he could give her. There was no hurry now, no threat of danger. His mouth pulled into a taut line, somewhere between a smile of pleasure and a grimace of agony, as she pressed her hips against him.

The silent language she shared with him brought tears to his eyes. Susannah wasn't passive. No, she responded, initiated, and matched his hunger for her. When her hands drifted down across his waist and caressed him, he trembled violently. His world, always held in tight control, began to melt as her lips molded against his and her hands ignited him. He surrendered to the strength of this woman who loved him with a blinding fierceness that he was only beginning to understand.

As he slid his hand beneath her hips, Susannah closed her eyes, her fingers resting tensely against his damp, bunched shoulders. Her world was heat, throbbing heat, and filled with such aching longing that she gave a small whimper of pleading when he hesitated fractionally. The ache intensified. Without thinking, guided only by her desire to give and receive, Susannah moved with a primal timelessness that enveloped them. They were like living, breathing embers, smoldering, then blazing to bright, hungry life within each other's arms.

As Killian surged powerfully into her, he gripped her, as if she represented his one tenuous hold on life. In those spinning, molten moments when they gave the gift of themselves to one another, he felt real hope for the first time since he had lost his family. Glorying in his burgeoning love for Susannah, Killian sank against her, breathing raggedly.

Gently he tamed several strands of her sable hair away from her dampened brow. His smile was vulnerable as she opened her eyes and gazed dazedly up into his face. What right did he have to tell Susannah he loved her? Did he dare hope that she could stand the brutal terrors that plagued him night after night? Was he asking too much of her, even though she was willing to try?

Tasting again her wet, full mouth, Killian trembled. He didn't have those answers—as badly as he wanted them. There was so much to say to Susannah, to share with her. He lost himself in her returning ardor, for now unwilling to look beyond the moment.

With a groan, Killian came to her side and brought her into his arms. "You're sunlight," he rasped, sliding his fingers through her tangled hair. "Hope and sunlight, all woven together like some kind of mystical tapestry."

The words feathered through Susannah. Sean held her so tightly—as if he were afraid that, like the sun, she would disappear, to be replaced by the awful darkness that stalked him. With a trembling smile, she closed her eyes and pressed the length of herself against him. He'd used the word *hope*. That was enough of a step for now, she thought hazily. The word *love* had never crossed his lips. But she had to be patient and wait for Sean to reveal his love for her, if that was what it was after all. Susannah didn't try to fool herself by thinking that, just because they shared the beauty of loving each other physically, it meant that Sean came to her with real love. She would have to wait and hope that he loved her in return. Whispering his name, she said, "I'm so tired...."

"Sleep, colleen. Sleep," he coaxed thickly. As much as he wanted to love her again, to silently show her his love for her, Killian knew sleep was best. He might be a selfish bastard, but he wasn't that selfish. Refusing to take advantage of the situation, he absorbed her wonderful nearness, wanting nothing more out of life than this exquisite moment.

Lying awake for a good hour after Susannah had quickly dropped off to sleep, Killian stared up at the plaster ceiling. How could she have known that he needed this? Needed her in his arms? Her soft, halting words, laced with tears, haunted him. Susannah loved him—without reserve. Didn't she know what she was getting into? He was a hopeless mess of black emotions that ruled his nights and stalked his heels during the day.

His mouth tightening, Killian absently stroked her silky hair, thinking how each strand, by itself, was weak. Yet a thick group of strands was strong. Maybe that was symbolic of Susannah. She was strong right now, while he'd never felt weaker or more out of control.

Sighing, Killian moved his head and pressed a chaste kiss to her fragrant hair. He'd cried tonight, for the first time in his life. Oddly, he felt cleaner, lighter. His stomach still ached from the wrenching sobs that had torn from him, and he absently rubbed his abdomen. The tears had taken the weight of years of grief away from him. And Susannah had paid a price to reach inside him to help him.

Closing his eyes, his arms around Susannah, Killian slid into a dreamless sleep—a sleep that was profoundly deep and healing. His first such sleep since the day he'd become a soldier in the French Foreign Legion.

Killian awoke with a start. *Susannah?* Instantly, he lifted his head and twisted it to the right. She was gone! Sunlight poured in through the ivory sheers—a blinding, joyous radiance flooding the room and making him squint. Quickly he sat up. The clock on the dresser read 11:00. *Impossible!* Killian muttered an exclamation to himself as he threw his legs across the bed and stood up. How could it be this late?

Fear twisted his heart. *Susannah.* Where was she? Had she left him after awaking this morning? Had she realized just how much of a liability he would be in her life? Bitterness coated his mouth as he quickly opened the door and strode across the hall to his bedroom. He wouldn't blame her. What woman in her right mind would stay around someone like him?

Killian hurried through a quick, hot shower and changed into a pair of tan chino slacks and a dark blue polo shirt. He padded quickly down the hall and realized that not only were the heavily draped windows in the living room open, they were raised. A slight breeze, sweet and fragrant, filled the house.

"Susannah?" His voice was off-key. Killian quickly looked around the living room and found it empty. He heard no sound from the kitchen, but hurried there anyway. Each beat of his heart said, *Susannah is gone.* A fist of emotion pushed its way up through his chest, and tears stung his eyes. Tears! Killian didn't care as he bounded into the kitchen.

Everything looked in order. Nothing out of place— and no Susannah. Killian stood there, his hand pressed against his eyes, and gripped the counter for support. She was gone. The shattering discovery overwhelmed him, and all he could do was feel the hot sting of tears entering his closed eyes as he tasted her loss.

The laughter of women vaguely registered on his spinning senses. Killian snapped his head toward the window. Outside, down by the lawn leading to the oceanfront, Susannah stood with his gardener, Mrs. Johnston.

His fingers whitened against the counter, and it took precious seconds for him to find his balance. Susannah hadn't left! She'd stayed! Killian stood rooted to the spot, his eyes narrowing on the two women. Susannah wore a simple white blouse, jeans, and sensible brown shoes. Her glorious hair was plaited into one long braid that hung between her shoulder blades. She stood talking animatedly with the gray-haired older woman.

Relief, sharp and serrating, jagged down through Killian. Susannah was still here. He hung his head, feeling a mass of confused emotions boiling up within him. He loved Susannah. He loved her. As he raised his head, he felt many things becoming clear. Things he had to talk to Susannah about. What would her reaction be? He had to tell her the truth, and she had to listen. What then? Killian wasn't at all sure how Susannah would judge him and his sordid world. What he did know was what he wanted: to wake up with this woman every morning for the rest of his life. But could he ask that of her?

Susannah waved goodbye to Mrs. Johnston as she left. Turning, she went through the front door of the beautifully kept cottage. In the living room she came to a startled halt.

"Sean."

He stood near the couch. The surprise on her features turned to concern. Killian searched her face ruthlessly for any telltale sign that she had changed her mind about him since last night. He opened his hand.

"When I got up, you were gone. I thought you'd left."

Susannah saw the suffering in his dark eyes. "Left?" She moved toward where he stood uncertainly.

"Yeah, forever." Killian grimaced. "Not that I'd blame you if you did."

Susannah smiled softly as she halted in front of him. Killian was stripped of his worldly defenses, standing nakedly vulnerable before her. Sensing his fragile state, she gently reached out and touched his stubbled cheek.

"I'm in for the long haul," she said, holding his haunted gaze. "If you'll let me be, Sean."

A ragged sigh tore from him, and he gripped her hand

in his. "Then we need to sit down and do some serious talking, Susannah."

"Okay." She followed him to the couch. When he sat down facing her, she tucked her legs beneath her. Her knees were touching his thigh. His face was ravaged-looking, and his eyes were still puffy from sleep.

"Last night," Killian began thickly, reaching out and grazing her skin, "I could have hurt you." He felt shaky inside, on the verge of crying again as he rested his hand on her shoulder. "After my parents were murdered, Meg and I were given to foster parents to raise. I guess we were lucky, because we had no family left back in Ireland, so Immigration decided to let us stay. Our foster parents were good to us. Meg really blossomed under their love and care."

"And you?"

Sean shrugged. "I was angry and moody most of the time. I wanted to kill the two boys who had murdered our parents. I didn't do well at school. In fact, I skipped it most of the time and got mixed up in gang activities. Meg, on the other hand, was doing very well. She began acting in drama classes at high school, and she was good. Really good."

Susannah saw the pain in Sean's features. No longer did he try to hide behind that implacable, emotionless mask. His eyes were raw with uncertainty and his turbulent emotions. Reaching out, she covered his hand with hers. "How did you get into the Foreign Legion?"

"I joined the French Foreign Legion when I was seventeen, after running away from home. I had a lot of anger, Susannah, and no place to let it go. I was always in fights with other gang members. I saw what I was doing to my foster parents, to Meg, and I decided to get out of their lives.

"The Legion was hard, Susannah. Brutal and hard. It kills men who don't toughen up and walk a straight line of harsh discipline. By the time they found out my real age, I'd been in a year and survived, so they didn't kick me out. Most of my anger had been beaten out of me by that time, or released in the wartime situations we were called in to handle.

"I was only in a year when my company was sent to Africa to quell a disturbance." Killian withdrew his hand and stared down at the couch, the poisonous memories boiling up in him. "I won't tell you the gory details, but it was bloody. Tribesmen were fighting one another, and we had to try and intercede and keep the peace. For three years I was in the middle of a bloodbath that never stopped. I saw such inhumanity. I thought I knew what violence was, because I'd grown up in Northern Ireland, where it's a way of life, but this was a hundred times worse."

"And a hundred times more haunting?"

Her soft voice cut through the terror, through the revulsion that dogged him. When she slid her hand into his, he gripped it hard. "Yeah—the basis for most of my nightmares.

"The Legion has no heart, no feelings, Susannah. No one in the company slept well at night—everyone had nightmares. To combat it, to try to find an escape, I took up karate." He released her and held up his hand, his voice bleak. "All I did was learn how to kill another way. I was a natural, and when my captain realized it, he promoted me and made me an instructor to the legionnaires stationed with me. Just doing the hard physical work took the edge off my time in Africa.

"And then, *Sous-Lieutenant* Morgan Trayhern was transferred into my company as an assistant company commander. He had a lot of problems, too, and we just kind of gravitated toward each other over a period of a year. We both found some solace in each other's friendship. Morgan kept talking about creating a private company of mercenaries like ourselves. He wanted to pursue the idea once his hitch was up with the Legion.

"I liked the idea. I hated the Legion, the harsh discipline. Some of the men needed that kind of brutality, but I didn't. I was getting out after my six-year obligation was up, so I began to plan my life for the future. I told Morgan I'd join his company if he ever wanted to try it." Gently he recaptured Susannah's hand, grateful for her silence. She was absorbing every word he said.

"Then we had trouble in Africa again, and my company parachuted into a hot landing zone. It was the same thing all over again—only the tribes' names had changed. But this time both tribes turned on us and tried to wipe us out."

Susannah gasped, and her fingers closed tightly over Killian's scarred hand.

His mouth twisted. "Morgan was facing a situation similar to the one he had in Vietnam. We lost eighty percent of our company, Susannah. It was a living hell. I thought we were all going to die, but Morgan pulled us out. I saved his life during that time. Finally, at the last moment, he got the air support he'd requested. We were all wounded. It was just a question of how badly. Before both tribes hit us with a final assault, we were lifted out by helicopter." His voice grew bitter. "All the rest, every last valiant man who had died, were left behind."

"How awful..."

Killian sighed raggedly. "Last night I lay awake a long time with you in my arms, reviewing my life." He gently turned her hand over in his, realizing how soft and feminine she was against him. "I was born into violence, colleen. I've done nothing but lead a violent life. Last year, Morgan sent three of us down to work with the Peruvian police to clean up a cocaine connection. Wolf, a member of our team, got captured by the local drug lord. I went in to save him, and I ended up getting captured, too."

Susannah's eyes widened. "What happened?"

"The drug lord was real good at what he did to us," was all he would say. He still wanted to protect Susannah, somehow, from the ugliness of his world. "He had us for a month before Jake, the third member of our team, busted in and brought down the drug lord. Wolf was nearly dead, and I wasn't too far behind him. We got flown stateside by the CIA, and we both recuperated in a naval hospital near the capital. As soon as Wolf regained consciousness, he told Morgan he wanted out, that he couldn't handle being a mercenary any longer."

With a little laugh, Killian said, "At the time, I remember thinking Wolf had lost the edge it takes to stay alive in our business. He's part Indian, so he stayed pretty much to himself. So did I. But I admired his guts when he told Morgan 'no more.' Morgan didn't call him a coward. Instead, he saw to it that Wolf got a job as a forest ranger up in Montana."

With a shake of his head, Killian whispered, "I envied Wolf for having the courage to quit. I wanted to, but I thought everyone would see me as a coward."

Hope leaped into Susannah's eyes, and it was mirrored in her voice. "You want to quit?"

"I can't," Killian said quietly, searching her glowing features, clinging to the hope in her eyes. "Part of my check goes to pay for my sister's massive medical bills. But..."

"What?"

He gripped his hands, thinking how small, yet how strong, she was. "I'm messed up inside, Susannah. Maybe I've done this work too long and don't know any other way." His voice grew thick. "Last night, when I held you, I realized that I needed to get help—professional help—to unravel this nightmare that's eating me alive from the inside out. I swore I'd never put you in that kind of jeopardy again."

With a little cry, Susannah threw her arms around Killian's shoulders. "I love you so much," she whispered, tears squeezing from her eyes. She felt his arms slide around her and bring her tightly against him. Killian buried his face in her hair. "It can be done, Sean. I know it can."

He shook his head, and when he spoke again his voice was muffled. "I don't know that, Susannah."

She eased away just enough to study his suffering features. "I'll be here for you, if you want...."

The words, sweet and filled with hope, fell across his tightly strung nerves. He searched her lustrous eyes. "I don't know...." How badly he wanted to confess his love to her, and yet he couldn't. "Let me feel my way through this."

"Do you want me to leave?" She hated to ask the question. But she did ask it, and then she held her breath.

"I— No, not really." He held her hand tightly within his. "That's the selfish side of me speaking. The other side, the nightmares... Well, you'd be better off staying at a nearby hotel—just in case."

Susannah had faith that Killian would never harm her, no matter how virulent his nightmares became, but she knew it wasn't her place to make that decision. "I have the next three weeks off, Sean. My principal gave me the time because he felt after all the trauma I'd gone through I needed time to pull myself together again."

Killian's heart thudded, and he lifted his head. "Three weeks?" Three weeks of heaven. There was such love shining in her eyes that he clung to the tenuous shred of hope that had begun burning in his chest when he loved Susannah last night.

"Yes...."

He compressed his lips and studied her long, slender fingers. The nails were cut short because she did so much gardening, Killian realized. Susannah had hands of the earth, hands that were in touch with the primal elements of nature—and her touch brought out so much in him that was good. "I'll take you to a hotel in downtown Victoria," he told her quietly. "I want you to stay these three weeks if you want, Susannah." He lifted his gaze and met hers. "No promises."

She shook her head, her mouth growing dry. "No... no promises. A day at a time, Sean."

Susannah gave him a trembling smile and framed his lean, harsh face between her soft hands. "You slept the whole night last night without those dreams coming back?"

Killian nodded. "It was the first night I've slept that hard. Without waking up." He knew there was awe in his voice at the revelation.

Susannah gave him a tender smile. "Because you trusted yourself on some level. The situation was important enough for you to reach out and try to change it."

There was food for thought in her assessment. A little more of the tension within him dissolved. "I want to live now, in the present,'' he told her, capturing her hands. ''I want to take you sailing this morning, if you'd like.'' He gestured toward the wooden dock at the edge of the water. ''I've got a forty-foot yacht that I've worked on for the past eight years, between assignments. I've always been good with wood, so I began to build the boat as something to do when I got back here.''

''Because you couldn't sleep?'' Susannah's heart broke for him.

''Partly.'' He managed to quirk a smile. ''Then I put in the rose garden around the house. I find keeping busy keeps me from remembering.''

''Then let's go sailing. I've never done it before, but I'm willing to try.''

Sunlight glanced off the dark blue of the ocean as the yacht, the *Rainbow,* slipped cleanly through the slight swells of early afternoon. Susannah sat with Killian at the stern of the yacht. He stood proudly at the helm, his focus on the sails as the wind filled them, taking them farther away from the coast of the island. The first time the yacht had heeled over on her side, Susannah had let out a yelp of fear and surprise, thinking the boat would flip over and drown them. But Killian had held her and explained that the yacht would never tip over. Over the past two hours, Susannah had relaxed and enjoyed his company, the brilliant sunlight and the fresh salt breeze that played across the Strait of Juan de Fuca, where they were sailing.

''Here, hold the wheel,'' he said. Killian saw the surprise in her wide eyes. He smiled and held out his hand. Just being on the water helped to clear his mind and emotions.

''But—''

"I need to change the sails," he explained, reaching down and gripping her fingers. "Don't you want to learn about sailing?" he said teasingly as he drew her to her feet and placed her beside him at the wheel.

"Sure, but—"

Killian stood directly behind her, his body providing support and shelter for her as he placed her hands on the wheel. His mouth near her ear, he said, "I'm going to shift the sails from port to starboard. Be sure and duck when the boom comes across the cockpit. Otherwise, you'll be knocked overboard, and I don't want that to happen."

"Are you sure I can do this?" Susannah was wildly aware of Killian's body molded against hers. The feeling was making her want him all over again. As she twisted a look up at him, she felt her heart expand with a discovery that nearly overwhelmed her. His hair was ruffled by the breeze, and there was real joy in his deep blue eyes. For the first time, she was seeing Sean happy.

"Very sure." He leaned down and pressed his lips to her temple. The strands of her hair were silky beneath his exploration. Susannah invited spontaneity, and Killian reveled in the quick, hot kiss she gave him in answer.

"All right, I'll try," she said, her heart beating hard from his closeness.

"Just remember to duck," he warned, and left her in charge of guiding the yacht.

At two o'clock, they dropped anchor in a small crescent-shaped bay. Thrilled with the way the day was revealing itself, Susannah helped Sean tuck the sails away before the anchor was dropped. He motored the vessel into the dark blue bay, which was surrounded by tall evergreens on three sides. A great blue heron with a seven-foot wing span had been hunting frogs or small fish in the shallows, and it took off just as their anchor splashed into the water.

Susannah watched in awe as the magnificent bird swept by, just above the mast, and headed around the tip of the island. She turned just in time to see that Killian was watching the huge crane, too.

"She was breathtaking," Susannah confided as she moved toward the galley. Killian had promised her lunch, and she was hungry.

Sean nodded. "What I'm looking at is breathtaking," he murmured, and he reached out and captured her. The yacht was very stable at anchor; the surface of the bay smooth and unruffled. Susannah came willingly into his arms, closed her eyes and rested against his tall, lean form. His voice had been low and vibrating, sending a wonderful sheet of longing through her.

Killian absorbed Susannah against him, her natural scent, the fragrance of her shining sable hair, intoxicating him. "I feel like a thief," he murmured near her ear, savoring the feel of her arms tightening around him. "I feel like I'm stealing from you before I get thrown back into the way things were before you stepped into my life."

Gently disengaging from him, just enough that she could meet and hold his gaze, Susannah nodded. Her love for him was so fierce, so steadfast, that she wasn't threatened by his admission. "I remember a number of times in my folks' marriage when they went through stormy times," she confided. "They love each other, Sean, and Ma often told me when I'd grown up and we talked about those stormy periods that love held them together. I like the way Ma sees love, Sean. She calls it a fabric that she and Pa wove together. Some threads were very strong. Others were weak and sometimes frayed or even broke. She saw those weak times as fix-it times. It didn't mean they weren't afraid. But the one thing they clung to throughout those times was the fact that they loved each other.''

He rested his jaw against her hair, absorbing her story. ''I've never thought of love as a fabric.''

''Look at your parents,'' Susannah said. ''Were they happy together?''

He nodded and closed his eyes, savoring her nearness and allowing her husky voice to touch his heart. ''Very happy.''

''And did they fight from time to time?''

''Often,'' he chuckled, suddenly recalling those times. ''My mother was a red-haired spitfire. My father was dark-haired and closed up tighter than the proverbial drum. When she suggested we emigrate to America, my father balked at the idea. My mother was the explorer, the person who would take risks.''

''And your father was content to remain conservative and have the status quo.''

Killian nodded and grazed her flushed cheek. Susannah's sparkling gray eyes made him aware of just how much she loved him. ''Yes. But in the end, my mother pioneered getting us to America. It took many years to make her dream for all of us come true, but she did it.''

Susannah asked soberly, ''Do you blame your mother for what happened a year after you emigrated?''

Killian shook his head. ''No. I wanted to move as much as she did.''

''You're more like your mother?''

''Very much.''

''A risk-taker.''

''I guess I am.''

Susannah held his thoughtful gaze. She could feel Sean thinking, weighing and measuring things they'd spoken about from the past and placing them like a transparency on the present—perhaps on their situation. Did he love her? He'd never said so, but in her heart, she felt he must—or as close as he could come to loving someone in his present state.

"I like," she said softly, "thinking about a relationship in terms of a tapestry. Ma always said she and Pa wove a very colorful one, filled with some tragedy, but many happy moments, too."

Gently Killian moved his hands down her slender arms, and then back up to rest on her shoulders. "A tapestry is a picture, too."

"Yes, it is."

"How do you see the tapestry of your life?" he asked quietly.

She shrugged and gave a slight smile, enjoying his rough, callused hands caressing her. "I see teaching handicapped children as important to my life. I certainly didn't see getting shot and being in a coma or having a contract put out on me, but that's a part of my tapestry now." She frowned. "I guess, having that unexpected experience, I understand how precious life is. Before, Sean, I took life for granted. I saw myself being a teacher, someday meeting a man who would love me, and then marrying. I want children, but not right away. I saw my folks' wisdom in not having children right away. It gave them a chance to solidify and work on their marriage. By the time Denny came along, they were emotionally ready for him. By the time I came along, they were more than ready." She smiled fondly. "I had a very happy childhood compared to most children. But I feel part of it was my parents' being older and more mature, more settled and sure of who they were."

"A tapestry that had the scales of life woven into it," he mused, holding her softened gaze.

"I never thought of it in symbolic terms, but yes, a balancing between doing something I love and having a husband and children when we're both ready for them, for the responsibility of raising them the best we can."

"You've brought balance into my life," Killian admitted, watching her eyes flare, first with surprise, then with joy. "I fought against it."

"Because you were scared."

"I still am," he told her wryly, and eased away.

Susannah followed him into the tight little galley below. There was a small table with a wraparound sofa, and she sat down to watch him fix their lunch at the kitchen area.

"I was scared to come and see you," she admitted.

Twisting a look over his shoulder as he prepared roast beef sandwiches, he said, "I couldn't believe you were standing there, Susannah."

"Your head or your heart?"

Her question was as insightful as she was about him. His mouth curved faintly as he forced himself to finish putting the sandwiches together. Placing the plate of them on the table, he brought over a bag of potato chips. "My head."

Susannah watched as he brought two bottles of mineral water from the small refrigerator built into the teakwood bulkhead. His entire face was relaxed, with none of the tension that was normally there. Even his mouth, usually a hard line holding back some emotional barrage, was softer.

"And your heart?" she asked in a whisper as he sat down next to her.

"My heart," he sighed, "in some way expected to see you." As he passed the sandwich to her, he met and caught her gaze. "I'm finding out that talking about how I feel isn't so bad after all."

With a little laugh, Susannah said, "Silence is the bane of all men. This society has bludgeoned you with the idea that you shouldn't feel, shouldn't cry and shouldn't speak of your emotions. It's a learned thing, Sean, and it's something you can change. That's the good news."

As he bit into his sandwich, Killian felt another cloak of dread dissolve around his shoulders. "You make it easy to talk," he admitted. "It's you. Something about you."

Melting beneath his intense, heated gaze, Susannah forced herself to eat the sandwich she didn't taste. Would Sean make good on his decision to send her away tonight? Or would he have the courage to let her remain? Her heart whispered that if he would allow her to stay with him tonight, his trust in himself and in her was strong enough that he could come to grips with his night-mare-ridden nights very quickly.

Nothing was ever changed in one day, Susannah re-minded herself. But life demanded some awfully big steps if one genuinely wanted to heal. If Sean could trust in her love for him, never mind the fact that he might not return her love in the same measure, he could use her support in healing his past.

Only tonight would tell, Susannah ruminated. Being a victim of violence had taught her about the moment, the hour, the day. She would take each moment with

Sean as a gift, instead of leaping ahead to wonder what his decision might be.

Just as they entered Sean's home, his phone rang. Susannah saw him frown as he hurried to the wall phone in the kitchen to answer it.

"Hello? Meg?" Killian shot a glance over at Susannah, who stood poised at the entrance to the living room. Surprised that his sister had called, he saw Susannah smile and disappear. She didn't have to leave, but it was too late to call her back. Wrestling with his shock over his sister's call, Killian devoted all his attention to her.

Susannah wisely left the kitchen. Going to her bedroom, she slowly began to pack her one and only bag to leave for the hotel in Victoria. She'd seen shock and puzzlement register on Sean's face over Meg's call. Didn't they talk often? Her heart wasn't in packing her clothes. The bed where they had lain, where they had made love, still contained the tangle of covers. Susannah ached to stay the night, to show Sean that two people could help his problem, not make it worse.

Killian was just coming out of the kitchen after the call when he saw Susannah placing her suitcase by the door. He shoved his hands into his pockets and moved toward her.

Straightening, Susannah felt her heartbeat pick up as Killian approached her. He wore a quizzical expression on his face, and she sensed that something important had occurred. She curbed her questions. Sean had to trust her enough to share, and not make her pull everything out of him.

"The funniest thing just happened," he murmured as he came to a halt in front of her. "Meg just called. I can't believe it." He shook his head.

"Believe what?"

"Meg just told me that she contacted Ian. She's asked him to fly to Ireland to see her." He gave Susannah a long, intense look.

"Wonderful!" Susannah clapped her hands together. "That's wonderful!"

"Yes...it is...."

"What led her to that decision?" she asked breathlessly, seeing the hope burning in Killian's dark eyes.

"She said he'd somehow found out where she was living and sent her a long letter. He talked about his love being strong enough to support both of them through this time in her life. All along, Meg loved Ian, but she was afraid he'd leave her as soon as he saw her disfigurement." Again Killian shook his head. "I'll be damned. The impossible has happened. I'm really glad for her. For Ian. They're both good people, caught in a situation they didn't make for themselves."

Reaching out, Susannah gently touched his arm. "The same could be said of you. Of us, Sean."

He stood very still, hearing the pain, the hope, in Susannah's voice, and seeing it reflected in her eyes.

Risking everything, she whispered, "Sean, you could send me away, just as Meg sent Ian away. Only you would be sending me away just for the night hours that you fear so much. She sent him away for several years, because of her fear that she would be rejected. In a way," she said, in a low, unsteady voice, "you're doing the same thing to me. You're afraid if I stay, you'll hurt me."

Her fingers tightening around his arm, Susannah stepped closer. "I know it isn't true, but you don't. At least not yet. But if you're searching for proof, Sean, look at last night. You didn't have nightmares haunt you after we slept in each other's arms, did you?''

''No...I didn't....'' He stood there, assimilating the urgency in her heartfelt words. Realization shattered him in those moments. Meg had finally realized that Ian's love for her was steady—that it wasn't going to be pulled away from her, no matter how bad the situation appeared. He studied Susannah intently. He wasn't really questioning her love for him; he was questioning his ability to love her despite his wounding. Just as Meg had done, in a slightly different way.

Running his fingers through his hair, he muttered, ''Stay tonight, Susannah. Please?''

Her heart leaped with joy, but she remained very quiet beneath his inspection. ''Yes, I'd like that, darling, more than anything...''

With a groan, Killian swept her into his arms. He buried his face in her hair. ''I love you, Susannah. I've loved you from the beginning, and I was too stupid, too scared, to admit it to myself, to you....''

The words, harsh with feeling, flowed across Susannah. Murmuring his name over and over again, she sought and found his mouth. The courage to admit his love for her was, perhaps, the biggest step of all. Drowning in the heated splendor of his mouth, being held so tightly that the breath was squeezed from her, Susannah returned his fire. Tears leaked from beneath her closed eyes, dampening her lashes and then her cheeks.

As Killian eased from her lips, he took his thumbs and removed those tears of happiness. His own eyes were damp, and the relief he felt was sharp and deep. ''I want to try,'' he rasped as he framed her upturned face. ''It isn't going to be easy.''

''No,'' she quavered, ''it won't be. But our tapestry

will be strong, because of our courage to grow—together, darling.''

"I'm afraid of tonight, colleen."

"We'll be afraid together. We'll hold each other. We'll talk. We'll do whatever it takes, Sean."

She was right. "One day at a time. One night at a time." Never had Killian wanted anything to work as much as he did this. He'd never admitted loving another woman. He'd been too fearful to do that. Susannah's strength, her undiluted belief in him, was giving him the courage to try.

"There will be good nights and bad ones, I'm sure," Susannah warned. "We can't expect miracles."

He smiled a little. "You're the miracle in my life. I'll do whatever I have to in order to keep you."

His commitment was more than she'd ever dreamed of hearing from him. Somehow Meg's courage to release her past had helped him see his own situation differently. "Just trying is enough," Susannah told him simply. And it was.

Epilogue

Susannah's heart wasn't in her packing. Her three weeks on Vancouver Island had fled by like a blink of the eye. Killian was quieter than usual as he helped her take her clothes out of the closet.

He was thinking about something important, and she could feel it. The days had been wonderful days of discovery, of joy and exploration. The nights had been a roller-coaster ride of good and bad. Together they had managed to confront Killian's nightmare past, and with some success.

More than anything, Killian knew he needed professional help to completely change for good. They'd talked about it and agreed that Susannah couldn't be the linchpin of his healing. He saw her as a loving support, his primary cheerleader. But it wasn't her responsibility to heal him. It was his.

The suitcase was packed, and she snapped it shut. As she turned around, Killian brought her into his arms.

"I've got a few phone calls to make before I take you to the airport."

"Okay." One day at a time, she reminded herself. Sean had not spoken of anything beyond her three weeks at his house. As badly as Susannah wanted to know his future plans and how they included her, she didn't ask.

"I want you to be there when I make the call."

She searched his shadowed face. "Who are you going to talk to?"

"Morgan."

Her heart thudded once. "Morgan?"

"Yes."

"Why?"

Killian cupped her face and looked deep into her wide, loving eyes. "To tell him I'm asking for permanent reassignment to the U.S. only. I'm also telling him I want jobs that don't involve violence. He's got some of those available. Mercenaries are more than just men of war. Sometimes a mercenary is needed just to be eyes and ears. I'm going to tell him I want low-risk short-term assignments." He smiled uncertainly. "That way, I can make my home in Glen, Kentucky, and keep putting my life back together with you."

Tears jammed into her eyes. "Oh, Sean..." She threw her arms around his shoulders.

"It's not going to be easy," he warned her grimly, taking her full weight.

"We'll do it together," Susannah said, her voice muffled against his chest.

Killian knew it could be the worst kind of hell at

times, but Susannah's unwavering support, her love for him, had made the decision easy. He held her tightly. "Together," he rasped thickly. "Forever."

* * * * *

COMMANDO

To my brothers and their families:
Gary, Debby, Brian and Kimberly Gent,
and Brent, Jeanne, Erin and Lauren Gent.
A sister couldn't get luckier, believe me.

Prologue

"Mr. Trayhern, I want my daughter out of the Amazon jungle. Now. No questions asked."

Morgan Trayhern eyed the man who stood tensely in front of his large desk. Ken Travers, a millionaire real estate developer, wore a Saville Row suit; his black hair was peppered with a few white strands. Right now, he looked angry. Morgan rested his finger against his chin and allowed his instincts to take over. Travers might be rich and influential, but Morgan didn't like his attitude.

"Mr. Travers—"

"Call me Ken."

Morgan allowed a brief, perfunctory smile to cross his mouth as he eased forward in his leather chair. He clasped his hands in front of him and rested them on top of his cherrywood desk.

"All right. Ken. Perseus doesn't do anything without

asking a lot of questions first. You come bursting into my office without an appointment, and—''

''Yes, yes, and I apologize.'' Travers raked his hand through his short hair, his blue eyes narrowing. ''It's just that my daughter, Shah, has no business being down in the Amazon! She's headstrong and opinionated.'' Travers paced for a moment, halted and pinned Morgan with a glare. ''On top of that, she's half Sioux, and wears it like a damned badge of honor. She calls herself a warrior for Mother Earth. What rubbish! She's a hellion who goes off half-cocked on ridiculous, fanatical quests.''

''Please, Ken, sit down and let's discuss this matter intelligently.'' Morgan wondered which of his Perseus employees might be available for the assignment. Marie Parker, his intrepid assistant, kept him supplied with a complete, updated list of who was open. Quickly perusing the list, Morgan noted the ''not available'' status of Wolf Harding, who had recently quit. At least he was happy with his ranger's job in Montana—and he would be marrying Sarah Thatcher shortly. Marie had penned a date in the margin near Wolf's name to remind Morgan that he and Laura would be attending that wedding.

Hiding a smile, Morgan's gaze moved down the list. Killian had requested only American assignments, and low-risk ones at that. Judging from Ken Travers's agitated state, this potential assignment was probably not low-risk. Besides, Killian was still on his requested three-month leave, working to get his life back together, and Morgan respected that request. With Morgan's own sister-in-law, Susannah Anderson at his side, and his recent move to Glen, Kentucky, to be with her, Killian's focus was on the personal right now, anyway.

Morgan was nearly to the end of the list when he noticed that one of his men, Jake Randolph, was due to come in off an assignment today. That meant he'd be checking in with Marie tomorrow morning as a matter of course. Every employee, after coming off an assignment, wrote up a detailed report at the main office to be submitted to Morgan. Then the employee was given two weeks—or more, if he or she requested it—time off to rest and regroup.

Frowning, Morgan sat back in his chair, rubbing his jaw. Jake had been on a brutal assignment in Peru. He'd been responsible for getting all the parties together regarding the contract on Susannah Anderson by José Santiago's drug cartel. If it hadn't been for Jake's brazen approach to Santiago's estate, demanding that those now in command talk with the Peruvian government, as well as with U.S. officials, the contract would never have been lifted from Susannah's head. Yes, Jake had clearly been a key to saving Susannah's life.

Jake would be tired, Morgan knew. He'd risked his life time and again, carrying messages to the drug cartel on behalf of the U.S. government when the cartel officials refused to talk directly. Quickly glancing to the end of the list, Morgan realized that Jake was the only operative potentially free to take this assignment for Travers.

But would he? Morgan looked up at Travers. "I've got one of my operatives coming off an assignment tomorrow morning. Why don't we discuss some of the details of what you want done, and we'll have a meeting with him tomorrow?"

Travers nodded brusquely. "Fine with me. I just want this thing settled. I want my daughter the hell out of Brazil."

Chapter One

"Welcome home, Jake," Marie said with a smile.

Wiping his eyes, Jake Randolph smiled tiredly as he got off the elevator that led directly to the main office of Perseus. "Hi, Marie." He moved slowly across the thick rose-colored carpeting toward her desk. "Got something you've been wanting."

With a smile, she took his report. "Handwritten, no doubt?"

"Yeah. You know me—I can't type to save my soul." He stretched and yawned. "I'm taking that two weeks off. I'm beat."

"Not so fast," Marie murmured apologetically. "Morgan left word for you to come directly to him when you came back."

"Oh?"

"Yes. I'm afraid he's got another assignment, and you're the only person available to take it."

Jake frowned. "Listen, I'm wiped out from that Peruvian fiasco."

"I know you are. Just go in and talk to Morgan, will you? There's a gentleman in there with him. They've both been waiting for you to show up."

Groaning, Jake rubbed his face, which needed a shave. "Okay, but I'm turning it down."

Marie smiled understandingly and pressed the button on the intercom that sat on her desk.

"Jake is here, Mr. Trayhern. Shall I send him in?"

Jake opened the door to Morgan's spacious office and entered. Morgan looked up and nodded to him.

"Come in, Jake. Meet Ken Travers. Ken, this is Jake Randolph. Jake's our Brazilian specialist. He knows Portuguese, the language of the country, and he's been there on assignment a number of times in the past few years."

Travers leaped from the couch like an overwound spring and held his hand out.

"Mr. Randolph."

Jake sized up the lean, restless-looking businessman, taking an immediate dislike to him. It was an intuitive thing, Jake thought as he extended his hand to shake Travers's manicured one. Intuition had saved his life on a number of occasions, and he wasn't about to dismiss a gut feeling.

"Mr. Travers."

Jake turned to Morgan, whose face showed no expression. Not unusual, Jake thought—Morgan knew how to keep his feelings hidden until the proper time. Jake noted Travers's expensive suit, his perfect haircut, the gold watch on his wrist—and his arrogance. Hiding a wry smile at the thought, Jake realized that he must look like a country bumpkin by comparison. He wore jeans, rough-out boots and an off-white fisherman-knit sweater. November in Washington, D.C., was cold, and there was a threat of snow today.

"Have a seat." Morgan gestured to a wing chair positioned to one side of his desk.

Jake nodded, his attention still on Travers. There was a feeling of electricity in the air, and it was coming from him. Jake had learned a long time ago to say little and observe a lot. Travers was pacing like a caged animal, his hands behind his back and his brow furrowed. His full mouth was set in a line of decided aversion. But aversion to whom? Morgan? Him? Probably both of them, he surmised.

Marie, dressed in her tasteful and conservative navy suit with white piping, came in moments later bearing a silver tray that contained coffee and a plate of cookies for the three men. She set it on the coffee table in front of the couch.

"Please call my wife," Morgan told her, "and tell her I have to cancel my luncheon date with her."

"Yes, sir. Shall I order in the usual lunch from the restaurant?" Marie asked.

Morgan glanced over at Jake. "Would you like something to eat?"

"No, thanks. My stomach's still on Peruvian time."

Morgan grinned. "How about you, Ken? Hungry?"

"No!"

"Just bring me the usual," he told his assistant.

"Yes, sir." Marie gave Travers a deadly look, turned and left.

Jake was fascinated by Travers's snappish mood. He was like a pit bull waiting to eat someone alive. Fighting jet lag, Jake got up and ambled over to the coffee table, where Morgan was already helping himself to a cup of coffee. He needed help keeping himself awake. Originally he'd planned to drop his report off at Morgan's office and then make his way home to his condo in Alexandria, Virginia, not far from the office that he used only when necessary. Jake's real home was located in Oregon.

Travers paced while the two men got their respective cups of coffee and sat down again. Jake saw amusement in Morgan's eyes, and he realized the look was for him alone. With a slight nod, Jake spread out his long legs in front of him. Holding the dainty gold-edged white china cup in one of his large, scarred hands, a cookie in the other, he leaned back and relaxed.

"Ken, why don't you start from the beginning?" Morgan suggested, sipping the black, fragrant Brazilian coffee.

Agitated, Travers came to a halt, his hands planted imperiously upon his hips. "I just don't like having Mr. Randolph here. This is strictly private."

"Mr. Travers," Morgan told him, his voice a deep rumble, "if you want Perseus to help you, we need to know the facts. Furthermore, I'm not sure we *can* help you. You're in luck that Jake is here, because, *if* we decide to take your case, Jake will be the man sent on the mission. So why don't you sit down and start from the beginning?"

Jake watched as Travers vacillated. The man acted as if he were going to explode.

"Very well." Travers strode to the couch and sat down, his spine as rigid as the rest of him.

"My daughter, Shah Sungilo Travers, is down in Brazil. She's thirty years old, and a damned fanatic!"

Morgan tipped his head. "Fanatic? In what sense of the word?"

Grinding his closed fist into the palm of his hand, Travers snapped, "She's a damned ecology fanatic. She's down there in the midst of all the hell breaking loose about the Amazon Basin trees being cut down. Global warming, and all that scientific garbage. Shah could be killed!"

"How long has she been down there?" Morgan asked.

"Three months."

Jake raised his eyebrows. "And you're just getting around to asking for help?"

Travers scowled, and his gaze dropped to his expensive-looking black leather shoes. "I didn't know. I— Oh, hell, I'm divorced from Shah's mother. I happened to be in Rapid City, South Dakota, on business, and I decided to drive out to the Rosebud Sioux reservation to visit Shah, who lives with her mother. But she wasn't there. That's when I found out she'd galloped off on another damned windmill-tilting adventure. Only this time it's to Brazil, and it could get her killed."

Travers stood up, his voice tight. "I want her out of there. She's in danger. It's that Sioux blood of hers. She loves a fight. She sees herself as a protector. A steward, she says."

Jake sat up, his interest piqued. A woman with Sioux blood and an unusual name like Shah interested him. But the picture Travers was painting didn't sound quite accurate. He gave Morgan a searching look.

"You can ask him anything you want," Morgan said, reading the question in Jake's eyes before he could voice his request.

"Mr. Travers, if your daughter is thirty years old, she's old enough to realize if she's in danger or not," Jake pointed out.

Travers gave him a withering look of pure disgust. "You don't know my headstrong daughter, Mr. Randolph. This isn't the first time Shah has been in the thick of things. Her mother named her Shah Sungilo, which means Red Fox in the Sioux language. She's got a temper to match any fox's red coat, and she's as clever as the damned animal she's named after." And then, with a snort, Travers added, "You'd think she would pick some worthwhile cause, and not put her life on the line for some lousy trees in Brazil!"

"What's her educational background?" Jake asked, realizing he wasn't going to get many facts from Travers under the circumstances. The man was clearly fit to be tied. But who was he angry at? Shah? Jake could understand a father being concerned about his daughter possibly being in danger, but where was this anger coming from? His gut told him there was a hidden agenda here, but could he get it out of Travers?

"Although she was born on the Sioux reservation, my daughter has had the finest education my money could buy. She has a master's degree in biology from Stanford University in California. I tried to persuade her to go after her Ph.D., but she said there was no time left, that Mother Earth was dying. Hell!" Travers raked his fingers through his hair again. "She's got her mother's firebrand temper and stubbornness. She's bullheaded and won't listen to anyone!"

He turned away and stared out the windows at the distant city. "Shortly after I divorced Shah's mother, I went to court to have my ex-wife pronounced an unfit mother. I didn't want my daughter raised on a Depression-level Indian reservation. Unfortunately, my ex-wife won. Shah spent the first eighteen years of her life on a damned reservation. What kind of place is that? They're backward there. Shah's mother is a medicine woman, and she forced Shah to live the old ways of her people. She was raised a heathen—never baptized. I should have—''

"Your daughter is a biologist down in Brazil," Jake said impatiently. "Is she on an assignment?"

"Yes. For a television station in Los Angeles that has paid her to investigate the destruction of the tropical rain forest in Brazil. Shah is an environmental activist. She thrives on confrontation." He shook his head. "She just won't back down."

Jake cast a look at Morgan, who was listening intently. "In a businessman, those attributes are often applauded," he noted mildly.

Travers glared at him. "Believe me, I tried to force my daughter to follow in my footsteps, but she didn't want anything to do with real estate. I tried to tell her it was about land, which she's so close to, but she said no Indian would ever sell the land, because it isn't ours to sell. She asked me one time, 'How can you sell Mother Earth? We're her children. All we can do is steward, not greedily buy and sell it.' Can you imagine? My own daughter calling me greedy because I buy and sell land?"

"Sounds like a cultural difference of opinion," Morgan murmured.

Jake liked Shah's attitude. He didn't particularly care for greedy people, whatever their business. "What makes you think your daughter's in trouble?" he asked.

Travers snorted and came over to them. He put his hands on his hips. "Shah goes out of her way to get into trouble. This isn't the first time, you know. She married that no-good half-breed Sioux when I told her not to— that it was a mistake. Well, it turned out to be one hell of a mistake. Shah's divorced from him now, but she had to be put in the hospital by that alcoholic husband of hers before she came to her senses.'' He nailed Jake with a dark look. ''My daughter lives for confrontation. Being physically attacked doesn't bother her. It's almost as if she expects it. Well, I've put too much money into her education to let her waste it, or herself, on some damned trees in the Amazon!''

''Calm down, Ken,'' Morgan ordered. ''Do you know what her exact assignment in Brazil is?''

''No. As I said, I just found out from my ex-wife that Shah left a month ago for Brazil.''

''And what do you want us to do?'' Morgan asked quietly.

''Bring her home! Get her out of there!''

''If she has a valid passport, approved by the Brazilian government, and she wants to stay, there's nothing we can do,'' Jake pointed out.

''Kidnap her, then!''

Morgan grimaced. ''Mr. Travers, we're not in the kidnapping business. We're in the business of providing protection and help to those who ask for it. But in this case, your daughter isn't asking us for help, you are.''

''I can't believe this! I'll pay you any amount of money to bring her out of Brazil! Shah should be home!''

Ordinarily, so soon after returning from a mission, Jake would be falling asleep in his chair, but this time he wasn't. He liked what he heard about Shah—a woman who evidently believed deeply and passionately in something beyond herself. It was too bad more Americans didn't have that kind of commitment.

''Maybe,'' Jake said, glancing over at Morgan, ''I could go down there and be a bodyguard of sorts.'' He turned to Travers. "I won't bring back your daughter against her will. Kidnapping is against the law in every nation in the world. What I can do is be there to protect her *if* she gets into trouble."

Morgan nodded. "Okay, that's what we can do, Mr. Travers. Jake is ideal for the mission, and I don't see a problem in him being a bodyguard for your daughter. What I want you to understand is, Jake won't haul her out of Brazil unless she wants to go."

Looking defeated, Travers spun on his heel. "I guess it's better than nothing," he muttered. He halted and turned his head in Jake's direction. "But I want you to do your damnedest to convince her to leave Brazil as quickly as possible. Can you do that?"

With a shrug, Jake finished off the last of the coffee and cookie. "No promises, Mr. Travers. Your daughter is an adult, mature and educated enough to know what she's doing. All I can do is wage a diplomatic campaign to try to get her to see your side of the issue."

"Then," Travers said unhappily, "I guess that's what I'll have to settle for." He took a photo out of his wallet and handed it to Morgan. "That's my daughter. You'll need to know what she looks like."

Morgan got up and came around the desk. "My assistant will have a number of papers for you to fill out and sign. She'll take you to another office to complete them. When you're done, we'll talk some more."

"Fine."

Jake watched Travers leave. Marie entered with Morgan's box lunch and set it on his desk. When she'd left, Jake stood up and placed his coffee cup on the silver tray.

"That guy has problems," Jake began seriously. He returned to his chair by Morgan's desk. Curiosity was eating him alive as he leaned forward to look at the small color photo of Shah Sungilo Travers.

Morgan smiled. "I don't care for his abrasive attitude, that's for sure. Go on, take a look at her."

Jake picked up the photo and studied it intently. Shah looked Native American, from her braided black hair to her light brown eyes, high cheekbones, full mouth and oval-shaped face. The photo was a close-up, but Jake could see that she was wearing a deerskin dress that was beaded and fringed. In her hair was a small eagle feather, along with several other decorations that hung to one side of her head. Her braids were wrapped in some kind of fur.

"She looks like she stepped out of the past," Jake said, more to himself than to Morgan.

"Doesn't she?"

"If she's half-white, she doesn't look it."

Morgan nodded and continued slowly eating his sandwich. "You looked interested, Jake," he noted after he swallowed.

"Maybe."

With a chuckle, Morgan wiped his mouth with a linen napkin. "That's one of your many traits that I like, Jake—you're noncommittal."

Jake had to admit that he was feeling anything but noncommittal as he continued to study the photograph of Shah. She wasn't smiling; she had a very thoughtful look on her face. Pride radiated from her in the way she stood, shoulders squared, with a glint of defiance in her wide, intelligent eyes. But there was something else, something that Jake sensed and felt but couldn't put his finger on. What was it? Was that a haunted look he saw in her eyes?

"I wonder how old she was when this photo was taken."

"Why?"

"Dunno." Jake laid the photo back on Morgan's desk. "Travers is hiding something from us," he said.

"I think so, too."

"But what?"

"I don't know." Morgan offered Jake some potato chips. Jake took a handful and munched methodically, frowning as he considered the question.

"Travers seems more angry than anything else," Morgan offered.

"Not exactly what I'd call the concerned-parent type," Jake agreed dryly.

"He's posturing, that's for sure," Morgan said. "It's obvious he's a real controller and manipulator."

Jake chuckled. "Yeah, and it sounds like his daughter rebelled very early on and leads her life the way she sees fit."

"Travers is also prejudiced against Indians."

"Noticed that, did you?" Jake rolled his eyes.

"I know you're a walking encyclopedia of knowledge...." Morgan said.

"I prefer to think of myself as a philosopher," Jake corrected, "despite being an ex-marine."

"And a mercenary," Morgan added. "So how much do you know about Indians?"

"Native Americans is the preferred term," Jake noted. "A little. Enough to realize that Shah is like some of the younger generation of Native Americans who are trying to reclaim their heritage. Her fierce pride isn't unusual."

"Ever been on a reservation?"

"Once, a long time ago. I had a marine friend who

was Navajo, and I went home with him for Christmas one year. His folks lived near Gallup, New Mexico, and they had a hogan made out of wood and mud. I stayed with them for nearly two weeks, and learned a hell of a lot.''

"You had a good experience?''

"Yeah.''

"Sounds like Travers didn't.''

"Travers,'' Jake intoned, "would hate anything or anyone who disagreed with him or got in his way.''

With a grin, Morgan finished off his sandwich. "Once Travers fills out the papers, I'm going to have a security check run on him.''

"Good idea. He looks a little too slick to me—one of those greedy eighties business types.''

"Sounds like his daughter is just the opposite of him—clear ethics, strong morals, and decided values.''

"I agree.''

"So, if all of our info comes back in order on Travers, do you want to be a bodyguard for a while?''

Jake shrugged. He tried to appear nonchalant, but his protective feelings had been aroused. He looked down at the photo. "Yeah, I'll go to Brazil and see what's going down.''

"She's a very pretty young woman.''

"The earthy type,'' Jake agreed.

Jake sat there for a long time, simply feeling his way through the photo of Shah. There was an ageless quality to her, as if all the generations of the Sioux people were mirrored in her classic Indian features. She didn't have a common kind of model's prettiness, but Jake never went for that cookie-cutter type, anyway. He liked women who had their own special and unique features.

Character, as far as he was concerned, should be reflected on a person's face, and Shah's face intrigued him.

Unconsciously he rubbed his chest where his heart lay.

"Memories?" Morgan asked quietly, breaking the comfortable silence of the office.

"Huh? Oh, yeah." Jake loved Morgan like a brother. They had both served as marines, and that bound them in an invisible way. Once a marine, always a marine—that was the saying. Even though they hadn't served together, they'd come from the same proud service. Marines stuck together, and supported each other and their families. Maybe that was why Jake liked working for Morgan so much—he understood Jake's tragic loss, and, like any marine brother, supported him as much as possible.

He gave Morgan a quick glance. "Bess was always spunky, too," he whispered, his voice strained. "Shah kinda reminds me of my wife in some ways."

"You always want me to give you assignments that deal with drugs," Morgan said. "This one won't involve drug trafficking."

"It's okay." Jake tried to shake off the old grief that still clung to his heart. "Maybe I need a change of pace. Something different."

"I feel this assignment may be more than it appears to be on the surface," Morgan warned him.

"What else do I have to do with my life?" Jake said, pretending sudden joviality. "Go home to an empty log house? Sit and watch a football game and drink a beer? No plants in the house. No animals..." *No family. No wife.* Not anymore. The grief grew within him, and he got up, rubbing his chest again. He saw Morgan's face, which was no longer expressionless. Morgan knew about personal loss as few men ever would. Jake stood there, unable to put into words the feelings unraveling within him.

"Well," Morgan said softly, "maybe it would do you good to have this kind of assignment, then." He attempted a smile. "Where you'll be going, there'll be plenty of plants and animals."

Jake nodded and moved to the windows. The November sky was cloudy, and it looked like either rain or the first snowfall of the year for the capital. "Brazil is having their springtime," he said, as much to himself as to Morgan. "It'll be the dry season down there, and the jungle will be survivable."

"Just make sure *you* survive this mission," Morgan growled.

Jake rubbed his jaw. "I always survive. You know that."

Morgan nodded, but said nothing.

Jake turned toward him. "You've got a funny look on your face, boss."

"Do I?"

"Yeah."

With a slight smile, Morgan said, "Well, maybe I'm hoping that Shah and her situation can lighten the load you've been carrying by yourself for so long, that's all."

Jake halted at the desk. "Well, time heals all, right?"

Morgan sat back. "Time has been a healing force for me, Jake. I hope it will be for you, too."

With a grimace, Jake ran his finger along the highly polished surface of Morgan's desk. "You know what William Carlos Williams said about time? He said, 'Time is a storm in which we are all lost.' I agree with him. I've never felt so lost since Bess's and the kids' deaths."

"I know."

Jake forced a smile he didn't feel. "Well, who knows? Maybe this storm surrounding Shah will be good for me. It can't get any worse."

Chapter Two

Manaus was the Dodge City of Brazil, Jake decided as he left the seedy-looking gun shop. Less than an hour ago, he'd stepped off the plane into the sweltering noontime heat that hung over the city. Now, standing on a cracked and poorly kept sidewalk outside the shop, Jake looked around. Disheveled houses, mostly shacks, lined both sides of the busy street. Odors in the air ranged from automobile pollution to ripe garbage to the muddy scent of the two mighty rivers that met near the city.

Sweat was rolling off Jake, but that wasn't anything new to him. Manaus sat at the edge of the Amazon Basin, home to one of the largest rain-forest jungles in the world. Rubber trees had been the cause of Manaus's rise to fame—and its downfall. Once chemical companies had learned to make synthetic rubber better than what the trees of the Amazon Basin provided, the city's boom had ground to a halt, leaving Manaus destitute.

Jake flagged down a blue-and-white taxi and climbed in.

"Take me to the docks. I need to hire a boat to take me down the Amazon," he said in Portuguese to the old man who drove the cab.

Nodding, the driver grinned and turned around.

Jake sagged back against the lumpy rear seat as the cab sped off. The asphalt highway leading to the docks was bumpy at best. Not much had changed in Manaus, Jake decided. Skinny brown children with black hair and brown eyes played along the edge of the road. Dilapidated houses lined the avenue. Although Manaus was struggling to come out of the mire of depression that had hit it so long ago, it had remained intrinsically a river town, filled with a colorful assortment of characters, greedy money-seekers willing to turn a quick dime and the now-impoverished "wealthy" who had depended upon their income from the rubber trees to keep them that way.

The docks came into view after about half an hour. Up ahead, Jake could see the wide, muddy ribbons of the Solimoes and the Rio Negro coming together to create the enormous Amazon. A number of boats—some small, some fairly large—dipped and bobbed, their prows either resting on the muddy river bank or tied off with frayed pieces of rope to some rotting wooden post on one of the many run-down wharves. As the taxi screeched to a halt, Jake paid the driver in cruzeiros, Brazil's currency, and climbed out. His only piece of luggage was a canvas duffel bag that was filled, though only partially, with clothes and other essential survival items.

Standing off to one side where the asphalt crumbled

to an end and the muddy slope began, Jake reached into the duffel bag and pulled out a large knife encased in a black leather sheath. He put the scabbard through his belt loop and made sure it rode comfortably behind his left elbow. Tying a red-and-white handkerchief around his throat to use to wipe the sweat from his face, Jake rummaged in the duffel bag again and came up with a few badly crumpled American dollars that he'd stuffed away in a side pocket.

Recession had hit Brazil big-time, and over the past few years inflation had risen from three hundred to six hundred percent. One American dollar was worth hundreds of cruzeiros, and Jake knew he'd have no trouble finding a willing skipper to take him where he wanted to go if he showed he had American money.

Jake also had a huge wad of cruzeiros stashed in a hidden leg pouch. Americans weren't common in Brazil, and those who did come were seen by the local populace as being very rich. Jake wasn't about to become one of the robbery or murder statistics on a local police roster. Manaus was a wide-open city, and it paid for any foreigner to be watchful and take nothing for granted. All of Brazil's large cities held areas of homes surrounded by huge wrought-iron fences, sometimes ten feet tall, to protect them from thievery, which was rampant in Brazil.

Pulling the leather holster that contained a nine-millimeter Beretta out of his bag, Jake strapped it around his waist. He wanted the holster low, so that he could easily reach the pistol. Because of the constant high humidity, Jake wore khaki pants and a short-sleeved white shirt, already marked with sweat.

Looking around from his position just above the muddy bank of the river, Jake smiled faintly. The cottony white clouds, heavy with moisture, barely moved above the jungle that surrounded Manaus. The noontime sun was rising high in the pale blue sky, shafting through the fragments of clouds. As Jake zipped up the duffel and slung it across his shoulder, he knew that for the next couple of days he'd be adjusting to the brutal combination of ninety-degree temperatures and ninety-percent humidity.

He heard cawing and looked up. A flight of red-and-yellow macaws flew across the river, barely fifty feet above the surface. They looked like a squadron of fighter jets, their long tails and colorful feathers in sharp contrast with the sluggish brown headwaters. Watching his step, Jake gingerly made his way down to what appeared to be the most seaworthy craft available, a small tug. The captain was dressed in ragged cutoffs. His legs were skinny and brown. His feet were large in comparison to his slight build, and he wore no shirt, pronounced ribs showing on his sunken chest. He was balding, and his brown eyes turned flinty as Jake approached.

"I need a ride," he called to the captain, "to a Tucanos village about three hours down the Amazon. Think that tub will make it that far?"

The captain grinned, showing sharp and decayed teeth. "This boat of mine isn't called the *Dolphin* for nothin'. She floats even when we have the floods!"

Jake stood onshore, haggling with the captain over the price of such a trip. In Brazil, everyone bargained. Not to engage in such efforts was considered rude. Finally, when Jake flashed a five-dollar American bill in the captain's face, negotiations stopped. The captain grabbed the money and held out his hand to Jake, a big, welcoming grin splitting his small face.

"Come aboard."

With an answering grin, Jake hefted himself onto the small tug. It had once been red and white, but lack of care—or more probably lack of money—had prevented upkeep on the paint. With a practiced eye, Jake slowly walked the forty-foot tug, checking for leaks.

"You know the name of this village?" the captain called as he slid up onto a tall chair that was bolted to the deck in front of the wooden wheel.

"Yeah, they call it the village of the pink dolphins."

Nodding sagely, the skipper waved to the children on-shore, who, for a few coins, would untie the tug and push it away from the wharf. "I know the village. There's a Catholic hospital and mission there."

Jake dropped his duffel bag on the deck and moved up front as the tug chugged in reverse. The hollow sound of the engine, and the blue smoke pouring from it, permeated the humid air. Narrow strips of wooden planking served as benches along the tug's port and starboard sides. Jake sat down near the captain and looked out across the bow.

"What else do you know about the village?" Jake asked.

The captain laughed and maneuvered the tug around so that the bow was now pointed toward the huge expanse of the headwaters, which were nearly a mile in width. "We hardly ever see an American who speaks fluent Portuguese." The man eyed the gun at Jake's side. "You go for a reason, eh?"

"Yeah." Jake decided the skipper wasn't going to answer his question—at least not on the first try.

The crystal-clear tea-colored water of the Solimoes was beautiful in its clarity. Its color was caused by the tannin contained in the tree roots along its banks, which seeped out and tinted the water a raw umber. The Solimoes's temperature was far lower than the Rio Negro's. As a result, the river's depths were clear, icy and pretty in comparison to the milky brown waters of the warmer Rio Negro, which Jake could see beginning to intersect it up ahead. Soon, the water surface around the tug mingled patches of tea-colored water with lighter, muddied water, reminding Jake of a black-and-white marble cake Bess used to bake.

"They say there's trouble at that village," the captain said as he maneuvered his tug against the powerful currents of the two rivers mixing beneath them.

So the skipper *was* going to answer him, if obliquely. Jake was pleased. "What kind of trouble?"

The captain shrugged his thin shoulders, his hands busy on the wheel as he kept the tug on a straight course for the Amazon River. "Pai Jose—Father Jose—who runs the Catholic mission there at the village, is said to have trouble. That's all I know."

Rubbing his jaw, which needed a shave, Jake nodded. He knew that the Catholic missionaries had had a powerful influence all over South America. The Indians had been converted to Catholicism, but the numerous missions along the rivers of the Amazon Basin were places not only of worship, but also of medical help—often the only places such help was available.

"You know this priest?" Jake asked.

"Pai Jose is balding," the skipper said, gesturing to his own shining head, "like me. He's greatly loved by the Indians and the traders alike. If not for his doctoring, many would have died over the years." The skipper wrinkled his nose. "He is a fine man. I don't like what I hear is happening at the Tucanos village where he has his mission."

Jake ruminated over the information. Communications

in this corner of the world were basically nonexistent outside of Manaus, except by word-of-mouth messages passed from one boat skipper to another. Few radios were used, because the humidity rusted them quickly in the tropical environment. Was Shah involved with Pai Jose? Was she even at the village? Jake didn't know— the information Travers had provided was sparse.

"They doing a lot of tree-cutting in this area?" Jake wanted to know.

"Yes!" The man gestured toward the thick jungle crowding the banks of the Amazon. "It brings us money. My tug is used to help bring the trees out of the channels along the Amazon to the Japanese ships anchored near Manaus."

It was a booming business, Jake conceded—and the money it supplied could mean the difference between survival and death to someone like the skipper.

"Besides," the man continued energetically as he brought the tug about thirty feet away from the Amazon's bank, where the current was less fierce, "the poor are streaming out of the cities to find land. They must clear the trees so that they can grow their own vegetables. No," he said sadly, "the cities are no place for the peasants. They are coming back, and we need the open land. Manaus no longer needs the rubber trees, and the farmers need the land. So, it is a good trade-off, eh?"

Jake didn't answer. He knew that the terrible poverty of Brazil, both inside and outside the cities, was genuine. Here and there along the muddy banks he could see small thatched huts made of grasses and palm leaves. Curious children, dressed in ragged shorts or thin, faded dresses, ran out to stare at them. He looked out across the enormous expanse of the Amazon. It made the Mississippi River look like a trickle.

"Look!" the skipper shouted with glee. "Dolphins!"

Sure enough, Jake saw three gray river dolphins arc into the air then disappear. They were playful, and soon they saw many more.

"This is a good sign," the skipper said, beaming. "Dolphins always bring luck. Hey! If you are truly lucky, you may get to see a pink dolphin near that village! They are very rare."

"What do the Indians say about pink dolphins?" Jake was enjoying the antics of the sleek, graceful gray animals that were now following the tug, playing tag.

"There is an old legend that if a pink dolphin falls in love with a beautiful young village girl, he will, at the time of the full moon, turn into a handsome youth. Once he has legs and lungs, he leaves the river to court this beautiful girl. He will lie with the girl, get her with child, then walk back into the water to become a pink dolphin again. A girl who has such an experience is said to be blessed."

Jake wondered about that legend, but said nothing. The legend could have been created to explain a young girl's sudden and unexpected pregnancy. Heaving a sigh, he allowed himself to relax. There was nothing to do for the next two and a half hours, until they reached the village. Stretching out on the narrow wooden seat, Jake decided to see if he could catch some badly needed sleep.

"Hey!" the skipper called. "We're here!"

Groggily Jake sat up. He was damp with sweat. He untied his neckerchief and mopped his face and neck. The tug was slowing, the engine's forward speed checked as they aimed at a dilapidated wooden dock where several Tucanos children waited.

Wiping sleep from his eyes, Jake stood up and rapidly sized up the small village huts thatched with palm fronds. The tall trees of the Amazon still lined the riverbanks, but just inside them the land had been cleared for homes for the Tucanos. He counted roughly fifty huts, and saw a number of Indian women near fires tending black iron cooking kettles. The women were dressed in colorful cotton dresses, their black hair long and their feet bare. The children raced around, barely clad. The short, barrel-chested, black-haired men held blowguns. Machetes hung on belts around many of their waists.

The odor of wood smoke combined with the muddy stench of the river. As the tug gently bumped the dock, Jake could also smell fish frying. About a dozen Tucanos children gathered, wide-eyed as Jake leaped from the tug to the dock. He set his duffel bag down on the gray, weathered surface of the poorly made dock.

"How can I get a ride back up the river to Manaus?" he asked the skipper.

Grinning toothily, the skipper pointed to the village. "Pai Jose has a radio. He knows the name of my tug. He can call the wharf at Manaus, and someone will find me."

That would have to be good enough, Jake thought. He lifted his hand to the skipper and turned to find the Indian children looking solemnly up at him, curiosity shining in their dark brown eyes. They were beautiful children, their brown skin healthy-looking, their bodies straight and proud. He wondered if Shah, because of her native ancestry, felt at home in the village.

"Pai Jose?" he asked them.

"*Sim! Sim!*" Yes! Yes! The oldest, a boy of about ten, gestured for Jake to follow him.

Slinging his bag over his shoulder, Jake followed the

boy through the village. The ground consisted of a whitish, powdery clay base that rose in puffs around his boots. Most of the village was in the shade of the trees overhead, and the smoke purled and made shapes as it drifted through the leafy barrier. Shafts of sunlight filtered through the trees here and there, and Jake's skin burned. Tropical sunlight was fierce.

A well-worn path through the vegetation wound away from the village and up a small incline onto a rounded hill that overlooked the river, and Jake could see a rectangular adobe brick structure near the top of it. Palm trees, both short and tall, bracketed the path. The calling of birds was nonstop, and sometimes, Jake would catch sight of one flitting colorfully through the brown limbs and green leaves of the thousands of trees.

The path opened into a small, grassy clearing. At the other end was the mission. It wasn't much, in Jake's opinion—just a grouping of three or four structures with a white cross on the roof of the largest building. That had to be the church. The place was well kept, and the path obviously had been swept, probably with a palm-leaf broom. Pink, white and red hibiscus bloomed around the buildings in profusion. Orchids hung down from the trees, turning the air heady with their cloying perfume.

Just as the Indian boy stopped and pointed at the church, Jake heard angry, heated voices. One was a woman's. He turned, keying his hearing to the sound. Giving the boy a few coins in thanks, Jake set his duffel bag on the ground and followed the sound. Turning the corner, he spotted a small wooden wharf down by the river, with several canoes pulled up onshore nearby. Five people stood on the wharf.

Frowning, Jake lengthened his stride down the sloping

path. As he drew closer, he recognized Shah Travers in the center of the group. His heart started to pound, and it wasn't because of the suffocating humidity or because of fear. Shah was tall—much taller than he'd expected. Her hair hung in two black, shining braids that stood out against the short-sleeved khaki shirt she wore. Mud had splattered her khaki trousers, and she wore calf-high rubber boots that were also covered with the thick, gooey substance.

What was going down? Jake saw the Catholic priest, an older man with wire-rimmed glasses, dressed in white pants and a shirt, plus his clerical collar, standing tensely. The other three made Jake uneasy. Two of them looked like goons hired by the well-dressed third man. Shah's husky voice was low with fury, and he couldn't catch what she said, but she was squaring off with the man in the light suit and white panama hat.

"I will not stay off that land!" Shah told Hernandez heatedly. "You can't make me!"

Hernandez's thin-lipped smile slipped. He touched the lapel of his cream-colored linen suit, where a small purple-and-white orchid boutonniere had been placed. "You have no choice, Miss Travers! That is my land, and I can do whatever I please with it—and that includes cutting down the trees!"

Shah tried to control her anger over the confrontation. She saw both of Hernandez's bodyguards come forward, trying to intimidate her. Well, it wouldn't work! She was aware that Pai Jose was wringing his hands, wanting to make peace. Her own heart was pounding with fear. She dreaded this kind of conflict. She'd been raised in a family of screaming and shouting, and she hated it.

"Look," she said between gritted teeth, "you can't

stop me from going onto that land! I know my rights, and I know Brazil's laws!''

Hernandez glowered down at her. "You are impertinent, Miss Travers. You Americans think you can come down here and cause trouble. Well, you can't! I forbid you to come into the area where we are going to log.'' He turned and looked at his men. "And if you so much as set foot on my land, I can assure you, my men will take care of you!''

Permanently, Shah thought. Before she could respond, the larger of the two men, a blond, German-looking hulk, moved forward. He gripped her by the collar of her shirt. Gasping, Shah froze momentarily. She heard Pai Jose give a cry of protest.

"Please," Pai Jose begged, "this isn't—''

Suddenly a hand appeared on the hulk's shoulder. "Now, where I come from, you treat a lady like a lady," the new man growled, pinching the man's thick muscles enough to let the lout know he meant business.

Shah's eyes widened considerably. Who *was* this man? Confusion clashed with her shock. He was tall. Taller than any of them, and bigger, too, if that was possible. Momentary fear sent a frisson of warning through her. He looked like an American, yet he'd spoken in fluent Portuguese. Her heart pounding hard in her chest, Shah gulped. His face was rugged and lined. When her gaze flew to his, something happened. Her heart snagged, a rush of wild feelings tunneling through her. His gray eyes were narrowed and nearly colorless, and for a brief second, Shah saw them thaw and felt an incredible sense of safety.

Instantly her heart and head denied those feelings. Men didn't protect, they abused. "Get your hand off me!'' she snapped at the blond man, and started to take a step back.

Jake jerked the hulk's shoulder just enough to force him to release Shah. The other bodyguard, a leaner, meaner-looking man, whirled toward him, his hand on the butt of the machete he carried in a long leather sheath at his side.

''Now,'' Jake drawled in Portuguese, ''I don't think any of us should behave like ruffians, do you? This is a lady, and we have a priest here. I know you boys have manners. How about showing them to me?'' Jake stepped away, his hand moving to the butt of his Beretta in a not-so-subtle warning that didn't go unnoticed.

Hernandez hissed a curse and spun around. ''Who are you?'' he demanded.

Jake smiled, but the smile didn't reach his eyes. Both goons were statues, waiting for orders from their thin Brazilian boss. ''I'm Ms. Travers' bodyguard,'' he said levelly.

Shah's mouth fell open. ''You're *what?*'' The word came out like a croak.

''Darlin', you stay out of this for now. This is male business.''

Shah's mouth snapped shut. Fury shot through her. ''Why—''

Jake barely turned his head. ''Pai Jose, why don't you take Miss Travers back to the mission? I'll finish the conversation with these boys alone.''

Hernandez jerked a look toward Shah. ''A bodyguard?''

''Well, you've got a couple, from the looks of it,'' Jake pointed out mildly, giving Hernandez a lazy smile. ''Why shouldn't she have one?''

''Well—'' Hernandez sputtered, then glared at Shah.

"It won't do you any good! You hire this, this American pig, and—"

"Hernandez, I didn't hire him!" Shah protested, straightening her shirt and collar. Who was he? Too much was at stake, and she wasn't about to get away from the point of Hernandez's unexpected visit. "And even if I did, I would still go onto that parcel of land where you're going to cut down the rain forest trees. It's my right to film anything I want. You can't stop me."

Jake saw Shah's cheeks flush. Her skin was glistening from the humidity, and she was simply breathtaking. Her body was ramrod-straight, her shoulders were thrown back proudly, and he wanted to applaud her courage. Still, under the circumstances, it obviously was a fool-hardy stance to take. This character Hernandez clearly hated everything Shah stood for. In Brazil, he knew women were frequently considered second-class citizens. Too many Brazilian men viewed women merely in terms of how many children they could bear, proof of a man's macho ability.

"Let's call an end to this discussion," Jake suggested amiably. He opened his hands and gestured toward Hernandez and his henchmen. "What do you say, gentlemen?"

Intimidated by the hardware Jake was carrying and by his size, Hernandez snarled, "Come!" at his goons, and they moved back into a dugout canoe with a small motor attached to the rear.

Shah remained tensely beside Pai Jose, breathing hard. She was still shaking inwardly from the man grabbing her by the collar.

"Thank God," Pai Jose whispered. He clasped his hands in a prayerful gesture and nodded to Jake. "I don't know who you are, *senhor,* but you have surely saved Shah.''

Shah watched as Hernandez's canoe sputtered noisily away from the dock, heading across the wide river. Then she turned to the American. "Who *are* you?"

Jake held up his hands. "Easy, I'm a friend. Your father sent me down here to—"

A gasp broke from Shah. "My father! Oh, brother, this is too much!" She leaped from the wharf. Once on the bank, she shouted, "Stay away from me! Just leave!" and hurried up the slope.

Nonplussed, Jake watched Shah head for the mission. He turned to the priest.

"Did I say something wrong?"

"My son," Pai Jose said in a sorrowful voice, "you just broke open a festering wound in her heart." He mustered a sad smile and offered his thin hand. "I am Pai Jose. And you?"

Disgruntled, Jake introduced himself. He noticed that the priest's hand was not only thin, but frail, as well. Pai Jose was probably close to seventy years old. His hair was silvered, and his small gold-rimmed glasses slid down on his hawklike nose. There was a kindness to the man, and Jake was glad he wasn't angry with him, too.

"Mr. Randolph, may I ask the nature of your visit?" the priest asked as he walked slowly off the dock with him.

"I'm here to take Shah home. Her father doesn't want her down in the Amazon. He's afraid she'll be hurt."

With a soft chuckle, the priest shook his head. "My son, Shah Travers is committed to saving our precious rain forest. God help her, but she isn't about to go home with you. And certainly not because her father sent you."

His mouth quirking, Jake followed the unhurried priest up the path toward the mission. "What do you mean, Father?"

"It's not really my place to speak of Shah or her personal problems." At the top of the knoll, huffing slightly, Pai Jose pointed to a small white adobe house that sat on the other side of the mission. "Shah is working with me on cataloging many of the medicinal plants used by the Tucanos shamans of the village. She has a hut down there, but it's my guess that she went back to the lab to work on some more plant specimens. Why don't you speak to her? I'm sure Shah can answer all of your questions."

But would she? Jake had his doubts. He nodded to the old priest. "Any chance of paying you to put me up here at the mission?"

"Of course, my son. You may stay with me at the cleric house."

"Money isn't any object."

"A donation would be satisfactory, my son, with our thanks. Red Feather, a dear Tucanos boy who helps me at the hospital and mission, will take your luggage and place sheets on a spare cot for you."

"Thanks, Father. Look, I've got to talk to Miss Travers."

"Of course." The priest smiled, his face wrinkling like crisp, transparent paper. "Dinner is at 8:00 p.m."

Jake nodded. He placed his duffel bag in front of the door the priest had indicated, then walked down another cleanly swept path toward the lab. He couldn't shake the image of Shah's face from his mind's eye—or his heart, to be brutally honest with himself. The photograph of Shah completely failed to do her justice. She had an earthy beauty. And beautiful *was* a word that Jake would use to describe her. Although their meeting had been fleeting, her facial features were forever branded on his memory. Her eyes were a tawny gold color, more intriguing than the light brown indicated in the photo. The Amazonian sunlight gave her eyes the color of the expensive golden topaz that was found and mined in Brazil. Her hair, thick and black, held captive in two braids that nearly reached her waist, was the inky bluish color of a raven's wing. Was it her mouth that intrigued him the most, that made him feel hot and shaky inside? In the photo, her lips had been compressed, but in person her mouth was full and lovely, reminding Jake of the luscious beauty of the orchids that hung in profusion around the mission from the tall, stately pau trees.

He slowed his step as he approached the lab. Shah was a strong-willed woman, there was no doubt about that. She hadn't screamed, fainted or backed down when that goon grabbed her. No, she'd stood her ground, her chin tilted upward, her mouth compressed and her eyes defiant. Jake had been in Brazil three other times, and on one occasion he'd come face-to-face with the most feared of all predators—the jaguar. He'd never forgotten that cat's golden eyes widening, the ebony pupils shrinking to pinpoints. The power he'd felt as he'd momentarily locked gazes with that cat was similarly etched in his memory. Shah's eyes were like the jaguar's: huge, alive with intelligence, and containing a spark of fierceness that he was sure was a gift from her Sioux heritage.

Shaking his head, Jake placed his hand on the lab's doorknob. Suddenly this was more than an assignment. It was an adventure—an adventure called "life." For the last four years he'd been living in a barren desert of grief. Now, with Shah impacting him like a hurtling meteor filling the night sky with its overwhelming brilliance, Jake felt guarded and uneasy. And, simultaneously, he was afraid—afraid that Shah would hate him and ask him to leave. Would she? He knocked on the wooden door with his knuckles to let her know that he was coming in.

Chapter Three

As Jake stepped into the lab, he heard the click of a pistol being cocked. The telltale click made him snap his head to the left. Shah stood behind a table covered with plant specimens, both hands wrapped around a deadly-looking .45.

"I told you to leave," she gritted out, glaring at him.

Jake's mouth fell open. Her voice was as low as a jaguar's growl. Her golden eyes were narrowed, just like the jaguar's.

"But—"

"I'm surprised my father was stupid enough to send someone else down to try to kidnap me."

His eyes widening, Jake slowly raised both his hands. Shah wasn't kidding around, he decided. She was fully capable of pulling that trigger. "Look," he told her, "we need to talk. Why don't you lower that gun, and we can—"

"Oh, sure," Shah said sarcastically. "Last time, Father sent two jerks who threw a gunny sack over my head and started dragging me toward the river, to a canoe they had hidden in the brush." She pressed her lips together and fought a desire to lower the gun. The man, whoever he was, looked genuinely upset and contrite. She was drawn to his eyes, whether she wanted to be or not. They looked terribly sad, and there were haunted shadows in their recesses. Whoever this hulking giant of a man was, something very painful must have happened to him. Angry at herself, at her tendency to always fall for the potential underdog, Shah hardened her voice. "My father sent you. That's all I need to know! Now get out of here, go back to Manaus, and leave me alone!"

Jake heard the real distress beneath the hardness that she was trying to bluff him with and slowly lowered his hands. "Where I come from, we introduce ourselves. I'm Jake Randolph. I work for Perseus, an organization based in Washington, D.C. It sends people around the world to help those who are in trouble."

With a twist of her lips, Shah moved carefully, the gun still pointed at Jake. "As you can see, Mr. Randolph, I'm not in trouble."

"You were a few minutes ago, lady."

"I could have handled Hernandez!"

"That big goon of his was going to pick you up by your collar and probably throw you into the Amazon. Then what would you have done? Gotten eaten by piranhas?" Jake was teasing her, hoping she'd lower the gun.

Scowling, Shah kept the long wooden table covered with plant specimens waiting to be cataloged between them. The lab had no electricity and had to rely on the natural light that filtered through the three large windows. "I swim in the Amazon and the channels all the time, and the piranhas don't attack me."

Allowing himself a bit of a grin, Jake said, "Because you're the meanest junkyard dog in the neighborhood?" He liked Shah. He sensed she was trying to bluff her way out of the situation. But in her eyes he could see a gamut of very real emotions bubbling close to the surface. He saw fear, real fear, in her eyes, a little anger, and a whole lot of wariness. More than anything, he liked the soft fullness of her lips and those flawless high cheekbones. Her wide, lovely eyes took on a slightly tilted appearance in her oval face. Jaguar eyes.

Jake Randolph's teasing lessened some of Shah's primal fear of him. She ignored his smile and tried to pretend she didn't like the strong shape of his mouth. Despite his craggy features, there was a gentleness to him that threw her off guard. How could anyone who looked that harsh have a gentle bone in his body? Her experience with men had taught her that none of them were to be trusted, anyway—regardless of their looks. "Sit down. Over there, in that wooden chair. And don't try any funny stuff."

Jake nodded, moving unhurriedly so as not to alarm her. He quickly scanned the lab. It was swept clean, and the walls were whitewashed, but green mold still clung stubbornly to the corners near the ceiling, speaking eloquently of the tropics' high humidity. The building held many tables, as well as a microscope and other scientific equipment. He saw a small glass of water with a lovely pink-and-white strand of small orchids in it. It gave off a faint perfume that was light and delicate—like Shah. He sat down.

"Now, with your left hand, very slowly take that gun

out of your holster and place it on the floor. Kick it away from you with your foot.''

"I'm a southpaw,'' he offered, giving her a slight smile.

Irritated, Shah moved closer, always keeping the table as a barrier between them. "Then use your right hand.''

Jake unsnapped the leather safety, withdrew the Beretta and laid it at his feet. "See? If I was really out to get you, I wouldn't have told you that, would I?''

"On the other hand,'' Shah snapped waspishly, "you could be lying. You could really be right-handed. Most people are.''

He straightened and laughed. It was a deep, rolling laugh that filled the lab. "Your logic is faultless.'' He held her distrustful gaze. "You know, you ought to think about working for Perseus. They could use someone like you. You think like a marine.''

Shah fought to shake off his sudden and unexpected laughter. She saw the light dancing in his gray eyes, as if he truly enjoyed their repartee. Her hands were sweaty, and the gun was heavy. Shah hated guns, but they were a way of life down here in the Amazon. "If that's supposed to be a compliment, then I don't accept it. Now, push that gun away with the toe of your boot.''

Jake gave the Beretta a healthy shove, and the pistol slid across the wooden floor. He watched as Shah started to move toward it. If he was going to get her to realize he wasn't her enemy, he had to earn her trust.

"Don't you want me to put my knife on the floor and kick it away, too?''

Shah halted and frowned. "Yes—I guess so. Do it— please.''

"Right or left hand?''

There was amusement in his eyes, and Shah knew he

was playing her for a fool. "When you get done laughing at me, you can use your right hand."

"I wasn't laughing at you."

"Really?"

Jake placed the knife on the floor. "It's rude to laugh at people. At least that's what my mother taught me."

"Then what did I see in your eyes?"

"Admiration."

Shah watched him kick the knife away. It landed near the pistol. This Randolph stymied her. "Now you stay still while I pick up your weapons," she told him. "One move and I'll blow your head off."

Jake didn't believe Shah's blustering. To disarm her distrust of him, he said, "I admire your courage under the circumstances. Not many women would be living in the Amazon jungle alone." She was shaken, he could tell, and he saw the pistol tremble in her hand. Carefully she moved toward his weapons, all the while keeping her gun trained on him.

With the toe of her boot, Shah kicked the weapons beneath the table. Finally she lowered the gun. There was a good ten feet between the two of them. "Father must have really gotten lucky snagging you. His last two tries failed miserably, so he must have put up a lot of money to hire the best kidnapper he could find—you." She allowed the pistol to hang at her side as she wiped her sweaty brow with the back of her left hand. "Too bad he couldn't have put all that wasted money into a nice donation to save the rain forest here, instead. But then, he wouldn't do that."

"He's sent two other teams down here to kidnap you?" Jake asked. There was indignation in his voice—and anger, too. He and Morgan instinctively hadn't trusted Travers. Now he was beginning to understand why.

Wearily Shah leaned against the wall, tense and on guard. "I don't know why I'm wasting my time talking with you. I've got a million things to do. Just stand up and go back down to the wharf. I'll have Red Feather take you by canoe to the nearest village where the tugs dock when they're working for Hernandez, pushing the logs down the river."

"I don't want to go."

Her spine stiffened, and she glared at him. "You don't have a choice!"

"Sure I do." Jake held up his hands in a peace-making gesture. "I'm not here to kidnap you. Your father hired me to try to *talk* you into coming home."

With a bitter laugh, Shah said, "Sure he did! He's a cold, hard businessman, Randolph. Anyone who gets in the way of his greedy progress is a liability, and he gets rid of them pronto. I'm a liability."

"Why would he want you out of here?" Jake asked reasonably, purposely keeping his voice low and soothing. Every minute spent with Shah convinced him that he should stay around. For the first time, Jake saw the slight shadows beneath her glorious golden eyes. There was tiredness around her mouth, too. Even the clothes she wore seemed a size too big for her. Was she working herself to death down here?

"Because," Shah said wearily, "he probably wants to protect his investment. I'm fighting a one-woman war to stop the destruction of the rain forest. Not that I'm the only one. There are other groups. But this area is especially important. Hernandez is particularly adept at slash-and-burn techniques."

Jake gave her a long look. "That's a hell of an indictment against anyone, especially your father."

Just the roughened tone of his voice soothed Shah's frayed nerves. He had a way of defusing her, and it made her relax. She straightened, making sure the pistol fit snugly in the palm of her hand. She couldn't trust this giant of a man. He could jump her if he got her off guard. His size alone would overwhelm her ability to defend herself and escape.

"Unfortunately, I am his daughter, but that's where any connection between him and me ends," Shah told him tightly. "My mother divorced him when I was twelve years old, and I couldn't have been happier."

"Why?"

Shah gave him a wide-eyed look. "Why would you want to know?"

"Because I care."

He did. It was on the tip of Shah's tongue to deny Randolph's words, but she saw genuine caring in his eyes, and felt that same powerful sense of protection emanating from him that she had on the dock when Hernandez's bodyguard grabbed her. Fighting the feeling, because it was foreign to her, Shah resurrected what little anger was left and snapped, "You care because he's paid you some fantastic sum of money! I know your kind, and I'm not about to trust you, so forget it! Now stand up!"

"I'm telling you the truth, Shah." Jake purposely used her first name to defuse her intent. It worked. He saw a startled expression momentarily flit across her features.

"Truth!" Shah spit out. "The only truth I see is you're a hired gun of my father's!"

"What was it someone said? Truth hurts, but it's the

lie that leaves scars? Why can't you believe me? I'm not here to kidnap you. Your father asked me to try to persuade you to come home, but if I couldn't, then I was to become your bodyguard instead.''

Rolling her eyes, Shah moved behind the table. She placed the heavy gun on the wooden surface. Her hand had grown tired from holding it. Wiping the sweat from her upper lip, she glared at him. ''Don't quote philosophy to me. The most dangerous kind of lie is the type that resembles the truth!''

''Who said that?'' Jake asked, truly impressed by her philosophical bent. He was delighted with the discovery; it was just one more amazing facet to Shah Travers.

''Oh, please! I had six years of college. Don't you think I took a course or two in philosophy? Kant? Descartes?''

''Great, we have a lot more in common than even I thought. We'll get along fine.''

''You aren't staying!''

''Now, Shah, I told you the truth. It's obvious to me you need me to stay. Fine. I'll just hang around like a big guard dog and protect you from the likes of Hernandez and his goons.'' Jake grinned, but inwardly he felt sorry for Shah. She appeared unsettled and exhausted. And why shouldn't she feel that way? Hernandez had been ready to have her beaten up if Jake hadn't arrived in the nick of time. She knew it, too, he suspected. Shah was nobody's fool.

''You can't stay because I don't want you to stay.''

''I can be of help to you.''

''I suppose you have a degree in biology?''

''No, but I have a degree in philosophy.''

''That doesn't get these plants identified and cataloged.''

"I'm a fast learner."

"You're impossible!"

"Thank you."

"It wasn't a compliment, Randolph, so don't sit there preening about it."

He tilted his head. "Are you mad at all men, or just your father?"

The question, spoken so softly, caught Shah off guard. The adrenaline from the confrontation with Hernandez was wearing off, and she felt shaky, mushy-kneed. She pulled over a four-legged wooden stool and sat down. What was it about Jake Randolph that threw her off-balance? Maybe it was his grave features, which looked carved out of granite, or his powerful physical presence. One look into those light gray eyes and Shah had realized she was dealing with a highly perceptive man. She had no experience with his type, so she didn't know how to react to him. Instinctively, she felt him trying to get her to relent and trust him.

Rubbing her brow, Shah muttered, "My track record with men isn't great. I don't trust any of them farther than I can throw them."

"Beginning with your father?" Jake needed to know the truth about Shah's background. It would give him understanding of her distrust toward him.

"I don't owe you my life story."

"That's true." The corners of his mouth lifted slightly. "I was born and raised in the Cascade Mountains of Oregon. Now, I don't know if you've ever been there, but it's one of the most beautiful places on the face of Mother Earth."

Shah's eyes narrowed. He'd used the term *Mother Earth.* What was Randolph up to? No one used that term unless they were Native American or some of the ecologically responsible people who believed in the Gaia theory, which held that the planet was indeed, a living being.

Ah, success! Jake mentally patted himself on the back for using the term *Mother Earth*. Shah had sat up. He had her full, undivided attention. Perhaps the more he revealed of himself the more she'd learn to trust him. Inwardly Jake laughed at the thought. He had been a typical male bastion of silence before marrying Bess. He'd been unable to communicate, unable to share what he was feeling with her. However, Bess wouldn't stand for the one-way communication system, and she'd insisted he open up. He was glad, because their marriage had deepened with joy and sharing as a result. Still, he wasn't used to baring his soul to just anyone, and on one level Shah was a stranger to him. On another level, however, Jake sensed, with a knowing that frightened him, that they were very much alike.

"I grew up on a small farm in a valley where my dad made a living for us by growing pears. We had a huge orchard, and my two sisters and I worked with him when we didn't have school. Dad was a real philosopher. He saw everything in terms of seasonal changes, the earth being alive, and respecting the environment. We never dumped oil on the ground, threw away a battery in the woods or put fertilizer on the soil. Instead, we had a couple of cows for milk, three horses because we kids liked to ride, and plenty of rabbits and chickens for food. He used to compost all the garbage from our household and spread it through the orchard twice a year as fertilizer. Dad had the finest pears in Oregon."

"You said 'Mother Earth,'" Shah growled, uncomfortable.

Jake nodded, placing his hands on his knees. He saw

the curiosity burning in her eyes and realized he'd struck a responsive chord in Shah. Jake hadn't felt so excited in years. Shah was a challenge, yet he sensed a fierce, caring passion lurking just beneath her prickly exterior. She had a passion for living life, Jake realized, and that excited him as little had since Bess's and the children's deaths.

"Yes, I did."

"Are you Native American?"

"No, just a combination of Irish, Dutch and English."

"Then why did you use that term?"

"Because my parents always spoke about the planet that way."

Shah sat back, trying to gauge whether Randolph was giving her a line or was really telling her the truth. "Oh..." she murmured.

Pleased that Shah was softening toward him, Jake continued in his rumbling voice. "I think Mom might have had a little Native American in her. Cherokee, maybe, somewhere a long ways back."

"Then that would give you some Native American blood."

Chuckling, Jake held up his hand. "Darlin', I'm about as white as a man can get. No, if I've got a drop of Cherokee in me, it's so washed out that it wouldn't matter."

Shah pointedly ignored the endearment that rolled off his tongue. It had felt like a cat licking her hand. "But it does," she said fervently. "It's a gene type. Even if you have just a drop of Cherokee blood, it would be enough. Genes have memory, and it's possible that your Cherokee gene is a dominant gene, which would give you an understanding that our planet is more than just a planet. She's alive. She communicates, and she breathes, just like us.''

There was such burning hope in her eyes that Jake couldn't bring himself to argue with her. Then again, she was a biologist, and she knew all about genes and such, so she could be right. If that meant something important and vital to Shah, then Jake was willing to go along with her logic. ''Well, I feel what matters is what we do on a daily basis,'' he demurred.

''Your walk is your talk. That's a Lakota saying.'' Thrilled that she was actually communicating with him, Jake heaved an inner sigh of relief. The gold in Shah's eyes danced with sunlight now, as if she'd met a brother of like mind. However, Jake didn't want to be her brother. Far from it.

''Lakota?'' he asked, fighting back his less-than-professional thoughts.

''Yes.''

''What's that?''

''Whites call us Sioux, but that's an Iroquois word that means 'enemy.' We call ourselves Lakota, Nakota and Dakota. There are three separate tribes, depending upon where you were born and the heritage passed down through your family. My mother is Santee, and that's Lakota.''

''I see.'' Jake smiled. ''I like learning these things.''

''In Brazil,'' Shah went on enthusiastically, ''the people are a combination of Portuguese, African and native. Brazil is a melting pot, and they certainly don't worry what color you are. And on top of that, the largest concentration of Japanese outside of Japan live in São Paulo. Did you know that?''

''No.''

''I like Brazil because of that. You aren't judged on

your skin color down here.'' Shah held out her hand.
''My skin looks tan in comparison to yours. But a Brazilian wouldn't care.''

''You have golden skin,'' Jake told her. Her skin was
a dusky color, and he wondered what it would be like
to lightly explore its texture—to slide his fingertips along
her arm. The thought was so powerful that Jake was
stunned into silence. There was such innocence to Shah,
to her simplified outlook on life in general.

Heat fled into Shah's face, and she looked away from
his kind gray eyes, momentarily embarrassed by her reaction to his statement. ''Well,'' she muttered, more defensively, ''you know what I'm saying. Lakota people
judge others by their walk being their talk.''

''It's a good philosophy,'' Jake said, meaning it. ''So
why don't you let me prove myself to you the same
way?''

Shah frowned. ''What do you mean?'' Why did she
have the feeling that behind this man's dangerous looks
there was a steel-trap mind?

With a lazy shrug of his shoulders, Jake said, ''I've
already told you the truth about why I'm here. I accept
that you don't want to go home. So why don't you let
me be your bodyguard? It's obvious you need one, with
Hernandez around.''

Getting up, Shah began to pace nervously back and
forth. ''No!''

''I can't go home,'' Jake told her reasonably, opening
his hands. ''Your father has paid me for a month's worth
of work down here. I'm not the type to gyp someone
out of work they've already paid me to do.''

''You should have been a lawyer,'' Shah charged
heatedly.

''Thanks. Was that a compliment?''

"You know it wasn't!"

His grin was broad and forgiving. "Calm down, Shah. I'm not your enemy. If I was, why didn't I side with Hernandez earlier? You know, I took a hell of a risk by entering that lopsided fray. If your father really wants you out of here, I could have stood aside and let Hernandez do his dirty deed."

Halting, Shah ruminated over his observation. She eyed him intently, the silence thickening in the lab. "Why should I believe you?" she asked him heatedly.

He held her golden gaze. He could see that she was fraught with indecision. Everything was so tenuous between them, and Jake had never wanted anyone's trust more. He wanted this woman's trust so badly he could taste it. "You're right," he told her quietly. "If your father has had others try to kidnap you, then you've got reason to be paranoid. But I can't prove myself to you except on a minute-by-minute basis, Shah. You'll have to be the judge and jury on whether I'm for real or not."

"I hate men like you!" she gritted out. "They say all the right things. You confuse me!"

"Truth is never confusing."

"Actions are a far better barometer of whether someone's lying," Shah snapped. Worriedly she paced some more. "I don't need you around. I've got enough responsibilities, Randolph. Tomorrow morning I'm going to take my video camera and canoe down the river. I'll make a landing on the parcel where Hernandez has a permit to cut down the rain forest trees. I need that film for the television station that's funding my work."

"Let me go along, then."

She stopped pacing and wrapped her arms against her chest. "No."

"Why not?"

"Because you could throw my video equipment into the river and—"

"I wouldn't do that, Shah," he told her sincerely. "I know you're jumpy about my presence, but I can't go home." He didn't want to, either. Shah fascinated him. She was an amalgam of fire, spirit and passion—all linked with innocence.

"Pai Jose said I could stay at the mission," Jake told her in a soothing tone, "and I'll do that. He said you live in the village. Let's take this relationship of ours one day at a time. I'll be your gofer. I'll do whatever little odd jobs or piddly tasks come up." Looking around, he added, "And judging from the way this lab looks, you need about five biology assistants helping you." Indeed, there were at least a hundred plant specimens in open plastic bags on the four tables. "I'm a pretty quick learner. Just see me as your right-hand man for a month."

Shah sat down, weary as never before. She didn't know what to do or say. Her heart was pleading with her to believe Randolph, while her head was screaming nonstop that he was lying, despite that roughened tone of his voice that sent a tremor of some undefined longing through her. And his eyes! She sighed. The man could melt icebergs with those eyes of his. There was such seemingly sincere gentleness contained in them that Shah had the ridiculous urge to throw herself into his arms and let him hold her.

Of all things! Shah berated herself. Men meant hurt, that was all. Lies and hurt, and not necessarily in that order. Randolph was too smooth, and far too intelligent, and Shah felt she'd more than met her mental match.

"We have a lot in common," Jake said, breaking the brittle silence. "I probably have Indian blood, however

little it might be. My parents raised my family to respect
Mother Earth.'' He gave her an imploring look, because
her face mirrored her indecision. ''What do you say? A
day at a time? Let my walk be my talk?''

She glared at him. ''A day at a time? Randolph, I'm
going to be monitoring your every move one minute at
a time.''

''No problem.''

Pointing to his gun and knife, Shah acidly added,
''And these weapons stay with me!''

''Fine.''

The man was infuriating! He was unlike any man
she'd ever met. He didn't try to argue with her or belittle
her decisions. ''Just who are you?'' Shah asked irritably,
sliding off the stool. She holstered her gun, picked up
his weapons and stalked around the table. Jerking open
the door, she turned and added, ''Never mind. I don't
want to know. Just leave me alone, Randolph, and we'll
get along fine. Stay up here with Pai Jose. The Great
Spirit knows, he needs all the help he can get. He'd love
to have a hardworking American around for thirty
days.''

She was gone. As Jake looked around, the lab suddenly seemed darker. Shah reminded him of blinding
sunlight; her presence was riveting and undeniable. Rising slowly to his feet, he rubbed his sweaty hands
against his pants. A slight smile lurked at the corners of
his mouth. Well, their first skirmish had ended in a decided victory for him. As he ambled out of the lab and
quietly closed the door behind him, Jake whistled softly.
Yes, the world was suddenly looking brighter. Shah was
like sunshine on water; scintillating, ever-changing.
There was an underlying tenderness to her, too. He
hadn't been wrong about her earthiness, either—not

judging from all the plants and flowers in the lab, and her work to catalog them and save the valuable information for the world at large.

Shah Travers had many fine qualities, Jake decided as he walked over to the mission. His duffel bag was gone, carried inside by Red Feather, the Tucanos boy who worked with Pai Jose. He stopped in the center of the small yard enclosed by the mission buildings and looked around. The profusion of color, the songs of the birds and the many scents mingling in the humid air made Jake smile broadly. The Amazon could be a cruel killer, he knew. But right now, the area was clothed in a raiment of beauty, because Shah Travers cared—deeply, passionately—for something outside of herself.

Whistling merrily, Jake decided to take a walk around the place. His mercenary side was always close at hand. He didn't trust Hernandez. Although he didn't know the local politics, he wanted to map out the village for his own satisfaction. He felt naked without his knife and pistol, but he was convinced that sooner or later Shah would trust him enough to give the weapons back.

But first things first. Reconnoitering the village like the recon marine he had once been was at the top of his list. Were these Indians friendly? Were they used to white men? Or would they use blowgun arrows tipped with deadly curare to kill him? There was a lot to discover, Jake conceded with a frown. Maybe the Tucanos accepted Shah because she carried native blood in her veins. Maybe Pai Jose was allowed to stay here because of his unceasing humanitarian work with them. He wasn't sure at all.

The dangers of the Amazon were many and real. Jake knew that from his other missions, although he'd never before spent so much time in the rain forest. On guard,

he tucked away the warm feelings lingering in his heart
regarding Shah. He was astonished by those emotions,
because for the past four years he'd felt nothing, numbed
by the loss of his family. Shah's unexpected entrance
into his life had been responsible for that change. But
what was he going to do about it? He wasn't sure. He
wasn't sure of anything right now.

Chapter Four

The Tucanos village was a long, haphazard affair that hugged the dry, cracked bank of the Amazon River. At first, Jake was jumpy about the Indians, but soon he had fifteen children following him as if he were the pied piper. The few men present were the old ones, and the women were busy working over their cooking pots. The younger men were probably out hunting during the daylight hours. They were a handsome people, Jake conceded, short but with robust bodies and clean features. Everywhere he walked, the old men and women would look up and stare at him, and some would give him a shy smile. He did the same.

The thatched huts were circular and varied in diameter, depending, Jake supposed, on the number of people living in them. Fires were kept outside of the homes, and Jake spotted woven mats placed on the dirt floor in several of them. The Tucanos people were primitive, without many civilized amenities. There was no electricity, except for what was produced by a gasoline-fed generator that Pai Jose kept behind the small infirmary next to the church. Jake doubted the old priest used it often—perhaps only when light was needed at night for a surgery.

Jake saw that he was coming to the end of the village. One small thatched hut with a dried brown palm-leaf roof sat off by itself. The huts were placed among the tall trees to take advantage of the shade. He slowed, and was about to turn around when he saw Shah emerge from the more isolated hut. Not wanting another confrontation with her, he started to turn, but it was too late.

Shah caught sight of Randolph, walking near her hut. "What are you doing? Snooping around?" she challenged as she walked toward the riverbank, where her dugout canoe was beached. She felt upset to see that Randolph was still around, still so close. Somehow, she hadn't wanted him to know where she was living.

"I was looking around." Jake shoved his hands in his pockets and smiled down at the assembled children in faded cotton shorts who trailed after him. He, too, moved toward the canoe. "It's an old marine habit," he offered.

"Marine?" And then Shah chastised herself for her curiosity. Randolph looked military, she acknowledged. Still, despite his size and his craggy features, she simply didn't feel threatened by him. Unable to understand why, she became angry with herself. She stopped at the canoe. Bento, her Tucanos helper, had found six new orchids along one of the lesser-used channels and brought them back for her to identify. But they had to be properly cared for if she was to try to find out what species they were. She had taught the Indian to place the plants in moist palm-fiber baskets to keep them safe and alive.

Jake stopped at the bow of the canoe and watched as she got down on her knees to gently and carefully gather up a multipetaled yellow flower. Perhaps conversation would ease the scowl on her broad brow.

"I was in the Marine Corps for sixteen years before I joined Perseus," he explained.

Shah glanced up. His towering figure was back-lit by the sun. The shadows deepened the harshness of his features, which would have been frightening if not for his boyish expression. She placed the orchid in a large plastic bag.

"You're a warrior, then." Somehow that fitted him. Shah couldn't picture him in a suit and tie.

He nodded. "Yeah, we saw ourselves as that. Your people were known as warriors, too."

Shah gently lifted the orchid and set it outside the canoe. She took a rusty tin can and walked to the river for water.

"The Lakota recognize that men *and* women can be warriors. It isn't gender-related."

"I didn't know that."

She gave him a dark look, then knelt down, her knees bracketing the orchid. Pouring water around the roots, she muttered, "Nowadays every woman has to be a warrior, to stand up and be counted, because we're the only ones who can save Mother Earth." She lifted her chin, challenge in her low voice. "It's the men who have polluted, poisoned and ruined our Earth in the name of greed, politics and self-oriented policies."

Jake looked up at the slow-moving Amazon. The muddy river's surface was like glass. He considered Shah's impassioned words. Looking back down at her, he realized she was waiting for his reaction. *Good.* He sensed her interest in him; he desperately needed to cultivate that fragile trust.

"I wouldn't disagree with you, Shah. Men have been raping Mother Earth for centuries. Everything's coming due now, though. It's payback time."

"*Rape* is the right word," she muttered, closing the plastic bag around the orchid's stem. She glanced at him, surprised that he agreed with her. Perhaps he was just stringing her along, trying to get her to believe he was really on her side. She was standing, ready to lift the heavy container, when Jake came forward.

"Here, let me carry that for you." He saw her golden eyes flare with surprise. Taking the plant container, he said, "I'm a great gofer. Tell me where you want this plant."

Stunned, Shah jerked her hands away from the container as he slid his large, scarred hands around its circumference. "Well, I...in my hut. I was going to try to look up these species before night fell." She dusted off her hands.

Jake walked toward her hut. It would give him the excuse he needed to see her living conditions—and to see how vulnerable her hut might be to attack. Shah hurried and caught up with him. There was a bright red cotton cloth over the front of the door, and she pulled it aside for him.

"Just set it next to the other ones," she told him, pointing to the far wall.

"This orchid smells great," Jake said as he bent low to enter the hut. Obviously it had been built for the short Tucanos people, not for tall Americans.

"I think it's a Mormodes orchid, but I'm not sure," Shah murmured as she followed him into the hut. He was so large! In fairness to him, though, the hut was one of the smallest made by the Tucanos—the type usually meant for an elderly person—and Shah had taken it because of that fact. She didn't want the generous Tucanos people giving up one of their family-size huts just for one person.

Jake's gaze took in the entire hut as he settled the flowering plant next to others against the wall. There was a wonderful scent of orchids mingled with the dry odor of the grass and palm leaves that made up the hut. He noted that a stack of flower identification books, all wrapped in plastic to protect them from the humidity and rain, sat nearby. Furnishings were sparse. Jake straightened to his full height. A grass mat that seemed to serve as Shah's bed lay on the dry dirt floor, topped by a light cotton blanket and a small pillow. Cooking utensils were near the door, for use over the open fire outside the hut. A woven trunk made of palm fiber was the only actual article of furniture.

"Nice place."

"If you like camping out," Shah said, moving back out through the door. She tried to calm her pounding heart. Was it because of Randolph's nearness? *Impossible.*

With a rumbling chuckle, Jake followed her. "I was a recon marine most of the time I was in the corps, and your hut is like a palace compared to what we had out in the bush."

"What do you mean?" Shah wished she could put a clamp on her mouth. Curiosity had been a catalyst throughout her life—too often landing her in hot water. Randolph was an enigma to her, and she tried to rationalize her curiosity about him: after all, if she knew more about him, she might be able to make a final decision on whether he was friend or enemy.

Jake ambled down the bank with her toward the canoe. "Recons are dropped behind enemy lines to gather needed information on troop movements, stuff like that," he explained. "We would sleep in trees, hide on the ground and generally be unseen while we collected the data we needed for the Intelligence boys."

Shah was impressed but didn't say anything, afraid her curiosity would be viewed as interest. But wasn't it? She tried to ignore her questioning heart. "I can get these other orchids," she protested.

"No way. I watched what you did. Why don't you go do something more important?"

Torn, Shah watched him take out the next flowering orchid. She was constantly amazed by the counterpoint of Randolph's size to his obvious gentleness. He picked up the orchid as if it were a vulnerable infant—surprising in such a big, hairy bear of a man. She tried to ignore his blatant male sensuality, the dark hair of his chest peeking out from the khaki shirt open at his throat. His arms were darkly sprinkled with hair, too. Shah swallowed convulsively. Despite his size, he wasn't overweight. No, he reminded her of a man who was not only in his physical prime, but in the best of condition, too.

"Oh, all right." Shah watched as several Tucanos children followed Jake to the canoe. They watched him with solemn brown eyes, and she smiled. She loved the Tucanos, who had welcomed her as one of their own. Once they'd found out that she was an "Indian," too, she'd been adopted by the chief of the village—a great honor.

"Do you like children?" Shah raised her hand to her mouth. Now where had that come from?

Jake frowned, hesitated and drew the next orchid, a

purple one, out of the canoe. "Yeah, I like the little rug rats."

"Rug rats?" Alarm entered her voice.

"That's an old Marine Corps term for kids. It's an affectionate term, not a bad one," he assured her as he put the water into the plastic bag that would keep the root system from drying out.

Shah saw his partial smile slip, and when he looked up at her she detected darkness in his gray eyes. There was an incredible sadness that settled around him, and it was overwhelming to her. She was highly intuitive, and had always had an ability to sense a person's real feelings. Her heart went out to him. "Kids mean a lot to you, don't they?" she pressed softly.

With a sigh, Jake gathered up the orchid. As he turned and met Shah's serious gaze, something old and hurting broke loose in his heart. "Well, I..." It was those golden eyes swimming with unshed tears that shook him. Why should she show such compassion for him? She was unaware of his past, of his family's tragic death. He stood there stupidly staring down at her, absorbing her understanding like a plant starved for water. The seconds eddied and halted around them, and Jake felt ensnared within the unspoken emotional web that surrounded him like an embrace.

Shaken by her unexpected understanding, he dipped his head and frowned. "Where do you want this orchid? Next to the others?" he demanded gruffly.

Shah swallowed convulsively. What had just happened? It felt as if they both had been suddenly surrounded by heightened and unexpected emotions. But the mesmerizing feeling had evaporated when Jake became gruff. Blinking, Shah stammered, "In—in my hut, with the rest..."

It hurt to feel, to think. Jake felt himself rebuilding old walls to defend his grieving heart. Adding to the hurt, the Indian children followed him like happy, playful puppies as he retrieved the rest of the orchids for Shah. He was grateful that she seemed aware that children were a sensitive topic for him. His mouth dry, tears burning the back of his eyes, he placed the last orchid on the floor of the hut.

Shah was outside, crouched over a small cooking fire, her tripod and kettle suspended above the coals. Giving him a quick glance, she went back to stirring the contents with a stick. Her heart beat faster as he approached. Suddenly shaky for no reason, Shah refused to look up at him.

"Are you psychic or something?" he demanded.

A small smile touched Shah's mouth, and she forced herself to look up at him. What she saw tore at her heart. There was such raw anguish in Randolph's eyes that she nearly cried out for him, for the pain he carried like a living thing within him. The Indian children had gathered around them. One small girl tucked herself beneath Shah's arm and leaned her small head against her shoulder.

"I'm intuitive," she admitted, and hugged the little girl fiercely, letting her know that she loved her.

Jake considered Shah with a renewed intensity. The little Indian girl looked as if she belonged to Shah. Both of them had shining black hair, brown eyes and golden skin. The child, no more than six years old, put her fingers in her mouth and smiled shyly up at him. It hurt to breathe in that moment, because the girl's expression resembled that of his eldest daughter, Katie, bringing back a flood of wonderful memories—and torment.

Without a word, Jake spun around and stalked away.

Nonplussed, Shah watched him leave. She had seen the questions in his eyes about her intuition. But she had also seen the devastation and bleakness in their depths. Slowly rising to her full height, Shah continued to hold the little girl close. Gently she ran her hand across the girl's long black hair and sighed. What was going on between her and Randolph? It was crazy, she decided finally. Daylight was fading quickly, and in its wake the sky had turned pale lavender and gold. Patting the little girl's shoulder, Shah asked her to stir the fish stew she had made. She needed to get to the identification books to find out if these orchids had been officially discovered before the light failed entirely.

Jake couldn't sleep. He lay on his back, his hands behind his head, in the austere mission room, which resembled a boxcar in size and shape. The palm-thatched door was open to allow what little cross-breeze there was from his open window. The cot wasn't long enough for him, but it didn't make much difference. The boards beneath him were covered by a thin, lumpy mattress that had seen too many years of ser7ice. All the night sounds—the calls of the howler monkeys, the insects buzzing outside the open window—provided a soothing chorus to Jake's frayed nerves.

Every time he closed his eyes, the image of Shah's lovely face, her large eyes filled with tears, struck at his wounded heart. After four years he'd thought that most of the loss was behind him, but that one poignant moment when Shah held the little girl in her arms had struck at him with savage intensity. With a sigh, he stared up at the wooden ceiling. If not for the quarter moon low in the night sky, the place would have been plunged into a darkness so inky that he wouldn't be able to see his hand in front of his face.

Although he wore only drawstring pajama bottoms, Jake's body was bathed in a sheen of sweat from the unrelenting humidity. Glancing at his watch, he realized it was four in the morning. He knew he had to get some sleep, but he was too tightly wound from being around Shah. Everything in the Amazon jungle seemed so quiet and serene in comparison to him.

There was no doubt that Shah loved children. He had seen it in her eyes, that special adoration she held for the little Tucanos girl. Shah was in touch not only with the soil beneath her bare feet, but also with the life she held in her arms.

With a soft curse, Jake slowly sat up, his bare feet touching the wooden floor. He buried his face in his hands. Why now? Why? He had to leave his past behind him, but it refused to be buried. Not that he tried to forget, but wouldn't there ever be a reprieve from the loss and the cutting loneliness he felt twenty-four hours a day? Jake raised his head to stare out the open door. He could hear Pai Jose snoring brokenly in the room next to his. Red Feather slept on a grass mat in the room across the hallway. There were three patients recovering from an assortment of ailments in the mission's small hospital wing, and Jake heard some snores drifting down the corridor from them, too. He was envious of the others' ability to sleep while insomnia stalked him.

Getting up, he rubbed his damp-haired chest with his hand. Maybe he needed to take a quick walk around the premises—to get some fresh air. Jake tugged off his pajamas and put on trousers, boots, and a dark green shirt with short sleeves. He missed his knife and pistol, because Pai Jose had warned him that at night, even this more settled area of the Amazon came alive with predators. Jaguars hunted the dangerous wild pigs; cougars, cousins to North America's mountain lions, also combed the tropical rain forest for unsuspecting prey.

Just as Jake came out of the mission doorway, he heard what at first sounded like a string of firecrackers popping. The sound came from the direction of the village, near the riverbank. Jake tensed—he recognized the sound of gunfire when he heard it. Running around the end of the building, he halted, his eyes widening. Fire erupted and exploded in the night sky. Some of the huts were on fire! Between the shadowy trees, Jake could see several men running with torches in hand through the Tucanos village.

Shah! Jake dug his feet into the sandy ground and sprinted down the hill. The village seemed so far away. More gunfire erupted. The cries of the Tucanos, startled out of sleep, spilled into the night air. The gunfire continued.

Suddenly Jake realized that whoever these invaders were they weren't Indian. No, they looked like the men Hernandez had hired. As he tore down the path, the wind whipping past him, Jake's mind spun with options. He was unarmed—unable to defend himself, much less Shah or the unarmed villagers. Veering off to the left, tearing through the jungle itself, Jake decided to hide by skirting around the village. He had to get to Shah's hut! His pistol was there, and so was she.

Shah groggily awoke, the sound of screams filling her ears. Sitting up, her hair cascading around her like a curtain, she smelled suffocating smoke. Firelight danced outside her window. What was going on? She scrambled to her feet, her knee-length cotton nightgown hampering her movement. Just as she reached the window, gunfire slammed through the hut. With a cry, Shah dropped to the floor, covering her head with her hands. What was going on? Who was attacking?

As she began to get up again, a hulking figure appeared in the doorway, jerking the cotton barrier aside. Shah screamed.

"It's me!" Jake rasped. He dropped to his knees. "Where the hell is my gun? We're under attack."

Frantic, the cries of the Tucanos shattering her composure, Shah groped for her trunk. "Here," she told him, fumbling in the darkness. "They're in here...."

"Get them!"

Obeying wordlessly, Shah's hands shook as she located the holster and pistol. "Here—"

"Stay down," Jake whispered savagely, and he forced her to lie on the ground. "Whoever's doing this is playing for keeps."

Sobbing for breath, Shah felt the strength of Jake Randolph's hand in the center of her back as he forced her to lie flat on the floor. "Who is it?" she cried.

"I don't know," Jake breathed as he hitched the holster around his waist. He could take a Beretta apart and put it back together again blindfolded. Despite the lack of light, he quickly drew the pistol from the holster, snapped off the safety and placed a round in the chamber. Getting up, pistol in hand, he went to the entrance.

"Don't you move," he growled to Shah.

She opened her mouth to tell him to be careful, but found that she couldn't speak. Her throat was choked with tears of outrage and terror over the attack. Who was setting fire to the village? Who was firing guns? Why?

Jake pounded down the bank of the Amazon toward

five dugout canoes tied to the dock. Each of them had a small motor mounted in the rear, and Jake's suspicion that Hernandez was involved grew. Ten men were fleeing the raging inferno of the village, running hard for the canoes. The shrieks of the Indians hammered at Jake as he halted, got down on one knee and aimed his Beretta.

Suddenly bullets whipped and whined all around him. Hitting the ground, Jake jerked his attention to the left, where the bullets were coming from. He couldn't see who was shooting at him; everything was dark and shadowed by the roaring flames and smoke that clouded the village. More sand whipped up in geysers around him. Someone had targeted him! Jake knew the other men were getting away. He wanted to capture one of them, but right now he had to protect himself. Whoever was firing at him was serious.

Sliding down off the bank, Jake moved into the tepid river up to his waist so that he'd present less of a target and the bank could provide cover. In moments, the firing stopped. Jake turned on his side, his Beretta aimed toward the dock. All but one of the canoes had left. Damn! Out of the corner of his eye, he saw the hulking figure of a man sprinting toward the remaining boat, followed by another, more slightly built man. The big man was the one who had grabbed Shah!

Scrambling out of the water, Jake leaped onto the bank. The big blond man was the one who had had him pinned down! Taking careful aim, he fired the pistol once, twice, three times. The man let out a cry and fell to the dock. Satisfaction soared through Jake as he scrambled to his feet and lunged forward. A tree root caught and captured the toe of his boot. With a grunt, Jake slammed down on the bank. Cursing, he got to his feet, but not in time. The canoe was leaving the dock, with both men in it. Damn!

Jake stood, torn between going after them and helping the Tucanos put out the raging fires that were consuming several of their huts. Shoving the pistol back into its holster, Jake decided to help the Indians. Many were running back and forth to the river with buckets. As he angled through the trees and headed for the first hut, he heard a moan. Looking to his left, he saw a Tucanos man writhing in pain. The light was poor, but Jake knew the man had been wounded in the fray.

He stopped, knelt beside the groaning Indian and tried to reassure him. He drew back his hand. It was covered with blood. Jake frowned. The wounded needed care first. Speaking to him in Portuguese, and trying to persuade the Indian that he was a friend, not his enemy, Jake picked the man up. The Indian was ridiculously light in his arms as he headed toward the hospital up on the knoll. Was Shah safe? Had a bullet found her, too? Jake hurried at a fast walk, weaving around the burning huts, dodging the running Indians who were trying to save their homes. He made his way up to the mission, where he handed the man over to Pai Jose for medical treatment. That done, Jake knew he had to locate Shah.

Jake's heart pounded unevenly in his chest as he approached Shah's hut.

"Shah?" he shouted as he neared it. "Shah? Are you okay? Answer me!"

His heart rate soared along with his anguish when only silence answered him. He broke into a trot, his face grim, his throat constricted, as he tried to prepare himself for the scene he'd see. He envisioned Shah wounded and bleeding on the floor of her hut. Other scenes, scenes from his ugly past, bludgeoned him. He halted at the hut and tore the cotton barrier aside.

Breathing hard, he stood in the doorway, looking frantically for Shah. She wasn't there! Relief cascaded through him, and then, on its heels, sheer terror. What if Shah had been kidnapped by those men? What if she hadn't listened to his orders and had run out of the hut? She could be hurt and bleeding anywhere in the village! The possibilities were too real, and Jake spun around.

Half running, half stumbling back toward the center of the village, he saw that the Tucanos had taken the brunt of the attack. Firelight danced and twisted in grotesque shapes as the huts continued to burn wildly out of control. The Indians were doing their best to put the fires out with the buckets of water, but Jake knew they needed to conserve their efforts for the nearby huts, which could easily catch fire from the sparks floating like red, winking fireflies in the night air.

He grabbed an older man, ordering him in Portuguese to use the water to save the other, vulnerable huts. It took a few minutes, but finally the Indian understood. Jake then raced to form a bucket brigade line, his arms waving, his voice thundering above the roar of the inferno for attention.

The new tactics spread quickly through the populace, and soon buckets of water were being thrown on the roofs and sides of nearby huts. Jake blinked the sweat from his eyes and looked around. He saw several men lying wounded. Gesturing to a couple of Indians, Jake got them to help him take the wounded up to the hospital. Where the hell was Shah? The bitter taste of fear in his mouth wouldn't leave.

Dawn was crawling over the crimson-and-gold horizon as Jake made his last swing of the village looking for Shah. He hadn't found her. Rubbing his mouth with the back of his hand, Jake suddenly felt weary as never before. The fires had died down—but five of the huts had burned completely to the ground. Smoke hung heavily over the area, mingling with the humid mist that stole silently in and around the trees as dawn continued to push back the night.

The place was eerie, with the mixture of fog and smoke hanging at rooftop level, Jake decided as he tiredly tramped through the village looking for Shah. Perhaps he'd missed her. The darkness had hampered relief efforts, and the hysteria of the Indians hadn't helped, either. Jake couldn't blame them for their reaction, though. At least ten Indians had been wounded at the hands of Hernandez's men.

Shah was nowhere to be found. Jake stood outside her hut, tears stinging his eyes. He tried to attribute them to the stringy smoke that hung in the air like a thick blanket. Glumly he headed back to the mission, where he knew he could be of some help. His steps were heavy, and he felt a bone-tiredness that reached clear to his soul. Jake didn't try to fool himself; he realized it was depression and grief over Shah being missing. Had she been kidnapped? Why hadn't he paid more attention to the men running for those dugout canoes? he chastised himself. But he knew the answer: he'd been pinned down by gunfire. He couldn't possibly have watched the canoes, much less identified who occupied each one.

At the top of the knoll, Indians were racing madly around the mission buildings. The cries of women and sobs of children rent the air. Thick fog blanketed the knoll as Jake slowly made his way through the crowd of relatives waiting to hear about wounded family members.

Bright light from bulbs strung in Christmas-tree fashion around the perimeter of the hospital wing momentarily blinded Jake. He raised a hand to protect his eyes while they adjusted to the change.

"Jake!"

He froze. He pulled his hand away from his eyes. There, not more than ten feet away, working with Pai Jose, was Shah! Realizing his mouth was hanging open, he snapped it shut. Never had Shah looked so lovely, despite her haggard appearance. Her hair hung loose about her body like a raven cloak. Her face was smudged with charcoal, and her white nightgown was splattered with mud and blood. At first Jake thought she'd been wounded, but then he realized she was helping Pai Jose dress the injuries of the Indian lying on the surgery table.

He took a step forward, but then halted, relief surging through him. Euphoria rose in him, and all he could do was stand there helpless beneath her golden gaze. Her huge eyes were shadowed with exhaustion, he noted.

"We need help," Shah pleaded, her voice cracking. "Do you know first aid?" She tried to deny the feelings racing through her, tried to ignore her overwhelming relief at seeing that Jake Randolph was safe. When he'd left her on the floor of the hut, Shah had feared for his life. And when she hadn't seen him throughout the past three hours, she'd feared him dead. The look of astonishment and joy mirrored in his eyes now shook Shah.

"I can help," he told her as he closed the distance between them. "Just tell me what you want done."

Shah reached into a box filled with sterile surgical gloves. "Go scrub over at the sink. Pai Jose can use your help. I'll go help some of the others who are hurt less. Hurry, please!"

Jake nodded to the old priest, whose hair was as white

as the surgical gown that covered his clothing. For a
moment Jake thought that Pai Jose's silvery hair, glowing in the light, might be a halo around the old man's
head. The priest worked quickly over the man who lay
on the table before him.

Jake's hands shook beneath the thin stream of water
coming weakly out of the faucet. The soap smelled clean
and good amid the stench of sweaty bodies, the lurid
smell of blood and the odor of antiseptics. Jake felt as
if he'd stepped back a century in time. As he scrubbed
up, he checked out the antiquated facilities. There was
very little here except the most necessary of equipment
and medicines, he realized as he gazed at the glass cabinet above the sink. He glanced around the room and
saw with growing anger that whoever had attacked the
village had hurt at least twenty people. Sickened, he hurried over to where Shah stood waiting for him. Expertly
she slipped the surgical gloves onto his hands.

"There are two more men who are seriously hurt,"
she told him breathlessly. "Pai Jose is so tired. You'll
have to watch him, Jake. His hands aren't as steady..."

He smiled tiredly down at her. "I'll take care of this,
darlin'. You go do whatever else needs to be done."

Darlin'. The endearment gave Shah sustenance and
strength when she felt as if her knees were going to cave
in beneath her. She lost herself momentarily in the warm
gray of Jake's gaze—that same feeling of powerful protection again embracing her. But this time she didn't
fight it or deny it. Absorbing Jake's care, she felt like a
plant welcoming sunlight onto its leaves for the first
time. Then, forcing herself to snap out of the inexplicable magic that bound them, she stepped away from
him.

"I'm glad you're okay," she quavered.

He gave her a grim smile. "You're the one I was worried about."

Shah knew they didn't have time to talk; there were too many wounded to be attended to. Turning away, she blinked back tears. Tears! Her emotions frayed and raw from the attack, Shah didn't try to rationalize them away this time: they were tears of relief that Jake wasn't dead. She headed toward the wall, where several of the less seriously wounded sat or stood, waiting patiently for treatment. A gamut of emotions smothered Shah, making her dizzy. How could Jake Randolph have come to mean so much to her in so short a time? He was the *enemy*.

Chapter Five

"Shah, let me take you to your hut. You're ready to keel over."

The instant Jake's hands curved around her slumped shoulders where she sat at a table in the hospital, Shah capitulated. The heat of the day was rising, and although all the windows were open to allow air to flow sluggishly through the long, rectangular area, the room was stifling. For an instant, she rested against his large, caring hands, but just for an instant. Straightening, she pulled away from the contact with him and got to her feet.

"I guess most of the emergencies are over," she said wearily.

Jake put his hands on his hips and surveyed Shah intently. It was nearly noon, and help had arrived from another mission nearby. Five nuns were now caring for the wounded, but he knew that Shah would stay on to help unless someone made her take care of herself.

"For now," he agreed quietly. Her hair, once loose, was now captured by a rubber band behind her head, the ebony strands drawn into a ponytail that almost reached her waist. He watched as Shah, with some difficulty, pulled the once-white surgical gown off her shoulders. Her golden eyes were dark with anguish.

"Here, I'll take that. One of the Tucanos women is out back with a big black kettle, boiling the hell out of anything used for the surgeries."

Shah forced a tired smile—one that she didn't feel but felt Jake deserved. "Thanks. You sound so chipper—as if nothing had happened." She looked up into his harsh features. Jake's eyes were red-rimmed, as she was sure hers must be, and his mouth was a slash, holding back the unexpressed feelings she knew he carried.

Taking a huge risk, Jake reached over and settled his hand again on her shoulder. "I've been through this kind of thing a few times more than you have," he said. "Come on, I'll walk you down the hill to your hut."

His hand was at once supportive and sheltering. Shah wanted to surrender to the powerful care that emanated from him like a beacon of light slicing through the darkest night. But she couldn't; she didn't dare. Long ago she'd learned that no matter how nurturing a man appeared outwardly, later he would change—withdraw that care and hurt her. Her spongy mind screamed at her to resist, but her instincts persuaded her to accept Jake's attention, just this once. Without a word, she nodded and left the antiseptic smells of the ward behind.

The tropical sunlight lanced through the triple canopy of rain-forest trees, producing bright splotches on the otherwise shaded ground. Everywhere Shah looked, she saw distraught expressions on the Tucanos's faces. Her heart ached for them, for their loss.

"How many died last night?" Jake asked. He forced himself to allow his hand to slide off Shah's shoulder. Every fiber of his being screamed that she needed to be held, but, much as he wanted to draw Shah into the circle of his arms, Jake knew she'd fight him.

"Two. Thank the Great Spirit it wasn't more," she murmured tiredly. The once-swept path was littered with leaves, small branches that had fallen from overhead, and many impressions from bare feet.

"Pai Jose is sleeping," Jake told her. Shah was weaving unsteadily, and he started to reach out, but forced his hand back to his side.

With a slight laugh, Shah said, "He ought to be! He's seventy-two, but he has such strength for his age. I'm sure it's his faith that gives him the grit to keep going when most people would have folded."

"Yeah," Jake agreed, constantly surveying the area. "He was something of a miracle himself last night and this morning. I didn't know he was a doctor."

"Well," Shah said reluctantly, "he isn't a medical doctor, but he's been so isolated out here for the past fifty years that he's had to learn more than just basic first aid." She gazed wonderingly up at Jake. "And you. You never told me you were a paramedic."

He flushed and avoided her admiring gaze. "All part of being a recon marine," he assured her.

"Between you and Pai Jose, the people are going to be fine." Shah walked carefully down the slope, dizzy from fatigue. Swallowing hard, she risked a look up at Jake. "This is all my fault," she choked out softly. "I realize now it was Hernandez and his men who did this. It was a warning for me to leave or else."

Grimly Jake pulled her to a halt. Without thinking, knowing she needed his touch, he swung her around to face him. Her golden eyes were filled with tears of self-incrimination. "Now look," he said gruffly, grazing her cheek with his fingers, "this attack *wasn't* your fault." He tried to ignore the fact that her skin felt like the lush velvet of an orchid petal.

Jake's brief touch sent Shah's senses spinning. She stepped away from him, closed her eyes and inhaled a sudden breath of air. She heard the barely contained emotion in his rumbling tone, the raw feelings that lay just beneath it, and knew that he could shatter her defenses with the intimacy he'd automatically established with her.

Forcing her eyes open and swallowing her tears, Shah tried to resurrect the tough barricade she'd presented to him yesterday. "This *is* my fault!" she insisted. "I should have realized that Hernandez would come back. Sometimes I'm too stubborn, too blind." She held her hand against her trembling lips. "I should have placed these people's welfare ahead of my own ideology! They're the ones who have suffered. What about the two men who are dead? Their families will never see them again, and I'm responsible for that!"

Jake winced inwardly at the logic of her words. He stepped forward, gripped her by the shoulders and gave her a tiny shake. "Listen," he growled, "stop blaming yourself, Shah. You had no way of knowing Hernandez would do this."

Shah tried to pull away, but Jake's fingers tightened their grip. Her voice rose. "I've been here three months, and I knew all about Hernandez! Everyone said he was a killing bastard. Well, he is! The Indians never had a good word to say about him. I should have listened to them, Jake." Sobbing, she tore out of his grip. She stumbled backward, off-balance, then caught herself. Tears streamed down her cheeks as she forced herself to look up into his grim features. "I should have listened," she sobbed again, and spun away.

Jake stood there, angry and helpless, as Shah walked hurriedly down the path toward the carnage in the village below. He wanted to run after her, to grab her and hold her. That was what she needed right now—a quiet harbor in the terrible storm that surrounded her. His wife had taught him about the safety of an embrace early on in their marriage, and he'd never forgotten that wonderful facet of their relationship.

Kicking at sand with the toe of his boot, Jake decided to go on into the village anyway. He wanted to see if the six-year-old girl who had been in Shah's arms yesterday was safe. He hadn't seen her up at the hospital, so he figured she was fine, but he wanted to make sure. He knew that he needed sleep, too, but his nerves were taut and his senses were screamingly alert. Anyway, he wouldn't put it past Hernandez to try another attack tonight. First, he'd check on the little tyke, then he'd grab a quick nap, and then he'd talk to the chief about preventing another surprise attack by Hernandez.

Frowning, Jake shoved his hands into his pockets. What he really wanted to do was go after Shah. But she needed sleep, and perhaps when she was more rested she would realize that this carnage wasn't her fault. Throughout the dawn hours and into the morning, he'd watched her work tirelessly with the survivors at the hospital, always offering a kind word, a soft smile, her healing touch. He believed that her passion for protecting Mother Earth was just as fierce and genuine as her compassion for the people around her, and that was admirable. At first, Jake had been concerned that she might be one of those ecofanatics who couldn't see beyond their own narrow views, but she'd proved that theory wrong. No, Shah Travers was a woman of incredible courage linked to a giving heart. That discovery did nothing but make Jake want to know her—to explore her, to chart the vast, hidden territory of her compassionate heart.

When Shah awoke, sunlight was slanting low through the western window. With a groan, she eased herself into a sitting position on the grass mat that served as her bed. She rubbed her eyes, which were puffy with sleep, and allowed the village sounds to filter into her awakening senses. She didn't hear the usual sounds of children's laughter, dogs barking and the singsong Tucanos language filling the air. Glancing at her watch, Shah was alarmed to discover it was nearly 4:00 p.m.

How could she have slept so long? Hurriedly she got to her knees and opened the trunk where she kept her toiletry items. Retrieving a pair of tan gabardine slacks and a white tank top, she rummaged around some more and found a pair of white cotton socks. Her hair was a tangled mass that desperately needed to be washed and combed. Forcing away her sleepiness, Shah got to her feet and pulled the cotton away from the door.

"You're up."

Shah jerked to a halt. Her eyes widened momentarily. Jake Randolph sat on a decomposing log not more than fifty feet from her hut.

"Jake…"

Jake smiled when he heard her use his first name, glad that the previous stiffness that had existed between them was no longer there. Perhaps it was because she had just awakened. Her features were softened, her lids half-open to reveal drowsy golden eyes. Disheveled, her hair mussed, Shah looked absolutely beautiful, in a natural sort of way.

"I figured I'd play bodyguard," he said teasingly.

"I don't need one," Shah groused in return. She frowned and walked toward a small, makeshift shower enclosed by three sheets of plywood. A large piece of black plastic suspended above the shower caught and contained rainwater.

Jake got up and slowly followed her. He watched as she placed a yellow terry-cloth towel on a nearby tree branch and stepped behind the enclosure.

"How are you feeling?"

Shah stripped out of her smelly, damp clothes and tossed them outside the shower. "Like hell."

"You don't look like hell. Now me, that's another thing." He ruefully rubbed his prickly jaw, aware that he needed a shave.

Releasing the small clothespin from the tubular plastic shower head, Shah quickly wet her body and her hair. Just Jake's nearness made her feel safer. Then all conversation ceased for the next fifteen minutes as she cleaned and scrubbed away the horror of the night before.

Jake sat down on another log and clasped his hands between his thighs. The muddy Amazon was so wide that it boggled his mind. If Americans could see this mighty river, they'd think the Mississippi was a stream in comparison. A grizzled smile touched his mouth. Oddly, he felt happier than he could recall feeling in a very long time. Maybe it was because of Shah.

Keying his hearing to Shah, who was showering behind his back, Jake continued to peruse the Amazon and its banks. There was tension in the air, thick enough to cut with a machete blade. The Tucanos were fearful, but

Jake had helped to allay some of that fear by setting up a watch by guards who would switch every two hours tonight to prevent another surprise attack. The old chief had been grateful for Jake's suggestions, and Jake was glad he could offer these gentle people a plan. Pai Jose, who had slept only a little, then come down to survey the needs of the village, was also grateful for Jake's ideas. He'd backed Jake's efforts enthusiastically, which had helped convince the Tucanos that it was the right way to protect themselves from Hernandez.

When he heard the shower shut off, Jake straightened. "Feel a little better?" he called over his shoulder.

Shah towel-dried her hair. "Yes, much better, thanks." She pulled on the slacks and tank top. Hanging the towel on a branch, she emerged moments later, brush and comb in hand.

"I feel a hundred percent better," she told Jake. He was sitting on the log that she usually sat on to pull on her socks and hiking boots. Shah sat down at the other end. The hungry look that suddenly gleamed in Jake's eyes sent a tremor of fear rippling through her. He quickly looked away, and she felt heat flood her neck and face. With trembling hands, she quickly moved her thick, heavy hair across her shoulder and began to ease the snarls out of it with the brush.

Jake berated himself. He'd stared at Shah like a slavering wolf—and he'd seen the instant terror in her eyes. Cursing his own weakness, and upset at frightening her, Jake moodily stared at the Amazon's quiet surface. He cast around for a safe topic of conversation, because the invisible tension had risen between them once again.

"Things have quieted down and more or less gotten back on track," he said, giving her a quick glance. It was his undoing. Shah sat combing her thick, luxuriant hair, looking fresher and more beautiful than he ever could have imagined. She wore no makeup, yet her skin had a golden glow and her cheeks a heightened rosiness. He stared, mesmerized, as she combed her hair, the sunlight glancing off it, bringing out blue and black highlights. He swallowed convulsively and quickly looked away, his heart pounding like a freight train.

Shah saw surprise, tenderness and then desire in Jake's eyes as he watched her comb her hair. She continued to ease the knots and snarls out, taming half her hair into a braid. Looking toward the village, she saw the Indians working to clean up the area where the five huts had been burned to the ground. A lump formed in her throat, and she tried to swallow it. This was all her fault.

"When I get done here, I'm going to leave," she said shakily.

Jake's head snapped up, and he turned, disbelief in his eyes. "What?"

Shah eyed him grimly. "Hernandez wants me out of here. It's obvious now that he'll do anything to accomplish his goal. I'll leave so that these people can get on with their lives. I've caused them enough pain."

Jake held her level gaze and saw that her mouth was set in stubborn determination. "Where will you go?" He knew enough about Shah already to recognize that arguing with her was a useless exercise.

With a sigh, Shah tied off a braid with a rubber band. "I'm going to take my canoe and load it with my video camera and tapes." She pointed down the Amazon. "Hernandez's parcel is three miles down the river. I intend to go down there, set up camp and begin secretly filming his operation."

Jake held on to his patience. "You'd be walking right into the lion's mouth by doing that."

"I didn't come here to turn tail and run, Jake."

"Parking in his backyard isn't cowardly, it's fool-hardy."

Shah ignored the low fury in his voice. "Well, it's not your problem, is it?"

"Why the hell isn't it?"

"Because you don't believe in what I'm trying to do, that's why! You're not committed to anything."

Anger frayed his patience, but Jake remained sitting on the log. He knew that if he got up and towered over Shah, it would only make her more defensive. "You don't know me well enough to say that," he answered, struggling to keep his tone even. "In fact, you've gone out of your way to pretend I don't exist."

Shah quickly braided the rest of her hair. Her fingers were trembling, and she wondered if Jake saw just how much he affected her. She knew for a fact that if not for Jake's shadowy presence in all their lives, more people might have died last night—during the attack, or later, in the hospital. Still, she couldn't admit it.

"I came down here to get proof that these land barons are destroying our rain forest," she insisted. "Not only that, I *know* that Hernandez is illegally using chain saws to cut down those trees. That's against Brazilian law, you know." She glared at Jake. "I want to nail that slimy bastard's hide to the wall with his own country's laws. I want him taken off the board as a player. But I need proof. All of these barons use illegal chain saws instead of axes or hand-held saws. My plan is to seek them out, videotape them and land them in jail. I may not be able to single-handedly stop the destruction of this basin, but I sure can slow it down."

Jake assimilated Shah's impassioned explanation, forcing himself not to speak for several minutes, allowing the tension to dissolve. She'd finished braiding her hair and was putting on her white cotton socks when he finally spoke.

"I didn't know it was against Brazilian law for these guys to use chain saws. In the U.S., all the loggers use them."

Shah jerked laces through the eyelets of her hiking boot. "Brazil is caught between a rock and a hard place, Jake. They've got millions of poor in the cities, and they're hurting. To try and ease the situation, the government gives them small parcels of farmland. These people can cut down trees with axes or saws, to clear the land for farming. That might be all right, but greedy businessmen have been buying up the small plots from the poor and contracting countries like Japan to buy the trees. It's a very big, *very* profitable business."

Shah quickly finished lacing up her boots. With a frustrated sound, she faced Jake. "Brazil is taking a lot of heat from the world scientific community and from ecological groups. But they've got runaway inflation, and the people are in turmoil. Brazil is getting squeezed inside and out by groups and factions. I see myself as a stopgap measure, Jake. I can help buy time for the rain forest in hopes that more pressure and education will make the Brazilian government realize they've got to stop destroying the Amazon Basin. I did it before on the Rio Negro, with another Brazilian realtor who was out to rape Mother Earth. He's in jail right now in Rio."

Jake's eyes narrowed. "Does Hernandez know about this?"

"Kind of obvious he does, don't you think?" Shah

gestured toward the village. "Why else would he have attacked?"

With a nod, Jake rested his hands against his chin. "I think you're right."

"I know I am."

Jake glanced at her out of the corner of his eye. "You're a pretty courageous woman."

"I'm a warrior, Jake. I've always been one. It doesn't mean I'm not afraid. I live with fear daily. All kinds of fear. The difference is, despite my fear, I'll move forward and act on my beliefs. I won't allow it to stop me." She made a helpless gesture with her hand, her voice filled with frustration. "Ever since I was born, I've been in hot water of one kind or another. First, it was with my father, who is a closet alcoholic. He'd never admit he's got a problem, but my mother and I sure know he does." Shah stood suddenly, realizing she'd said too much. To reveal the pain she carried to a near stranger— who was in the employ of her father!—was dangerous, to say the least.

"Wait!" Jake leaped to his feet and covered the distance between them. He reached out and drew her to a halt. "Wait," he entreated her softly. "Tell me more about your father."

His touch was branding. The ache it sent through Shah was like a raw, unsettling current of longing combined with desperation. She pulled out of his grasp and looked up into his gray eyes, trying to ferret out whether he was sincere in his request.

"Why should I?" she asked challengingly.

"Because you know I care."

"I don't know that."

Jake smiled slightly and relaxed. Shah stood rigidly,

as if she were going to run at any moment. "Yes," he said softly, "you *do* know that."

Shah took several steps away from him, unable to hold his burning gray gaze or accept the tenderness he seemed to offer. "It doesn't matter," she said waspishly.

"You matter, Shah."

A tremor passed through her, and she closed her eyes briefly, then turned away. "Words, just words. You men are so good with words. It's actions that count with me, not your damnable words."

He felt a rift in the tension, and seized the moment. Approaching Shah slowly, he kept his hands at his sides—the last place he wanted them to be. Shah was openly suffering. He could hear the anguish in her husky voice.

"My actions of the past twenty-four hours should prove something to you," he began, his voice raw. "It sounds as if you've been fighting pitched battles by yourself all your life, Shah." His eyes darkened. "This time you don't have to fight alone."

The gritty sound of his voice wrapped around Shah like a protective blanket. She drew in a shuddering sigh and slowly raised her head. She met and held the gaze from his narrowed gray eyes, eyes that were banked with some heated, indefinable emotion. "What are you talking about?"

His smile became grimmer. "I'll go with you down the Amazon. We'll find a good place to make camp, then we'll get that tape you want."

Stunned, Shah gasped. Her mind spun with questions, but her heart told her that Jake Randolph was more sincere than any man she'd ever met.

"Why would you do that?"

"Because I believe in your cause. I believe in you."

She frowned. "My father is paying you."

"So?" Jake shrugged. "My orders were to be a body-guard if you decided to stay down here, and that's fulfilling my assignment as far as Travers is concerned. He didn't tell me what to do with my time. If I want to help you, I will."

"If he knew what you wanted to do, he'd hit the ceiling," Shah growled. "He wants me out of this place permanently."

"Guess he won't get his way, will he?"

Jake's teasing broke the terrible tension she carried in her shoulders. Shah searched his harsh features ruthlessly for any sign that he was lying. Men had always lied to her.

"I don't trust men," she warned him throatily.

"Why?" Jake asked the question so softly that he wasn't sure she'd heard him at first.

Her mouth compressed, Shah wrapped her arms across her chest and looked out at the river. "I never talk about my past."

"Most kids who come from alcoholic families feel that way," Jake said gently.

Shah's eyes narrowed. "I suppose you've got a degree in psychology, too, besides philosophy?"

Grinning bashfully, Jake shook his head. "I got trained a long time ago to be more aware of other people's feelings and motivations." Memories of Bess pooled in his heart, and he shrugged. "An incredible woman with a heart as big as yours helped me open up and see a lot more than most men do about people and their problems."

Curiosity stalked Shah. For just a moment, she'd seen Jake's face lose its harsh cast. Underneath, she'd seen a man of immense sensitivity. Then that cloak of grief had surrounded him again. She swallowed hard. "You're married?"

Jake was wrestling with real, unresolved pain. "I was...but that was a long time ago." It hurt to breathe in that moment, and hot, unexpected tears momentarily blurred his vision, dissolving Shah's taut features. Blinking them back, he tried to steer the conversation back to her. When he spoke, his voice was rough. "So how long did your mother tolerate your father's alcohol problem?"

Caught off guard by the tears she saw in Jake's eyes, Shah stood very still. She felt her way through the ravaged, haunted look on his face. She'd never seen tears in a man's eyes before. The only tears she knew were ones shed in hurt and pain by women and children. Were Jake's tears due to some memory, a past he couldn't put to rest? His features remained open and accessible, and the words, the feelings, tumbled out of Shah's mouth before she could stop them. "My mother was very young—and very beautiful—when my father met her. She was waiting tables at the best hotel in Rapid City, South Dakota, and he fell in love with her. My mother was a medicine woman in training at the time, and she tried to explain that to my father. She lived in the traditional ways of our people, but he didn't care or want to know about my mother's beliefs.

"My father shrugged off her explanations, dazzled her with beautiful gifts, fine food at the best restaurants, and within days they were married. I guess I was conceived the first night. But when my father wanted my mother to move away from the Rosebud reservation, where our family has land and homes, my mother said no. Her medicine teacher was there, as she'd tried to tell him days earlier. One day she'd be a medicine woman helping her people, and she couldn't leave the reservation.''

''Your mother is a healer?'' Jake asked, seeing all too clearly the suffering that speaking about her past was causing Shah.

''Yes, but that didn't matter to him. My father started drinking, flew into a rage and beat my mother senseless. When she came to, they were driving to Denver, where he lived.'' Shah's voice died in her throat, and she shook her head. ''My mother was a virtual prisoner at my father's estate. He was jealous and guarded her. She could never go anywhere without a private detective in plain sight. He was a Jekyll-and-Hyde personality, and when he drank, he beat her.''

Jake shut his eyes, buffeted by her pain. When he opened them again, he stared grimly into her distraught features. ''I'm sorry,'' he rasped. It took every bit of Jake's control not to reach out and touch Shah in a gesture of humanity, but he knew that, given her distrust, she might wrongly interpret his action. The ache in his heart for her, for the tragedy that surrounded her, grew.

Shah pushed the grayish-white sand around with the toe of her boot. So much misery was surfacing as she spoke. ''My mother convinced my father to let her give birth to me on the reservation. Living with him for nine months, she'd figured out how to manipulate him without making him angry enough to beat her. I was born in my grandmother's cabin at Rosebud, and three days later we were taken back to our prison in Denver.

''I don't have a lot of memories until I was about six years old. I do remember this huge, cold estate that was like a fortress. My father hated me. He told my mother to keep me out of his sight, to keep me quiet because he hated to hear a child crying. I remember being held by my mother, her hand pressed to my mouth if I started to cry. She used to press my face against her breast, hold me very tightly and pray that father didn't hear me.''

Biting back a curse, Jake stood helplessly. Shah's lower lip was trembling. It tore heavily at his own grieving heart to hear how much abuse she had endured.

''Until I was twelve years old, I remember living in a nightmare war at his house. I went to school, came home and went to my room. I had my meals served there, I did my homework there, and I played with my dog out in the big yard, which was enclosed by a black wrought-iron fence.'' Shah wearily touched her brow. ''As I got older, I became aware that sometimes my mother would have terrible bruises all over her. One time…one time I saw my father beating her in a drunken rage. I flew down the staircase, screaming and shouting at him to leave her alone….'' Shah made a strangled sound and fell silent.

Jake moved over to her and slid his hand along her slumped shoulder. His mouth moved into a thin line as he thought of the daily suffering Shah had lived with. The anger he felt toward Travers ballooned tenfold. No wonder Shah was combative. ''What happened? What did he do to you?'' he asked, his voice cracking.

Shah felt Jake's fingers tighten on her shoulder, and gathered the strength to go on. ''I— Well, I was like a wild animal attacking him, I guess. I don't really remember what happened, to tell you the truth. Mom told me about it later—after I woke up in the hospital with a severe concussion.''

''My God,'' Jake choked out, reeling with shock.

She gave him a cutting look. ''In those days, hospitals didn't question a child being beaten. My mother took me to the emergency room. She was in tears when she told them that I'd fallen down the stairs. I was in the hospital for three days. On the third day, my mom came and got me. I found out later she'd stolen money from my father's wallet and bought two bus tickets for Rosebud. We escaped. I remember being wrapped up in a nice, warm star quilt that my grandmother had made for me when I was younger. I was still dizzy, and I couldn't walk straight, but it was sure nice to be held in her arms on that bus trip. I was so happy to be going home, I cried most of the time. My grandmother...well, she's a wonderful woman. She loved me and my mother with a fierceness that defies description.''

Unconsciously Jake slid his hand back and forth along Shah's shoulder. He forced out a question that he didn't want to ask—because he wasn't sure if he could handle hearing the answer. ''Did it end there?''

''No.'' She sighed. ''Once we got on the res, we were legally safe from my father. He tried to get the tribal council to give him permission to take us back to Denver, but a reservation is like a foreign country, Jake. We have our own laws and ways of doing things. My mother filed for a divorce the day she arrived, and the tribal council supported her decision to stay at Rosebud. From the age of twelve until I was eighteen, I never left the res, for fear that one of father's hired detectives might try to kidnap me. I went to the missionary school over in St. Francis, about fifteen miles from where we lived.''

''At least your mother protected you,'' he said, his voice raspy with emotion. ''What did Travers do next?''

''After he got over the initial rage that his money couldn't buy us back, I guess my father started feeling guilty about what he'd done to me and my mom, so he sent money for me to go to college. By that time, I didn't fear him trying to kidnap me, so I took his money and went to Stanford. I got a master's degree in biology, because I wanted to serve Mother Earth and her people as my mother continues to do in her capacity as a healer at the res.''

Jake allowed his hand to drop, because he was afraid that if he didn't he would fold Shah in his arms and hold her, try to protect her against the pain that was clearly etched on her face. When she lifted her chin and stared up at him, he saw the extent of the devastation her father had wreaked upon her.

''Saying I'm sorry seems useless in the face of what you went through,'' he whispered roughly. Travers better hope he never crossed his path again, he thought grimly.

Shah's mouth pulled into a slight, pained smile. ''Men feel it's their right to beat women,'' she told him bitterly. ''When I was at Stanford, I got mixed up in politics. I met my husband, Robert, who's half Lakota. He'd been raised over at the Pine Ridge reservation. I was so lonely for my people and for our way of life that I let the infatuation go to my head. I married Robert in my third year.''

''Are you still married?''

''No.'' Shah shook her head sadly. ''I repeated my mother's mistakes. Can you believe that? Robert was an alcoholic, too. At first he used to manipulate me mentally and emotionally. He tried to make me feel unworthy because I was a woman. He thought I should be serving him. Well, that didn't go over too well with me. By then my mother was a full-fledged medicine woman, and she'd taught me that women are sacred to the Great Spirit.

''Robert tried to demean me over the next two years. When I wouldn't break and become a victim, he finally attacked me. The moment he laid a hand on me, I was out of there. I filed for divorce the next day. I wasn't about to get beat up the way my mother had. Enough was enough.''

Jake nodded, a bitter taste in his mouth. ''Now I understand why you don't trust men.''

Shah pulled back and gave him a measuring look. ''I have a bad track record,'' she agreed. ''And I've still got a lot of anger toward men that I'm trying to work out,'' she warned.

''Rightfully so,'' Jake conceded. He was dying inside, for Shah, for the brutal way she'd been treated.

Shah weighed his words, the sincerity of them. ''I'd like to believe you, but I can't, Jake.'' She gave a helpless shrug. ''Too much water under the bridge between me and men. I'll pack up and leave in about an hour. I don't want to be a noose around Pai Jose's neck here. You go home. This isn't your battle—it's mine.'' With a sad little smile, she added, ''After hearing about my life, no man in his right mind would stay around me, anyway.''

For the first time since his family's death, Jake felt the numbness leave his heart, all of it. In its wake came a vibrant, living mass of emotions bubbling through him, emotions that were both good and bad. He stared at Shah, unable to put his tangled feelings into words. She'd suffered just as grievously as he had, he realized. Perhaps even more so, because she'd been a child, caught in a trap, with no safe place to hide, and no escape.

Clearing his throat, he said, ''Well, this time you aren't alone, Shah. We'll take care of Hernandez together, whether you can trust in me or not.'' He wanted to add, *You're too special, Shah, too important, to be* putting your neck on the line by yourself. Jake held up his hand when she began to protest. "No argument on this," he told her firmly. "You're stuck with me, whether you like it or not."

Chapter Six

"What is this nonsense about you leaving, Shah?" Pai Jose demanded as he halted on the dock next to her.

Shah looked guiltily up at the old priest. She stopped packing the canoe and got up off her hands and knees. Rubbing her hands against her trousers, she said, "I can't stay here, *Pai*. I've caused all of this." She gestured toward the village. "Hernandez wanted to scare me off."

The priest gave a sorrowful shake of his head, resting a thin hand on Shah's shoulder. "No, child. Don't go. You've been here three months. The people love you. You belong here, doing your work on the medical herbs with the shamans."

Shah saw Jake coming down the bank. Had he told Pai Jose she was leaving? Still wrung out from last night's ordeal, she patted the priest's hand and captured it between her own.

"*Pai,* I love you and the Tucanos people enough to keep you safe from Hernandez. Please try to understand that."

Pai Jose frowned, his silvery, caterpillarlike eyebrows moving downward. He gripped Shah's hand. "I can see your mind is made up. We'll pray for you, my child."

Prayer, no matter who did it—or from what religious or spiritual base—was not only good, but powerful, in Shah's opinion. "That's wonderful. Thank you," she answered softly.

"Father, did you talk her out of going?" Jake asked as he drew to a halt. He had an olive green canvas knapsack slung across his shoulder. Glancing at Shah, he saw her staring accusingly in his direction.

"No, my son, I didn't." Pai Jose turned to him. "At least you're going along."

Shah snorted softly and knelt down to finish her packing. "My father hired him, *Pai,* so don't be so sure he isn't waiting to jump me from behind, drag me off to Manaus and throw me on a plane bound for North America."

Pai Jose chuckled indulgently as he stood there, his hands clasped against his body. "I would think that after Mr. Randolph's magnificent work helping us save lives you would see him in a kinder light."

Shah gave a sharp, derisive laugh. "*Pai,* you're a man, therefore you trust other men. I'm a woman, and I don't."

Making the sign of the cross, Pai Jose blessed each of them. "God be with you, my children. Will you be coming back here once you've gotten the film you want?"

Shah, who was wrapping her camcorder tightly in

plastic for the trip down the Amazon, paused for a moment. "I don't know, *Pai*..."

"We'll probably stop here for supplies," Jake said.

"If you get into trouble," Pai Jose told Shah seriously, wagging his finger in her direction, "you come home. You come here."

Home. The word formed a lump in Shah's throat. She blinked back the tears and got to her feet. Wordlessly she stepped over to the priest and embraced him.

"No promises, but we'll try," she whispered, her voice cracking.

Jake smiled to himself. Shah had used the word *we* instead of *I.* Good. Unconsciously she was accepting his presence on this foolhardy expedition. Jake wouldn't have had it any other way. It was obvious to him that Shah did trust the old priest, even if he was a man. That gave him renewed hope as he watched her turn away to wipe the tears from her eyes. If she trusted Pai Jose, she might trust him. *Let it be so,* Jake prayed. *Let it be so.*

"Ready?" Jake asked when he saw that Shah had completed her packing. The sun was heading for the western horizon, and it was nearly 4:00 p.m. Shah had planned to use the two hours of light that remained to get down the Amazon, dock the canoe and make camp. Three miles downstream wouldn't be a problem; but coming back would be more difficult. They would have to paddle the canoe by hand, since it didn't have a motor.

Shah nodded. She put the valuable camcorder and some extra videotapes in a small knapsack that she shrugged over her shoulders. Waving goodbye to the many Tucanos who stood on the bank silently watching, Shah felt like crying all over again. These people had openly accepted her as one of their own. Jake moved beside her and sat on the edge of the dock, removing his boots. He placed them inside his knapsack.

"I learned the hard way that wearing boots in a canoe is a stupid idea, when I got dumped in the Orinoco," he told her ruefully.

Shah moved beside him to sit in the rear of the canoe.

"Wait," he said. "You move to the bow and paddle. I'll sit in the rear and be the rudder."

Shah hesitated. "I suppose you know how to paddle this kind of canoe, too?"

"A little," he admitted sheepishly. Shah's features were dark and wary. "Hey," he told her playfully, trying to ease her worry about his presence, "the biggest, strongest guy always sits in the stern to paddle and be the rudder. You know that. I outweigh you by a lot."

Wasn't that the truth? Shah said nothing as she slipped carefully into the canoe, her bare feet touching the bottom's roughly hewn wood. Kneeling in the stern, Jake handed her one of the two paddles. Her heart was in utter turmoil, and so was her head. Jake was acting as if he were going along with her on some kind of picnic. Did he realize the danger they would be in? Hernandez had proved himself capable of murder. And he wanted her dead. A part of her that she was trying desperately to ignore didn't want Jake in the line of fire. Not that he couldn't take care of himself, she admitted grudgingly. Still, she was agitated by the possibility that he could be hurt on her account. She couldn't bear that thought.

"Cast off," Jake called as he unhitched the loop of rope that tethered the canoe to the dock. He saw Shah turn and give him a questioning look, then straighten to face the bow of the canoe. He saw the shadows in the recesses of her eyes, but said nothing. Raising his hand, he waved to the people on the shore, then picked up his own paddle.

Jake used his paddle as a rudder, maneuvering the twenty-foot-long dugout only a little way offshore to avoid the swift currents that lurked beneath the seeming calm surface of the Amazon. The bank curved, the lush rain forest like a lumpy green velvet ribbon bracketing the huge river. His ears were keyed for any out-of-place sounds, because he didn't trust Hernandez in the least. Ahead of them, an osprey wheeled, looking for unsuspecting prey swimming close to the surface.

Shah did little paddling, because the canoe moved slowly but surely along with the flow of the river. Jake admired her straight, long back, wondering what it would be like to glide his fingers down that proud spine and feel her respond. Jake frowned, castigating himself. Where was all this wishful thinking coming from? In four years, he'd been around plenty of other women, but none of them had engaged his heated imagination. Until now.

Jake watched her graceful movements as she moved the paddle from one side of the canoe to the other. She reminded him of a long-limbed ballerina, her every economical movement gliding into the next.

"You ever take ballet lessons?"

Startled, Shah twisted a look across her shoulder at Jake. "What?"

He flushed. "I just wondered if you'd ever taken ballet lessons?"

With a soft laugh, Shah returned to her paddling. "No."

Jake's paddle dipped into the water. Suddenly an image of Katie, his ten-year-old daughter, flashed before him. She was running toward him in her pink tutu. She was laughing, excited about the plans for a recital. The memory hit Jake like a punch to the gut. Kneeling there in the stern, he paddled for a long time without speaking as deeply closeted emotions from the past overwhelmed him. He'd pushed away so much about his family, because it had been too painful to remember. Now his past seemed to be surfacing, and he didn't know what was going on.

Shah relaxed as the first mile slipped behind them. The scents of the rain forest were many and complex. Sometimes she'd get a whiff of an orchid, or the odor of decaying leaves on the sandy soil of the forest floor. Brightly colored blue-and-yellow parrots hid in the tall, stately pau trees that hung over the bank, their dark green leaves like an umbrella over the muddy Amazon. The vines were numerous, varying from thin snakelike ones to some as thick as Jake's muscular arms.

Shah remained hyperaware of Jake's silent presence behind her. Sometimes she could almost feel his eyes boring into her—but then she would shake off the silly feeling. But no matter what she did, she couldn't completely ignore him. What was it that drew her to him? Frowning, Shah tried to figure it out. His size, at first, had frightened her, bringing back memories of the violence done to her by her father and then her husband. Jake's hand alone was nearly twice the size of her own.

Yet he didn't swagger like most males. He didn't have that shallow arrogance she'd seen too often. Shah swallowed and remembered the sadness in Jake's eyes when he'd seen her hold the little Tucanos girl in her arms. She recalled the frantic emotion in his voice last night when he'd charged into her hut to see if she was safe. Shah rested the paddle across the canoe, in front of her, deep in thought. Yes, Jake had shown his feelings to her—in many ways. The only feelings she'd ever seen from a man on a consistent basis were such negative ones as anger, envy and jealousy—until now.

Jake was different, her heart whispered. Shah closed her eyes and hung her head momentarily, feeling the impact of that realization, absorbing it. Jake scared her. Badly. He *was* different from most men she'd met, in ways she had absolutely no experience with. She'd never realized someone like Jake even existed! A small part of her still questioned his motives for being here. She felt torn apart inside. Time would be the true test of Jake's intentions, the only test. A frisson of panic shot through Shah. To make matters worse, she acknowledged, her heart was responding of its own accord to Jake, and there didn't seem to be anything she could do to stop it. Jake's vulnerability was like a magical key able to unlock Shah's closely guarded heart, and it made her feel as exposed as a deer caught in the cross hairs of a hunter's lethal rifle.

"Shah?"

Her head snapping up, Shah jumped at the unexpected sound of Jake's lowered voice. Her hand moving to her pounding heart, she twisted around. "What?"

"I didn't mean to scare you...." Jake said apologetically.

"I'm just naturally jumpy when a man's behind me," she said. Shah saw darkness in Jake's gray eyes, but he quickly hid his reaction. "I got jumped by my husband from behind, and some part of me has never forgotten it," she explained, realizing he was upset for her, not with her. That was another new discovery—a man caring about her.

"I understand," Jake said, noticing how Shah's face had paled, her eyes widening enormously. He could see not only her fear, but, even more moving, her vulnerability, as well. "You were deep in thought."

She tried to smile, but didn't succeed. Her hand was still pressed to her heart. "Yes..."

The overwhelming desire to blanket Shah in all the warmth and tenderness he possessed threatened to be Jake's undoing. He understood Shah's fragility where men were concerned, now that he knew where it had originated. His mouth curved slightly. "Maybe canoe rides invite people to think long and hard," he offered.

"They always do for me," Shah admitted. She purposely kept her voice low for fear of discovery—just in case some of Hernandez's men were nearby, invisible in the thick jungle.

"How do you want to approach this area where Hernandez is being allowed to cut down trees? Is it on this side of the river or the other?"

"This side. I tied a piece of red cloth to a bush hanging near the edge of the water. Once we see that, we can make camp anywhere nearby."

"Don't you feel it would be wiser to camp outside of Hernandez's area and hike in? He could have sentries patrolling the river where that parcel's located."

Shah shook her head. "If you've been in Brazil before, you know that this jungle—" she pointed to the trees with her finger "—is thick with vegetation. It would slow us down too much. I want to be as close as possible to the area where he's going to be cutting."

Jake conceded to her reasoning. Most of the rain forest was overrun with vines that hung like giant pieces of spaghetti off trees that towered well over a hundred feet above them. Add to that many gnarled roots of bushes and trees, exposed by six months of rain on sandy soil—ready to quickly trip a person. Jungle hiking was slow and tedious, requiring the utmost focus. "Okay," he said, "we'll land when you spot that red cloth."

Jake didn't like hugging the bank of the river. When the hair on the back of his neck began to stand up in warning, he used the paddle as a rudder to guide the canoe about a hundred feet farther into the river.

"What are you doing?"

"We're too close to the bank."

Shah frowned. She could feel the current begin to snag and pull the canoe farther out. "It's dangerous to get out too far, Jake! The Amazon makes huge whirlpools. If we're caught in one, we could be killed! We might not be able to paddle hard enough to break the hold of the current. I know the river looks calm and safe on the surface, but it's not, believe me."

"I know that, darlin'. Now, just relax. I'll get us safely back to shore."

Shah couldn't shake her sudden tension. The truth was, she wasn't a good swimmer. Believing that each living thing had a spirit, she never entered the Amazon without offering it a gift of tobacco to ask for safe transit. She gripped the sides of the canoe, her knuckles whitening as Jake continued to guide the canoe farther from shore.

"I'm a lousy swimmer, Jake! If we tip over, I'll be a liability." Shah turned around. "I could never make it to shore from here."

Jake felt bad for having frightened her. "This is for our safety, Shah," he explained, keeping his voice low and calm. "What if Hernandez has his goons along the bank where we want to land? Do you think they're going to welcome us with open arms? My bet is they'll draw a bead on us and kill us."

Shah lowered her head, biting nervously on her lower

lip. "I— Okay, it makes sense. I don't know what I'm more scared of—bullets, or trying to survive being dumped in this river. A lot of people have drowned here. The current's just too swift. It pulls you down. You don't have a chance, Jake."

"Take it easy," he said soothingly, reading the panic in her voice. Shah was gripping the sides of the canoe like a person who was sure she was going to drown. "I'm an ace swimmer," he told her, trying to get her to relax. "In the recons, I had to swim a mile with a forty-pound pack strapped on my back, wearing combat boots. So don't worry. I don't trust Hernandez. I'd rather face this river than hot lead. We can survive this river, but if we get wounded, we could die. There's no medical help out here if we get hurt, Shah."

Jake was right—again. Embarrassed by her sudden display of weakness, Shah whispered, "So much for me being a warrior."

Jake laughed pleasantly, using the paddle expertly in the swift, powerful current. "A smart warrior admits his or her fear. I've been afraid plenty of times."

Shah nodded jerkily. "I've always found that no matter how bad the fear, it's important to keep moving ahead."

"That's right," he agreed. "Recognize it, make it your friend, but for God's sakes, keep moving forward."

With a tight little laugh, Shah felt some of her terror drain away. "That's what the Lakota believe. You'd make a good warrior among them, Jake." She made a conscious effort to stop digging her fingers into the rough sides of the dugout. It was obvious from the way he deftly maneuvered the canoe through the water that he knew how to deal with the lethal currents. His adventures must have taught him a lot.

Jake said, "There's an old Moorish proverb that says, 'He who fears something gives it power over him.'"

"I like an Irish saying better," Shah responded. Maybe talking would help ease her fear of the current turning the canoe over. "'Fear is a fine spur, so is rage.'"

"You've known both," Jake murmured, his heart reaching out to Shah. He watched her battle her very real fear of the water, and admired her ability to stay levelheaded despite it, not giving away her power. In fact, the discovery that Shah had an Achilles' heel only made him respect and desire her more.

With a dip of her head, Shah nervously touched her paddle. "A spur makes a horse jump forward to avoid the pain of it. I guess I grew up like that horse. I guess that's why I'm so jumpy now...."

"Well," Jake said, "maybe in the next week or so I can help you change your view of men as spurs in your side." When he saw her twist her head to give him a look, he added, "Hey, I'm not such a bad specimen of a male. I kinda pride myself on being a little more sensitive toward women than most guys—even if I was in the Marine Corps for sixteen years. We're not all ogres, you know."

No, Jake was far from an ogre, Shah admitted silently. Belatedly she realized that he was teasing her, trying to get her to trust his judgment of the situation. Grimly she said, "I want you to know this is the first time I've ever let a man call the shots." She jabbed her finger down at the milky brown water. "And I can't swim worth a damn!"

Jake chuckled indulgently, then smiled. "You're doing just fine, darlin'. Didn't you know? A good relationship always requires give-and-take by both partners."

Now where the hell had that come from? Jake chastised himself. What relationship? And why had he used the word *partners?* Unconsciously he saw Shah as his partner, he grudgingly admitted. If only these unexpected feelings would stop surfacing. If only he would think before he inserted his foot in his mouth. Shah gave him a strange look, but turned around and said nothing. The humidity had frayed her hair along her temples, giving her angular face a softer look.

Jake studied Shah's clean profile as she looked across the water toward the bank. She opened her mouth to say something, then seemed to think better of it, and turned away without saying a word. Had she been about to deny that she was his partner? Jake thought so. Every moment spent with Shah was tearing down those defensive walls she hid behind to protect herself. Jake wished mightily that she would reach out and try trusting him. He wouldn't take advantage of her. Well…

Laughing harshly to himself, Jake forced an honest appraisal. Shah was a beautiful woman, and suddenly his body was behaving like that of an unruly sixteen-year-old. He liked Shah's independent streak, her vitality and unapologetic passion for life. There weren't many people, man or woman, who would knowingly put their life on the line for their ideals. That was true courage, in Jake's estimation—something badly needed in this world today.

Nightfall stalked them as they neared the boundary of Hernandez's land. The sun had set long ago, leaving only a lavender strip of color on the horizon above the silhouetted jungle. Howler monkeys could be heard here and there, their cries mingling with the songs of night birds. A chill worked its way up Jake's spine as he began guiding the canoe closer to shore—a powerful warning that shook him into renewed alertness. He tried to penetrate the misty dusk toward the darkened bank of the river. Was he allowing his imagination to get the best of him? he wondered. He almost thought he saw the shapes of several men with submachine guns standing there, waiting for them.

Shaking his head, Jake chastised his overactive imagination and kept searching the jungle as he paddled strongly to break the current's hold on the canoe. Then a noise coming from far away caught his attention.

Shah whirled around. "Do you hear that?" Her voice was high, off-key.

"Yeah? What is it?"

Shah frantically searched the dusk sky. "It's a helicopter! Hernandez has one."

Jake cursed under his breath. That was it. That was the sound. The noise drew closer. An ugly feeling snaked through Jake.

"Shah—"

The sound of gunfire erupted from the shore. Jake jerked his head to the left. He saw the winking of the submachine guns, heard the popping sounds filtering and echoing across the river toward them.

"Duck!" he yelled, and leaned down, moving the canoe sharply out toward the center of the river again.

Too late! Bullets whined and whizzed around them. Bark flew and exploded as several slugs slammed into the hull of the dugout. He realized with horror that these weren't ordinary bullets—they were dumdums, the type of bullet that expanded as they struck their quarry, tearing huge holes as they wreaked their damage. Jake heard Shah give a sharp cry as she flattened down in the canoe for protection. Had she been hit?

From the darkening sky above the jungle a small helicopter suddenly loomed. The sound of its rotor blades cut thickly through the humidity, pounding heavily against Jake's ears. The dugout was rapidly filling with water. Gaping holes had been torn in the sides by the bullets. They were sinking! Realizing it as Jake did, Shah frantically began using her hands to bail out the canoe, exposing herself too much to gunfire from the nearest bank.

Jake's eyes narrowed on the approaching helicopter. His heart ached in his throat. No! He saw light machine guns mounted on both of the aircraft's skids. ''Shah! Jump! Jump!''

Gunfire erupted from the helicopter as it swept thirty feet above the surface of the river, coming straight at them. Jake saw Shah hesitate. Bullets were marching in two lines, right for them, making explosive geysers rise from the surface of the water. If they didn't jump now, they'd be killed!

With a grunt, Jake lunged forward, grabbing Shah and throwing her over the side. The bullets whipped closer. Jake jumped, too, diving deep into the river.

Shah's scream was cut short as the powerful current caught her legs, yanking her downward. With the heavy camcorder in her knapsack on her back, she flailed frantically, her nose and mouth filling with water, her breath cut off. For several seconds, she panicked, swallowing water. Then a large, strong arm grabbed her and wrenched her upward. Shah shot upward breaking the surface, choking and coughing.

''Hang on!'' Jake gasped. He clutched Shah to him as she blindly threw out her arms in terror. He maneuvered her away from his neck where she threatened to cut off his own air with her death grip. Kicking out strongly, he saw the helicopter sink the canoe with a withering hail of bullets. Three men ran along the edge of the bank, continuing to fire in their direction.

"H-help!"

"Shah," Jake gasped, "don't panic!" Keeping them both afloat in the arms of the current, he tugged at Shah's knapsack until it came off her shoulders, then fastened the snap of the camcorder to the side strap of the knapsack he wore. His mind was working like a steel trap now, because he knew that if it didn't they were going to die. The thought of Shah being killed by these bastards shattered Jake with anger. And the anger gave him the necessary strength to keep them afloat in the powerful, deadly current.

Shah gripped at Jake's neck, and she felt him trying to loosen her fingers. What was he doing? She gave a little cry, panic seizing her again, water funneling into her nose and mouth. No! She was going to drown!

Grimly Jake transferred Shah's clawing hands to his shoulders. The current kept trying to suck them downward. He kicked hard with his bare feet, grateful that he'd had the intelligence to take off his boots. His recon training was going to come in handy.

"Hold on to my knapsack, Shah!" he croaked. "Hold on and I'll get us to shore!"

Trying desperately to contain her panic, Shah clung to Jake's shoulders. She twisted her head, hearing the helicopter turning around to come after them again.

"Oh, no!" she cried. The helicopter was bearing down on them, barely twenty feet off the water. She saw a floodlight on the nose of the aircraft flash on, the glaring white light skimming the surface of the water.

Jake's eyes widened. The bastards had a spotlight, and they were hunting for them! He stopped moving and began to tread water.

"Shah, we're going to have to dive when that light gets near. Take a deep breath and hold on!"

"But—"

"If we don't, they'll find us and kill us!" he yelled.

She didn't have time to argue, with the helicopter roaring down upon them. The water's surface lifted in a huge circle of fine spray ahead of the approaching aircraft. Her eyes widening, Shah took a huge gulp of air, digging her fingers frantically into the knapsack on Jake's back. Jake dived deep and fast, and she was jerked along, the raw, physical power of his dive overwhelming her as they spiraled downward. Her eyes closed, she buried her head against the knapsack, clinging wildly to him.

The current tugged and played with them. Shah heard pinging sounds all around them. Bullets! Jake was still diving, and she wondered if she had managed to gulp enough air to last for the duration.

A minute later, they broke the surface with a gasp, both choking on the brackish water.

"Shah?" Jake gasped, his voice cracking. He reached frantically for her. "Shah! You all right?" The helicopter was moving farther downstream, away from them, the floodlight still searching the dark water.

"I... Yes..." She clung to the knapsack, coughing violently, retching up the water she'd swallowed.

"Hang on," Jake ordered. He knew it would be impossible to land nearby with Hernandez's henchmen waiting for them on the shore.

"What—what are you doing?" Shah couldn't believe it. Jake was striking out toward the center of the wide river!

"We can't land now," he gasped. "We're gonna have

to let the current carry us a mile or two downstream before we go ashore.''

Fear clawed at Shah. The darkness was complete now, except for the dazzling light from the helicopter, now a good half mile away from them. ''C-can you make it?''

''I think so. Don't struggle anymore. Kick your feet and help me.''

Her panic subsided, replaced with the very real fear of drowning. The river was filled with schools of piranha that, if they caught the scent of blood, would descend upon them in a feeding frenzy and strip the flesh from their bones. Shah wondered bleakly if Jake was wounded. Was she? There was no way to know. The current was frighteningly potent—but so was Jake's constant, seemingly tireless swimming stroke.

The dreaded jacare, the Amazonian crocodile that could grow to more than twenty feet in length, prowled near the shores. Any kind of splashing would alert the reptile to their presence. The jacare had no fear of man. It didn't even fear the dreaded jaguar, lord of the rain forest. Gulping convulsively, Shah tried to do as Jake instructed, kicking with her feet.

Her thoughts were clashing with her heart. How long was Jake going to stay in the center of the river? How long could he remain afloat? She prayed fiercely to the Great Spirit and begged the spirit of the river to have mercy on them, to let them get safely to shore.

In the ensuing minutes, as Shah clung to Jake's knapsack, she slowly began to realize just how strong he really was. The current was deadly, constantly moving around their legs and trying to pull them under. But each powerful stroke of his arms and legs kept their heads above the water's surface. And each stroke gave Shah a little more hope. But then, up ahead, she saw the helicopter stop and hover at the bend in the Amazon.

"Oh, no!" she cried. "They're coming back toward us!"

Chapter Seven

Relief coursed through Shah as Hernandez's helicopter missed them completely on its second pass. Instead of searching the center of the Amazon, the pilot flew low near the left bank. As the aircraft swept past them, Jake grunted and struck out strongly toward the same shore.

Shah's panic eased as she felt his steady strokes begin to pull them out of the grip of the current. And their luck changed markedly when a six-foot-long log drifted by them.

''Grab it!'' Jake gasped.

Shah trusted him with her life now, and without thinking she lunged toward the log, which was as thick as a man's middle. Instantly she was buoyed upward by the floating log. Jake followed, maneuvering the log so that he gripped the end of it. With forceful kicks of his legs and feet, he was quickly able to guide them toward shore.

Light was fading fast, and Shah clung to the log, her teeth chattering. At night, the temperature in the forest dipped, and it actually got cold—at least by the standards of the thin-blooded natives. She'd lived here long enough to have become acclimated to the steamy Amazon weather, so she knew she was going to be terribly chilled once they got to shore. *If* they got to shore.

"Jake!" she croaked. "When we get near the bank, look out for crocodiles. They're around this time of night, hunting for food."

"Yeah…okay…" Exhaustion was pulling at Jake. The adrenaline charge that had helped him remain afloat with Shah clinging to him had begun to dissolve. With a nod, he blinked, the water running in rivulets down his face. His fingers were numb from holding and guiding the stubborn log. The current was tricky, trying to lure the log back toward the center of the river, and he had to kick damn hard. But with each kick, the current's grasp seemed to grow weaker.

Glancing upstream, Jake saw the helicopter bank and move back over the rain forest. Soon it disappeared from view, and the sound of the blades faded. Even straining his eyes, he could barely make out the shore. They had less than three hundred yards to go. Every muscle in his body screamed in protest. He knew he needed to rest, but if he tried, the current would snag him and haul them back out. And if that happened, they would surely die, because he knew he didn't have the necessary strength left to fight the Amazon's power all over again. Jake also knew about the fierce, aggressive jacare that plied the waters of the Amazon. He knew about the piranha, which often numbered in feeding schools of a hundred or more. He had no idea if he or Shah was cut and bleeding. The smell of blood could draw the savage little silver-and-red fish with their razor-sharp teeth.

Drawing huge gulps of air into his lungs, Jake concentrated on making it to shore. He'd worry about the local jacare once they got there. His main concern was for Shah. Had she been hit by a bullet? Broken a bone? She clung to the log, her face contorted in silent terror. At least she wasn't panicking, and for that Jake was grateful.

As they got close to shore, Jake stopped making large, loud kicks that spewed water high into the air. The jacare were drawn to churning water, honing in on the splashes like radar. Instead, he made scissorlike kicks beneath the water, making no sound at all. Suddenly his feet hit the sandy bottom, and he stood up. His knees wobbly, he used his upper-body weight to send the log toward the bank. As he staggered out into the shallows, he felt all his joints burning with pain from overexertion.

Stooping down, he hooked his arms beneath Shah's armpits and helped her to stand. She was shaking badly. "It's all right," he said, turning her around and bringing her tightly against him to keep her from falling. His knees were none too steady, but hers were like jelly. Jake couldn't blame her for her reaction; a weak swimmer had every right to fear the Amazon. It crossed his groggy mind that Shah might rebel and push his arms away, but he needed her in that moment. He'd almost lost her. The instant she sank against him, her arms moving around his waist, her head against his chest, Jake released a low groan. How right Shah felt against him. He held her with all of his remaining strength.

Closing his eyes, he rested his head against her wet hair. He could feel Shah's heart pounding against his chest, her breathing coming in ragged sobs. Unconsciously he pressed a kiss to her tangled hair and moved one hand down across her back in an effort to soothe away her terror.

"We're safe…safe…" he said unsteadily. She was so slender. Slender and strong. He felt her woman's strength renew itself in his arms, in his protective embrace. Nothing in the past four years had felt so right to him.

Gradually, the minutes flowing by as they stood in the ankle-deep water getting their second wind, Shah felt strength returning to her shaking knees. With each trembling stroke of Jake's hand up and down her spine, she felt him giving her renewed energy. She understood better than most the transfer of energy, because that was what a healer did for a sick patient—transferred the vitality of life. Jake was doing the same thing for her, whether he realized it or not. Her shorted-out mind awed by the discovery, Shah could only humbly receive the warmth that flowed from him to her, receive it with unspoken gratitude.

Jake forced himself to lift his head. He wanted to kiss her lips, to taste and feel her life mingling with his as his mouth met hers. Against his bulk, she was like a slender arrow. In that moment, Jake realized that Shah presented a powerful presence to the world because of her height and the way she carried herself. But holding her in his arms, he had discovered her fragility, and the discovery made his heart open like petals on a flower. Despite being a warrior for Mother Earth, Shah was decidedly human, and that gave him hope. No matter how strong someone appeared, how invincible, Jake knew from personal experience that everyone had faults and weaknesses. He was glad Shah was able to share her weaknesses with him, as well as her strengths.

"Better?" he asked, leaning down, his mouth inches from her ear. Jake felt Shah nod. He gave her a small squeeze, wanting to feed her hope that they would be safe now. Purposely he kept his voice very low, fearing discovery by Hernandez's roving henchmen. He had no idea if they were still on Hernandez's parcel of land.

The light was sparse as Jake lifted his head to survey the place where they'd come ashore. He felt Shah pull away, and he opened his embrace so that she could step out of his arms if she wanted. However, still not convinced she could stand, he kept his hand around her waist—just in case. If Shah minded his action, she didn't show it, and Jake savored the soaring joy that swept through him. To his surprise, Shah kept her arm around his waist and rested against him as they faced the rain forest together.

Shah tried to grapple with her receding terror. They had survived the Amazon River unscathed, and she sent a prayer to the spirit of the river in thanks for its having spared them. Looking up into Jake's harsh, shadowed features, she met his turbulent gray gaze.

"We need to find a tree," she told him, her voice scratchy. "We'll have to sleep up in one, or the jacare will find us. It's not safe to sleep on the ground."

With a nod, Jake pointed to a rubber tree about fifty feet inland. With proper pruning and shaping, rubber trees grew straight and tall. However, in the wilds of the rain forest, the trees spread their smooth-barked limbs in all directions, often looking like grotesque, twisted caricatures of octopuses.

"What about that one?" Jake asked. The trunk of the tree rose a good eight feet straight up, then its limbs flowed outward like tentacles. Jake thought it looked like a candelabra.

"Yes." Shah hated to leave Jake's embrace, but she knew that now that they were on land it was her responsibility to help. Jake hadn't lived in the rain forest, as she had. Or had he? They climbed the riverbank together. As Jake shed the heavy knapsack, Shah asked, "What do you know about survival in a rain forest?"

"Probably not as much as you," Jake admitted. Shah's hair, once braided, was coming undone, sheets of the drying strands like a dark cloak against the curve of her small breasts.

"The Tucanos have taught me a lot about this place, Jake." Shah turned. "That rubber tree is a good place to sleep tonight." She frowned, flexing her hands. Her fingers were stiff from the death grip she'd had on the log. "The only thing we've got to worry about is the jaguar. She's the only tree-climber."

"We've got a pistol and a knife," Jake said. "We'll be safe enough."

Shah moved carefully through the knee-deep vegetation. Transferring all her focus to her feet, she felt for vines and exposed roots that might trip them on their way to the tree. Shivering as the night became cooler by the minute, Shah wrapped her arms around herself. She had no change of clothes. And with the high humidity, the wet clothes they wore would dry only slowly, and probably not completely. Trying to stop her teeth from chattering, she halted at the base of the rubber tree.

When Jake joined her, Shah pointed upward. "We're in luck. See those two branches that criss-cross like a large loop on a high-backed chair?"

Squinting, Jake could barely make out the thick branches that tangled together. "Yeah..."

"That's like a cradle, Jake. It's strong enough and wide enough to hold you. All you have to do is ease back into the tree's branches like a hammock. You'll be able to sleep comfortably, and you won't fall.''

"What about you?" he asked. Searching the rest of the tree, he could find no limbs that would give Shah that kind of guaranteed safety. And, more than anything, they needed a good night's sleep to ready them for the trials that lay ahead tomorrow.

"I'll just find a branch and lean up against the main trunk," Shah assured him.

"Like hell you will," Jake growled. He shrugged out of the knapsack and tied it to an overhanging limb. Taking Shah's, he tied it next to his. "Come on, I'll boost you up," he ordered.

Surprised at Jake's sudden authoritative tone, Shah allowed him to lift her into the rubber tree. She watched as he gracefully hefted himself up on the opposite limb.

"Follow me," he said, and began the climb toward the cradle of limbs.

Perplexed, Shah followed him. The rubber tree's bark was smooth, and the oval leaves were large and waxy. The cacophony of night sounds surrounded them like a swelling orchestra. Her teeth chattering uncontrollably now, Shah watched as Jake settled gingerly back into the limbs that would hold him safe for the night. He tested the makeshift bed for strength, satisfying himself that the limbs weren't going to break.

"Come here," he said.

Shah was transfixed. "What?"

"I said, come here."

She frowned as he held out a hand to her. "Jake, I can't stay with you!"

"Sure you can." He gestured for her to come over to him. "I don't want you falling thirty feet and breaking something, Shah. If you fall asleep, you're liable to lose your balance against the trunk.''

A new kind of panic struck at Shah. Her mouth grew dry. "Jake...I can't!''

"No arguments, Shah. Now come on.''

The grimness in his eyes and mouth warned her not to debate his decision. Her heart beating wildly in her breast, Shah hesitated. "How am I going to sleep with you?'' she demanded in a high, off-pitch tone.

"In my arms.'' Jake patted the smooth, thick limb beside him. "I'll be your mattress. My arms will be around you, so you won't fall.''

"But—''

Jake held on to his patience. The alarm in Shah's voice was real. He understood her hesitancy, but under the circumstances he couldn't be swayed by it. "I'll hold you,'' he said patiently, "and we'll sleep. I'm not going to hurt you, Shah.''

She moved toward him and gripped his hand. "This isn't right!''

"It will be okay,'' Jake told her. In his heart, he knew it was the right thing to do. Hadn't he wanted to hold Shah, sleep with her? Taking her hand, he guided Shah toward him. "Now, turn around and sit down in my lap,'' he instructed her. The crisscrossed branches behind his back supported him completely.

Shah's heart was beating so loudly that she thought Jake must surely hear it as she settled stiffly on his broad thighs. His hands gripped her upper arms to steady her. A different fear raced through Shah—the fear of herself and her response to Jake as a man. He must have sensed her tension, because he squeezed her arms.

"You're safe,'' he murmured, pulling her toward him until her back rested against him. She was stiff in his arms. "Here, turn on your side. Just think of me as a big, lumpy mattress, with my shoulder as a pillow for your head…"

His teasing broke through her panic. She slowly turned so that her left side was ensconced against Jake's body.

"I'm afraid the limbs will break!" she protested. "We could fall and be killed!"

Reaching out, Jake stroked her damp hair. "You're so wild and untamed," he murmured. "We're not going to fall, Shah. This tree is old and strong, like me." He chuckled softly at his own joke.

Just the touch of his fingers against her head, caressing her as if she were an animal caught in a snare, calmed Shah to a degree. Her teeth chattered, and she had to admit she was freezing, and in need of shared body heat. Physical exhaustion stalked her in earnest now, and she had no choice but to lay her head against his broad, capable shoulder and press her brow to the column of his neck.

"Old?" she muttered. "How old are you?"

"Thirty-eight. And you?"

"Thirty."

He smiled. "You're young."

"And you aren't?" Her voice was softening as the fight went out of her.

"That's it," Jake whispered, and he groaned inwardly as Shah finally capitulated and eased against him. Her arm moved hesitantly around his waist. "You're cold," he whispered, wrapping his arms around her for warmth.

Shah shut her eyes and surrendered to Jake. This was the second time in her life that she'd truly trusted a man. The first time had been with her husband, who had proven quickly that he wasn't worthy of her trust. A shiver raced through her, and Shah felt her legs jerk of their own accord.

"Just lie here. I'll warm you up a little," Jake soothed, and he took his hand and began vigorously rubbing her wet trousers across her thigh and hip. Despite the danger they were in, Jake had to admit that nothing had ever felt more right than the weight of Shah nestled deep in his arms.

"Wh-why aren't you cold?" she chattered.

With a rumbling chuckle, Jake said, "I've got you in my arms, darlin'. The right woman always makes a man feel warm."

Shah's eyes flew open. He was teasing her, wasn't he? She moaned a little as his hand created warmth across her thigh and hip. He had to be teasing! Pursing her lips, she muttered, "I'm not any man's woman!"

"You can be."

"No one would want someone like me, Jake Randolph! I'm mean-tempered, defensive, and in general I don't care for men!"

"You're such a wildcat, Shah." Jake stopped rubbing her, because she'd ceased shivering. Wrapping his arms around her, he gave her a light squeeze. "You've got a lot of fine points about you," he whispered close to her ear. "And not every man is going to be scared off by your past or that tough-broad act you put on."

Confused and exhausted, Shah couldn't decide whether Jake was teasing or serious. She closed her eyes and pressed against him, absorbing his heat. How he could be so warm when she was freezing was beyond her. "I've been wounded too many times, Jake," Shah warned him, realizing her words were slightly slurred. "I don't trust men."

Jake smiled in the darkness and slowly began to undo

the rest of her braid so that her thick, silky hair could cover her. It was one more way to keep her warm. "Darlin'," he said softly, "we've all been wounded one way or another by love."

She stubbornly shook her head. "I suppose that's a quote from some famous philosopher."

His teeth were white against the darkness. "Yeah, a hell of a guy said it. I think Jake Randolph was his name."

All the tension Shah had been holding within her snapped. She giggled a little, and covered her mouth with her hand so that the sound wouldn't carry far. Just the simple act of Jake unbraiding her hair and allowing it to flow across her like a coverlet had been her undoing.

"What?" he asked teasingly. "You're not familiar with that famous philosopher?"

The darkness was complete now, and Shah allowed herself the luxury of enjoying Jake's embrace. She lifted her hand and rested it against the column of his neck. "You're good for morale," she murmured, "and I'm not going to comment one way or another about your philosophy."

Chuckling indulgently, Jake sighed and rested his head against the tree. "We've all been wounded," he told her softly. "But wounds should be allowed to heal, Shah."

"They still leave scars," she muttered with a frown.

"Nothing wrong with that. Scars are memories, but they shouldn't stop you from trying to reach out and live again." Jake laughed harshly at himself. Had he thought he'd ever laugh again? Ever love again? After his family had been taken from him, Jake had truly known the bleakness of a future without hope. Not until he'd met Shah, not until he'd held her in his arms, had he found hope again. She fit against his length like a missing piece of a puzzle. A piece he had never envisioned finding.

Warmth was beginning to seep back into Shah. Jake was like a huge furnace, and surrendering to him had been right. She laughed at herself for having thought she'd never trust a man again. Jake's rumbling voice flowed across her, bringing an unfamiliar ache to her heart. In some way, he was able to get through her complex defenses to touch her—gently, without engaging her fear. Yet Shah did fear the future. At some point, would Jake, like all the rest of the men in her life, turn on her? Abuse her? Take advantage of her?

Shah squeezed her eyes shut. She didn't know the answer, and not knowing left a helpless feeling in her heart. Jake absently stroked her arm, as if it were the most natural thing in the world. His touch, unlike any other man's that she'd known, was quieting and healing, and that amazed her.

Wearily Shah nuzzled against Jake's neck, and felt an instant response, his arm tightening around her just enough to let her know he liked her trust in him. "I'm so tired, Jake...."

"Go to sleep," he urged her huskily. "I'll hold you safe and warm tonight."

A soft smile tugged at Shah's mouth. "I can't believe a man could make me feel this safe...."

Those last words chased around in Jake's head most of the night. Sleep, though badly needed, wasn't on his list of priorities tonight. The need to stay alert, not only for four-legged predators, but for two-legged ones, as well, kept him thoroughly awake. The Amazon was like a lover in some ways, Jake thought as he lay there through the hours of darkness, experiencing the rich sounds of insects and animals and the heady fragrance of nearby orchids. His body throbbed with the knowledge that he wanted to make love with Shah. She slept deeply, like a lost child in his arms, her hand curled against his chest, over his heart.

Jake's attention was torn between keeping watch and succumbing to Shah's presence. The thrill of her trust was keeping him awake on another, more physical level. The ache deep within him surprised him even as it made him hungry in a way he'd thought he would never know again. He absorbed each soft, moist breath she released, felt her breasts lightly rise and fall, and devoured the sensation of her body resting against his. He almost laughed aloud at the thought that if she could read his mind she'd fly out of his arms.

A quarter moon rose silently in the sky, lending a misty luminescence to the landscape. Jake marveled at the hazy beauty of the rain forest, which seemed to be more magical than real. He watched wisps of mist twist slowly, like graceful hands and arms, through the branches overhead. The Amazon, now a wide black ribbon, shone like an ebony mirror in the moonlight. Several times he saw the sleek, dark shapes of dolphins as they leaped out of the river, made a quick splash and dived beneath the surface again. Never had Jake felt as fulfilled as he did at this moment.

Somewhere near dawn, Jake dropped off to sleep, his head tipped back against the tree, his arms wrapped around Shah. But his dreams were torrid and heated, instead of being filled with his usual cutting feelings of loneliness and grief.

Shah awoke slowly, feeling warm and safe. The scent of a man entered her nostrils, and she inhaled it as if it were some forgotten perfume that only her heart recognized. The bristles of Jake's beard chafed pleasantly against her brow, and she released a sigh of pleasure. The weight of his arms made her feel secure. The entire length of her body followed his, and as she flexed and moved her fingers, which lay against his powerful chest, she felt the smooth flow of muscles beneath his damp shirt. Jake had a hidden power, she decided groggily, and she didn't want to wake up, wanting instead to stay contained in the safe haven of his arms.

Jake's broken snoring made her smile softly. At some point in the night he had shifted just enough to allow his head to rest against her hair, and now his moist breath was flowing down across her. Forcing her eyes open, Shah blinked and allowed her senses to open up to the sounds and smells surrounding her. A huge part of her wanted to lift her head and explore Jake's mouth. What would it be like to kiss him? Would he overwhelm her with his superior strength? Or would he be tender and sharing with her? Shah tried to berate herself for her idealism. Her mind told her that men had no capacity for sharing, but her heart argued that Jake had already shown her his tenderness in many small, meaningful ways.

Ribbons of mist lay across the Amazon, and transparent, gauzy clouds of humidity floated just above the triple-canopied rain forest. The mist darkened the trees so that everywhere she looked the jungle seemed ethereal— as if it were a floating, moving mirage that could, at any moment, disappear before her very eyes. This was what she loved about the Amazon—its mysteriousness, the way it appeared and disappeared in these haunting white mists that reminded her of ever-moving curtains. Trees were silhouetted, then blotted out by a thick cloud moving silently across them, only to reappear later. Sounds were muted by the humidity and mist moving sensuously through the trees.

Shah heard a loud hiss from beneath the tree. Instantly she froze.

Jake jerked awake, his embrace tightening around Shah. "What?" he muttered, startled.

"Don't move," Shah breathed, craning her neck. "There's a huge jacare right under the tree, Jake."

At the base of the tree was a fifteen-foot jacare, its jaws open, the pink of its mouth and rows of white, pointed teeth showing. The reptile hissed again and whipped its tail, thumping it hard against the jungle floor.

Jake sat up, holding Shah hard against him. Sleep was torn from him as he stared down at the nasty-looking creature. They were safe. There was no way the jacare could climb the tree. He shifted his awareness to Shah, who was leaning forward.

"Don't fall," he warned.

"I won't." Shah gulped and decided it was time to get out of Jake's embrace. If she stayed, the temptation to kiss him, to explore his mouth, would overwhelm her. "Let me go."

Jake released her, scowling. "What are you doing?"

Shah moved slowly to the opposite side of the tree. "Trying to get rid of the jacare," she muttered. The jacare followed her movement, sluggishly turning in a half circle as she moved out onto another, smaller limb.

"Dammit, Shah, get back here!" Jake launched himself upward and gripped an overhead limb. What was she doing?

"Stay there," Shah ordered. She retrieved a hefty piece of limb that had fallen from a pau tree and lodged in the rubber tree. "Do you want to stay up here all day with him waiting for his meal to come down to him, or do you want him to leave?"

"Just tell me what you've got planned," he growled.

"I'm going to get rid of him. You can't shoot him. The noise will tell Hernandez we're alive and in his territory." She twisted her head toward Jake, who had a thundercloud look of disapproval on his darkly bearded face. Didn't he think she could help?

Retrieving the four-foot limb, Shah whispered, "Give me your knife."

Jake grudgingly handed it to her, butt first. Her logic was faultless.

Leaning down, Shah pricked two of her fingers with the tip of it.

"What the hell are you doing?" Jake demanded, alarmed.

"Relax." Shah allowed the blood to drip over the end of the limb. Then, satisfied that there was enough, she wiped her fingers on her trousers and handed Jake his knife. He was glaring at her.

"Jacare have lousy eyesight," she informed him testily, "but they've got noses like bloodhounds." She held up the limb. "They can smell blood half a mile away in the water. Unless you want to get down and wrestle this guy, this is the best way to get rid of him! The Tucanos showed me this trick."

Disgruntled, Jake watched as Shah clambered down to the lowest limb of the tree. The jacare heard her and whipped around with amazing speed for such an unwieldy creature. Shah took the limb and poked it down toward the hissing jacare, waving it back and forth in front of him. The crocodile tested the air with his long, thin snout, making several loud whuffing sounds. Shah chuckled.

"He's got the scent," she whispered excitedly. Then, with all her strength, she hurled the limb toward the bank of the river. Scowling, Jake watched Shah sit down on the limb and wait. Within a few minutes, the jacare lifted its dark green snout again, sniffed the air and slowly trundled toward where the limb lay on the bank.

Shah grinned expectantly as the jacare got within a few feet of the limb and attacked it, scooping it up in his massive jaws. Within moments, the reptile made a waddling run for the river and slid back into the muddy Amazon waters, disappearing beneath the surface with the limb. She tossed a triumphant look up at Jake.

"That jacare is going to have one heck of a bellyache after he eats that wood," she said with a chuckle.

Admiration for Shah flowed through Jake. He forced himself to stop scowling. "That's a pretty neat trick," he congratulated her. "How are your fingers?" It had hurt him as much to see her prick them as if they'd been his own.

She held them up and smiled. "Fine." Standing gingerly, Shah looked around, then back at him. Her smile faded. "Well, I guess we'd better start planning our day." She pointed to the north. "Hernandez's land is that way. If my camcorder isn't ruined, we'll be in luck."

A scowl instantly formed on Jake's brow. "What the hell are you talking about, Shah?"

She eased out of the tree and lowered herself to the ground. "You're sure grouchy when you first wake up, you know that? Are you always like that? Or is this something special for my benefit? Maybe you need a cup of good, thick Brazilian coffee..." Shah retrieved Jake's knapsack and laid it on the ground. To her delight, the camcorder was not only undamaged, but dry, as well.

Jake dropped to the ground next to her. "I only get grouchy when I think someone's going to make a fool out of herself." He hunkered down opposite Shah. "You aren't still planning to film Hernandez cutting down those trees, are you?"

Glancing up as she gently pulled the plastic wrap aside, Shah said, "Of course I am."

Jake stared at her in shock. "After what he's done?"

Heaving a sigh, Shah held his gaze. "Especially after what he's done," she said grimly. "I know the score with him, Jake. I know he'll try to kill me."

"Us."

"You don't have to go. I'm not asking that of you."

He held on to his thinning patience. "You nearly drowned yesterday!"

"Don't shout, Jake."

He frowned. "I'm shouting because I care, Shah. I care about your neck. Okay? It's too dangerous to go after Hernandez now. The smartest thing we can do is get our butts out of this sling, get back to Pai Jose's mission, make a radio call for police help and have them arrest Hernandez for attempted murder."

Shah tried to placate Jake. "Yesterday, I was on your turf, the water. Today—" she looked around the rain forest "—you're on my turf, Jake. I've been trained by the Tucanos. I know how to survive here. Look, you don't have to go along with me. I know the way back to the mission from here. I've got an excellent sense of direction, and I never get lost."

"That's not the point," Jake gritted out, feeling completely helpless beneath her stubborn determination. On one hand, his protective instincts were getting the best of him. On the other, he respected Shah's knowledge of the area. What he didn't want to deal with any more than was necessary was Shah's life being in danger again. "Dammit, Shah, I care about you! I want you safe!"

His words cut through Shah, and she slowly stood. Jake cared for her. His gray eyes were turbulent with feeling, and she heard the undisguised emotion in his voice. "Don't," she pleaded. "Don't care about me, Jake. It's no good. I'm not a good bet. Don't you understand?"

Jake rose, towering over her. How beautiful Shah looked with her long, loose hair flowing across her shoulders like an ebony cape. Her mouth was soft and parted, and her lovely golden eyes were filled with pain. He reached out, just barely grazing her cheek. "I don't have a choice," he rasped. "I don't want a choice, Shah."

She stood there looking up at him, stunned by his low, trembling admission. She looked around helplessly, then took a step away from his presence. "I— No, Jake. This isn't good—"

"That's what your head is telling you. What does your heart say, Shah?"

Stunned by Jake's insight, Shah felt nakedly vulnerable as never before. How could he read her true thoughts so easily? Panicking, she cried out softly, "It doesn't matter how I feel! Just go home, Jake! Go home to America and leave me here! This isn't your battle, it's mine!"

The tears in her eyes tore at him. Shah was frightened of him—of the connection he was offering her. Jake didn't have time to analyze why he'd said what he'd said. He wanted to take back the words, but it was too late. Shah wasn't ready to hear the depth of his feelings. Her fear regarding men was well-founded, and he was a man. It was that simple—and that complex.

"I'm not leaving you out here alone," he told her grimly.

"Because my father paid you?"

"Your father doesn't have a thing to do with this now, and you know it!"

Angry and frightened, Shah tensed. "I'm a lousy risk, Jake. So just—"

"You're a risk I want to take," he snapped. "And that's my decision, Shah." He jabbed a finger at her and instantly regretted the action. "You're stuck with me. Don't be bullheaded about this. Let's go to the mission first and report the incident."

"No," Shah said firmly. "No. Hernandez thinks he's killed us. Now he'll bring out those chain saws and let his men use them because he thinks we're not around to catch him on tape." She knelt again by her knapsack and pulled the last of the plastic away so that she could thoroughly examine the video equipment.

With a growl, Jake leaned down and gripped her by the shoulder. He used very little real strength, because of her fear of violence from men. "Then we'll do this together," he rasped.

Jake's hand was like a hot, searing iron against her flesh. Shah looked up, lost in the thundercloud blackness of his eyes, surrounded by his emotions. *Together.* Tears pricked her eyes, and she lowered her lashes. "You don't deserve this, Jake," she said, her voice wavering. "You're a good man. One of the best I've ever met. Please, just go home."

"No way, Shah," he whispered as he straightened. Jake had seen her tears and understood them. A part of her wanted him to stay; he'd seen it mirrored in her topaz eyes. Another part of her was so frightened of him and her feelings for him that she would rather risk her neck alone against Hernandez than have him around. Jake felt helpless and angry. But he was damned if he was going to abandon Shah. She'd been betrayed by men too many times before and for once he was going to show her that a man could be counted on to stick it out with her—even under threat of death.

Chapter Eight

"Look!" Shah whispered excitedly. "There's Hernandez!" Hidden deep in the shoulder-high bushes, she glanced over as Jake quietly crept up beside her. To her surprise, trekking through the rain forest hadn't been as bad as she'd thought. There was comparatively little underbrush, because smaller plants had difficulty surviving in the shade of the triple canopy of the trees overhead.

Shah pointed toward an area a quarter-mile down the slight hill they were kneeling on. Jake nodded but said nothing as he intently studied the situation. Shah could see three bulldozers and at least forty workers. Already the tall and the medium-sized trees had been taken down, leaving only the shortest trees still to fall to the buzzing chain saws wielded by the workers. The hillside looked stripped, and soon would be bare. Shah wondered if any of them realized that with the root system no longer holding the soil the earth would flow into the

Amazon when the summertime rainy season began. Losing the foot-and-a-half layer of topsoil that had accumulated in the past million years would have dire consequences. Once upon a time, in a prehistoric era, the Amazon Basin had been a vast desert wasteland. Now, only that precious layer of decayed leaves and trees on top of the sand base created the fragile barrier between life and death. If the destruction of the rain forest was allowed to continue unabated, the Amazon Basin would once again be a desert, incapable of sustaining life.

Without thinking, Shah gripped Jake's arm. "Chain saws!" The air rang with their sound; at least thirty of the men were using them against the last of the standing trees.

Looking around, Jake realized that daylight was slipping away from them. They had hiked at least three miles to the northeast, and there was no doubt that they were now on Hernandez's parcel of land.

"Yeah, but look," he growled, pointing out three men walking along the periphery of the work detail. All three were carrying submachine guns.

With a nod, Shah took off her knapsack, which contained the camcorder. "I promise we'll get the photos and get out, Jake. I don't want to get shot at again any more than you do." She kept her voice low so that they wouldn't be detected by the guards.

Edgy, Jake said nothing, but helped Shah prepare the camcorder for recording Hernandez and his men illegally using chain saws. Sweat ran down his face, and he wiped it away with the back of his arm. Shah seemed impervious to the steamy heat, but then, Jake reminded himself sourly, she had already become accustomed to the demands of the tropics.

"Ready?" he asked.

With a nod, Shah slowly stood, the camcorder balanced on her left shoulder. She moved to a nearby araba tree whose five-foot-tall roots resembled flying buttresses. Each root was less than an inch thick at the top, with a wedge shape that thickened to sometimes two to three feet in width as it breached the ground. Shah hid herself behind one of the dark brownish-gray barriers, just her head and the video camera visible above it. Leaning against the root's stability, Shah began to tape, her heart pounding a steady, heavy beat of triumph.

Jake remained alert, scanning the area for any sign of trouble as Shah continued to shoot the necessary footage. He tried to ignore the carnage that Hernandez's men were wreaking below them. He wondered what animal species were being displaced and, worse, what potentially life-saving medicinal plants were being destroyed before they could ever be discovered.

The sunlight was almost gone now, brief beams cutting through the rain forest only occasionally. In another two hours it would be dark, and Jake wanted to be a long way from this particular area. Detection by Hernandez's guards was still a very real possibility.

After forty minutes of taping the timber cutting operation, Shah knelt down behind the buttress root and shut off the camcorder. Jake joined her and took the videotape she proffered. Slipping it into an airtight plastic bag, he made sure the tape was well protected, hidden deep within his knapsack.

"We've gotta hightail it out of here," he muttered near her ear. "It's getting dark, and we've got to find a safe place to sleep before nightfall."

"No argument," Shah said, giddy with excitement, with the knowledge that she could put Hernandez behind bars with the tape. She looked up and met Jake's darkened gaze. He'd been testy and grouchy all day, and she couldn't blame him—this was dangerous work. "You've been wonderful!" she said, and spontaneously threw her arms around him and gave him a quick, hard embrace.

Surprised, Jake had no time to react—at least not the way he would have liked to. The glow in Shah's eyes told him of her joy, and he smiled crookedly.

"Glad to see there's a little of the child left in you," he said teasingly as he rewrapped the camcorder in protective plastic.

Years of weight seemed to lift off Shah's shoulders as she stared up at Jake. His smile was that of a bashful boy, and if her eyes weren't deceiving her, there was a new ruddiness in his cheeks. "Jake, you aren't blushing, are you?" She laughed softly with delight at her discovery.

"Hey," he muttered, "it's been a long time since a beautiful lady hugged me." Jake felt the heat nettling his bearded cheeks. He was thankful that the darkness of his two-day beard probably hid the worst of the flush, but he still felt vulnerable to Shah's observation. When had he last blushed like a teenager? Jake couldn't even recall. His neck and shoulders still tingled where Shah had touched him. The ache to love her, to make her his, nearly overwhelmed him. But the feelings he held for her, though heated, were tender. He smiled into her dancing gold eyes, losing himself in her happiness.

The danger of their situation was still very real, and Shah was well aware that they couldn't sit and chat. Within moments they were slipping out of the area, undetected. Their plan called for heading back to the banks of the Amazon, then simply walking along it to shorten their journey back to the mission, instead of moving inland and fighting the rain forest all the way back. The inland route would be safer, but they'd weighed that against the time factor and decided that speed was their best asset, so they'd chosen the river route.

Grateful that Jake was ahead of her, Shah made a mental note to ask him about his past sometime. He'd once referred obliquely to not being married. Why had he blushed? He was a thirty-eight-year-old man with obvious experience with women. Dividing her attention between where she was placing her feet and the sounds around her, Shah decided to ask her questions tonight, after they made camp.

To Shah's delight, they came upon a mango tree, the fruit ripe and edible. She had already collected edible berries that had dropped to the damp jungle floor, and she knew they'd eat well once they camped. Jake remained tense, and Shah had to admit that she had no idea whether they were still on Hernandez's land.

Again she selected a rubber tree with grotesque limbs to support them during sleep, and Jake nodded at her choice. Was he disappointed that she wouldn't sleep in his arms tonight? Last night had been one of the best nights of sleep Shah had ever experienced. Confused, she tried not to think about it—or Jake. She watched as he moved like a shadow upstream through the rain forest while she made camp for them in the tree. The trunk rose almost ten feet straight up, and then began to spread out its twisted, gnarled limbs.

Standing on a nearby log to tie both knapsacks high in the tree, Shah looked up to see the pale pink sunset along the western horizon. The color was softened and muted by the ever-present mist, which was beginning to return in earnest now that the sun had set.

Near dark, she sensed Jake nearby from her tree perch

and strained to see him. Or was it Jake? Shah wasn't sure, and remained parallel to the trunk so that she took on the shape of the tree as camouflage.

Jake appeared silently. He looked up and raised his hand without a word.

Relieved, Shah sighed and returned his gesture. She watched as he jumped to grip the lowest-hanging limb, then moved easily up into the tree. Jake's face had a dangerous look to it with his two-day growth of beard. His gray eyes looked darker, and more lethal, and the harsh planes of his face were emphasized. Shah smiled happily when he sat down on the limb opposite her, the tree trunk between them.

"Anything?" she asked in a whisper as she handed him a mango to eat.

"No, it's quiet." Jake sank his teeth into the juicy flesh of the mango. They'd lost their food pack when the canoe overturned. If not for Shah's knowledge of the rain forest, they'd have starved today. Jake was trained to live off the land, but the rain forest had many deadly forms of plants and berries, not to mention the multitude of poisonous mushrooms that grew in the dampness of the jungle floor. Shah had learned her lessons well from the Tucanos shaman she had worked with finding the medicinal plants. Throughout the day, she'd gathered berries or nuts that had fallen from last year and lay partly hidden by the damp leaves.

They ate in silence, watching as the sunset turned a bloodred, then slowly dissolved into the swiftly approaching cloak of darkness. Shah shared the last of the berries with Jake. The night sounds of insects rose around them, and she felt a good kind of tiredness. She was still on a high from getting the video of Hernandez's illegal operation.

"A penny for your thoughts," Jake said. He wiped his long, strong fingers across his thighs. Shah was positively glowing with happiness, and he felt fortunate to see this side of her. He'd never realized how beautiful she really was until she'd smiled; now he'd never forget it. More than anything, he wanted to be the one to make her smile like that again.

"Oh..." Shah sighed softly, resting her head against the trunk. "I'm just so happy, Jake. I think I'm floating on air."

He grinned. "I like seeing you happy."

She lifted her chin and held his searching gaze. "You've been wonderful today, too. I couldn't have done it without you."

"Can I get that in writing?" He chuckled indulgently. He liked Shah's thoughtfulness and ability to share. She made him feel a part of her team effort. Yes, she was a good leader.

Shah reached out and slapped his hand lightly. "Jake, you're such a tease!"

He relaxed a little, wanting badly to devote all his attention to Shah. Jake estimated it would take roughly a day and a half, maybe two days, of walking to reach the mission. He desperately wanted this time alone with Shah. There was a natural, powerful intimacy that sprang up between them, and he wanted more of these moments with her. He caught Shah's hand in midair and held it for just a moment. The surprise in her eyes wasn't fueled by fear, he realized, but by desire. Hope beat strongly in his chest. Was it a desire for him?

Shah's hand tingled where Jake had touched it. "Jake?"

"Hmm?"

"Are you tired?"

"Yeah. You?"

"No, not really. I guess I'm too excited."

Jake felt exhaustion pulling at him. Tonight he'd have to sleep in spurts if he was going to maintain security around them. "Do you always get like this?"

"What?"

"Excited when you get what you want?"

Her smile was large. "Yes." The seconds fled by, the silence lengthening. Shah sobered a bit. "Jake, may I ask you a personal question?"

Jake suddenly grew very alert, the exhaustion torn from him. He'd hoped beyond hope that Shah would reach out and establish a more personal relationship with him. Maybe this was his opportunity. "Sure," he mumbled, trying not to sound too eager.

Shah sat nervously for a long moment and stared down at her clasped hands in her lap. Torn, she finally offered, "I have a terrible case of curiosity. It always gets me in trouble. If you think I'm getting too personal—"

"I'm an open book to you," Jake said, and he meant it.

Shah glanced over at his shadowy features. "I don't see how you can be so vulnerable. It scares me to open up."

"That's because you've been hurt every time you did it," Jake offered gently.

"I guess…" Shah said. Then she made an exasperated sound. "You're so trusting and open, Jake. I've never met a man like you. Sometimes I feel you're from another planet."

Chuckling, Jake said, "Believe me, I'm no alien. I'm very male. You just haven't run into my bad side yet."

"I think you're bluffing, Jake. Somewhere along the

line, you learned that manipulation and control of a woman wasn't right. I guess that's what I wanted to know. You said you aren't married now. Are you divorced?''

Of all the questions Shah could have asked, this was the most unexpected. He felt his gut tighten, as if someone had sucker-punched him. For a moment, it was hard for him to breathe, much less talk.

Shah watched Jake wrestle with a multitude of emotions plainly etched on his grim features. She saw the torture appear in his eyes, and, too late, she realized that she had stepped into a very painful topic for him. ''Jake, I—''

''No,'' he said, his voice raw, ''I'll tell you, Shah.'' He swallowed back a lump that threatened to shut off his breathing. ''I want to tell you.''

The words were charged with emotion, and Shah felt uneasy. Unconsciously she reached over and touched the hand that he'd clenched into a fist against his powerful thigh. ''I'm sorry....''

Jake turned his hand and gripped her long, slender fingers. How small Shah's hand was in comparison to his. He expected her to pull out of his grasp, but, to his surprise, she didn't. He was heartened by that. Jake needed Shah's compassion and understanding in that moment in order to answer her question honestly. He knew what it had cost Shah to make this overture to him, and he owed it to her to be just as brave.

''Four years ago,'' he croaked, ''I was married. But I have to go back to the beginning, I guess. I went into the Marine Corps when I was eighteen. I was a real hell-raiser then, footloose and fancy-free. I never wanted to be married or tied down.'' Jake studied Shah's hand, barely able to see it in the darkness. Soon the moon would rise and he'd be able to see her better. Still, the darkness gave him the courage to go on. He didn't want Shah to see his face as he related his past.

"Five years later I met Bess at a USO club in Los Angeles. At the time, I was stationed at Camp Pendleton, and a couple of the guys and I decided to go up there for a change of pace." Jake shut his eyes. "I walked into that place and felt like lightning had struck me. Bess was a 'donut dolly,' one of the girls who serve food to the servicemen and women. She was twenty-three also, fresh out of college, and beautiful—with light brown hair, brown eyes, and a pretty smile that made me feel ten feet tall."

Shah felt Jake's pain. Something had happened to Jake and his wife. Automatically she clasped his hand a little more tightly.

Jake began to move his fingers back and forth across the top of Shah's hand, lost in the bittersweet memories, caught up in the old pain and grief. "Bess had a degree in economics, and she was sharp as hell. I courted her for a year before she'd marry me. At the time, I was getting my college degree, even though I was still an enlisted marine." Jake shook his head as the memories swiftly welled up. "Bess was a lot like you," he went on in a hushed tone. "She had the love of the land, of nature, and she wanted children more than anything. Nine months to the day after we got married, Bess had Katie…"

Wrestling with a gamut of new emotions, Jake hung his head and clung to Shah's hand. "Katie," he choked out, "looked a lot like that Tucanos girl you held in your arms a few days ago. She had my dark hair and her mother's pretty brown eyes and smile." Taking a deep breath, Jake plunged on. "Two years later, we had

Mandy, and she had her mother's light brown hair and my gray eyes. Things were going well for us, and we were happy. I eventually got my degree, went to Marine Officer's Candidate School and came out a lieutenant.

"To make a long story real short, after almost eleven years of marriage, Bess and the girls were in the wrong place at the wrong time." Anger, white-hot and suffocating, flowed through Jake. "I was stationed near Miami, part of a multiservice drug enforcement team that worked closely with the Coast Guard. We'd made a couple of big busts, and the boys down in Colombia were plenty angry. Somehow," Jake said bleakly, "information was leaked on all of us, our names, our addresses, where we lived...."

"Oh, no," Shah cried softly.

Jake bowed his head, holding Shah's hand as if to release it would be to lose control of himself and his violent, grief-stricken emotions. "A drug lord down in Peru had his men come up to the States to even the score. He had the bastards plant a bomb under my car," he rasped. "I was sick at home that day with the flu, and Bess had to take both girls for ballet lessons, so she took my car, because it was parked outside the garage." Tears dampened Jake's eyes, and he shut them. When he spoke again, his voice was trembling. "I was asleep up in the bedroom.... The next thing I knew, the whole damn side of the house was blown off in the explosion. I— It was a nightmare...."

With a little cry, Shah withdrew her hand and stood up. She couldn't endure the anguish in Jake's voice, and she knew he needed to be held. Carefully she moved around the tree until she could sit down beside him, her back supported by another branch so that she couldn't fall.

"Come here," she choked out, and gently drew her arms around Jake's broad shoulders. Her eyes blinded by tears, she felt Jake's arms slide around her waist, and she felt the air rush out of her lungs as he held her tightly against him. As he buried his head next to hers, Shah whispered brokenly, "I'm so sorry, Jake. So sorry..." The rest of the words died in her throat as it closed up with tears, and she sobbed.

Shah's unexpected compassion broke Jake's hold on his grief. He'd cried off and on throughout the years since losing his family, but there had remained a stubborn part of his grief that he'd never been able to reach. Shah's simple act, placing her slender arms around him, holding him with her woman's strength, shattered that last bastion of grief. Her hair was like a silken curtain that he could bury his face in. Somewhere in his cartwheeling mind, he realized how much courage it had taken Shah to come to him, to hold him.

The first sob, like a fist shoving violently upward through the center of him, slammed into his throat and lodged there. He tried to fight it, but Shah's trembling, soothing hand across his hair broke through his control. Jake had always cried alone. Cried when no one was around. The Marine Corps didn't see tears as strong or good—only as a sign of weakness.

"Cry," Shah whispered near his ear. "Cry for all you've lost, Jake. I'll hold you.... I'll just hold you...." And she did, with all her strength and all her love. Shah felt another sob rack Jake's body, and she held him even more tightly. This bear of a man she'd been so afraid of, so distrusting of, before, was hauntingly human now as she held him in her arms. As she sat rocking him ever so slightly, much as a mother would a hurt child, she cried with him. She cried for his terrible loss, unable to imagine how much it must continue to hurt him. The closest comparison Shah could imagine was her mother being torn brutally and suddenly out of her life. She thought how terrible that loss would be, and she was able to transfer that understanding to Jake. But only he knew the full emotional impact of losing his family.

The moments melted into one another. The darkness was so complete that Shah couldn't see anything. It didn't matter, anyway, because the tears flowing from her eyes were blinding her. She continued to stroke Jake's head, shoulders and back. If only she could take away some of his grief. And then she laughed softly to herself as Jake expended his heartache within her arms. Amazingly, all her fear of him as a man had dissolved. As she sat there in the aftermath, a half hour after the storm had broken within Jake, Shah watched the moon rise in the east. She saw the soft, luminescent light silently spreading across the dark, silhouetted rain forest, as the symbolic light of a new day.

Intuitively Shah understood that she had been a catalyst in Jake's healing process. The moon was a woman's symbol, a feminine one, and the light from the silvery sphere was always gentle and nonintrusive. She prayed to the Great Spirit that her questions hadn't been damaging to Jake, but had served instead as a catharsis for further healing.

Leaning down, she pressed a kiss against his heavily bearded cheek. Jake's scent entered her nostrils, and she inhaled it deep into her lungs. The bristles of his beard were wet from his tears. Or were they her tears, too? Shah was lost in the textures, scents and awareness of Jake as a vulnerable human being. As she pressed a second kiss to his cheek to console him, she felt his hands frame her face.

A soft breath escaped Shah as Jake opened his eyes and looked deep into her soul. Her breathing suspended, she felt her world tilt out of control. Vividly she recalled that her ex-husband had always called her cold, unable to respond. Hesitating fractionally, she wondered if she had anything to offer Jake. Another part of her urged her to try, despite that knowledge. Her lips parting, she leaned forward to meet and touch Jake's mouth. Never in all her life had anything felt so right.

Shah's entire existence centered on Jake's questing mouth, touching her lips, sliding gently against them. The bristles of his beard were a counterpoint to the strength of his mouth as it molded and captured hers. With a moan, she melted against him, drowning in the splendor of his mouth as it moved with a reverence that made tears squeeze beneath her lashes. His hands, large, scarred and rough, held her gently as he touched, cajoled and silently asked Shah to participate in the beautiful dance of life their kiss was creating. It was life, she realized hazily, all her senses moving in a rainbow of vibrant feelings as she hesitantly returned his kiss.

The steamy Amazon jungle caressed them like a lover, and Shah's breathing increased as she felt his tongue move across her lower lip. There was such a ribbon of pleasure beneath each touch. Jake proceeded to explore her slowly, deliberately—as if each contact were an exquisite gift. And to Shah it was. Her mind was no longer functioning. She was aware only of Jake, of his tenderness and his coaxing. With each small kiss, each nip, each touch with his tongue, she yielded, like a flower opening for the first time. Reality mingled with euphoria, with the fragrance of the orchids that surrounded them, with the singing sounds of the night that embraced them, and with Jake's ragged breath flowing moistly across her face.

How long Shah clung to his mouth, allowing him to explore her fully, to kiss her reverently, she had no idea. She felt bereft when Jake drew inches away, his breathing uneven, his hands still framing her uplifted face. Slowly opening her eyes, Shah lost herself in the silver glitter of his narrowed ones. Her body felt on fire, a bubbling volcano ready to explode, and it left her trembling and anticipating. Anticipating what? She had no idea. All she knew was that Jake had made her feel more alive, more of a woman, with that single kiss, than in all her experience with her ex-husband combined.

Gently Jake leaned down and brushed Shah's parted lips one more time. He knew he'd reached the limit of his control. If he continued to kiss her, continued to teach her that love, real love, was not painful, but something so beautiful it could make a man cry, he'd take her to the jungle floor and make love to her there. Shah's eyes were lustrous with desire, and the moonlight was radiant and lovely on her upturned features. With her hair loose, she looked like a magical part of this rain forest—a goddess, perhaps, flowing like the silent mists through the jungle.

Jake felt as if someone had taken a bottle brush to his insides, leaving him miraculously lighter. The load he'd unconsciously carried for so long was gone. Blinking away the last of his tears, he smiled down at Shah, who clung to him as if she might fall out of the tree. There was such beauty in her dazed-looking eyes, and Jake knew that the kiss they'd shared had been wonderful— for both of them. Caressing her high cheekbones with his thumbs, he erased the last of her tears there. More tears were beaded on her thick lashes, and Jake felt such a fierce love for Shah that it left him stunned in its wake.

As he sat with Shah resting against him, her hands pressed against his chest as she looked up at him, Jake assimilated the discovery. He loved Shah. And then he realized that from the moment he'd met her he'd been falling in love with her. There wasn't anything not to love about her, Jake decided as he continued to dry her cheeks with his thumbs. Weren't they both terribly scarred by past battles with life? Was it possible not only to feel like living again, but to want to love again? Shocked by the prospect—a silly dream he'd never envisioned coming true—Jake could do nothing but lose himself in Shah's golden eyes, eyes that spoke of her love for him. Was she aware of it? Jake, humbled by the realization that they could have shared so much in such a short space of time, had no answers.

There were no words he could say, so Jake took the ultimate risk and folded his arms around Shah. They would sleep here, together, with him leaning against the trunk of the tree, holding her safe in his arms. Shah could lean against him. To his surprise, she eased into his arms, her body meeting his, molding against it. He shut his eyes, and a low sound, like a groan, escaped his lips. As her arm went around his waist and she nestled her head in the crook of his shoulder, Jake knew he was the luckiest man alive.

Too shaken by the grief he'd expressed, Jake's mind refused to work coherently. Exhaustion and lack of sleep overtook him, and in minutes he slept. A nagging thought flitted through his spongy senses as he surrendered to sleep. How would Shah react to him tomorrow morning? Would she run away from him because he was a man? He loved her with a fierceness that defied description. As he rested there, with Shah secure in his arms, he knew that he was being given a second chance—and nothing short of dying was going to keep him from taking the risk of loving Shah without reservation. But did she love him? Could she ever fall in love again?

Chapter Nine

Shah awoke first, wrapped in a warm, secure feeling she'd never felt anywhere except in Jake's arms. It was barely dawn, not light enough yet to travel, so she relaxed and absorbed the moment at his side.

The mists moved slowly and sensuously through the rain forest's branches, seeming to symbolize Shah's own life: the twists and turns she'd taken, some of them by her own choice, most of them not, and where they had led her at this moment. The kiss Jake had branded her lips with lingered hotly in her body, like a fever that refused to subside. It was a new and unfamiliar sensation, one that Shah basked in. There was a gnawing ache within her, and she didn't know where it was coming from, or why it was there. The entire lower region of her body felt like a simmering cauldron ready to overflow. Because Shah was Native American, she had grown up seeing life in terms of symbols, and understanding that everything was connected to everything else. This new and wonderful yet disturbing feeling in her triggered her curiosity. Would Jake know what it was? What she was feeling? She had long since recognized his perceptiveness about human beings in general. If anyone would know, Jake would, she decided.

The sky, a veil of thick and thin curtains of mist, took on an ethereal glow as the night eased its grip on the rain forest. The horizon, covered with magnificent pau trees stretching for the sky with their arms, became a panorama of golden hues and darker tones. Shah lay there, her head pressed to Jake's chest, the slow beating of his heart soothing the chaotic feelings that were moving through her like a wild, unmanageable river that had escaped its banks.

She felt Jake jerk awake. Lifting her head, she sat up and brushed the hair away from her face. Never had she felt more vulnerable than in the moments before she forced herself to meet and hold Jake's gaze.

Jake reached over, laid his hand on her arm. He saw the terrible uncertainty in Shah's face. "Don't go," he rasped, and his fingers closed gently around her arm.

"I—" Shah gulped unsteadily as she anxiously searched Jake's sleep-clouded eyes. His raw voice had sent a shiver of need through Shah that tore at her fear of rejection. "No... I'm not going anywhere...." she whispered.

Fighting to regain wakefulness, Jake hungrily absorbed Shah's innocent gestures. Her lips were still slightly swollen, proof of his need of her. All his focus, his world, narrowed on her as he eased into a sitting position. The bluish sheets of her hair moved in a rippling wave, and he captured some of the thick strands and tucked them behind her shoulder so that he could have a good look at her profile. Shah's nervousness touched him deeply.

"It's all right," he assured her, sliding his hand along her arm and capturing her fingers.

Shah shrugged and looked down at his large hand. The hand that had been so incredibly gentle with her the night before. The hand that had wiped the tears from her face. "I feel mixed up inside, Jake," she admitted hoarsely. "I'm sorry I asked you about Bess…about your family." She risked a glance up at him. "I don't understand how you survived with that happening to you. I—I'd go crazy. I'd kill the bastards. I'd do something…."

He sighed and nodded. "What I didn't tell you was that I left the Marine Corps shortly after it happened. I wanted to kill the men responsible for my family's murders. The only place I could go was Perseus, the company I work for now. Morgan Trayhern, who runs it, let me take assignments having to do with drug dealers here in South America. I'd been in Peru and Columbia on a number of missions, putting the bastards out of commission, usually in jail. I had one assignment that put me on the Orinoco River, close to the Brazilian border. For the past four years I've been waging a one-man war against the drug dealers. It's helped me settle past debts."

Shah gauged him in silence. "A one-man war." She laughed, a little self-consciously, glad that Jake was holding her hand. "I've always seen myself as waging a one-woman war down here with a different kind of criminal—an ecological one."

"I know," Jake whispered, and managed a lopsided smile. "We have a lot more in common than you first thought."

"Yes..." Shah bit down on her lower lip. "What I don't understand is why you took my father's assignment. This has nothing to do with drug dealers, Jake."

He held her shimmering golden gaze, touched as never before, because Shah was completely open to him, without any of her old defenses in place. Had their kiss been the reason? Jake didn't know, and he desperately wanted to find out. Caution made him move slowly, however, because he sensed that so much of what Shah had experienced last night was new to her. How could it be? She was thirty years old—a grown woman with experience. *Patience,* he ordered himself. *Be patient with her.*

"I just happened to have come off an assignment for Perseus and was in the office when your father and Morgan were talking. Morgan called me in because I was the only available agent who spoke Portuguese and had South American experience." Jake watched Shah's expressive features, his gaze centered hotly on her parted lips. The kiss they'd shared had been unlike any other. "I didn't like your father or his attitude, and neither did Morgan. At first, because of your father, I wasn't going to take the assignment. Besides, I needed a rest, and I didn't want to get sent out this soon after my last mission."

Shah frowned. "What changed your mind?"

He smiled gently. "I saw the photo your father had of you. Morgan isn't stupid. He knew I wasn't going to take the mission, because of your father's abrasive attitude. Neither of us could figure out why he was angry with you. We could understand why he'd be concerned and worried, but not angry. Pieces of the puzzle didn't fit. Of course, when I got down here and found out your father had botched two other attempts to have you kidnapped, then I figured it out.''

''Chances are,'' Shah whispered bitterly, ''that my father has stock in some Brazilian lumber company or something. It would be just like him. He always wants to make a quick buck at the expense of Mother Earth and all her relatives. He doesn't care.''

''I know,'' Jake said soothingly, sliding his fingers across the back of her hand. Shah's pain was no less real than his. ''I still have questions I want to ask him when I get back. When I get to Manaus, I'm going to call Morgan and get him to check on your father's business interests. Then we'll see what cards he's holding. I feel that will explain the rest of the missing pieces to us.''

Shah cringed inwardly. Jake was leaving for Manaus? When? She was afraid to ask. She was afraid of her own feelings for him. ''So my photo convinced you to take this mission?''

Jake nodded. ''Yeah. Morgan's like a brother to me, and he knows me pretty well. All he had to do was slide that photo of you into my hands, and he knew I'd take the mission; no questions asked.''

She smiled hesitantly. ''Morgan sounds like a decent human being.''

''Even if he is a man?'' Jake teased gently.

''I guess I had that coming, didn't I?''

''Don't ever apologize for how you feel, Shah,'' Jake told her in a low, vibrating tone. ''What happened to you has shaped your life and your actions.''

''I'm trying to get rid of my anger toward men,'' Shah admitted, looking away from Jake's burning gray gaze. ''I really am. I know it doesn't seem like it most of the time....''

''Listen to me.'' Jake took Shah by the arms and made

her look at him. "No one knows better than me what pain can do to a person. It's taken me four years to crawl out from beneath all that grief over losing my family. I tried, the other night, to put myself in your shoes, to try and feel what it might be like to be a kid growing up in that kind of brutal, violent environment."

"I walked on eggshells," Shah admitted. "Mother did, too. We tried to find out what kind of mood Father was in as soon as possible so we could plan how we were going to behave for the rest of the day."

Jake shook his head. "Sweetheart, you're a survivor of a war. I don't know if you realize that or not, but you are. You were in a dangerous war zone for twelve of your most formative years." He gave her a small smile of encouragement. "From my vantage point, I'd say you've made something worthwhile out of your life, despite the lousy start you had. There are lots of kids who come out of that same kind of environment and end up on drugs or in prison. Look at you. Look at how you're helping the world. I'm proud of you."

Shah turned her head away to wipe her eyes free of the tears that had gathered unexpectedly.

"No, you don't," Jake rasped, and he captured her chin, forcing her to meet his gaze. "Don't ever be ashamed to cry in front of me, Shah. How can you feel that way after I cried in your arms last night?"

He was right, Shah acknowledged. "Jake... You—all of this—it's so new to me. I'm so confused."

"What do you mean?" He gently wiped the tears from her cheeks. There was such hope burning in Shah's eyes; this was a look he'd never seen in them before. Perhaps sharing that load he'd carried alone for so many years had been the most right thing he'd ever done.

"It's you!" When Shah realized she'd raised her

voice above a whisper, she clapped her hand over her lips and sent Jake a silent apology. She looked around, and when she was finally convinced there were no humans nearby to hear her, she said, in a strained undertone, "It's you, Jake. You're different. You aren't like the men I've known."

"All you've known are the violent bastards, the ones who would strip your soul from you because you're a woman." He grimly held her wavering stare. "I know all about that type, Shah. They're weak little men with low self-esteem, and the only way they feel powerful is to keep a woman or a child under their thumb. That makes them feel powerful when nothing else does. Men know they've got more physical strength than a woman, and so they'll use it to keep you captive, to keep you docile."

"But by hurting a woman they are hurting themselves!" Shah whispered, her voice choked with emotion. "The Lakota believe that within each of us is the spirit of both man and woman." She touched her breast. "If a man despises and fears women, he despises his own gentleness, his ability to cry, to reach out and nurture someone other than himself."

"That's right," Jake agreed. "Our society has suppressed women's feelings and strengths."

"But why?" she asked, her voice cracking. "Women know how to cry, how to be creative, how to be in touch with Mother Earth."

He saw the terrible sense of loss in Shah's eyes, and he understood her pain. "Listen," he said. "I don't have all the answers, Shah. Each woman is going to have to find the courage within herself to stand up and say that she will no longer be controlled. Each man has to have the courage to allow women to be their true selves."

She shook her head in awe. "Jake, before meeting you, I never realized any man could understand what we women see so clearly." Then she corrected herself. "Well, some women see it. Others are just starting to awaken to the imbalance and unfairness of it all."

"Yes, and still others are asleep," Jake agreed.

"Or," Shah said softly, "too frightened to make the change, even though they're aware of the unfairness."

"As I've always said," Jake told her grimly, "it doesn't take much just to exist a day at a time, but it sure as hell takes the rawest, purest kind of courage to *live* your life. Living life means changing and growing. And change is frightening to most people."

"I just wish women would realize that the unknown future will be a better one than they're in right now," Shah said. "My mother was like that, you know. At first she was so afraid of my father that she cowered like a dog. Over the years, she never grew less afraid of him, but she began to put my safety and welfare ahead of her own."

"Yes, your mother thought she couldn't help herself, but she felt you were worth saving."

"It's called being a victim," Shah rattled. "I know— I used to be one myself, in my marriage with Robert."

Jake stroked her hair in an effort to take away her obvious shame over her lack of fearlessness. "But you chose to grow instead of becoming trapped like your mother. That took real courage, Shah. The rarest kind."

"My marriage was a travesty," she admitted painfully. "I let Robert beat me down, and I started to believe I was as worthless as he said I was. Talk about brainwashing." She smiled bitterly, not feeling very proud of herself. "I swallowed everything he said to me. It never occurred to me he might be wrong."

Jake wanted to tread carefully, but he had to know the truth regarding Shah's marriage. "Did you love Robert?"

"Yes and no. At first I did, but, Jake, it was a stupid infatuation, that's all. I woke up one morning six months later realizing Robert and I had very little in common." And then she muttered, "I wasn't any good in bed, either."

Jake's eyes narrowed. "Who told you that?"

Shah refused to look at him, too humiliated by the admission. Once Jake had cried in her arms, she'd become helpless to erect defenses against his questions, and now she was blathering like the village idiot. But she couldn't help herself—the words just came tumbling out in a hurtful torrent.

"I was a virgin when I married Robert. I guess he'd been around a lot, and he—" Shah swallowed, because the words were sticking in her throat "—he said I was lousy in bed. I didn't know what I was doing, and he said I was too stupid to learn. He said I was cold...."

Jake stared at her in disbelief. He remembered hotly how her mouth had opened to his. He'd tasted her sweetness and felt her passionate response to his kiss. "What?" The word escaped before he could take it back.

"Frigid," Shah said in a strangled voice. She cast a glance over at Jake and saw the thundercloud blackness in his eyes. Was it aimed at her? Had her kiss been that bad? Had Robert been right?

"Answer me something," Jake demanded heavily. He forced Shah to hold his gaze. "After you divorced Robert, did you have any lovers?"

Blinking, Shah said, "No."

Jake's hands tightened around Shah's upper arms.

"The bastard. The lowlife bastard." He snapped his mouth shut. He saw the confusion in Shah's eyes and realized she wasn't sure if he was angry at her or at her ex-husband. Getting hold of his escaping emotions, he whispered tautly, "Robert is wrong, Shah. Do you hear me? He's wrong."

"I— Well, how would you know?"

He smiled grimly. "Sweetheart, anyone who kisses like you do, who makes me feel like I'm melting in a hot fire, isn't frigid—believe me."

"Oh..." Shah sat looking up at Jake in the moments that followed. The heat of a blush stung her cheeks, and she gave a little laugh of embarrassment, placing her hands against her face. "Look at me! I'm blushing like a girl!"

Jake allowed his hands to drop away. "Every woman should have a bit of girl in her," he whispered. "It makes you beautiful, Shah." He savored the mixture of embarrassment and sudden hope he saw burning in Shah's eyes. If he never did anything else for her in this lifetime, he'd at least given her back a piece of her soul, her womanhood, by helping her realize how wrong her ex-husband had been. He ached to teach her about love between a man and a woman. He ached to feel her open and blossom beneath his hands and body, like a lovely, fragrant orchid opening to the misty Amazonian sunlight for the first time. But those were all dreams, Jake realized sadly. And dreams, as he well knew, could shatter unexpectedly and be destroyed before one's very eyes. It had happened once. It could happen again.

It took long minutes for Shah to gather her strewn composure. The dawn brightened, light gliding silently across the rain forest. Birds began to sing, the sound echoing the song in Shah's heart. Jake's arm remained around her shoulders as she sat, her hands pressed to her cheeks.

"Talk to me," Jake urged her finally as he saw her drop her hands to her lap and clasp them nervously. "What are you feeling?"

She gave a startled little laugh. "Feeling? Everything! I feel like I'm in chaos, Jake."

"Happy? Sad?" He held his breath, cherishing the intimacy strung gently between them.

"Both," she admitted, and she glanced over at him, a sad smile pulling at the corners of her mouth. "I feel sorrow for myself, because once again I fell for Robert's lies." She frowned and stared down at her hands. "There were a couple of times—not many—when other men walked into my life. They weren't bad men, and I got interested in them. But the moment they tried to take me to bed, I froze." Shah frowned and admitted, "That was when I was younger, and I ran."

Gently he rubbed her shoulders. "That's over now. You're more mature and settled."

With a nod, Shah said, "Yes."

"What are you happy about?"

She hesitated. "*Scared* would be a better word."

"About?"

Uncomfortable, Shah finally said, "Us."

His hand remained still on her shoulder, the thick silk of her hair beneath his fingers. He yearned to take her into his arms and kiss her until she melted like sweet nectar in his hands, his body. "What about 'us'?"

"Well," Shah mumbled, "it's probably just me, not you. I have no right to assume anything. Especially when we haven't known each other that long, and—"

Jake grimaced. "Shah, you can tell me anything. I'm not like Robert. I'm not going to judge how you feel."

Closing her eyes, Shah remained silent. The words got stuck in her throat and congealed there. She was struggling to say them, and she could feel Jake's tension, too. Finally she rubbed her temples in a nervous gesture. "I—I didn't want to like you, Jake. At first, I thought you were like all the men I've known."

He studied her intently, praying for her to tell him that she liked him even half as much as he loved her. Jake couldn't stand the tension, but he realized Shah was genuinely struggling to overcome her fear. Robert had taken advantage of Shah's innocence. He'd placed her in a cage and nearly broken her magnificent spirit.

Gently Jake smoothed the damp fabric across her back. "Look," he told her huskily, "don't force anything, Shah. Let's you and I take it one day at a time."

Touching her throat, Shah gave him a pleading look. "I—I just can't say the words, Jake. I'm afraid. Afraid…"

So was he. Just as much as she was, and maybe more. "It takes guts to admit even as much as you already have," he murmured. Glancing up, he said, "It's light enough to travel. What do you say we finish off those last two mangos for breakfast and hightail it back to the mission? When you feel like talking, you can. In the meantime, we've got work to do, darlin'."

Grateful for Jake's understanding, Shah fought the desire to throw her arms around his neck and embrace him. Would that one heated kiss he'd shared with her ever be repeated? She couldn't tear her gaze from his strong, mobile mouth, which was drawn into a wry smile. If Jake realized she was gawking at him, he didn't say anything. Instead, he eased off the limb and dropped to the jungle floor below.

He held his hands open to her. "Come on."

* * *

The day fled swiftly, as far as Shah was concerned. They had made good progress toward the mission. With each hour, Jake relaxed, feeling that Hernandez and his henchmen were far behind them. However, he cautioned Shah to speak in low tones and not make any undue noise.

Sometimes, to Shah's delight, Jake would drop back and capture her hand, and they'd walk beside each other. It was as if he had read her mind, understanding her doubts about the kiss they'd shared last night—as if he were silently trying to convince her that his feelings toward her weren't short-term. Jake's hand was warm and reassuring, and Shah savored those moments when he'd look down at her with such warmth that she felt as if she were walking on air.

Water was a problem in the forest—drinking from the Amazon would have given them parasites and germs— so Shah showed Jake the liana vines, about one inch in diameter. Whenever they needed water, they would carefully cut a vine open and drink from the water stored within it. He praised her knowledge of survival, and she felt like a true team member, not just some bothersome burden to Jake.

Jake's own jungle training came in handy when he spotted a certain type of palm that, when stripped of leaves, yielded a sweet inner core that supplied them with lunch. Heart of palm was a delicacy in Brazil, often pickled and sold for a high price in the cities. They sat hidden in the rain forest, eating the sweet, juicy heart of palm and exchanging smiles over the pleasure of sharing such a stolen moment together. As the day began fading and dusk set in, they looked for another tree to act as bed and security against the denizens of the Amazon night. Jake spotted a rubber tree about a hundred feet inland from the bank of the Amazon. Taking off his pistol and laying it on a stump next to Shah, who was shelling some nuts she'd found, he went in search of the makings of a better bed for them tonight. Moving around the immediate area, Jake found a number of broken limbs that had probably been torn off in the sudden thunderstorms that constantly occurred in the Amazon Basin.

Satisfied with the platform he'd made out of the branches, Jake cut a number of palm leaves to create a mattress. If they had to spend another night in a tree, it might as well be in relative comfort, he rationalized. Satisfied with his handiwork, he leaped off the finished platform and dusted off his hands.

Shah was sitting by the tree stump, having just finished dividing their larder, when she heard a sharp squeal. Her eyes widened enormously.

"Jake!" she screamed, and leaped to her feet, pointing behind where he stood.

Startled, Jake whirled and crouched. He'd heard the almost human squeal, too, and he was expecting an attack from a man. Instead, the green vegetation thirty feet away shook and trembled, and a brown, furry boar with long, curved white tusks exploded out of the jungle, charging him. Jake started to move, but the fifty-pound boar, with small red eyes and a long snout, shifted course, aiming directly for him.

Time slowed down to a painful, crawling clarity. Jake knew his only safety was the tree, which was a mere ten feet away. He saw the boar's mouth open, froth spilling from the corners of it, his lethal, razor-sharp tusks glinting with saliva. What about Shah? She was even more vulnerable to attack by the angered beast. The moment's hesitation cost Jake. He could have turned and made it to the safety of the tree in three strides. But he'd have left Shah defenseless. Grimly he stood his ground.

The boar smashed into him, knocking him down. With a shrieking squeal, the animal whirled around and charged into him again, then again. Each angry movement of his tusks slashed long, deep cuts through Jake's torn pant legs. Floundering, he tried to keep the boar at bay by using his feet to kick out at the animal. Jake yelled for Shah, but the squeals of the furious boar drowned out his cry.

Shah jerked the Beretta out of its holster. She watched in horror as the boar ruthlessly attacked Jake. She saw blood staining his legs, and she rushed forward. The boar whuffed and grunted as he butted Jake's feet, pushing them aside to again attack his extremities. Shah aimed the pistol, praying she wouldn't hit Jake. The Beretta jerked once, twice, three times. The roar of the pistol shattered her eardrums. And then there was silence.

Sobbing, Shah allowed the pistol to drop from her hands. "Jake!" she cried. "Jake!"

Chapter Ten

A cry tore from Shah as she raced to Jake. The boar lay dead near his boots. Falling to her knees, her mouth contorted in a silent cry, she touched his shoulder. At first she thought he must be dead, but then she saw Jake's eyes flutter open.

Pain was beginning to replace the initial numbness Jake had felt during the savage boar's attack. He forced himself to focus on speaking. "I'm okay," he choked out, and made an effort to rise. Shah helped him sit up. He watched as she moved toward his legs. The boar had cut his pants to ribbons and Jake realized with a sinking feeling that the fabric was stained with blood. His blood.

"Jake, you're hemorrhaging!" Shah barely touched the surface of his trousers with her shaking fingertips. The boar had opened some thirty wounds in Jake's legs. If Jake hadn't had the coolness to use his heavily protected feet to keep the boar from getting to other, less protected parts of his body, he might be dead.

"Take my knife," he ordered Shah sternly, "and cut my trousers off at the knee." Leaning to one side, Jake unsnapped the knife from his belt and handed it, butt first, to Shah. Her face was pale, and her eyes were dark with shock. Jake knew he was in shock himself, because he was acting too calmly. They had to act fast, before the initial shock wore off. "Cut off my trousers," he repeated to Shah, and she took the knife with shaking hands.

"The wounds...they're terrible, terrible..." Shah whispered as she surveyed the damage to Jake's legs.

"I'm alive," Jake said, supporting himself with his arms behind him. He tried to prepare himself for how badly damaged his legs were as Shah cut away the fabric to expose the extent of his wounds. His mouth turned downward as he realized that it looked as if someone had taken a razor blade and slashed indiscriminately at his flesh from his ankles to his knees. He saw Shah trying not to cry, trying to be brave.

"You're doing fine," Jake told her in an unsteady voice. He was starting to feel light-headed, the first effects of the adrenaline charge in his bloodstream beginning to wear off. "Shah," he called as he lay down, "put something, anything, under my feet. Get the blood back to my head. I'm feeling faint...."

Those were the last words he spoke. Before Shah could get off her knees, Jake passed out. Alarmed, she made sure his head was tipped back enough to allow air to flow in and out of his lungs. Blood was soaking into the decomposed leaves all around his legs. Shah shoved her own unraveling feelings aside. She had to think swiftly and clearly now. She had to think for both of them, or Jake might bleed to death.

Getting to her feet, she found a small log and placed it beneath his ankles, elevating his legs by six inches so that the blood would begin to flow back toward his upper body and to his head. Then she ran to their knapsacks, wondering what, if any, first-aid kit she'd find in Jake's pack. Because he had been a recon marine and a para-medic, she thought he might have packed medical items; she'd packed only aspirin and Band-Aids in her own pack.

She tore at the buckles and the leather straps, her breath coming out in sobs. Where had that boar come from? Why hadn't she remembered how dangerous the wild boars of the Amazon Basin were? And, worse, why hadn't she warned Jake about them? They were the only animals she'd failed to tell him about.

Tears blurred Shah's eyes as she rummaged quickly through the pack, throwing things out in a desperate search for a first-aid kit. The wild pigs lived in small and large groups, always lorded over by a huge older boar, and they were feared by the Indians for their savagery and their willingness to attack anyone who entered their foraging territory. Oh, why hadn't she told Jake about them?

Her fingers closed over a large metal container. Shah froze for an instant. She was down to the bottom of Jake's pack, and there was nothing else left in it. If this wasn't a first-aid kit, they were in trouble. Gulping, she yanked the rectangular box out of the knapsack. Her eyes widened when she saw that it was white, with a large red cross painted on its smooth surface.

Trying to talk herself out of her panic, Shah set the kit down on the ground and unlatched it. To her relief, she found huge rolls of gauze, ace bandages, scissors, iodine and adhesive tape. Shutting her eyes, she hung her head and sent a prayer of thanks to the Great Spirit.

Getting up on unsteady legs, Shah forced herself to calm down and try to think coherently. It was almost impossible, because in those horrifying moments when the boar had attacked Jake, she had realized something that she knew would change her world. Dropping to her knees, she quickly examined the wounds that criss-crossed Jake's exposed extremities. The curved slashes scored his flesh, but as Shah looked closely at them, relief began to trickle back and give her hope.

She hadn't had much medical training—all she knew was what Pai Jose had taught her over the past three months, when she'd helped him at the mission hospital—but she knew that Jake's loss of blood wasn't life-threatening. He would need a great many stitches—perhaps a hundred or more on each leg—and she couldn't do that. Taking the iodine, she poured it liberally into the wounds on both legs and hoped that Jake remained unconscious during her efforts to bandage them.

Shah's head spun with options. She had no idea how badly the boar had cut into Jake's legs, or if his muscles had been damaged. If they had, he wouldn't be able to walk, and she'd have to leave him here to rush back to the mission for help. But the mission was still maybe half a day away. Unrolling the thick gauze, Shah reassured herself that Jake's wounds, while serious, wouldn't be fatal. What was potentially life-threatening was the fact that she had no antibiotics to stop any infection that would occur as a result of the attack.

She glanced down at Jake's booted feet, then studied the boar's bloodied tusks. Dirt and stains marred their curved length, and she was convinced that bacteria must have been transferred to Jake's many wounds. Urgency thrummed through her as she quickly wrapped his legs in swaths of gauze. The pristine whiteness of the dressing stood out starkly against the dark, damp leaves on the floor of the jungle.

Rubbing her brow with the back of her hand, Shah stood up. She went to the river and quickly washed her hands. As she hurried back to Jake's side, she heard him groan and watched him weakly raise his hand. Kneeling and placing her fingers against his shoulder to orient him, Shah realized with a clarity that frightened her that she loved Jake Randolph. The boar's attack had ripped away all her defenses against her feelings. Now, as she watched him slowly become conscious, Shah felt her heart contract beneath the weight of the discovery. Jake could die before she could get him to the mission. If she left him here and went alone, a jaguar or jacare could find Jake, because of the powerful smell of blood. Infection would set in quickly, due to the humid climate, and could make him feverish and delirious within the next twelve hours. Worst of all, Jake could have blood poisoning, which would mean a race against time before the lethal bacteria reached his heart and caused it to stop beating forever.

Her fingers tightened on Jake's shoulder as his lashes lifted to expose his bewildered gray eyes.

"Jake, you're all right," Shah told him, her voice shaking. "You're safe, and the boar's dead."

Fighting the faintness rimming his blurred vision, Jake homed in on Shah's husky voice. He felt her strong, slender hand on his shoulder. Weakly he captured her hand and held it. Flashes of the boar coming out of the jungle and attacking him forced him to recall why he was lying on the ground feeling light-headed. As the minutes crawled by, the pain drifting up from his legs forced him into full consciousness. The smarting, jabbing pains were like thousands of hot needles being poked into his flesh.

Jake looked up into Shah's anguished face. Her eyes were huge and dark with suffering, and her lips were compressed as if she were about to burst into tears. His mouth stretched, but the smile twisted into a grimace. Squeezing her fingers, he rasped, "I'm alive."

"Y-yes."

He frowned and lifted his head. "How bad?"

"Maybe thirty or so cuts on each leg, Jake. The boar's tusks were like razors."

"How much blood did I lose?" he asked, craning to look at his bandaged legs. The effort was too much for him, and he sank back to the ground.

Shah glanced anxiously down at him. For Jake's sake, she wanted to sound calm. She didn't want to alarm him. "I don't know. Maybe half a pint, a full pint. I'm not a nurse. I don't know."

With a nod, Jake clung to her hand. "If I'd lost a lot, I'd be feeling a hell of a lot more light-headed than I do," he muttered. "I'm in shock right now."

"I know...."

"Just let me lie here for another half hour, Shah, and I'll start coming out of it."

"Are—are you cold?"

He was, but he knew there were no blankets to put over him. "A little, but I'll be okay." He heard the terror in Shah's voice, although it was obvious she was trying to hide her panic. He loved her fiercely for her courage.

"That was one hell of a pig," he joked wearily. "I think I'd rather see my pork all nicely wrapped in a package in a grocery store. What do you think?"

Shah wiped the tears off her face. "This isn't funny,
Jake. He must weigh close to sixty pounds," Shah told
him. "Old and big. Oh, Jake, I'm sorry I didn't tell you
about the wild pigs. If I had—"

Forcing his eyes open, Jake met and held her tearful
gaze. "Honey, even if you had, it couldn't have prepared
me for his charge. I didn't know he was there, and neither did you."

"But you hesitated!" Shah cried. "Why? You could
have jumped up in the tree and been safe! Why didn't
you?"

A loose, pained smile crossed Jake's mouth. He
squeezed her fingers. "Because he'd have gone after you
with me out of the way. There was no place for you to
go, Shah. I didn't have my pistol on me, or I could've
shot the bastard. I didn't want to jump into the tree and
leave you the target."

Shah digested his logic. It was true: she'd had absolutely nowhere to go to escape the boar's charge. The
animal could have outrun her easily—and boars were
strong swimmers, too, so it wouldn't have helped to
jump in the river. Jake had made a conscious decision
to be the boar's target to save her from his attack. Kneeling next to him, she held his warm gaze. It was marred
by pain.

"You should have saved yourself," she whispered.

"I'm your bodyguard, remember? It's my job to keep
you safe," he joked wearily. Then he sighed heavily.
"You've been a target all your life, Shah. I was damned
if I was going to be like every other man in your life
and leave you open for attack. No way."

Shaken, Shah hung her head and forced back the tears
that threatened to fall. Her love for him welled up
fiercely within her, and she fought the urge to tell him

exactly that. Several minutes passed before she was able to control the feelings rampaging through her.

Jake watched Shah's reaction to his reasoning, seeing disbelief then confusion in her eyes. Didn't she realize she was worth saving? There had been such damage done to Shah by her father and her ex-husband. Little men with brittle egos who had used her as a scapegoat for their own shortcomings. He lifted her hand toward his mouth and kissed her fingers.

"We need to plan what we're going to do," he said with an effort. Night was beginning to fall, turning the Amazon a misty gray and making the rain forest a dark silhouette against the sky.

With a jerky nod of her head, Shah agreed. Jake's lips upon her fingers sent a ribbon of warmth through her pounding heart. Despite the pain he must be in, he was trying to soothe her! Shah knew she had to be strong for both of them if she was going to get Jake back to the mission alive. Time was the enemy now.

"We've got to get you up on that tree platform," Shah said, her low voice off-key. She wondered if the pistol shots she'd fired had been heard by Hernandez's men. The rain forest was thick and absorbed sounds quickly, so it was unlikely. Still, there was always a possibility of further threat from the land baron.

Jake agreed. "Take the limb out from under my feet and help me get up," he said.

Shah removed the limb and gently placed his booted feet on the ground. She watched Jake's face carefully, realizing that he had an extraordinary ability to master pain. Perhaps it was because he'd been a recon marine.

"I'll help you sit up," she whispered, placing her arm beneath his neck and pulling him up.

Biting back a groan, Jake sat up. Dizziness assailed

him, and he leaned forward, resting his brow on his knees to draw the blood back to his head. He felt Shah's hands on his shoulders, steadying him.

"Put your arm around my shoulders," she told him as she crouched next to him. "You can lean on me as we get you to your feet."

Jake didn't know the extent of his injuries. If that old boar had slashed deeply enough into his legs, his Achilles tendon might be cut, leaving him unable to walk. Bothered, but keeping that knowledge to himself, Jake did as she instructed. He knew she wasn't strong enough to support his full bulk and weight. No, he had to use his own inner fortitude to stand up.

But as Shah straightened, Jake realized that he'd underestimated her strength. Despite her slenderness, she was like a steel cable supporting him as he rose to a standing position. Dizziness might have felled him if not for Shah holding him steady.

"You're stronger than I thought," he rasped, his head resting against her hair.

Shah nearly blurted out, *My love for you has made me strong.* The discovery that she loved Jake was so new, so overwhelming, that she hadn't had time to react to the knowledge. Too many more important things had to be addressed before she could sit quietly and examine her feelings. "How do your legs feel?" she asked.

Jake slowly raised his head and leaned heavily against Shah until he got his bearings. "They smart like hell, but I need to see if I can walk."

Her fear magnified, as she silently agreed with his judgment. She knew he was aware of the ramifications if he couldn't walk. "Take just a small step," she pleaded hoarsely, praying that he wouldn't fall.

His mouth tight against the pain that attacked him in

ever-growing waves, Jake gripped her shoulder and moved his right foot. Biting back a groan, he lifted his leg and took that first step.

"Okay?" Shah demanded breathlessly, watching his rugged profile anxiously.

"Yeah...sore but usable," he rasped. "Let me try the left one." He lifted it and then slowly placed his full weight on it. His leg didn't buckle beneath him. Jake released a long-held breath. "No muscle damage. Or, if there is, it isn't going to cripple me."

The words were sweet to Shah's ears. "Thank the Great Spirit," she murmured. Their next challenge was to get Jake up on the platform for the night. With each step, Jake seemed to grow a little bit stronger, a little more stabilized. As they passed the dead boar, Jake stopped and looked down at the animal.

"Three shots?" He looked at Shah.

"Yes. I fired three times." She gulped. "I was so worried I'd hit you instead of the boar."

He squeezed her shoulder. "Who taught you to shoot like that?"

"I used to belong to the pistol team at Stanford," Shah muttered.

Impressed, Jake smiled slightly. "With the way that boar was moving around, there was every chance you could have nailed me instead."

With a shake of her head, Shah said unsteadily, "I know...."

"The tree's next," Jake said, and they began a slow walk toward the platform.

Shah's admiration for Jake soared in the next few minutes. She watched him heft himself onto the platform with his powerful arms. The pain he must be feeling didn't stop him from lifting his legs high into the air and landing with a thunk on the platform of palms and branches he'd built earlier. Unable to assist him, she stood on the ground, watching him maneuver himself around until he lay down.

"You okay?" she called, amazed.

"Yeah," Jake grunted. His legs were hurting like hell, but he wasn't about to let Shah know it. She was shaken enough by the incident. "Just get the knapsacks, the pistol and our food. It's getting dark." Then he said weakly, "You don't need to be jaguar bait." He lay down, dizziness forcing him to close his eyes and lie still. He'd probably lost close to a pint of blood, he thought. But if he could sleep tonight, his body should revitalize enough for the trek back to the mission tomorrow morning. His mind spun with options. The worst, Jake knew, would be if his legs were infected. Iodine would kill a certain amount of bacteria, but not all of it. No, he needed powerful third-generation antibiotics, or he'd more than likely be a dead man within the next day or two.

As he lay in the gathering darkness, contemplating the gloomy limbs and leaves above him, Jake knew he didn't want to die. Not this way, and not now. He loved Shah. For a long time, he'd walked numbly through life, not really caring whether he lived or died. Now, for the first time since his family had been torn from him, Jake desperately wanted to live.

As Shah climbed up to the platform with the knapsacks, he studied her in the growing dusk. There was such determination written on her features. Jake saw the guilt and anguish in her eyes and realized she felt responsible for his wounds. With time, he told himself as he threw his arm against his sweaty brow, he could ease Shah out of the overresponsible attitude she had toward people in her life. There was so much he wanted to share with her, to teach her—and have her teach him—he thought as she left the platform to retrieve their food.

Night fell rapidly after Shah climbed up on the platform with their cache of food. She had cut several liana vines, knowing that Jake would grow thirsty throughout the night, as a fever was sure to set in soon. Placing the vines against the trunk of the tree, she moved over to him.

"How are you feeling?" she asked in a low voice, touching his shoulder.

"Better," Jake said. It was a lie.

"Really?"

He heard relief and surprise in Shah's voice. Jake believed in white lies, lies that hurt no one and sometimes kept the damaging hurt of truth at bay—if only for a little while. "Yeah, I'm dizzy, but that's about all. A good night's sleep will set me up for tomorrow's hike."

A gasp escaped Shah. "Jake, do you really think you can walk back to the mission?"

"Do I have a choice?" he asked wryly.

"You could stay here," she began hesitantly, "and I could run back and get help."

Jake shook his head. "It wouldn't work, sweetheart." He reached out and gripped her hand, which was resting lightly against his chest. Barely able to make out her features now, Jake said, "One thing recons are taught is that no matter how much pain you're in you can walk. My wounds aren't life-threatening, Shah. Another thing they taught us is that you go in as a team, and you come out as a team. A marine never leaves a squadmate behind. No, we'll go back together." That was partly a white lie. He knew his wounds could very well be life-threatening. "You did a hell of a good job wrapping my legs. It was smart putting the ace bandages over the dressing. They'll hold everything in place until we get back to the mission.''

Shah didn't have the courage to mention the possibility of infection. It scared her too much to speak about it. ''You have enough courage for ten men,'' she said, and placed her hand against his broad forehead. His flesh was damp, but Shah didn't know whether it was the first sign of fever or just the normal humidity and temperature that was causing Jake to sweat.

''You're the reason I want to make it back to the mission, Shah.'' He absorbed the light, cool touch of her hand on his brow. Just that simple connection stabilized his out-of-control world. She possessed a serenity that calmed him no matter how much danger swirled around them. She was checking for fever, and he knew it. Jake loved her even more for trying to protect him against the worst that might happen. He watched her grow quiet over his statement.

Stunned by Jake's whispered admission, Shah could say nothing. Taking her hand away, she said, ''I want you to eat the two mangos—and no argument, Jake. You've lost a lot of fluids, and we need to replace as much as we can before we start back. I've got plenty of liana vines for water for you.''

Exhaustion stalked Jake as they ate and then settled down for the night. Shah insisted on keeping the pistol and taking the watch, for fear of a jaguar getting the scent of his blood and coming to investigate. Jake didn't argue. He obediently took two aspirin with a little water. So far, he wasn't feeling feverish, but he knew it was only a matter of time. Neither of them broached the subject, but he could feel the tension in Shah. Her worry was like a tangible thing.

As the aspirin dulled some of his pain, Jake fell asleep. He couldn't roll on his side the way he wanted; his legs were too badly cut up for him to stand them touching each other. The last thing he saw was Shah leaning against the tree, her knees drawn upward toward her body, the pistol nearby.

Jake was jerked out of his sleep at dawn by a shattering, screaming cry that rocked the forest around them. Sitting up, he saw Shah leap to her feet, the pistol in hand. Her attention was riveted on the rain forest behind them.

"What—?" he mumbled groggily.

"Jaguar," Shah breathed. "It's the jaguar...."

Shaken, Jake froze. "How close?"

"N-not far," she stammered. Shah's eyes burned. She hadn't slept at all. Trying to steady her hammering heart, she whispered, "She's been around most of the night. I've heard her from time to time." Licking her dry lips, Shah tried to penetrate the shadowy darkness of the rain forest. If only there were more light! "She's close, Jake. Very close."

Feeling helpless, Jake took his knife from its scabbard and held it firmly in his hand. His eyes wouldn't adjust to the darkness so that he could try to spot the cat. "Will she attack?"

"I don't know," Shah said, holding the pistol ready. Now and then throughout the night she'd felt her back crawl with shivers. Intuitively she'd sensed the jaguar's presence. The cat's scream unnerved her, but she knew she mustn't panic. She glanced over at Jake. His face was pasty, with a sheen of sweat across it. Her heart dropped when she realized that he was looking feverish.

"Tell me about jaguars," Jake demanded, trying to sit up in a position that wasn't so painful for him.

"They hunt at night and sleep during the day. That's what we have going for us," she told him. "It's going to be daylight soon, and maybe she'll go home to her tree and sleep."

"Unless she's really hungry and sees me hobbling along the riverbank," Jake muttered.

Shah nodded wearily, gazing hard at the vegetation. "I hope she's not that hungry."

Jake sat there another fifteen minutes, tense and alert. The dawn grew brighter, and the birds began singing in the distance, but not near them—a strong indication that the jaguar was still close by. "Maybe," he joked weakly, "if we give her this platform, she'll stay here instead of tailing us."

Her arms tired and heavy, Shah slowly allowed the pistol to drop to her side. Pushing her hair away from her face, she realized how tangled it had become. She glanced over at Jake. Forcing a slight smile, she said, "Why don't we try it?"

Staying here might mean their demise, and Jake knew it. "Okay, partner, let's saddle up and blow this joint. What do you say?"

Shah avoided his feverish gaze. Jake had such courage. He was the one who could die, and yet he was trying to lift her spirits by teasing her. As she silently gathered the items to put into the knapsacks, Shah allowed the word *partner* to touch her heart. Oh, if only she could be! Throughout the hours of darkness, Shah had ruthlessly examined the contents of her heart. For thirty years she'd experienced only the negative side of men. Now, when she'd least expected it, Jake had come along, epitomizing the positive male. He'd walked into her life and turned it upside down.

Shah made a silent promise to Jake that if they both survived this journey she would find the courage to tell him she loved him—regardless of his reaction. She didn't know if Jake loved her. She knew he liked her, but for Shah that wasn't enough. From the moment the boar had attacked Jake, her heart had belonged to Jake forever. She knew with a certainty that shook her soul there would never be another man for her. Jake was a gift from the Great Spirit—a second chance to live life happily.

Avoiding Jake's red-rimmed eyes, Shah busied herself with the preparations for their journey. She left the camcorder behind to lighten their load, along with everything else except the first-aid kit, the pistol, and the videotape that incriminated Hernandez.

"Good move," Jake praised her. "Bare essentials."

Shah forced a grin. "I'm not lugging you *and* the knapsacks. Something had to go."

Rallying beneath her indefatigable courage, Jake took hope. Fever was stalking him in earnest now, and he had realized earlier that his legs were puffy and swollen—a sure sign of infection. "Nice to know I'm more important than what's going to be left behind," he teased.

Shah moved over to the edge of the platform. "Jake Randolph, I'd never hear the end of it if I left you behind. Knowing you, you'd haunt me from the other world. Come on, we've got some hiking to do today— together."

Chapter Eleven

"*Pai*, is he going to be all right?" Shah stood anxiously next to the priest as he injected Jake's limp arm with a hefty dose of antibiotics. Jake lay unconscious on a gurney. Night was falling, and a nun who had been a surgical nurse, Sister Bernadette, stood opposite them. Despite her exhaustion, Shah's gaze moved from the priest to the sister. Jake had collapsed a quarter of a mile from the Tucanos village, falling unconscious from a high fever and delirium. Luckily, several Indians fishing nearby had spotted them from their canoes. The short trip back to the mission had brought Jake safely home. *Home.*

"It's too early to tell, child," Pai Jose whispered as he handed the empty syringe to the sister. "Sister Bernadette will change his dressings, scrub out all his wounds and then dress them again." The priest placed his hand gently on Shah's shoulder. "Come, you're nearly ready to fall over. How long has it been since you ate any food or drank any water?''

Blearily Shah answered, ''I made Jake eat the food and drink the water.'' She touched her brow, on the verge of tears. Jake's face was pale, frighteningly pale. Had she gotten him to the mission in time? The sister, a pleasant-faced woman in her sixties who wore a gray-and-white habit, took up a pair of surgical scissors and began to cut off the blood-soaked dressings on one of Jake's legs. Unable to stand the sight of the festered wounds, Shah turned away. His infected legs had turned puffy, and the smell made her gag.

''Come,'' the priest told her, more firmly this time, and he guided her out of the ward and toward his small residence. ''First, you must eat. Then I want you to take a shower, change clothes and sleep.''

Tears stung Shah's eyes. ''*Pai,* I'll eat, shower and change. But after that I'm coming back here. Jake needs me.'' *And I need him.* Throughout the day, Shah had seen the raw courage that Jake possessed. He had grown delirious toward afternoon, but he had clung to her voice, leaning heavily on her and trusting her implicitly. They'd kept going despite the overwhelming odds against them. The jaguar had stalked them—quietly, out of sight, but Shah had known the cat was never more than a few hundred yards away at any given time. Twice she'd fired the pistol in hopes of scaring the hungry cat away. Afterward Shah could feel that the cat had left, but then, a little later, her back would crawl with cold shivers of warning and she knew the jaguar had returned to stalk them.

''You need sleep, child,'' the priest murmured.

Shah knew she hadn't slept for thirty-six hours, but it didn't matter. She felt anything but sleepy. The possibility that Jake could die, that the antibiotics had been given to him too late, shook her as nothing else ever could have. *"Pai,"* she whispered, her voice cracking, "I love Jake. I want to be at his side. He could die. Don't deny it. I know enough about this rain forest. I've seen a small cut become so infected that it caused blood poisoning. No, I want to be with him, pray for him..."

"We'll all pray for him." Pai Jose patted her shoulder gently. "I'm sure Sister Bernadette will be finished with her duties with Jake by the time you get back to the ward."

"If blood poisoning doesn't get him, gangrene could. He could lose his legs," Shah whispered as she halted in front of the priest's small room.

Pai Jose barely nodded his silvery head. "If blood poisoning has set in, that's a possibility," he agreed somberly. Placing his hands on her slumped shoulders, he added, "He could die, too. Losing his legs to gangrene would be terrible, but not fatal."

"We don't even have the capacity to get him to a hospital from here," Shah said, blinking back the tears. The radio, old and worn, wasn't working at the moment—their only tie with the outside world.

"Now, now, child. I've already sent Red Feather upstream to where the tugs dock with a message to bring a boat down here to transport Jake back to Manaus."

Shah threw her arms around the old priest. "Oh, thank you!" she cried, swallowing against a sob.

The priest patted her consolingly. "You pray to your Great Spirit," he told her, "and I'll pray to God. Between our prayers, Jake will make it."

The dim night light outlined Jake's sweaty, harsh features. Shah numbly wrung out a cloth again from the nearby bowl of water and gently wiped down his face, neck and shoulders. It was nearly midnight, and she was fighting back tears of terror. The rest of the ward was quiet; a few snores of the Tucanos still recovering from their wounds and the chirping of crickets were the only sounds to soothe her fear. Moving the damp cloth across Jake's powerful chest, she prayed steadily.

Sister Bernadette had confirmed her worst fears. Jake had blood poisoning. Now he wore only boxer shorts, the rest of his body unclothed to try to cool him from the fever's effects. Shah could see those dangerous red lines moving up his long, powerful thighs. It was only a matter of hours, perhaps a day at the most, before they would reach his magnificent, giving heart and stop it from beating.

The sister had given Jake the largest dosage of antibiotics allowed—any more, and that could kill him, too, she had warned Shah earlier. Shah gripped Jake's hot, sweaty arm and stared at his face. She understood as never before why Jake's face was lined, with brackets carved deep around his partly opened mouth and furrows across his brow. There were many laugh lines at the corners of his eyes, too. She wondered if she'd ever see him smile again, or hear that booming laughter rumbling up out of his chest like thunder.

Jake's temperature hovered at 104 degrees, and since their return to the mission it hadn't moved downward, not even with all the antibiotics he'd been given to combat his massive infection. There was no ice available, so all Shah could do was continue to use a damp cloth to wipe the sweat from him—and pray. Luckily, they had IVs, and two of them were replacing the necessary liquids Jake was losing via sweat due to his high fever.

"Fight," Shah whispered to him. She gathered up his

hand and pressed his limp fingers to her lips. "Jake, fight for yourself. Fight—" she choked "—for me. Jake, I love you. Do you hear me? I love you!" Her raspy voice flowed into the silence. Shah pressed her fingertips against Jake's massive wrist. His pulse was fast and hard, symbolizing the fight his body was valiantly waging against the blood poisoning.

Pressing her brow against Jake's damp, naked shoulder and clinging to his hand, Shah released a shuddering sigh. She was beyond exhaustion, beyond any sense of time. The only thing she felt was her heart bursting with an agony she'd never encountered in her life. She alternately prayed, cooled Jake down and caught brief snatches of sleep.

Toward morning, Shah jerked upright. She was disoriented for a moment, but then she realized that Jake was moaning and muttering. Her hands shaking, she touched his glistening chest. Beads of sweat stood out all over his skin as she pressed her hands against him. His skin was cooler! Gasping, Shah turned and took the thermometer from the glass of alcohol on the bedside stand and slipped it beneath Jake's armpit. It was the longest three minutes of her life. All of Shah's awareness narrowed on that thermometer. Jake was muttering and turning his head slowly from one side to the other. The IVs would soon need to be replaced, Shah noted, for they were nearly empty of their lifesaving contents.

Taking the thermometer from his armpit, Shah stood up and held it under the night-light at the head of the bed to read it. Her blurry eyes stung with the effort. Blinking several times, frustrated by the tiny markings, Shah tried to steady her trembling hands. A gasp tore from her.

The thermometer read 102! She gave a little cry and

lurched back to her chair. She had to sit down before she fell down. Jake's fever had broken! The antibiotics had done their job, turning back the raging poisons that had threatened to overwhelm his body's defenses. Quickly, Shah rinsed out the cloth and wiped the sweat from Jake's body. Euphoria raced through Shah. Tears streamed down her cheeks, but she didn't care. All those prayers had helped turn the tide and she knew it.

A hand settled on her shoulder, and Shah twisted a look upward. Sister Bernadette's sharp but kindly features came into view.

"And how is our patient?" she asked.

Sniffing, Shah showed her the thermometer. "Look," she said, her voice the merest quaver, "Jake's going to live. He's going to live...."

Jake heard Shah's voice, low and husky, near his ear. Was he dreaming again, or was it real? He wasn't sure. Thirst vied with his focus on her lovely voice. The darkness he rested within was comfortable, and he felt no pain. Flashes of the boar attacking him, of Shah screaming, raced across his closed eyelids. He felt a woman's hand in his, her fingers interlaced with his own. Shah. It had to be Shah! His heart galloped at the revelation. Jake fought the darkness, fought against the unconsciousness that tried to hold him prisoner.

Shah sat tensely as she watched Jake struggle to become conscious. She sat now on a metal chair next to Jake's hospital bed. Did he have any idea that two days ago he'd been transported by tug and then by ambulance to the best hospital in Manaus? Probably not. The urgency to see Jake open his eyes, to talk with him, nearly overwhelmed her.

"Jake? Can you hear me? It's Shah. Come on, it's

okay to wake up. You're safe...." She bit back the need to speak of her love to him. His lashes fluttered, dark brown spikes against his pasty complexion, and she felt his fingers move weakly in her hands. Breaking into a smile of relief, Shah stood up and placed a hand on his damp brow. She hated the sterile smell that inhabited the hospital room, but was grateful for the cleanliness that surrounded them. Leaning down, she pressed one small kiss after another on Jake's brow. He desperately needed a shave; his dark beard accentuated his harsh looks.

"Jake?" she whispered, and, following her heart's bidding, she lightly placed a kiss on his stubbly cheek and then on his mouth. His lips were slightly parted, dry and cool to her touch. Shah couldn't help herself; she pressed her lips more firmly against Jake's mouth, breathing her life, her love, into him. There was such fragility to life, Shah realized as she shared her sweetness with him. When she felt him respond, his mouth moving weakly against her own, her heart soared with joy. Caught in the web of love created by his courage, her defenses gone, she drowned in the returning strength of Jake's mouth as he took hers.

As his hand lifted to caress her neck and then her cheek, Shah sighed against his mouth and eased inches away. She smiled down into his dark gray eyes and pressed her hand against his. The words *I love you* begged to be spoken. But she was too emotional, too grateful for Jake's life, to speak.

Jake sighed and closed his eyes. He savored Shah's kiss; her lips were soft and beckoning, pulling him out of the darkness. He felt her velvety flesh beneath the palm of his hand and felt her cool hand upon his. "I love you," he whispered, his voice rusty from disuse. "God, I love you, Shah." And then he sank back into semiconsciousness, aware of her presence, her touch, never happier.

Shah felt Jake's hand begin to slip from her cheek, and she caught it and gently placed it across his belly. Had she heard right? Had Jake whispered that he loved her? Or had it been her exhausted, starved imagination? She stood there, holding his hand, unsure. She'd slept very little—only snatches here and there over the past four days. She touched her brow, and her mind coldly informed her that she was imagining Jake's words. Simultaneously her heart cried that she'd heard him correctly.

Torn, Shah could do nothing but watch Jake float in his semiconscious state. The doctors had warned her that it would take a long time for him to become completely conscious after his close brush with death. He would drift in and out of consciousness, muttering and perhaps not very coherent. She held his hand, moving her fingers slowly up and down his forearm, caressing him, letting him know in the silent language of touch how much she loved him.

The door to the private room opened, and she turned her head. A man with neat black hair, wearing a dark gray pinstripe suit, stood hesitantly at the entrance. Shah felt the power around him, met his hard, intelligent gaze, and knew that it must be Morgan Trayhern, Jake's boss. He was a tall man, powerfully built. Despite the veneer of civilization provided by the expensive clothes he wore, Shah knew him for what he was—a warrior. She offered a slight smile of welcome.

"Mr. Trayhern?" Her voice was charged with emotion, with relief that Jake was going to live.

"Yes." He entered the room and quietly shut the door

behind him, giving her a slight, strained smile. "You must be Shah Travers." He held out his hand to her.

For a moment, Shah was on guard against Trayhern, but then his eyes thawed, and the same kind of warmth that Jake possessed surrounded her. She released Jake's hand and turned. "Yes, I'm Shah Sungilo Travers. I'm the one who called you." She returned to Jake's side and picked up his hand again. "When they gave me Jake's clothes and belongings, a business card fell out of his wallet. Your name and phone number were on it. I knew Jake worked for you, and I figured you'd want to know his condition."

Morgan nodded. "I'm glad you did." He frowned and moved around to the opposite side of Jake's bed. His dark brows drew down in worry as he studied his friend. "How is he?"

"Have you talked to his doctors?"

"I don't speak Portuguese," Morgan said.

"Oh, of course. Well, he tangled with a wild boar four days ago, as I told you on the phone. The doctors didn't know at first whether Jake would lose his legs or not. That's when I called you." Shah gave a shrug. "I'm sure I must have sounded like a blithering idiot, but I was worried…"

Morgan smiled gently. "You made perfect sense to me on the phone, Shah. I'm just grateful you called."

"He needs the best medical attention possible," she went on quickly. "The doctors say he will recover, but I worry…" She bit down on her lower lip, unable to finish.

Morgan gazed around the spare, clean room. "When one of my people gets hurt out in the field, we always try to bring them back home for treatment and recuperation, Shah. I've brought the company jet. With your help, we'll get Jake out of here today and flown stateside to Bethesda Naval Hospital, in Maryland. It's one of the best, and they have an extensive knowledge of tropical infections, thanks to the Vietnam War.''

Shah gasped. She had hoped for help, but she had never imagined that Morgan Trayhern had this kind of power and influence. She saw his smile deepen, his eyes warm and thoughtful, as he held her gaze.

"Will you act as my interpreter? I'll need help getting the release from his doctors and clearance from the airport authorities to place Jake in our charge.''

Our charge. Shah blinked belatedly. "But—''

"I've got a doctor, one of my employees, standing by in the jet. She's fully qualified to take care of him on the trip back to Andrews Air Force Base. I don't leave my people stranded on a mission if I can help it.''

Overwhelmed by the sudden turn in events, Shah was speechless. Jake as going to be taken home. He was going to be torn from her. She couldn't possibly afford the thousand-dollar one-way fare to the States to follow him. All her money—what little there was of it—had been donated to the fund to save the rain forest, because Shah had needed so little to live at the Tucanos village. She stood, stunned, unable to think of a way to go home with Jake. Her mother was poor and always gave away most of her money to those on the reservation who were in greater need than she was. And she would never call her father and beg for money. *Never.*

"Well, I— Yes, of course I'll help,'' she whispered, her heart breaking into a thousand pieces. "Jake needs the best medical attention he can get. He almost died.'' She turned away so that Morgan couldn't see the tears in her eyes.

Her emotions had been brutalized over the past four

days, but from somewhere Shah gathered the strength to force herself to fulfill her promised obligation, despite her pain. Blindly heading for the door, she whispered, ''I'll go find his doctors and get things started, Mr. Trayhern.''

''Fine. Thank you.''

Shah didn't return for nearly forty-five minutes. She didn't dare. After getting the release signed by the doctors, Shah went to the nurse's station and used the phone to call the American embassy in Brazilia, the capital city. The embassy official she spoke to told her there should be no problems with the Brazilian authorities, and promised to call the Manaus airport immediately to explain the situation and make sure Jake could be placed on the jet as soon as he arrived from the hospital. Shah then saw to it that an ambulance was available to transport Jake to the airport. That done, she walked slowly down the highly polished hall toward Jake's room, weaving slightly with exhaustion. She knew she needed sleep, long, uninterrupted sleep, in order to throw off her dizziness, her confusion in her mind, and see the situation with some clarity.

A lump formed in her throat, and she fought the urge to cry. Jake was leaving within the hour, conscious or not. She loved him, and now he was being torn from her. But he needed the care that an American hospital could give him if he was to make a complete recovery. She wasn't angry at Morgan Trayhern—just the opposite. There weren't many businessmen who would spend corporate money to rescue one of their employees.

Slowly opening the door, Shah tried to prepare herself emotionally. But it was impossible. When she entered, she saw Morgan standing next to Jake's bed. And Jake was awake. Shah let go of the door, stunned. Jake's ravaged face looked angry, and his gray eyes were flashing with thunderstorm darkness. Her heart sank.

"What's wrong?" Shah managed, standing tensely.

Morgan moved aside, looking uncomfortable. "I think I'll come back in about fifteen minutes," he said, and left the room.

In shock, Shah watched Morgan leave, as quietly as he'd come. Slowly she turned to Jake, who sat up in bed, the white sheet draped haphazardly around his waist. His fists were wrapped in the bedding. Joy clashed with fear as she met and held his dark eyes. "Jake, what's wrong?"

He winced. "Come here," he ordered gruffly, his voice sounding like sandpaper. As weak as he was, he lifted his hand, his fingers stretched outward. "Come here, Shah...."

Numbly Shah walked toward him. She realized the effort it cost Jake to lift his hand. Her fingers outstretched, she caught and held it. She swallowed the lump in her throat. "Why are you so upset? Are you in pain?"

"Pain's the right word," Jake muttered, closing his fingers around Shah's hand. "I just woke up, and Morgan said you were getting authorization to send me stateside."

"Well...he has a jet standing by, with a doctor on board, and—"

"Dammit, I don't want to go!" He looked up at her drawn, pale face and saw her lower lip tremble. "I told Morgan to shove his plane and his doctor." His hand tightened on hers. "I'm not leaving you behind, Shah. I can heal here just fine. I'm not letting you go. Do you understand that?"

She stared at him, her mouth dropping open. As weak as he'd become, Jake still had the strength to hold her hand in a painful grip. Clearing her throat, she tried to control her wildly fluctuating emotions. "Don't I have anything to say about this?"

"What the hell are you talking about?" Jake demanded, breathing hard.

"Morgan came in here and told me what he was going to do. He's right, Jake. You stand a better chance of full recovery at a hospital that knows how to treat wounds like yours."

"Morgan told me I've been unconscious for four days. Is that so?"

"Y-yes."

"Tell me what happened. I don't remember."

For the next five minutes, Shah outlined the series of events that had brought him to the hospital in Manaus. He was glaring at her, his chest rising and falling with exertion, and she couldn't understand why he was so upset. He was going home. Wasn't that what he wanted?

Jake ruthlessly examined Shah's suffering features. Hadn't she heard him say he loved her? He knew he'd spoken the words, and he knew she must have heard them. Why was she behaving like this? Why was she acting so unsure? That last day, as they'd hiked toward the mission, their closeness had melted into a oneness Jake had never before experienced. His anger was ballooning, and so was his frustration, and his fear of losing her.

"Did Morgan ask you to come with us?"

"No. Why should he?"

"Shah, don't turn away. Look at me, dammit. Look at me!"

She turned and sniffed, her eyes filling with tears.

"What do you want?" she cried. "What have I done wrong?"

Her cry tore at his heart. Jake pulled her closer, until she stood next to his bed. Tears blurred his vision. "I'm not leaving you behind, Shah." His fingers tightened painfully around her hand as he tried to steel himself against the answer she might give to the question he was going to ask. "Will you come home with me? Back to America?" His heart aching, Jake held his breath as he anxiously searched her distraught features. He hadn't meant to make Shah cry. Tears dripped into the corners of her mouth, and she sniffed.

"Home?" she asked scratchily. "With you?" She saw his reddened eyes fill with tears. Afraid to ask why, she saw him nod once.

"Too much has happened too fast," he told her, in a rough, emotional tone. "We need time, Shah. You've got the proof against Hernandez you wanted. You can send a copy of the video to the Brazilian embassy in Washington. I know Morgan will help you." He took a deep, ragged breath, wanting so badly to tell her again that he loved her. But he'd told her before, and it was obvious to him that he needed her more than she needed him. "Please," he said, his voice hoarse, "just see me home. That's all I ask. I know it's more than I deserve, but I need you, Shah."

Need. She took a deep, halting breath and covered his hand with hers. Didn't Jake realize how much she needed him? Perhaps even more than he did? "Yes," she murmured, "I'll fly back with you."

Shaken by her soft, anguished tone, Jake closed his eyes, relief flowing through him. "Thank you," he said unsteadily.

* * *

Jake was agitated. He lay on a comfortable, clean gurney on the corporate jet, which was being flown by two Perseus pilots. Morgan was sitting at a small desk just behind the cockpit, phone in hand, talking to someone stateside. To Jake's left was the medical doctor, Anne Parsons, a woman in her early thirties with short black hair and blue eyes. She had offered a warm, welcoming smile when they'd come aboard earlier at the Manaus airport.

Jake twisted his head and tried to look back toward the rear of the cabin. Dr. Parsons raised her head from a report she was filling out on Jake's medical condition.

"May I get you something, Mr. Randolph?"

"No." Jake craned to catch a glimpse of Shah, who had moved to the rear of the plane after takeoff. "Is Shah okay?"

Dr. Parsons smiled and nodded. "She's asleep, Mr. Randolph." Putting her clipboard aside, she rose. "Matter of fact, I think I'll put a blanket over her. It's a little chilly in the cabin. Are you cold?"

Jake grunted a "No" and turned around. Both his arms had IVs in them, and he felt like a fly caught in a spiderweb. He was agitated because Shah had appeared not to really want to come along. He'd whispered his love to her, but she hadn't responded. Heartsick, frustrated, Jake lay back, his mouth compressed against pain much worse than that in his legs.

He knew he was going to live now. Shah had told him on the way to the airport how close he'd come to dying: Jake knew the prayers of many people had pulled him through, but he also knew that his love for Shah was a powerful part of his will to survive. Shutting his eyes, eaten up by frustration and anger over his medical condition, he tried to fall asleep. As he spiraled downward, somewhere in that twilight zone between sleep and wakefulness, Jake felt Shah's lips tenderly touching his own, felt her moist breath fanning across his face, felt the gossamer touch of her mouth sliding across his. He dreamed of Shah, of loving her, sharing laughter with her and helping her birth their babies. They were such powerful dreams, wishes, hopes, that Jake fell into a deep, healing sleep.

Shah awoke slowly, the slight vibration of the corporate jet surrounding her, the low growl of the engines at the tail of the aircraft filtering into her consciousness. As she sat up, the blanket slid off her shoulders and pooled around her waist. The cabin was dimly lit and gloomy. Looking out the small window, she saw it was pitch black outside. What time was it? How long had she slept?

The watch on her wrist read 4:00 a.m. They had been in the air for a long time. On a commercial flight, it took nine hours for a jet to fly from Miami to Rio de Janeiro. Morgan's jet, because it was much smaller, couldn't hold that sort of fuel load and had to fly back via the long route, up through Brazil and Mexico and then into the U.S. Had they landed and taken on fuel that she hadn't been aware of? More than likely. That told Shah just how deep her sleep had been.

All of Shah's awakening attention shifted to the gurney that bore Jake in the center of the cabin. Directly across the aisle Dr. Parsons was curled up in a chair that had been pulled out into a reclining position. Everyone was asleep, except the two pilots up in the cockpit.

Lying back down, Shah sighed and closed her eyes again. The vibration of the plane gave her a faint sense of security, though she felt none in her heart. Why had

Jake asked her to come along? Shah refused to believe that she'd heard him whisper that he loved her after she'd kissed him. Her spongy mind, after having gone without sleep for days, had merely made it up. She turned on her side, gripping the blanket, and curled into a fetal position. If only Jake did love her. She loved him. He had nearly given his life for her by standing in the way of that charging boar.

Shah was confused, and she realized that she was still in desperate need of sleep. And what she needed even more was to sit down and have a long, uninterrupted talk with Jake. But she knew that wouldn't happen soon. According to Dr. Parsons, Jake would need immediate surgery. At least six of the boar's slashes had torn into leg muscles, and they would all have to be repaired. How Jake had managed to overcome the terrible suffering he must have felt with every step, Shah didn't know. She was in awe of Jake's ability to master his pain. Maybe, she thought, losing his family had been the worst possible pain in the world for Jake to survive, and physical agony was nothing in comparison.

Snuggling down into the pillow—the blanket a poor substitute for Jake's nearness—Shah fell asleep, dreaming of Jake, of his kisses, of his incredible tenderness....

Chapter Twelve

Shah stood uncertainly at the nurse's desk on the surgical floor of Bethesda Naval Hospital. Morgan had called at her hotel room at eight o'clock this morning. She'd still been asleep. Jake had come through the leg operation just fine and wanted to see her now that he was out of recovery and in his private room. Gripping the bouquet of flowers that she'd bought downstairs, Shah found out Jake's room number and slowly walked down the white tiled hall. Nurses and doctors and a few patients and visitors passed her, but she barely saw them.

Last night they'd landed at Andrews Air Force Base, outside Washington, D.C. Shah had accompanied Jake by military ambulance to the prestigious hospital in Maryland, not far from the air force base. They'd held hands all the way to the hospital, few words exchanged between them because of the presence of Dr. Parsons and a military paramedic.

Trying to gather her strewn emotions, Shah slowed her step even more after she spotted Jake's room. She had entered the emergency room with Jake last night, only to be shuffled quickly out of the way as Jake's gurney was surrounded by medical personnel. Jake had tried to call to her, but Shah had moved out the doors and into the visitors' lobby, reeling with emotional stress and exhaustion. Morgan had come by half an hour later in a rented car, gotten her a posh hotel room near the hospital and taken her there. He'd told her that since Jake would be going directly into surgery there was no use waiting for him at the hospital. What she needed, he'd said, was a shower and sleep, in that order.

Everyone seemed to know what was best for her, and Shah was too numb to fight back. She'd surrendered to Morgan's assessment of the situation and allowed him to take over. The only clothes she had were the ones she wore, inappropriate for the cold, snowy East Coast.

Morgan had tactfully asked if she had money, and, when Shah had shown him the ten dollars she had in her pocket, he'd slipped three hundred-dollar bills into her hand and told her to buy some clothes at one of the boutiques in the hotel lobby. Shah had protested at first, but Morgan had patiently explained that Jake would want him to help her.

A terrible uncertainty haunted her waking and sleeping hours. This morning, she'd gone to the hotel lobby and purchased a pair of dark brown wool slacks, a camel-colored turtleneck sweater and sensible brown socks and shoes. Luckily, the hotel provided shampoo and conditioner for her hair, and beneath a scaldingly hot shower she had cleansed her hair and her body until she was free of the damp smell of the Amazon.

Now her hair hung in ebony sheets, loose and flowing

across the lightweight red nylon jacket she'd also purchased. The paper around the flowers crinkled under the tight grip of her nervous fingers. She lifted her hand to knock, hesitated, then lightly struck the door with her knuckles. Hearing no sound from within, Shah thought Jake might be asleep. Pushing the door open, she peeked around the edge of it.

"Shah?"

She froze. Jake was propped up in bed, a breakfast tray nearby. She tried shakily to smile, and forced herself to move into the room. He looked terribly pale, and both his legs were suspended by a set of cables that kept them inches off the bed.

"Hi... How are you feeling?"

Jake stared at her hungrily. "Better than I was a moment ago," he groused. Shah looked positively frightened. He waved her into the room. "Come over. I want to know how *you're* doing." He almost said that she looked like hell, but it wasn't true. Shah looked beautiful in the clothes, the brown earth tones complementing her dusky skin, her black hair and her lovely golden eyes.

Shyly Shah handed him the flowers. "Here, these are for you." And then she laughed a little, nervously, as the small bouquet was swallowed up in his large hands. Hands that had touched her, made her body sing and her heart take flight. Swallowing, Shah choked out, "I guess you need a vase. I'll go get one from the nurses' desk, and—"

"Don't go."

She halted, a few feet from the door. It was agony to be with Jake, to be around him. Taking a ragged breath, Shah turned back.

"I can ring for a nurse to come in." Jake examined the flowers and smiled. "That was thoughtful of you, but then again, I'm finding out you're that way with everyone. It's a nice trait, Shah. Take off your coat and stay a while.''

Like a robot, Shah took off her coat and hung it over the chair beside Jake's bed. The room was large and comfortable, painted pale blue rather than a cold hospital white. Outside the window, the trees were coated with a light dusting of snow—the first of the season, she'd heard from the bellman in the hotel lobby who'd called a cab for her.

Jake watched Shah in silence. He laid the pretty bouquet of yellow mums and purple asters on the tray by the bed and pushed them aside. She was so nervous, clasping and unclasping her hands, wringing them unconsciously. The darting look in her eyes told him she felt like a trapped animal. He patted the side of the bed.

"Come over here and sit down," he coaxed. "We need to talk."

The words sent a cold, splintering sensation through Shah. Trying to steel herself against what Jake might say, she turned and moved to the side of his bed. Sitting gingerly on the edge, she saw that his eyes were dark with pain and, although he'd recently shaved, his cheeks were gaunt, testament to his recent operation and past week of physical stress. Shah picked up a corner of the blue bedspread and played with it, still unable to meet his searching eyes.

"How do you feel?" she asked, casting frantically about for some safe topic of conversation.

"Lousy. But what really hurts is my heart, Shah."

Her head snapped up, her eyes widening. The blue spread fell from between her fingers. "What?"

Jake longed to reach out and caress her suddenly rosy cheek. "I said," he told her quietly, "my heart hurts."

"But...your legs were cut up by the boar..."

Patience, Jake cautioned himself. "My heart's taking a worse beating, if you want to know the truth." He looked deeply into Shah's golden eyes and tried to gauge the depth of her inability to believe that someone could love her. Jake knew in his heart that Shah had heard him say those words to her in Manaus. He'd spent all morning replaying the sequence of events, feeling his way through it.

When Jake reached over and claimed her hand, Shah swallowed convulsively. "I don't understand," she whispered.

"I know. At least I think I know." Jake's heart started a slow, almost painful pounding. "Tell me something. Did your father ever say he loved you?"

Startled by the question, Shah laughed a little. "Him? No. His way of showing his love was taking off his belt to punish me, and telling me it was going to hurt him worse than it was going to hurt me." She gave a bitter laugh. "I never understood that one."

Jake scowled heavily. "What about Robert? Did he say he loved you?"

"Yes."

"But you knew six months later that he really didn't."

"I guess I wanted to believe he loved me, Jake. I guess the truth is, he said it to get me into bed. When I realized that, I felt betrayed. He lied to me. He used the word *love* to lure me into his arms. I never forgave him for that." Shah compressed her lips. "That lie made me realize how little men value the word."

Jake held on to his very real anger at the callousness of the men in Shah's life. "I thought so."

She tilted her head. "Jake, what's going on? You're going somewhere with this conversation, I can tell."

He lifted her hand to his mouth and kissed it. Instantly he saw the golden fire flare in her eyes. Jake took hope, and plunged forward with his plan. "In Manaus, when I was just coming awake after you kissed me, I whispered something to you, Shah." He looked up and captured her startled gaze. "What did I say to you?"

The silence deepened, and Shah sat transfixed. A part of her, a large part, wanted to run. Just as she had run from Robert, and, earlier, from her father. She watched as Jake took her hand and gently stroked it with his fingers. The tingling sensation went all the way up her arm, and she pulled in a strangled breath.

"What did you hear me say to you?" he repeated quietly.

Licking her lips, Shah whispered, "I—I'm not sure, Jake. I thought I was making it up."

"You didn't make it up."

Oh, what if she'd heard it wrong? What if her heart and her foggy brain had made up what she wanted to hear, and it wasn't what Jake had said at all? She was going to appear to be a bigger fool in Jake's eyes if she mouthed those words. Bowing her head, Shah closed her eyes and whispered, "I think you said you loved me...."

Tipping her chin up so that she was forced to meet his patient gaze, Jake said, "That's right, I did." He watched surprise flare in her eyes. Why surprise?

"I didn't want to believe you said it, I guess."

"Why?"

Shah gave an embarrassed shrug, unable to hold his burning, intense gaze. "I was so tired. You have to understand, Jake, I'd gone without sleep for almost three days. When I kissed you, it was wonderful. When you woke up, I was so happy. I didn't see how someone like you could love someone like me. So I thought I'd made it up in my groggy head..." Her voice trailed off.

Jake whispered her name and framed her face. "I love you, Shah Sungilo," he said, his voice cracking with emotion. "I love you with my heart and all of my soul." He caressed her cheek. "This time, you know your mind didn't make it up. This time, you can't deny it."

With a little cry, Shah pressed her hand against her lips. Jake's mouth curved into a tender smile, and she could only stare at him in the silence.

"All your life," Jake began heavily, "men have abused you in one form or another, sweetheart. I couldn't, for the life of me, understand why you didn't respond when I said I loved you. This morning—" Jake shook his head and gazed around the room "—I lay here a long time trying to figure out why you hadn't heard me. And then I realized, you had, but you've been so hurt so many times by men who were incapable of loving that you didn't believe your ears. Am I right?"

Ashamed of herself, Shah hung her head. "Yes..."

With a sigh, Jake captured her clasped hands in his. "Only time can prove to you that I love you, Shah. Not because I want you beside me in bed. I want that, too, but sex is only a small part of what love is all about. You need to know that I love you for you, not for what you can give me, or what I can take from you." He saw tears forming in her eyes.

"I have a plan I want to share with you. The doc told me I'll need two months to recuperate. I want to go home, Shah. Home to the Cascade Mountains of Oregon. And I want you there, with me." He watched her face closely. "In a way, we both need to heal from a lot of wounds we've accumulated in the last decade. I need to come to terms with the loss of my family—and you need to realize that you can trust me," he added with a small, hopeful smile. "I can't undo what your father and Robert did to you, Shah, but I can show you a whole new world, a place where love is shared. Let me give you that chance to heal."

Shah sat for a long time, assimilating Jake's words and, more important, the feelings behind his words. Her heart burst with such joy at the knowledge that she hadn't made up Jake's whispered words that she could barely think, much less talk. "I guess," she joked nervously, "I'm more Indian than I ever realized. I can't get out how I feel about this, Jake. We don't talk much, you know. We let our actions speak for us instead."

"Your walk is your talk. Fair enough," Jake told her. "Let me prove that my walk is my talk, too." And it would be. "Then you'll come home with me? To Oregon?" he asked again.

She gave a him a small smile. "If I didn't, who would take care of you? You're strung up like a Christmas goose ready to be baked in an oven, Jake Randolph."

He laughed. Every movement hurt his legs, but Jake didn't care. His laughter boomed and rolled around the room. Shah was going to come home with him! He loved her more than she could possibly know. He smiled up at Shah. Her face no longer seemed as haunted as before. There was happiness there, along with uncertainty. "I'm not going to be a very good patient," he warned her. "I hate being bed-bound."

"I think I can deal with your grouchiness," she told him seriously. The joy written on Jake's face simply amazed Shah. He was like a little boy who had gotten the most wonderful gift in the world. She didn't feel like a prize, though. In fact, she didn't know what he saw in her. "I'm not used to living with someone," she warned him.

"We'll take it a day at a time."

Shah hung her head as she felt her way through a myriad of emotions. "It's such a chance. I don't know if I'm capable of that kind of risk."

Patiently Jake said, "You risk your life all the time in the name of worthy causes. Don't you think *you're* a worthy cause?"

His insight into her wounded heart astonished her. Weighing his words, his observation, for several long, silent moments, she whispered, "I think I am worthy."

"So do I."

Rallying beneath his beaming smile, Shah felt as if the sunshine were coming out in her life for the first time. "Okay," she said with a shy laugh. She looked forward to Oregon, to seeing Jake's home there. And yet Shah couldn't help wondering if she was being trapped in a new and different way. Only time would tell.

"I still will work on rain-forest issues, Jake."

"Fine," he agreed. "Maybe I can do something to help you. You never know. I'll need something to keep me occupied while I'm mending. I have a fax, a computer, a modem and several phone lines for business purposes. You can use them all you want."

Shah was pleased and surprised by Jake's enthusiasm, and by the sincerity burning in his eyes. "Well," she stumbled, "I'd planned on working with the Sierra Club on this issue, getting petitions signed and learning to lobby Congress, once I came back to America."

"I was a little worried you might be bored out in Oregon, but I can see you'll be busy."

Shah was unable to stop staring at Jake's mobile mouth, which was wreathed in a contented smile. She longed to kiss him, to share the joy bubbling up through her. But to be fair to Jake, to be fair to herself, she couldn't succumb to the heated kisses that had kindled that unknown but welcome fire in her body. Robert had trapped her that way, and she had to prove to herself that Jake wasn't like that. Her paranoid head warned her that he knew she loved his touch, hungered for it and wanted more. Her heart, that soft voice that acted on feelings alone, told her that she loved Jake with a fierceness she'd never felt before, and that because it was such a new and overwhelming experience it was scaring her, making her overly cautious.

She trusted Jake to keep his word, and she understood that he wouldn't trap her. Reading between the lines of his offer, Shah realized that if she wanted him it was she who would have to take the initiative. For the first time in her life, she held power, her true power, in her own hands. It was a giddy, euphoric feeling to know that Jake wouldn't stalk her, manipulate her with words or touches to get her to do what he wanted. No, he'd respect her, give her the time she needed to be sure, first about herself, then about him.

"You'll be going from one extreme to another," Jake said, humbled, as Shah slid her hand into his. There was such intimacy between them, strong and good, that it left him shaken in the wake of it. "From the tropics of Brazil to the snow and winter of the Cascades."

With a little smile, Shah said, "My life's always been one of extremes. I'll adjust."

Jake wondered if Shah realized that such flexibility wasn't something a whole lot of people possessed. It was one of the reasons she'd survived thus far, and he applauded her ability to bend, not break, when new situations presented themselves to her. "I'm going to call the

Butterfields, who take care of the house for me, and tell them we're coming home." He squeezed Shah's slender hand, and an ache seized him. The need to love her, to introduce her to the realm of true love, was eating away at him. Jake knew he had to control his physical hunger for Shah, or he'd scare her away. "It's December first. You realize we're going to spend Christmas together?"

There was a wistful tone to his voice. Shah met his boyish smile. "Can we have a Christmas tree?"

"Just take a walk out into the front yard and take your pick," he chuckled. "That cedar A-frame of mine is stuck deep in the heart of big-tree country. We're surrounded by Douglas firs for as far as the eye can see."

"It sounds wonderful," Shah whispered, a little dazed by the sudden and unexpected turn of events. "Like a winter wonderland, a fairy tale..."

"You're my dream come true," Jake said, his throat tightening. "You're coming home with me. I never thought, I never imagined, that any woman would ever share that house with me."

Shah understood Jake's emotionally charged statement. He'd lost his family, he'd lost everything he'd ever loved. How many times had he come off a mission to be alone in that cedar A-frame? How many? Her heart bled for Jake, for the terrible loneliness he'd endured. As she sat there, Shah began to realize that they were very much alike in some ways. That small revelation tore down another barrier of Shah's fear, and she looked forward to going home with him with a new eagerness.

"If I have to spend one more day in this bed, I'm going to turn into a bear," Jake grumbled unhappily.

Shah grinned as she brought Jake his breakfast tray. "You've been home exactly two weeks, and I think you've already turned into a grumpy old bear, Jake Randolph.'' It was seven in the morning, sunlight barely showing on the horizon outside the window of the small first-floor bedroom where Jake stayed. He'd just awakened; his covers were in twisted heaps, and both his bandaged legs were exposed. Shah tried to keep from looking at his powerful, darkly haired chest. Jake had informed her once they got home that normally he didn't wear anything to bed, but in deference to her he'd wear pajama bottoms only. Shah had tucked her smile away and tried to be serious about it.

Placing the tray on the bedstand, Shah patiently smoothed the covers across his legs and tucked them around his waist. Jake was already sitting up, several goose-down pillows providing backing for him against the cedar headboard. Some of the grumpiness had left Jake's sleepy features when she'd entered his room.

"I'm going crazy," he muttered, taking the pink linen napkin Shah offered and spreading it across his naked torso.

"The doctor said fourteen days in bed, Jake. You've only got one more to go." She placed the tray on his lap. She found such joy in small things like making Jake's breakfast. Actually, Shah thought, laughing to herself, it wasn't that small: he ate enough for three people.

"This is a nice touch," he murmured. In a little white vase, Shah had placed a sprig of holly with red berries. "What did you do? Get up early and tramp outside in the snow to find them?"

"Yes. I had a lovely walk in the snow this morning. It was beautiful, Jake. The stars are so close at this altitude, so shiny and bright." She gazed out the window. The sky had been clear early this morning, but it had clouded over in the past hour, and now snowflakes twirled thickly through the gray morning sky.

"Wish I could've joined you," Jake said.

Shah smiled understandingly and sat carefully on the edge of the bed, facing Jake. She usually took her breakfast with him in his room. It was something she looked forward to, because Jake had insisted she take the lovely master bedroom up on the second floor. Shah felt cut off, being a story away from Jake when she went to bed at night. It was lonely in that big queen-size bed, with its massive cedar posts. All the furniture in the place, Shah had discovered, had been made by Jake. After the death of his family, he'd used the building of his home as therapy.

"One more day," she repeated patiently.

Jake dug hungrily into the stack of pancakes Shah had fixed for him. She'd put red raspberry syrup nearby, plus a small basket of well-fried bacon. "You're one hell of a cook, you know that?" He glanced up at her as he began eating the light, fluffy pancakes. "You get all this talent from your mother?"

"I guess. Actually, it was my grandma. Because my mother is a medicine woman, she's often traveling to people's homes, so my grandmother taught me how to cook and keep house."

"Your grandma still around?" Jake thought how beautiful Shah looked. She wore a bright red cable-knit sweater, and her long black hair was flowing around her. Her light tan slacks were loose, but still reminded him of her long thoroughbred's legs. She also wore a pair of lightweight hiking boots, a necessity for winter in the Cascades.

"Yes, and I hope you get to meet my whole family someday soon. Gram is ninety-four, but you wouldn't know it. She's sharp and spry.'' Shah surprised herself. Now, where had the invitation to meet her family come from? Glancing over at Jake, whose forkful of pancake had halted midway to his mouth, she realized her mouth was getting ahead of her brain—something that happened too frequently when she was around Jake.

"You mean that?" He saw a high flush come to her cheeks.

"Well...sure..."

With a smile, Jake popped the pancakes into his mouth, savoring them. Shah had put some piñon nuts in them; it was a trick that made even the most ordinary of pancakes taste great. "You're hesitating," he said with a grin, baiting her.

Clasping and unclasping her hands, Shah studied them intently. "Foot-and-mouth disease," she muttered.

"Oh, then you didn't mean the invitation?" Jake's grin widened. He hadn't teased Shah very often in the past two weeks, because coming here had been such an adjustment for her. Still, things were settling into a comfortable routine, and he saw her relaxing more and more every day. This morning he wanted to test Shah's security about being here with him.

"Sure I did!" she protested. "It's just that sometimes my heart gets ahead of my brain, and—"

"I thought you said Native Americans always speak from the heart, not the head."

Befuddled, and aware that Jake was teasing her, Shah managed a short laugh. "They do. I mean, they should. I mean, they don't always, but that's what my mother taught me. We're right-brained, and that side of the brain has no voice, like the left brain does. Did you know the left brain contains the nerves that lead to our voice? The right brain has no voice—at least not a loud one. Mother always said that our heart is this side of the brain's voice.'' Shah smiled fondly, recalling that particular conversation with her mother.

''No, I didn't know that. Sounds interesting,'' Jake murmured, impressed. He quickly finished off the pancakes and held out a strip of bacon to Shah. She took it and thanked him. The pleasure of sharing the morning meal with her was something Jake always looked forward to eagerly. But, then, he savored each and every moment with her. ''So, if Native Americans are right-brained and heart-centered, what does that make white men?'' he baited.

''Left-brained and vocal,'' Shah said with a wry grin. After finishing off the strip of bacon, she wiped her fingers on the pink linen napkin draped across Jake's torso. ''Except for you.''

''What am I?''

''I feel like you're a nice balance between the two,'' she answered seriously. Shah saw the dancing light in Jake's gray eyes. ''Somewhere along the line, you disconnected from the general male stereotype and embraced your heart and feelings.''

Jake handed her the tray with his thanks and watched as Shah stood up. She had such gazellelike grace that he never tired of simply watching her move. ''That happened when my family was killed,'' he told her quietly. ''Bess had been working on me for a long time, though, to get me unstuck from the male mode.''

Shah stood near the dresser where she'd placed the tray. ''I thought so,'' she said softly, not wishing to open up that wound. Lately Jake had talked more often about his family, and she could see that those conversations, though painful, were healing him before her very eyes.

"Do me a favor?" Jake pointed toward the upper level of the house.

"Sure." Shah saw his face grow pensive. What was he up to now?

"Go to the large cedar dresser opposite the bed. In the fourth drawer is a huge photo album. Bring it to me? There are some things I want to show you, share with you."

Suddenly shaky, Shah nodded and left. As she climbed the stairs that led to the huge master bedroom up in the loft, her heart started a slow pounding. As she gently opened the drawer and took out the leather photo album, she realized that this was about Jake's family. Her mouth dry, she descended the stairs, the album pressed protectively to her chest.

Jake's face mirrored vulnerability as she handed him the album. Her heart wouldn't stop its rapid beating as she sat on the edge of the bed next to him. He hesitantly touched the album, which was now resting in his lap.

"I've been wanting to share this with you for a long time," he rasped. "It's the family photo album." Running his fingers along the well-worn leather cover, Jake managed a sad smile. "It was Bess's idea—our beginning, middle and ending, she said."

Gently Shah reached over and placed her hand on top of his. Jake's voice trembled with emotion. She understood, and she hoped her look conveyed that as he risked a glance up at her before he opened the album.

Clearing his throat, Jake managed a weak smile. "I just never thought there would be an end," he said as he opened the album. "Bess was a lot more realistic about life than I was. Or maybe I ought to say that I was so in love with her that life's realities never really hit me until she was gone."

Words were impossible for Shah. All she could do was wrap her arm around Jake as he sat there with the album in his lap. Feelings were vibrating around them, and she understood as never before the depth of the love Jake had had for his family, for his wife. As he gestured to the first page of the album, Shah devoted her full attention, her heart, to what Jake was sharing with her.

"I never showed this album to anyone after they died. I couldn't look at these photos, our marriage, or the baby pictures of our kids." Tears blurred Jake's eyes, but he went on. It was so important that Shah understand his past. "Here's Bess and me on our wedding day."

"She was very beautiful," Shah said. The woman was petite, with light brown hair. Her white wedding dress emphasized the joy radiating from her oval face. Jake looked so very young, proud and tall in his dark blue Marine Corps dress uniform. "You both look so happy."

Jake smiled fondly. "We were. Young, idealistic, and carrying the hope of a happy future." Oddly, the tears left his eyes and a new kind of calm filled him as he went on to the next page of the album. "Katie was our firstborn. She weighed ten pounds at birth. Look at the head of hair on that kid."

The baby in the picture had dark hair, just like Jake. Shah smiled gently, because the photo had been taken with Jake at Bess's bedside, the baby cradled lovingly between them. "The three of you look very happy."

"Bess probably looks more relieved than anything," Jake commented dryly, meeting and holding Shah's warmth-filled gaze. "She swore up and down she'd never have another baby because the labor had been so long with Katie." He laughed appreciatively, feeling another weighted cloak dissolve from around his shoulders. "Of course, then Mandy came along, two years later."

"And did she weigh in like a ten-pound sack of potatoes?" Shah asked, smiling and feeling Jake's joy. It was as if showing her the album and talking about his family were healing him before her eyes. Grateful for whatever was happening, Shah felt the tension in the room dissolving. In its place came an incredible sense of subdued joy that they could share this album filled with happiness.

With a chuckle, Jake nodded and turned another page. "Mandy weighed in at exactly ten pounds. Bess blamed me for that, and I gladly took the blame. Look at her. Katie had my dark hair, and Mandy had Bess's lighter hair. The kid was a beauty."

And she was, Shah thought. Mandy had her mother's delicate features, but her eyes were Jake's in shape and color. Relaxing, her hand unconsciously moving up and down Jake's back, she listened as he shared his family years with her. On the last page, he became choked up.

"There's Katie in her pink tutu. She was crazy about becoming a ballerina. At ten years old, she was the star of her class." Gently he touched the picture of his smiling daughter. "This was taken by Bess just before the recital that Katie starred in."

"Were you able to see her recital?" Shah asked. She saw Jake's mouth compress into a thin line and knew the answer. Sliding her hand across his shoulder, she allowed him to lean upon her.

Jake felt Shah's hand move on his shoulder. He reached over and embraced her, the tears in his eyes going away as he held her, the pain from the past seeming to disappear beneath her healing touch and the love she held for him. In the moments that followed, poignant and bittersweet, Jake realized that sharing the album, his life and his family with Shah was a catharsis for him. It was as if he had finally been able to place the wonderful memories and feelings into a chamber of his heart to be held there forever. That was the past.

Somehow, he realized, meeting Shah and falling in love with her had helped bring his past full circle, to completion. As he drew her more deeply into his arms and felt her sigh and rest her head against his shoulder, Jake felt a new flow of feelings through him. The past, his past, had finally been healed. Now he was genuinely able to step forward and dare to dream of a future with her.

"Thanks," he told her gruffly, kissing first her cheek and then her brow, "for sharing this with me."

Easing out of his embrace, Shah fought back tears. With a soft, unsure smile, she whispered, "I wouldn't have it any other way, Jake."

"They're in my heart," he told her quietly. "Forever. But I'm at peace with myself now, thanks to you, to us."

Touched to the point of being unable to speak, Shah could only nod and grip his strong, scarred hand. She didn't want to break the beauty, the healing, of this moment, but there were chores that had to be attended to. "Peace is another word for healing, Jake. In our own ways, we're still healing from our pasts, but at least we know it's possible to do that." Then, sliding off the bed, she said, "I've got to get your legs taken care of."

Shah bent down, opened a drawer in the lovely cedar dresser that Jake had made and drew out clean dressings. The bandages on his healing legs had to be changed daily.

Jake brightened as Shah leaned down after he'd removed the covers from his legs. "Hey, how about I try a walk outside? I'm only a day away from when the doc said I could start moving around in earnest." Jake gestured toward the window. "I like cold weather. I like the snow." Every day he'd been puttering around the house, extending his time out of bed and exercising his newly healed muscles. Shah would catch him standing forlornly at a window, looking out with a wistful expression on his face. Jake really was an outdoor person, and her heart bled for him, because she knew how hard it must be for him to remain house-bound.

"You like anywhere but this bed," Shah reminded him as she expertly cut away the old dressings and put them aside.

"I warned you—I'm not one to be tied down. Especially when I'm sick."

She smiled absently and looked at the many curved pink scars on his leg. All the wounds had healed nicely, but she regretted the hundreds of stitches required to patch Jake back together again. The scars would be many, and most would never go away. Gently she ran her hand down the expanse of his calf.

"How do they feel today?"

Jake tried to smile. Every time Shah touched him like that, he wanted to groan with pleasure. Did she realize how healing her touch was? How lovely her slender hand was as it caressed his ugly, scarred flesh? "Great," he muttered, praying that he could control himself. The bulk of the covers would hide his reaction to Shah's touch, but Jake lived in fear that one day, she would discover what her light caress did to him. Thus far, he'd been able to keep his hands off Shah. Every day she touched him a little more, and that told him that his decision had been right—for both of them. Every day

Shah's confidence in herself, as a woman, as a human being who could show her feelings without threat, was increasing. To Jake, it was like watching her blossom before his very eyes.

"I want to put that calendula oil on them before I bandage them back up," she told him.

"Go ahead." He pointed to his leg. "The scars are a lot less noticeable since you've been putting that marigold juice on them."

With a smile, Shah brought the bottle of calendula, an essence of marigold, over from the dresser. "I'm glad I called my mother and she sent this to us right away," Shah said. She poured the glycerine that contained the brownish-colored liquid into the palms of her hands. Leaning down, she gently bathed Jake's leg with it. "Mother said it always took away scars if used early enough after an operation," she murmured. "And she was right."

"Your mother puts regular doctors to shame," Jake told her. Jake lay there in abject pleasure. Just being touched by Shah sent wave after wave of longing through him. All too soon she had replaced the dressings and was retrieving a pair of jeans and a dark green polo shirt from his closet for him.

"What's on your agenda today?" Jake wanted to know as he eased his feet to the golden-reddish cedar floor.

"I'm expecting a call from the Brazilian embassy today. They've got the video of Hernandez using chain saws." Shah frowned and laid the clothes next to Jake. Although his legs were outwardly almost completely healed, he was still weak. Each afternoon she worked with him on several exercises designed to strengthen his legs. "They're supposed to let me know if they'll send the police to arrest him. I just hope they'll prosecute."

Jake saw the frown on her face deepen. "They will," he assured her confidently. When she gave him a distrustful look, he grinned. "How about we go find a Christmas tree after you get that call? To celebrate your victory?"

"Jake, you're not supposed to be going outside yet! The doctors are afraid you'll slip on some ice and tear those newly healed muscles."

"Now, Shah..."

She watched Jake slowly get to his feet. His routine was to shave, dress, and then move into the den to watch television, which he hated doing for any length of time. Then he would read books to stay mentally engaged in something. At other times he'd play secretary on one of her projects, folding letters and licking envelopes and placing stamps on them. Her heart went out to Jake; he just wasn't the sedentary type. He groused because she split wood every morning for the huge earth stove that sat in the living room. He complained when she swept off the red-brick steps that led to the garage and the fieldstone sidewalk that led to the snow-covered dirt road. He groused a lot, but Shah knew it was because he considered those responsibilities his, not hers.

"Just one more day," she pleaded.

He glanced at her as he moved slowly around the bed. "We'll see," he said, and then smiled at her. "Did I tell you how pretty you look in red?"

She grinned. "Matches my temper, don't you think?"

"What a smart mouth you have, Ms. Travers."

Rallying beneath his teasing, Shah said, "I'll see you later. I'll be working in your office if you need me."

* * *

Jake stood at the floor-to-ceiling windows in the living room. The snow had stopped falling, the sky was a light shade of gray, and the evergreens were swathed in their white winter raiment. It was almost noon, and he was bored out of his skull. There was only so much television a man could watch, only so many magazines, newspapers and books he could read, before he got restless. Very restless.

He crossed his arms, well aware of what lay beneath his keen restlessness. He wondered when Shah would gather enough courage to lean over and kiss him again. How many times had he seen the desire in her lovely, shadowed eyes? The hesitation, the fear, the longing? His own body fairly boiled for her, and it was all he could do to force his mind onto anything other than making long, slow, delicious love with Shah. But it had to be on her terms, Jake reminded himself savagely—her time and her decision. Intuitively he knew that once he got her in his arms, in his bed, she would never leave again. It was just that first time, overcoming her fear from the past, that was the sticking point. Jake had lost count of how many times he'd cursed her father and her ex-husband.

He was feeling strong again. Strong and powerful and incredibly vital. Jake turned, a plan in mind, a slight smile working its way across his mouth. The Brazilian embassy had just called to inform Shah that Hernandez was under arrest, and that he would indeed go to trial. That meant they would be going back down to Brazil as witnesses, but not until at least three months from now. Shah had put down the phone, thrown her arms around Jake and laughed in triumph. He'd hugged her long and hard, and both of them had been a little breathless after he released her. Yes, the time was ripening.

Jake hummed softly, feeling lighter with each step he took. If only Shah would go along with his plan, he felt it might be the turning point in their relationship.

Chapter Thirteen

Shah had just entered Jake's office, euphoric over the fact that Hernandez was being indicted by the Brazilian government. She hummed softly as she drew a file from the file cabinet. The phone rang.

"Hello?"

"Shah? This is your father."

Her heart plummeted. Automatically her hand tightened around the phone. "What do you want?" she asked, standing stiffly. She'd been unprepared for the anger she'd heard in his voice.

"Want? You know what I want! How could you do this to me, Shah? You took those damned pictures of Hernandez cutting trees down with chain saws! How could you?"

Anger sizzled through Shah, and she sat down, her free hand clenched into a fist. "How could I? How dare you! You didn't want me down there in Brazil because

the stock you bought is all tied up with Hernandez and
several other landowners. And don't deny it. I have
proof that you bought heavily into the Brazilian rain forest timber trade."

"This is going to cost me millions! You don't care,
do you, Shah? You're just like your damned mother—
bullheaded, single-sighted, and you absolutely refuse to
see anyone else's point of view."

Her heart throbbed at the base of her throat, and when
she spoke again her voice wobbled. "You've lied to me,
you've tried over the last year to have me kidnapped out
of Brazil. Why couldn't you have told me the truth in
the first place?"

"Would it have done any good?"

"No, but at least there would be honesty between us.
That's a start."

"There is no start, Shah. I can't believe you would
be this disloyal to me."

Shah nearly choked. Every muscle in her body was
tense with fury. "Disloyal? What about your disloyalty
to Mother Earth?"

"Stop talking that drivel—"

"No!" Shah said tightly. "Father, you hate women
of any kind. You don't respect Mother Earth. You can't
even respect my mother, much less me."

"Cut it out, Shah. I called to ask you to remove your
charges against Hernandez. My company can't afford to
lose the millions we've invested in timber in Brazil."

"I'll *never* do that."

"Shah, you can't do this to me."

Tears marred Shah's vision, and she released a harsh
bark of laughter. "Do what? Allow you to continue to
rape our mother? Allow you to help alter the quality of
our air? Of life itself? I will never lift those charges

against Hernandez. Not for you, not for anyone.'' Shah was breathing erratically, and she was trying to stop the quaver in her voice, but she couldn't.

''If you love me, you'll drop those charges.''

Shah sat back and shut her eyes tightly. Gulping back a scream of pure frustration at his unfair tactics, she was silent for a good minute before she could control her voice and her feelings. ''Love?'' she whispered. ''You don't know the meaning of love, Father. You never did. You never loved my mother, or me. You never respected us as human beings. I won't allow you to use love as an excuse for forsaking everything I live for and believe in, just to please you.''

''You're just as fanatical as your mother!'' Travers snarled. ''Fine! I'll fight you in court on this, Shah. I'll use every penny I have to defend Hernandez and the other landowners in Brazil. This is war. You're not my daughter. You never have been.''

The words cut deeply into Shah's heart. She had known that one day this would happen. The hurt seared through her, and for long moments she grappled with the truth of the situation: Some men were incapable of being fathers, much less decent, kind ones, such as Jake had been. ''You do what you have to do,'' she said. ''You might be my biological father, but you've never been a real one to me. I'll see you in court—on the opposite side, as usual.''

Shah dropped the receiver back into the cradle and sat for a long time, allowing the grief, rage and hurt to flow through her. Hanging her head, she realized that Jake had given her the strength to stand up to her father. He was the polar opposite of Ken Travers in every way possible. She was so glad Jake had shown her that album, shown her that parents could really love and respect their children.

With a ragged sigh, Shah stood up on shaky knees. She locked them, her hand resting on the desk, until she got the strength to move. She wanted to find Jake and share the conversation with him.

Jake sat in the overstuffed chair, the magazine he'd been reading lying idle in his lap as he listened to Shah recounting the upsetting phone call from her father. She sat on the stool where his feet rested, almost doubled over, her elbows planted on her thighs, her chin resting on top of her clasped hands. When she'd finished, the silence ebbed and flowed around them. Such sadness and abandonment were clearly etched on her features that Jake ached for her.

Reaching forward, he gently eased her hands apart and held them in his own. Her golden eyes were marred by darkness, and he felt her grief and injury. "You did the right thing, Shah." Jake shook his head and gave her a gentle smile. "Sometimes life tests you on what you really believe in, and you've got to make choices. Hard choices. You made the right decisions for the right reasons. Your father was the one who was dishonest with you. Not vice versa."

Sniffing, Shah nodded. "It hurt so much when he said that if I really loved him I would withdraw the charges."

"I know.... Listen, when someone like him is stuck in such a dysfunctional state, everything he sees is interpreted with the same emotional skewing," Jake explained quietly. "Travers never knew what love was, Shah. The man can't love himself, and therefore he's incapable of knowing how to love others, even you."

The hurt in her heart mushroomed with Jake's calm words. "It's the alcoholism, Jake. That's the root of it."

"No, that's a symptom," he said. "I'll bet if you went into your father's past, the way he was raised, he was probably beaten the same way he beat you and your mother. Inside, the man's a cowering animal, hurt and frightened."

"Well, so am I, but I try not to take it out on others," Shah murmured.

"The difference is that you want to get well, Shah, and your father doesn't. And until he does, he's going to continue to play these kinds of games with you. He's using the word *love* when it's not really love at all, just a manipulation of you." He smiled a little and gripped her hands more firmly. "You didn't fall for his game, and I'm proud of you."

Shah held Jake's warm gray gaze, feeling his care wash across her raw feelings. "There's no easy end to this. No easy answers. My father sees me as this horrible villain ruining his life, his business."

"Maybe," Jake said, "someday, he'll realize he's got a disease that's poisoning not only himself and how he sees the world through those eyes, but his relationship with his daughter, his ex-wife, and probably everyone around him. Until he does, Shah, you'll remain the villain in his life. He won't win this court fight, even though he'll try. After he loses, he'll probably hate you until the next problem in the guise of a person comes along, and then he'll train his diseased focus on that poor target."

"And then he won't hate me as much," she muttered, seeing his faultless logic.

Pulling her forward, Jake guided Shah onto his lap. She came without fighting and he was grateful. As she settled in his lap, her arm went around his shoulders and she pressed her brow against his hair. He held her in an embrace meant to give her protection and love.

"It's so hard to know that he hates me. That he sees me as a bad person."

Jake patted her gently. "I know, honey, I know. But you have to listen to me, to your mother and your grandmother about how good a person you are. Try not to listen to your detractors—that will only tear you down, and if you buy into it heavily enough, it will end up destroying you." He closed his eyes, absorbing the vulnerability Shah was sharing with him. "You stick to the high road on these things, Shah. You didn't set out to deliberately or knowingly hurt your father. You happen to have a different reality about how to live your life, and that's allowed. You didn't try to manipulate him the way he did you. You stuck to your guns, your beliefs, and walked your talk."

She smiled a little and hugged Jake. "Sometimes I think you are part Native American. You seem to understand me so well."

He sighed and closed his eyes, content as never before. "That's because I love you, strengths and weaknesses combined. No one's perfect, Shah. And you can't march to someone else's idea of how you should live your life." Opening his eyes again, he said, "Come and help me find the right Christmas tree?" Shah lifted her head from where it was resting against him, her eyes widening at his request.

Jake held up his hand to stop the protest he knew was coming. "I know—I'm not supposed to start walking outdoors until tomorrow. But one day isn't going to kill me, Shah."

She laughed. "You're such a bad boy when you want to be. You know I can't stop you."

Jake wove invisible designs on her hip and thigh with his light touch. "I more or less had you contributing to helping me go outdoors." He sighed and looked around the large, airy room. "The place looks naked without a tree in the living room," he complained. "Christmas is always something special. I miss not having the tree decorated. Usually, the tree was set up around the first of December."

"You," Shah said accusingly, "could get a rock to walk if you wanted to, Randolph."

"It's not a rock I want at my side. It's you."

The instant Shah met and held his warm gray gaze, she felt a ribbon of heat flow through her. The last of the hurt over her father's phone call had evaporated. How could she say no to Jake? Did he realize how much sway he had over her? Placing both arms around his shoulders and giving him a quick hug, she muttered, "Oh, all right, Jake. You just keep chipping away at me until I break down and say yes!"

"I believe," he said, with a rather pleased expression on his face, "it's called nagging."

The snow was fresh, fine and powdery, and it was knee-deep in places as they walked in search of just the right tree. Shah remained close to Jake's left arm—just in case he should slip and start to fall. But she kept her worry to herself, because he was such a little boy about getting to go out in the cold, crisp winter air. Jake wore a brightly colored Pendleton wool jacket, a red knit cap thrown carelessly over his head, and a pair of warm gloves. His cheeks were ruddy from the temperature, which hovered in the high twenties. Each time he exhaled, a mist formed around his mouth and nose.

"Jake," Shah pleaded, "we're almost a quarter of a mile from the house. You shouldn't overextend yourself this first time. Dr. Adams is going to throw a shoe when he hears what you've done!"

Jake halted and turned. Shah wore her red nylon jacket with a dark green knit cap and gloves. Her black hair flowed around her shoulders like an ebony cape, in stark contrast to the jacket. She wiped her nose with a tissue and stuffed it back into her pocket. Without thinking, because he was overjoyed to be outdoors again, he caressed her flushed cheek.

"Maybe you're right," he murmured. Then he gave her a happy grin. "Which one do you think will make a good Christmas tree?" He swung his arm outward to encompass the thick stand of evergreens that surrounded them.

The worry Shah felt evaporated beneath Jake's touch. She ached to lean up and kiss his smiling mouth. Never had she seen Jake so happy, so vital, as now. The past two weeks had been a sort of living hell for Shah. She so desperately wanted to kiss Jake, to walk into his arms and discover the love he'd promised her. But she was afraid. Too afraid.

"How about that one?" She pointed to a seven-foot blue spruce.

Jake sized it up, his ax in his left hand. "Looks pretty good to me."

Shah moved over to the tree and gently touched its snow-covered needles. "Now, don't laugh at me, Jake, but if you really want this tree, we have to ask it permission to give its life for us." When she saw his brows lift, she added breathlessly as she stroked the evergreen's limb, "We believe everything has a spirit, Jake. And we never take without asking permission first. If the tree says no, we have to find another one. All right?"

He tramped over to where she stood. There was such anxiety in her eyes that he wanted to reassure her that he wouldn't laugh at her explanation. Leaning down, he kissed the tip of her cold nose. "I like the way Native Americans see the world. Yeah, go ahead. Ask it."

Her nose tingled from his brief kiss, breaking loose a portion of Shah's fear. She moved the few inches that separated them and threw her arms around his broad shoulders. Pressing herself against him, her face nestled against his shoulder, she whispered, "I knew you'd understand. Thank you..." She moved away quickly, before his arms could wrap around her. Though embarrassed by her boldness, Shah was struck by the sudden hunger and need she saw in Jake's narrowed gray eyes. It made her go weak with longing, and she struggled to stop herself from moving back into his arms.

Jake anchored himself. He ordered himself not to move a muscle after Shah's surprising embrace. It had happened so fast that it had caught him off guard. And then he smiled to himself, joyous over Shah's thawing toward him. Maybe it was the pristine air and the scent of the forest that encompassed him, but he was sure something special was happening. Sunlight broke through the low gray clouds, sending blinding, brilliant shafts across the mountain where they stood.

Shah closed her eyes and tried to concentrate, her hands gently touching the tree. For her, everything was alive, and everything had a voice. Maybe not one like a human being's, but a voice, a feeling, nevertheless. Shaken by her unexpected spontaneity with Jake, she tried to concentrate on mentally sending a message to the tree asking if it would give its life to them. Her heart was pounding, but gradually it slowed as she formed the explanation and the question for the tree.

Jake stood silent, watching as Shah closed her eyes, her hands reverently cupping one of the branches of the blue spruce. There was something natural and touching about Shah's belief system and her practice of it. How many spiders had she found and carried out to the garage? She wouldn't throw them out in the snow for fear of killing them. One didn't kill one's relatives. Moved, Jake wondered if Shah knew just how special she was. Probably not, but he longed to be the one to show her, to tell her.

"It's okay," she whispered after several minutes, opening her eyes. She dug into a small bag she always carried in her pocket. "This is tobacco. We always give a gift to the tree, no matter what its answer is." Shah liberally sprinkled the tobacco across the tree. With a smile, she tucked the leather pouch back into her pocket. "Ready?"

With a nod, Jake came forward. He approved of the respect Shah held for all living things. The gifting of tobacco was an added thoughtfulness. With quick, sure strokes, Jake cut the tree down. In minutes they'd shaken the limbs free of the snow. Taking the spruce by the trunk, they walked side by side down the long, gentle slope back toward the house.

Halfway down the slope, Shah slipped. With a little cry, she threw out her arms. She'd hit a patch of ice hidden beneath the snow. Jake reached over to try to catch one of her flailing arms. Instead, he slipped on the same patch of ice. Snow flew upward in an explosion as Shah landed unceremoniously on her back. The tree slid on by them. Jake landed on top of Shah.

She gasped as he fell on her. He rolled onto his side to keep his massive weight from striking her fully. Reaching out, he made a grab for her as she continued her slide down the hill. They ended up several yards down the slope, tangled in each other's arms and legs, covered with snow.

"Jake! Are you all right?" Shah had a horror of him tearing those just-healed muscles. She lay beneath him, excruciatingly aware of him as a man, his weight not alarming, but sending heated, urgent signals throughout her.

He grinned carelessly, enjoying the intimacy the accident had created. "I'm okay. In fact, I couldn't feel more right," he gasped, mist forming as he breathed. "And you? Are you okay?" Shah was in his arms, her body pressed against his. She'd lost her cap in the fall, and her eyes widened beautifully as he reached over with his gloved hand and slowly began to remove snow from her hair near her temple.

"I—I'm fine," she whispered breathlessly, hotly aware of his powerful body covering hers, his arms pinning her against him. Shah's heart was pounding like a wild bird's, and as she looked up and drowned in Jake's hungry gaze, she felt the last of her fear disappear. His smiling mouth intrigued her, drew her, and without hesitation she leaned upward. The smile on his mouth changed, and she felt his arms tauten, drawing her even more tightly to him. Her lips parted, and she leaned upward, closing her eyes.

The world focused for Jake as he covered her lips with his. He tasted the coolness of the air on her soft, opening mouth, tasted the evergreen and a sweetness that was only Shah. Their ragged breath met and mingled as he deepened his exploration of her ripe, willing mouth. Heat twisted and knotted deep within his body, and Jake groaned as Shah's arms slid shyly around his neck, drawing him down against her. The snow cradled them gently, the cold air in direct opposition to the heat he felt welling within him and Shah. Tipping her head back a little more, Jake unconsciously allowed his hand to move across her jacket, to caress the curve of her breast, and he felt her tremble. It wasn't out of fear, but out of a fiery longing that was consuming her.

Jake tore his mouth from hers, his eyes narrowed upon her dazed features. He saw the undeniable desire in Shah's half-closed eyes, saw the glistening softness of her parted lips asking him to kiss her again. Pain throbbed through him, the pain of wanting her more than life itself. With a shaking hand, he caressed her fiery red cheek.

"Let's go home and finish this," he murmured in a rough tone.

With a nod, Shah reached out, her gloved hand briefly resting against his cheek. "Oh, Jake, I love you so much.... I was so scared to say it...."

Those words echoed through him, the sweetest music he'd ever heard. He gave a little laugh of relief, rested his brow against her hair. "I know you do, and I know how scared you've been."

She clung to him. "I've been so blind. So stupid."

Jake kissed her with all the tenderness he possessed, and afterward he whispered against her lips, "Blind, maybe, but never stupid, Shah. We had to have the time to build our trust of each other."

Closing her eyes, her body like a vibrant, burning flame in a way she had never experienced, Shah whispered, "Love me when we get home, Jake? I know I'm not very good but—"

"Hush," he murmured against her lips, silencing her self-doubts as he captured her full mouth against his. Whatever Shah thought she lacked, Jake was going to try to show her she was wrong, today, this hour. Reluctantly he eased his mouth from her wet lips. "Come on," he coaxed, helping her sit up and brushing snow off her jacket, "let's go home. Together."

The tree was placed in the garage, and Shah held Jake's hand as he led her in the back door of the house. Her heart was pounding so hard that she thought she might be experiencing a cardiac arrest. Jake's smile, bestowed upon her as he allowed her to walk ahead of him, soothed her frantic anxiety. On the porch, they shed their outer gear and hung their coats on large brass hooks. Their boots were left there, too, and they padded in their stocking feet through the warm, fragrant kitchen.

"Sweetheart?" Jake pulled her to a halt at the entrance to the cathedral-ceilinged living room. He settled his hands on her shoulders. "This is your call all the way. Understand?" His voice was low, off-key. He wasn't trying to hide his feelings from her. The need to love Shah was nearly overwhelming, but his concern for her welfare tempered his needs.

She gazed up into his strong, harsh features. "No... everything is right about this, Jake," she whispered, "I'm ready.... I want this. I want you."

With a nod, he murmured, "Let's go upstairs."

Shah had already conceded that Jake's bedroom was the loveliest she'd ever seen in her life. Jake had made the stained-glass panes that graced the floor-to-ceiling windows. Broken sunlight shafted through them, lending a softened kaleidoscope of color to the large, open room. The gold-and-red cedar floor glowed as the sunlight slid across its polished surface, creating more warmth. Perhaps most touching to Shah was the dark green knitted afghan that served as a spread across the cedar bed. Jake had told her that his mother, who had died many years ago, had knitted it for him just before her unexpected death, and that he could never part with it, or the memory of her.

Sitting down on the edge of the bed, Shah ran her fingers across the worn expanse of the afghan. Jake knelt beside her and peeled one sock, then the other, off her feet.

"You have such pretty feet," Jake said quietly, and he ran his hands across them. "Strong, yet dainty." He lifted his head and smiled up at her. "Like you."

She framed Jake's face between her hands. "You find beauty in everything," she murmured, her thumbs caressing his cool cheeks. Drowning in his lambent gray eyes, Shah felt his hands slide up her arms and around her shoulders. In one smooth movement, he brought them both across the bed. She lay in his arms, looking up at him, her hand pressed to his chest, the soft polo shirt transferring delightful warmth to her palm.

Threading the thick strands of her hair through his fingers, Jake leaned over, caressing her lips. "Everything about you is beautiful," he murmured, moving his tongue to first one corner and then the other of her softly smiling mouth, teasing her, tempting her to respond. He felt her slight intake of breath, felt her fingers curl against his chest, and saw her eyes become a deeper gold. "Taste me if you want," he invited hoarsely. "Touch me like you want, Shah. Explore me. I'm yours...."

Dazed by the molten fire his mouth wreaked upon her lips, Shah drew him down until her lips met and fused with his. The instant they met and molded to each other, Shah relaxed bonelessly into Jake's arms. His body pressed against hers, urgent and hungry. Her breathing growing ragged, she felt his hand trail down her neck, eliciting tiny tingles, then turn hot and burning as it skimmed the crescent shape of her breast. A little gasp escaped her, kissed away by Jake as he continued to allow his fingers to linger, to caress her until she felt mindless with explosive needs she could no longer control.

Her hand moved of its own accord, and Shah longed to feel him, to tangle her fingertips in the dark, curling hair that covered his broad, massive chest. Sliding her hand beneath the green polo shirt, she felt Jake tense. He groaned as she boldly slid her hand across the flat, hard skin of his belly. Her fingertips slid upward to caress and outline his magnificent chest. The shudder that racked his body incited her, and Shah helped him tug off the shirt.

"You're just as beautiful," she whispered raggedly, her fingers buried in the fine, dark hair of his chest. She could feel the thundering beating of his heart, too, and his urgency spread through her.

Jake smiled a very male smile as he eased her back onto the bed. "I like your boldness, your courage," he told her thickly as he began to remove her red sweater. The moment his rough hand slid beneath the sweater, moving against her rib cage, he saw Shah's eyes grow drowsy with desire. His smile deepened as he nudged the sweater over her head and her black hair spilled around her like an ebony waterfall. To his surprise and delight, Shah wore no bra, just a white silk teddy. The thin fabric outlined her nipples and made her look even more desirable.

A sigh shuddered through Shah as Jake bent his head, his moist mouth capturing the peak of one nipple through the silken material. A little cry of pleasure tore from her, and she arched upward into his arms. The jagged heat, like powerful bolts of lightning striking down through her, made her weak, and she tipped back her head, surrendering to his caresses, to his loving. She forgot everything, wildly aware of the ache building in her lower body, the hunger stalking her. All she could do was frantically open and close her fingers against Jake's taut shoulders.

Winter sunlight burst through the stained-glass windows, the colors ripening and darkening across them. Shah felt the warmth of the sunlight, tasted the power of Jake's mouth upon her own, and felt his hand moving downward, releasing her jeans and nudging them away from her waist. Lost in the heat, the color, the amazing fragrance, she utterly surrendered herself to him. All she could do was react, incapable of thinking coherently enough to try to please him as he was pleasing her.

"That's it," Jake said, his voice an unsteady rasp, as the last of their clothing was swept off the bed. "Just enjoy it, Shah. Let me love you this time." Humbled as never before in his life, he felt her arch into his arms. Her little moans each time he caressed her drove him into a frenzy. She was like a highly sensitive instrument. Somewhere in his barely functioning mind, Jake had to remind himself that Shah had probably never experienced the enjoyment a woman could experience if the man took the time to bring her to that pinnacle of pleasure. Savoring her moans and responses, Jake absorbed the beauty of her half-closed eyes, the parted lips that were silently begging him to continue his intimate exploration.

As Jake's hand trailed down across her rounded belly, easing her thighs apart, Shah felt her world crack and splinter into a shower of rainbow colors. Each caress, each tender movement, made her cry out, wanting more of him. Frantic, she gripped Jake's shoulders, begging him for something she couldn't have defined. Speech was impossible; all she could do was move, press herself to his hard length and plead with her eyes. His smile was tender and knowing as he moved above her. Jake framed her face between his large hands, slowly allowing her to adjust to his greater weight.

Driven beyond her own barriers of fear, Shah arched upward, wanting, needing, Jake. The instant he met and filled her, she closed her eyes. The feeling was shattering, transforming and consuming. With each rocking movement of his hips, he moved deeper and deeper, until Shah truly understood the power of a man for the first time. But this was more than just physical sensation. As Jake slid his hand beneath her hip, angling her upward to meet his thrusts, pleasure burned and consumed Shah. Her head thrown back, a gasp drove through her. Her hands gripped him, and a cry, sweet and low, escaped from her lips.

Jake prolonged the pleasure for Shah, watching her face glow, the sudden flush covering her cheeks as her hands tensed against him. When he felt her begin to relax, only then did Jake release the hold he'd placed upon himself. Plunging deeply inside her, sweeping her uncompromisingly into his arms, he buried his face in her strong, soft hair and released his life within her loving, giving body.

Moments spun and glimmered together like rainbow beads of dew caught in the spiral circle of a spiderweb for Shah. She lay breathing raggedly, pinned by Jake's weight, his arms holding her tightly against him, his breath punctuating against her face and neck. Weak. She was as weak as a newborn kitten! Wave after wave of incredible pleasure sang through her newly awakened body. She felt Jake's mouth press against her damp temple, and she unconsciously inhaled his male scent, glorying in his tenderness in the aftermath. The beauty of their being one brought tears to her eyes that slipped out from beneath her dark lashes. Jake kissed each of them away.

Spinning in his embrace like sunlight captured by a cloud, Shah didn't want to open her eyes—she simply wanted to feel, and then feel some more. Jake's weight was like a heavy blanket across her. The thudding of his heart raced in time against hers. The power of him still filled her, reminding her that this was what true harmony was all about. Slowly she lifted her lashes. Jake's eyes were nearly colorless as he tenderly surveyed her, but his pupils were huge and black. His hair was damp, clinging to his brow, and her mouth stretched into a tender smile as she reached up and smoothed those damp strands away with her fingertips.

"I never knew," she whispered brokenly. "I never knew...." She slid her hands upward to touch and outline Jake's harsh-featured face. She watched his eyes narrow, and she felt his smile long before it appeared on his strong mouth.

"I didn't, either," Jake admitted, his voice rough. "Not like this. Not ever like this." He captured her full, sweet mouth against his in a long, cherishing kiss that brought a sound of pleasure from Shah. Her moan was like a song to him. Even as they lay there, still coupled, Jake felt himself growing strong within her once again. He eased his mouth from hers, drowning in the sunlight of her eyes. "I want you to be the mother of my children." He touched her hair, smoothing it away from her face. "I want to fill you, Shah, with myself, with my love. I want our love to grow in you."

The idea of having his children shimmered through her like a rainbow after a violent storm. Her eyes widened with surprise, and then grew lustrous with pleasure as she felt Jake move his hips. A soft smile touched her mouth as she slipped her arms around his shoulders.

"Yes..." she murmured. "Yes..."

Night had fallen long ago, and the firelight in the stone fireplace was dancing out across the large living room. Jake was in his blue terry-cloth robe, barefoot, and Shah stood in her pink chenille robe next to him. The Christmas tree standing in the middle of the huge room was now fully decorated, the lights bright and colorful.

Jake slipped his arm around Shah's waist, drinking in her shadowy beauty. The firelight graced her smooth features, emphasizing the clean lines of her face. It was a face softened by love, he realized humbly, the love she held for him alone. As he led her over to the large sheepskin rug that lay before the fireplace, Jake brought a bottle of white wine with him.

Just the idea, the hope, that Shah was pregnant with his child filled Jake with such euphoria and humility that he felt on the verge of tears. Loving Shah was like holding sunlight in his hands. Whatever fears she'd had, she'd relinquished earlier, in the heat of their loving. As she sat down next to him on the sheepskin, the firelight reflecting across them, Jake understood the courage she had shown.

He filled two crystal glasses with wine and handed one to Shah. Barely touching the rim of her glass with his own, he said, "To our love, and to the courage it took you to love me in return."

The words, like a warming blanket, enveloped Shah. She smiled up into Jake's shadowed features, feeling herself respond to the burning look of desire in his eyes. Holding her glass against his, she whispered, "And to the man who gave me the courage to love..." Taking a sip of the wine, she put it aside and touched Jake's cheek, now in dire need of a shave. The darkness of the stubble only made him look more dangerous, more alluring, to her.

"What if I am pregnant, Jake? We didn't take any precautions."

He shrugged and set the wine aside, drawing Shah into his arms. She came willingly and languished within his embrace, her head resting against his shoulder as they watched the fire dance before them. "Wouldn't bother me." He tipped his head so that he could see her expression, which was thoughtful, and perhaps a bit worried. "Would it you?"

She smiled tentatively. "No..."

"Then what has you worried?"

"I— Nothing, really. It's just all so soon, so new..."

Jake held her for a long time. "You're right," he admitted. "We love each other. We have the time now."

Turning in his arms, Shah faced him, his eyes dark with disappointment. "We do, but I don't feel you believe that."

He caught her hand and pressed a kiss to it. "I don't understand what you're saying."

Tears touched her eyes. "Jake, you had your family torn unexpectedly from you. I feel that now that you love me you're afraid something terrible will take me from you, too." Smiling gently, she caressed his cheek.

"I won't disappear on you, but you've experienced otherwise. You love children. And you were born to be a family man. It's written all over you."

Jake squeezed his eyes shut and hung his head, Shah's hand warm against his face. She was right on all counts. At the time, he hadn't thought of protection for Shah. Unconsciously he'd made the decision for both of them, and that hadn't been right. Raising his lashes, he stared into her wide, compassionate eyes. "You're right, sweetheart. We do have the time. I'm sorry."

"Never be sorry," Shah begged him. "I guess I'm just now understanding how very deeply you love me, Jake. You knew from the moment you met me. But I had to let you grow on me, because I was leery of you as a man." She leaned over and pressed a kiss to the grim cast of his mouth. "We'll grow together, Jake. A day at a time."

He nodded and ran his hand down the textured surface of her robed arm. "What if you are pregnant?"

"Then," Shah whispered, placing her arms around his neck and forcing him to look up at her as she knelt between his thighs, "you and I will be parents sooner rather than later." The joy she saw in his eyes made her heart break. Smoothing his hair, she added, "Did you know twins run on my mother's side of the family?" Grinning suddenly, Shah gave him a little shake. "Serve you right, Jake Randolph, if I do have twins! Instant family!"

With a rumbling laugh, Jake caught Shah in his arms and laid her gently on the rug. Her laughter was breathless, and undying love for him burned in her dancing eyes and in the sweet curve of her mouth. "Marry me, Shah."

The sincerity, the pleading, in his gaze tore whatever

hesitancy she had left within her completely away. The word whispered from her lips, low and trembling. "Yes…" She threw her arms around him and hugged him with all her womanly strength. He buried his head beside her, nuzzling into the silk of her ebony hair.

As Shah lay in Jake's arms, the firelight flickering over them, she had never felt more happy. Her heart was open, receiving, and Jake was responsible for it, for freeing her from the prison of her past. Shah realized that not every day would mean forward progress, because wounds took a long time to heal properly. As she lay there, feeling his heart's steady beating against hers and his powerful arms snugly around her, Shah felt a contentment she had never before known.

"I love you," she said, kissing him with all the tenderness she held within her. As she eased away from his mouth, Shah met and held his warm gray gaze. "Forever…"

*　*　*　*　*

SILHOUETTE *Romance*™

Escape to a place where a kiss is still a kiss...
Feel the breathless connection...
Fall in love as though it were
the very first time...
Experience the power of love!

Come to where favorite authors—such as
Diana Palmer, Stella Bagwell,
Marie Ferrarella and many more—
deliver heart-warming romance and genuine
emotion, time after time after time....

Silhouette Romance—
stories straight from the heart!

Silhouette®
Where love comes alive™